The BEST of Archie COMICS

DELUXE EDITION

BOOK THREE

The BEST of Archie COMICS

Publisher/Co-CEO:
Jon Goldwater

Co-President/Editor-in-Chief:
Victor Gorelick

Co-President:
Mike Pellerito

Co-President:
Alex Segura

Chief Creative Officer:
Roberto Aguirre-Sacasa

Chief Operating Officer:
William Mooar

Chief Financial Officer:
Robert Wintle

Director of Book Sales
& Operations:
Jonathan Betancourt

Production Manager:
Stephen Oswald

Lead Production Artist:
Carlos Antunes

Production Artist:
Rosario "Tito" Peña

Lead Designer:
Kari McLachlan

Assistant Editor/Proofreader:
Jamie Lee Rotante

Co-CEO:
Nancy Silberkleit

Published by Archie Comic Publications, Inc. 629 Fifth Avenue, Suite 100, Pelham, New York 10803-1242.

Printed in Canada.   First Printing.   ISBN: 978-1-68255-867-6

DELUXE EDITION

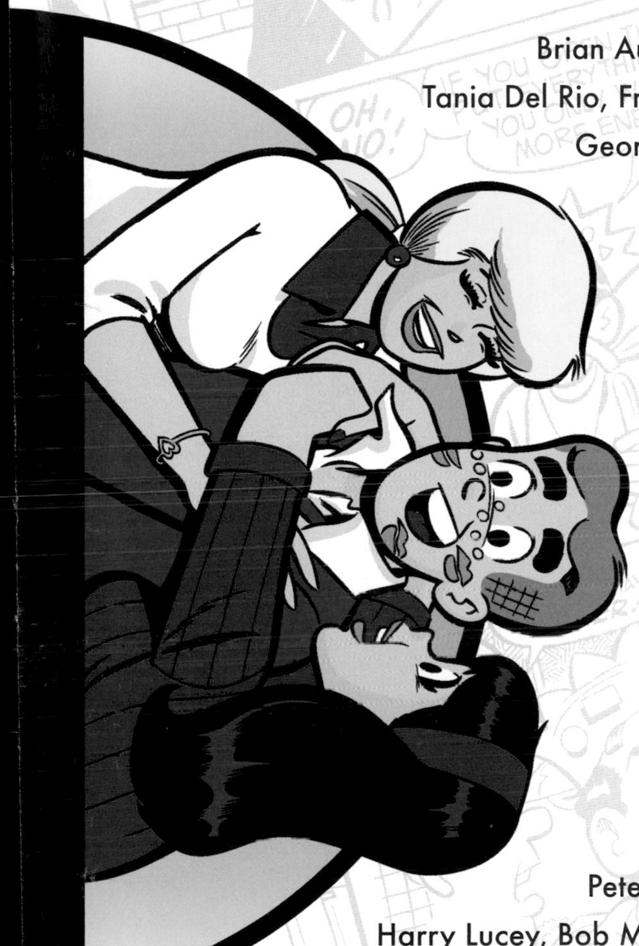

STORIES BY:

Brian Augustyn, Bob Bolling, Paul Castiglia, Tania Del Rio, Frank Doyle, Joe Edwards, Ian Flynn, George Gladir, Ed Goggin, Bill Golliher, Harry Lucey, Rich Margopoulos, Bob Montana, Dan Parent, Mike Pellowski, Tom Root, Mark Waid and Kathleen Webb.

ARTWORK BY:

Jim Amash, Bob Bolling, Jon D'Agostino, Dan DeCarlo, Dan DeCarlo Jr., Jim DeCarlo, Vince DeCarlo, Tania Del Rio, Joe Edwards, Marty Epp, Kelly Fitzpatrick, Ginger, Gisele, Barry Grossman, Matt Herms, Jason Jenson, Rich Koslowski, Peter Krause, Rudy Lapick, Rex Lindsey, Harry Lucey, Bob Montana, Audrey Mok, Jack Morelli, Dan Parent, Rosario "Tito" Peña, Jeff Powell, Ridge Rooms, Fernando Ruiz, Harry Sahle, Marguerite Sauvage, Henry Scarpelli, Samm Schwartz, Gregg Suchow, Rick Taylor, Nanci Tsetsekas, Bob White, Glenn Whitmore, Vickie Williams, Tracy Yardley, Bill Yoshida and Digikore Studios.

Welcome to the BEST of ARCHIE COMICS!

Here it is—a third volume of all-time favorite Archie stories! Thanks to readers like you, the *Best of Archie Comics* series continues to break records as our best-selling book line ever. Each time that we've invited artists, writers, editors, and fans to nominate their favorite stories, we've been delighted by the variety and quality of their choices from thousands and thousands of candidates.

The nominated stories have been pulled from the best available materials, usually from scans of the original black and white illustrations that we have then had digitally recolored. In some instances a favorite story's only available source material has been scans of the original printed comics, which in some cases date back 50 years or more and hadn't been in print since. We hope you enjoy the selection of rare classic stories from the '40s that showcase some of the best of Archie's broad slapstick beginnings. Until very recently, many of these stories had been only available to Golden Age comic book collectors. There's also a great mix of fun stories featuring Archie's pal Jughead. It's a treat to watch his character develop over the years under the expert hands of Archie's talented writers and artists.

Curl up in your favorite chair, and join us on another fun-filled, 75+ year journey through Riverdale!

Happy reading!

The BEST of Archie® COMICS

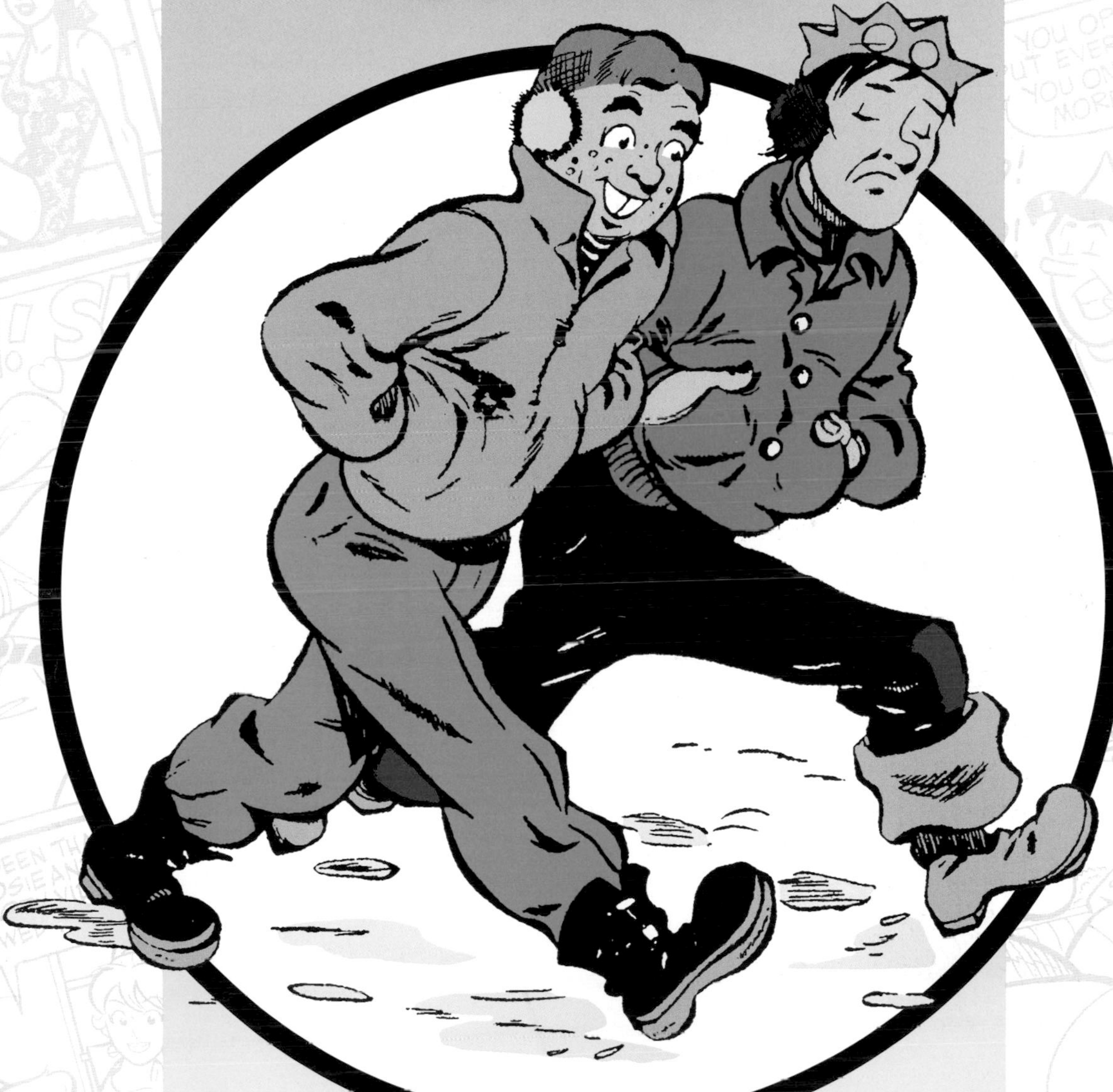

1940s

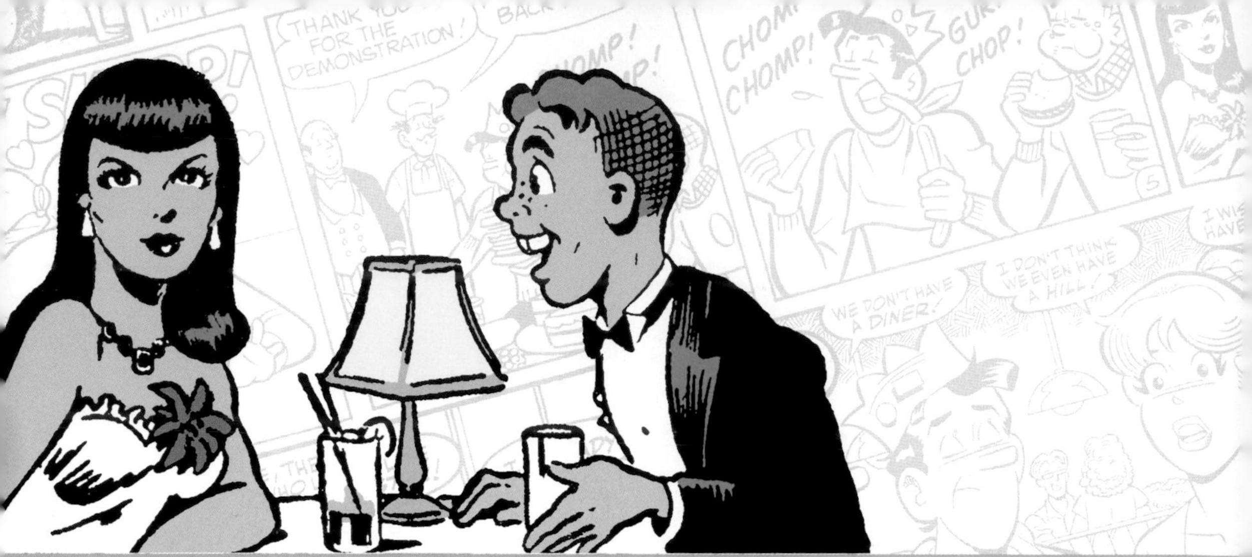
CHOMP! CHOMP!
WE DON'T HAVE A DINER!
I DON'T THINK WE EVEN HAVE A HILL!

ARCHIE
PEP #36, 1943
BY BOB MONTANA

The year was 1943 and we were right in the middle of World War II. Before you read this story, look at the sticker on the windshield of Archie's car in the first panel. It reads, "Keep em Flyin." This was a reminder to conserve much needed fuel for our airplanes.

Why I like this story: to start with, it's funny and Archie's character is at its best. Bob Montana gives insight into the characters in this story. Not only do you see the characters' individual personalities, but also how they interact with each other. I hope you enjoy this story as much as I did. For those of you who like to write, there are lessons to be learned when you read "The 3-11 Club."

—Victor Gorelick
Co-President/Editor-in-Chief,
Archie Comics

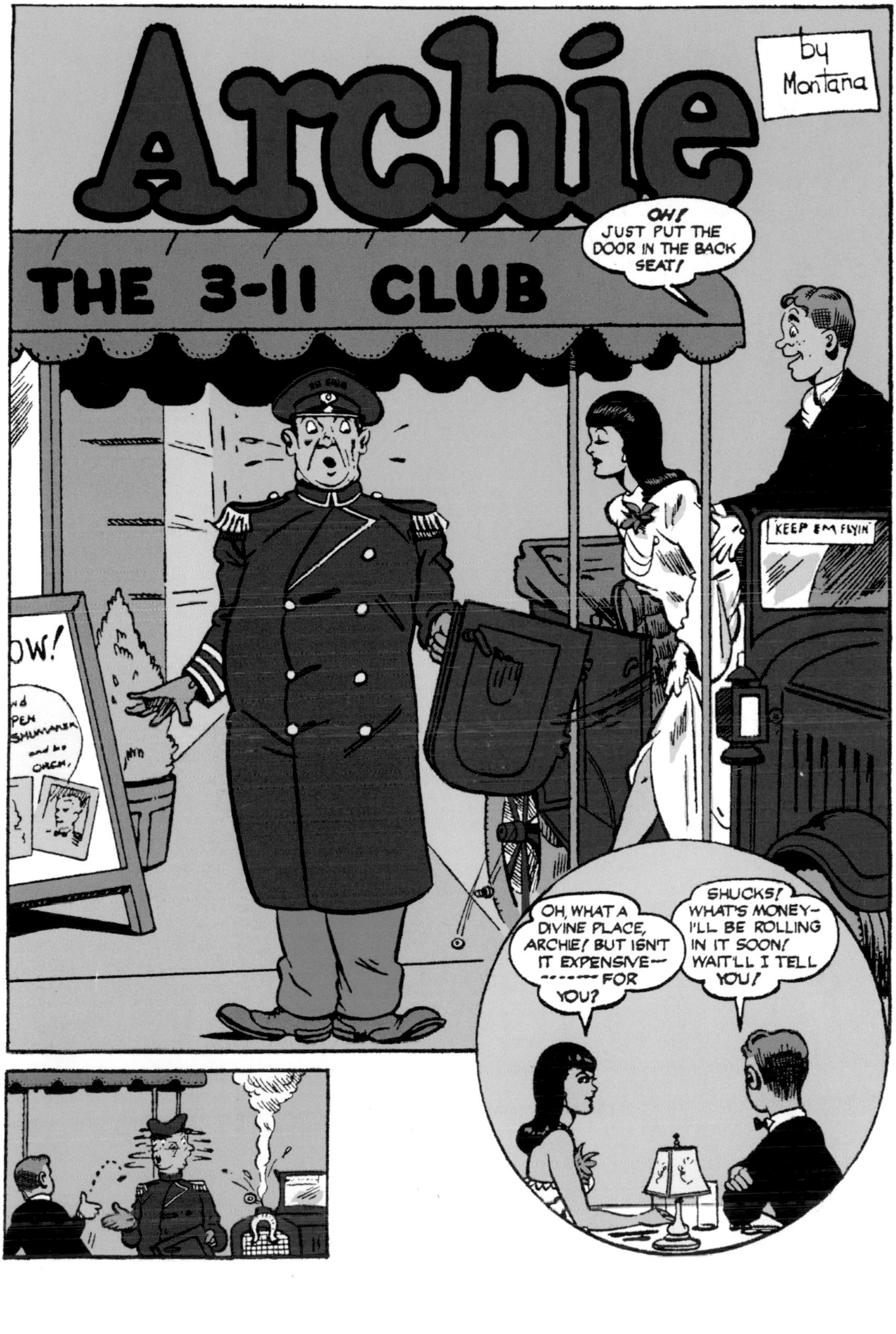

Archie
by Montana
THE 3-11 CLUB
OH! JUST PUT THE DOOR IN THE BACK SEAT!
KEEP EM FLYIN
OH, WHAT A DIVINE PLACE, ARCHIE! BUT ISN'T IT EXPENSIVE-- ------ FOR YOU?
SHUCKS! WHAT'S MONEY-I'LL BE ROLLING IN IT SOON! WAIT'LL I TELL YOU!

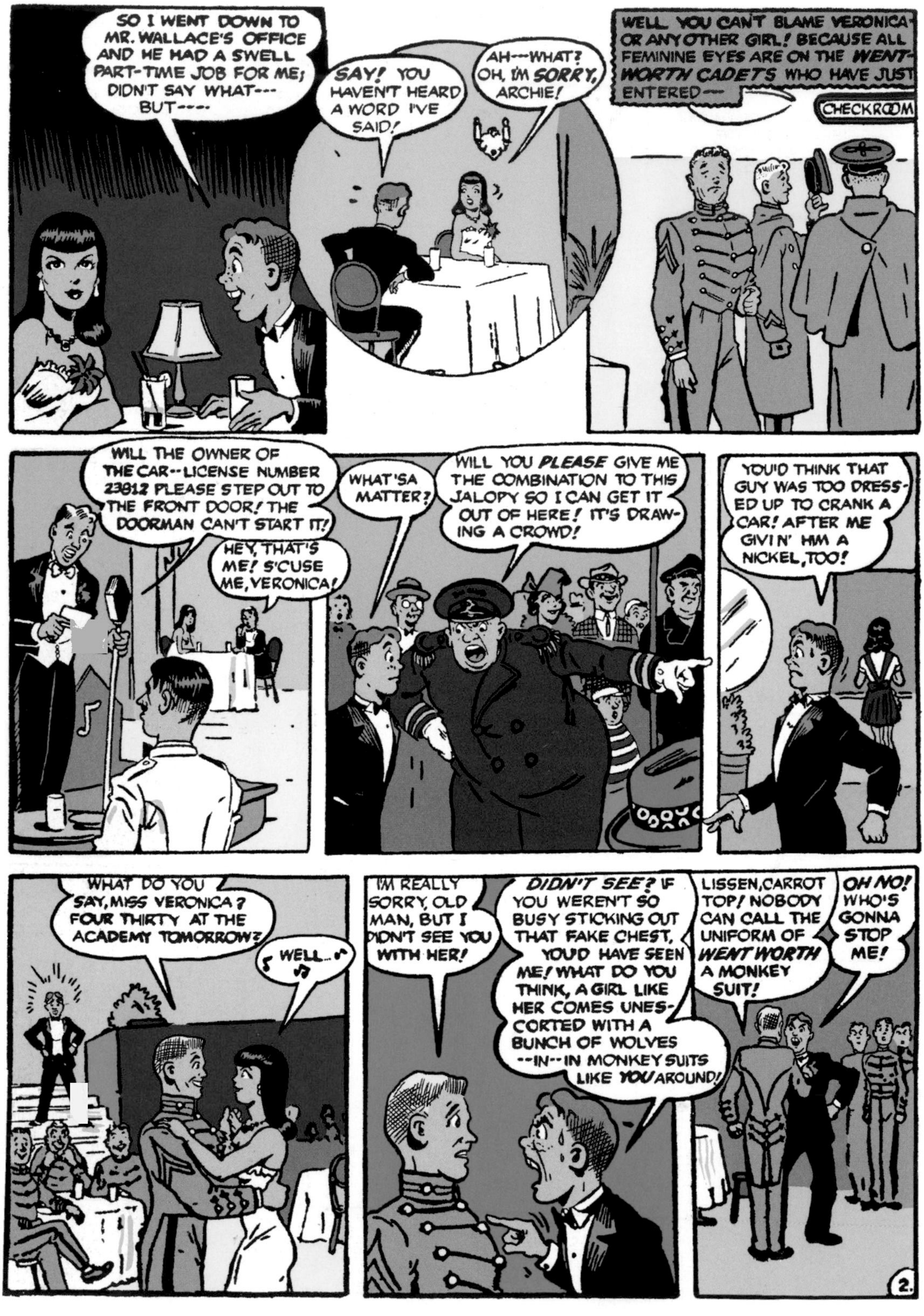
SO I WENT DOWN TO MR. WALLACE'S OFFICE AND HE HAD A SWELL PART-TIME JOB FOR ME; DIDN'T SAY WHAT--- BUT----
SAY! YOU HAVEN'T HEARD A WORD I'VE SAID!
AH---WHAT? OH, I'M SORRY, ARCHIE!
WELL, YOU CAN'T BLAME VERONICA OR ANY OTHER GIRL! BECAUSE ALL FEMININE EYES ARE ON THE WENTWORTH CADETS WHO HAVE JUST ENTERED--
CHECKROOM
WILL THE OWNER OF THE CAR--LICENSE NUMBER 23812 PLEASE STEP OUT TO THE FRONT DOOR! THE DOORMAN CAN'T START IT!
HEY, THAT'S ME! S'CUSE ME, VERONICA!
WHAT'SA MATTER?
WILL YOU PLEASE GIVE ME THE COMBINATION TO THIS JALOPY SO I CAN GET IT OUT OF HERE! IT'S DRAWING A CROWD!
YOU'D THINK THAT GUY WAS TOO DRESSED UP TO CRANK A CAR! AFTER ME GIVIN' HIM A NICKEL, TOO!
WHAT DO YOU SAY, MISS VERONICA? FOUR THIRTY AT THE ACADEMY TOMORROW?
WELL...
I'M REALLY SORRY, OLD MAN, BUT I DIDN'T SEE YOU WITH HER!
DIDN'T SEE? IF YOU WEREN'T SO BUSY STICKING OUT THAT FAKE CHEST, YOU'D HAVE SEEN ME! WHAT DO YOU THINK, A GIRL LIKE HER COMES UNESCORTED WITH A BUNCH OF WOLVES --IN--IN MONKEY SUITS LIKE YOU AROUND!
LISSEN, CARROT TOP! NOBODY CAN CALL THE UNIFORM OF WENTWORTH A MONKEY SUIT!
OH NO! WHO'S GONNA STOP ME!
2.

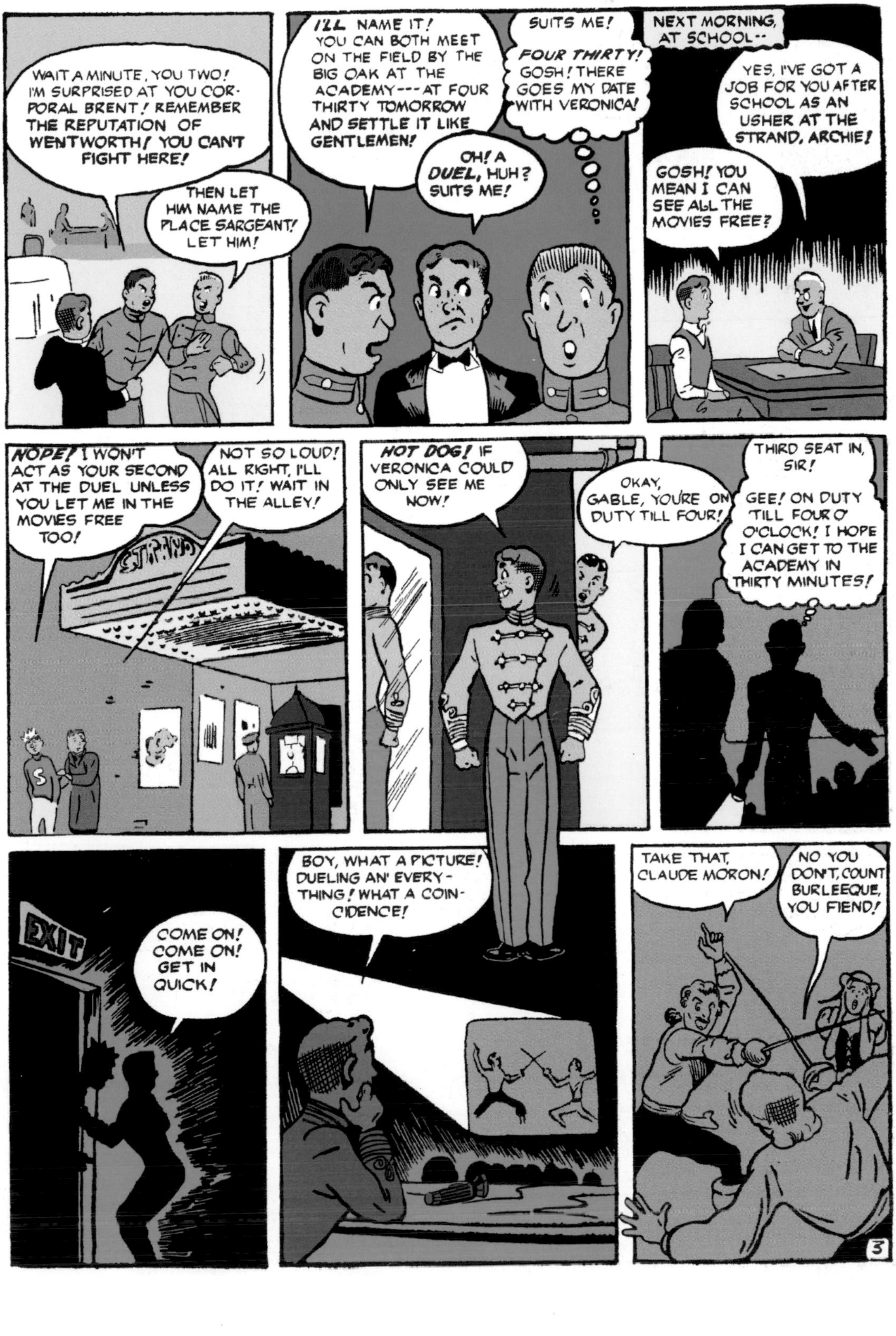
WAIT A MINUTE, YOU TWO! I'M SURPRISED AT YOU COR-PORAL BRENT! REMEMBER THE REPUTATION OF WENTWORTH! YOU CAN'T FIGHT HERE!
THEN LET HIM NAME THE PLACE SARGEANT! LET HIM!
I'LL NAME IT! YOU CAN BOTH MEET ON THE FIELD BY THE BIG OAK AT THE ACADEMY---AT FOUR THIRTY TOMORROW AND SETTLE IT LIKE GENTLEMEN!
OH! A DUEL, HUH? SUITS ME!
SUITS ME!
FOUR THIRTY! GOSH! THERE GOES MY DATE WITH VERONICA!
NEXT MORNING, AT SCHOOL--
YES, I'VE GOT A JOB FOR YOU AFTER SCHOOL AS AN USHER AT THE STRAND, ARCHIE!
GOSH! YOU MEAN I CAN SEE ALL THE MOVIES FREE?
NOPE! I WON'T ACT AS YOUR SECOND AT THE DUEL UNLESS YOU LET ME IN THE MOVIES FREE TOO!
NOT SO LOUD! ALL RIGHT, I'LL DO IT! WAIT IN THE ALLEY!
STRAND
HOT DOG! IF VERONICA COULD ONLY SEE ME NOW!
OKAY, GABLE, YOU'RE ON DUTY TILL FOUR!
THIRD SEAT IN, SIR!
GEE! ON DUTY 'TILL FOUR O' O'CLOCK! I HOPE I CAN GET TO THE ACADEMY IN THIRTY MINUTES!
EXIT
COME ON! COME ON! GET IN QUICK!
BOY, WHAT A PICTURE! DUELING AN' EVERY-THING! WHAT A COIN-CIDENCE!
TAKE THAT, CLAUDE MORON!
NO YOU DON'T, COUNT BURLEEQUE, YOU FIEND!
3

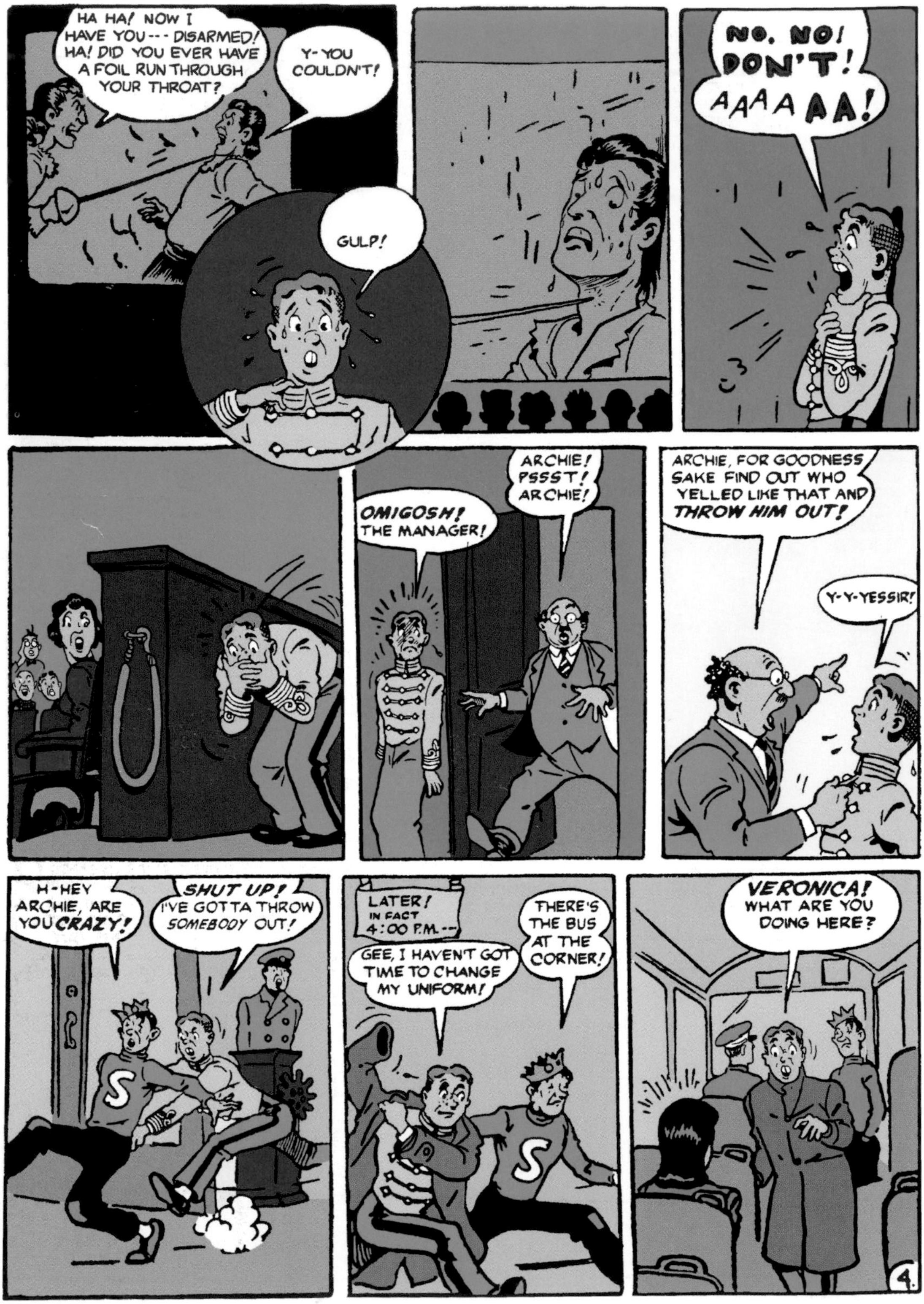
HA HA! NOW I HAVE YOU--- DISARMED! HA! DID YOU EVER HAVE A FOIL RUN THROUGH YOUR THROAT?
Y-YOU COULDN'T!
GULP!
NO, NO! DON'T! AAAAAA!
ARCHIE! PSSST! ARCHIE!
OMIGOSH! THE MANAGER!
ARCHIE, FOR GOODNESS SAKE FIND OUT WHO YELLED LIKE THAT AND THROW HIM OUT!
Y-Y-YESSIR!
H-HEY ARCHIE, ARE YOU CRAZY!
SHUT UP! I'VE GOTTA THROW SOMEBODY OUT!
LATER! IN FACT 4:00 P.M.--
GEE, I HAVEN'T GOT TIME TO CHANGE MY UNIFORM!
THERE'S THE BUS AT THE CORNER!
VERONICA! WHAT ARE YOU DOING HERE?
4.

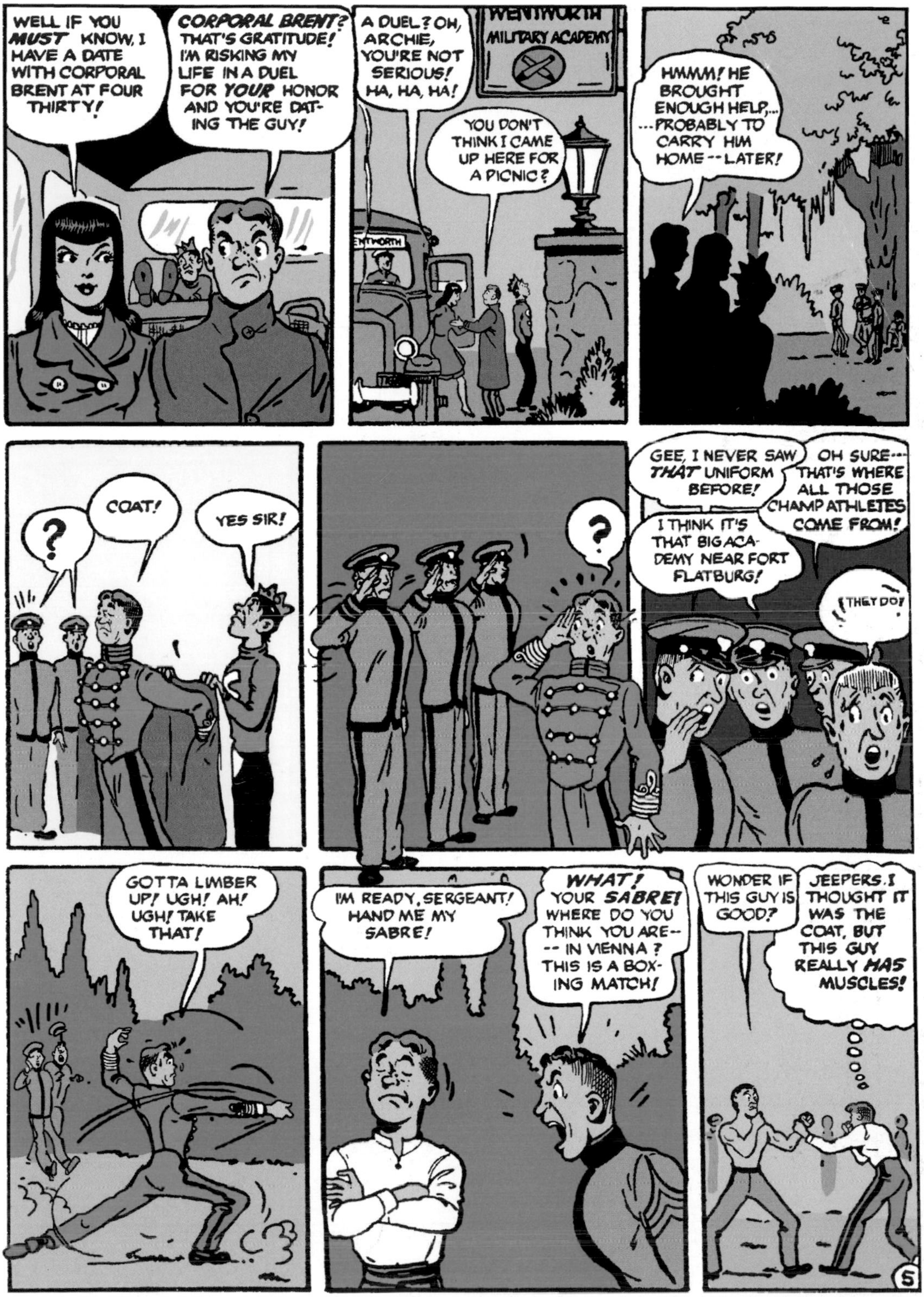

WELL IF YOU MUST KNOW, I HAVE A DATE WITH CORPORAL BRENT AT FOUR THIRTY!
CORPORAL BRENT? THAT'S GRATITUDE! I'M RISKING MY LIFE IN A DUEL FOR YOUR HONOR AND YOU'RE DATING THE GUY!
A DUEL? OH, ARCHIE, YOU'RE NOT SERIOUS! HA, HA, HA!
WENTWORTH MILITARY ACADEMY
YOU DON'T THINK I CAME UP HERE FOR A PICNIC?
WENTWORTH
HMMM! HE BROUGHT ENOUGH HELP... ...PROBABLY TO CARRY HIM HOME -- LATER!
?
COAT!
YES SIR!
?
GEE, I NEVER SAW THAT UNIFORM BEFORE!
I THINK IT'S THAT BIG ACADEMY NEAR FORT FLATBURG!
OH SURE--- THAT'S WHERE ALL THOSE CHAMP ATHLETES COME FROM!
THEY DO!
GOTTA LIMBER UP! UGH! AH! UGH! TAKE THAT!
I'M READY, SERGEANT! HAND ME MY SABRE!
WHAT! YOUR SABRE! WHERE DO YOU THINK YOU ARE-- -- IN VIENNA? THIS IS A BOXING MATCH!
WONDER IF THIS GUY IS GOOD?
JEEPERS, I THOUGHT IT WAS THE COAT, BUT THIS GUY REALLY HAS MUSCLES!
5

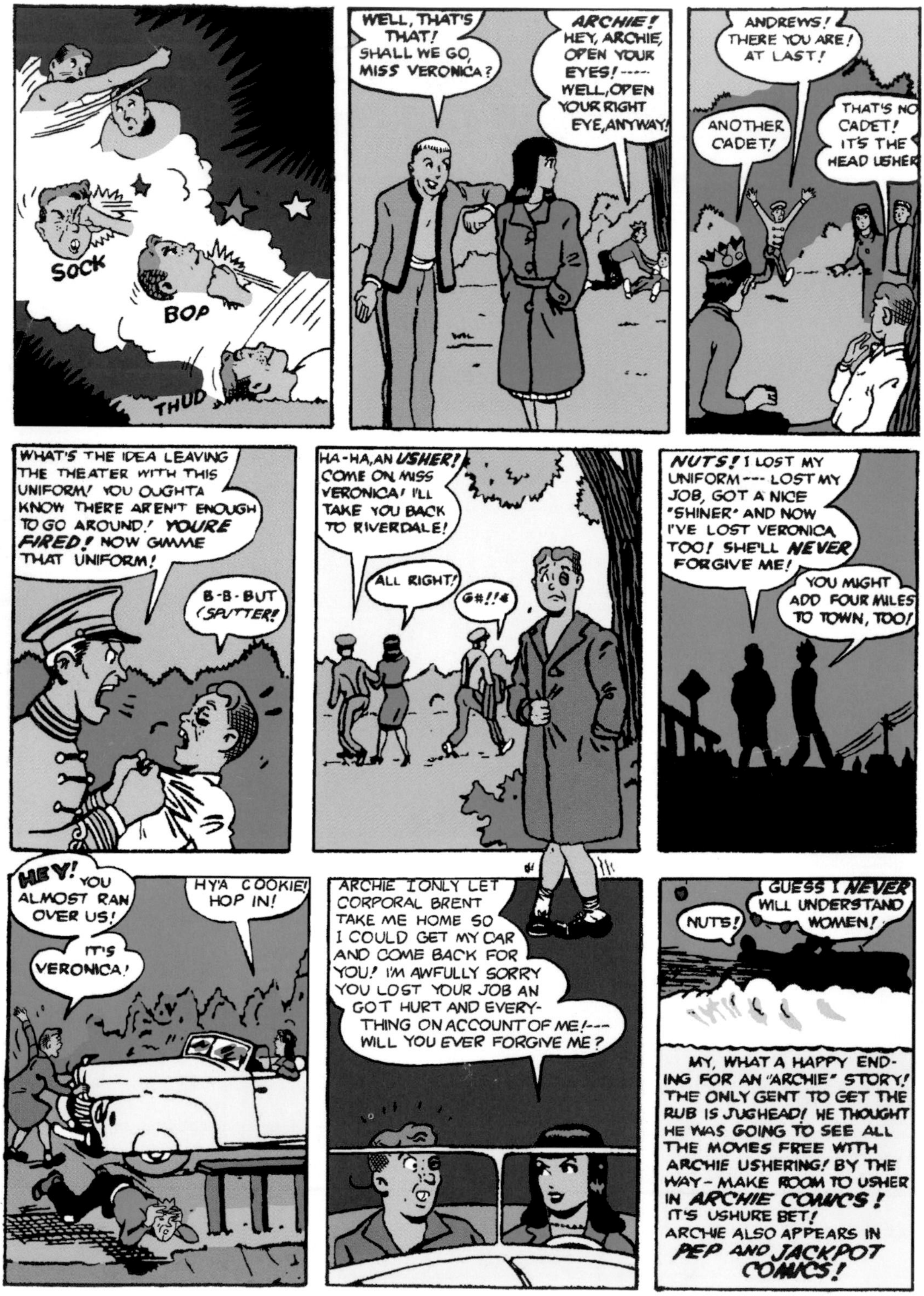
SOCK
BOP
THUD
WELL, THAT'S THAT! SHALL WE GO, MISS VERONICA?
ARCHIE! HEY, ARCHIE, OPEN YOUR EYES!---- WELL, OPEN YOUR RIGHT EYE, ANYWAY!
ANDREWS! THERE YOU ARE! AT LAST!
ANOTHER CADET!
THAT'S NO CADET! IT'S THE HEAD USHER
WHAT'S THE IDEA LEAVING THE THEATER WITH THIS UNIFORM! YOU OUGHTA KNOW THERE AREN'T ENOUGH TO GO AROUND! YOURE FIRED! NOW GIMME THAT UNIFORM!
B-B-BUT (SPUTTER!
HA-HA, AN USHER! COME ON MISS VERONICA! I'LL TAKE YOU BACK TO RIVERDALE!
ALL RIGHT!
G#!!$
NUTS! I LOST MY UNIFORM--- LOST MY JOB, GOT A NICE "SHINER" AND NOW I'VE LOST VERONICA TOO! SHE'LL NEVER FORGIVE ME!
YOU MIGHT ADD FOUR MILES TO TOWN, TOO!
HEY! YOU ALMOST RAN OVER US!
IT'S VERONICA!
HY'A COOKIE! HOP IN!
ARCHIE I ONLY LET CORPORAL BRENT TAKE ME HOME SO I COULD GET MY CAR AND COME BACK FOR YOU! I'M AWFULLY SORRY YOU LOST YOUR JOB AN GOT HURT AND EVERY-THING ON ACCOUNT OF ME!--- WILL YOU EVER FORGIVE ME?
NUTS!
GUESS I NEVER WILL UNDERSTAND WOMEN!
MY, WHAT A HAPPY END-ING FOR AN "ARCHIE" STORY! THE ONLY GENT TO GET THE RUB IS JUGHEAD! HE THOUGHT HE WAS GOING TO SEE ALL THE MOVIES FREE WITH ARCHIE USHERING! BY THE WAY- MAKE ROOM TO USHER IN ARCHIE COMICS! IT'S USHURE BET! ARCHIE ALSO APPEARS IN PEP AND JACKPOT COMICS!

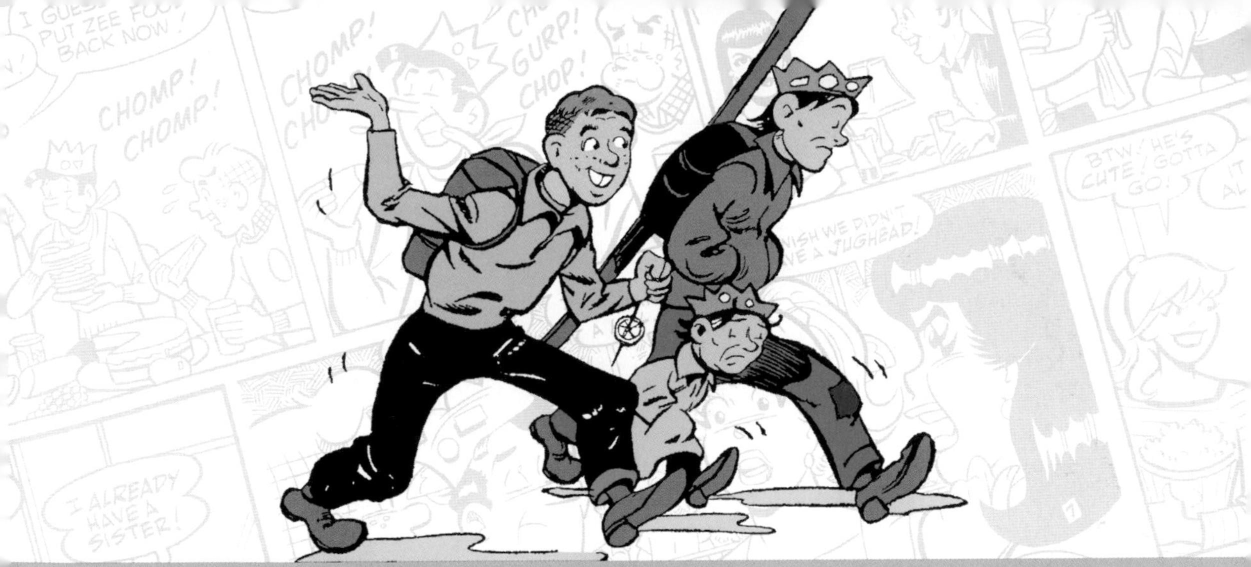
CHOMP!
CHOMP!
GURP!
CHOP!
I ALREADY HAVE A SISTER!

SPRING FEVER
ARCHIE #4, 1943
BY ED GOGGIN, HARRY SAHLE & GINGER

No, you're not seeing double, that's actually the first appearance of Jughead's young cousin Souphead. This is Souphead's first appearance in an Archie comic and he even made the cover of the issue. Souphead has shown up a lot over the years causing trouble, but his first appearance really sets the stage for this wild pre-teen. Written by one of the most prolific writers in Archie's early years, Ed Goggin. Goggin really seemed to thrive at these "simple solution creating bigger problems" stories which became a staple of Archie comics. The art is handled by Golden Age Archie great Harry Sahle, whose name started to show up often on Archie covers and titles really helped take and mold the look and feel of the Archie gang in those early years. Sahle often inked by "Ginger" was not only one of the best and busiest inkers of Archie stories but one of the first women working in comics.

—Mike Pellerito
Co-President,
Archie Comics

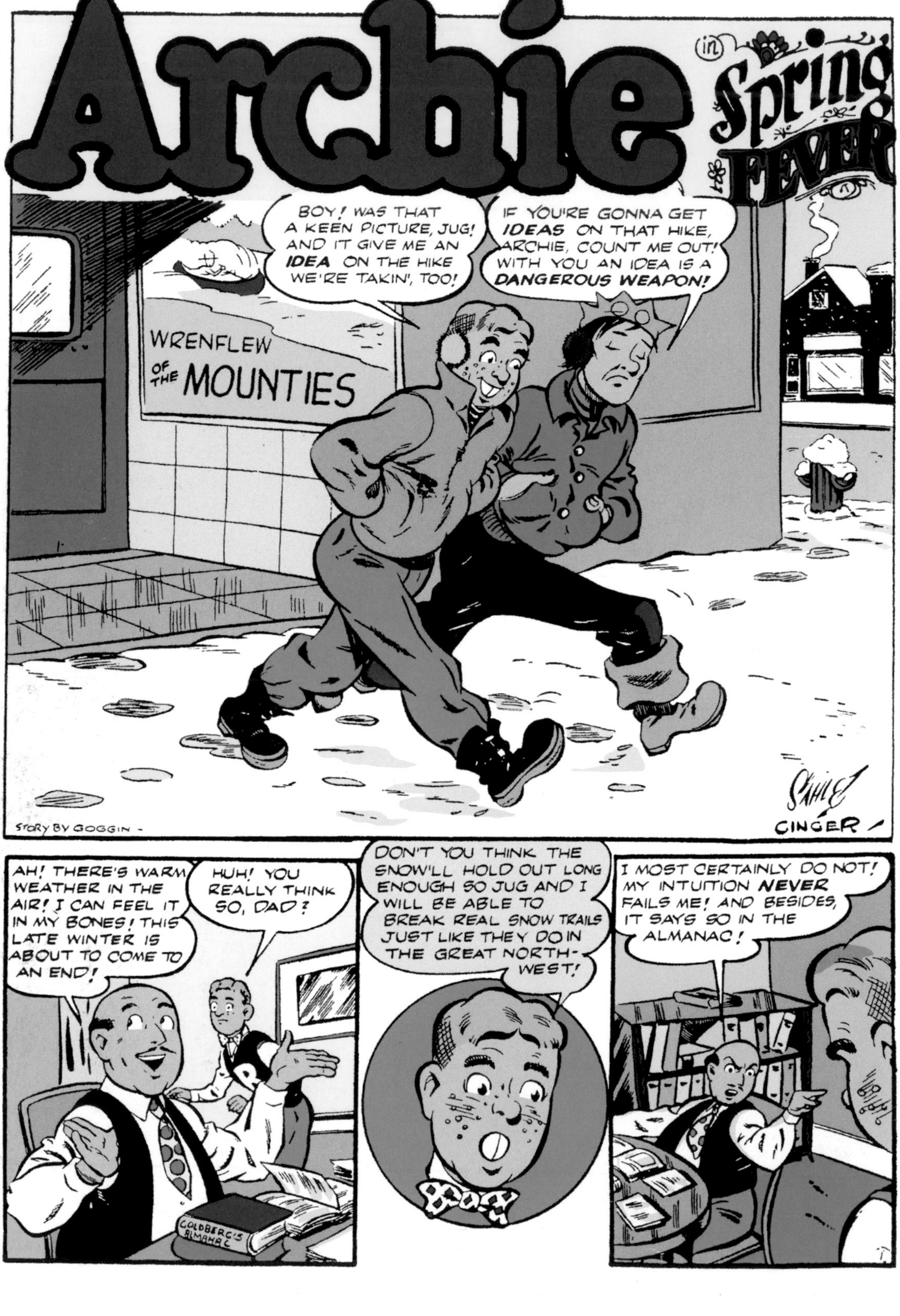
Archie
in
Spring Fever
BOY! WAS THAT A KEEN PICTURE, JUG! AND IT GIVE ME AN IDEA ON THE HIKE WE'RE TAKIN', TOO!
IF YOU'RE GONNA GET IDEAS ON THAT HIKE, ARCHIE, COUNT ME OUT! WITH YOU AN IDEA IS A DANGEROUS WEAPON!
WRENFLEW OF THE MOUNTIES
STORY BY GOGGIN
CINGER
AH! THERE'S WARM WEATHER IN THE AIR! I CAN FEEL IT IN MY BONES! THIS LATE WINTER IS ABOUT TO COME TO AN END!
HUH! YOU REALLY THINK SO, DAD?
GOLDBERG'S ALMANAC
DON'T YOU THINK THE SNOW'LL HOLD OUT LONG ENOUGH SO JUG AND I WILL BE ABLE TO BREAK REAL SNOW TRAILS JUST LIKE THEY DO IN THE GREAT NORTH-WEST!
I MOST CERTAINLY DO NOT! MY INTUITION NEVER FAILS ME! AND BESIDES, IT SAYS SO IN THE ALMANAC!

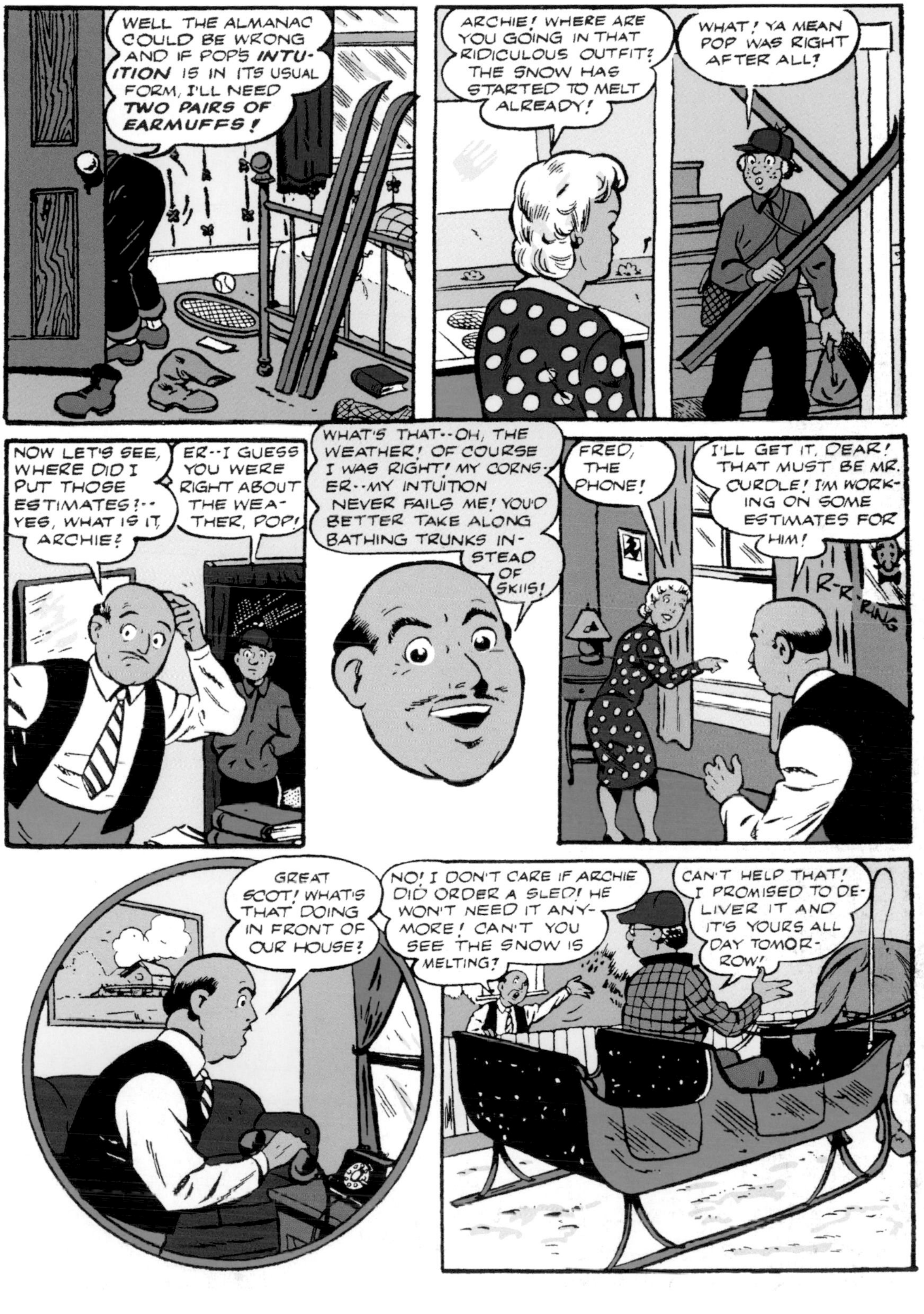
WELL THE ALMANAC COULD BE WRONG AND IF POP'S INTUITION IS IN ITS USUAL FORM, I'LL NEED TWO PAIRS OF EARMUFFS!
ARCHIE! WHERE ARE YOU GOING IN THAT RIDICULOUS OUTFIT? THE SNOW HAS STARTED TO MELT ALREADY!
WHAT! YA MEAN POP WAS RIGHT AFTER ALL?
NOW LET'S SEE, WHERE DID I PUT THOSE ESTIMATES?-- YES, WHAT IS IT, ARCHIE?
ER--I GUESS YOU WERE RIGHT ABOUT THE WEATHER, POP!
WHAT'S THAT--OH, THE WEATHER! OF COURSE I WAS RIGHT! MY CORNS-- ER--MY INTUITION NEVER FAILS ME! YOU'D BETTER TAKE ALONG BATHING TRUNKS INSTEAD OF SKIIS!
FRED, THE PHONE!
I'LL GET IT, DEAR! THAT MUST BE MR. CURDLE! I'M WORKING ON SOME ESTIMATES FOR HIM!
R-R RING
GREAT SCOT! WHAT'S THAT DOING IN FRONT OF OUR HOUSE?
NO! I DON'T CARE IF ARCHIE DID ORDER A SLED! HE WON'T NEED IT ANYMORE! CAN'T YOU SEE THE SNOW IS MELTING?
CAN'T HELP THAT! I PROMISED TO DELIVER IT AND IT'S YOURS ALL DAY TOMORROW!

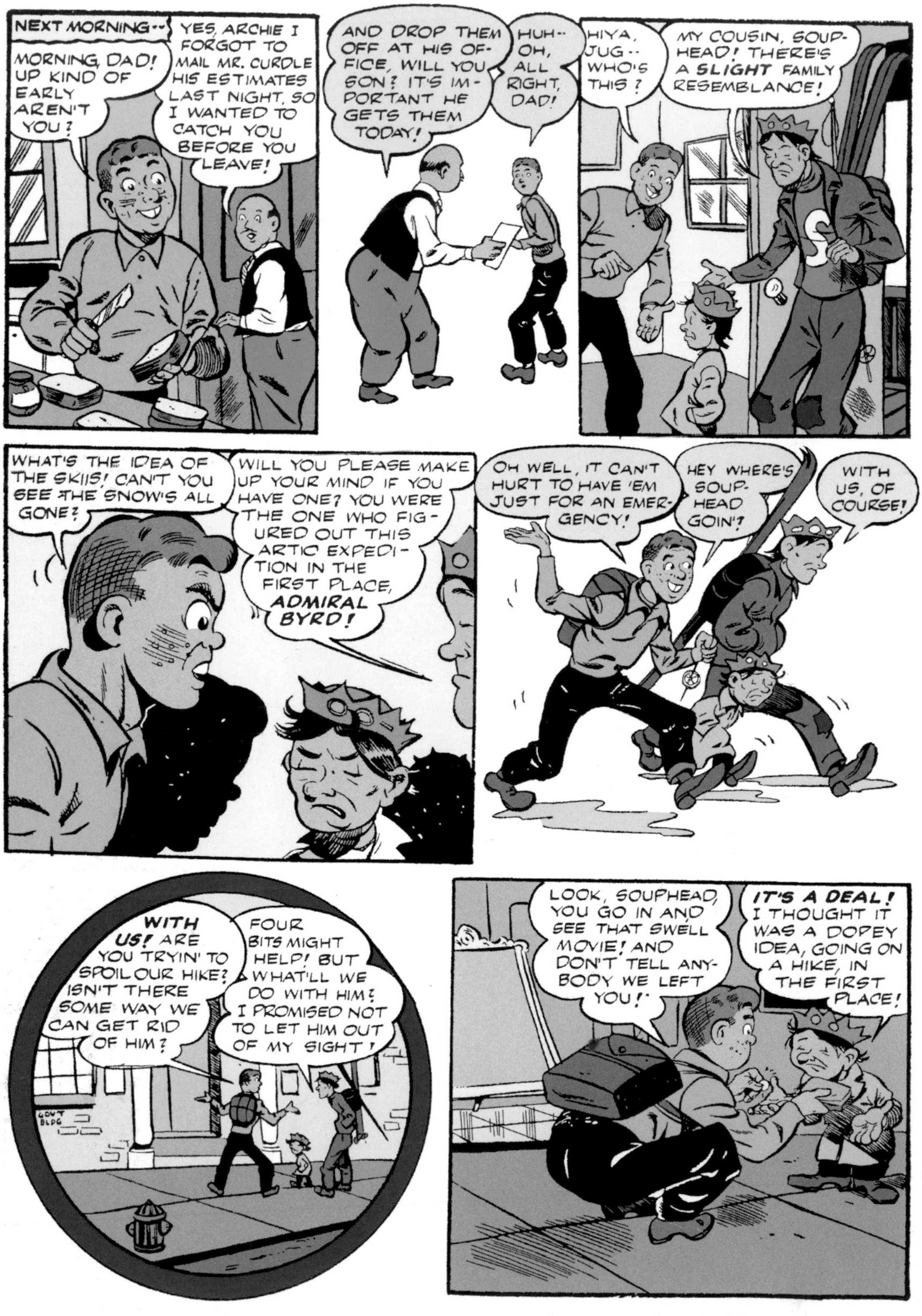
NEXT MORNING--
MORNING, DAD! UP KIND OF EARLY AREN'T YOU?
YES, ARCHIE I FORGOT TO MAIL MR. CURDLE HIS ESTIMATES LAST NIGHT, SO I WANTED TO CATCH YOU BEFORE YOU LEAVE!
AND DROP THEM OFF AT HIS OFFICE, WILL YOU SON? IT'S IMPORTANT HE GETS THEM TODAY!
HUH-- OH, ALL RIGHT, DAD!
HIYA, JUG-- WHO'S THIS?
MY COUSIN, SOUPHEAD! THERE'S A SLIGHT FAMILY RESEMBLANCE!
WHAT'S THE IDEA OF THE SKIIS! CAN'T YOU SEE THE SNOW'S ALL GONE?
WILL YOU PLEASE MAKE UP YOUR MIND IF YOU HAVE ONE? YOU WERE THE ONE WHO FIGURED OUT THIS ARTIC EXPEDITION IN THE FIRST PLACE, ADMIRAL BYRD!
OH WELL, IT CAN'T HURT TO HAVE 'EM JUST FOR AN EMERGENCY!
HEY WHERE'S SOUPHEAD GOIN'?
WITH US, OF COURSE!
WITH US! ARE YOU TRYIN' TO SPOIL OUR HIKE? ISN'T THERE SOME WAY WE CAN GET RID OF HIM?
FOUR BITS MIGHT HELP! BUT WHAT'LL WE DO WITH HIM? I PROMISED NOT TO LET HIM OUT OF MY SIGHT!
GOV'T BLDG
LOOK, SOUPHEAD, YOU GO IN AND SEE THAT SWELL MOVIE! AND DON'T TELL ANYBODY WE LEFT YOU!
IT'S A DEAL! I THOUGHT IT WAS A DOPEY IDEA, GOING ON A HIKE, IN THE FIRST PLACE!

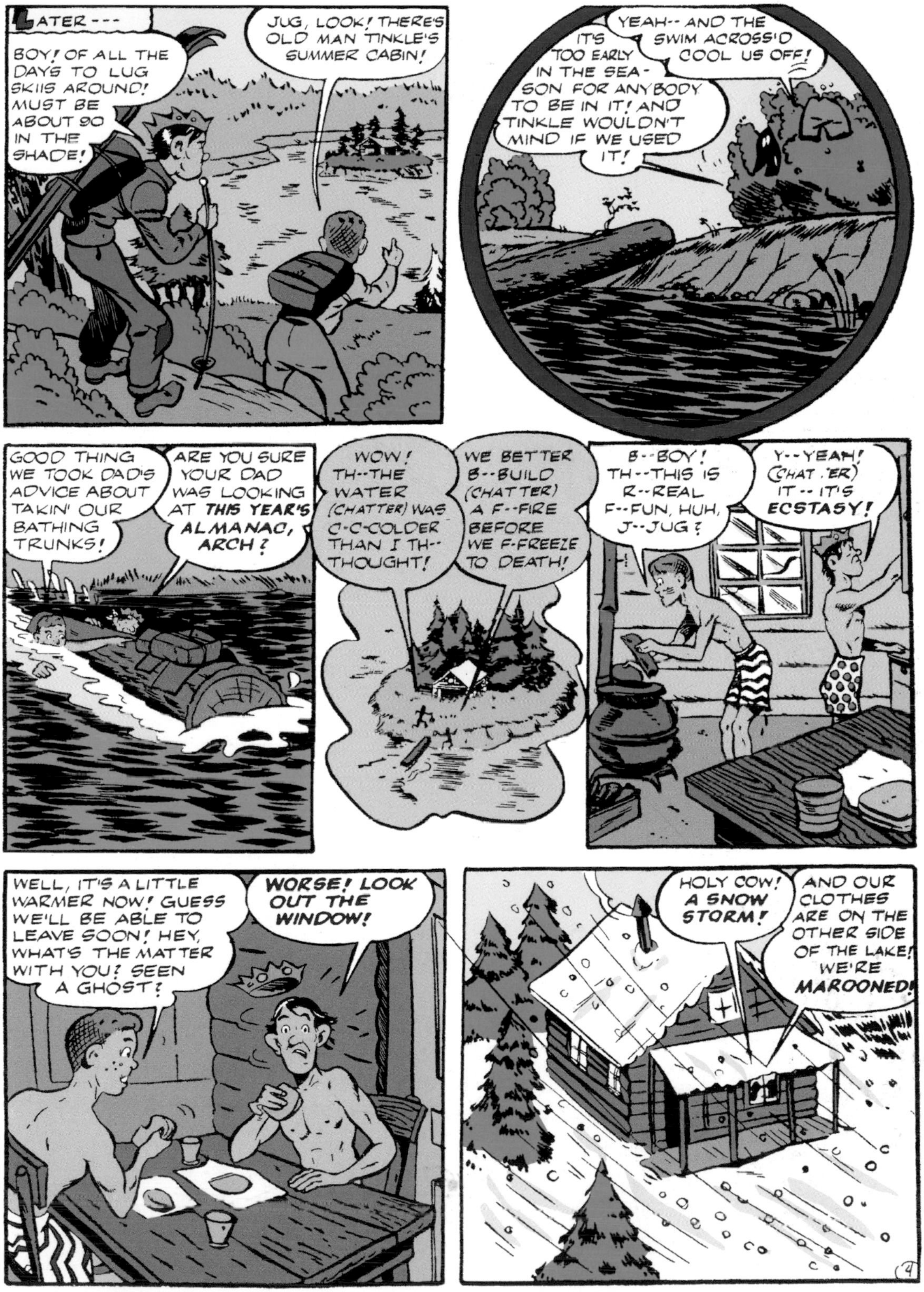
LATER---
BOY! OF ALL THE DAYS TO LUG SKIIS AROUND! MUST BE ABOUT 90 IN THE SHADE!
JUG, LOOK! THERE'S OLD MAN TINKLE'S SUMMER CABIN!
IT'S TOO EARLY IN THE SEASON FOR ANYBODY TO BE IN IT! AND TINKLE WOULDN'T MIND IF WE USED IT!
YEAH-- AND THE SWIM ACROSS'D COOL US OFF!
GOOD THING WE TOOK DAD'S ADVICE ABOUT TAKIN' OUR BATHING TRUNKS!
ARE YOU SURE YOUR DAD WAS LOOKING AT THIS YEAR'S ALMANAC, ARCH?
WOW! TH--THE WATER (CHATTER) WAS C-C-COLDER THAN I TH--THOUGHT!
WE BETTER B--BUILD (CHATTER) A F--FIRE BEFORE WE F-FREEZE TO DEATH!
B--BOY! TH--THIS IS R--REAL F--FUN, HUH, J--JUG?
Y--YEAH! (CHAT-'ER) IT-- IT'S ECSTASY!
WELL, IT'S A LITTLE WARMER NOW! GUESS WE'LL BE ABLE TO LEAVE SOON! HEY, WHAT'S THE MATTER WITH YOU? SEEN A GHOST?
WORSE! LOOK OUT THE WINDOW!
HOLY COW! A SNOW STORM!
AND OUR CLOTHES ARE ON THE OTHER SIDE OF THE LAKE! WE'RE MAROONED!
4

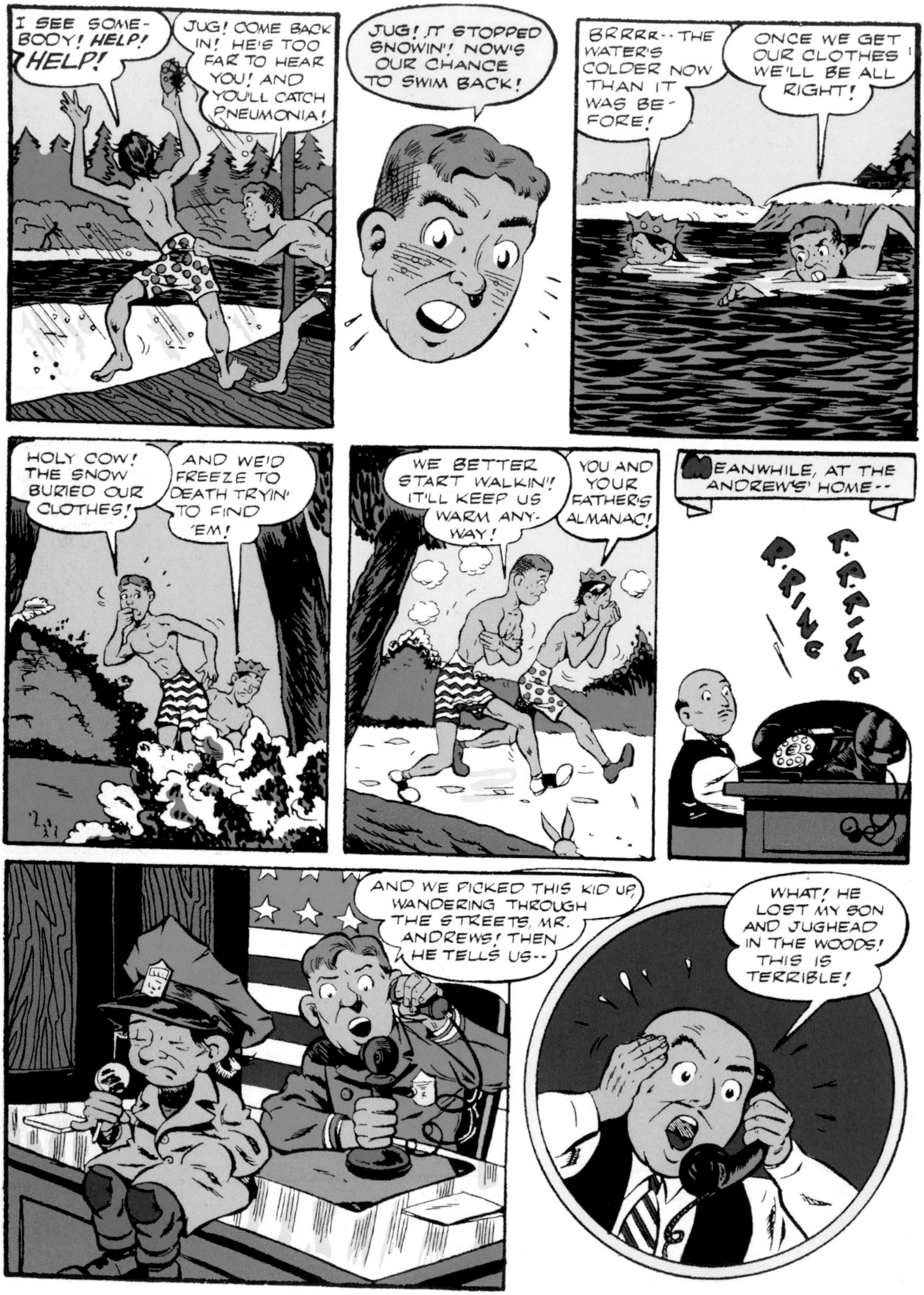
I SEE SOME-BODY! HELP! HELP!
JUG! COME BACK IN! HE'S TOO FAR TO HEAR YOU! AND YOU'LL CATCH PNEUMONIA!
JUG! IT STOPPED SNOWIN'! NOW'S OUR CHANCE TO SWIM BACK!
BRRRR-- THE WATER'S COLDER NOW THAN IT WAS BE-FORE!
ONCE WE GET OUR CLOTHES WE'LL BE ALL RIGHT!
HOLY COW! THE SNOW BURIED OUR CLOTHES!
AND WE'D FREEZE TO DEATH TRYIN' TO FIND 'EM!
WE BETTER START WALKIN'! IT'LL KEEP US WARM ANY-WAY!
YOU AND YOUR FATHER'S ALMANAC!
MEANWHILE, AT THE ANDREW'S' HOME--
R-RING
R-R-RING
AND WE PICKED THIS KID UP, WANDERING THROUGH THE STREETS, MR. ANDREWS! THEN HE TELLS US--
WHAT! HE LOST MY SON AND JUGHEAD IN THE WOODS! THIS IS TERRIBLE!

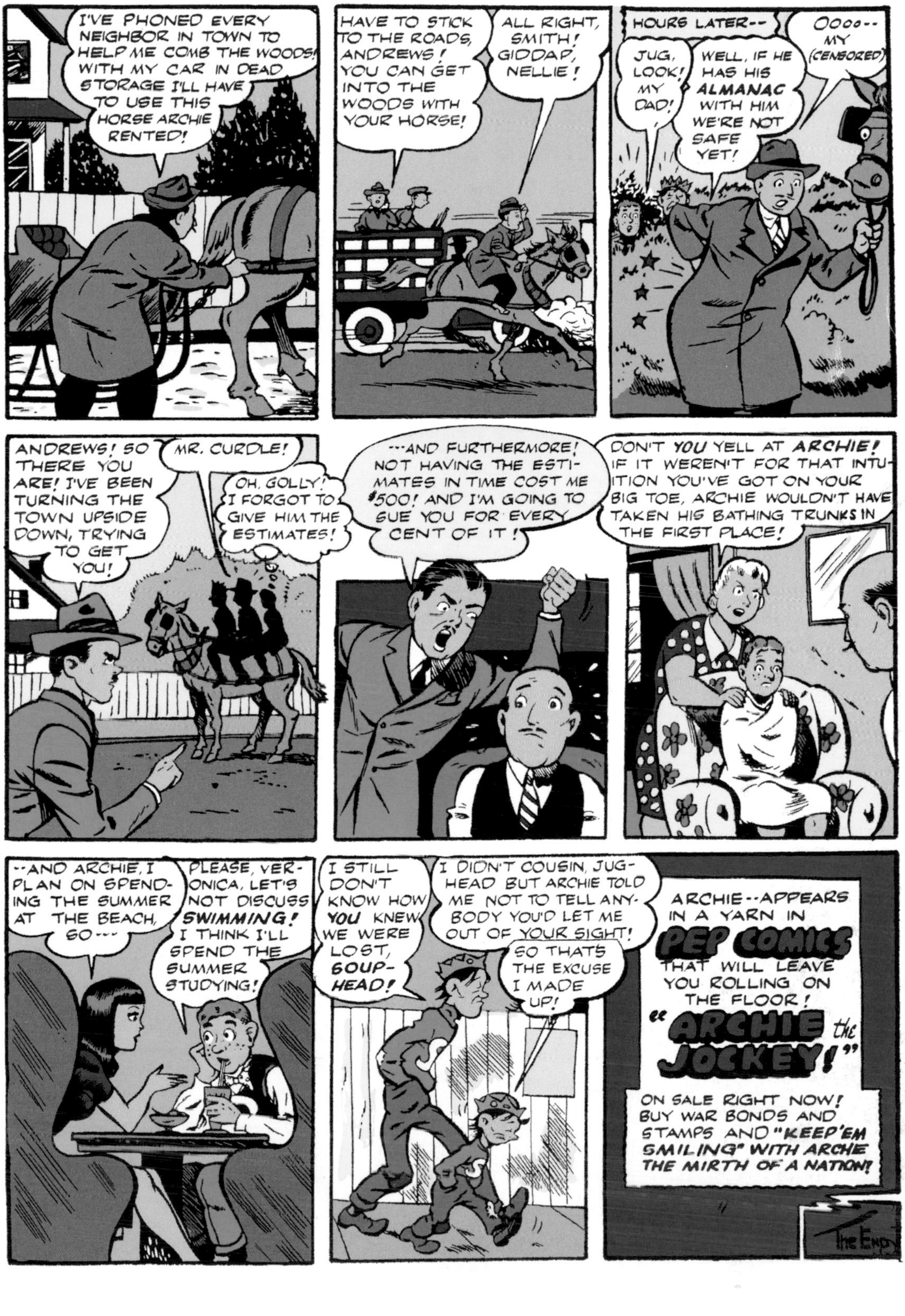
I'VE PHONED EVERY NEIGHBOR IN TOWN TO HELP ME COMB THE WOODS! WITH MY CAR IN DEAD STORAGE I'LL HAVE TO USE THIS HORSE ARCHIE RENTED!
HAVE TO STICK TO THE ROADS, ANDREWS! YOU CAN GET INTO THE WOODS WITH YOUR HORSE!
ALL RIGHT, SMITH! GIDDAP, NELLIE!
HOURS LATER--
JUG, LOOK! MY DAD!
WELL, IF HE HAS HIS ALMANAC WITH HIM WE'RE NOT SAFE YET!
Oooo-- MY (CENSORED)
ANDREWS! SO THERE YOU ARE! I'VE BEEN TURNING THE TOWN UPSIDE DOWN, TRYING TO GET YOU!
MR. CURDLE!
OH, GOLLY! I FORGOT TO GIVE HIM THE ESTIMATES!
---AND FURTHERMORE! NOT HAVING THE ESTIMATES IN TIME COST ME $500! AND I'M GOING TO SUE YOU FOR EVERY CENT OF IT!
DON'T YOU YELL AT ARCHIE! IF IT WEREN'T FOR THAT INTUITION YOU'VE GOT ON YOUR BIG TOE, ARCHIE WOULDN'T HAVE TAKEN HIS BATHING TRUNKS IN THE FIRST PLACE!
--AND ARCHIE, I PLAN ON SPENDING THE SUMMER AT THE BEACH, SO---
PLEASE, VERONICA, LET'S NOT DISCUSS SWIMMING! I THINK I'LL SPEND THE SUMMER STUDYING!
I STILL DON'T KNOW HOW YOU KNEW WE WERE LOST, SOUPHEAD!
I DIDN'T COUSIN, JUGHEAD BUT ARCHIE TOLD ME NOT TO TELL ANYBODY YOU'D LET ME OUT OF YOUR SIGHT!
SO THAT'S THE EXCUSE I MADE UP!
ARCHIE--APPEARS IN A YARN IN PEP COMICS THAT WILL LEAVE YOU ROLLING ON THE FLOOR! "ARCHIE the JOCKEY!"
ON SALE RIGHT NOW! BUY WAR BONDS AND STAMPS AND "KEEP'EM SMILING" WITH ARCHIE THE MIRTH OF A NATION!
The End

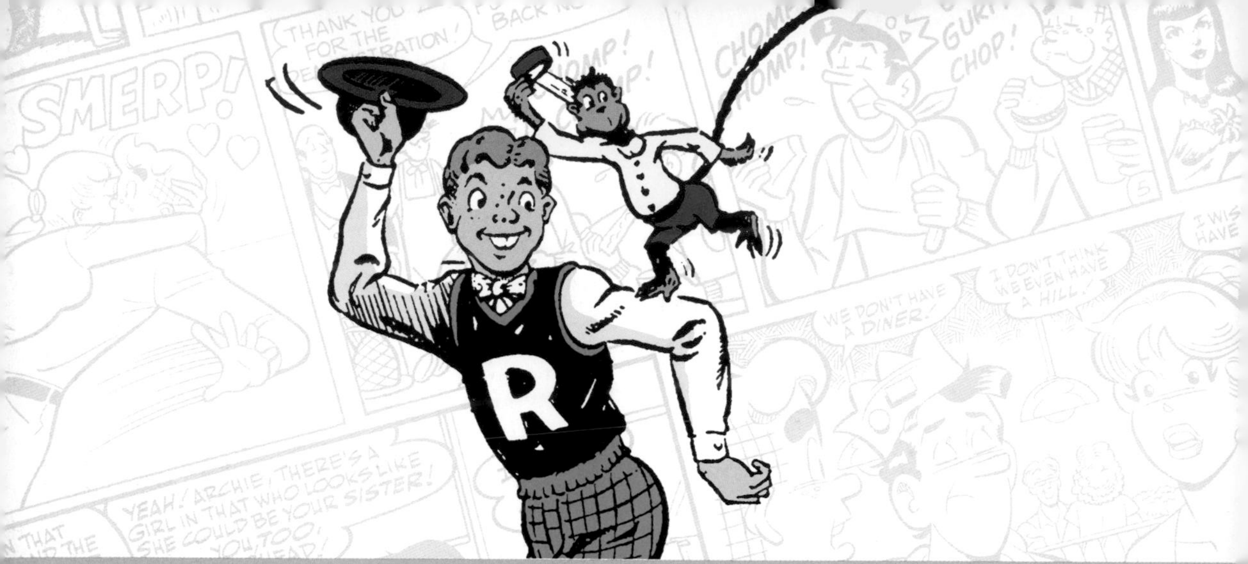
SMERP!
WE DON'T HAVE A DINER.
I DON'T THINK WE EVEN HAVE A HILL.

MONKEY SHINES
ARCHIE #16, 1945
BY BOB MONTANA

If comic book history has taught us anything, it's that people love primates. There's a long account of the success simians have on the covers and interiors of my favorite medium—and Archie Comics joins in the knuckle-dragging fun with this classic tale. Old-school Archie was always making poor decisions that wrecked his house, so what could possibly go wrong when he brings home a monkey? To put it briefly: the Andrews' household goes bananas! Soon enough, the little guy has mimicked his way through Riverdale in the most destructive game of "Monkey See, Monkey Do" ever! Learn how insincere imitation can be when it comes from the animal kingdom!

—Jonathan Betancourt
Director of Book Sales & Operations,
Archie Comics

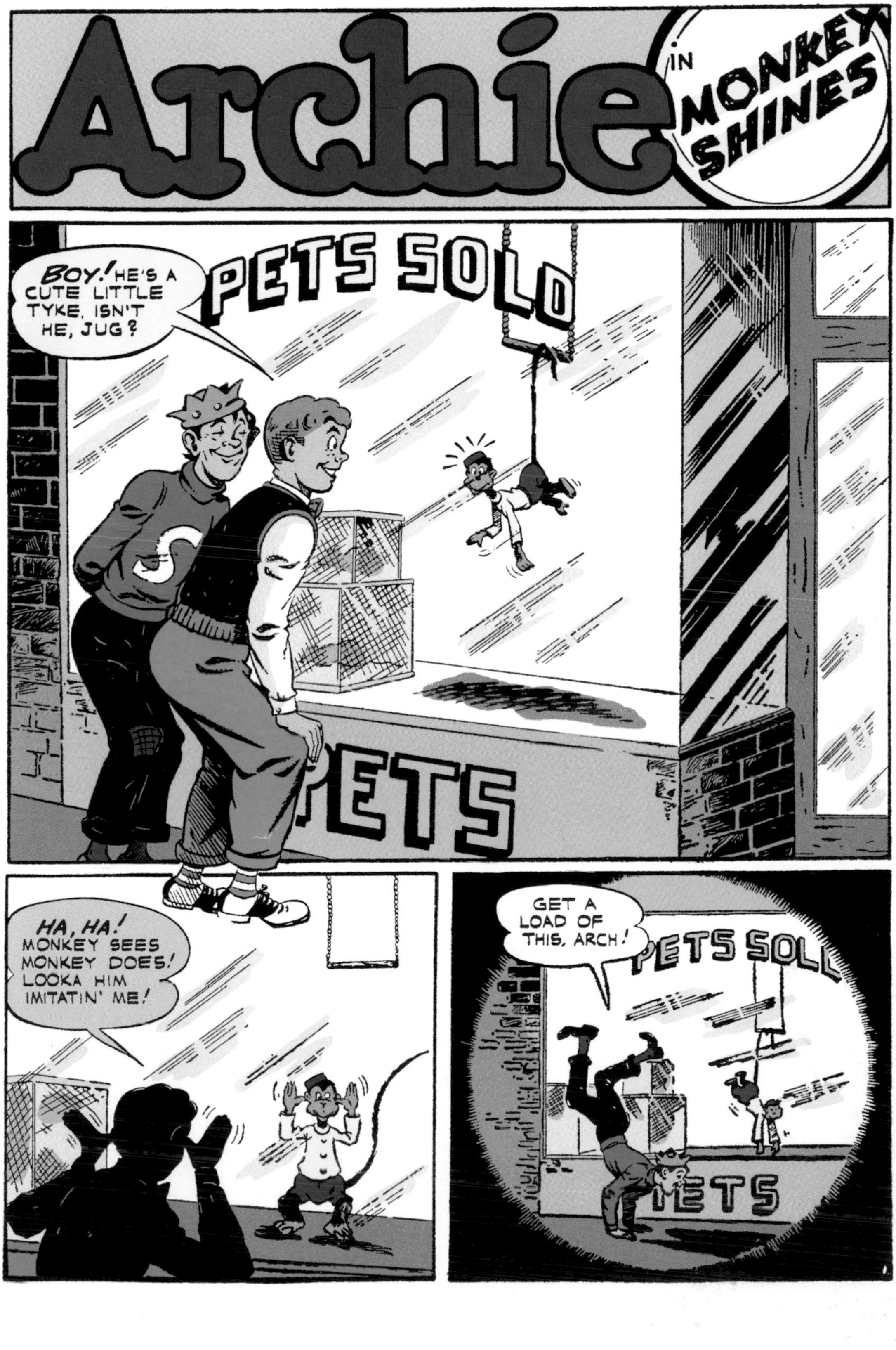
Archie
IN
MONKEY SHINES
PETS SOLD
BOY! HE'S A CUTE LITTLE TYKE, ISN'T HE, JUG?
PETS
HA, HA! MONKEY SEES MONKEY DOES! LOOKA HIM IMITATIN' ME!
GET A LOAD OF THIS, ARCH!
PETS SOLL
PETS

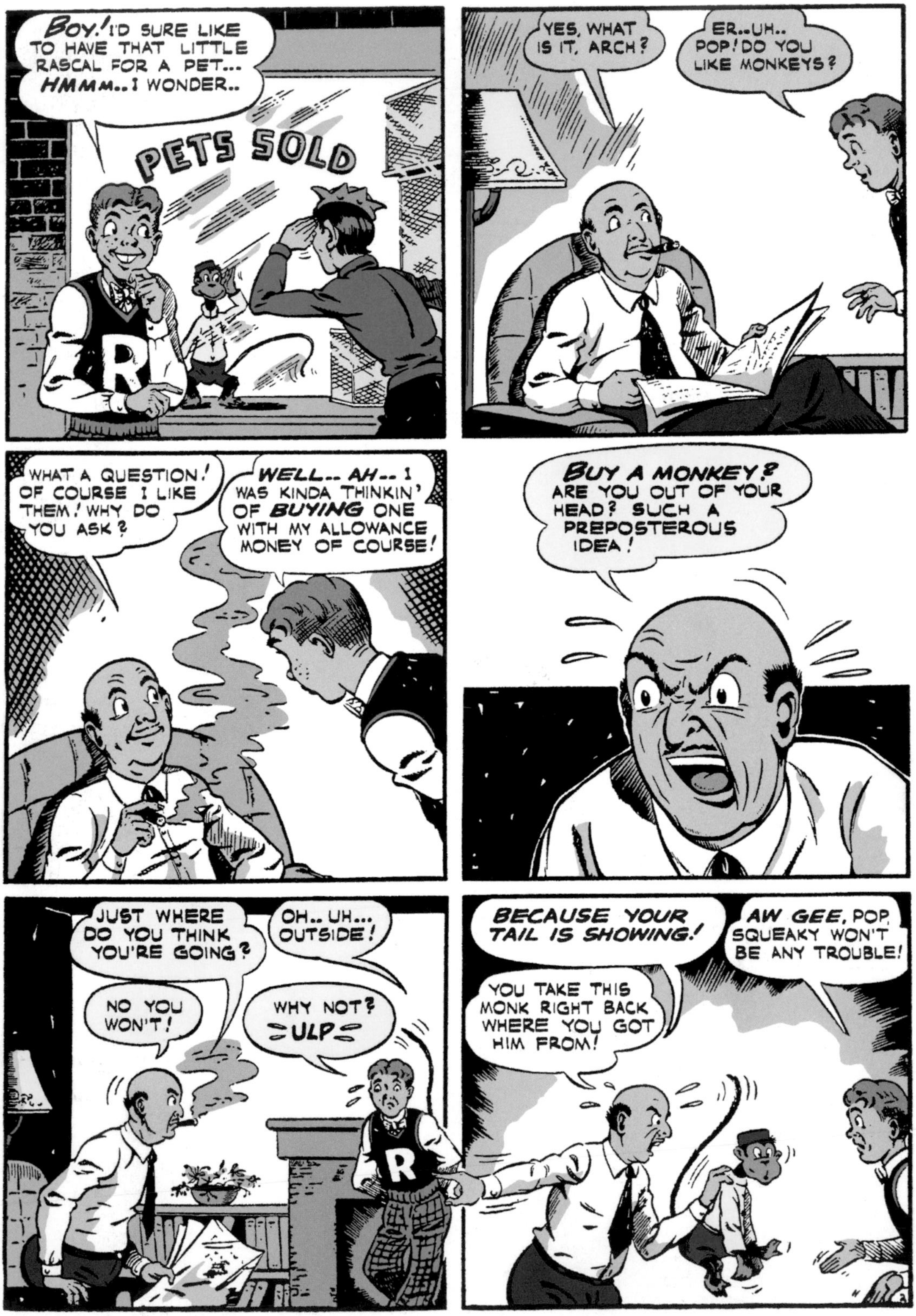
BOY! I'D SURE LIKE TO HAVE THAT LITTLE RASCAL FOR A PET... HMMM.. I WONDER..
PETS SOLD
YES, WHAT IS IT, ARCH?
ER..UH.. POP! DO YOU LIKE MONKEYS?
WHAT A QUESTION! OF COURSE I LIKE THEM! WHY DO YOU ASK?
WELL.. AH.. I WAS KINDA THINKIN' OF BUYING ONE WITH MY ALLOWANCE MONEY OF COURSE!
BUY A MONKEY? ARE YOU OUT OF YOUR HEAD? SUCH A PREPOSTEROUS IDEA!
JUST WHERE DO YOU THINK YOU'RE GOING?
OH.. UH... OUTSIDE!
NO YOU WON'T!
WHY NOT? ULP
BECAUSE YOUR TAIL IS SHOWING!
AW GEE, POP, SQUEAKY WON'T BE ANY TROUBLE!
YOU TAKE THIS MONK RIGHT BACK WHERE YOU GOT HIM FROM!

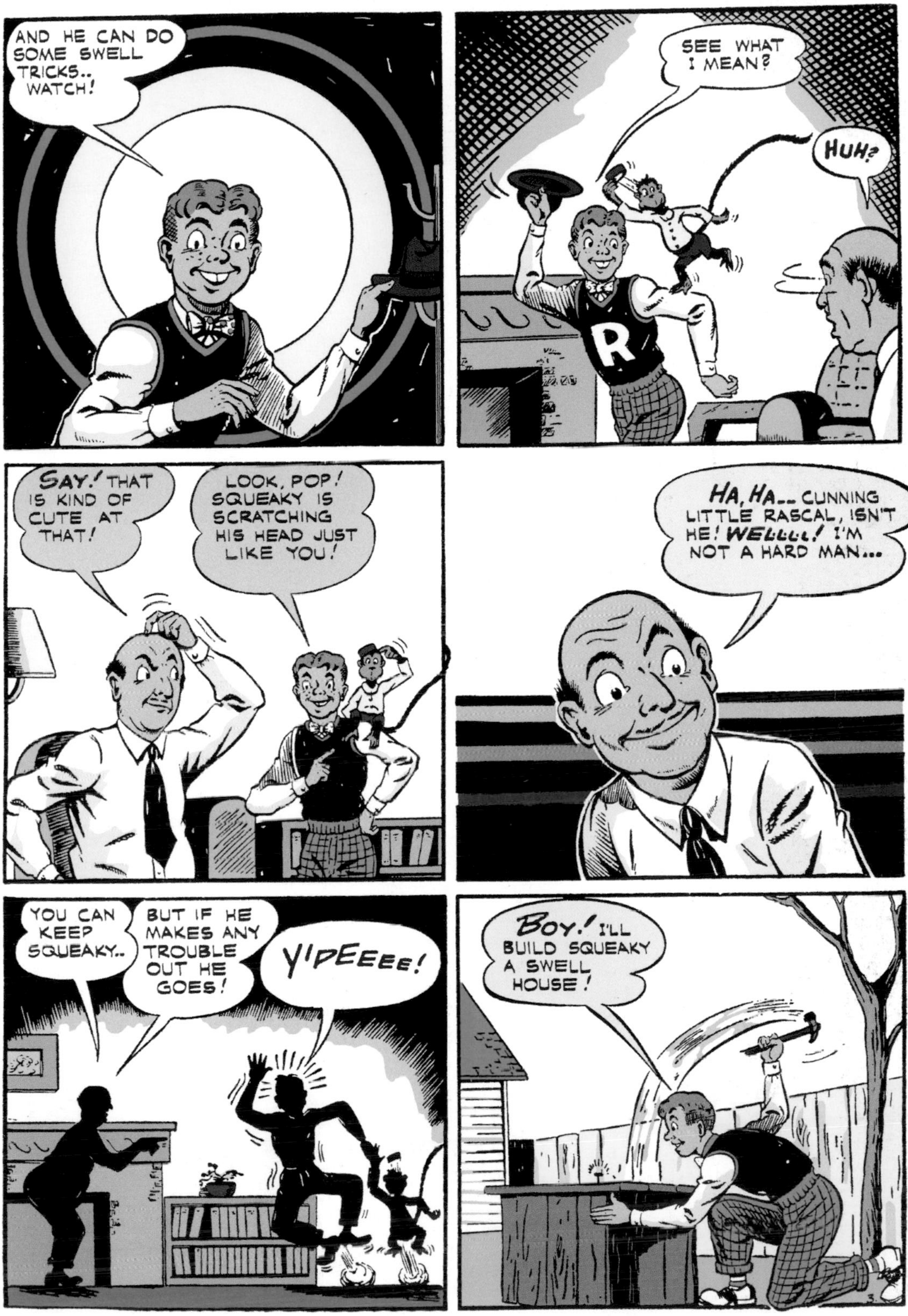
AND HE CAN DO SOME SWELL TRICKS.. WATCH!
SEE WHAT I MEAN?
HUH?
SAY! THAT IS KIND OF CUTE AT THAT!
LOOK, POP! SQUEAKY IS SCRATCHING HIS HEAD JUST LIKE YOU!
HA, HA... CUNNING LITTLE RASCAL, ISN'T HE! WELLLLL! I'M NOT A HARD MAN...
YOU CAN KEEP SQUEAKY..
BUT IF HE MAKES ANY TROUBLE OUT HE GOES!
Y'IPEEEEE!
BOY! I'LL BUILD SQUEAKY A SWELL HOUSE!

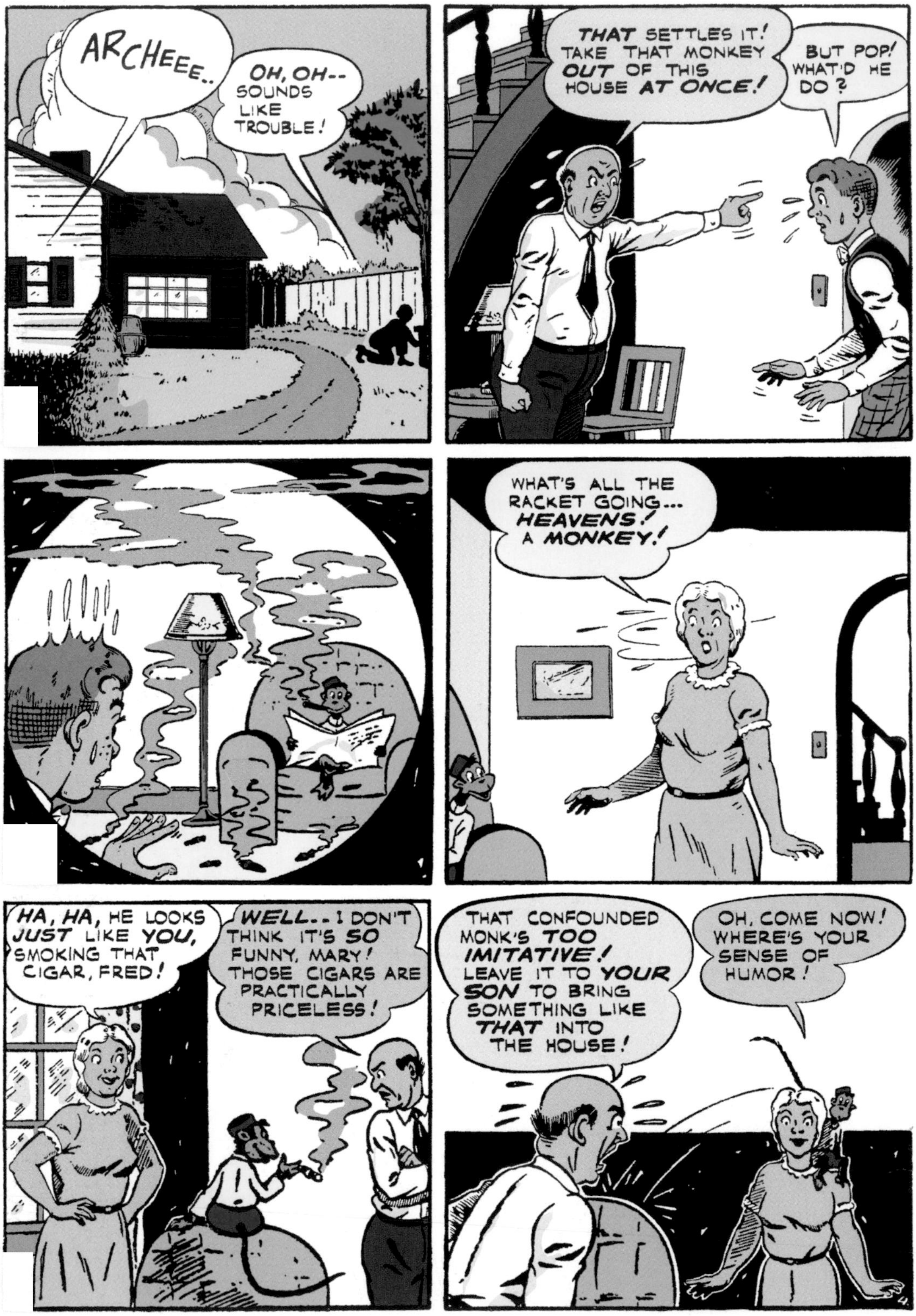
ARCHEEE..
OH, OH-- SOUNDS LIKE TROUBLE!
THAT SETTLES IT! TAKE THAT MONKEY OUT OF THIS HOUSE AT ONCE!
BUT POP! WHAT'D HE DO?
WHAT'S ALL THE RACKET GOING... HEAVENS! A MONKEY!
HA, HA, HE LOOKS JUST LIKE YOU, SMOKING THAT CIGAR, FRED!
WELL.. I DON'T THINK IT'S SO FUNNY, MARY! THOSE CIGARS ARE PRACTICALLY PRICELESS!
THAT CONFOUNDED MONK'S TOO IMITATIVE! LEAVE IT TO YOUR SON TO BRING SOMETHING LIKE THAT INTO THE HOUSE!
OH, COME NOW! WHERE'S YOUR SENSE OF HUMOR!
4.

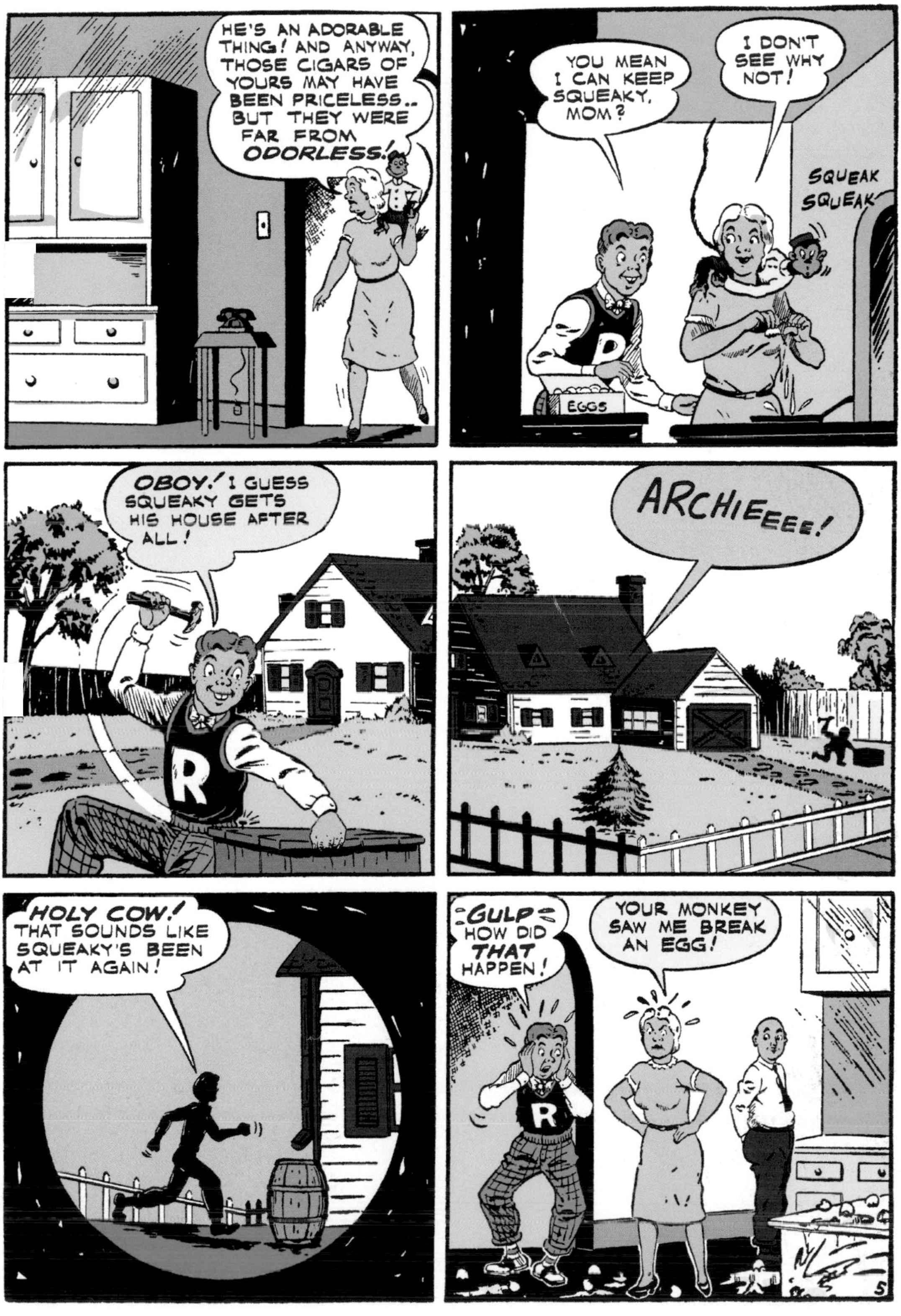
HE'S AN ADORABLE THING! AND ANYWAY, THOSE CIGARS OF YOURS MAY HAVE BEEN PRICELESS.. BUT THEY WERE FAR FROM ODORLESS!
YOU MEAN I CAN KEEP SQUEAKY, MOM?
I DON'T SEE WHY NOT!
SQUEAK SQUEAK
EGGS
OBOY! I GUESS SQUEAKY GETS HIS HOUSE AFTER ALL!
ARCHIEEEEE!
HOLY COW! THAT SOUNDS LIKE SQUEAKY'S BEEN AT IT AGAIN!
GULP HOW DID THAT HAPPEN!
YOUR MONKEY SAW ME BREAK AN EGG!
5

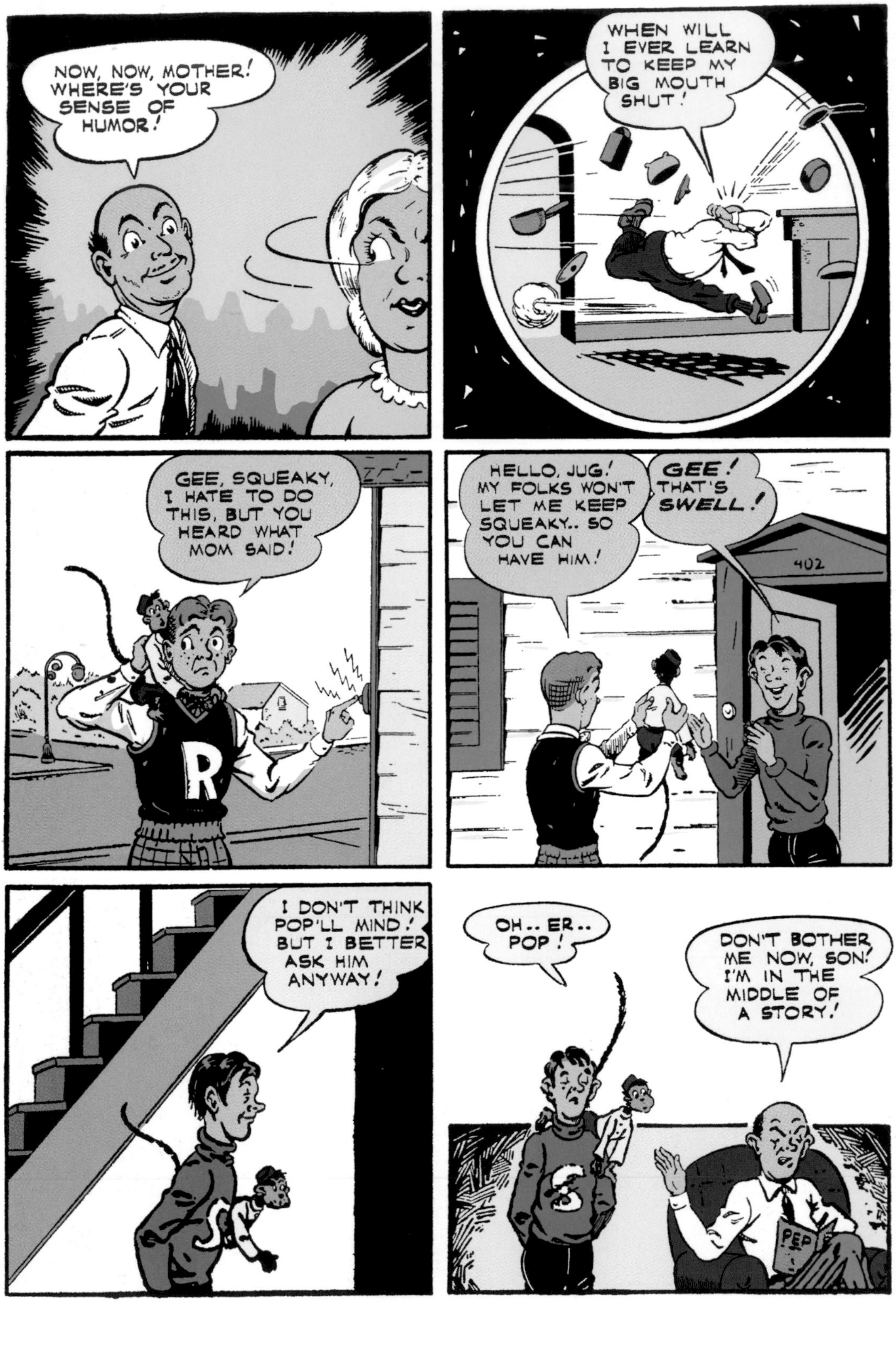
NOW, NOW, MOTHER! WHERE'S YOUR SENSE OF HUMOR!
WHEN WILL I EVER LEARN TO KEEP MY BIG MOUTH SHUT!
GEE, SQUEAKY, I HATE TO DO THIS, BUT YOU HEARD WHAT MOM SAID!
HELLO, JUG! MY FOLKS WON'T LET ME KEEP SQUEAKY.. SO YOU CAN HAVE HIM!
GEE! THAT'S SWELL!
402
I DON'T THINK POP'LL MIND! BUT I BETTER ASK HIM ANYWAY!
OH.. ER.. POP!
DON'T BOTHER ME NOW, SON! I'M IN THE MIDDLE OF A STORY!
PEP

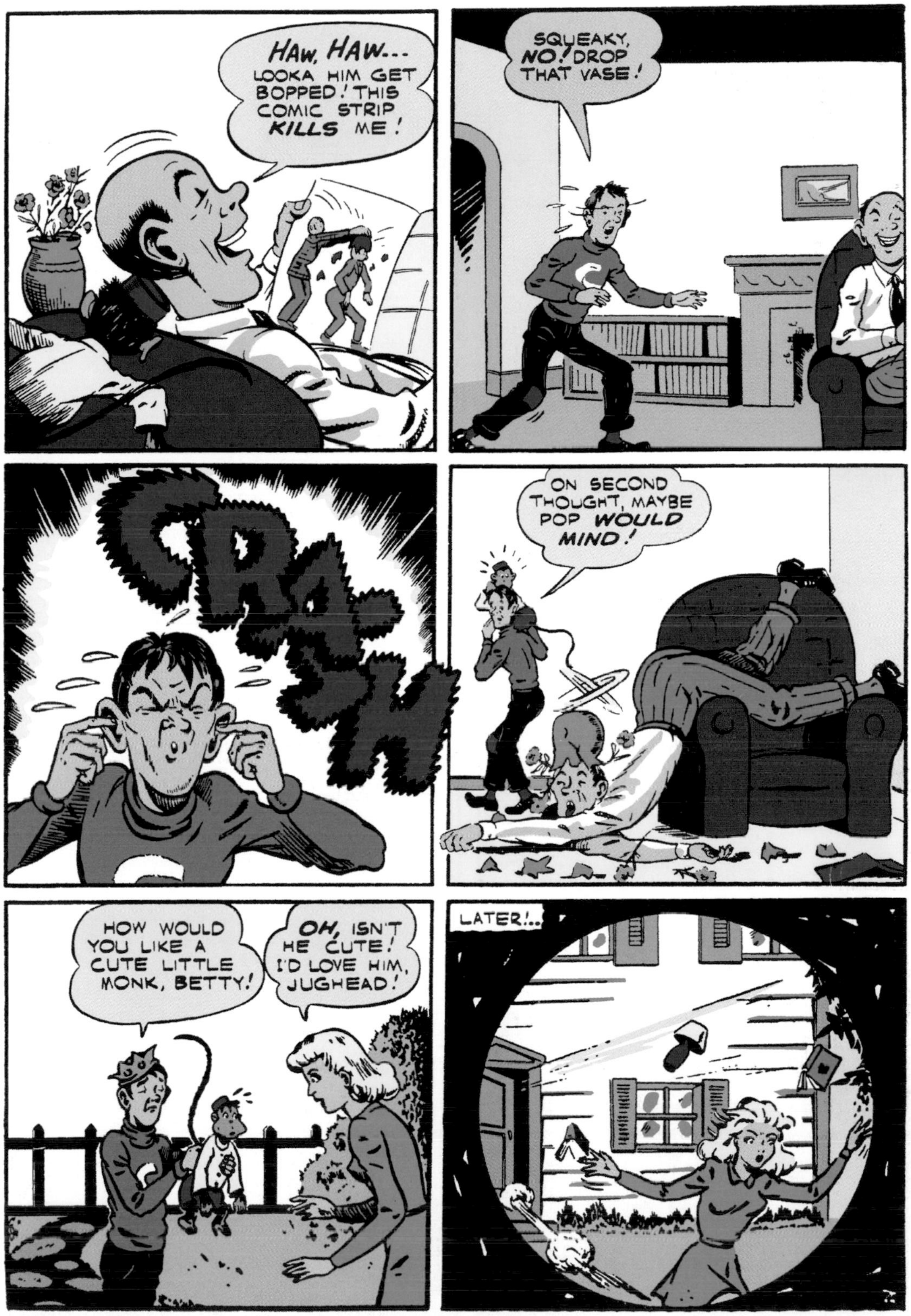
HAW, HAW... LOOKA HIM GET BOPPED! THIS COMIC STRIP KILLS ME!
SQUEAKY, NO! DROP THAT VASE!
CRASH
ON SECOND THOUGHT, MAYBE POP WOULD MIND!
HOW WOULD YOU LIKE A CUTE LITTLE MONK, BETTY!
OH, ISN'T HE CUTE! I'D LOVE HIM, JUGHEAD!
LATER!..

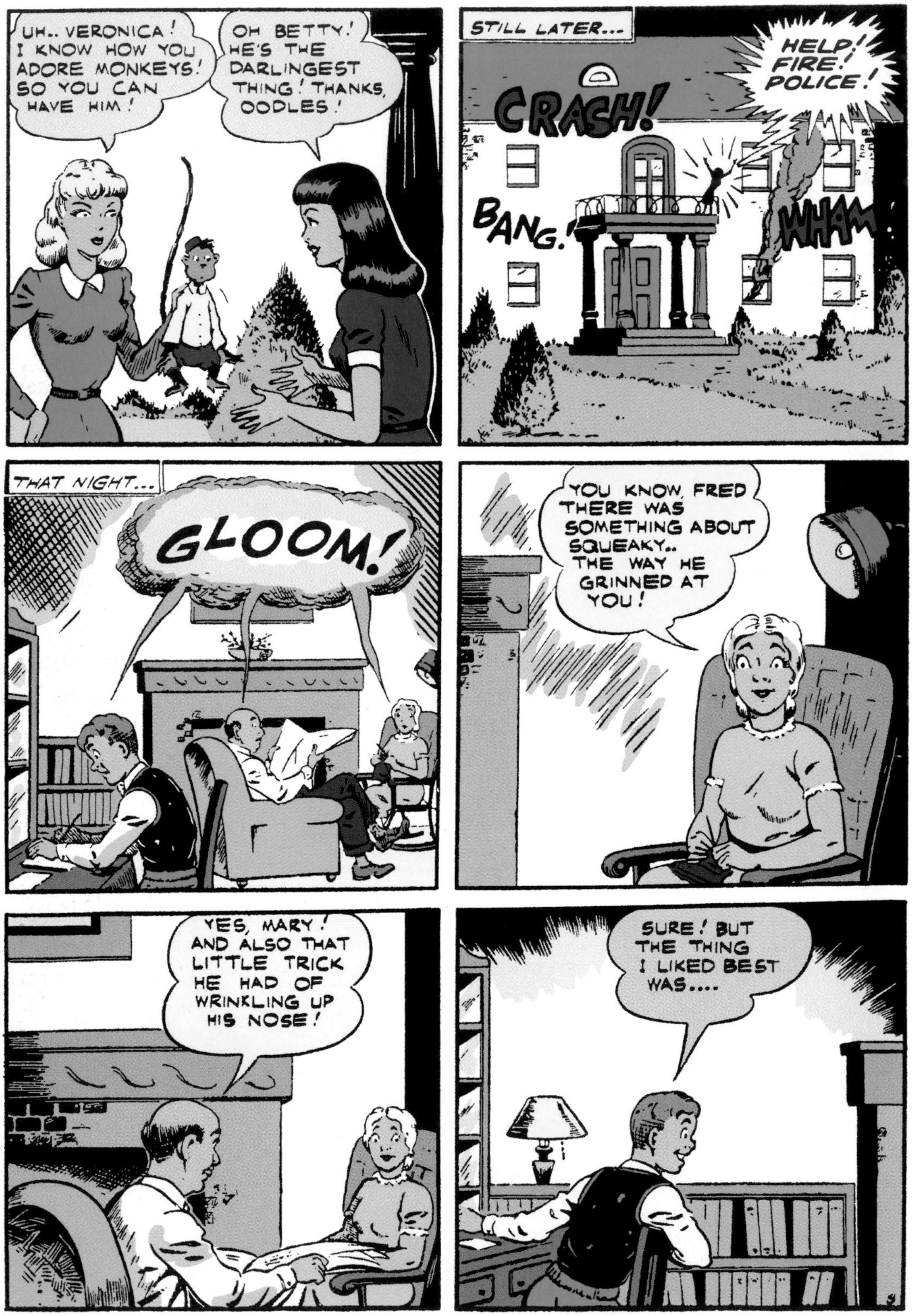
UH.. VERONICA! I KNOW HOW YOU ADORE MONKEYS! SO YOU CAN HAVE HIM!
OH BETTY! HE'S THE DARLINGEST THING! THANKS, OODLES!
STILL LATER...
HELP! FIRE! POLICE!
CRASH!
BANG!
WHAM
THAT NIGHT...
GLOOM!
YOU KNOW, FRED THERE WAS SOMETHING ABOUT SQUEAKY.. THE WAY HE GRINNED AT YOU!
YES, MARY! AND ALSO THAT LITTLE TRICK HE HAD OF WRINKLING UP HIS NOSE!
SURE! BUT THE THING I LIKED BEST WAS....

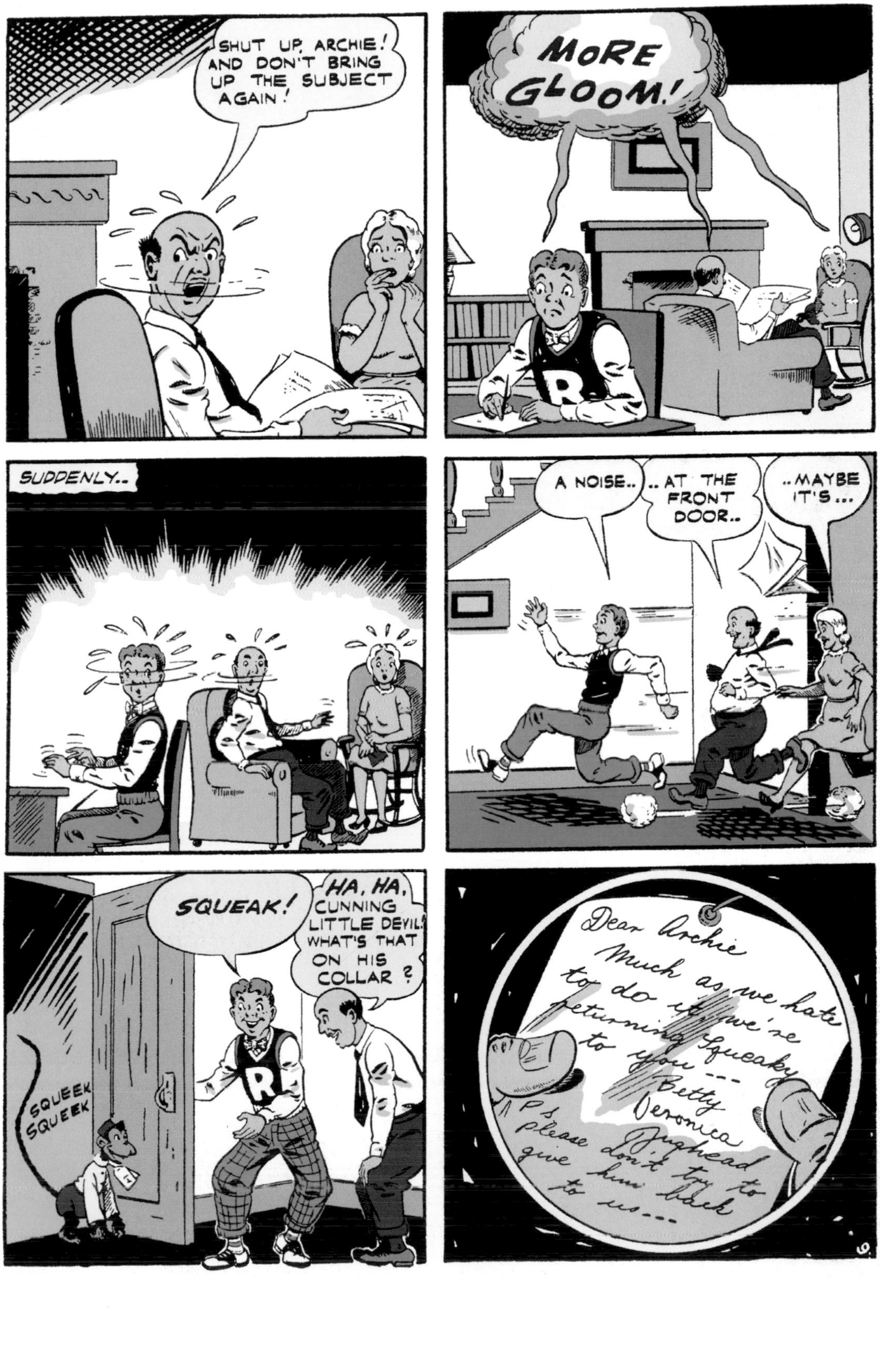
SHUT UP, ARCHIE! AND DON'T BRING UP THE SUBJECT AGAIN!
MORE GLOOM!
SUDDENLY..
A NOISE..
.. AT THE FRONT DOOR..
..MAYBE IT'S...
SQUEAK!
HA, HA, CUNNING LITTLE DEVIL! WHAT'S THAT ON HIS COLLAR?
SQUEEK SQUEEK
Dear Archie
Much as we hate to do it, we're returning Squeaky to you ---
Betty
Veronica
Jughead
P.S. please don't try to give him back to us ---

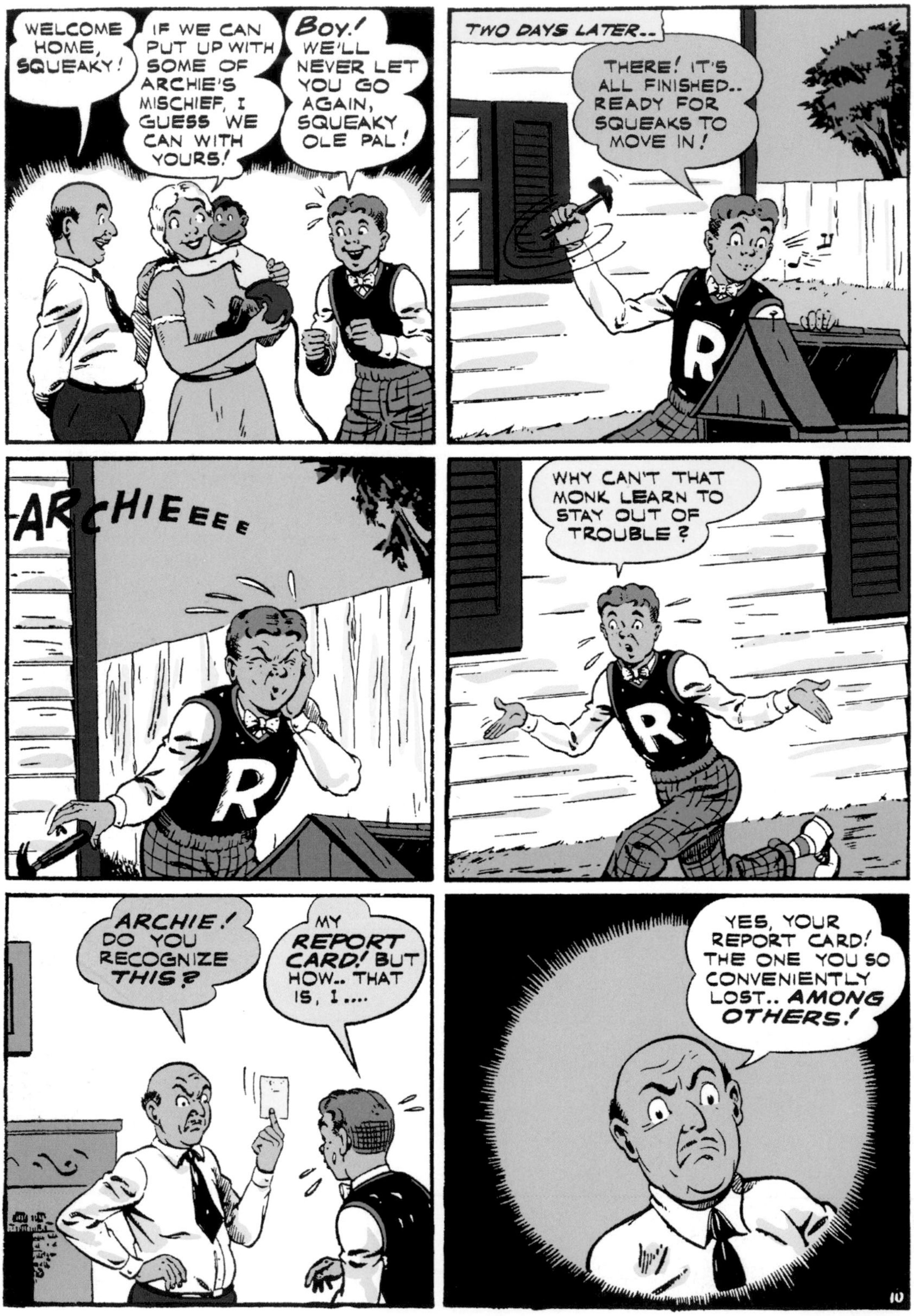
WELCOME HOME, SQUEAKY!
IF WE CAN PUT UP WITH SOME OF ARCHIE'S MISCHIEF, I GUESS WE CAN WITH YOURS!
BOY! WE'LL NEVER LET YOU GO AGAIN, SQUEAKY OLE PAL!
TWO DAYS LATER..
THERE! IT'S ALL FINISHED.. READY FOR SQUEAKS TO MOVE IN!
ARCHIEEEEE
WHY CAN'T THAT MONK LEARN TO STAY OUT OF TROUBLE?
ARCHIE! DO YOU RECOGNIZE THIS?
MY REPORT CARD! BUT HOW.. THAT IS, I....
YES, YOUR REPORT CARD! THE ONE YOU SO CONVENIENTLY LOST.. AMONG OTHERS!
10

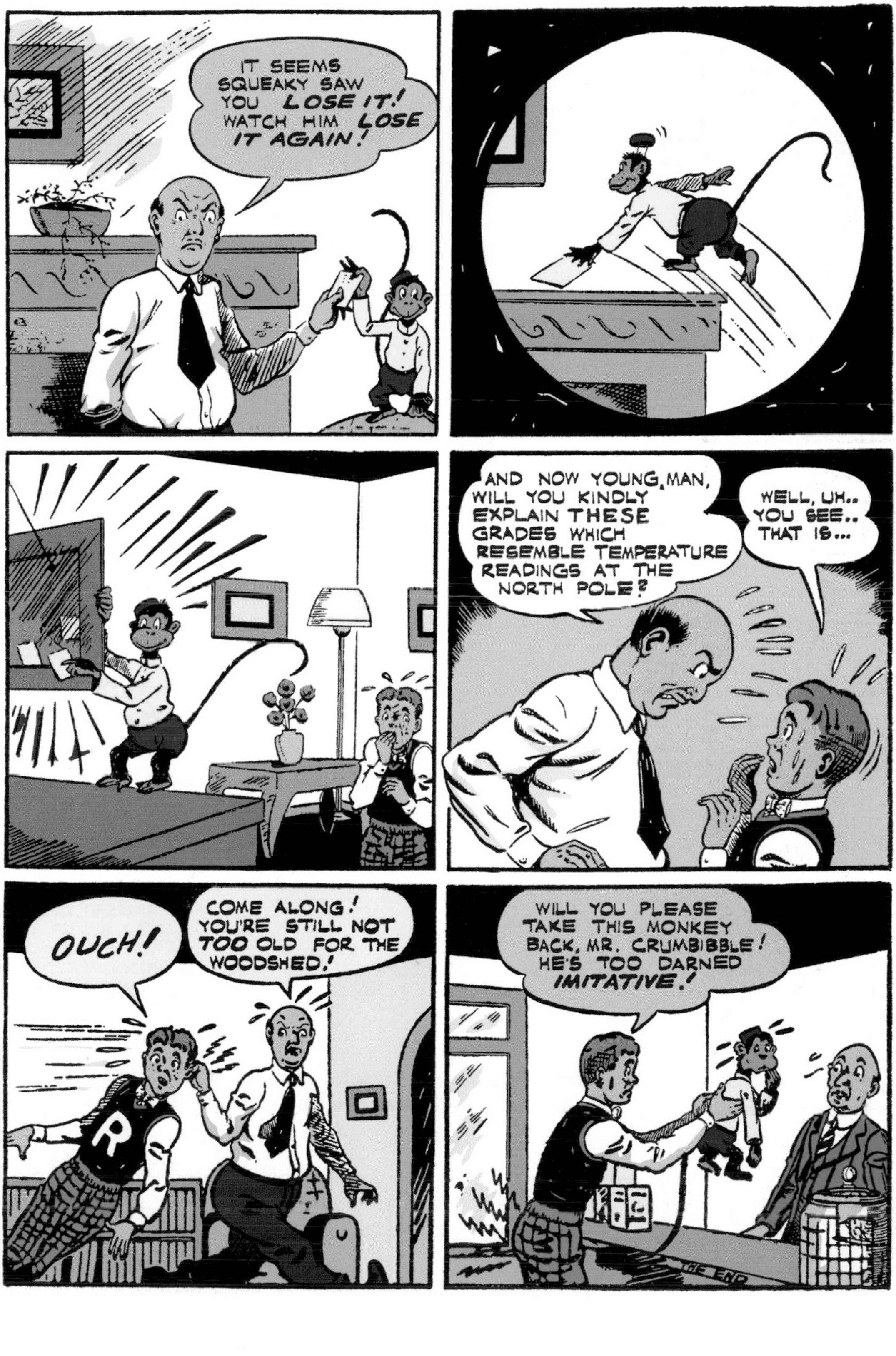
IT SEEMS SQUEAKY SAW YOU LOSE IT! WATCH HIM LOSE IT AGAIN!
AND NOW YOUNG MAN, WILL YOU KINDLY EXPLAIN THESE GRADES WHICH RESEMBLE TEMPERATURE READINGS AT THE NORTH POLE?
WELL, UH.. YOU SEE.. THAT IS...
OUCH!
COME ALONG! YOU'RE STILL NOT TOO OLD FOR THE WOODSHED!
WILL YOU PLEASE TAKE THIS MONKEY BACK, MR. CRUMBIBBLE! HE'S TOO DARNED IMITATIVE!
THE END

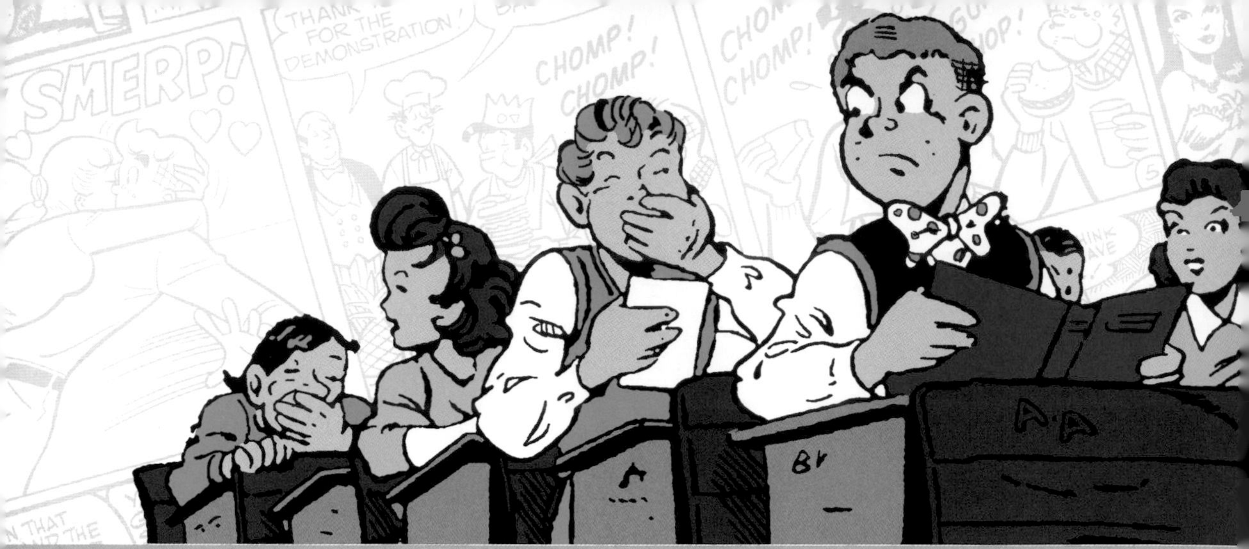
SMERP!
FOR THE DEMONSTRATION!
CHOMP! CHOMP!

TIME FOR TROUBLE
ARCHIE #7, 1945
BY HARRY SAHLE & GINGER

This tale's title could be the story of Archie's life! One of the themes the 1940s stories particularly excelled at was "misunderstandings." Amidst the chaos the script stays true to the characters and the art brilliantly fills each panel with exactly what's needed. An hysterical "comedy of errors"!

—Paul Castiglia
Writer & Archivist,
Archie Comics

CAMERA BUGS
PEP #48, 1946
BY ED GOGGIN, HARRY SAHLE & GINGER

One of the funniest stories of the 1940s! The entire plot hinges on a comedy of errors brought on by photos shot at incorrect angles. As such, there is the type of innuendo present that one would see in a Marx Brothers movie or later on in the sitcom *Three's Company*; and yet the sheer silliness of it all keeps it from being inappropriate for children. A great example of the mastery of Archie's writers and artists in creating stories that both adults and children could enjoy. BONUS: A caricature of 1940s Archie Comics editor Harry Shorten appears in one panel.

—Paul Castiglia
Writer & Archivist,
Archie Comics

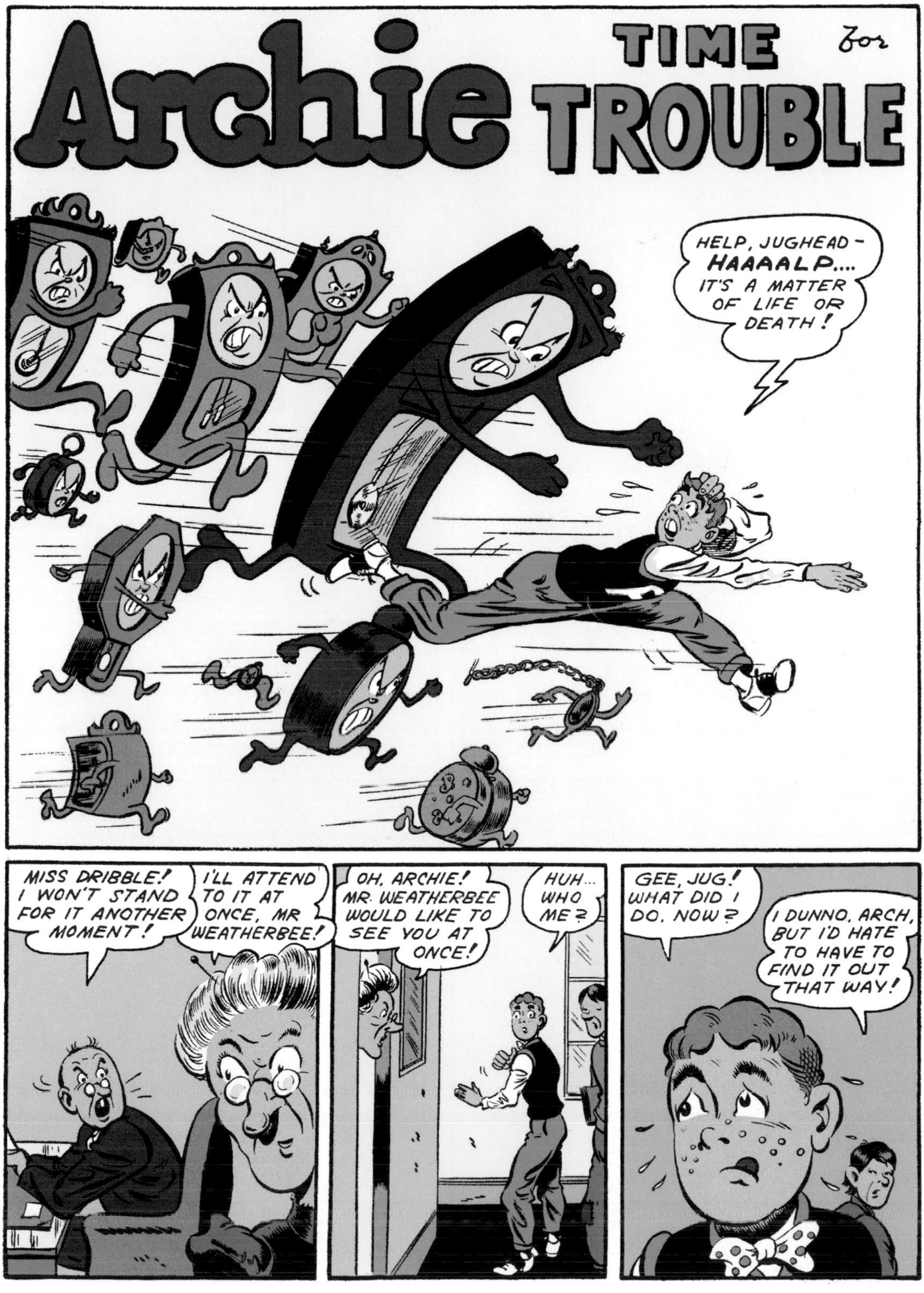
Archie
TIME for TROUBLE
HELP, JUGHEAD - HAAAALP.... IT'S A MATTER OF LIFE OR DEATH!
MISS DRIBBLE! I WON'T STAND FOR IT ANOTHER MOMENT!
I'LL ATTEND TO IT AT ONCE, MR WEATHERBEE!
OH, ARCHIE! MR. WEATHERBEE WOULD LIKE TO SEE YOU AT ONCE!
HUH... WHO ME?
GEE, JUG! WHAT DID I DO, NOW?
I DUNNO, ARCH, BUT I'D HATE TO HAVE TO FIND IT OUT THAT WAY!

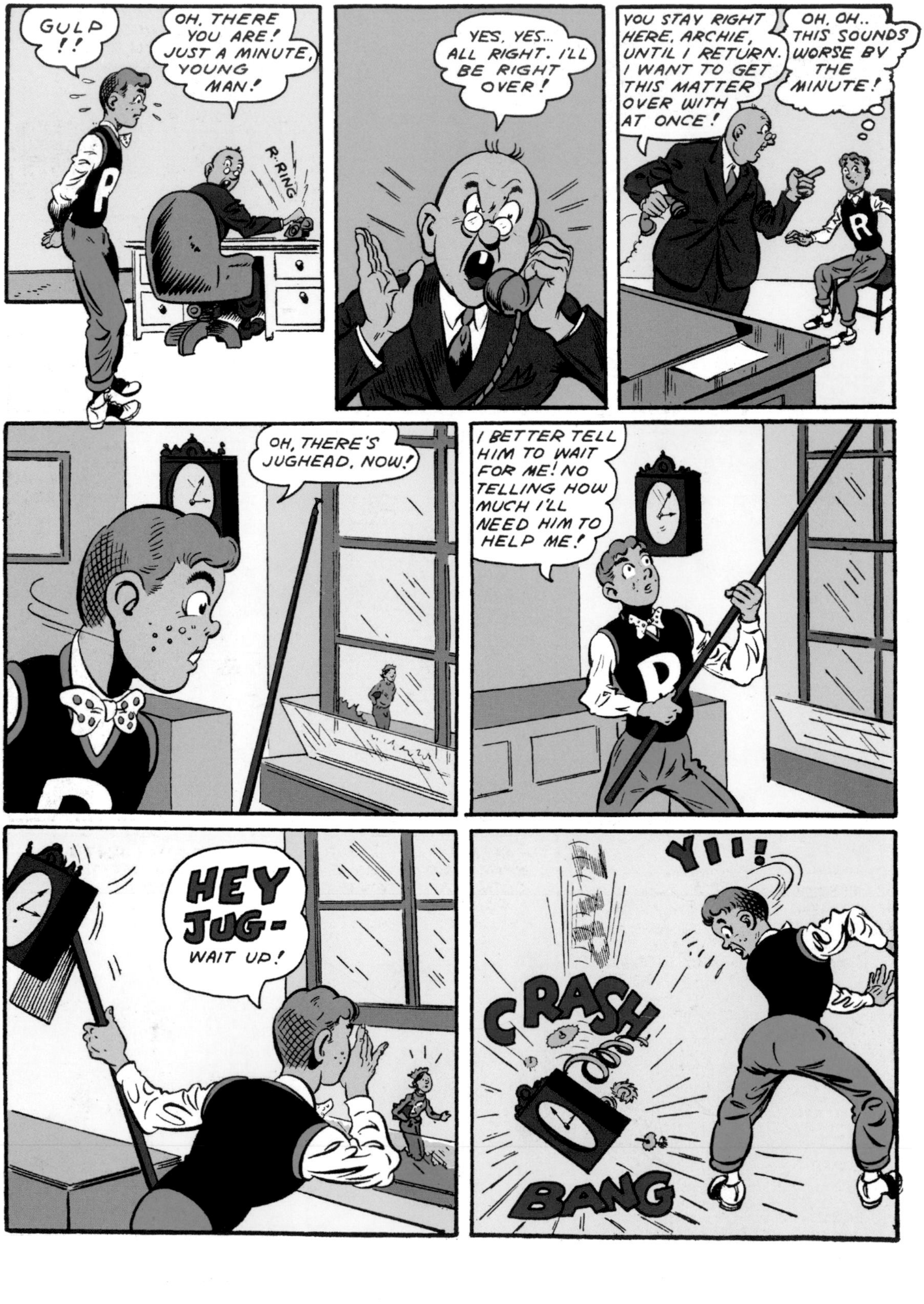
GULP !!
OH, THERE YOU ARE! JUST A MINUTE, YOUNG MAN!
R-RING
YES, YES... ALL RIGHT. I'LL BE RIGHT OVER!
YOU STAY RIGHT HERE, ARCHIE, UNTIL I RETURN. I WANT TO GET THIS MATTER OVER WITH AT ONCE!
OH, OH.. THIS SOUNDS WORSE BY THE MINUTE!
OH, THERE'S JUGHEAD, NOW!
I BETTER TELL HIM TO WAIT FOR ME! NO TELLING HOW MUCH I'LL NEED HIM TO HELP ME!
HEY JUG- WAIT UP!
YII!
CRASH
BANG

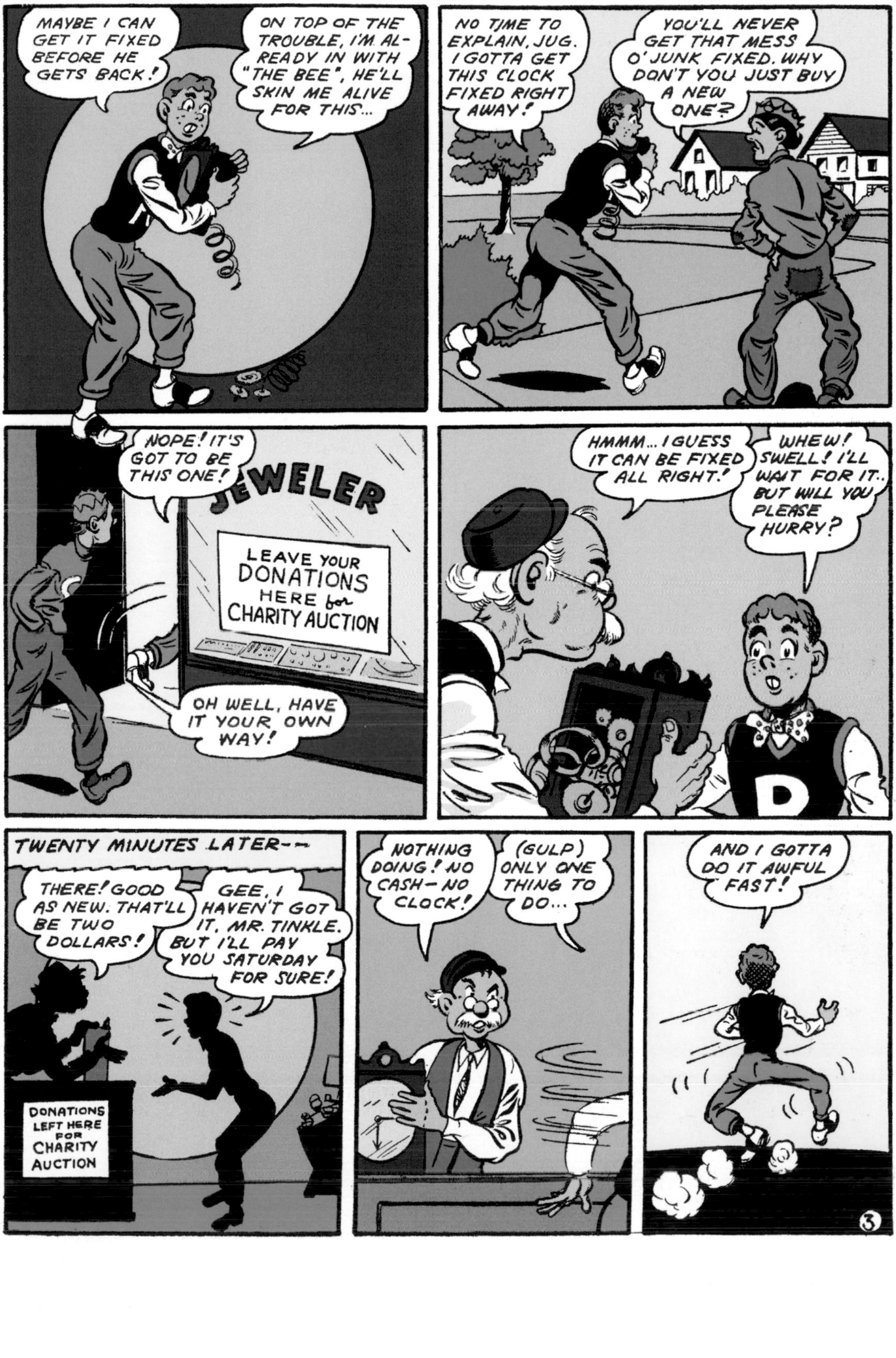
MAYBE I CAN GET IT FIXED BEFORE HE GETS BACK!
ON TOP OF THE TROUBLE, I'M ALREADY IN WITH "THE BEE", HE'LL SKIN ME ALIVE FOR THIS...
NO TIME TO EXPLAIN, JUG. I GOTTA GET THIS CLOCK FIXED RIGHT AWAY!
YOU'LL NEVER GET THAT MESS O' JUNK FIXED. WHY DON'T YOU JUST BUY A NEW ONE?
NOPE! IT'S GOT TO BE THIS ONE!
JEWELER
LEAVE YOUR DONATIONS HERE for CHARITY AUCTION
OH WELL, HAVE IT YOUR OWN WAY!
HMMM... I GUESS IT CAN BE FIXED ALL RIGHT!
WHEW! SWELL! I'LL WAIT FOR IT.. BUT WILL YOU PLEASE HURRY?
TWENTY MINUTES LATER--
THERE! GOOD AS NEW. THAT'LL BE TWO DOLLARS!
GEE, I HAVEN'T GOT IT, MR. TINKLE. BUT I'LL PAY YOU SATURDAY FOR SURE!
DONATIONS LEFT HERE FOR CHARITY AUCTION
NOTHING DOING! NO CASH—NO CLOCK!
(GULP) ONLY ONE THING TO DO...
AND I GOTTA DO IT AWFUL FAST!
3

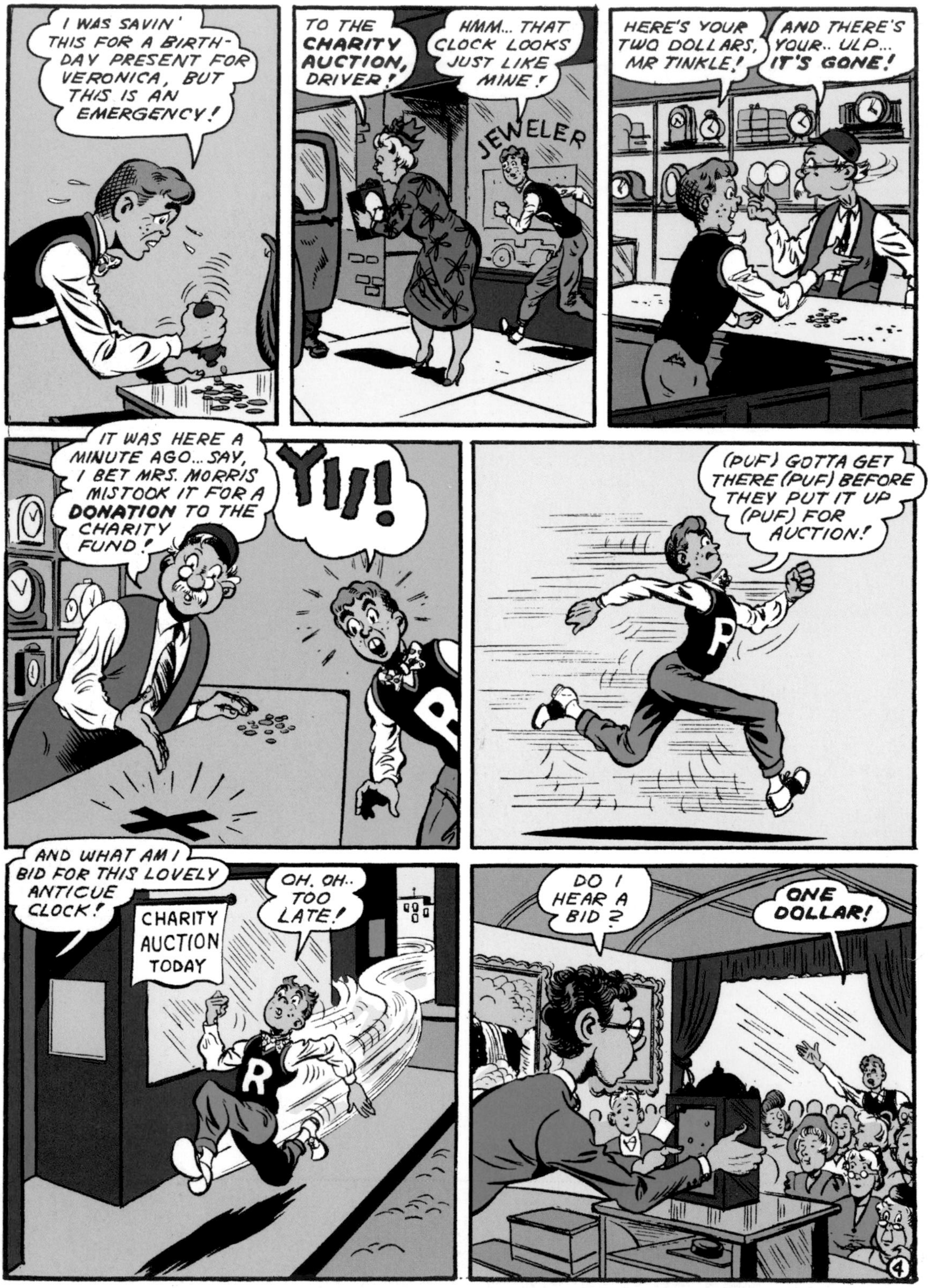
I WAS SAVIN' THIS FOR A BIRTH-DAY PRESENT FOR VERONICA, BUT THIS IS AN EMERGENCY!
TO THE CHARITY AUCTION, DRIVER!
HMM... THAT CLOCK LOOKS JUST LIKE MINE!
JEWELER
HERE'S YOUR TWO DOLLARS, MR TINKLE!
AND THERE'S YOUR.. ULP... IT'S GONE!
IT WAS HERE A MINUTE AGO... SAY, I BET MRS. MORRIS MISTOOK IT FOR A DONATION TO THE CHARITY FUND!
YI!!
(PUF) GOTTA GET THERE (PUF) BEFORE THEY PUT IT UP (PUF) FOR AUCTION!
AND WHAT AM I BID FOR THIS LOVELY ANTICUE CLOCK!
CHARITY AUCTION TODAY
OH. OH.. TOO LATE!
DO I HEAR A BID?
ONE DOLLAR!
4

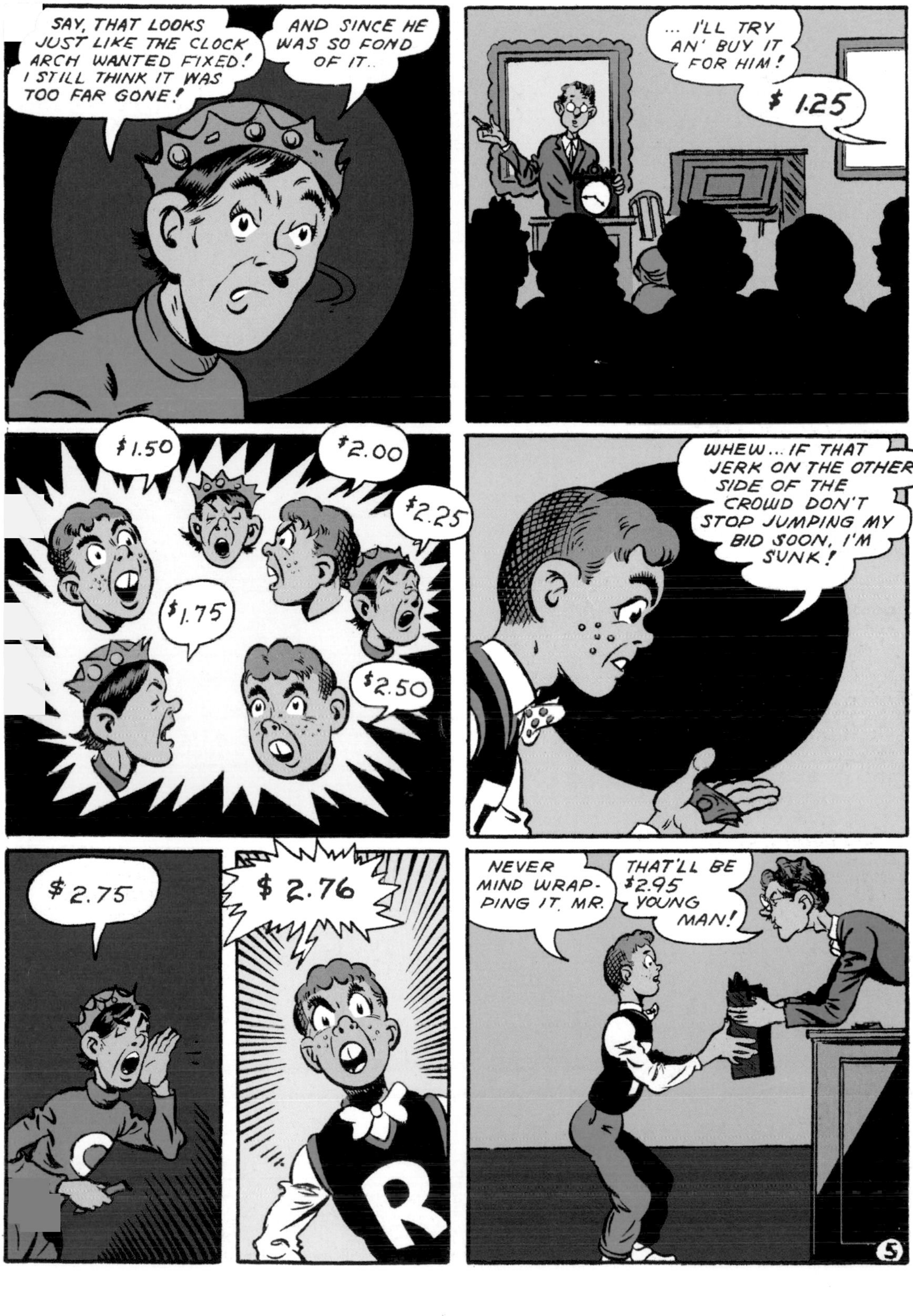
SAY, THAT LOOKS JUST LIKE THE CLOCK ARCH WANTED FIXED! I STILL THINK IT WAS TOO FAR GONE!
AND SINCE HE WAS SO FOND OF IT..
... I'LL TRY AN' BUY IT FOR HIM!
$ 1.25
$1.50
$2.00
$2.25
$1.75
$2.50
WHEW... IF THAT JERK ON THE OTHER SIDE OF THE CROWD DON'T STOP JUMPING MY BID SOON, I'M SUNK!
$ 2.75
$ 2.76
NEVER MIND WRAPPING IT, MR.
THAT'LL BE $2.95 YOUNG MAN!
5

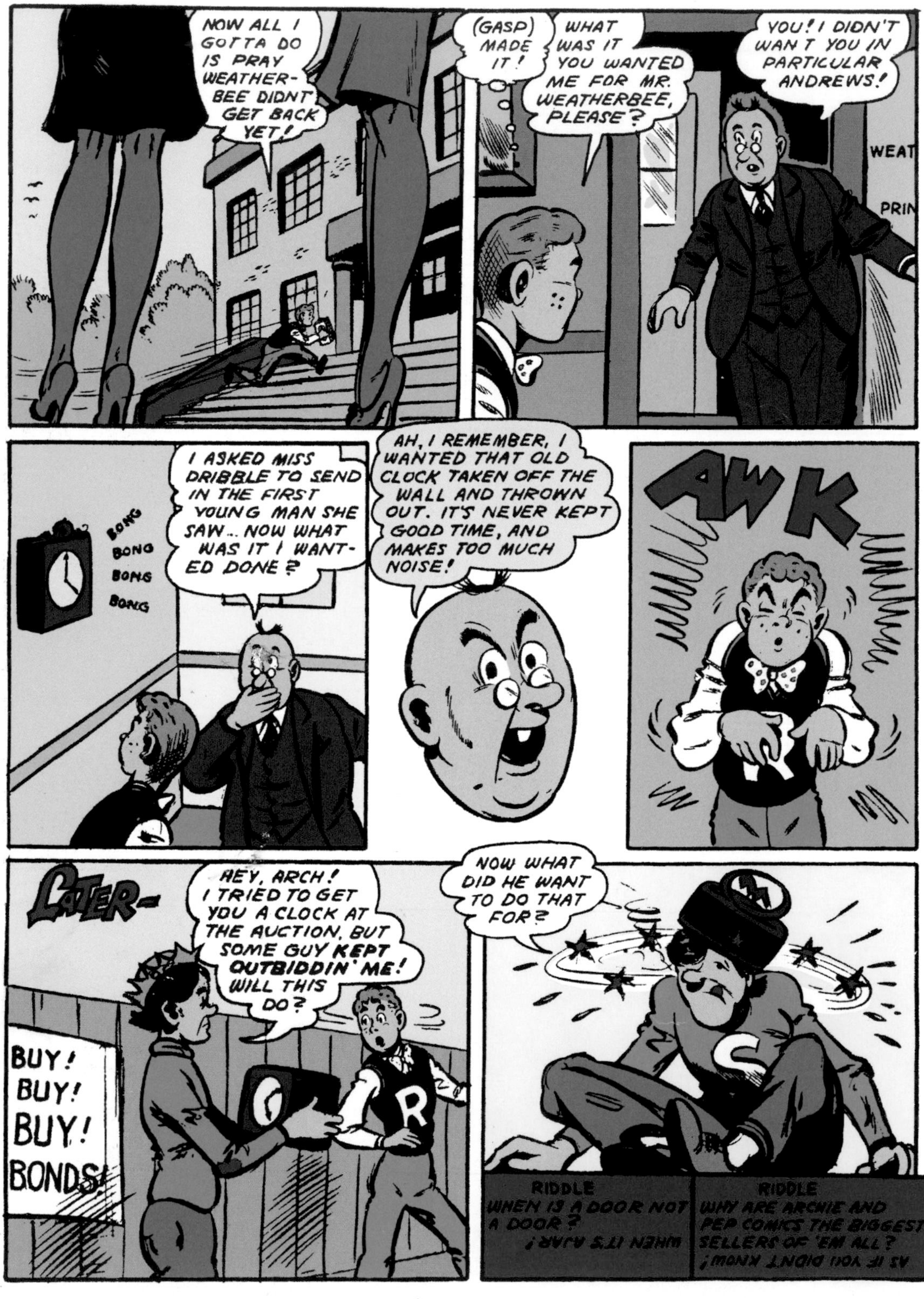
NOW ALL I GOTTA DO IS PRAY WEATHERBEE DIDN'T GET BACK YET!
(GASP) MADE IT!
WHAT WAS IT YOU WANTED ME FOR MR. WEATHERBEE, PLEASE?
YOU! I DIDN'T WANT YOU IN PARTICULAR ANDREWS!
I ASKED MISS DRIBBLE TO SEND IN THE FIRST YOUNG MAN SHE SAW... NOW WHAT WAS IT I WANTED DONE?
BONG BONG BONG BONG
AH, I REMEMBER, I WANTED THAT OLD CLOCK TAKEN OFF THE WALL AND THROWN OUT. IT'S NEVER KEPT GOOD TIME, AND MAKES TOO MUCH NOISE!
AWK
LATER—
HEY, ARCH! I TRIED TO GET YOU A CLOCK AT THE AUCTION, BUT SOME GUY KEPT OUTBIDDIN' ME! WILL THIS DO?
BUY! BUY! BUY! BONDS!
NOW WHAT DID HE WANT TO DO THAT FOR?
RIDDLE
WHEN IS A DOOR NOT A DOOR?
WHEN IT'S AJAR!
RIDDLE
WHY ARE ARCHIE AND PEP COMICS THE BIGGEST SELLERS OF 'EM ALL?
AS IF YOU DIDN'T KNOW!

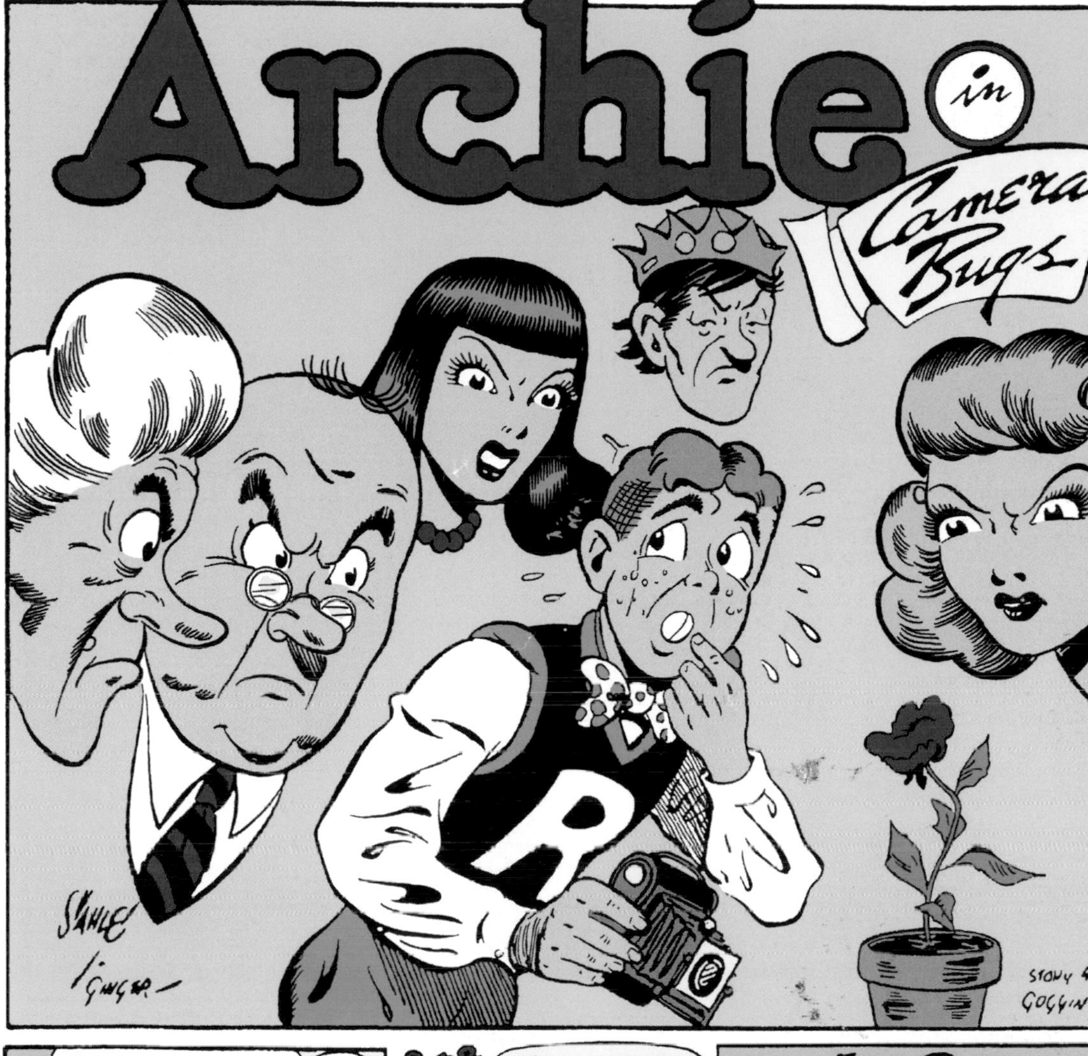
Archie in
Camera Bugs
STANLEY
GINGER
STORY BY GOGGIN

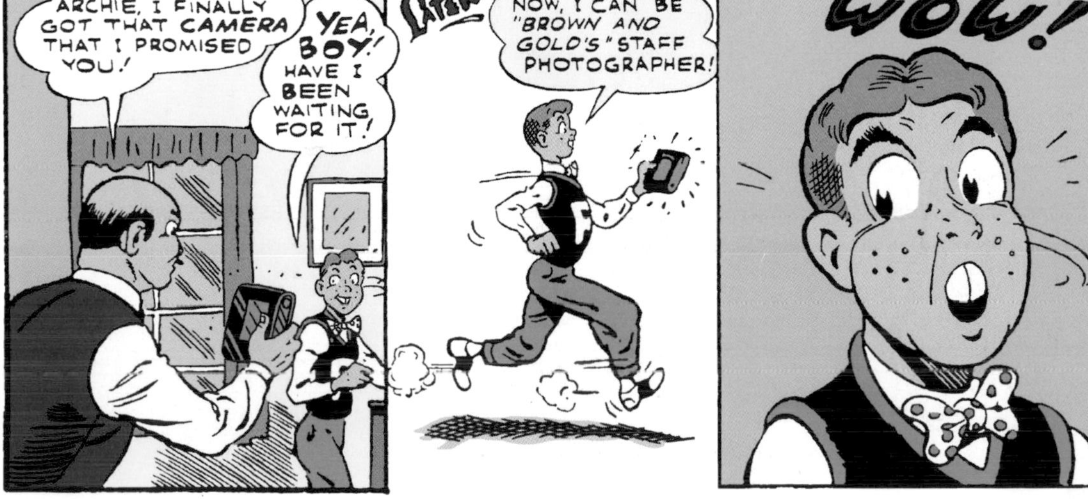
ARCHIE, I FINALLY GOT THAT CAMERA THAT I PROMISED YOU!
YEA, BOY! HAVE I BEEN WAITING FOR IT!
LATER
NOW, I CAN BE "BROWN AND GOLD'S" STAFF PHOTOGRAPHER!
WOW!

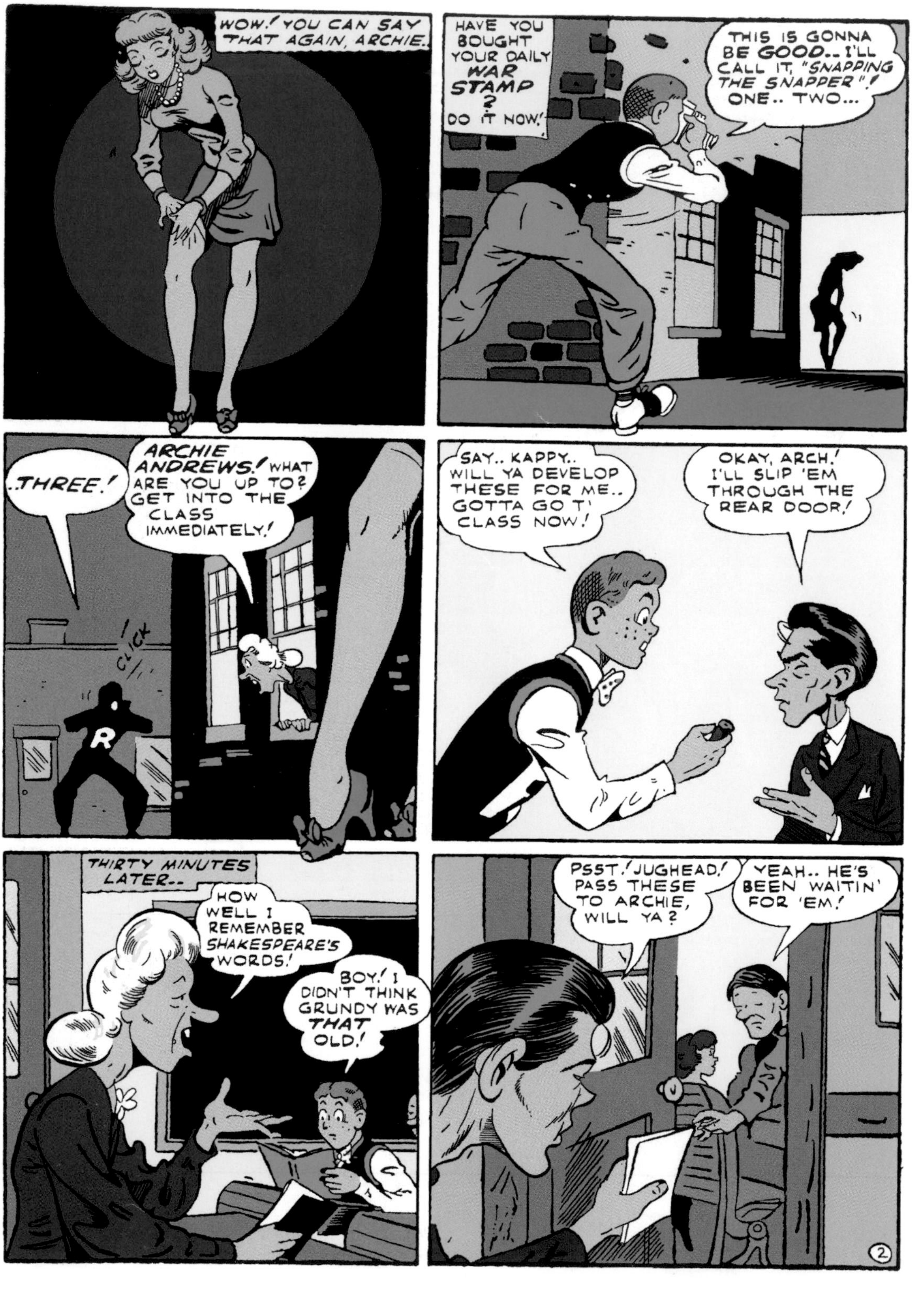
WOW! YOU CAN SAY THAT AGAIN, ARCHIE.
HAVE YOU BOUGHT YOUR DAILY WAR STAMP ? DO IT NOW!
THIS IS GONNA BE GOOD.. I'LL CALL IT, "SNAPPING THE SNAPPER"! ONE.. TWO...
..THREE!
ARCHIE ANDREWS! WHAT ARE YOU UP TO? GET INTO THE CLASS IMMEDIATELY!
CLICK
R
SAY.. KAPPY.. WILL YA DEVELOP THESE FOR ME.. GOTTA GO T' CLASS NOW!
OKAY, ARCH! I'LL SLIP 'EM THROUGH THE REAR DOOR!
THIRTY MINUTES LATER..
HOW WELL I REMEMBER SHAKESPEARE'S WORDS!
BOY! I DIDN'T THINK GRUNDY WAS THAT OLD!
PSST! JUGHEAD! PASS THESE TO ARCHIE, WILL YA?
YEAH.. HE'S BEEN WAITIN' FOR 'EM!
2

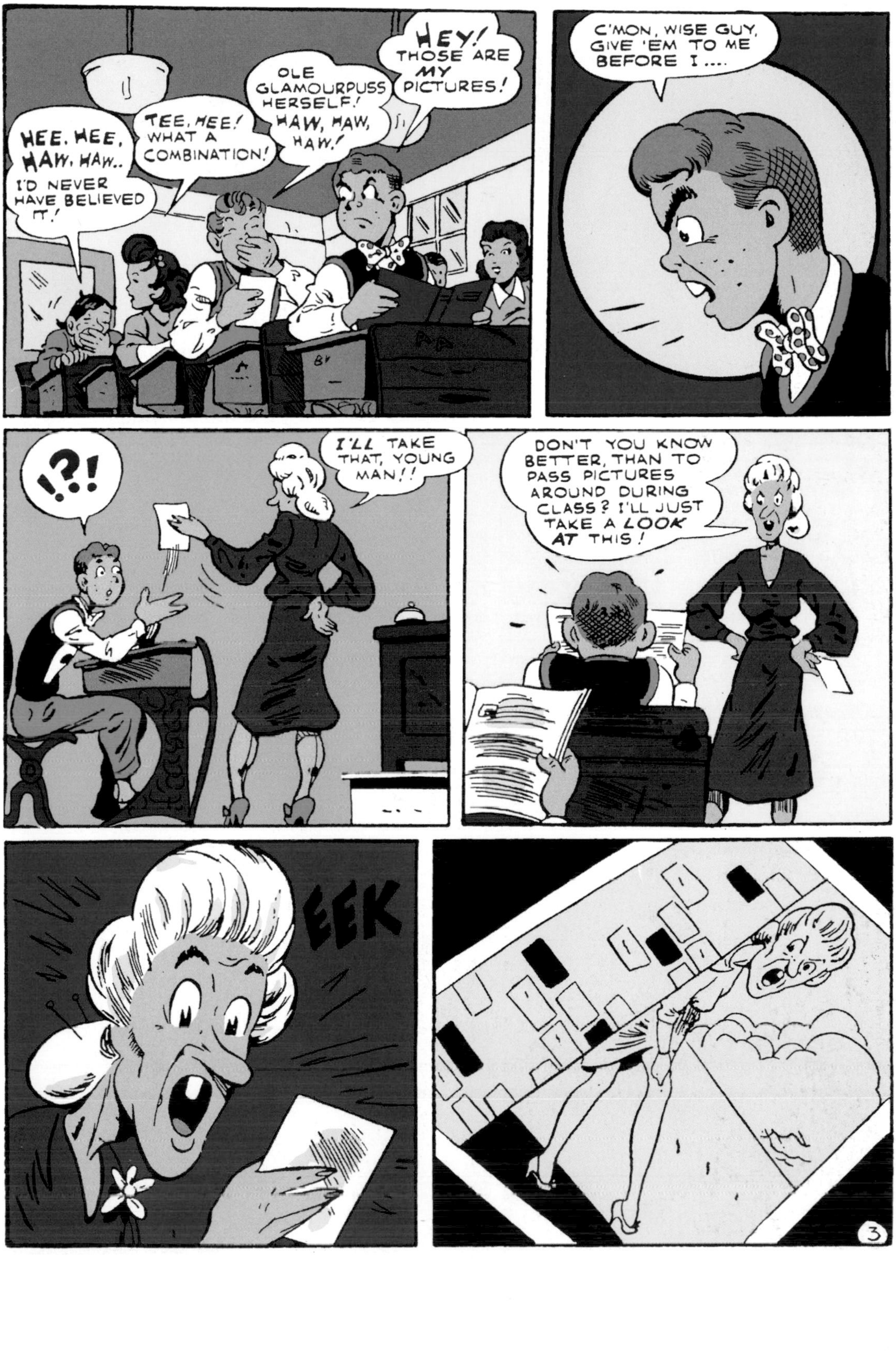
HEE. HEE, HAW. HAW.. I'D NEVER HAVE BELIEVED IT!
TEE. HEE! WHAT A COMBINATION!
OLE GLAMOURPUSS HERSELF! HAW, HAW, HAW!
HEY! THOSE ARE MY PICTURES!
C'MON, WISE GUY, GIVE 'EM TO ME BEFORE I....
!?!
I'LL TAKE THAT, YOUNG MAN!!
DON'T YOU KNOW BETTER, THAN TO PASS PICTURES AROUND DURING CLASS? I'LL JUST TAKE A LOOK AT THIS!
EEK
3

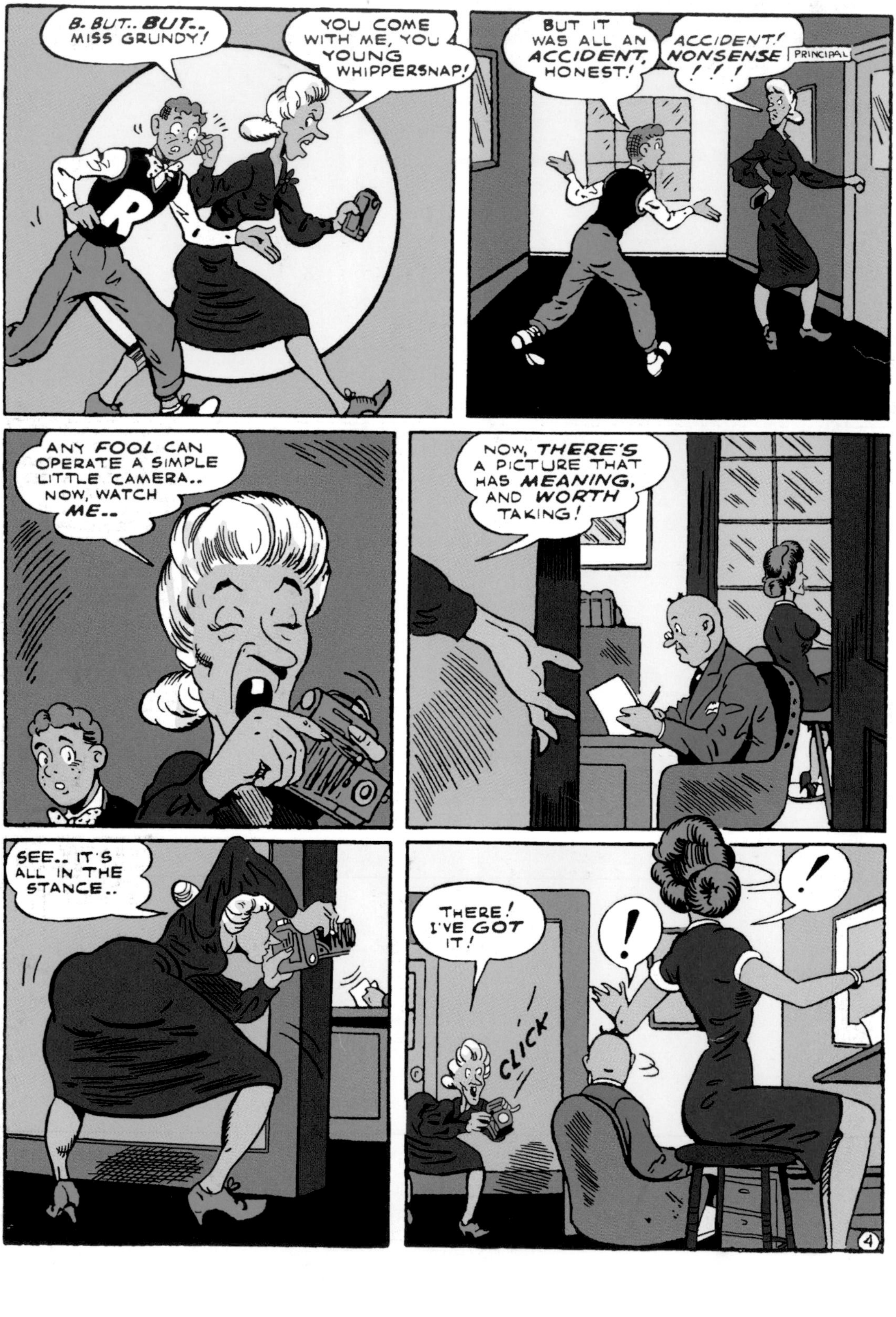

B. BUT.. BUT.. MISS GRUNDY!
YOU COME WITH ME, YOU YOUNG WHIPPERSNAP!
BUT IT WAS ALL AN ACCIDENT, HONEST!
ACCIDENT! NONSENSE !!!
PRINCIPAL
ANY FOOL CAN OPERATE A SIMPLE LITTLE CAMERA.. NOW, WATCH ME..
NOW, THERE'S A PICTURE THAT HAS MEANING, AND WORTH TAKING!
SEE.. IT'S ALL IN THE STANCE..
THERE! I'VE GOT IT!
CLICK
!
!
4

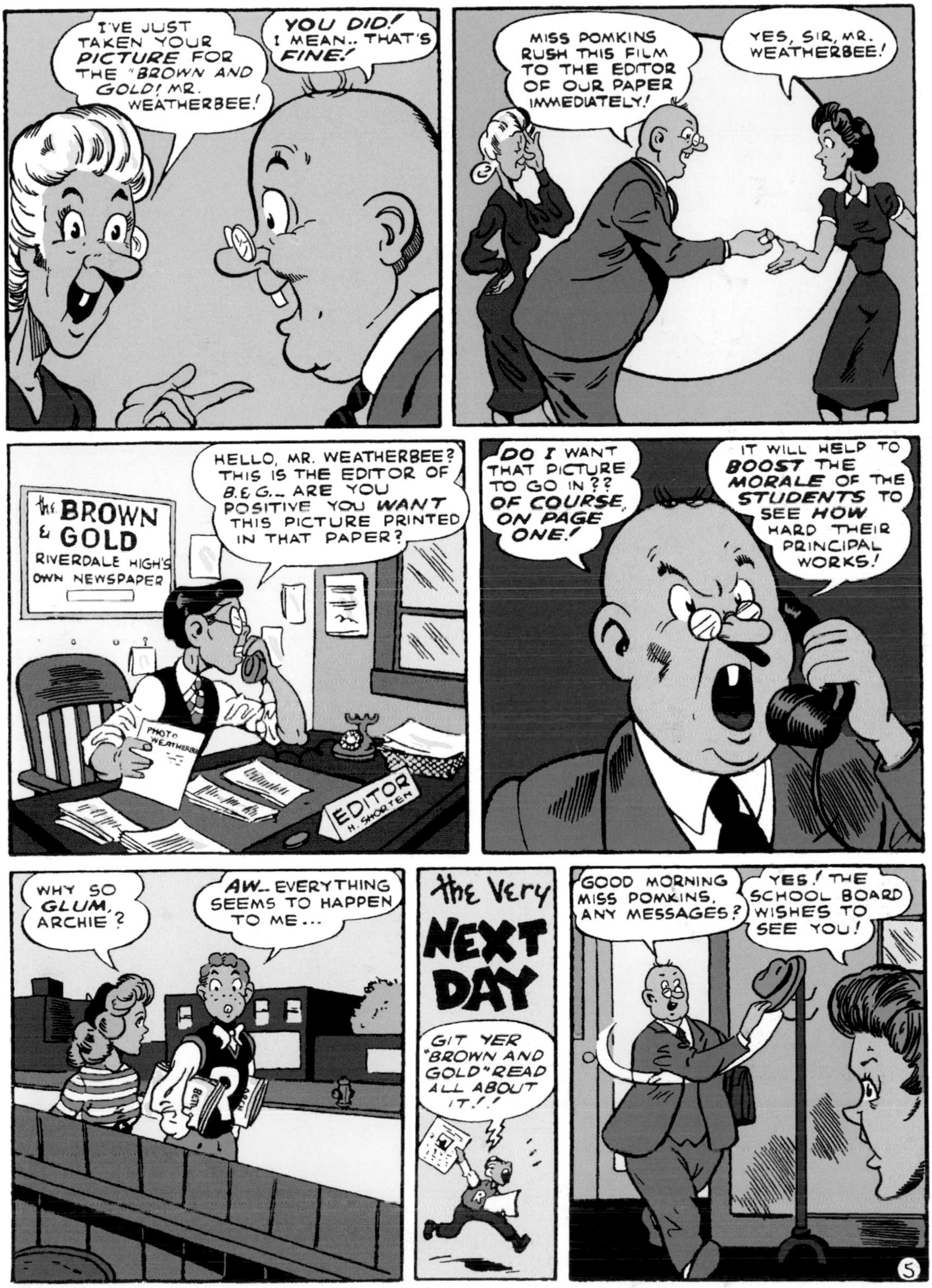

I'VE JUST TAKEN YOUR PICTURE FOR THE "BROWN AND GOLD," MR. WEATHERBEE!
YOU DID! I MEAN.. THAT'S FINE!
MISS POMKINS RUSH THIS FILM TO THE EDITOR OF OUR PAPER IMMEDIATELY!
YES, SIR, MR. WEATHERBEE!
HELLO, MR. WEATHERBEE? THIS IS THE EDITOR OF B.&G.. ARE YOU POSITIVE YOU WANT THIS PICTURE PRINTED IN THAT PAPER?
the BROWN & GOLD
RIVERDALE HIGH'S OWN NEWSPAPER
PHOTO WEATHERBEE
EDITOR H. SHORTEN
DO I WANT THAT PICTURE TO GO IN?? OF COURSE, ON PAGE ONE!
IT WILL HELP TO BOOST THE MORALE OF THE STUDENTS TO SEE HOW HARD THEIR PRINCIPAL WORKS!
WHY SO GLUM, ARCHIE?
AW.. EVERYTHING SEEMS TO HAPPEN TO ME...
the Very NEXT DAY
GIT YER "BROWN AND GOLD" READ ALL ABOUT IT!!
GOOD MORNING MISS POMKINS, ANY MESSAGES?
YES! THE SCHOOL BOARD WISHES TO SEE YOU!
5

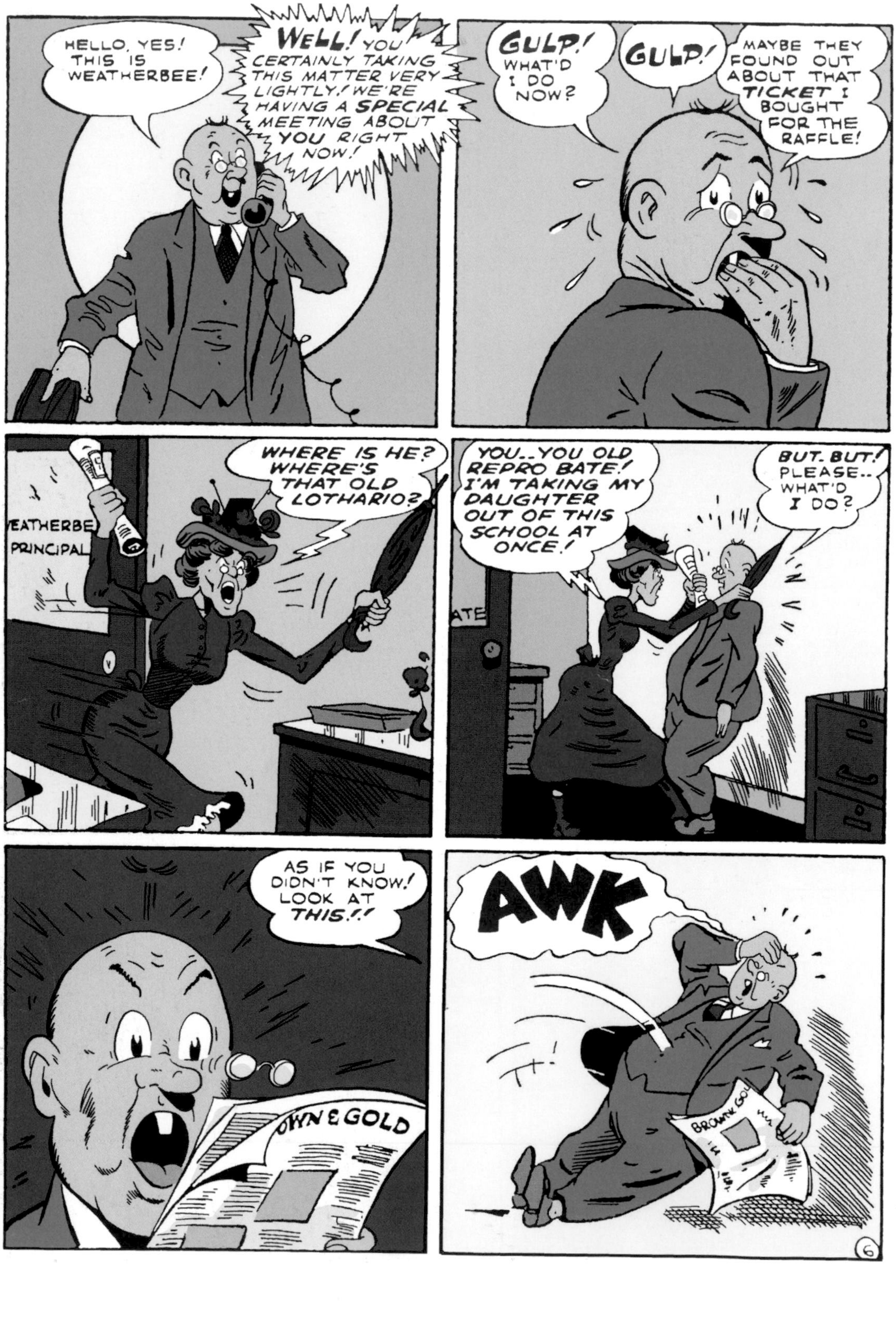
HELLO, YES! THIS IS WEATHERBEE!
WELL! YOU CERTAINLY TAKING THIS MATTER VERY LIGHTLY! WE'RE HAVING A SPECIAL MEETING ABOUT YOU RIGHT NOW!
GULP! WHAT'D I DO NOW?
GULP!
MAYBE THEY FOUND OUT ABOUT THAT TICKET I BOUGHT FOR THE RAFFLE!
WHERE IS HE? WHERE'S THAT OLD LOTHARIO?
EATHERBE
PRINCIPAL
YOU..YOU OLD REPRO BATE! I'M TAKING MY DAUGHTER OUT OF THIS SCHOOL AT ONCE!
BUT. BUT! PLEASE.. WHAT'D I DO?
AS IF YOU DIDN'T KNOW! LOOK AT THIS!!
OWN & GOLD
AWK
6

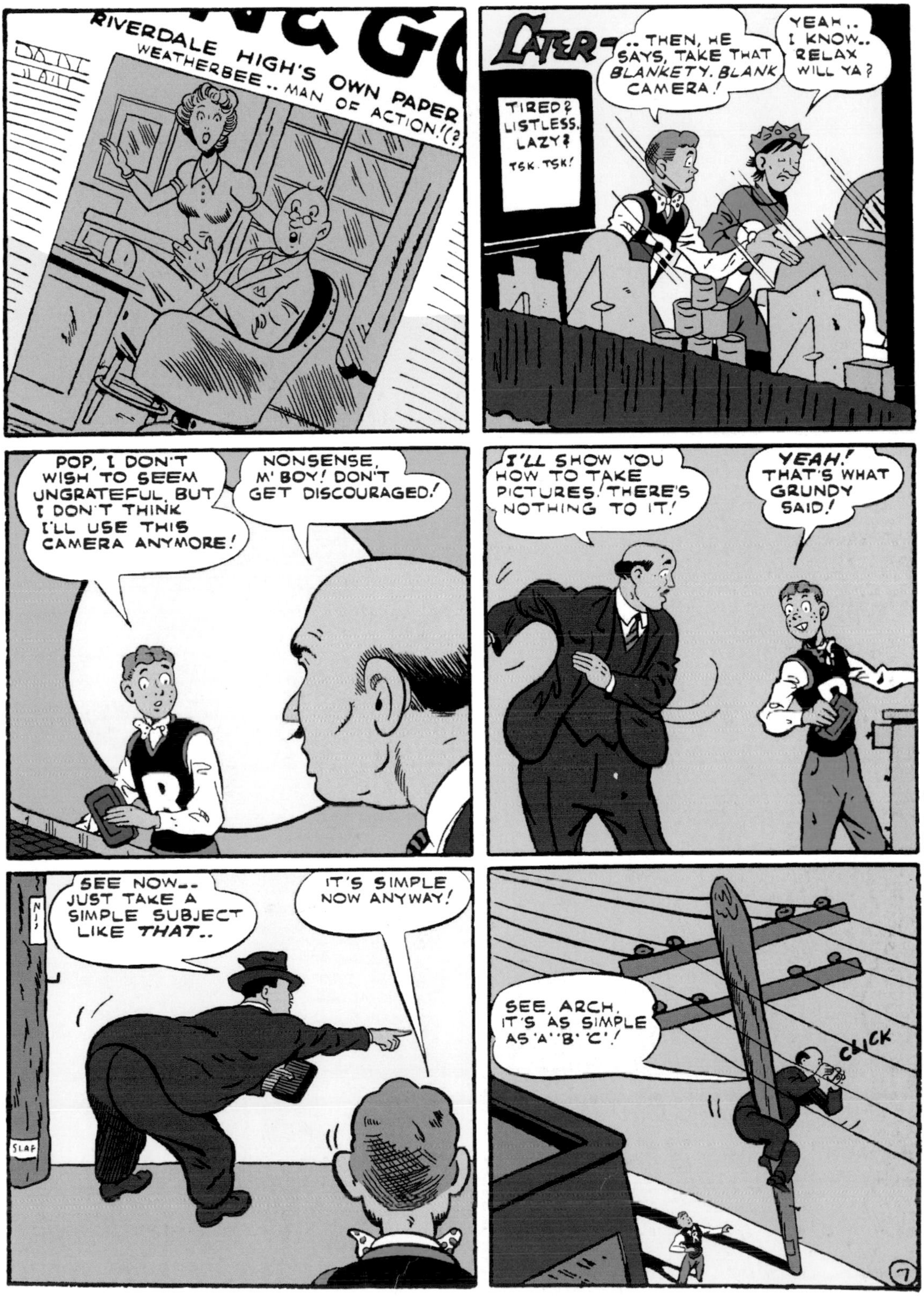
RIVERDALE HIGH'S OWN PAPER
WEATHERBEE.. MAN OF ACTION!(?
LATER-
.. THEN, HE SAYS, TAKE THAT BLANKETY. BLANK CAMERA!
YEAH.. I KNOW.. RELAX WILL YA?
TIRED? LISTLESS. LAZY?
TSK. TSK!
POP, I DON'T WISH TO SEEM UNGRATEFUL, BUT I DON'T THINK I'LL USE THIS CAMERA ANYMORE!
NONSENSE, M' BOY! DON'T GET DISCOURAGED!
I'LL SHOW YOU HOW TO TAKE PICTURES! THERE'S NOTHING TO IT!
YEAH! THAT'S WHAT GRUNDY SAID!
SEE NOW.. JUST TAKE A SIMPLE SUBJECT LIKE THAT..
IT'S SIMPLE NOW ANYWAY!
SEE, ARCH, IT'S AS SIMPLE AS 'A' 'B' 'C'!
CLICK
7

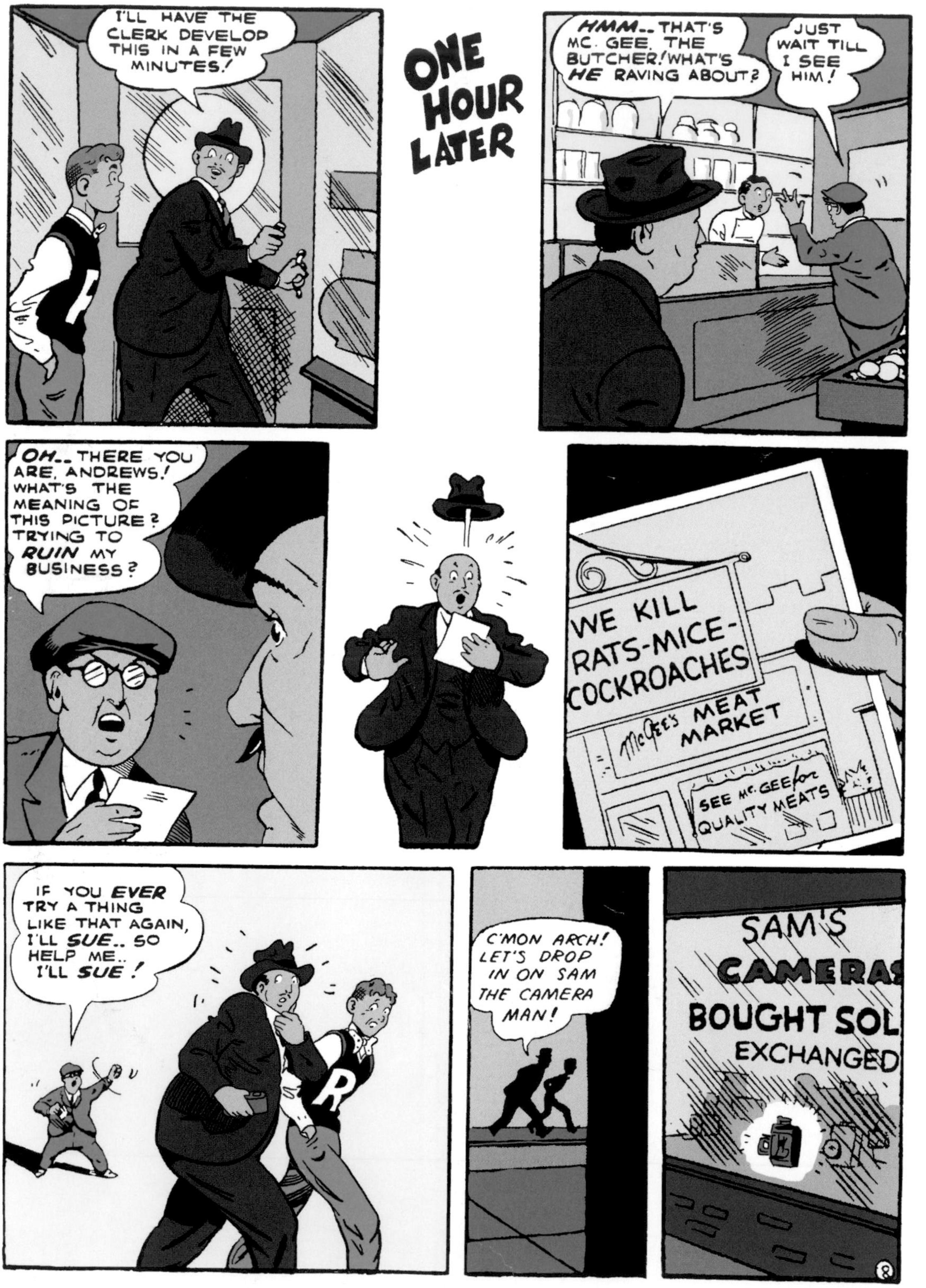
I'LL HAVE THE CLERK DEVELOP THIS IN A FEW MINUTES!
ONE HOUR LATER
HMM.. THAT'S MC. GEE, THE BUTCHER! WHAT'S HE RAVING ABOUT?
JUST WAIT TILL I SEE HIM!
OH.. THERE YOU ARE, ANDREWS! WHAT'S THE MEANING OF THIS PICTURE? TRYING TO RUIN MY BUSINESS?
WE KILL RATS-MICE-COCKROACHES
McGEE'S MEAT MARKET
SEE MC. GEE for QUALITY MEATS
IF YOU EVER TRY A THING LIKE THAT AGAIN, I'LL SUE.. SO HELP ME.. I'LL SUE!
C'MON ARCH! LET'S DROP IN ON SAM THE CAMERA MAN!
SAM'S CAMERAS
BOUGHT SOL
EXCHANGED
8

The BEST of Archie® COMICS

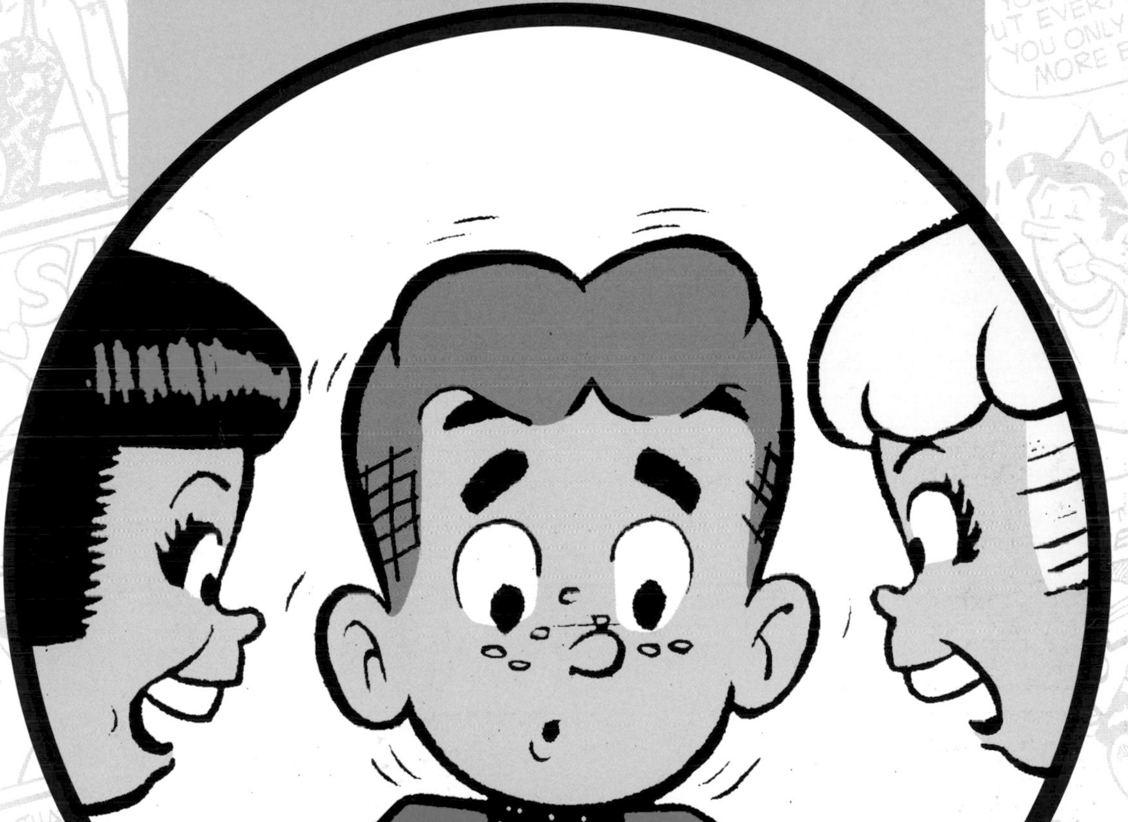

1950s

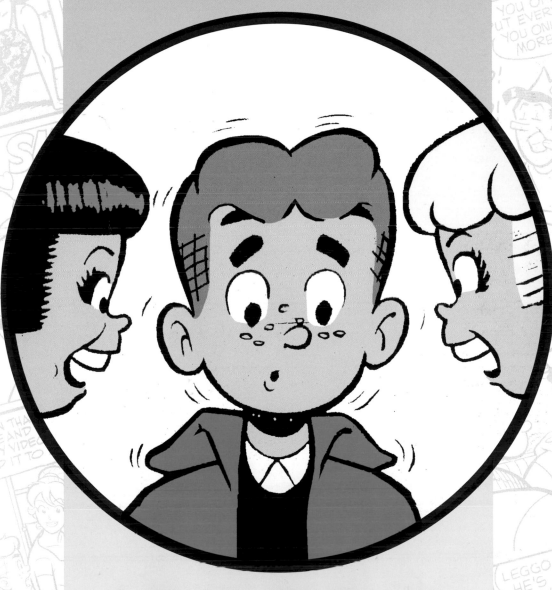

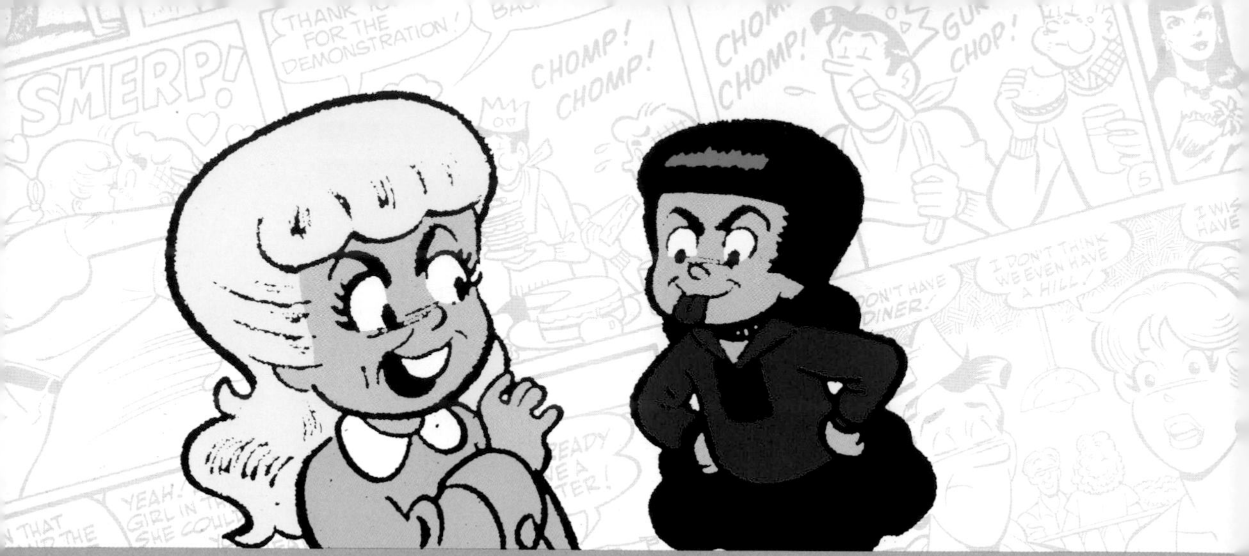
SMERP!
FOR THE DEMONSTRATION!
CHOMP! CHOMP!
CHOMP! CHOMP!
CHOP!
I DON'T THINK WE EVEN HAVE A HILL!

THE COOK-OFF
LITTLE ARCHIE #2, 1956
BY BOB BOLLING

I love this story because it's classic Little Archie AND classic Archie. Period. It's Betty and Veronica competing for Archie's affections. What's more Archie than that? The cover to the issue as well as the marrying theme are even more charming in the Married Life era. I can also spend hours just looking at Bolling's art. I think he's in his prime here. I just love these illustrations. The kids are so cute! I especially like the big teeth and cylindrical legs.

—*J. Torres*
Writer,
Archie Comics

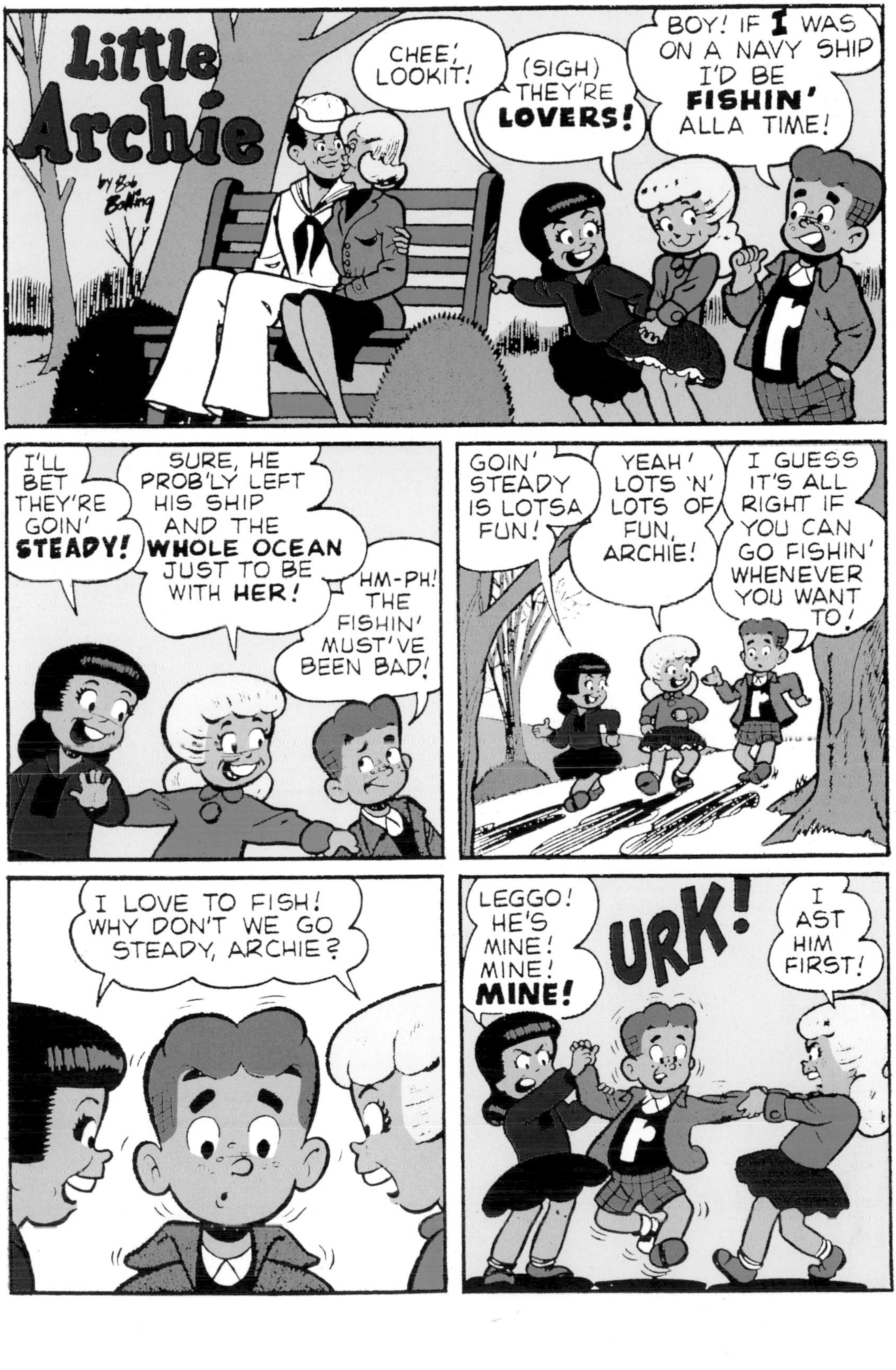
Little Archie
by Bob Bolling
CHEE! LOOKIT!
(SIGH) THEY'RE LOVERS!
BOY! IF I WAS ON A NAVY SHIP I'D BE FISHIN' ALLA TIME!
I'LL BET THEY'RE GOIN' STEADY!
SURE, HE PROB'LY LEFT HIS SHIP AND THE WHOLE OCEAN JUST TO BE WITH HER!
HM-PH! THE FISHIN' MUST'VE BEEN BAD!
GOIN' STEADY IS LOTSA FUN!
YEAH! LOTS 'N' LOTS OF FUN, ARCHIE!
I GUESS IT'S ALL RIGHT IF YOU CAN GO FISHIN' WHENEVER YOU WANT TO!
I LOVE TO FISH! WHY DON'T WE GO STEADY, ARCHIE?
LEGGO! HE'S MINE! MINE! MINE!
URK!
I AST HIM FIRST!

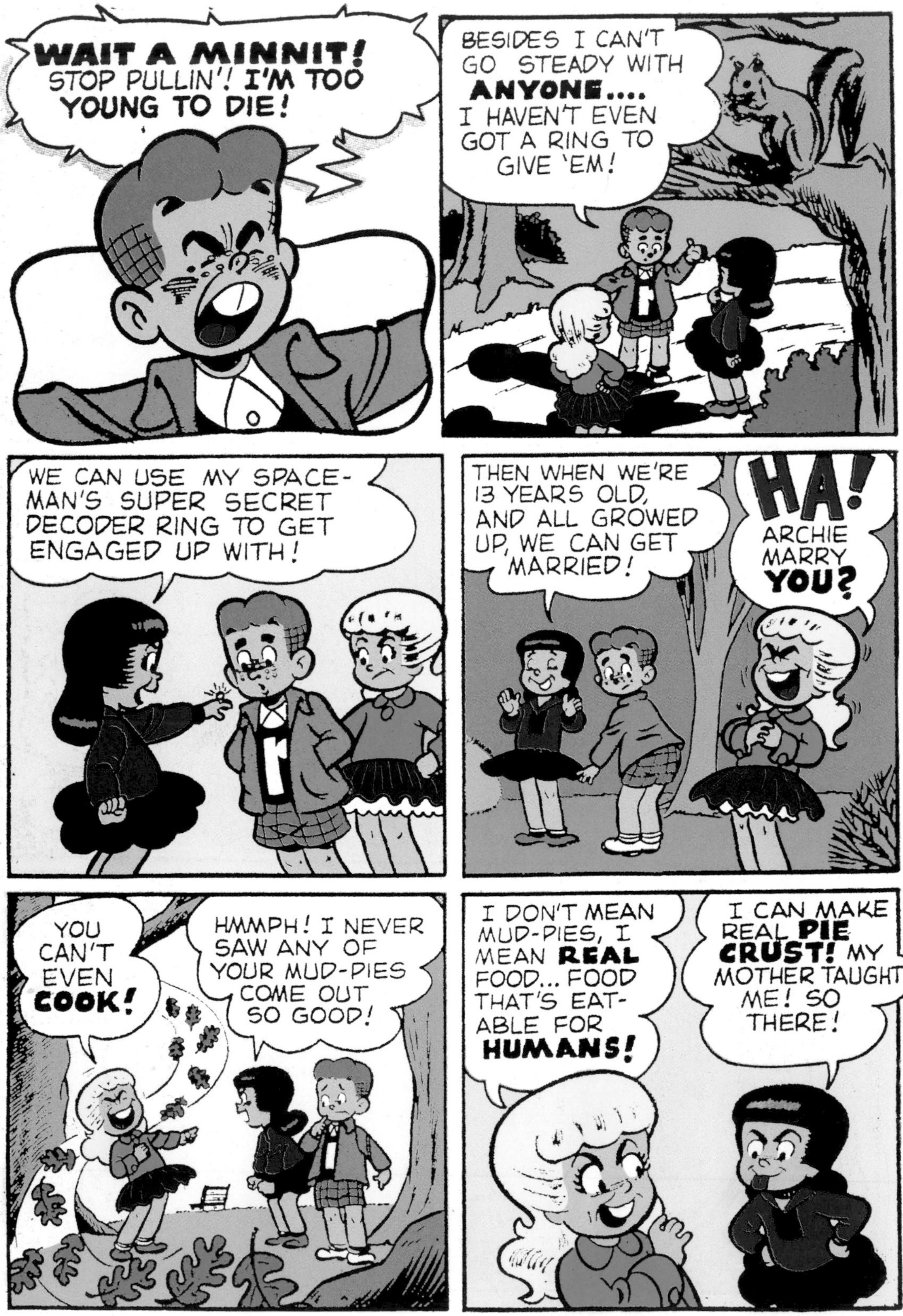
WAIT A MINNIT! STOP PULLIN'! I'M TOO YOUNG TO DIE!
BESIDES I CAN'T GO STEADY WITH ANYONE.... I HAVEN'T EVEN GOT A RING TO GIVE 'EM!
WE CAN USE MY SPACE-MAN'S SUPER SECRET DECODER RING TO GET ENGAGED UP WITH!
THEN WHEN WE'RE 13 YEARS OLD, AND ALL GROWED UP, WE CAN GET MARRIED!
HA! ARCHIE MARRY YOU?
YOU CAN'T EVEN COOK!
HMMPH! I NEVER SAW ANY OF YOUR MUD-PIES COME OUT SO GOOD!
I DON'T MEAN MUD-PIES, I MEAN REAL FOOD... FOOD THAT'S EAT-ABLE FOR HUMANS!
I CAN MAKE REAL PIE CRUST! MY MOTHER TAUGHT ME! SO THERE!

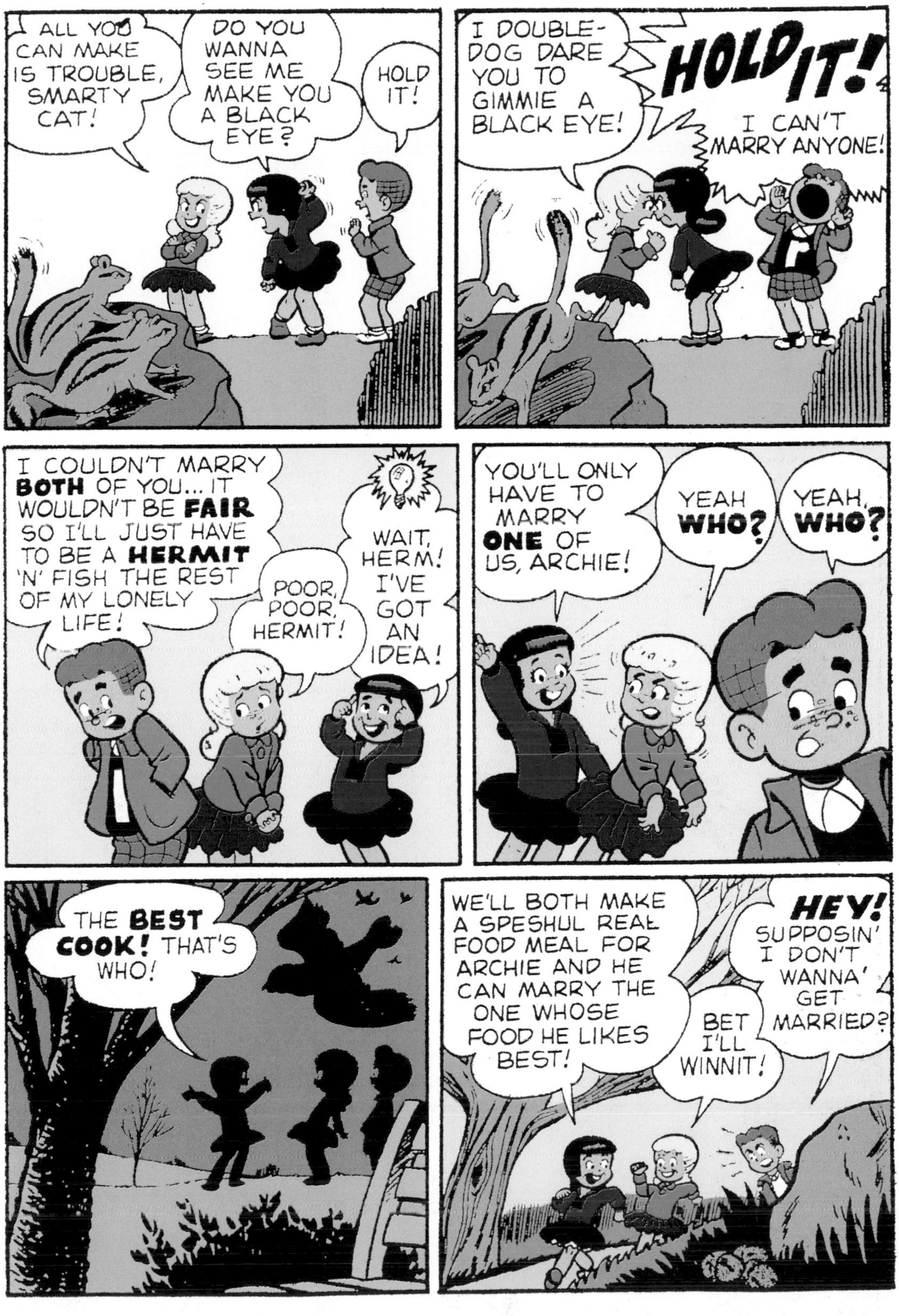
ALL YOU CAN MAKE IS TROUBLE, SMARTY CAT!
DO YOU WANNA SEE ME MAKE YOU A BLACK EYE?
HOLD IT!
I DOUBLE-DOG DARE YOU TO GIMMIE A BLACK EYE!
HOLD IT!
I CAN'T MARRY ANYONE!
I COULDN'T MARRY **BOTH** OF YOU... IT WOULDN'T BE **FAIR** SO I'LL JUST HAVE TO BE A **HERMIT** 'N' FISH THE REST OF MY LONELY LIFE!
POOR, POOR, HERMIT!
WAIT, HERM! I'VE GOT AN IDEA!
YOU'LL ONLY HAVE TO MARRY **ONE** OF US, ARCHIE!
YEAH **WHO?**
YEAH, **WHO?**
THE **BEST COOK!** THAT'S WHO!
WE'LL BOTH MAKE A SPESHUL REAL FOOD MEAL FOR ARCHIE AND HE CAN MARRY THE ONE WHOSE FOOD HE LIKES BEST!
BET I'LL WINNIT!
HEY! SUPPOSIN' I DON'T WANNA' GET MARRIED?

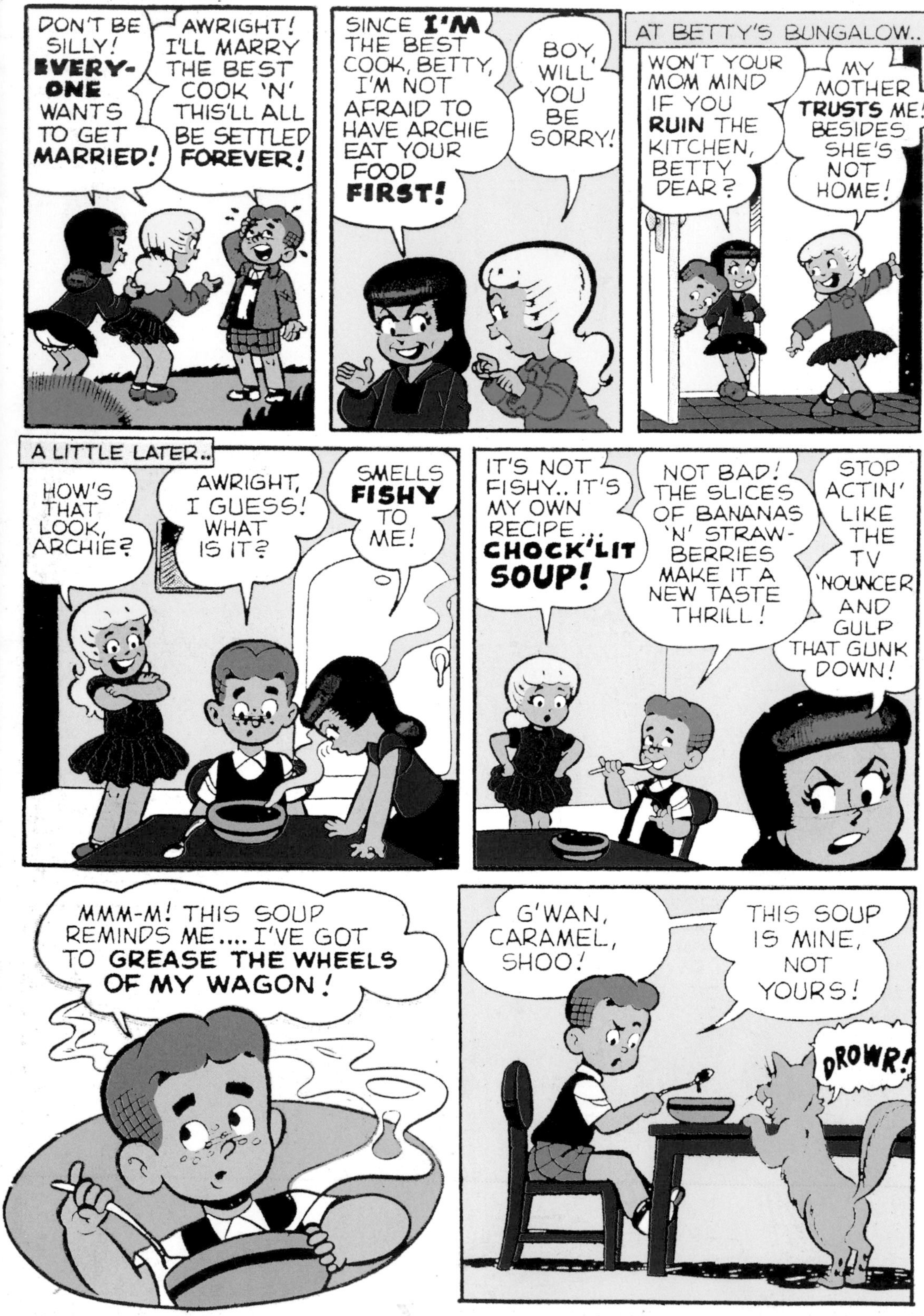

DON'T BE SILLY! EVERY-ONE WANTS TO GET MARRIED!
AWRIGHT! I'LL MARRY THE BEST COOK 'N' THIS'LL ALL BE SETTLED FOREVER!
SINCE I'M THE BEST COOK, BETTY, I'M NOT AFRAID TO HAVE ARCHIE EAT YOUR FOOD FIRST!
BOY, WILL YOU BE SORRY!
AT BETTY'S BUNGALOW..
WON'T YOUR MOM MIND IF YOU RUIN THE KITCHEN, BETTY DEAR?
MY MOTHER TRUSTS ME! BESIDES SHE'S NOT HOME!
A LITTLE LATER..
HOW'S THAT LOOK, ARCHIE?
AWRIGHT, I GUESS! WHAT IS IT?
SMELLS FISHY TO ME!
IT'S NOT FISHY.. IT'S MY OWN RECIPE... CHOCK'LIT SOUP!
NOT BAD! THE SLICES OF BANANAS 'N' STRAW-BERRIES MAKE IT A NEW TASTE THRILL!
STOP ACTIN' LIKE THE TV 'NOUNCER AND GULP THAT GUNK DOWN!
MMM-M! THIS SOUP REMINDS ME.... I'VE GOT TO GREASE THE WHEELS OF MY WAGON!
G'WAN, CARAMEL, SHOO!
THIS SOUP IS MINE, NOT YOURS!
DROWR!

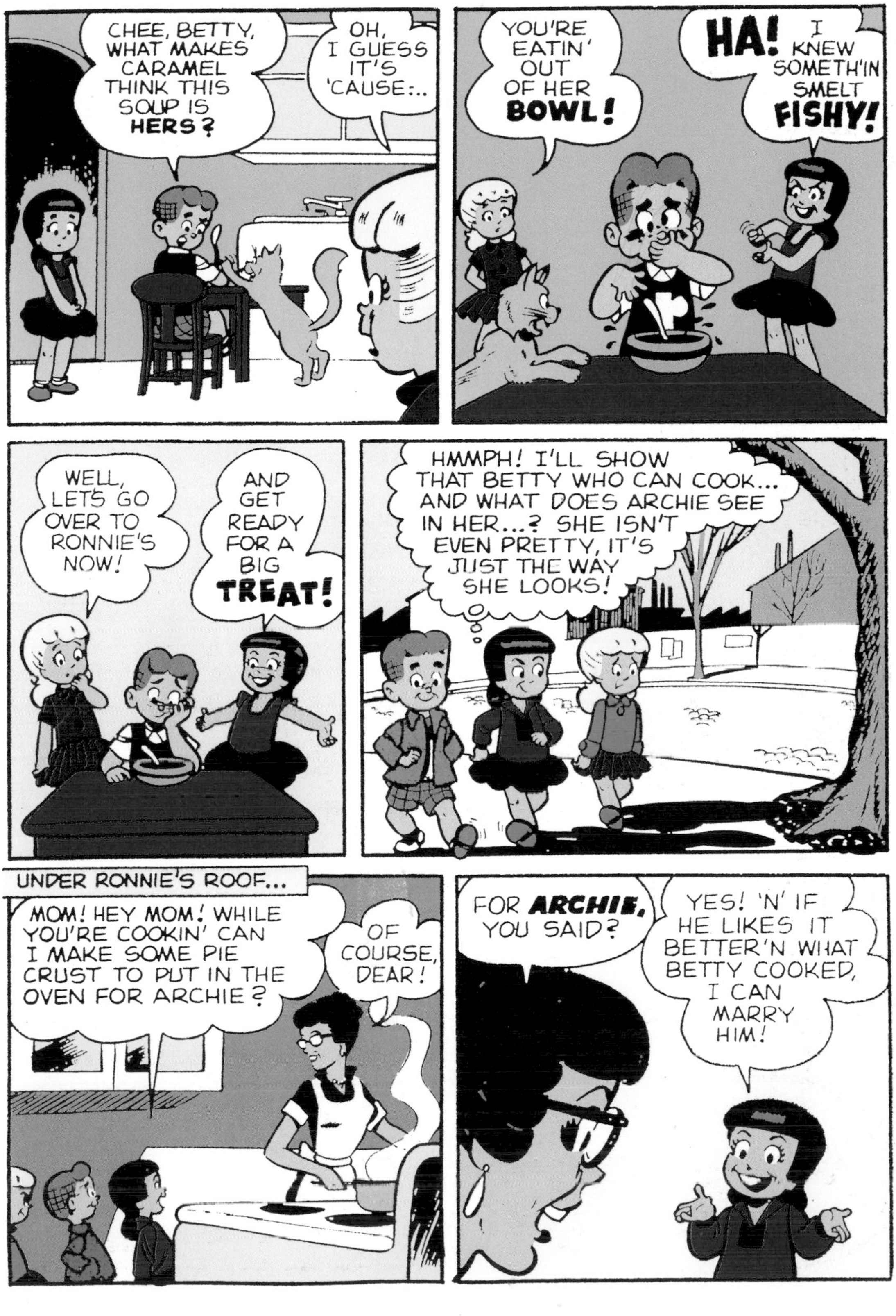
CHEE, BETTY, WHAT MAKES CARAMEL THINK THIS SOUP IS HERS?
OH, I GUESS IT'S 'CAUSE:...
YOU'RE EATIN' OUT OF HER BOWL!
HA! I KNEW SOMETH'IN SMELT FISHY!
WELL, LET'S GO OVER TO RONNIE'S NOW!
AND GET READY FOR A BIG TREAT!
HMMPH! I'LL SHOW THAT BETTY WHO CAN COOK... AND WHAT DOES ARCHIE SEE IN HER...? SHE ISN'T EVEN PRETTY, IT'S JUST THE WAY SHE LOOKS!
UNDER RONNIE'S ROOF...
MOM! HEY MOM! WHILE YOU'RE COOKIN' CAN I MAKE SOME PIE CRUST TO PUT IN THE OVEN FOR ARCHIE?
OF COURSE, DEAR!
FOR ARCHIE, YOU SAID?
YES! 'N' IF HE LIKES IT BETTER'N WHAT BETTY COOKED, I CAN MARRY HIM!

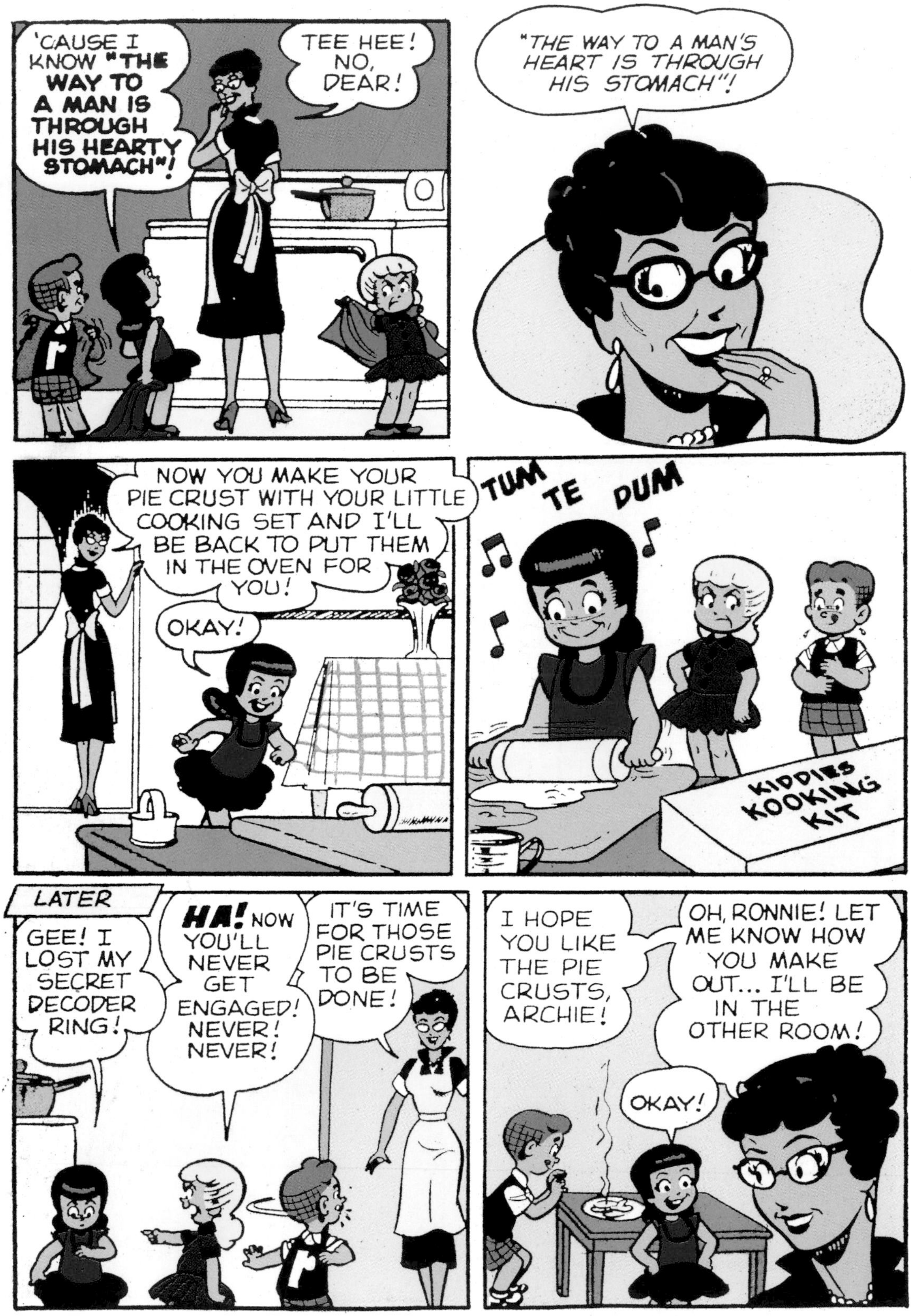
'CAUSE I KNOW "THE WAY TO A MAN IS THROUGH HIS HEARTY STOMACH"!
TEE HEE! NO, DEAR!
"THE WAY TO A MAN'S HEART IS THROUGH HIS STOMACH"!
NOW YOU MAKE YOUR PIE CRUST WITH YOUR LITTLE COOKING SET AND I'LL BE BACK TO PUT THEM IN THE OVEN FOR YOU!
OKAY!
TUM TE DUM
KIDDIES KOOKING KIT
LATER
GEE! I LOST MY SECRET DECODER RING!
HA! NOW YOU'LL NEVER GET ENGAGED! NEVER! NEVER!
IT'S TIME FOR THOSE PIE CRUSTS TO BE DONE!
I HOPE YOU LIKE THE PIE CRUSTS, ARCHIE!
OH, RONNIE! LET ME KNOW HOW YOU MAKE OUT... I'LL BE IN THE OTHER ROOM!
OKAY!

I KNOW YOU'LL LOVE 'EM, ARCHIE! THEY'VE GOT VITAMINS!
AW! I ALWAYS SPIT OUT THE VITAMINS!
MM-MM! GOOD!
KLUNK!
IS THAT A VITAMIN?
HOW CLEVER, ARCHIE, YOU FOUND MY DECODER RING!
HEY! I COULD'VE SWALLERED THAT!
THAT'D BE HORRIBUL!
YEAH, THEN THERE'D BE NO WEDDING! AND NO DECODING SECRET LOVE LETTERS!
WELL, I'VE DECIDED WHOSE COOKIN' IS BEST!
SPEAK RIGHT UP, ARCHIE, BETTY'LL BE A GOOD LOSER!
MY JAW STILL ACHES FROM THAT DECODER... SO I GUESS THE BEST COOK IS BETTY!
BAW! HA!
ER... WHO WON, DEAR?
THE CONTEST IS OVER, MOM!

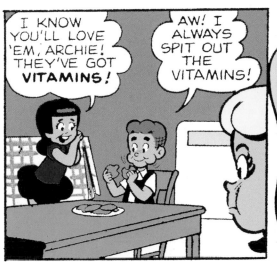

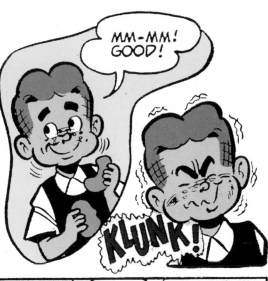

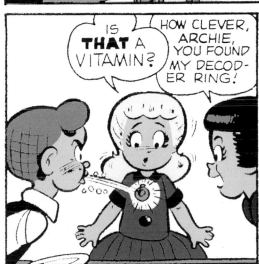

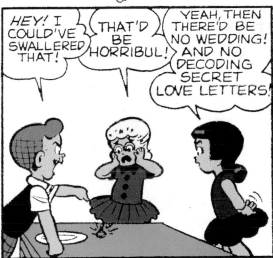

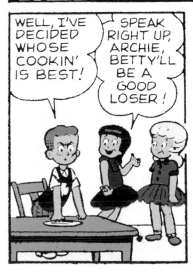

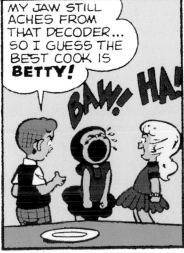

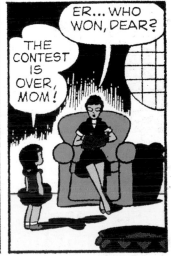

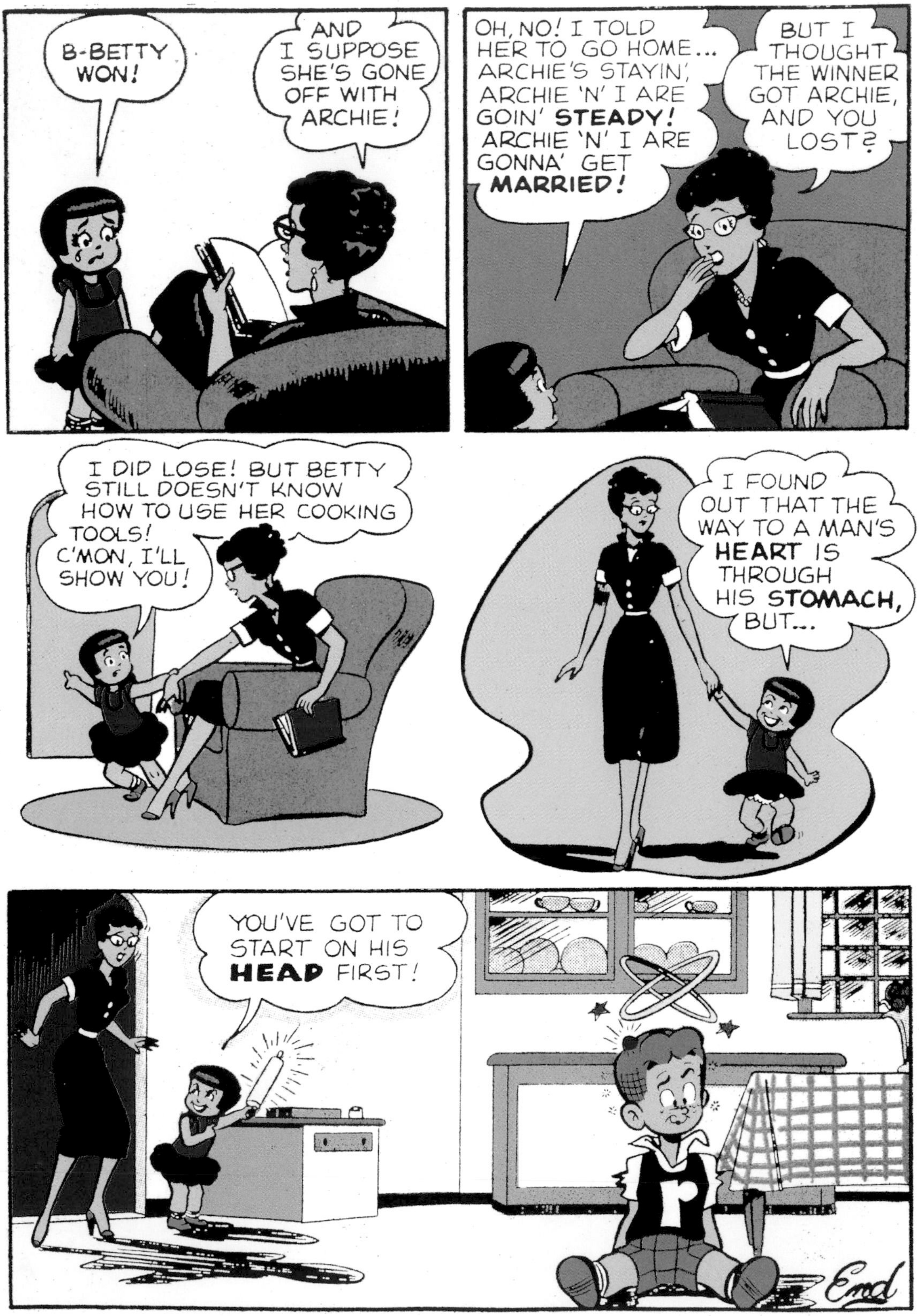
B-BETTY WON!
AND I SUPPOSE SHE'S GONE OFF WITH ARCHIE!
OH, NO! I TOLD HER TO GO HOME... ARCHIE'S STAYIN', ARCHIE 'N' I ARE GOIN' STEADY! ARCHIE 'N' I ARE GONNA' GET MARRIED!
BUT I THOUGHT THE WINNER GOT ARCHIE, AND YOU LOST?
I DID LOSE! BUT BETTY STILL DOESN'T KNOW HOW TO USE HER COOKING TOOLS! C'MON, I'LL SHOW YOU!
I FOUND OUT THAT THE WAY TO A MAN'S HEART IS THROUGH HIS STOMACH, BUT...
YOU'VE GOT TO START ON HIS HEAD FIRST!
End

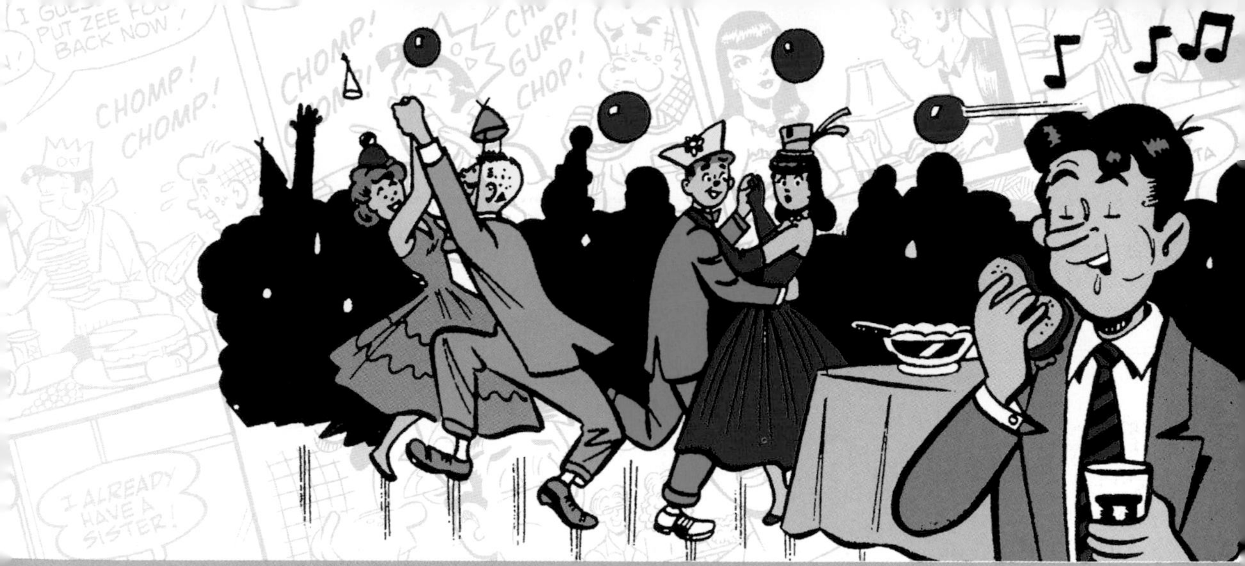
CHOMP! CHOMP!
GURP! CHOP!
I ALREADY HAVE A SISTER!

JUGHEAD'S FOLLY
JUGHEAD'S FOLLY #1, 1957
BY JOE EDWARDS

Jughead isn't JUST a burger-hungry teen. Turns out, he's the soul of Riverdale. While everyone around him is running around, boy/girl crazy, he's sensible. He's competent. He sees what the others don't, he can do what the others don't, and he is, I believe, kinder and more generous than any of them. He's the best of Riverdale, and he's the best of us. A character like that is hard to write—much harder than just "likes: food; dislikes: smooching"—but it's necessary if you're going to capture the core of who Jughead is. He's your best friend, and he'll always have your back.

—Ryan North
Writer, Archie Comics

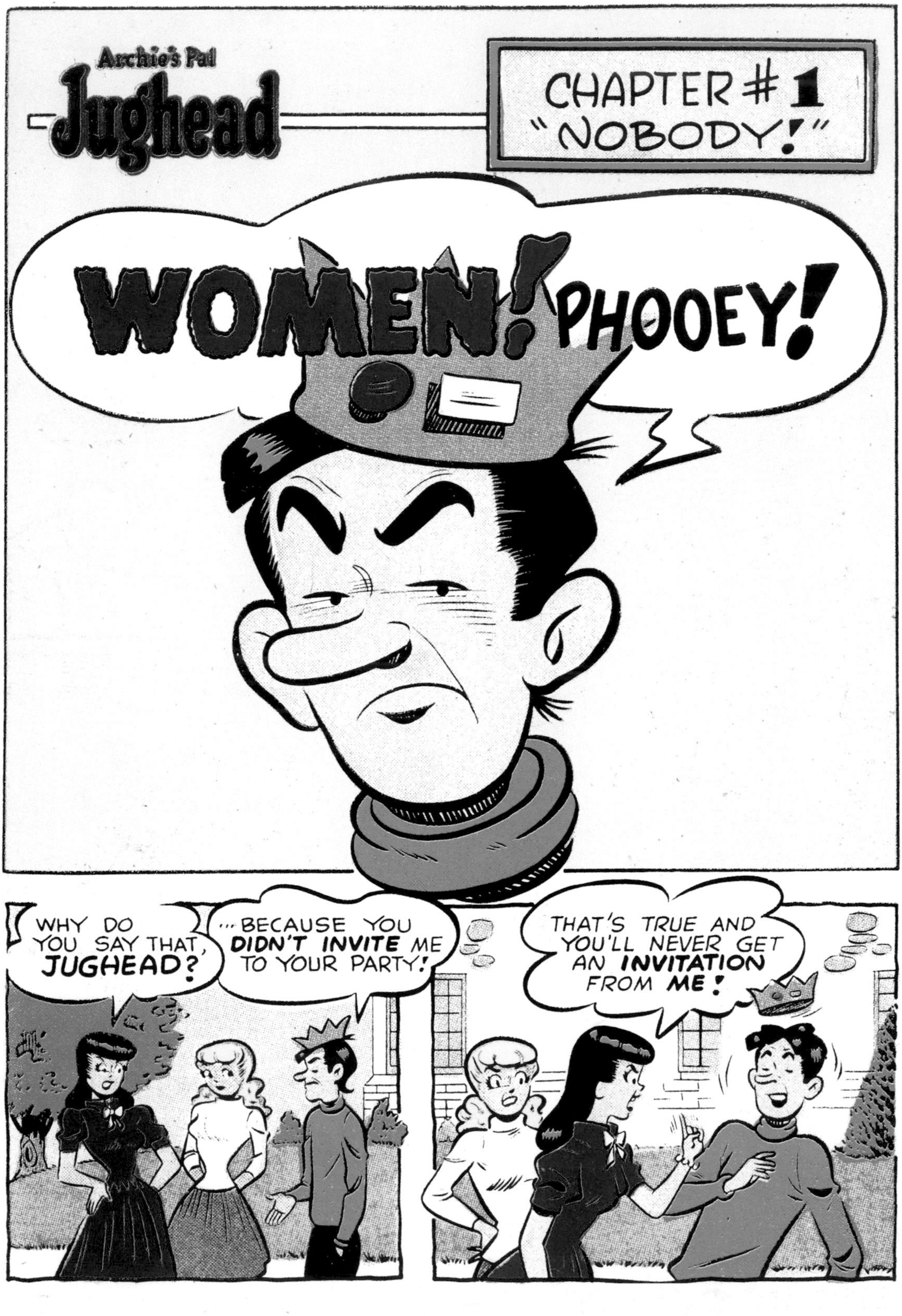
Archie's Pal Jughead
CHAPTER # 1 "NOBODY!"
WOMEN! PHOOEY!
WHY DO YOU SAY THAT, JUGHEAD?
...BECAUSE YOU DIDN'T INVITE ME TO YOUR PARTY!
THAT'S TRUE AND YOU'LL NEVER GET AN INVITATION FROM ME!

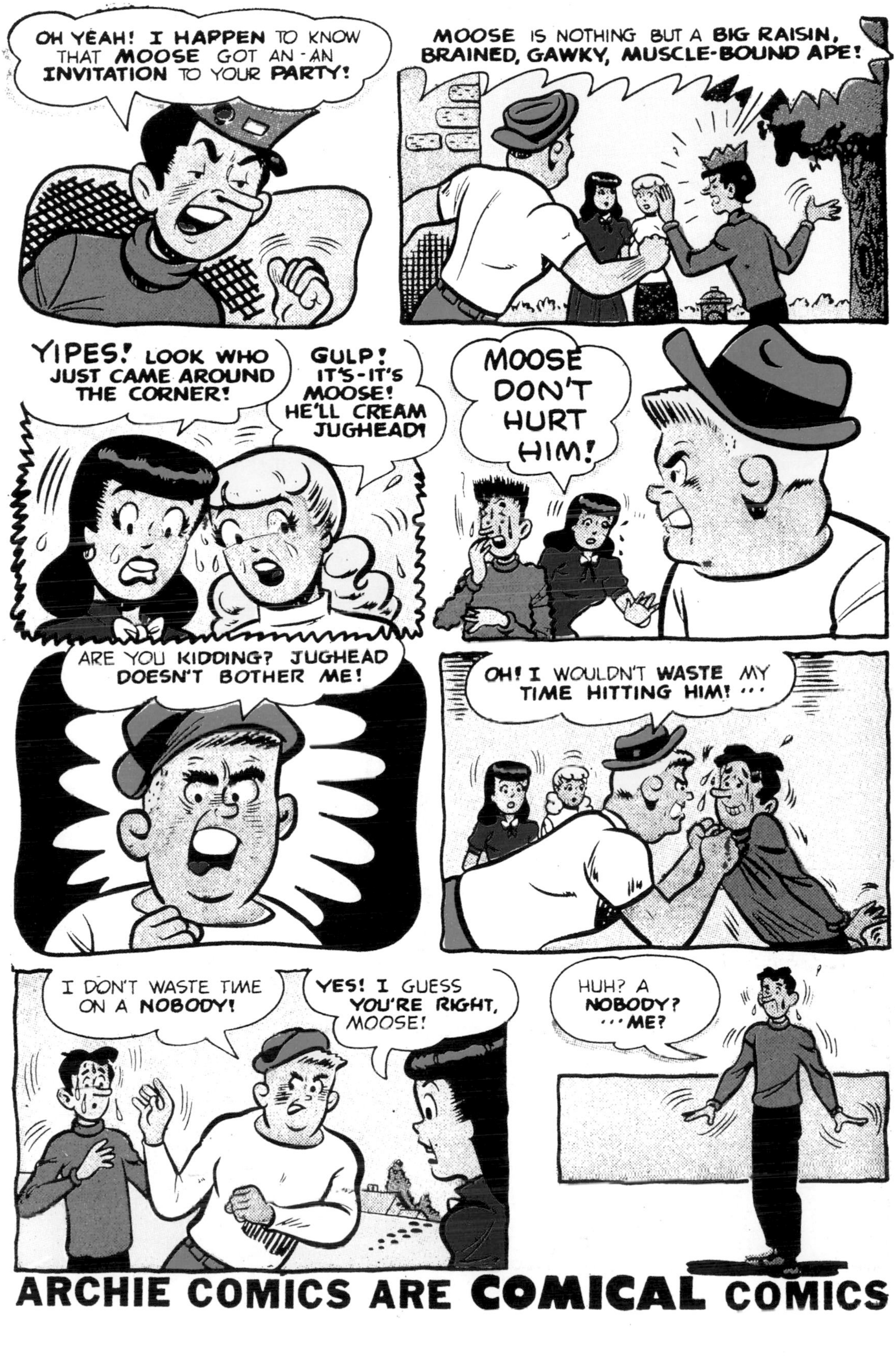
OH YEAH! I HAPPEN TO KNOW THAT MOOSE GOT AN - AN INVITATION TO YOUR PARTY!
MOOSE IS NOTHING BUT A BIG RAISIN, BRAINED, GAWKY, MUSCLE-BOUND APE!
YIPES! LOOK WHO JUST CAME AROUND THE CORNER!
GULP! IT'S-IT'S MOOSE! HE'LL CREAM JUGHEAD!
MOOSE DON'T HURT HIM!
ARE YOU KIDDING? JUGHEAD DOESN'T BOTHER ME!
OH! I WOULDN'T WASTE MY TIME HITTING HIM! ...
I DON'T WASTE TIME ON A NOBODY!
YES! I GUESS YOU'RE RIGHT, MOOSE!
HUH? A NOBODY? ... ME?

ARCHIE COMICS ARE COMICAL COMICS

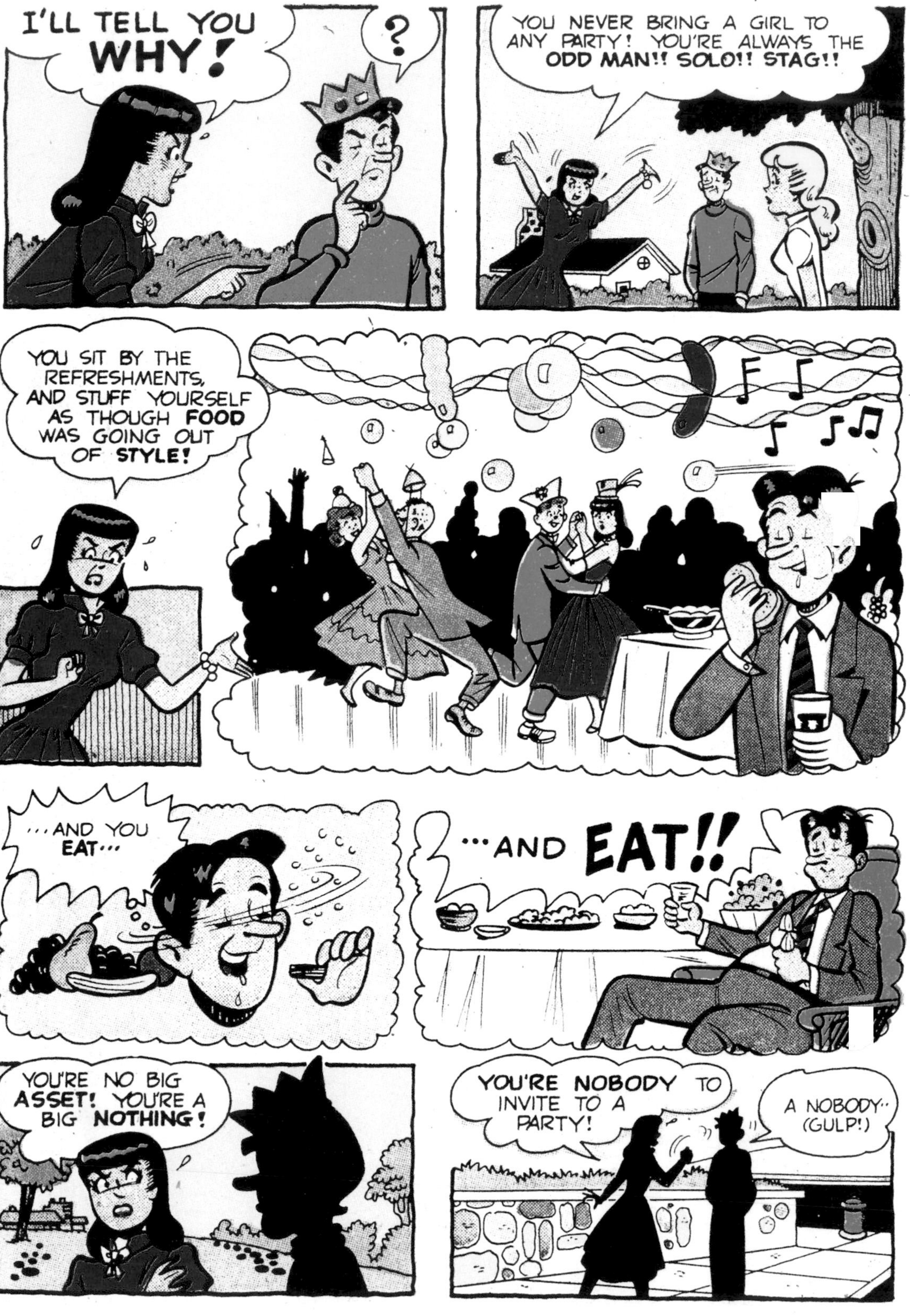

I'LL TELL YOU WHY!
?
YOU NEVER BRING A GIRL TO ANY PARTY! YOU'RE ALWAYS THE ODD MAN!! SOLO!! STAG!!
YOU SIT BY THE REFRESHMENTS, AND STUFF YOURSELF AS THOUGH FOOD WAS GOING OUT OF STYLE!
...AND YOU EAT...
...AND EAT!!
YOU'RE NO BIG ASSET! YOU'RE A BIG NOTHING!
YOU'RE NOBODY TO INVITE TO A PARTY!
A NOBODY.. (GULP!)

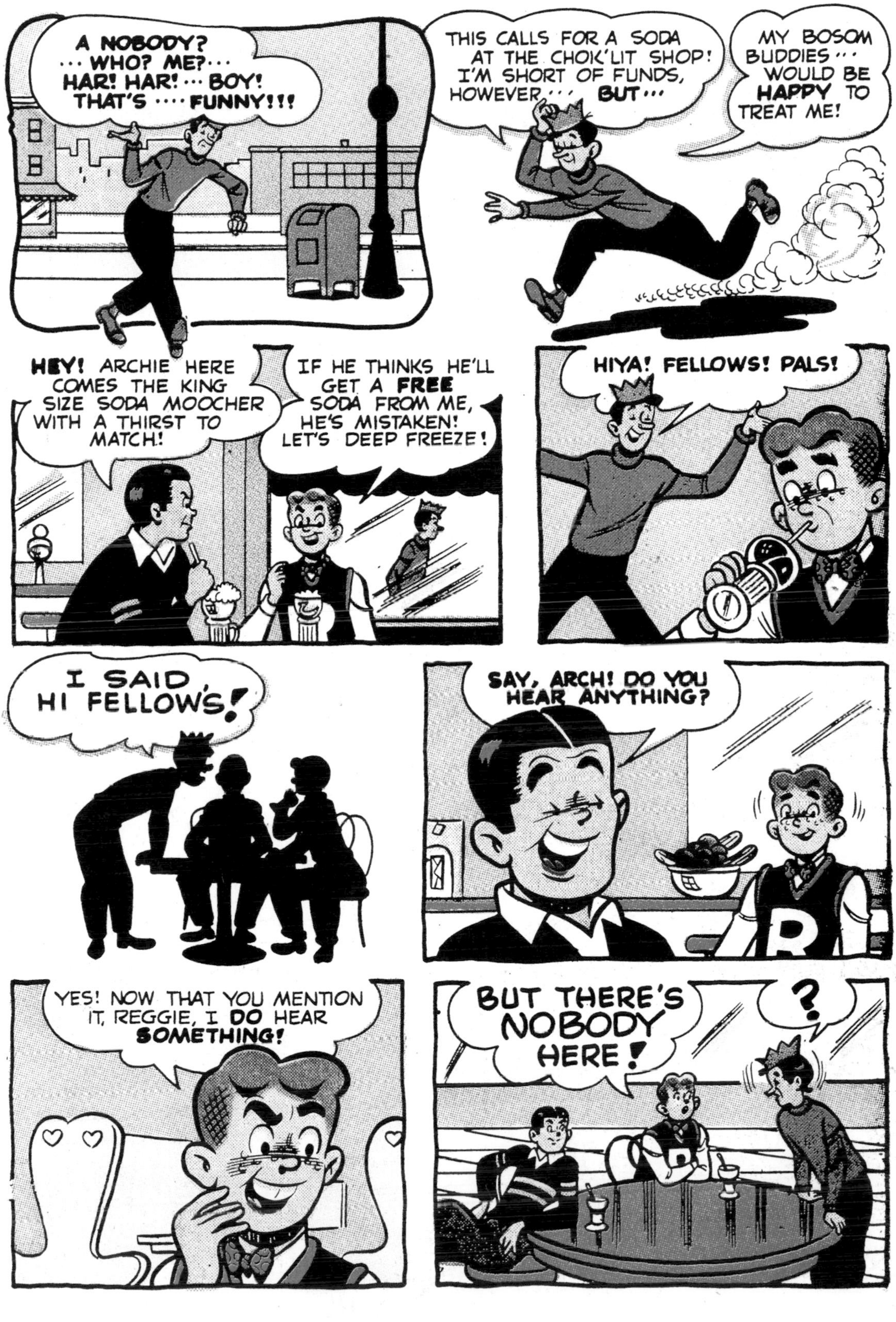

A NOBODY? ... WHO? ME?... HAR! HAR! ... BOY! THAT'S .... FUNNY!!!
THIS CALLS FOR A SODA AT THE CHOK'LIT SHOP! I'M SHORT OF FUNDS, HOWEVER... BUT...
MY BOSOM BUDDIES... WOULD BE HAPPY TO TREAT ME!
HEY! ARCHIE HERE COMES THE KING SIZE SODA MOOCHER WITH A THIRST TO MATCH!
IF HE THINKS HE'LL GET A FREE SODA FROM ME, HE'S MISTAKEN! LET'S DEEP FREEZE!
HIYA! FELLOWS! PALS!
I SAID, HI FELLOWS!
SAY, ARCH! DO YOU HEAR ANYTHING?
YES! NOW THAT YOU MENTION IT, REGGIE, I DO HEAR SOMETHING!
BUT THERE'S NOBODY HERE!
?

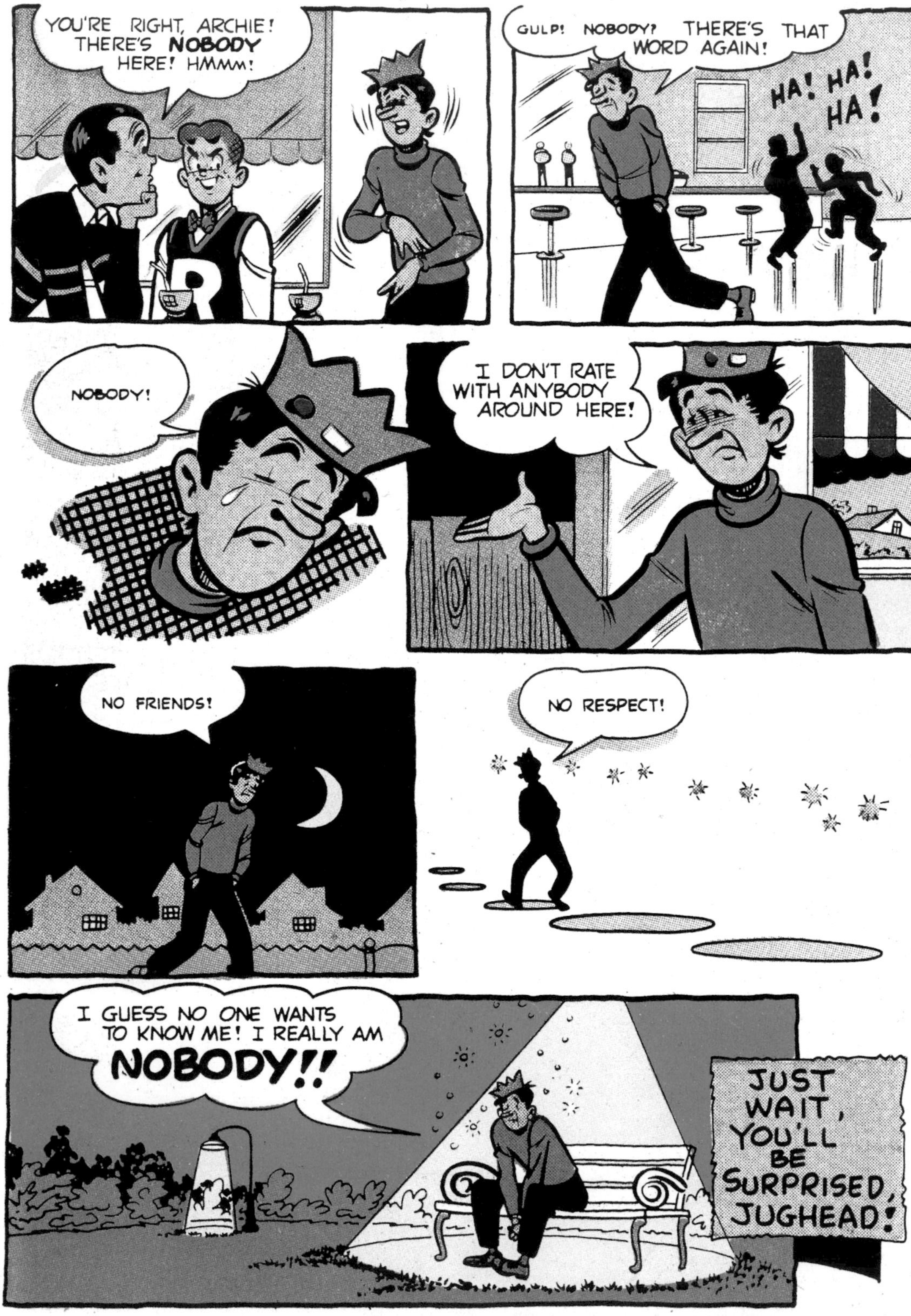
YOU'RE RIGHT, ARCHIE! THERE'S NOBODY HERE! HMMM!
GULP! NOBODY? THERE'S THAT WORD AGAIN!
HA! HA! HA!
NOBODY!
I DON'T RATE WITH ANYBODY AROUND HERE!
NO FRIENDS!
NO RESPECT!
I GUESS NO ONE WANTS TO KNOW ME! I REALLY AM NOBODY!!
JUST WAIT, YOU'LL BE SURPRISED, JUGHEAD!

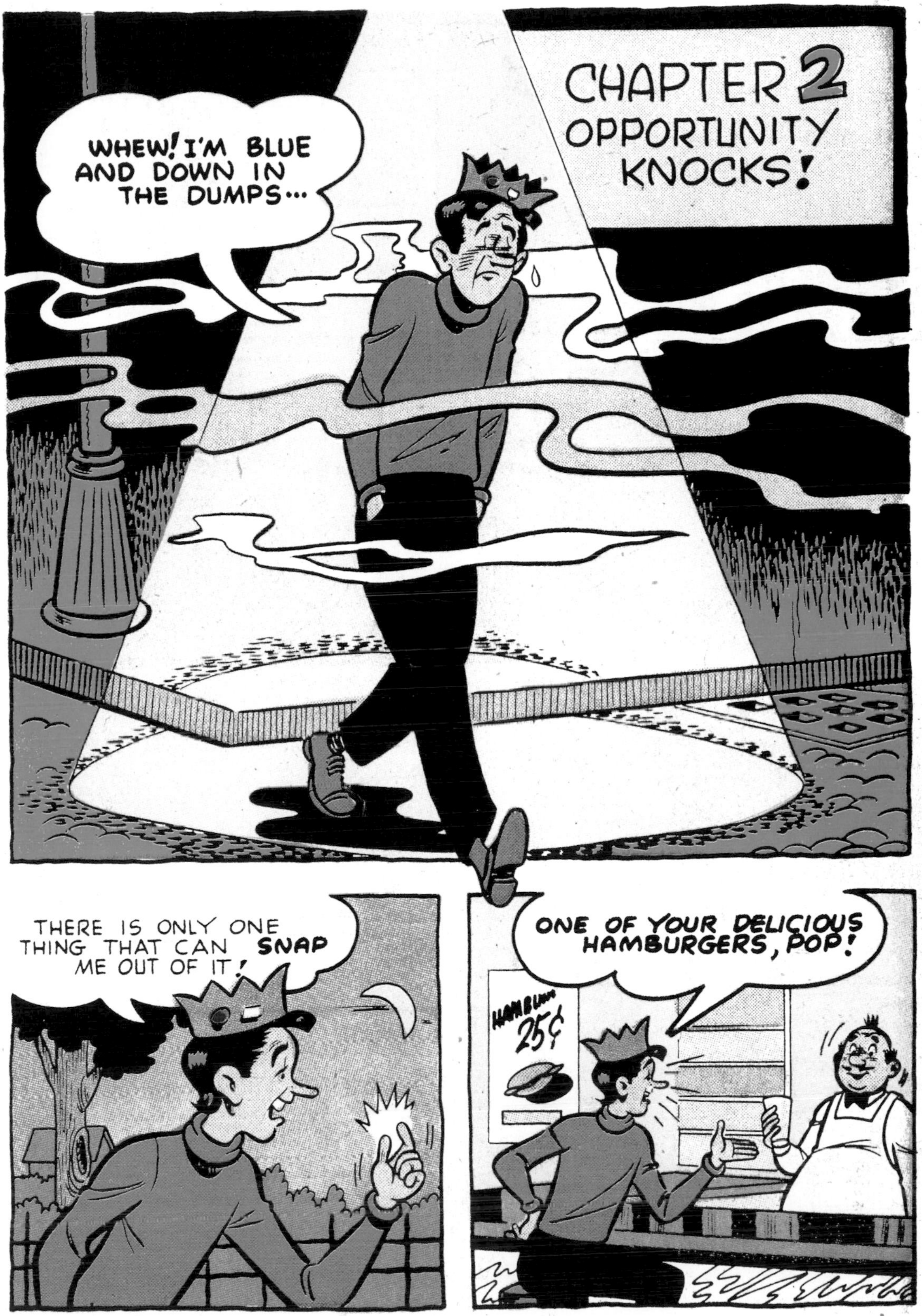
CHAPTER 2
OPPORTUNITY KNOCKS!
WHEW! I'M BLUE AND DOWN IN THE DUMPS...
THERE IS ONLY ONE THING THAT CAN SNAP ME OUT OF IT!
ONE OF YOUR DELICIOUS HAMBURGERS, POP!
25¢

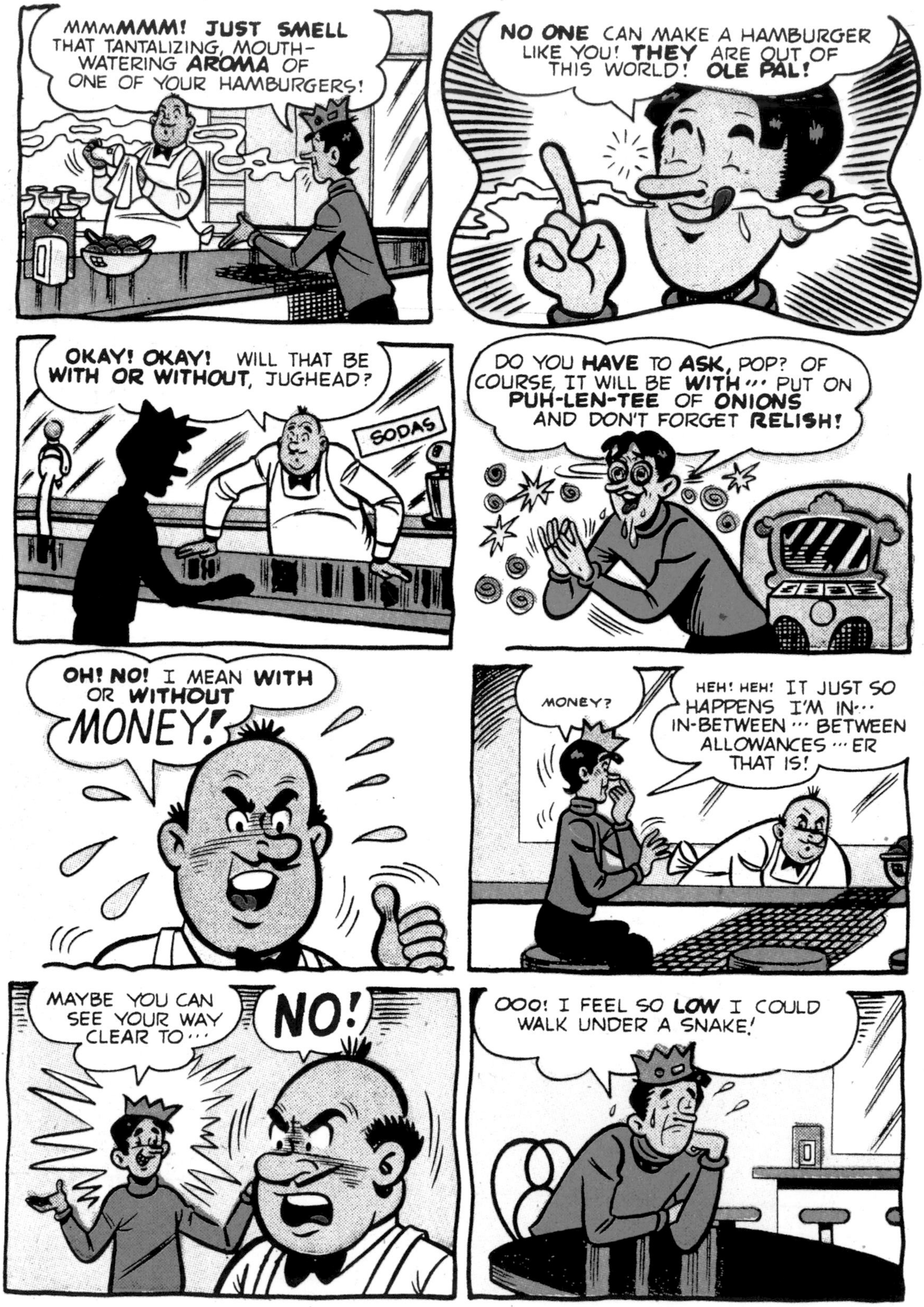
MMMMMM! JUST SMELL THAT TANTALIZING, MOUTH-WATERING AROMA OF ONE OF YOUR HAMBURGERS!
NO ONE CAN MAKE A HAMBURGER LIKE YOU! THEY ARE OUT OF THIS WORLD! OLE PAL!
OKAY! OKAY! WILL THAT BE WITH OR WITHOUT, JUGHEAD?
SODAS
DO YOU HAVE TO ASK, POP? OF COURSE, IT WILL BE WITH··· PUT ON PUH-LEN-TEE OF ONIONS AND DON'T FORGET RELISH!
OH! NO! I MEAN WITH OR WITHOUT MONEY!
MONEY?
HEH! HEH! IT JUST SO HAPPENS I'M IN··· IN-BETWEEN ··· BETWEEN ALLOWANCES ··· ER THAT IS!
MAYBE YOU CAN SEE YOUR WAY CLEAR TO···
NO!
OOO! I FEEL SO LOW I COULD WALK UNDER A SNAKE!

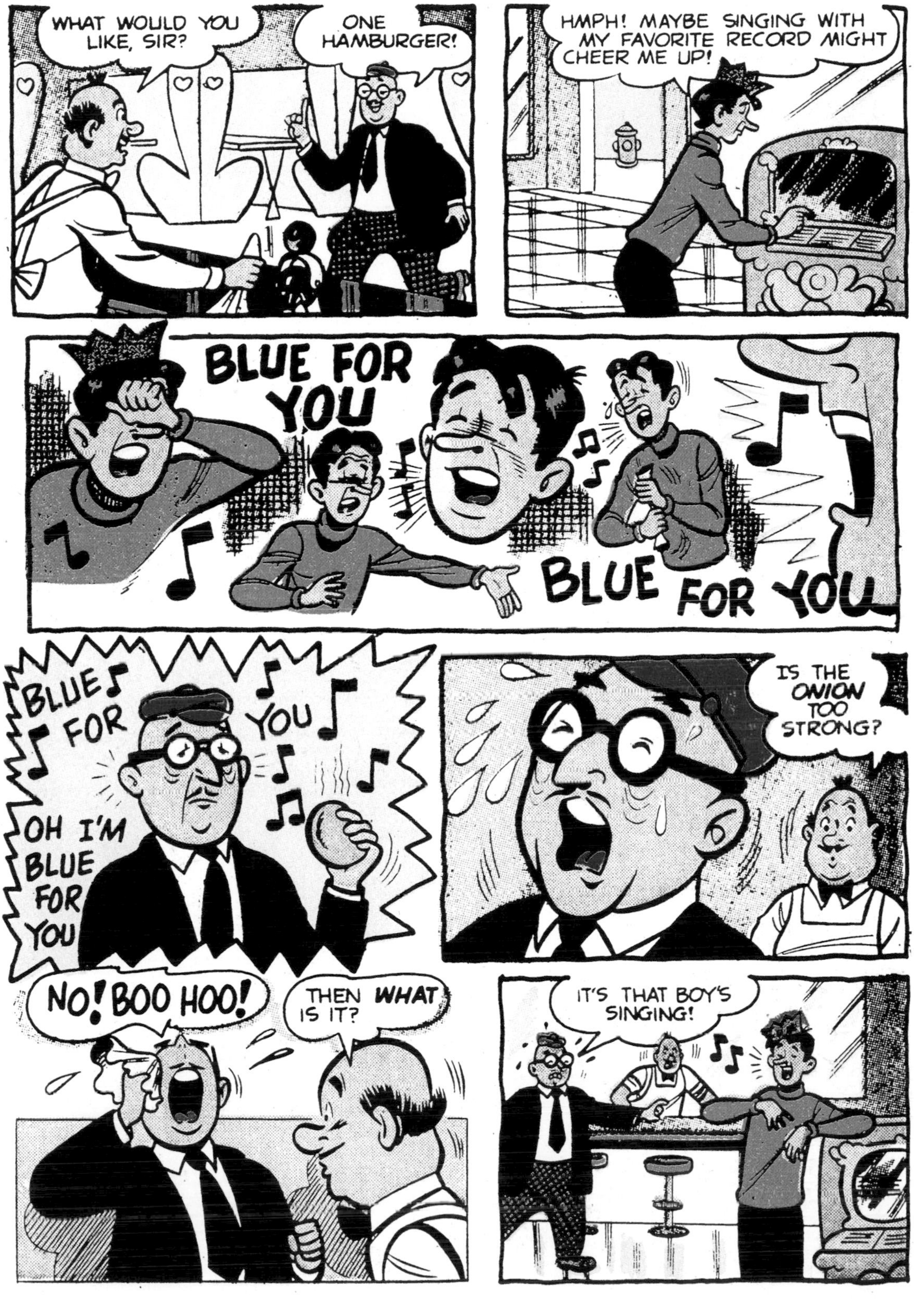
WHAT WOULD YOU LIKE, SIR?
ONE HAMBURGER!
HMPH! MAYBE SINGING WITH MY FAVORITE RECORD MIGHT CHEER ME UP!
BLUE FOR YOU
BLUE FOR YOU
BLUE FOR YOU
OH I'M BLUE FOR YOU
IS THE ONION TOO STRONG?
NO! BOO HOO!
THEN WHAT IS IT?
IT'S THAT BOY'S SINGING!

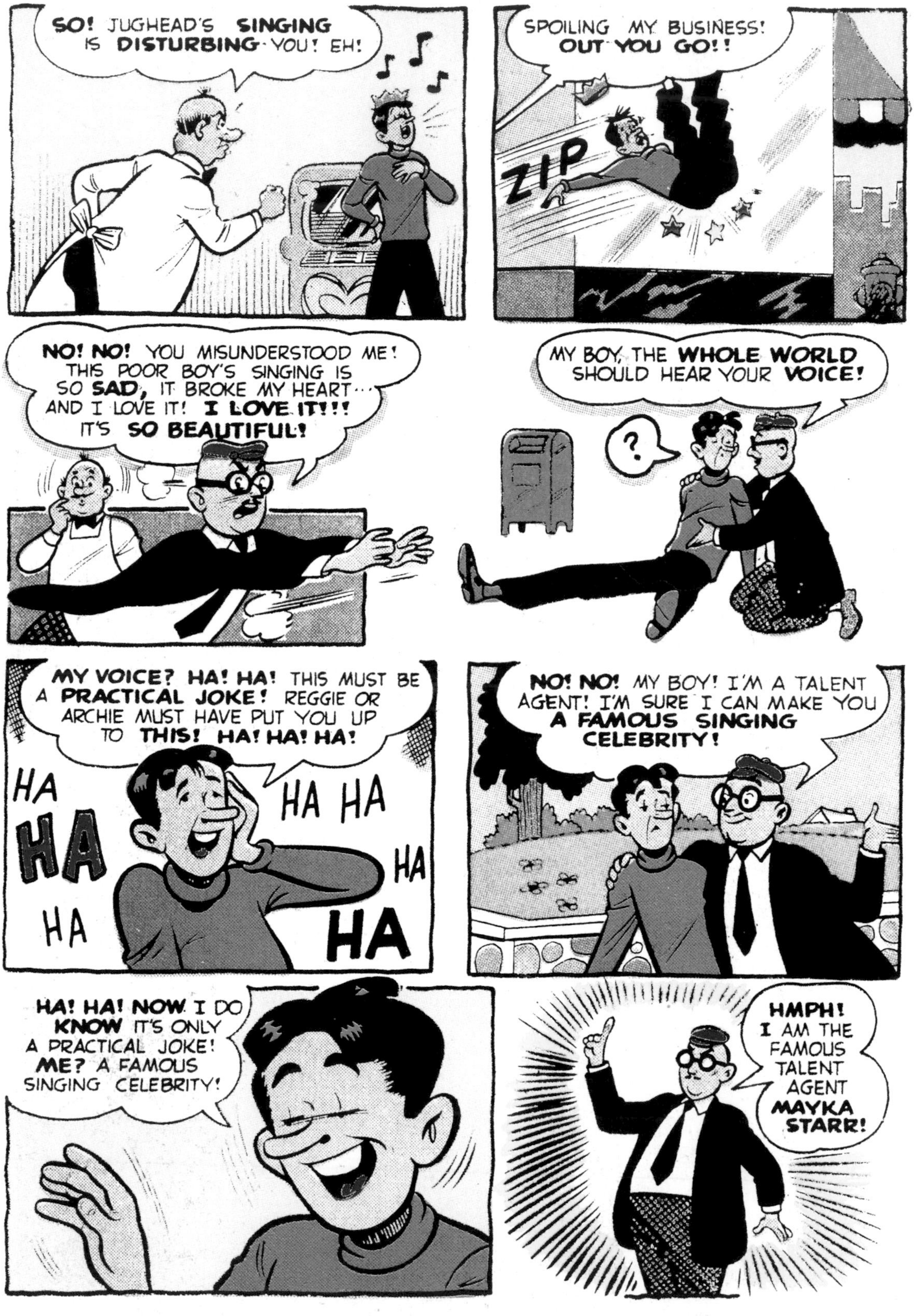
SO! JUGHEAD'S SINGING IS DISTURBING YOU! EH!
SPOILING MY BUSINESS! OUT YOU GO!!
ZIP
NO! NO! YOU MISUNDERSTOOD ME! THIS POOR BOY'S SINGING IS SO SAD, IT BROKE MY HEART... AND I LOVE IT! I LOVE IT!!! IT'S SO BEAUTIFUL!
MY BOY, THE WHOLE WORLD SHOULD HEAR YOUR VOICE!
?
MY VOICE? HA! HA! THIS MUST BE A PRACTICAL JOKE! REGGIE OR ARCHIE MUST HAVE PUT YOU UP TO THIS! HA! HA! HA!
HA HA HA HA HA HA HA HA
NO! NO! MY BOY! I'M A TALENT AGENT! I'M SURE I CAN MAKE YOU A FAMOUS SINGING CELEBRITY!
HA! HA! NOW I DO KNOW IT'S ONLY A PRACTICAL JOKE! ME? A FAMOUS SINGING CELEBRITY!
HMPH! I AM THE FAMOUS TALENT AGENT MAYKA STARR!

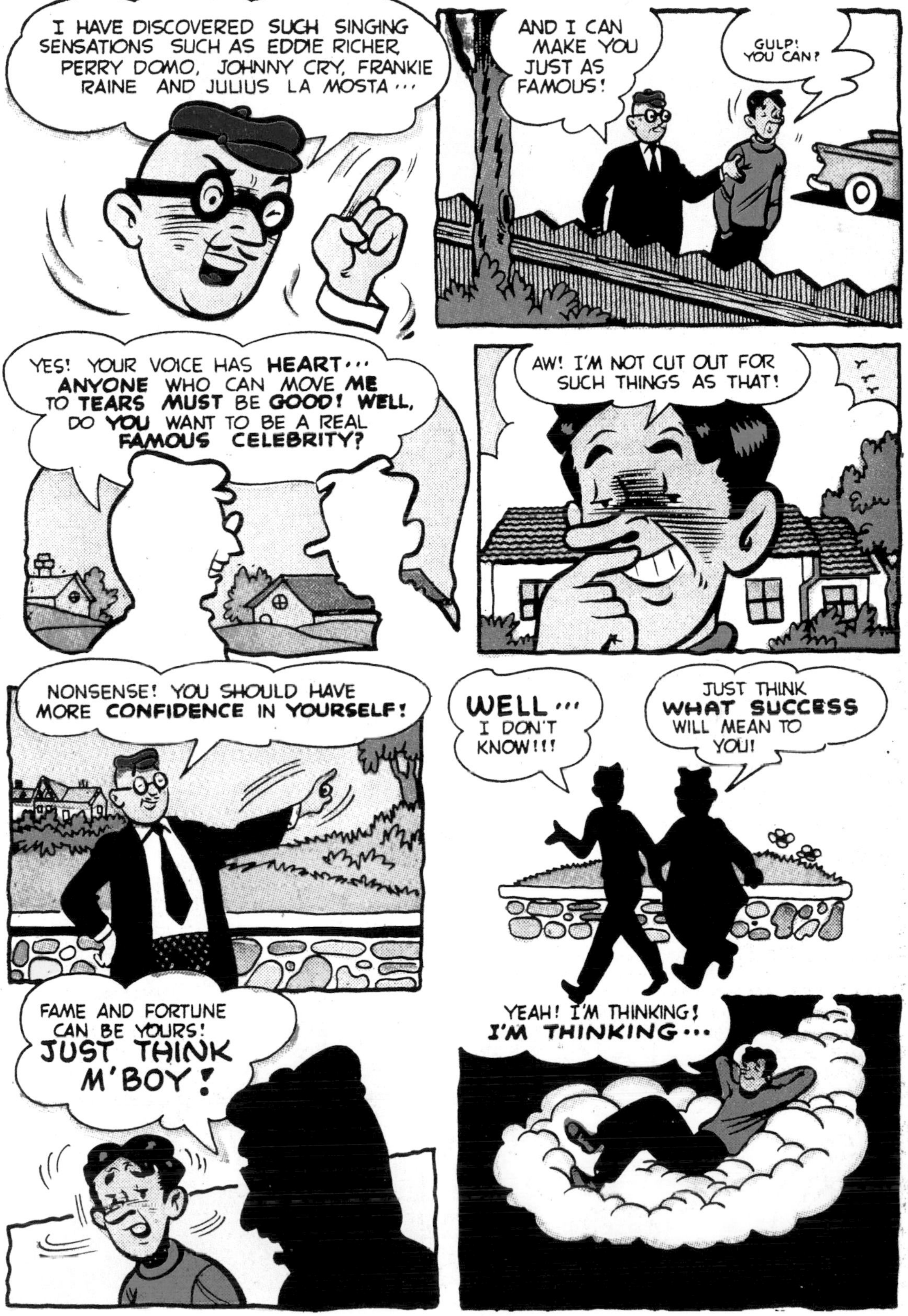
I HAVE DISCOVERED SUCH SINGING SENSATIONS SUCH AS EDDIE RICHER, PERRY DOMO, JOHNNY CRY, FRANKIE RAINE AND JULIUS LA MOSTA...
AND I CAN MAKE YOU JUST AS FAMOUS!
GULP! YOU CAN?
YES! YOUR VOICE HAS HEART... ANYONE WHO CAN MOVE ME TO TEARS MUST BE GOOD! WELL, DO YOU WANT TO BE A REAL FAMOUS CELEBRITY?
AW! I'M NOT CUT OUT FOR SUCH THINGS AS THAT!
NONSENSE! YOU SHOULD HAVE MORE CONFIDENCE IN YOURSELF!
WELL... I DON'T KNOW!!!
JUST THINK WHAT SUCCESS WILL MEAN TO YOU!
FAME AND FORTUNE CAN BE YOURS! JUST THINK M'BOY!
YEAH! I'M THINKING! I'M THINKING...

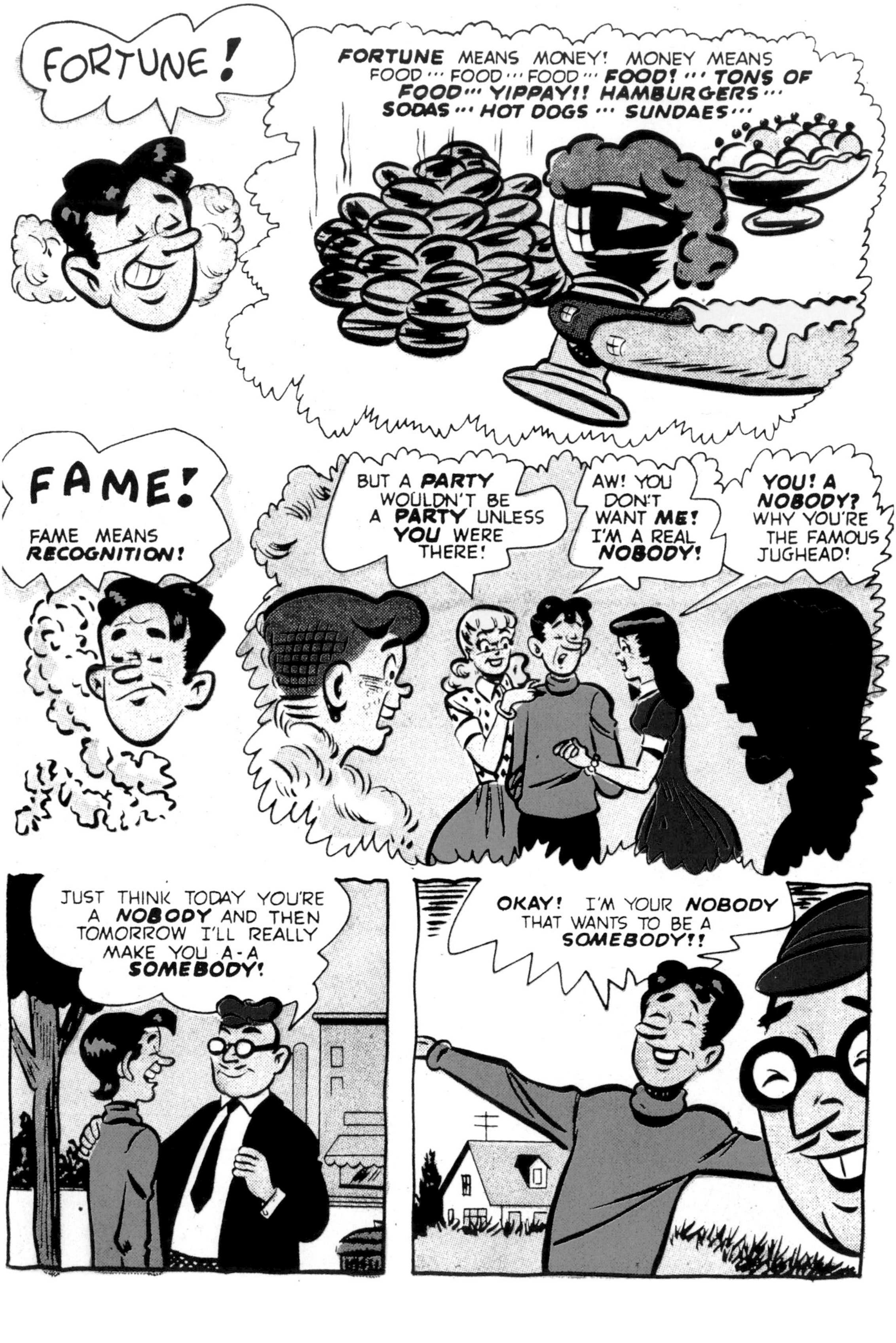
FORTUNE!
FORTUNE MEANS MONEY! MONEY MEANS FOOD... FOOD... FOOD... FOOD!... TONS OF FOOD... YIPPAY!! HAMBURGERS... SODAS... HOT DOGS... SUNDAES...
FAME!
FAME MEANS RECOGNITION!
BUT A PARTY WOULDN'T BE A PARTY UNLESS YOU WERE THERE!
AW! YOU DON'T WANT ME! I'M A REAL NOBODY!
YOU! A NOBODY? WHY YOU'RE THE FAMOUS JUGHEAD!
JUST THINK TODAY YOU'RE A NOBODY AND THEN TOMORROW I'LL REALLY MAKE YOU A-A SOMEBODY!
OKAY! I'M YOUR NOBODY THAT WANTS TO BE A SOMEBODY!!

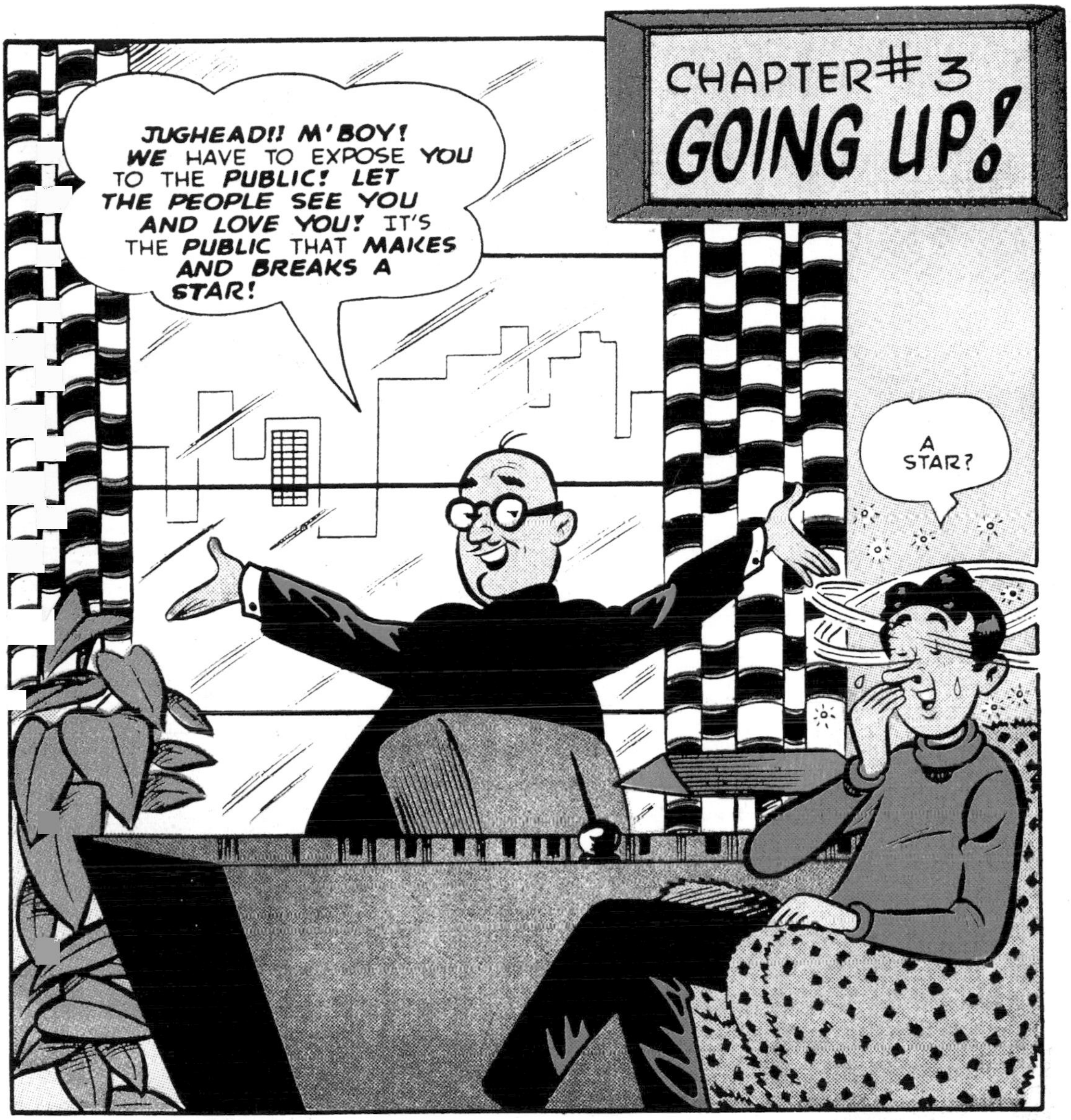
CHAPTER # 3
GOING UP!
JUGHEAD!! M'BOY! WE HAVE TO EXPOSE YOU TO THE PUBLIC! LET THE PEOPLE SEE YOU AND LOVE YOU! IT'S THE PUBLIC THAT MAKES AND BREAKS A STAR!
A STAR?

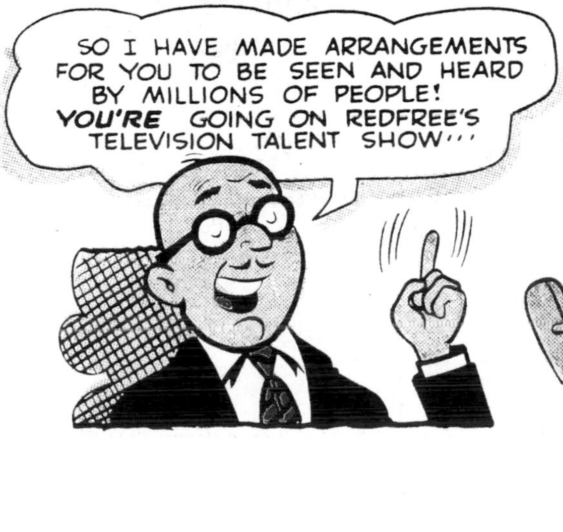
SO I HAVE MADE ARRANGEMENTS FOR YOU TO BE SEEN AND HEARD BY MILLIONS OF PEOPLE! YOU'RE GOING ON REDFREE'S TELEVISION TALENT SHOW...

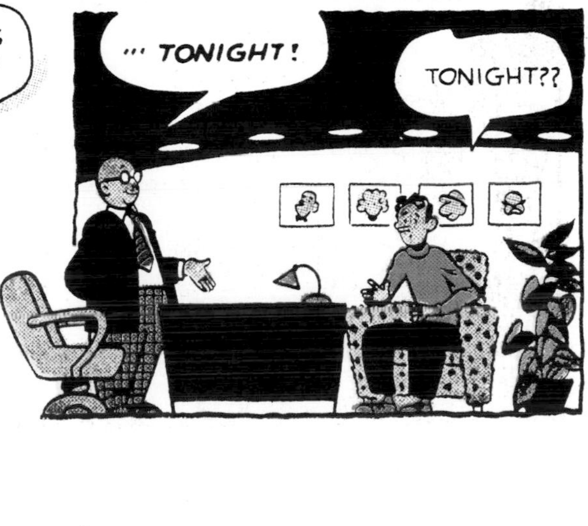
... TONIGHT!
TONIGHT??

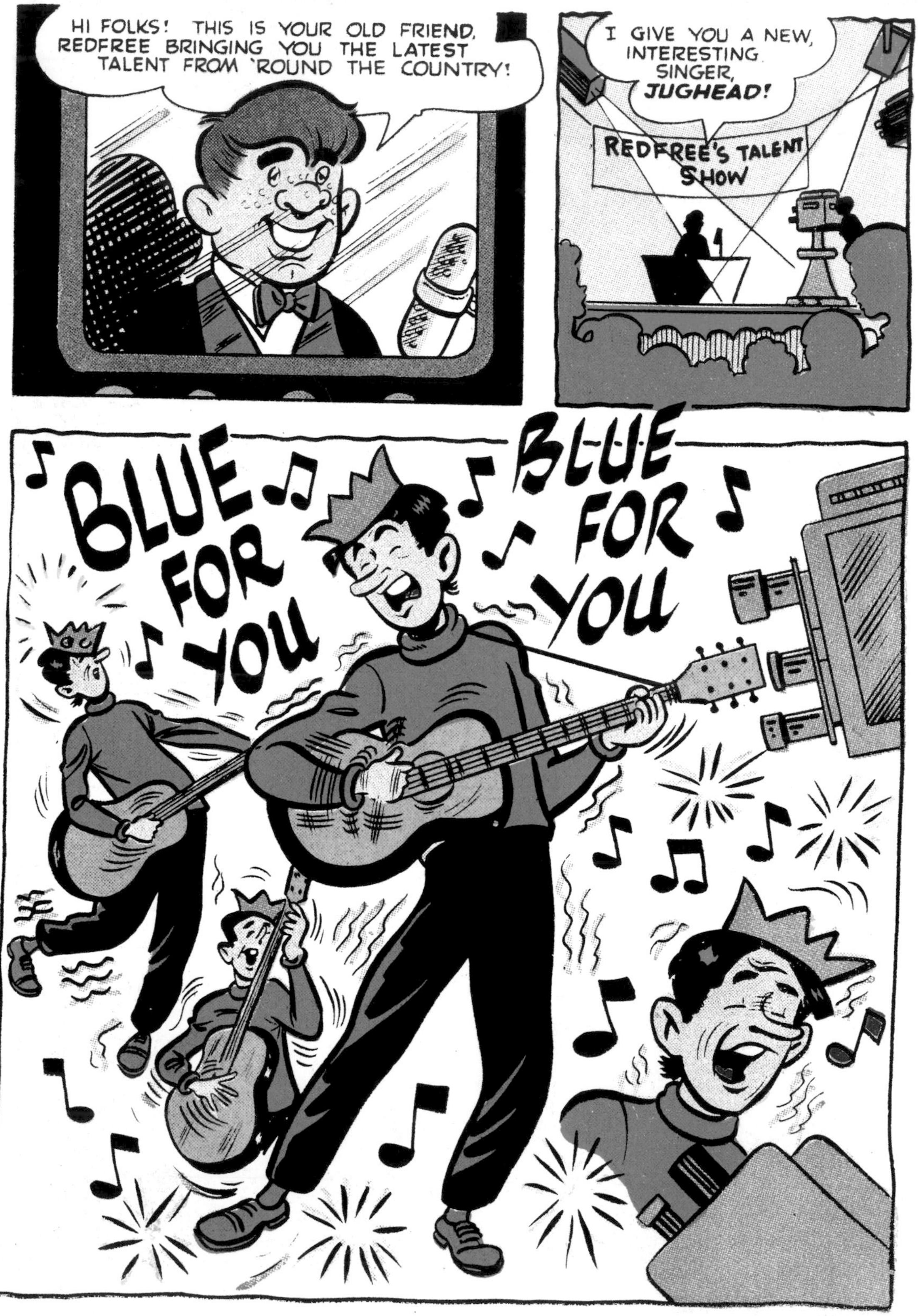
HI FOLKS! THIS IS YOUR OLD FRIEND, REDFREE BRINGING YOU THE LATEST TALENT FROM 'ROUND THE COUNTRY!
I GIVE YOU A NEW, INTERESTING SINGER, JUGHEAD!
REDFREE'S TALENT SHOW
BLUE FOR YOU
BLUE FOR YOU

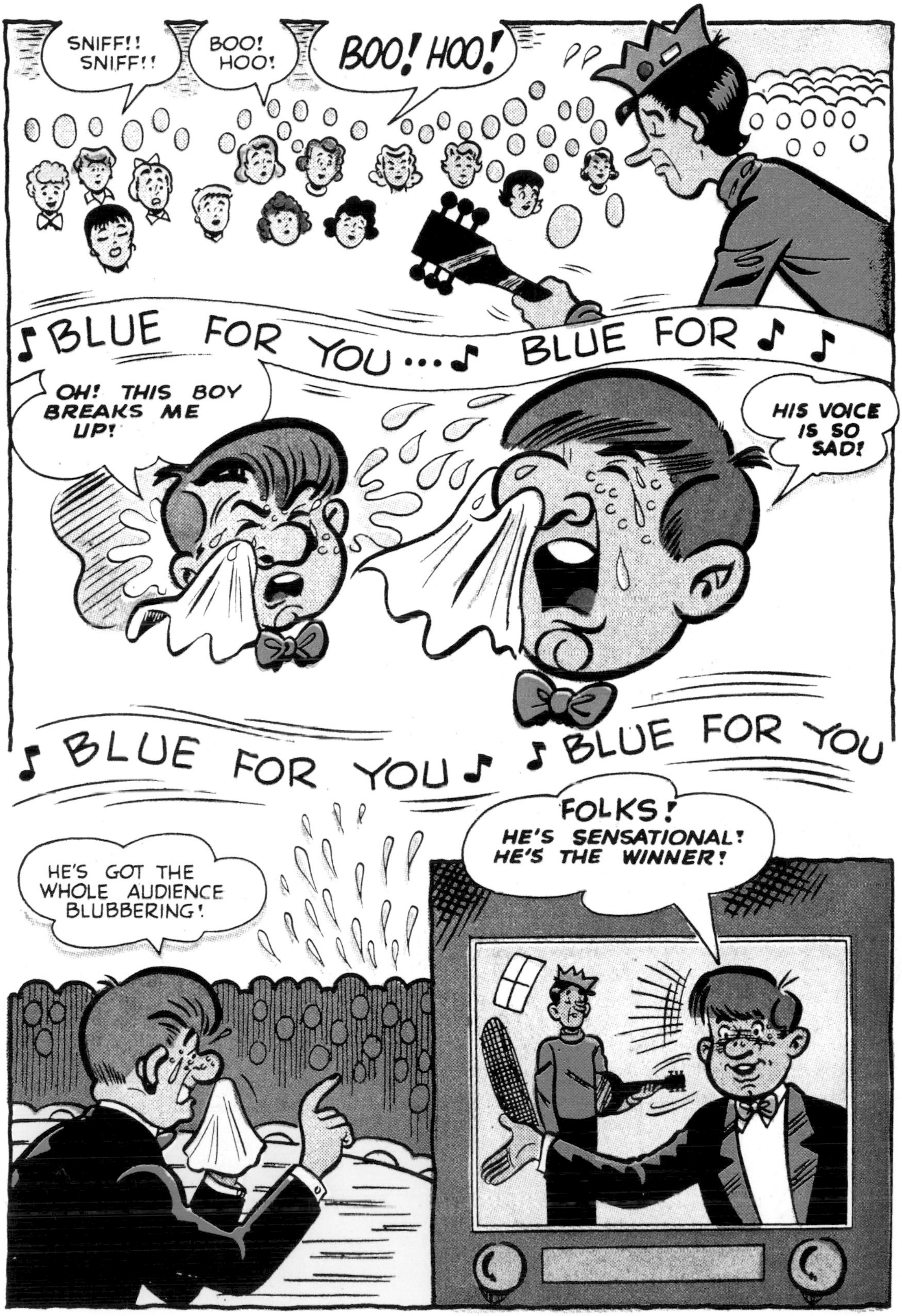
SNIFF!! SNIFF!!
BOO! HOO!
BOO! HOO!
♪ BLUE FOR YOU... ♪ BLUE FOR ♪ ♪
OH! THIS BOY BREAKS ME UP!
HIS VOICE IS SO SAD!
♪ BLUE FOR YOU ♪ ♪ BLUE FOR YOU
HE'S GOT THE WHOLE AUDIENCE BLUBBERING!
FOLKS! HE'S SENSATIONAL! HE'S THE WINNER!

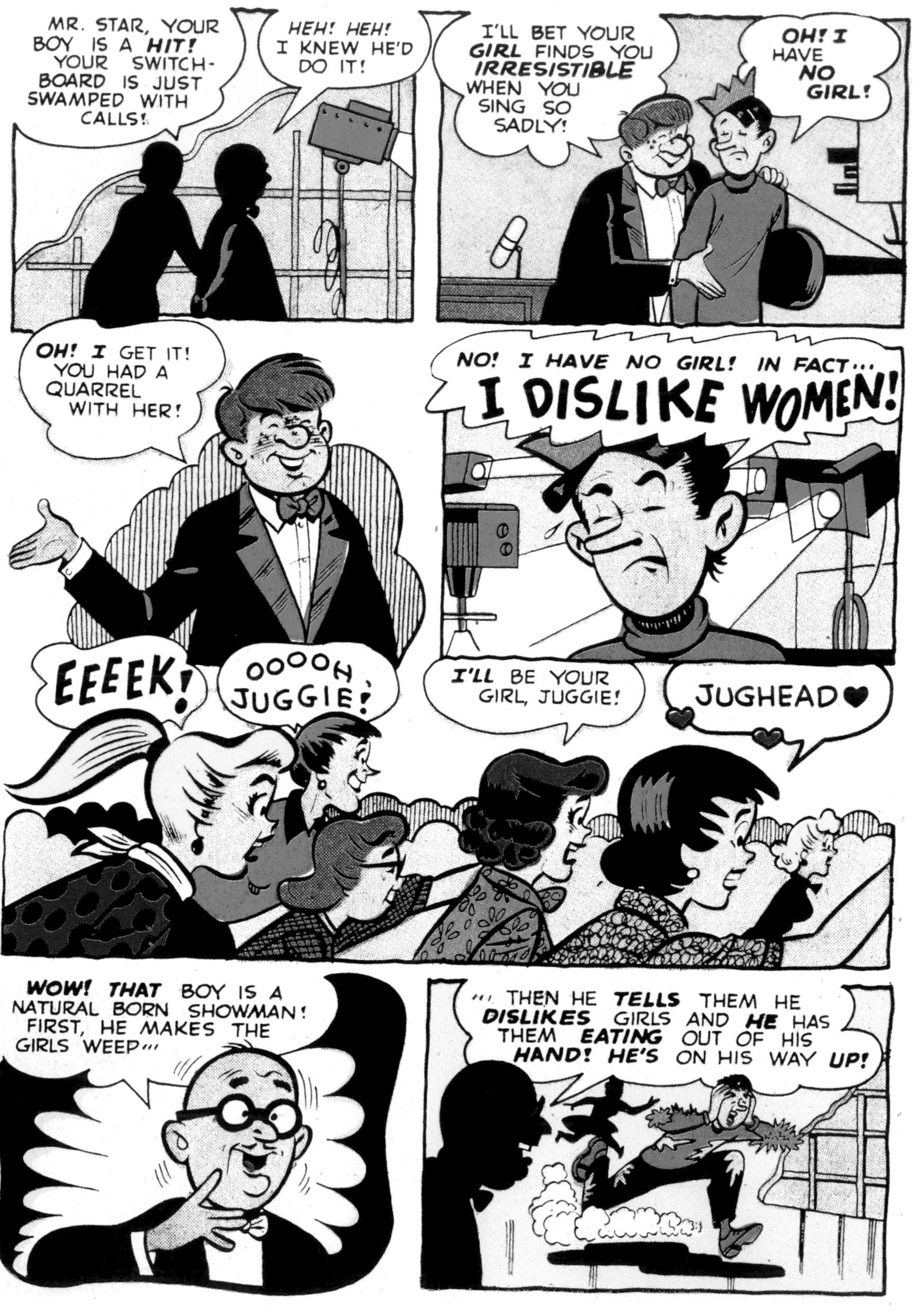
MR. STAR, YOUR BOY IS A HIT! YOUR SWITCH-BOARD IS JUST SWAMPED WITH CALLS!
HEH! HEH! I KNEW HE'D DO IT!
I'LL BET YOUR GIRL FINDS YOU IRRESISTIBLE WHEN YOU SING SO SADLY!
OH! I HAVE NO GIRL!
OH! I GET IT! YOU HAD A QUARREL WITH HER!
NO! I HAVE NO GIRL! IN FACT...
I DISLIKE WOMEN!
EEEEK!
OOOOH, JUGGIE!
I'LL BE YOUR GIRL, JUGGIE!
JUGHEAD
WOW! THAT BOY IS A NATURAL BORN SHOWMAN! FIRST, HE MAKES THE GIRLS WEEP...
... THEN HE TELLS THEM HE DISLIKES GIRLS AND HE HAS THEM EATING OUT OF HIS HAND! HE'S ON HIS WAY UP!

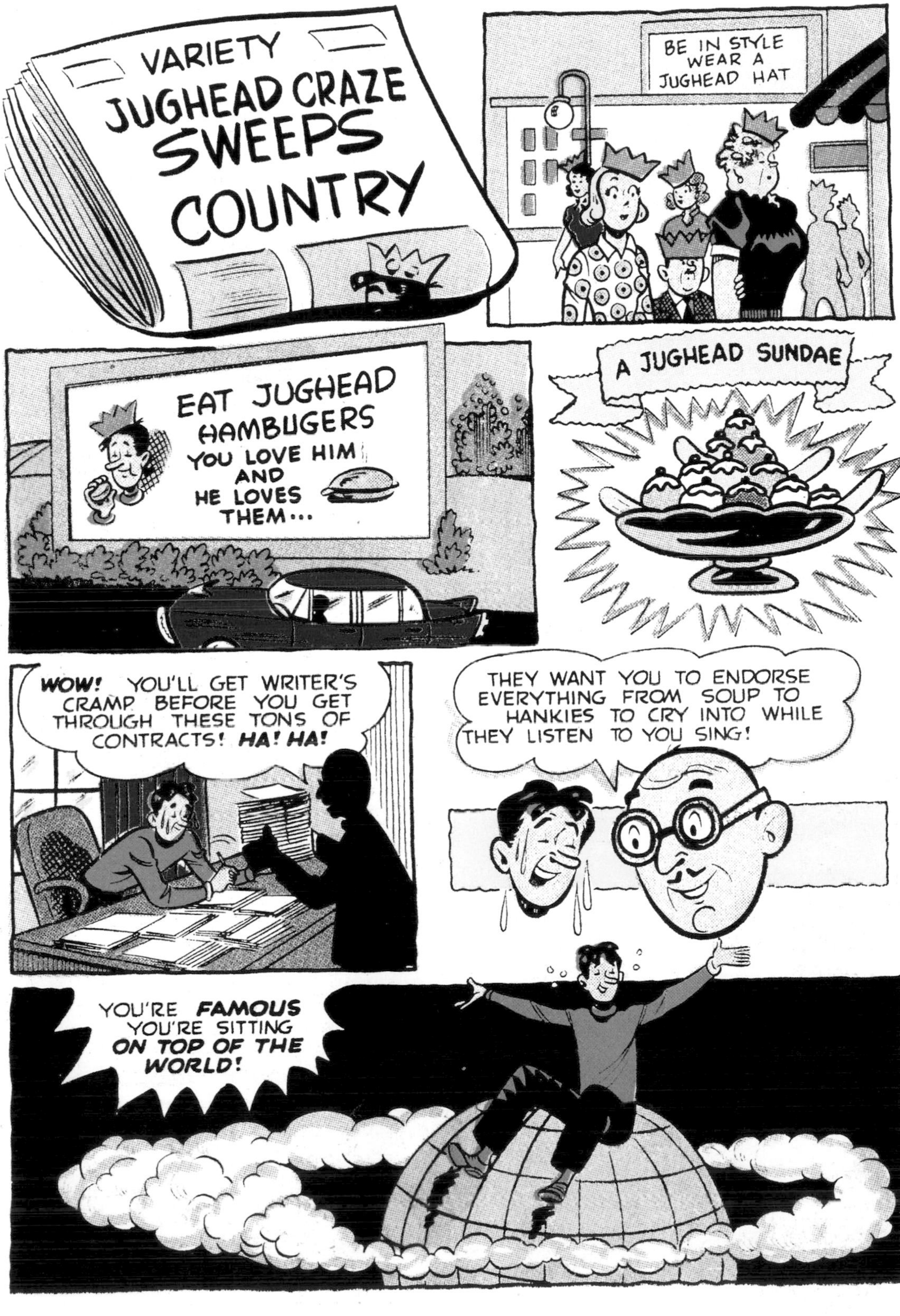

VARIETY
JUGHEAD CRAZE SWEEPS COUNTRY
BE IN STYLE WEAR A JUGHEAD HAT
EAT JUGHEAD HAMBUGERS
YOU LOVE HIM AND HE LOVES THEM...
A JUGHEAD SUNDAE
WOW! YOU'LL GET WRITER'S CRAMP BEFORE YOU GET THROUGH THESE TONS OF CONTRACTS! HA! HA!
THEY WANT YOU TO ENDORSE EVERYTHING FROM SOUP TO HANKIES TO CRY INTO WHILE THEY LISTEN TO YOU SING!
YOU'RE FAMOUS YOU'RE SITTING ON TOP OF THE WORLD!

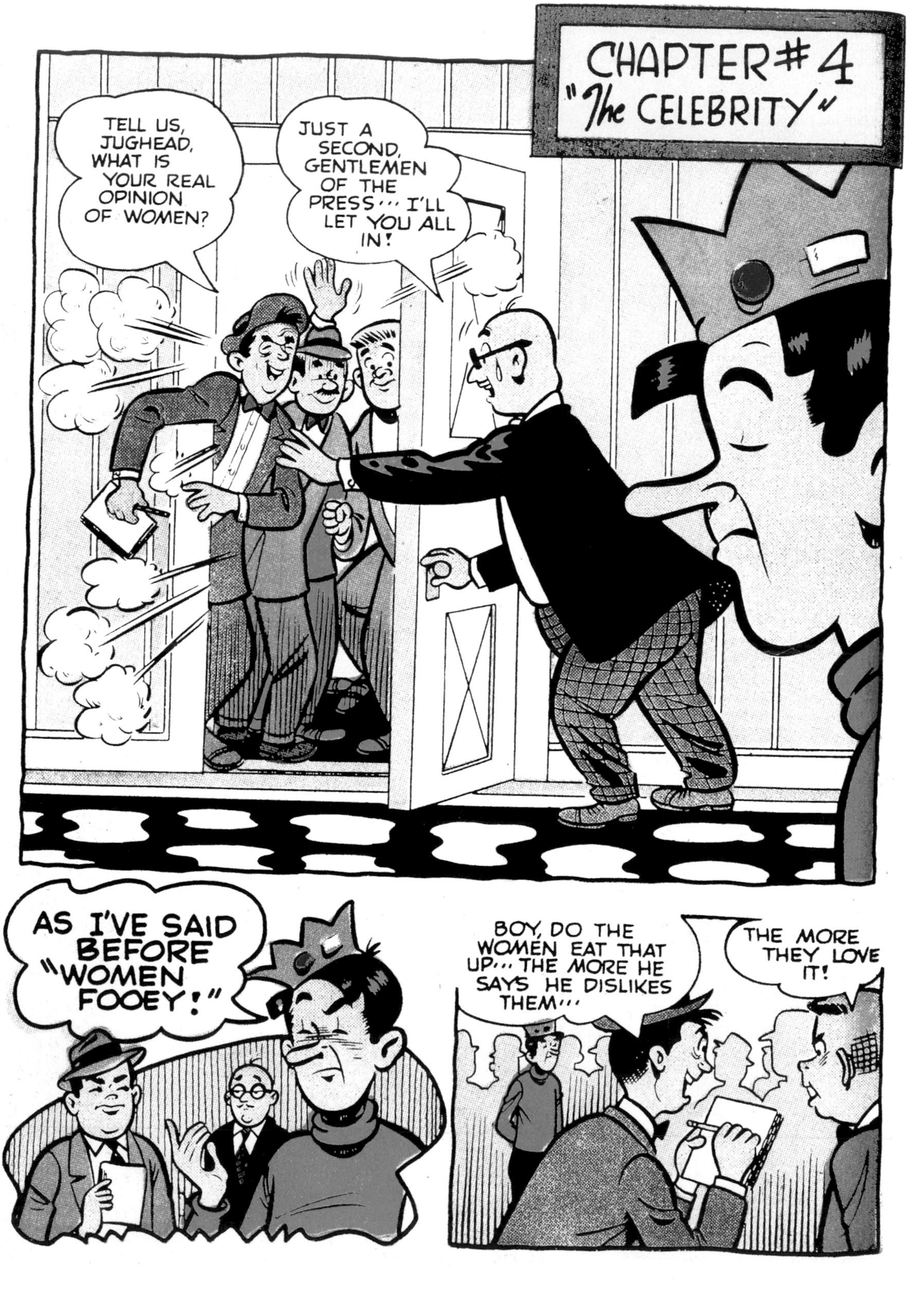
CHAPTER # 4
"The CELEBRITY"
TELL US, JUGHEAD, WHAT IS YOUR REAL OPINION OF WOMEN?
JUST A SECOND, GENTLEMEN OF THE PRESS... I'LL LET YOU ALL IN!
AS I'VE SAID BEFORE "WOMEN FOOEY!"
BOY, DO THE WOMEN EAT THAT UP... THE MORE HE SAYS HE DISLIKES THEM...
THE MORE THEY LOVE IT!

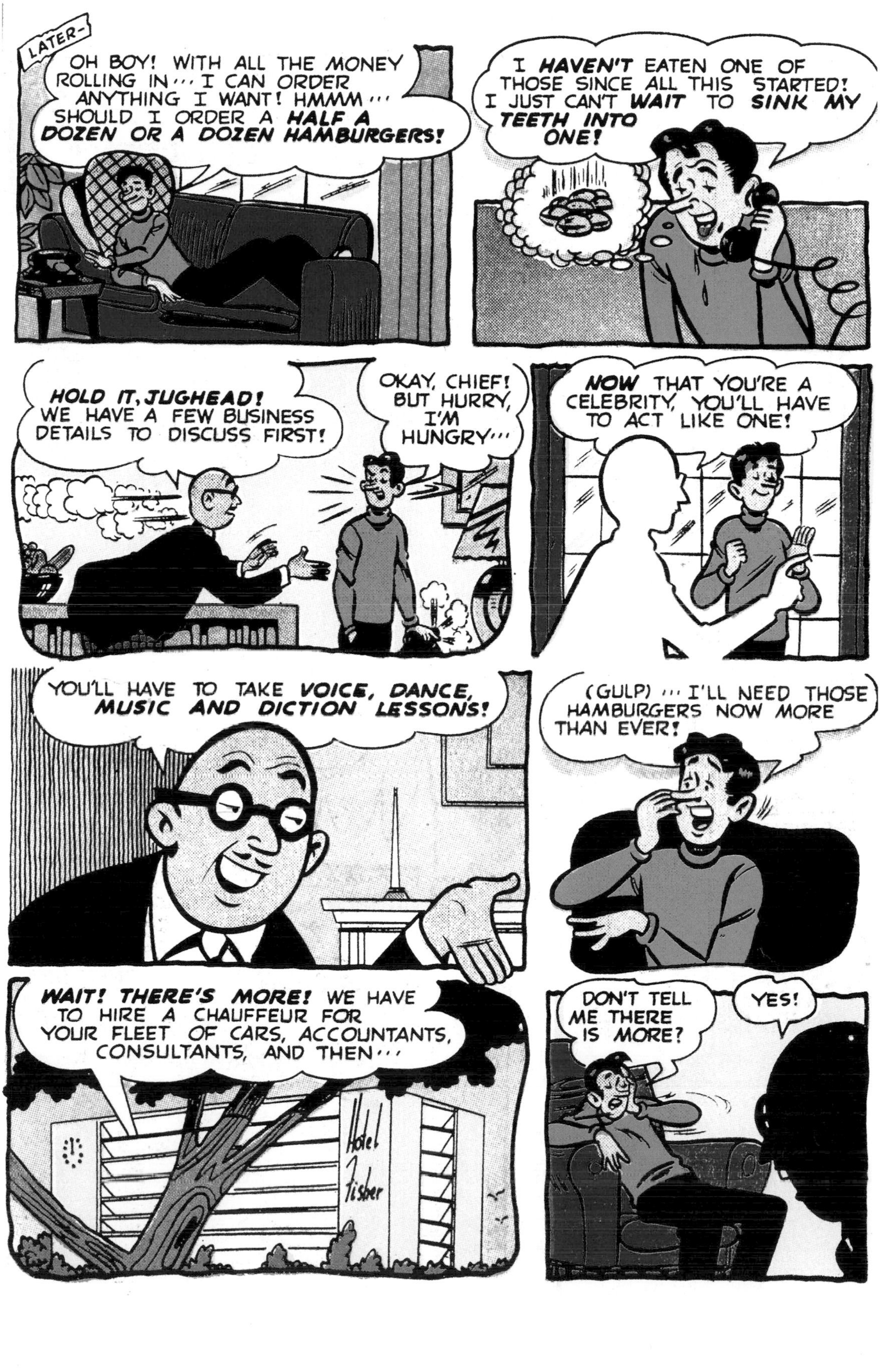
LATER-
OH BOY! WITH ALL THE MONEY ROLLING IN... I CAN ORDER ANYTHING I WANT! HMMM... SHOULD I ORDER A HALF A DOZEN OR A DOZEN HAMBURGERS!
I HAVEN'T EATEN ONE OF THOSE SINCE ALL THIS STARTED! I JUST CAN'T WAIT TO SINK MY TEETH INTO ONE!
HOLD IT, JUGHEAD! WE HAVE A FEW BUSINESS DETAILS TO DISCUSS FIRST!
OKAY, CHIEF! BUT HURRY, I'M HUNGRY...
NOW THAT YOU'RE A CELEBRITY, YOU'LL HAVE TO ACT LIKE ONE!
YOU'LL HAVE TO TAKE VOICE, DANCE, MUSIC AND DICTION LESSONS!
(GULP)... I'LL NEED THOSE HAMBURGERS NOW MORE THAN EVER!
WAIT! THERE'S MORE! WE HAVE TO HIRE A CHAUFFEUR FOR YOUR FLEET OF CARS, ACCOUNTANTS, CONSULTANTS, AND THEN...
Hotel Fisher
DON'T TELL ME THERE IS MORE?
YES!

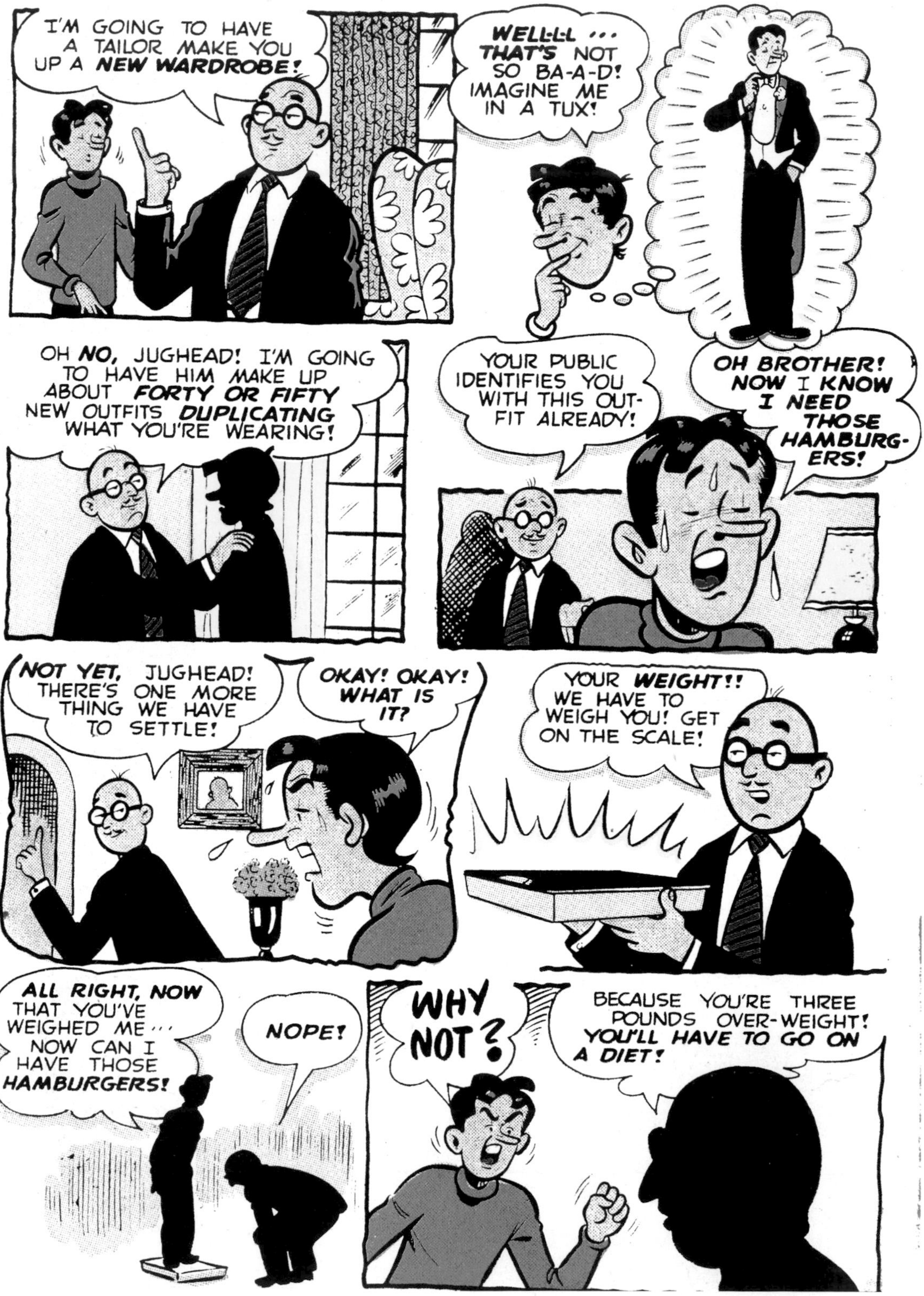
I'M GOING TO HAVE A TAILOR MAKE YOU UP A NEW WARDROBE!
WELL-L-L ... THAT'S NOT SO BA-A-D! IMAGINE ME IN A TUX!
OH NO, JUGHEAD! I'M GOING TO HAVE HIM MAKE UP ABOUT FORTY OR FIFTY NEW OUTFITS DUPLICATING WHAT YOU'RE WEARING!
YOUR PUBLIC IDENTIFIES YOU WITH THIS OUTFIT ALREADY!
OH BROTHER! NOW I KNOW I NEED THOSE HAMBURGERS!
NOT YET, JUGHEAD! THERE'S ONE MORE THING WE HAVE TO SETTLE!
OKAY! OKAY! WHAT IS IT?
YOUR WEIGHT!! WE HAVE TO WEIGH YOU! GET ON THE SCALE!
ALL RIGHT, NOW THAT YOU'VE WEIGHED ME ... NOW CAN I HAVE THOSE HAMBURGERS!
NOPE!
WHY NOT?
BECAUSE YOU'RE THREE POUNDS OVER-WEIGHT! YOU'LL HAVE TO GO ON A DIET!

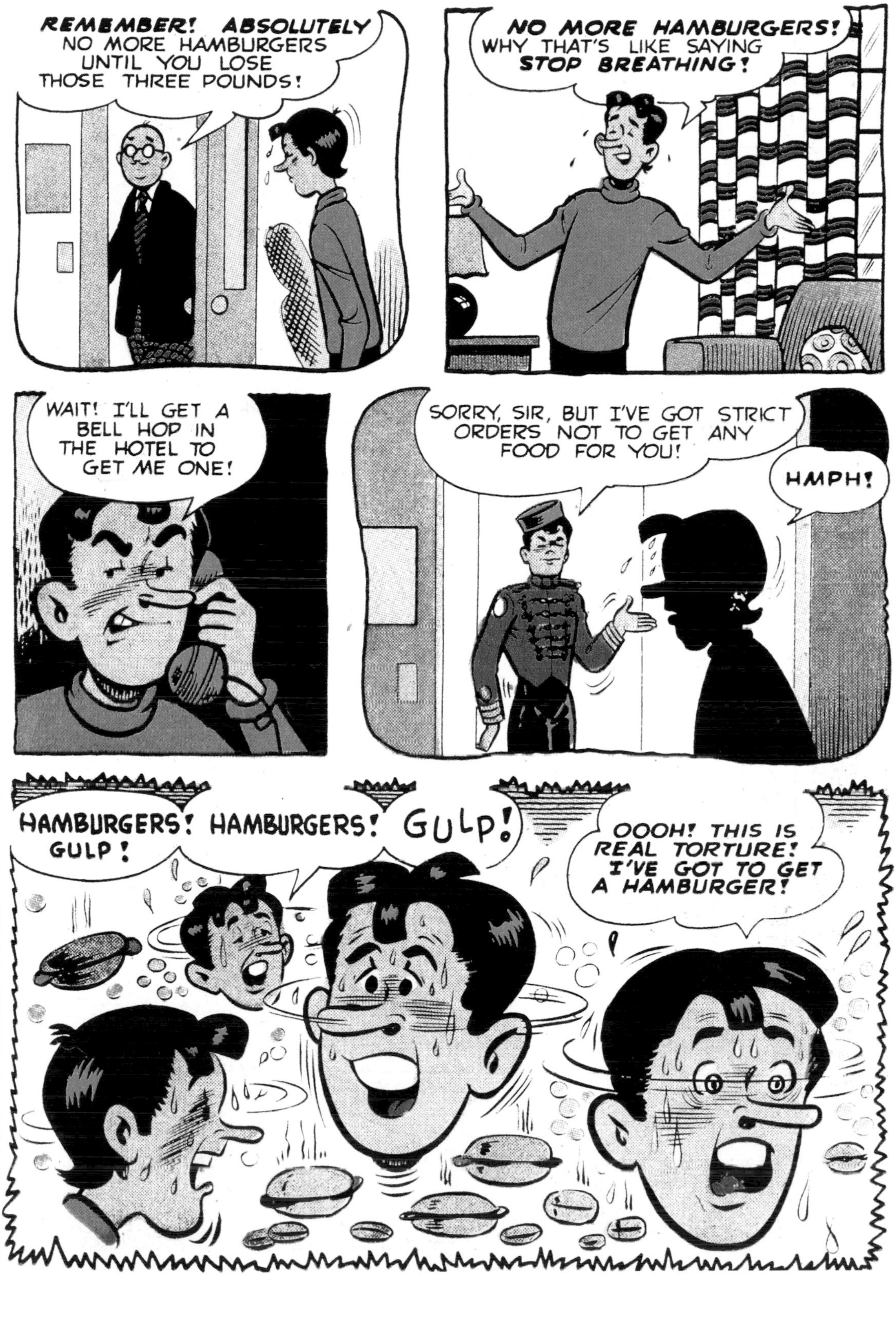
REMEMBER! ABSOLUTELY NO MORE HAMBURGERS UNTIL YOU LOSE THOSE THREE POUNDS!
NO MORE HAMBURGERS! WHY THAT'S LIKE SAYING STOP BREATHING!
WAIT! I'LL GET A BELL HOP IN THE HOTEL TO GET ME ONE!
SORRY, SIR, BUT I'VE GOT STRICT ORDERS NOT TO GET ANY FOOD FOR YOU!
HMPH!
HAMBURGERS! HAMBURGERS! GULP!
GULP!
OOOH! THIS IS REAL TORTURE! I'VE GOT TO GET A HAMBURGER!

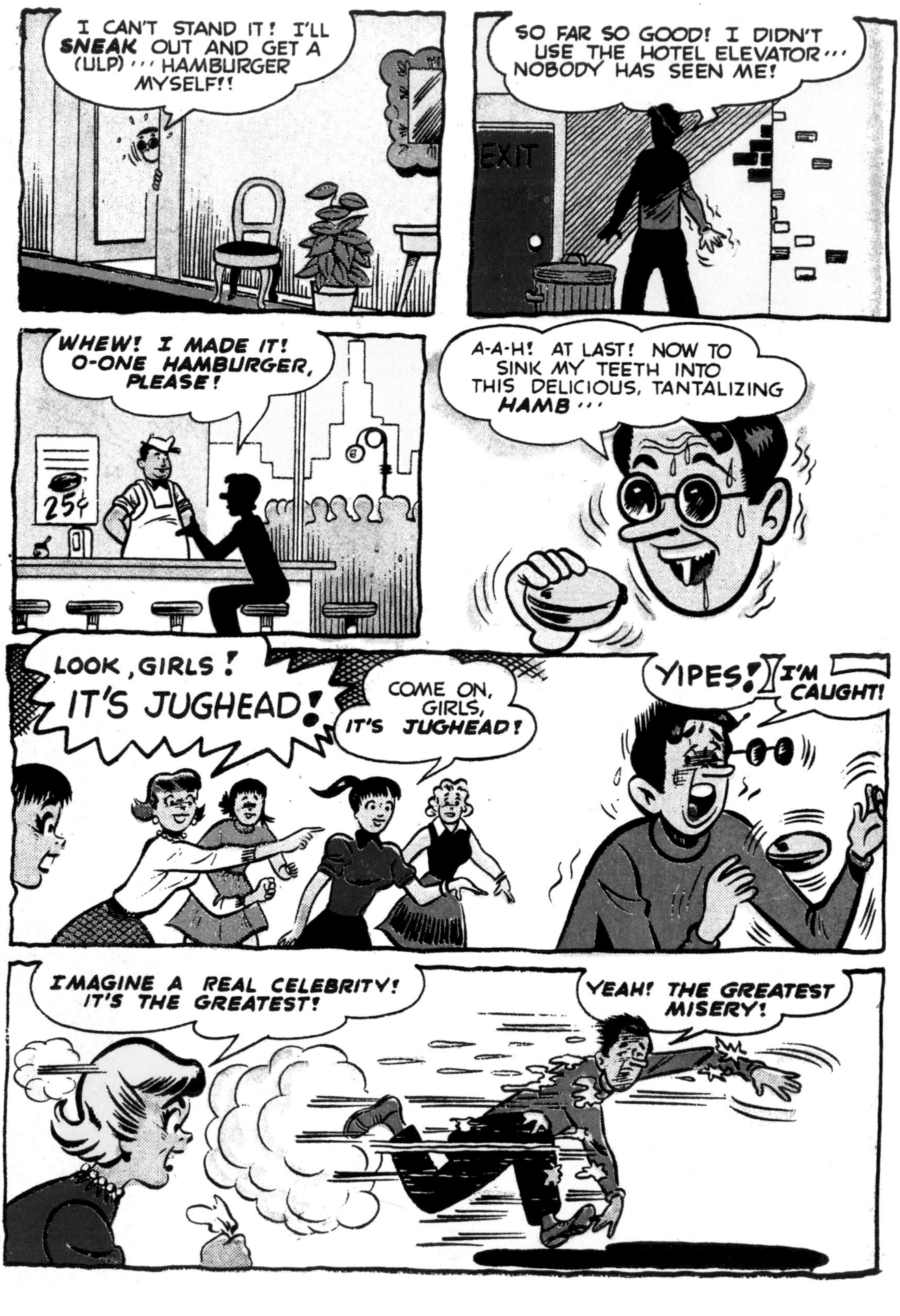
I CAN'T STAND IT! I'LL SNEAK OUT AND GET A (ULP)... HAMBURGER MYSELF!!
SO FAR SO GOOD! I DIDN'T USE THE HOTEL ELEVATOR... NOBODY HAS SEEN ME!
EXIT
WHEW! I MADE IT! O-ONE HAMBURGER, PLEASE!
25¢
A-A-H! AT LAST! NOW TO SINK MY TEETH INTO THIS DELICIOUS, TANTALIZING HAMB...
LOOK, GIRLS! IT'S JUGHEAD!
COME ON, GIRLS, IT'S JUGHEAD!
YIPES! I'M CAUGHT!
IMAGINE A REAL CELEBRITY! IT'S THE GREATEST!
YEAH! THE GREATEST MISERY!

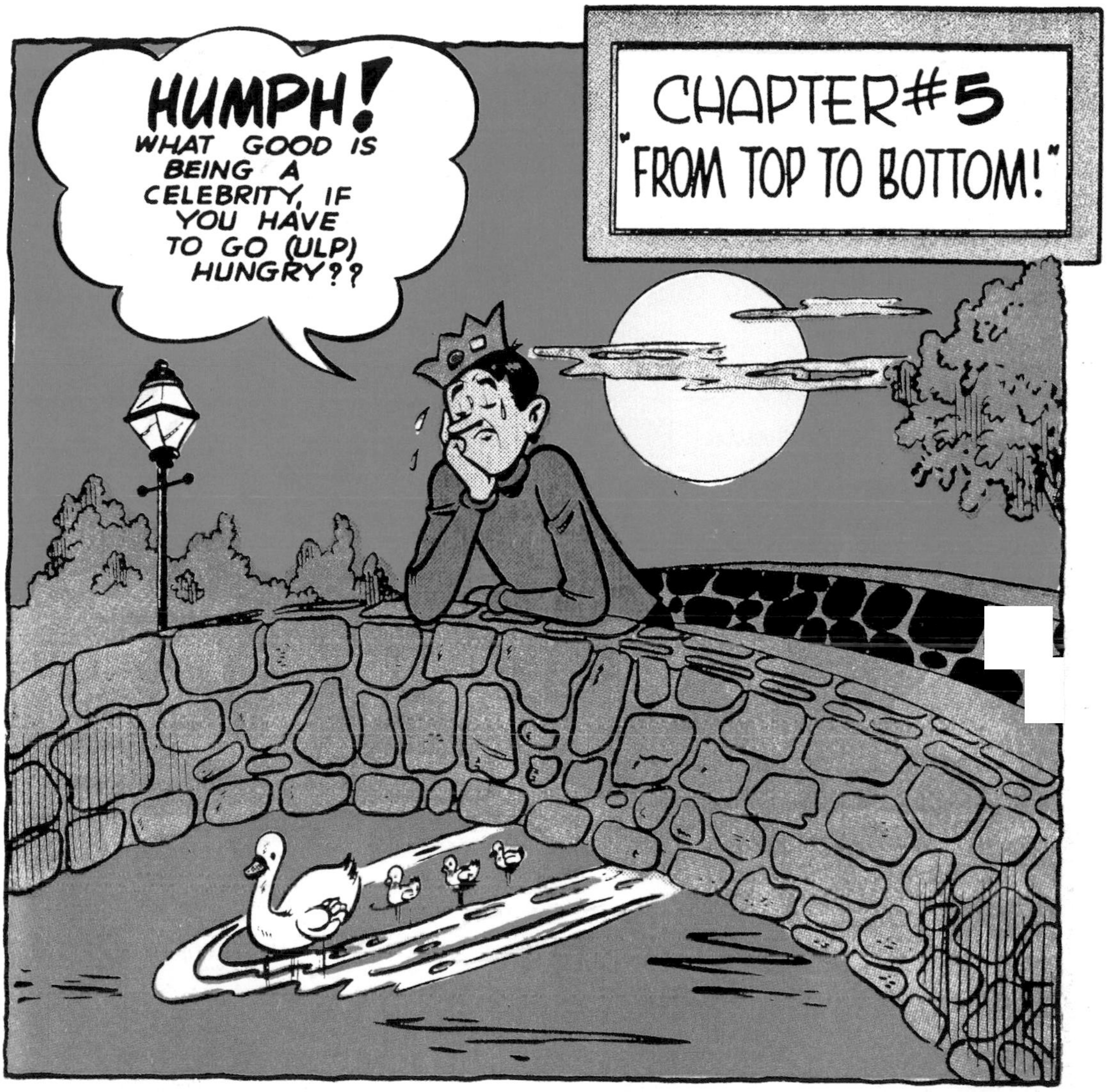
HUMPH! WHAT GOOD IS BEING A CELEBRITY, IF YOU HAVE TO GO (ULP) HUNGRY??
CHAPTER #5
"FROM TOP TO BOTTOM!"

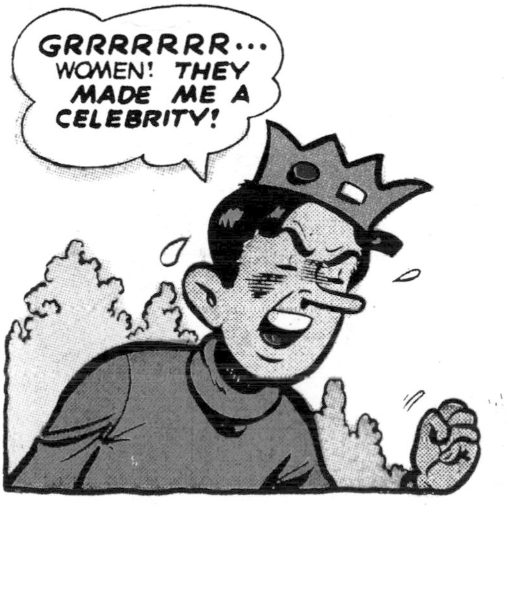
GRRRRRRR... WOMEN! THEY MADE ME A CELEBRITY!

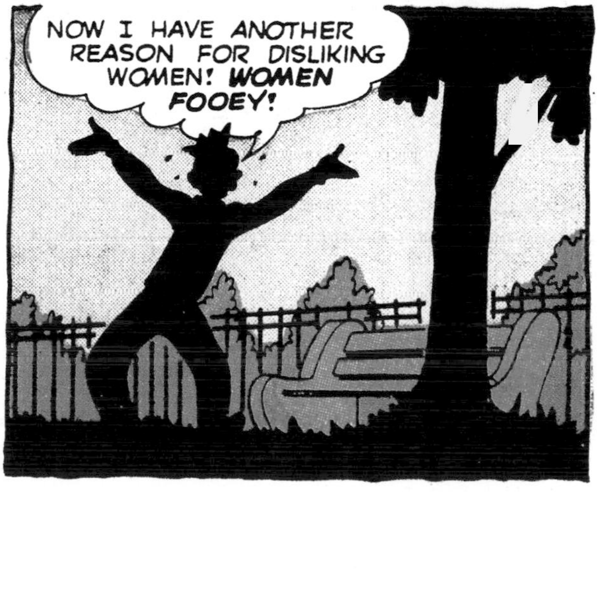
NOW I HAVE ANOTHER REASON FOR DISLIKING WOMEN! WOMEN FOOEY!

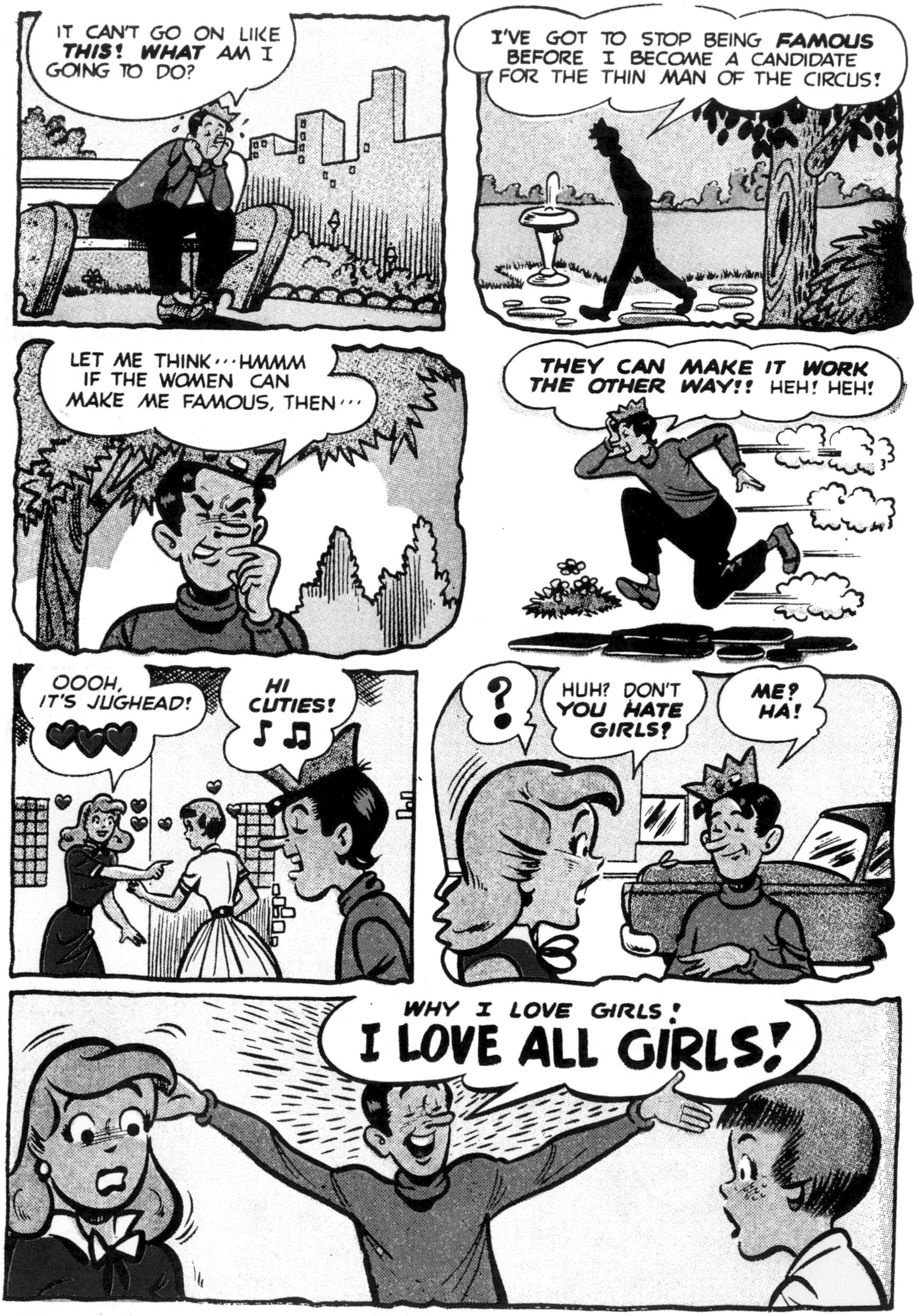
IT CAN'T GO ON LIKE THIS! WHAT AM I GOING TO DO?
I'VE GOT TO STOP BEING FAMOUS BEFORE I BECOME A CANDIDATE FOR THE THIN MAN OF THE CIRCUS!
LET ME THINK··· HMMM IF THE WOMEN CAN MAKE ME FAMOUS, THEN···
THEY CAN MAKE IT WORK THE OTHER WAY!! HEH! HEH!
OOOH, IT'S JUGHEAD!
HI CUTIES!
?
HUH? DON'T YOU HATE GIRLS?
ME? HA!
WHY I LOVE GIRLS!
I LOVE ALL GIRLS!

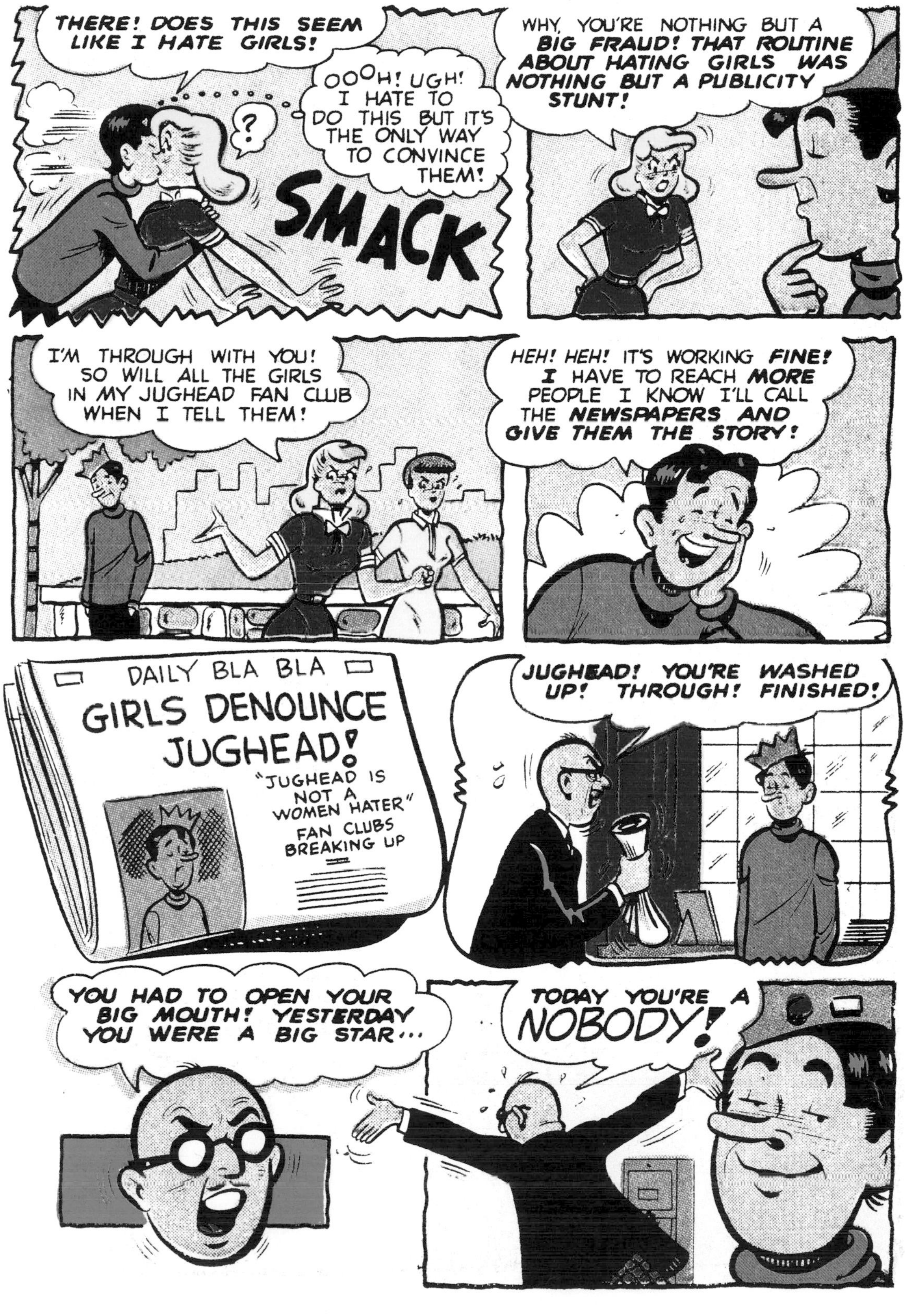
THERE! DOES THIS SEEM LIKE I HATE GIRLS!
?
OOOH! UGH! I HATE TO DO THIS BUT IT'S THE ONLY WAY TO CONVINCE THEM!
SMACK
WHY, YOU'RE NOTHING BUT A BIG FRAUD! THAT ROUTINE ABOUT HATING GIRLS WAS NOTHING BUT A PUBLICITY STUNT!
I'M THROUGH WITH YOU! SO WILL ALL THE GIRLS IN MY JUGHEAD FAN CLUB WHEN I TELL THEM!
HEH! HEH! IT'S WORKING FINE! I HAVE TO REACH MORE PEOPLE I KNOW I'LL CALL THE NEWSPAPERS AND GIVE THEM THE STORY!
DAILY BLA BLA
GIRLS DENOUNCE JUGHEAD!
"JUGHEAD IS NOT A WOMEN HATER"
FAN CLUBS BREAKING UP
JUGHEAD! YOU'RE WASHED UP! THROUGH! FINISHED!
YOU HAD TO OPEN YOUR BIG MOUTH! YESTERDAY YOU WERE A BIG STAR...
TODAY YOU'RE A NOBODY!

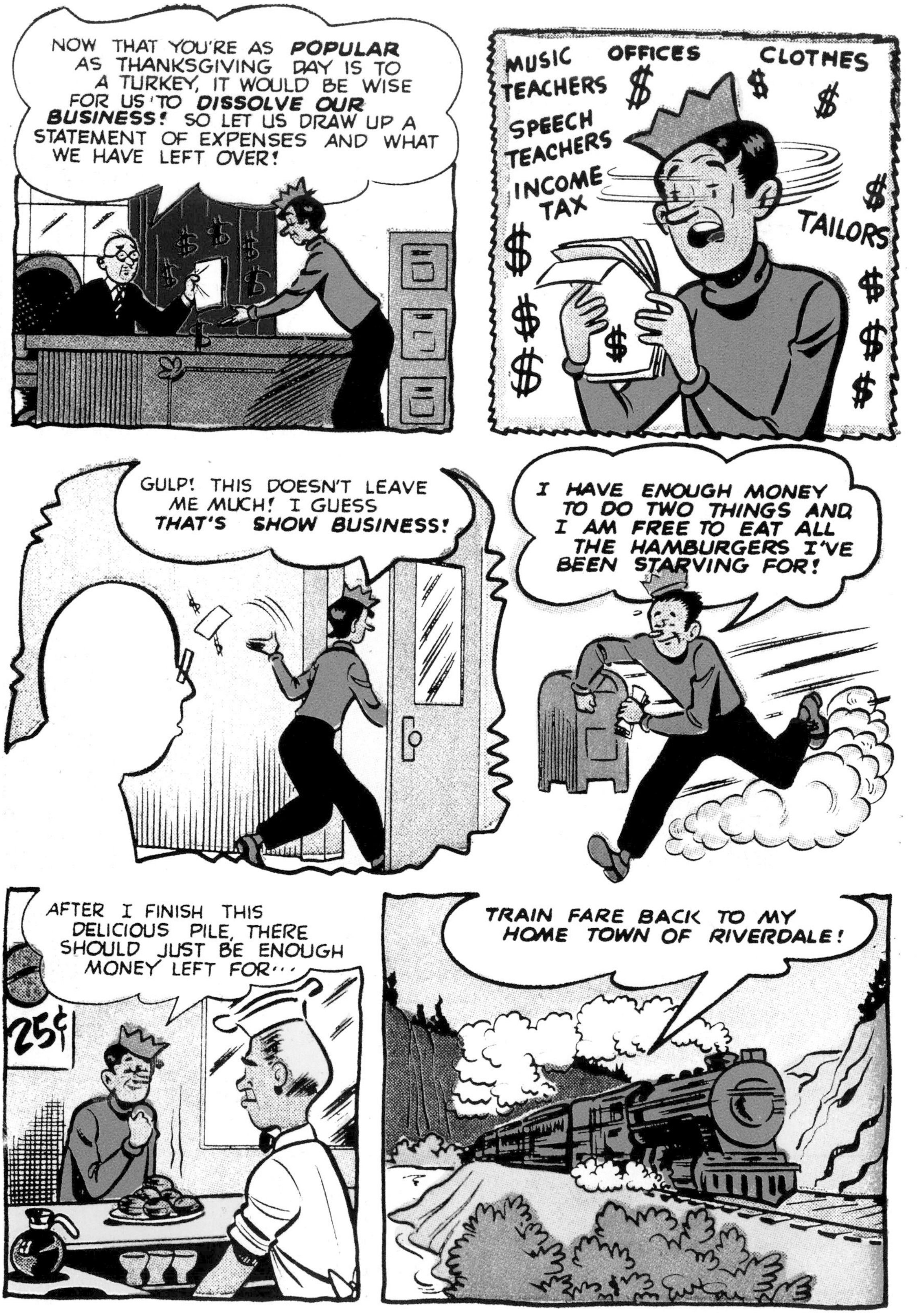
NOW THAT YOU'RE AS POPULAR AS THANKSGIVING DAY IS TO A TURKEY, IT WOULD BE WISE FOR US TO DISSOLVE OUR BUSINESS! SO LET US DRAW UP A STATEMENT OF EXPENSES AND WHAT WE HAVE LEFT OVER!
MUSIC TEACHERS
OFFICES
CLOTHES
SPEECH TEACHERS
INCOME TAX
TAILORS
GULP! THIS DOESN'T LEAVE ME MUCH! I GUESS THAT'S SHOW BUSINESS!
I HAVE ENOUGH MONEY TO DO TWO THINGS AND I AM FREE TO EAT ALL THE HAMBURGERS I'VE BEEN STARVING FOR!
AFTER I FINISH THIS DELICIOUS PILE, THERE SHOULD JUST BE ENOUGH MONEY LEFT FOR...
25¢
TRAIN FARE BACK TO MY HOME TOWN OF RIVERDALE!

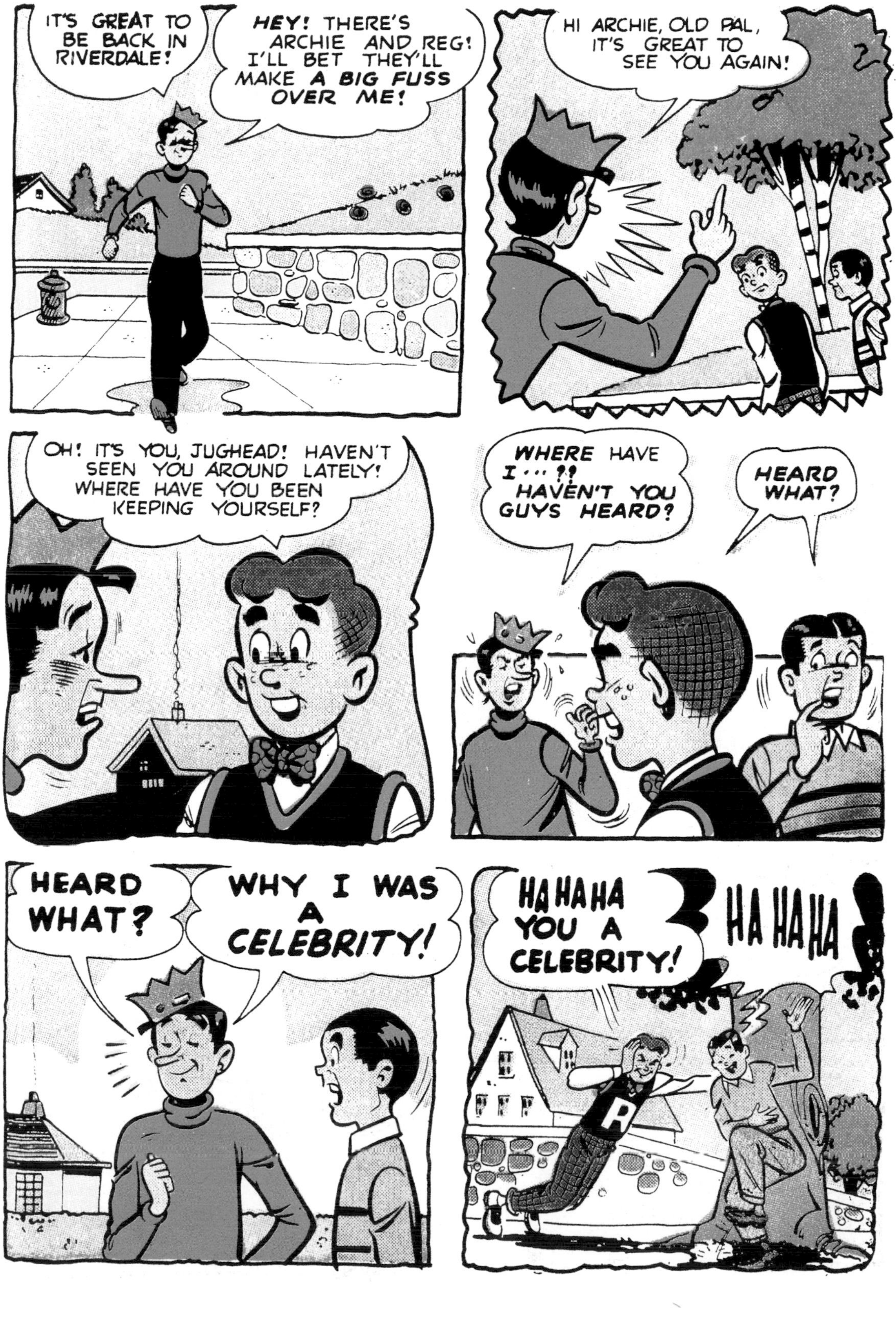
IT'S GREAT TO BE BACK IN RIVERDALE!
HEY! THERE'S ARCHIE AND REG! I'LL BET THEY'LL MAKE A BIG FUSS OVER ME!
HI ARCHIE, OLD PAL, IT'S GREAT TO SEE YOU AGAIN!
OH! IT'S YOU, JUGHEAD! HAVEN'T SEEN YOU AROUND LATELY! WHERE HAVE YOU BEEN KEEPING YOURSELF?
WHERE HAVE I...?! HAVEN'T YOU GUYS HEARD?
HEARD WHAT?
HEARD WHAT?
WHY I WAS A CELEBRITY!
HA HA HA YOU A CELEBRITY!
HA HA HA

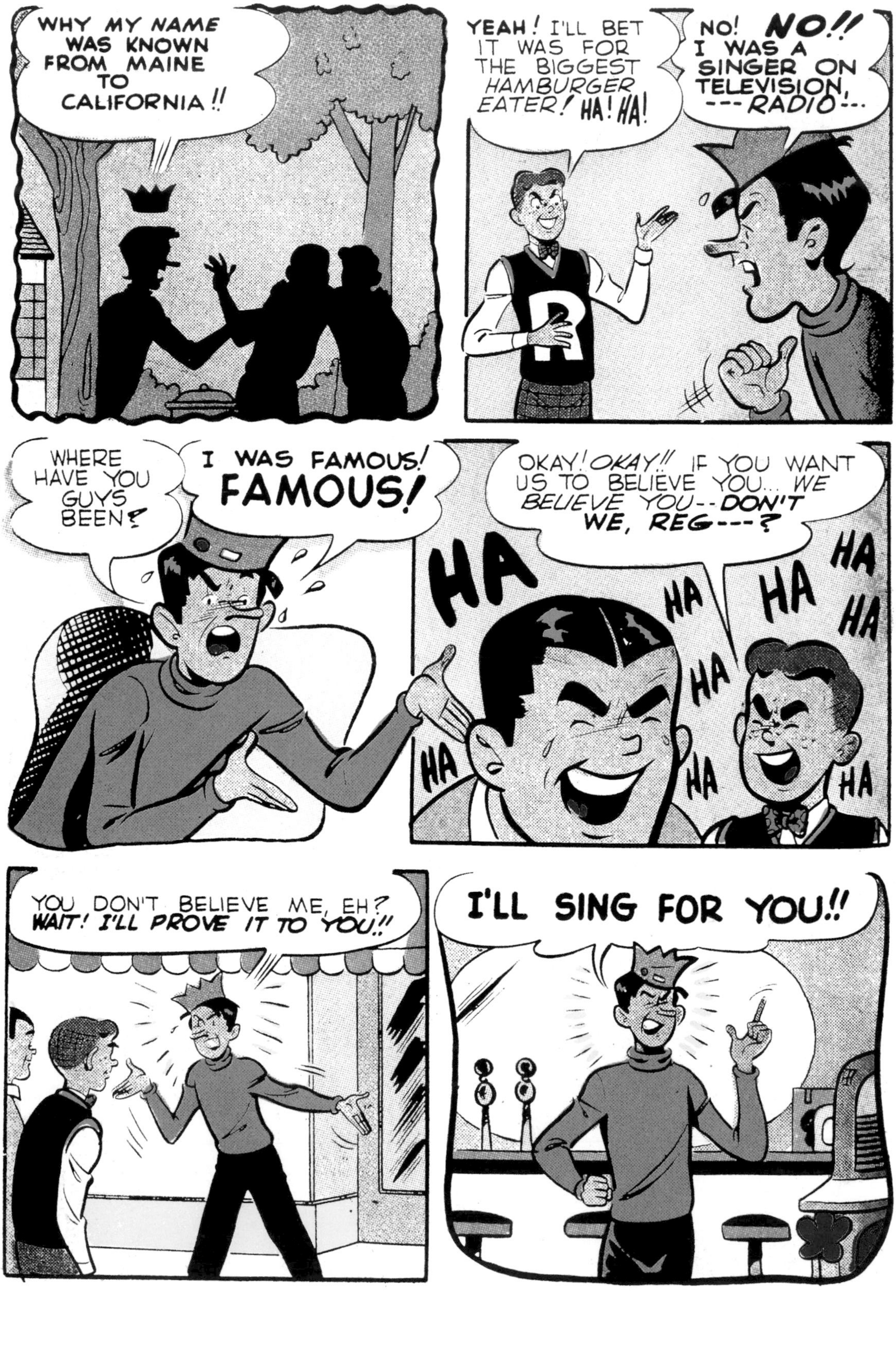
WHY MY NAME WAS KNOWN FROM MAINE TO CALIFORNIA!!
YEAH! I'LL BET IT WAS FOR THE BIGGEST HAMBURGER EATER! HA! HA!
NO! NO!! I WAS A SINGER ON TELEVISION, ---RADIO!--
WHERE HAVE YOU GUYS BEEN?
I WAS FAMOUS! FAMOUS!
OKAY! OKAY!! IF YOU WANT US TO BELIEVE YOU... WE BELIEVE YOU--DON'T WE, REG---?
HA HA HA HA HA HA HA HA HA
YOU DON'T BELIEVE ME, EH? WAIT! I'LL PROVE IT TO YOU!!
I'LL SING FOR YOU!!

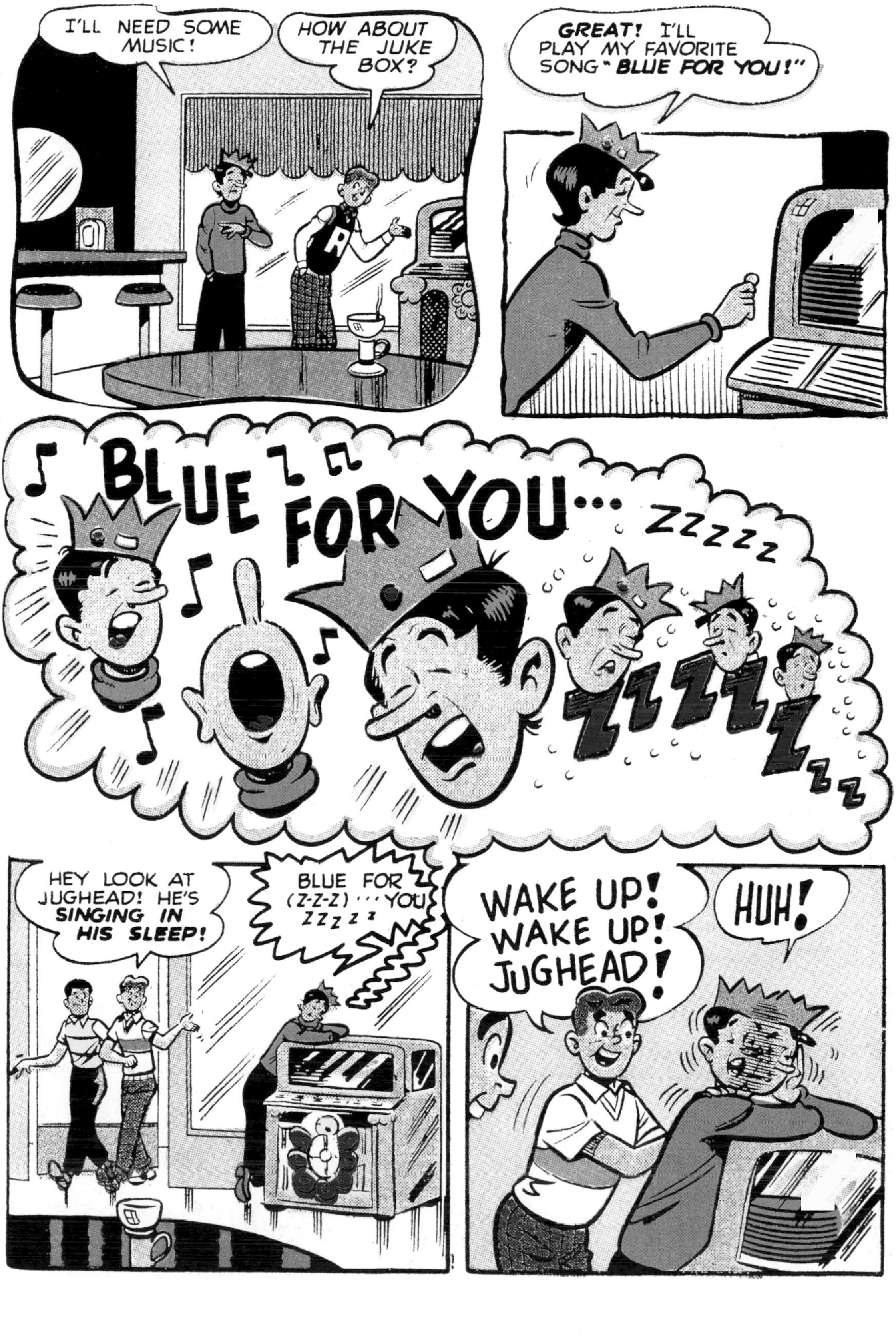

I'LL NEED SOME MUSIC!
HOW ABOUT THE JUKE BOX?
GREAT! I'LL PLAY MY FAVORITE SONG "BLUE FOR YOU!"
BLUE FOR YOU... ZZZZZ
HEY LOOK AT JUGHEAD! HE'S SINGING IN HIS SLEEP!
BLUE FOR (Z-Z-Z) ... YOU ZZZZZ
WAKE UP! WAKE UP! JUGHEAD!
HUH!

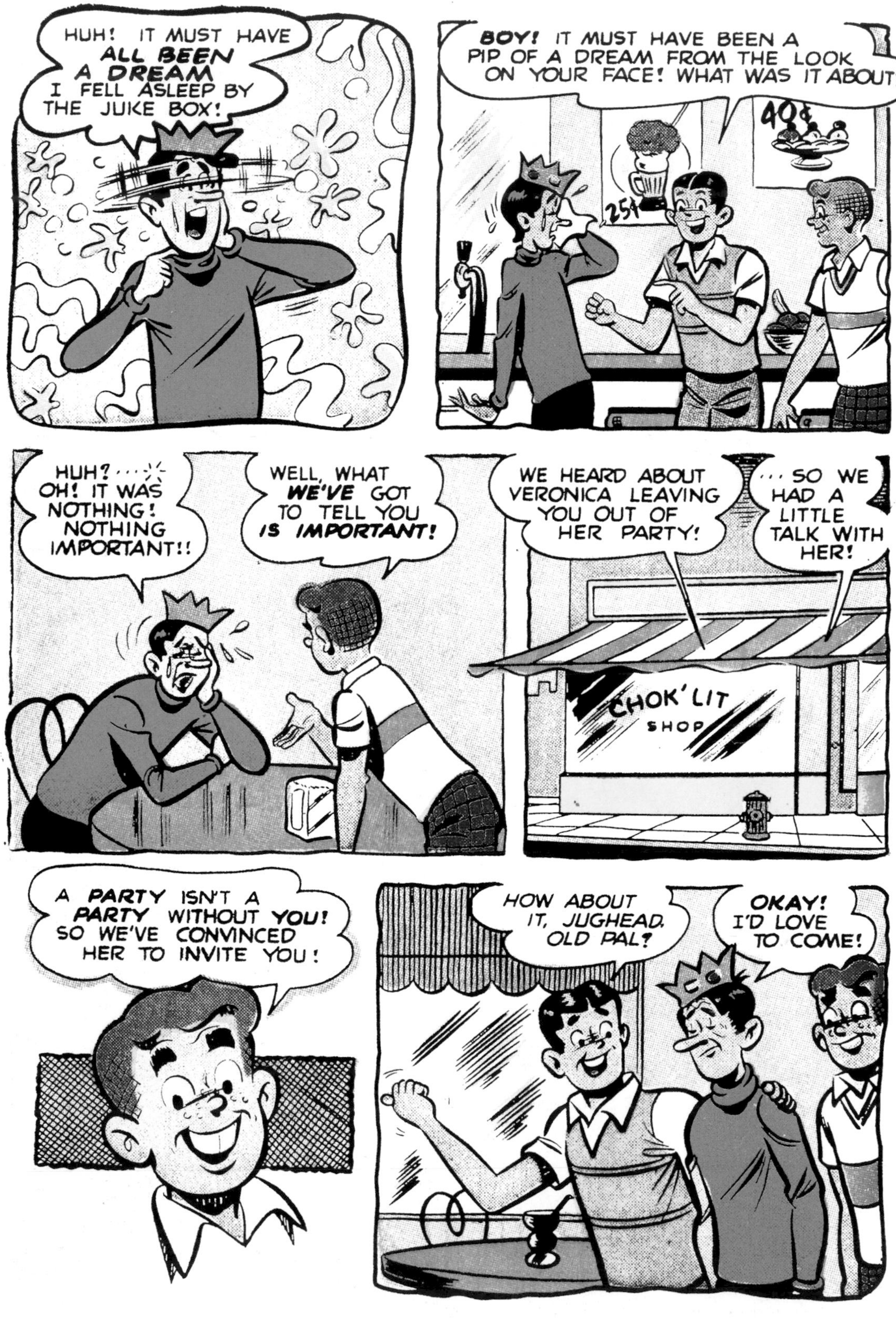
HUH! IT MUST HAVE ALL BEEN A DREAM I FELL ASLEEP BY THE JUKE BOX!
BOY! IT MUST HAVE BEEN A PIP OF A DREAM FROM THE LOOK ON YOUR FACE! WHAT WAS IT ABOUT?
40¢
25¢
HUH? ... OH! IT WAS NOTHING! NOTHING IMPORTANT!!
WELL, WHAT WE'VE GOT TO TELL YOU IS IMPORTANT!
WE HEARD ABOUT VERONICA LEAVING YOU OUT OF HER PARTY!
... SO WE HAD A LITTLE TALK WITH HER!
CHOK'LIT SHOP
A PARTY ISN'T A PARTY WITHOUT YOU! SO WE'VE CONVINCED HER TO INVITE YOU!
HOW ABOUT IT, JUGHEAD, OLD PAL?
OKAY! I'D LOVE TO COME!

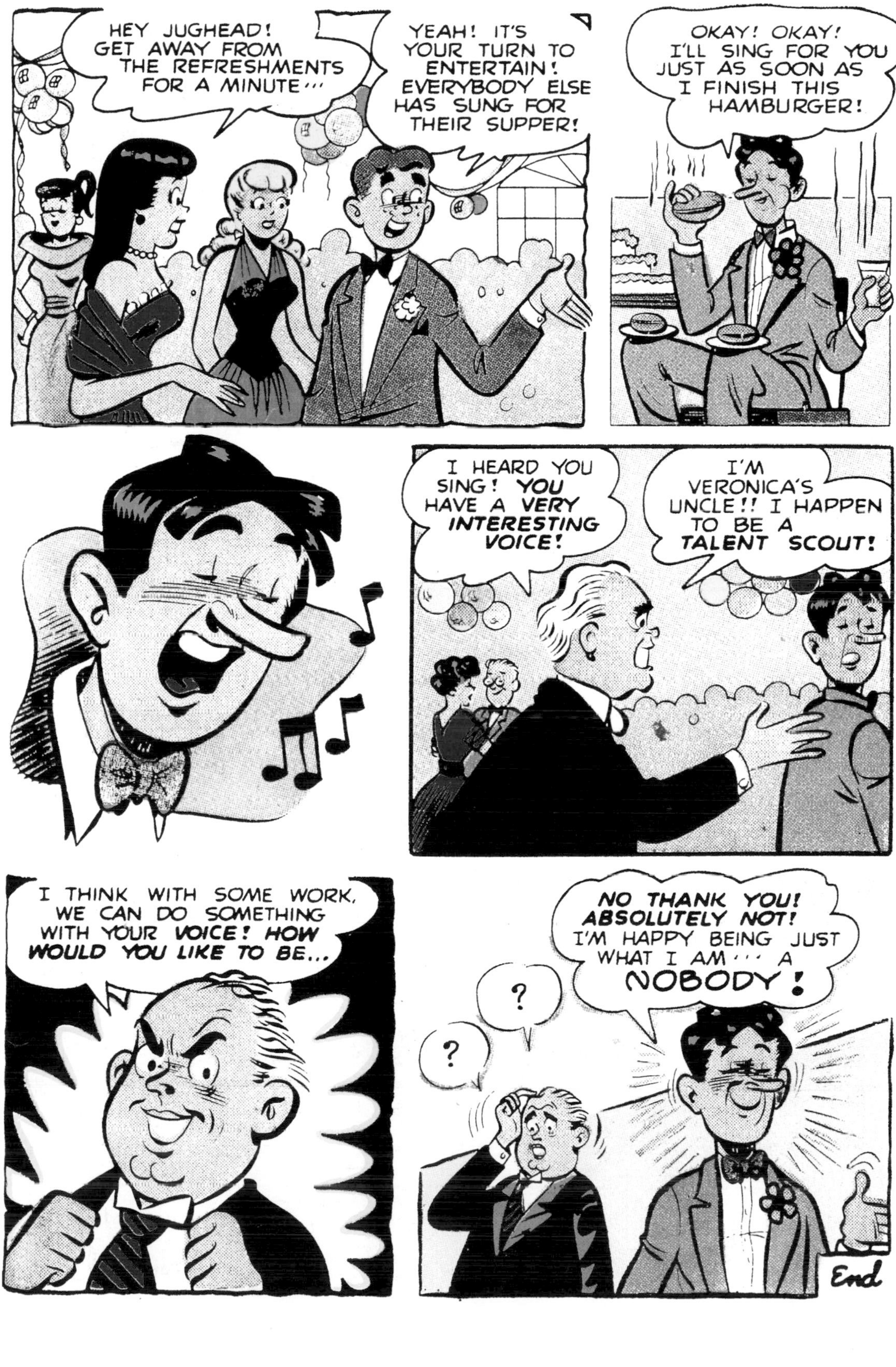
HEY JUGHEAD! GET AWAY FROM THE REFRESHMENTS FOR A MINUTE...
YEAH! IT'S YOUR TURN TO ENTERTAIN! EVERYBODY ELSE HAS SUNG FOR THEIR SUPPER!
OKAY! OKAY! I'LL SING FOR YOU JUST AS SOON AS I FINISH THIS HAMBURGER!
I HEARD YOU SING! YOU HAVE A VERY INTERESTING VOICE!
I'M VERONICA'S UNCLE!! I HAPPEN TO BE A TALENT SCOUT!
I THINK WITH SOME WORK, WE CAN DO SOMETHING WITH YOUR VOICE! HOW WOULD YOU LIKE TO BE...
?
?
NO THANK YOU! ABSOLUTELY NOT! I'M HAPPY BEING JUST WHAT I AM... A NOBODY!
End

The BEST of Archie COMICS

1960s

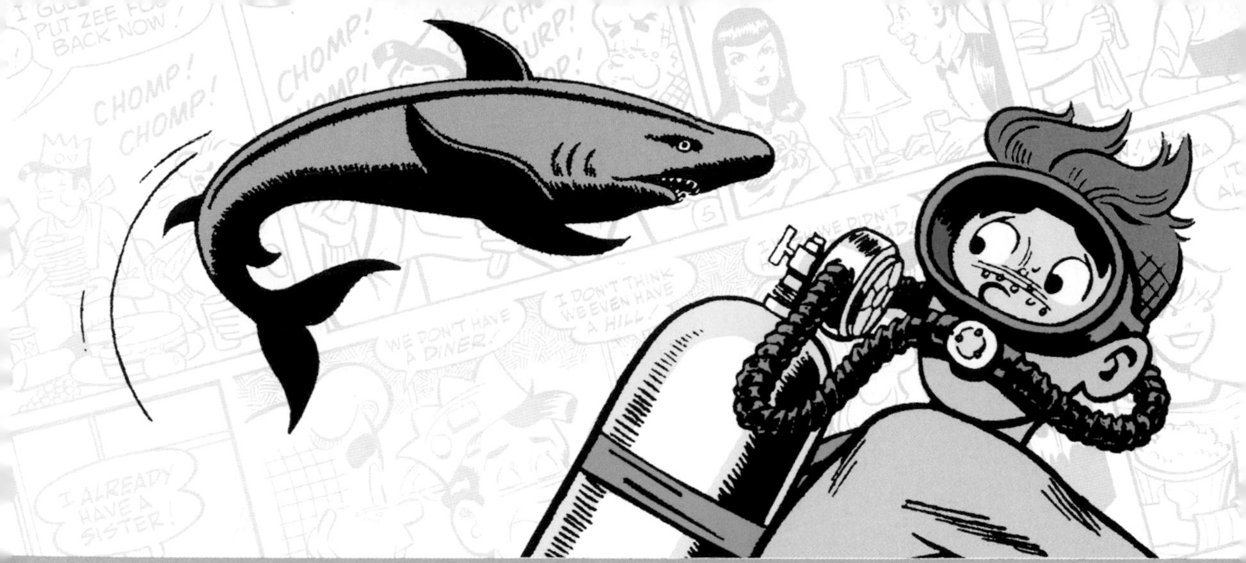
CHOMP! CHOMP!
CHOMP! CHOMP!
WE DON'T HAVE A DINER!
I DON'T THINK WE EVEN HAVE A HILL!
I ALREADY HAVE A SISTER!

HI-JINKS AND DEEP DIVERS

LIFE WITH ARCHIE #16, 1962

BY BOB WHITE

When I was growing up in the late '70s, the two things that most entertained me were Jacques Cousteau and Archie. Truth be told, this was a short window in my life. The early '80s would give way to *Star Wars* which would give way to baseball, but for a few short years my only concerns were what Jughead was up to and where Jacques Cousteau's next great exploration would be to.

Maybe it's for this reason that the Archie comic I remember best was "Hi-jinks and Deep Divers"! While these first appeared in *Life With Archie* #16 in 1962, my sister (whom I would've stolen it from) wasn't even born until 1965, so I'm pretty sure I read them both in one of her dozens of Archie digests. No matter! In one fell swoop, my two great loves came together, with Archie and the boys having one of their greatest adventures at the bottom of the ocean. And while the jellyfish sandwich offered to Archie sounded gross, I agreed with him when he was offered a sea foam soda and declared, "I'll try anything once!"

Years later, I'm now a trained scuba diver who's had the luxury of diving some awesome wrecks and seeing some amazing aquatic life, but I'm still waiting for the day when I find my own Neptunia, complete with mermaids!

—*Marcus Grimm*
Head of Tales,
NXT Book Media

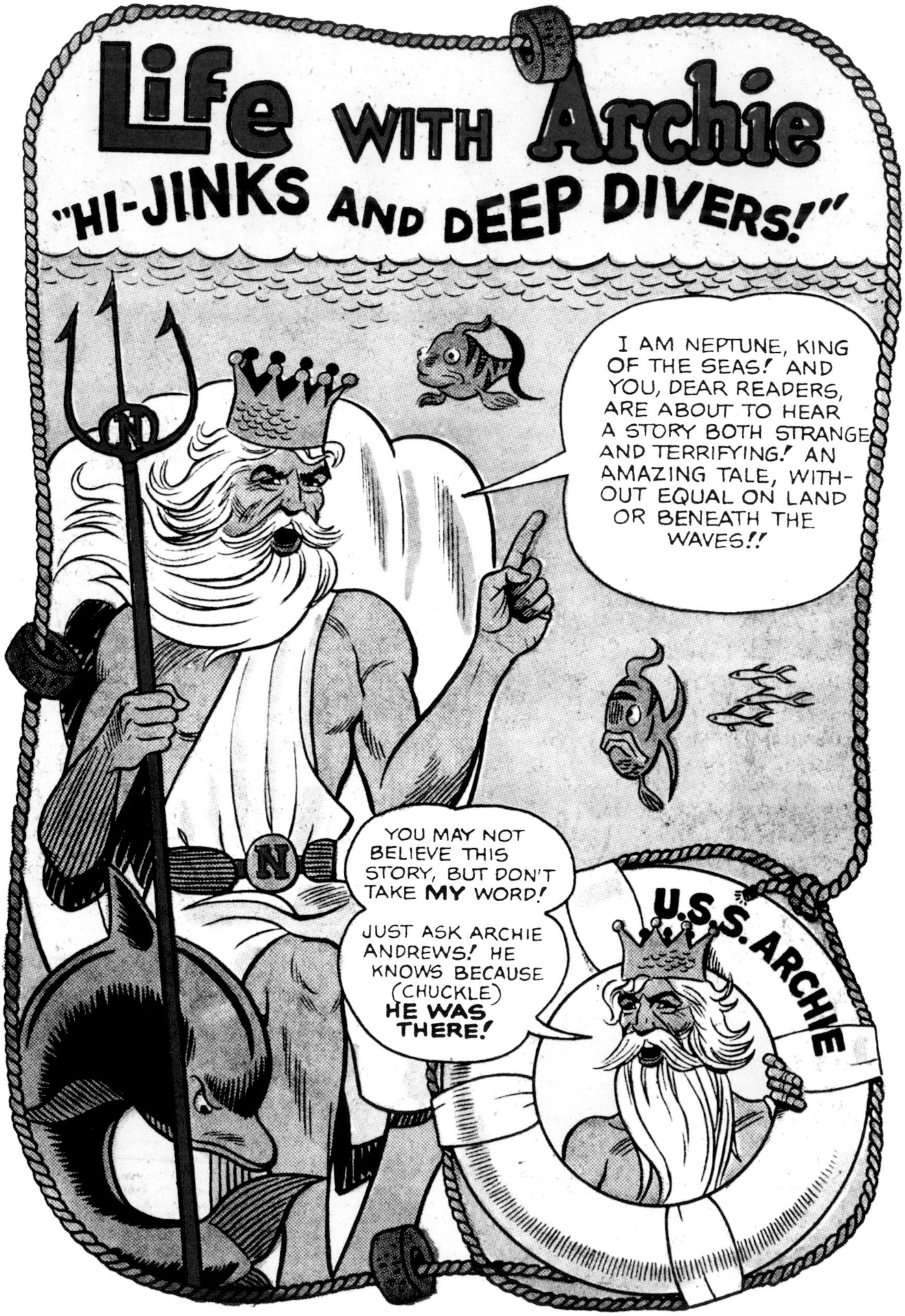
Life WITH Archie
"HI-JINKS AND DEEP DIVERS!"
I AM NEPTUNE, KING OF THE SEAS! AND YOU, DEAR READERS, ARE ABOUT TO HEAR A STORY BOTH STRANGE AND TERRIFYING! AN AMAZING TALE, WITHOUT EQUAL ON LAND OR BENEATH THE WAVES!!
YOU MAY NOT BELIEVE THIS STORY, BUT DON'T TAKE MY WORD!
JUST ASK ARCHIE ANDREWS! HE KNOWS BECAUSE (CHUCKLE) HE WAS THERE!
U.S.S. ARCHIE

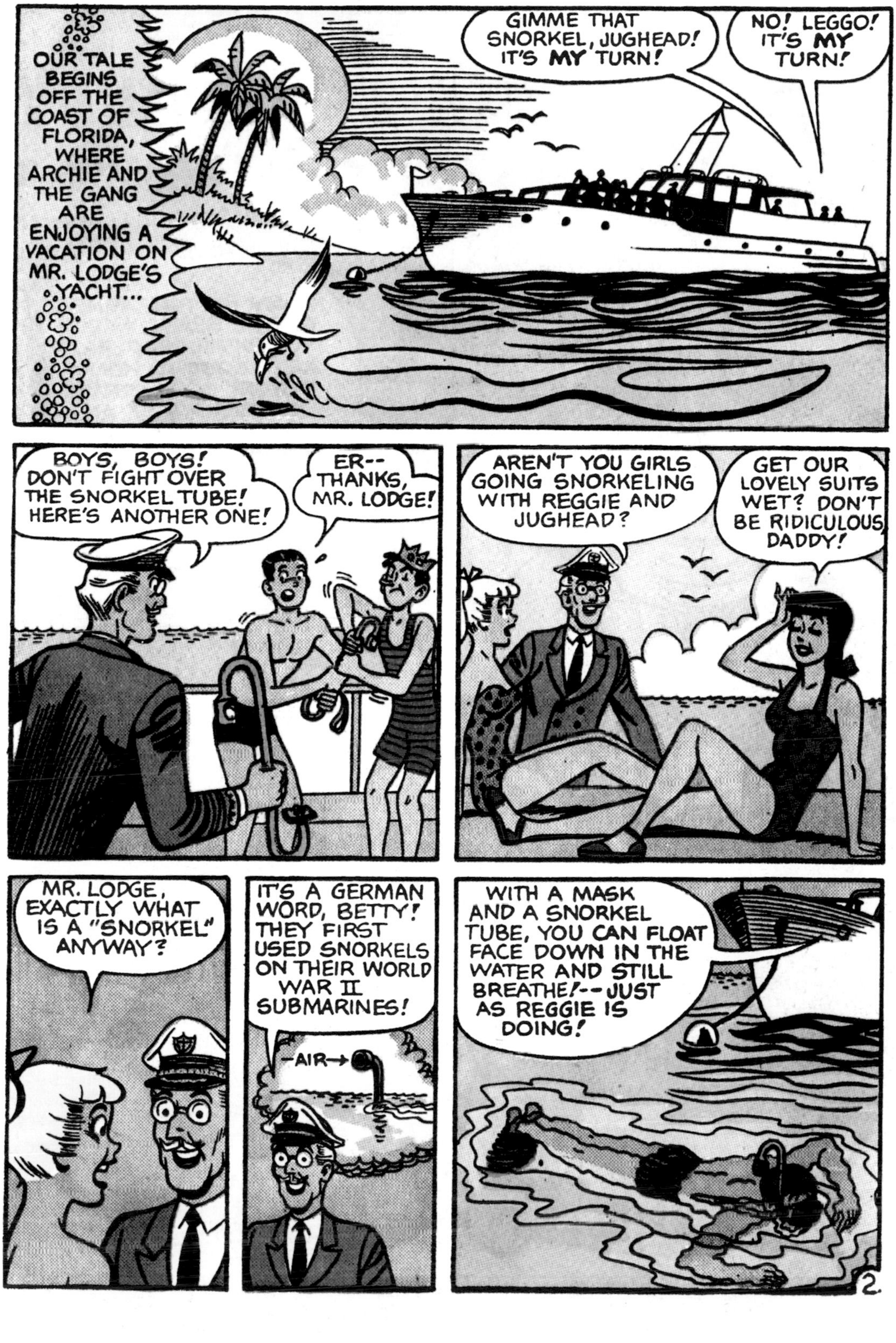
OUR TALE BEGINS OFF THE COAST OF FLORIDA, WHERE ARCHIE AND THE GANG ARE ENJOYING A VACATION ON MR. LODGE'S YACHT...
GIMME THAT SNORKEL, JUGHEAD! IT'S MY TURN!
NO! LEGGO! IT'S MY TURN!
BOYS, BOYS! DON'T FIGHT OVER THE SNORKEL TUBE! HERE'S ANOTHER ONE!
ER-- THANKS, MR. LODGE!
AREN'T YOU GIRLS GOING SNORKELING WITH REGGIE AND JUGHEAD?
GET OUR LOVELY SUITS WET? DON'T BE RIDICULOUS, DADDY!
MR. LODGE, EXACTLY WHAT IS A "SNORKEL" ANYWAY?
IT'S A GERMAN WORD, BETTY! THEY FIRST USED SNORKELS ON THEIR WORLD WAR II SUBMARINES!
—AIR→
WITH A MASK AND A SNORKEL TUBE, YOU CAN FLOAT FACE DOWN IN THE WATER AND STILL BREATHE!-- JUST AS REGGIE IS DOING!
2.

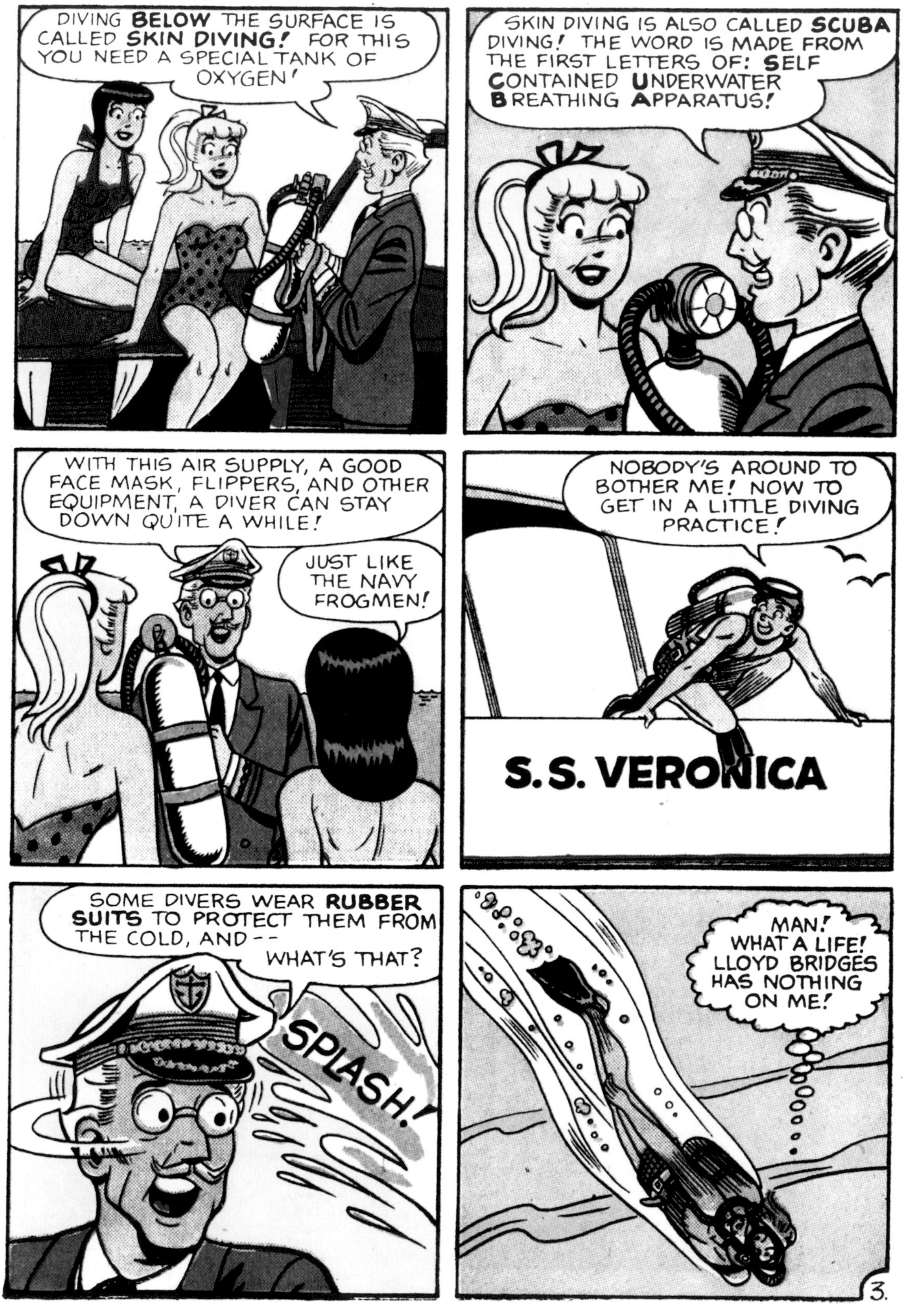
DIVING BELOW THE SURFACE IS CALLED SKIN DIVING! FOR THIS YOU NEED A SPECIAL TANK OF OXYGEN!
SKIN DIVING IS ALSO CALLED SCUBA DIVING! THE WORD IS MADE FROM THE FIRST LETTERS OF: SELF CONTAINED UNDERWATER BREATHING APPARATUS!
WITH THIS AIR SUPPLY, A GOOD FACE MASK, FLIPPERS, AND OTHER EQUIPMENT, A DIVER CAN STAY DOWN QUITE A WHILE!
JUST LIKE THE NAVY FROGMEN!
NOBODY'S AROUND TO BOTHER ME! NOW TO GET IN A LITTLE DIVING PRACTICE!
S.S. VERONICA
SOME DIVERS WEAR RUBBER SUITS TO PROTECT THEM FROM THE COLD, AND --
WHAT'S THAT?
SPLASH!
MAN! WHAT A LIFE! LLOYD BRIDGES HAS NOTHING ON ME!
3.

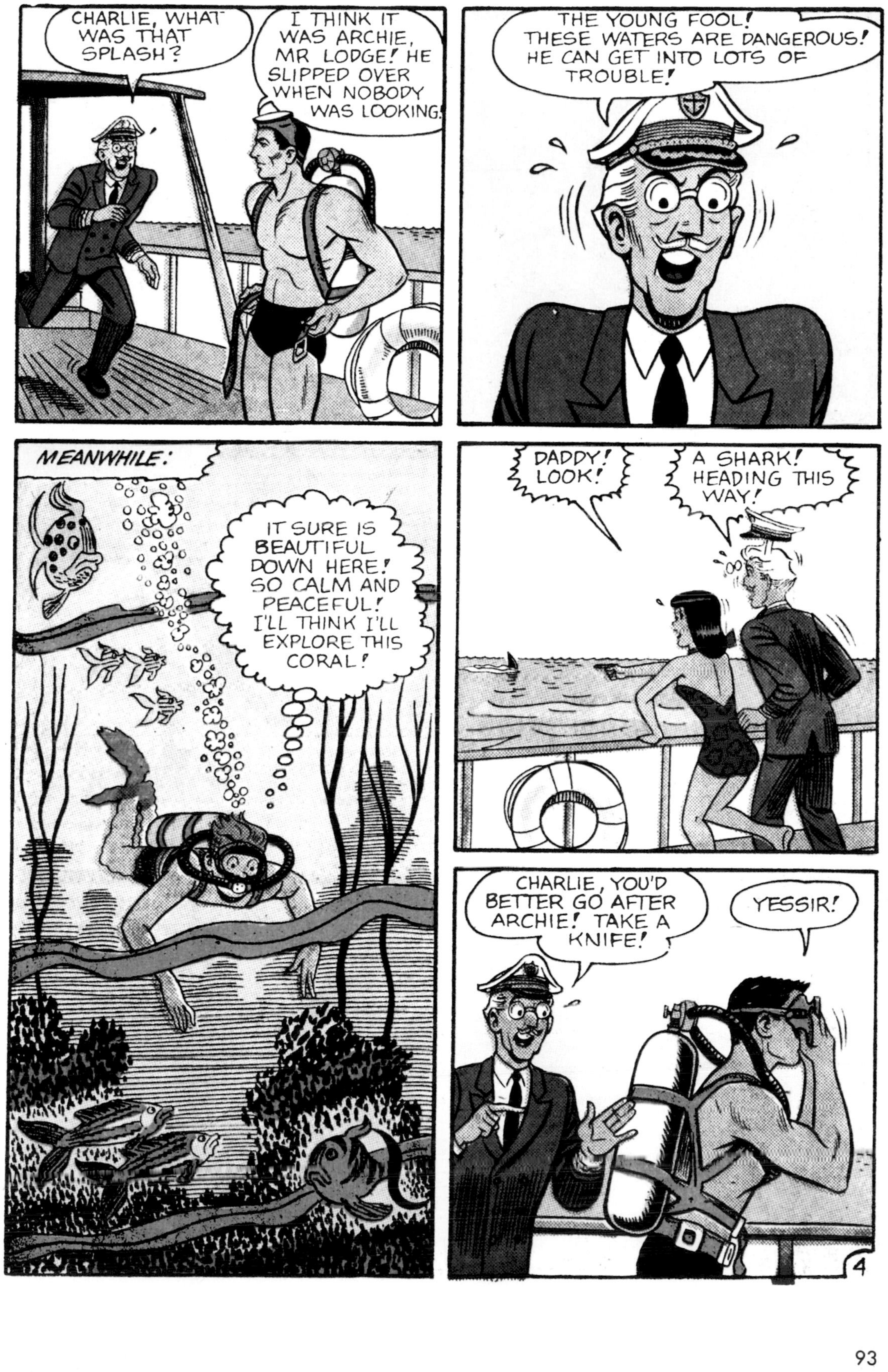
CHARLIE, WHAT WAS THAT SPLASH?
I THINK IT WAS ARCHIE, MR LODGE! HE SLIPPED OVER WHEN NOBODY WAS LOOKING!
THE YOUNG FOOL! THESE WATERS ARE DANGEROUS! HE CAN GET INTO LOTS OF TROUBLE!
MEANWHILE:
IT SURE IS BEAUTIFUL DOWN HERE! SO CALM AND PEACEFUL! I'LL THINK I'LL EXPLORE THIS CORAL!
DADDY! LOOK!
A SHARK! HEADING THIS WAY!
CHARLIE, YOU'D BETTER GO AFTER ARCHIE! TAKE A KNIFE!
YESSIR!
4

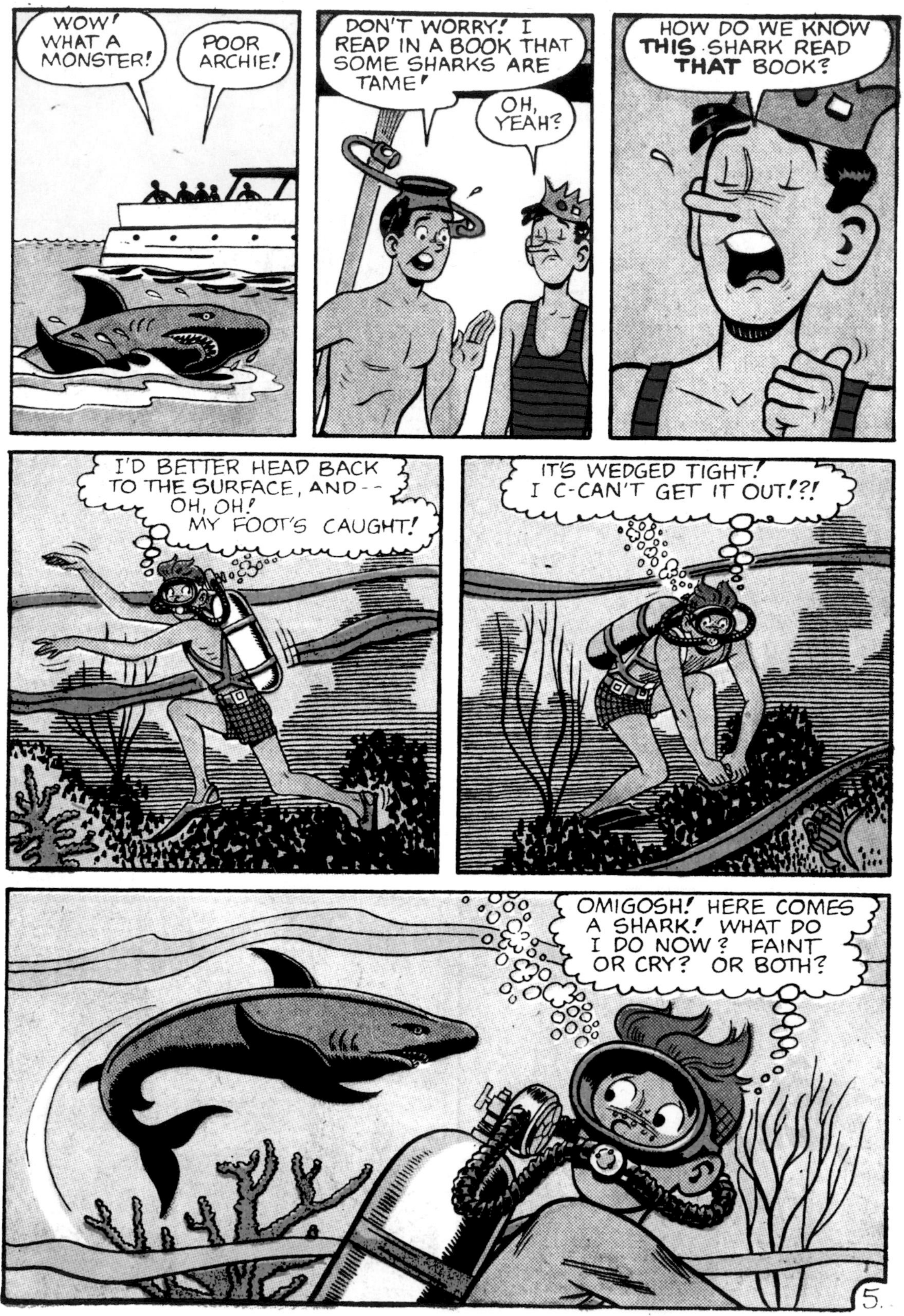
WOW! WHAT A MONSTER!
POOR ARCHIE!
DON'T WORRY! I READ IN A BOOK THAT SOME SHARKS ARE TAME!
OH, YEAH?
HOW DO WE KNOW THIS SHARK READ THAT BOOK?
I'D BETTER HEAD BACK TO THE SURFACE, AND-- OH, OH! MY FOOT'S CAUGHT!
IT'S WEDGED TIGHT! I C-CAN'T GET IT OUT!?!
OMIGOSH! HERE COMES A SHARK! WHAT DO I DO NOW? FAINT OR CRY? OR BOTH?
5.

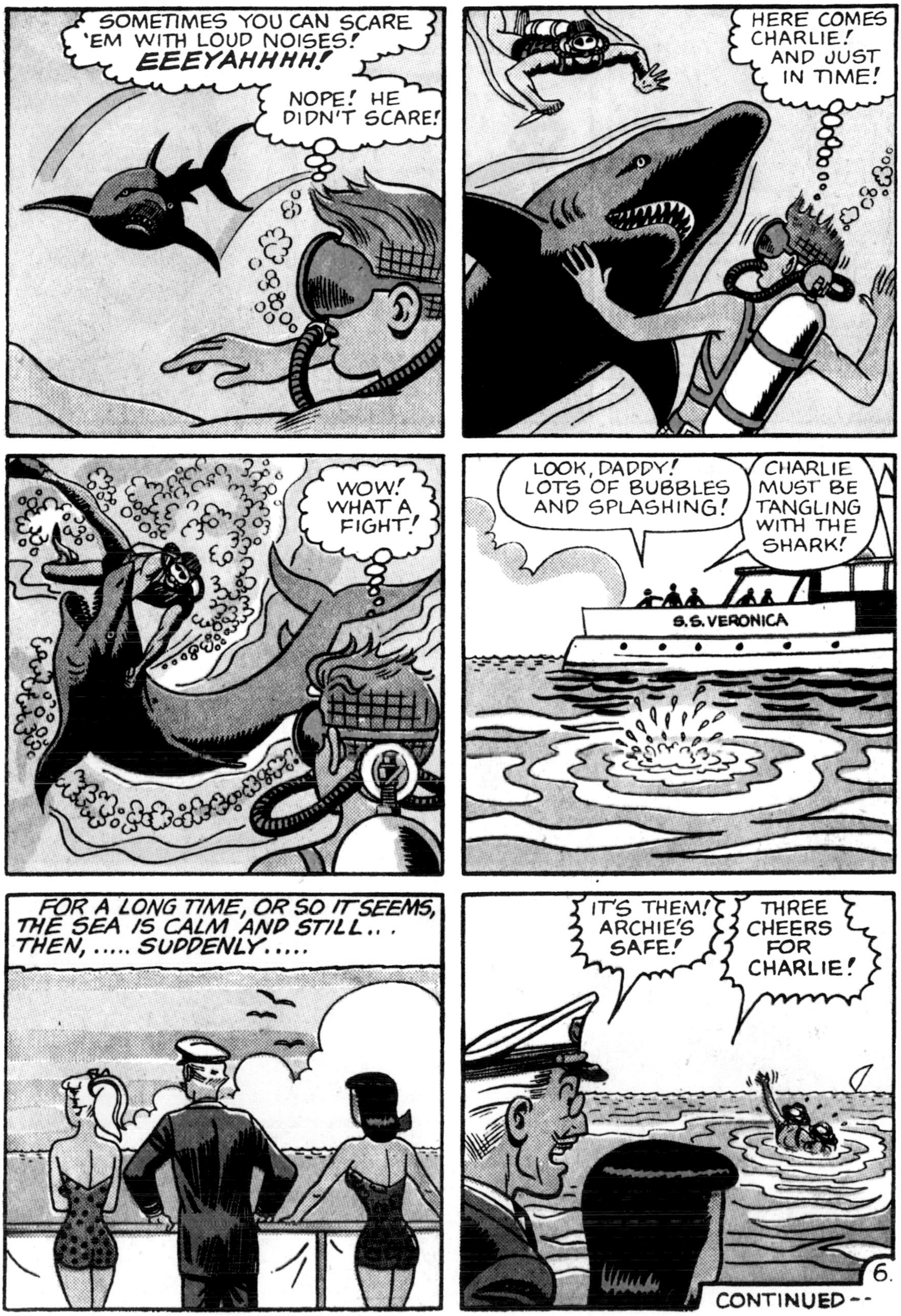
SOMETIMES YOU CAN SCARE 'EM WITH LOUD NOISES! EEEYAHHHH!
NOPE! HE DIDN'T SCARE!
HERE COMES CHARLIE! AND JUST IN TIME!
WOW! WHAT A FIGHT!
LOOK, DADDY! LOTS OF BUBBLES AND SPLASHING!
CHARLIE MUST BE TANGLING WITH THE SHARK!
S.S. VERONICA
FOR A LONG TIME, OR SO IT SEEMS, THE SEA IS CALM AND STILL... THEN, ... SUDDENLY.....
IT'S THEM! ARCHIE'S SAFE!
THREE CHEERS FOR CHARLIE!
6.
CONTINUED--

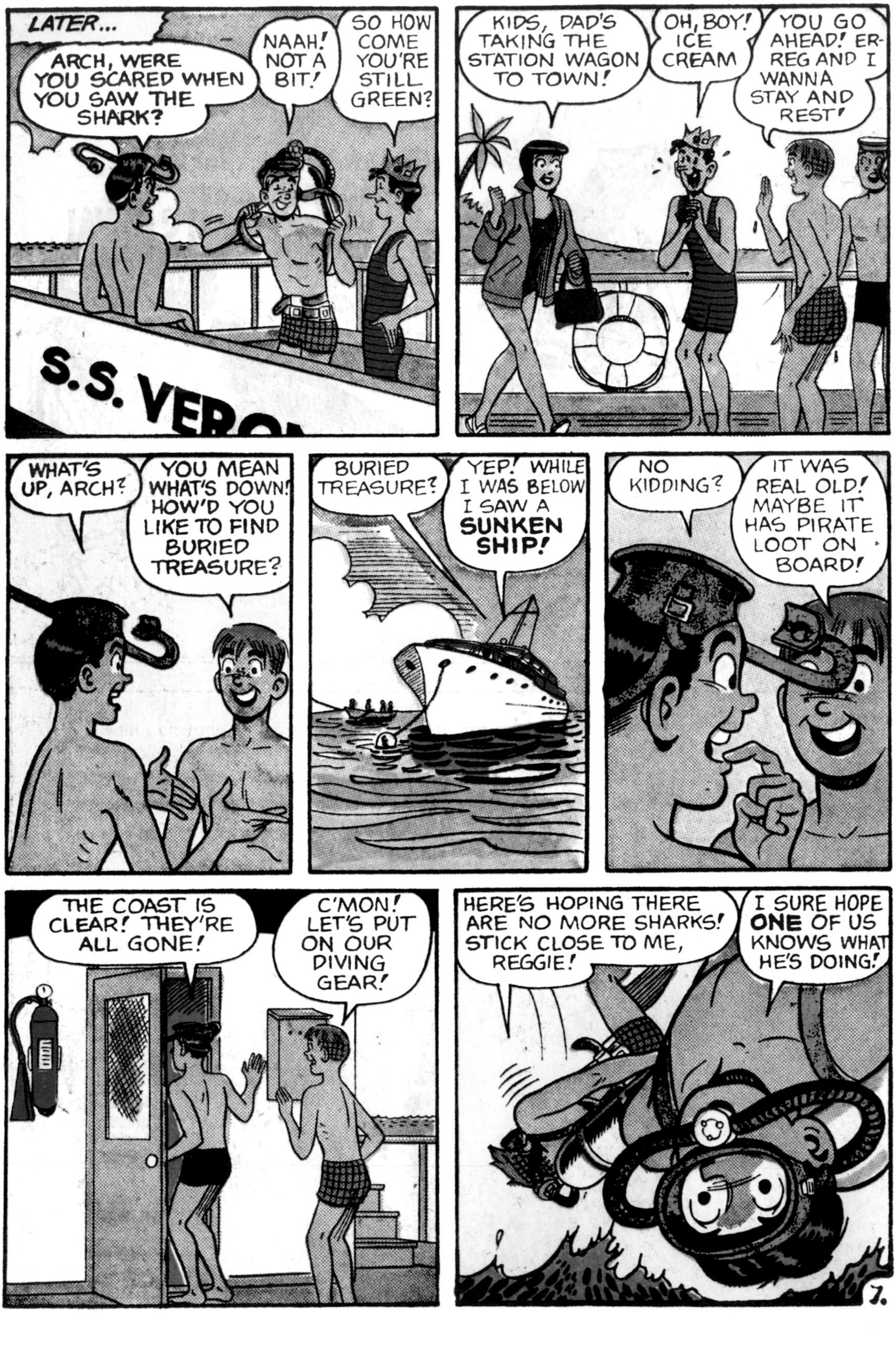
LATER...
ARCH, WERE YOU SCARED WHEN YOU SAW THE SHARK?
NAAH! NOT A BIT!
SO HOW COME YOU'RE STILL GREEN?
S.S. VERO
KIDS, DAD'S TAKING THE STATION WAGON TO TOWN!
OH, BOY! ICE CREAM
YOU GO AHEAD! ER- REG AND I WANNA STAY AND REST!
WHAT'S UP, ARCH?
YOU MEAN WHAT'S DOWN! HOW'D YOU LIKE TO FIND BURIED TREASURE?
BURIED TREASURE?
YEP! WHILE I WAS BELOW I SAW A SUNKEN SHIP!
NO KIDDING?
IT WAS REAL OLD! MAYBE IT HAS PIRATE LOOT ON BOARD!
THE COAST IS CLEAR! THEY'RE ALL GONE!
C'MON! LET'S PUT ON OUR DIVING GEAR!
HERE'S HOPING THERE ARE NO MORE SHARKS! STICK CLOSE TO ME, REGGIE!
I SURE HOPE ONE OF US KNOWS WHAT HE'S DOING!
7.

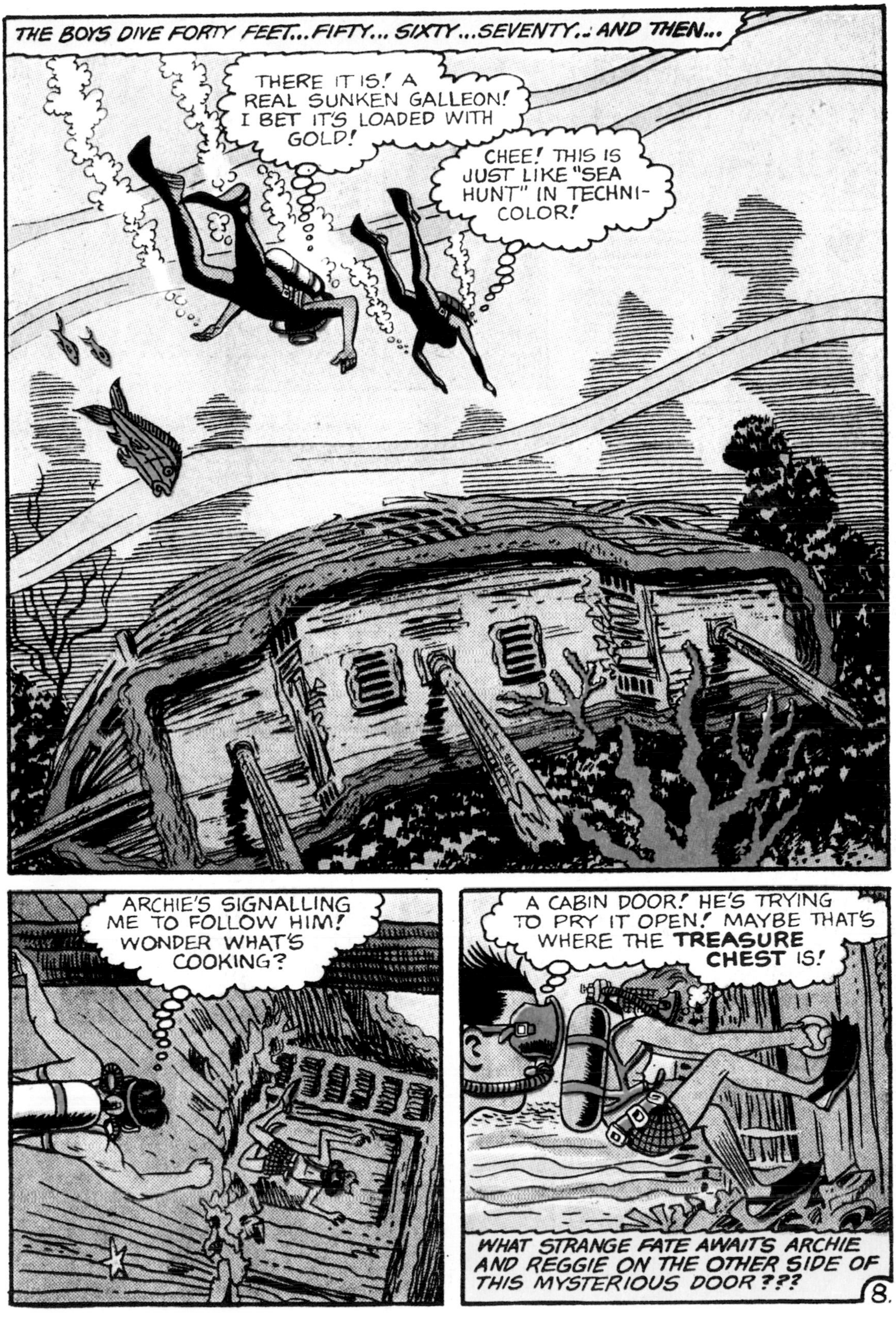
THE BOYS DIVE FORTY FEET... FIFTY... SIXTY... SEVENTY... AND THEN...
THERE IT IS! A REAL SUNKEN GALLEON! I BET IT'S LOADED WITH GOLD!
CHEE! THIS IS JUST LIKE "SEA HUNT" IN TECHNI-COLOR!
ARCHIE'S SIGNALLING ME TO FOLLOW HIM! WONDER WHAT'S COOKING?
A CABIN DOOR! HE'S TRYING TO PRY IT OPEN! MAYBE THAT'S WHERE THE TREASURE CHEST IS!
WHAT STRANGE FATE AWAITS ARCHIE AND REGGIE ON THE OTHER SIDE OF THIS MYSTERIOUS DOOR???
8.

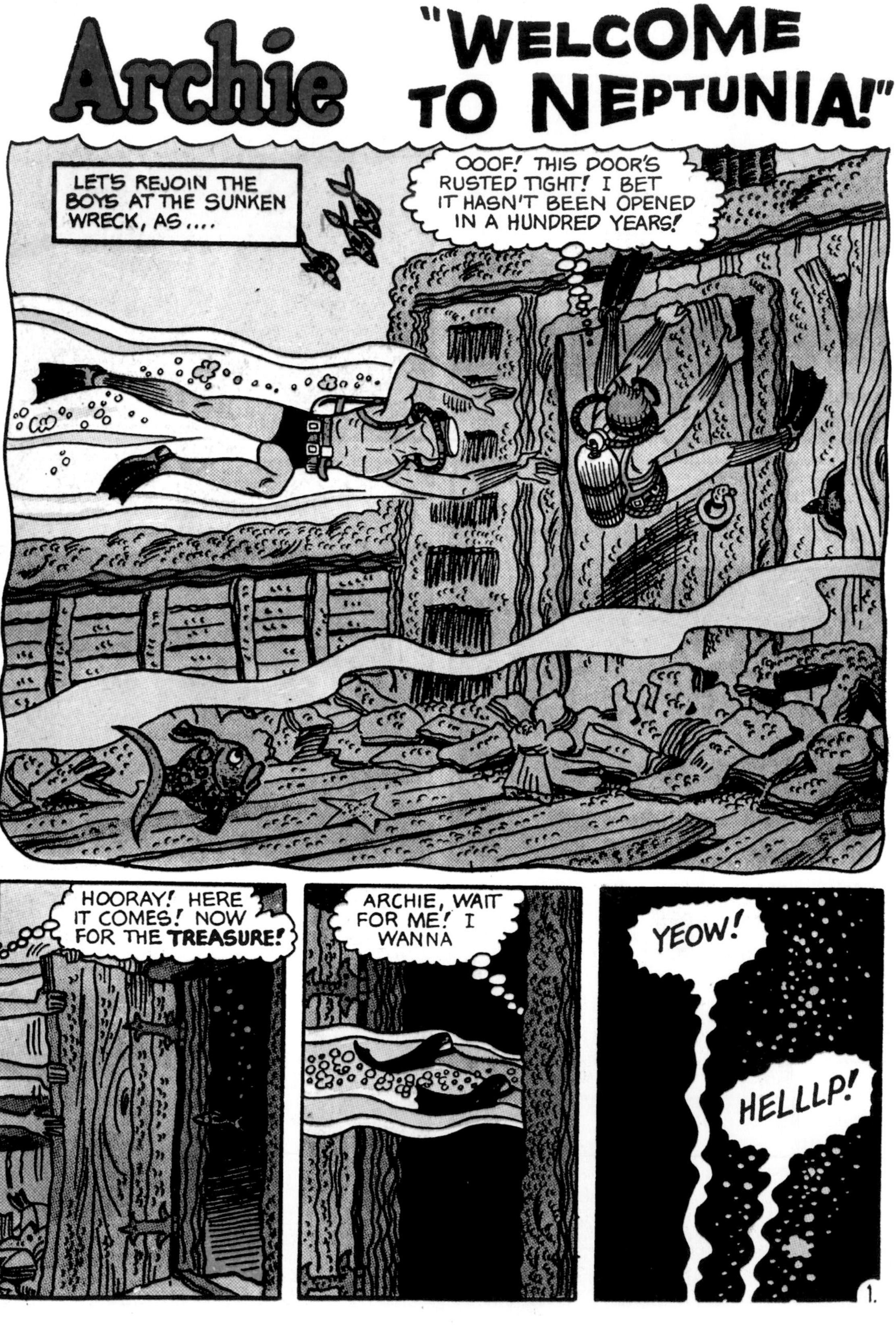
Archie
"WELCOME TO NEPTUNIA!"
LET'S REJOIN THE BOYS AT THE SUNKEN WRECK, AS....
OOOF! THIS DOOR'S RUSTED TIGHT! I BET IT HASN'T BEEN OPENED IN A HUNDRED YEARS!
HOORAY! HERE IT COMES! NOW FOR THE TREASURE!
ARCHIE, WAIT FOR ME! I WANNA
YEOW!
HELLLP!
1.

DRAWN BY AN INVISIBLE FORCE, THE BOYS PLUMMET DOWN A STRANGE, CORKSCREW CHUTE...

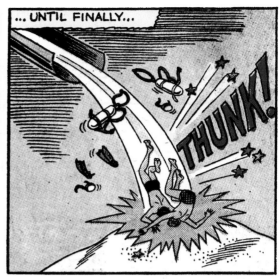

... UNTIL FINALLY...

THUNK!

THANK GOODNESS WE FELL ON A PILE OF SAND! WHAT HAPPENED TO OUR MASKS AND AIR TANKS?

WE MUST HAVE LOST THEM ON THE WAY DOWN!

ARCH! WE'RE B-BREATHING **FRESH AIR!** I DON'T GET IT!?

YEH! IT **IS** SLIGHTLY IMPOSSIBLE, AT THAT!

SNIFF!

SNIFF!

WELCOME TO NEPTUNIA, LADS!

???

!!?

YIPE!

ADD A "YIPE" FOR ME, TOO!

2.

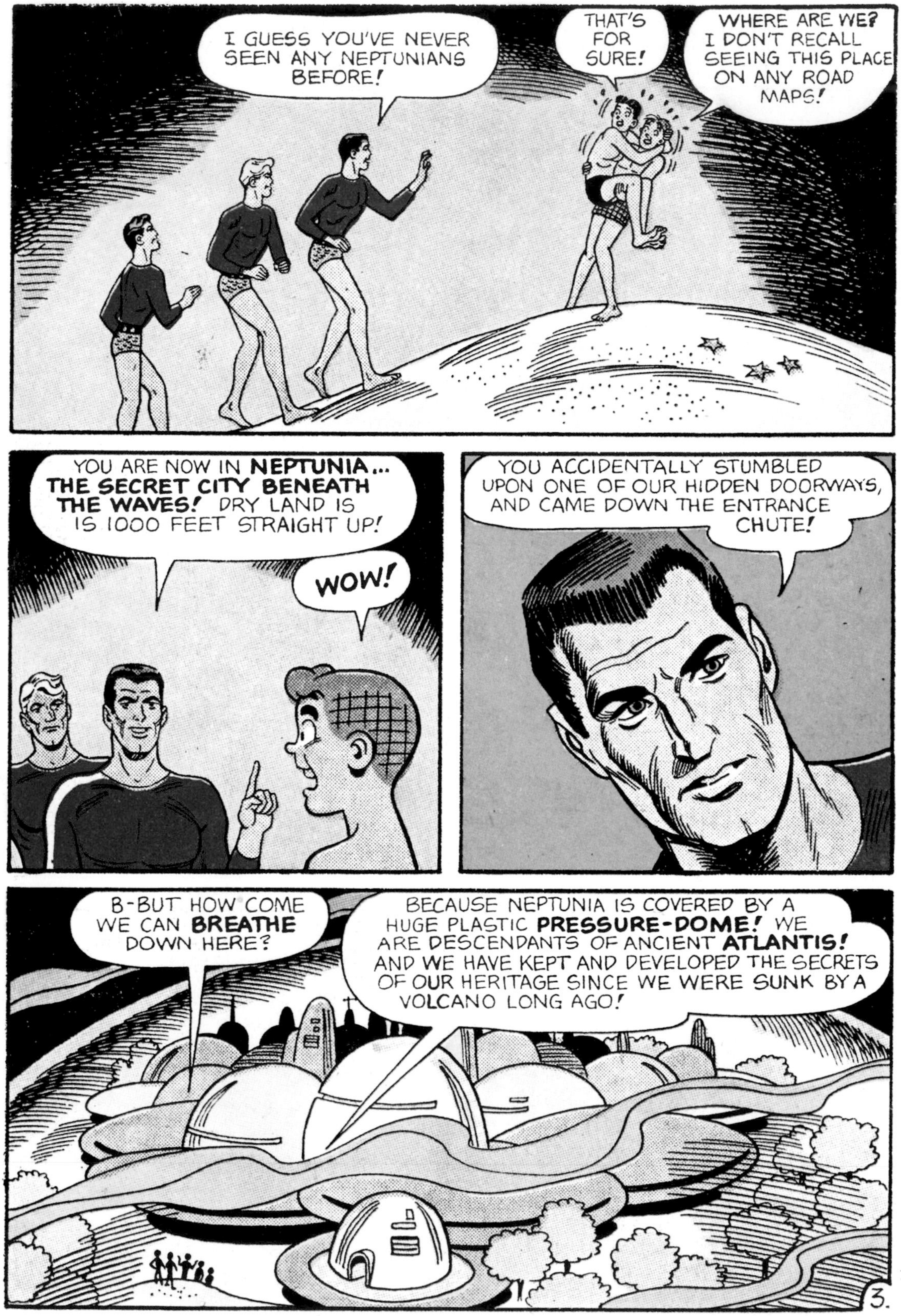
I GUESS YOU'VE NEVER SEEN ANY NEPTUNIANS BEFORE!
THAT'S FOR SURE!
WHERE ARE WE? I DON'T RECALL SEEING THIS PLACE ON ANY ROAD MAPS!
YOU ARE NOW IN NEPTUNIA... THE SECRET CITY BENEATH THE WAVES! DRY LAND IS IS 1000 FEET STRAIGHT UP!
WOW!
YOU ACCIDENTALLY STUMBLED UPON ONE OF OUR HIDDEN DOORWAYS, AND CAME DOWN THE ENTRANCE CHUTE!
B-BUT HOW COME WE CAN BREATHE DOWN HERE?
BECAUSE NEPTUNIA IS COVERED BY A HUGE PLASTIC PRESSURE-DOME! WE ARE DESCENDANTS OF ANCIENT ATLANTIS! AND WE HAVE KEPT AND DEVELOPED THE SECRETS OF OUR HERITAGE SINCE WE WERE SUNK BY A VOLCANO LONG AGO!
3.

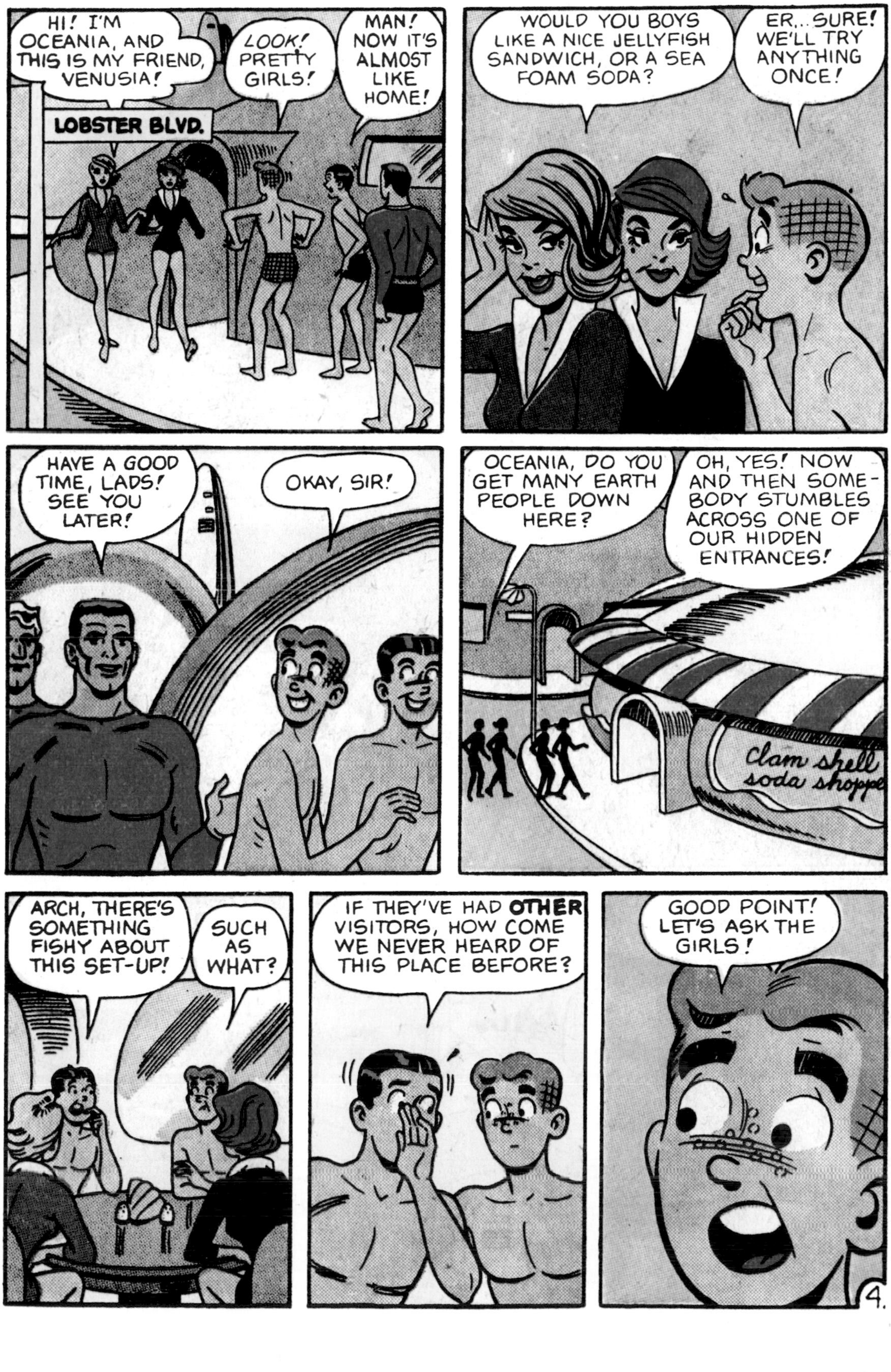
HI! I'M OCEANIA, AND THIS IS MY FRIEND, VENUSIA!
LOOK! PRETTY GIRLS!
MAN! NOW IT'S ALMOST LIKE HOME!
LOBSTER BLVD.
WOULD YOU BOYS LIKE A NICE JELLYFISH SANDWICH, OR A SEA FOAM SODA?
ER... SURE! WE'LL TRY ANYTHING ONCE!
HAVE A GOOD TIME, LADS! SEE YOU LATER!
OKAY, SIR!
OCEANIA, DO YOU GET MANY EARTH PEOPLE DOWN HERE?
OH, YES! NOW AND THEN SOMEBODY STUMBLES ACROSS ONE OF OUR HIDDEN ENTRANCES!
Clam shell soda shoppe
ARCH, THERE'S SOMETHING FISHY ABOUT THIS SET-UP!
SUCH AS WHAT?
IF THEY'VE HAD OTHER VISITORS, HOW COME WE NEVER HEARD OF THIS PLACE BEFORE?
GOOD POINT! LET'S ASK THE GIRLS!
4.

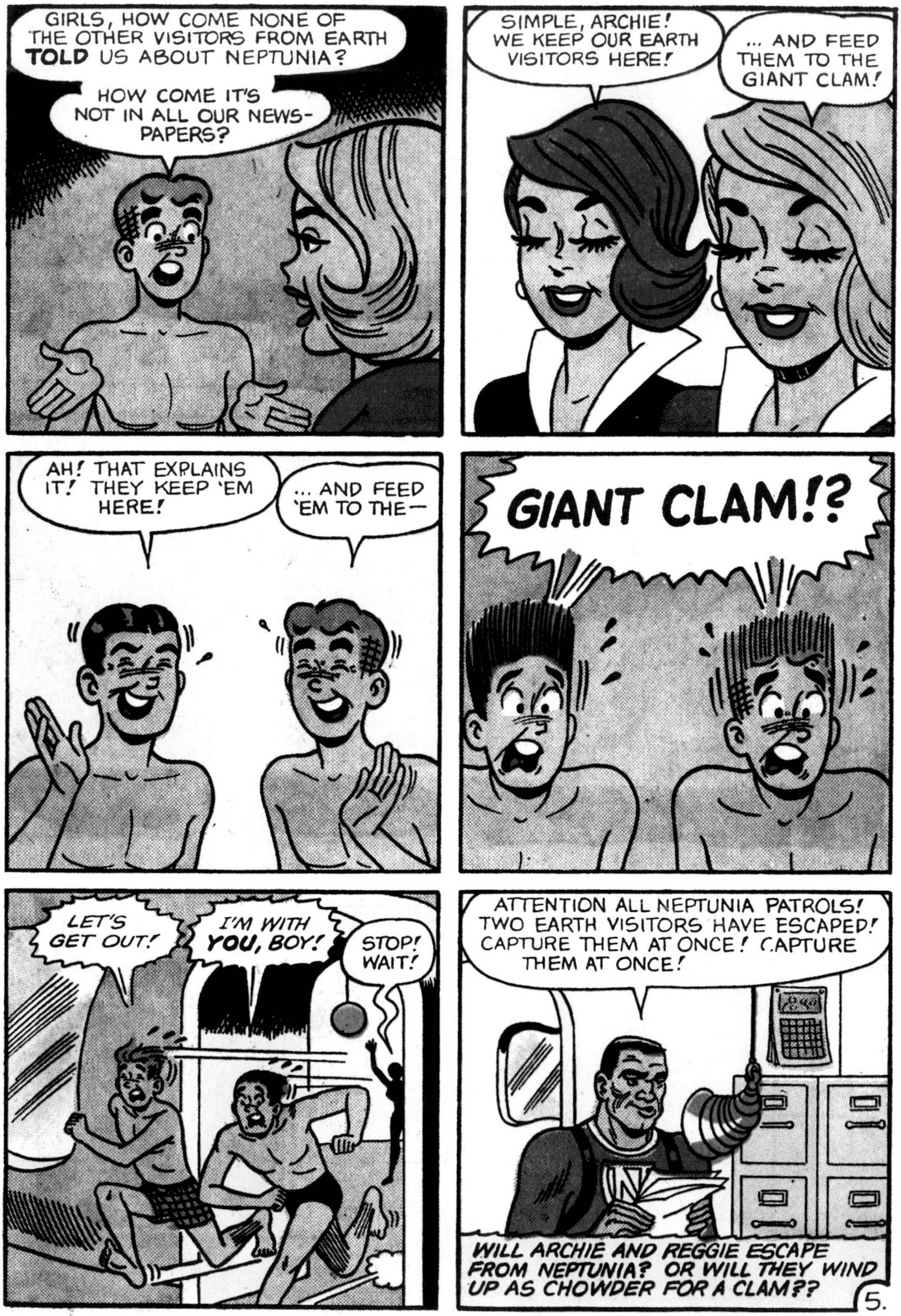
GIRLS, HOW COME NONE OF THE OTHER VISITORS FROM EARTH TOLD US ABOUT NEPTUNIA?
HOW COME IT'S NOT IN ALL OUR NEWS-PAPERS?
SIMPLE, ARCHIE! WE KEEP OUR EARTH VISITORS HERE!
... AND FEED THEM TO THE GIANT CLAM!
AH! THAT EXPLAINS IT! THEY KEEP 'EM HERE!
... AND FEED 'EM TO THE—
GIANT CLAM!?
LET'S GET OUT!
I'M WITH YOU, BOY!
STOP! WAIT!
ATTENTION ALL NEPTUNIA PATROLS! TWO EARTH VISITORS HAVE ESCAPED! CAPTURE THEM AT ONCE! CAPTURE THEM AT ONCE!
WILL ARCHIE AND REGGIE ESCAPE FROM NEPTUNIA? OR WILL THEY WIND UP AS CHOWDER FOR A CLAM??
5.

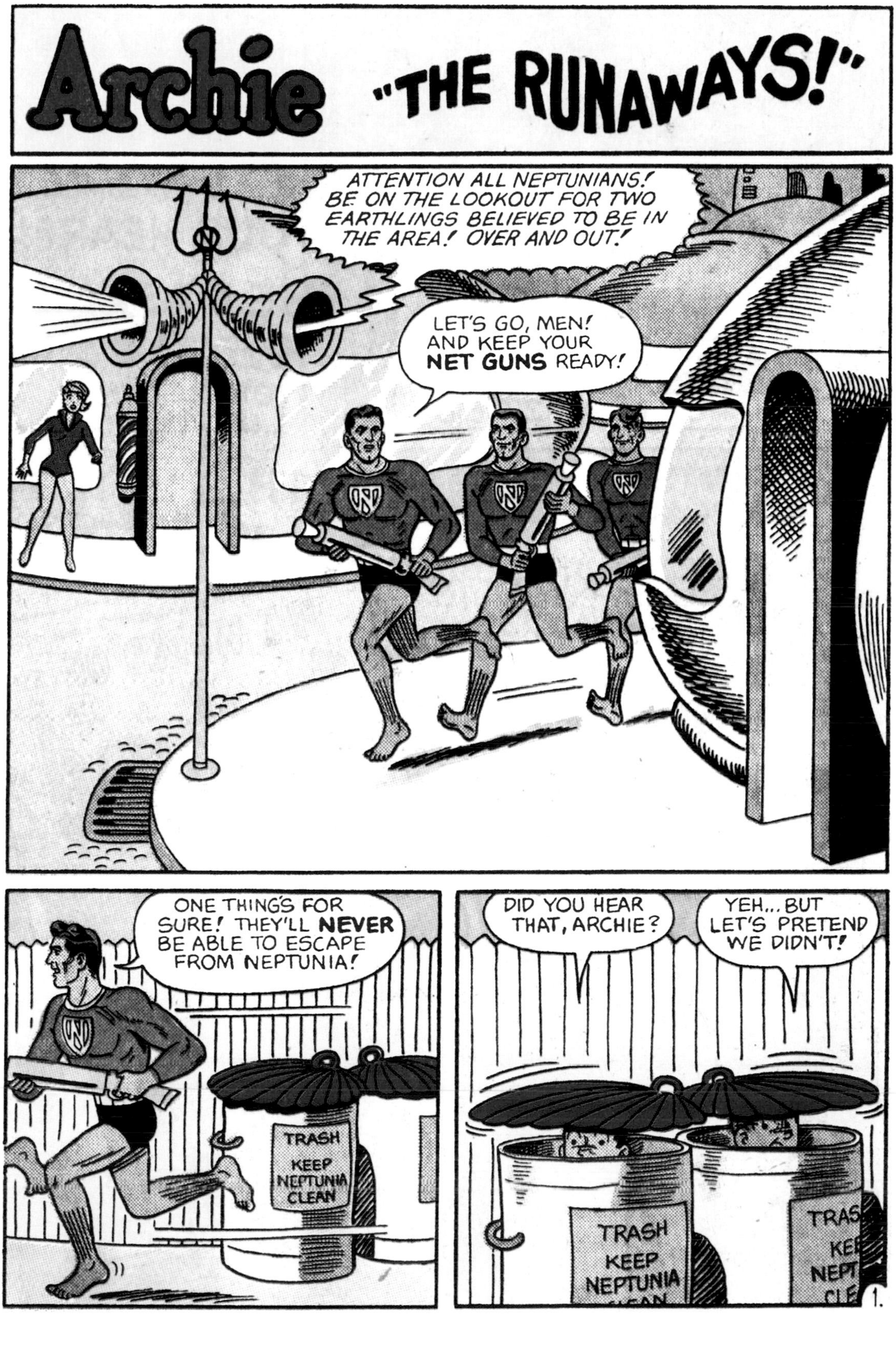

Archie
"THE RUNAWAYS!"
ATTENTION ALL NEPTUNIANS! BE ON THE LOOKOUT FOR TWO EARTHLINGS BELIEVED TO BE IN THE AREA! OVER AND OUT!
LET'S GO, MEN! AND KEEP YOUR NET GUNS READY!
ONE THING'S FOR SURE! THEY'LL NEVER BE ABLE TO ESCAPE FROM NEPTUNIA!
TRASH
KEEP NEPTUNIA CLEAN
DID YOU HEAR THAT, ARCHIE?
YEH... BUT LET'S PRETEND WE DIDN'T!
TRASH
KEEP NEPTUNIA
1.

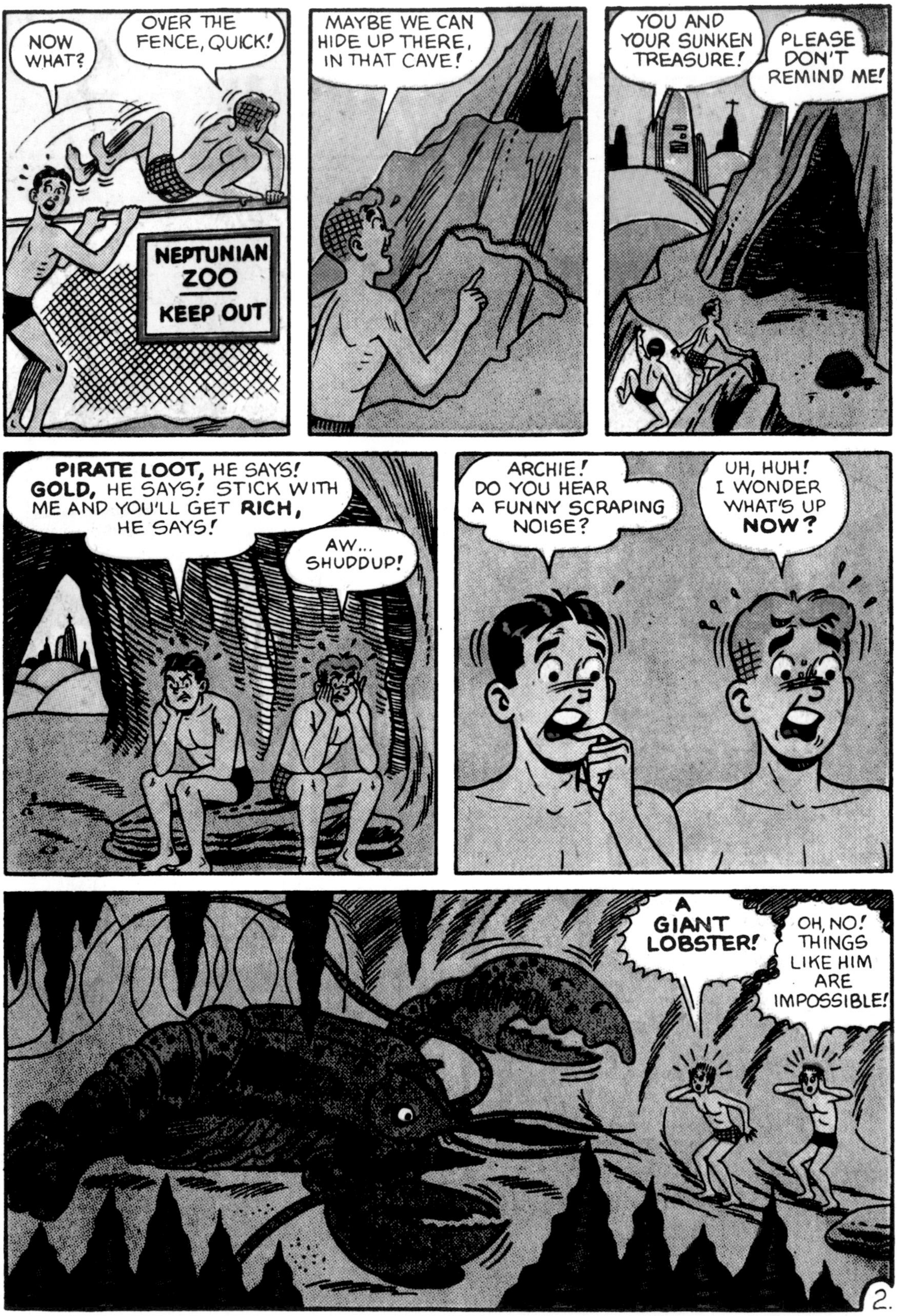
NOW WHAT?
OVER THE FENCE, QUICK!
NEPTUNIAN ZOO KEEP OUT
MAYBE WE CAN HIDE UP THERE, IN THAT CAVE!
YOU AND YOUR SUNKEN TREASURE!
PLEASE DON'T REMIND ME!
PIRATE LOOT, HE SAYS! GOLD, HE SAYS! STICK WITH ME AND YOU'LL GET RICH, HE SAYS!
AW... SHUDDUP!
ARCHIE! DO YOU HEAR A FUNNY SCRAPING NOISE?
UH, HUH! I WONDER WHAT'S UP NOW?
A GIANT LOBSTER!
OH, NO! THINGS LIKE HIM ARE IMPOSSIBLE!
2.

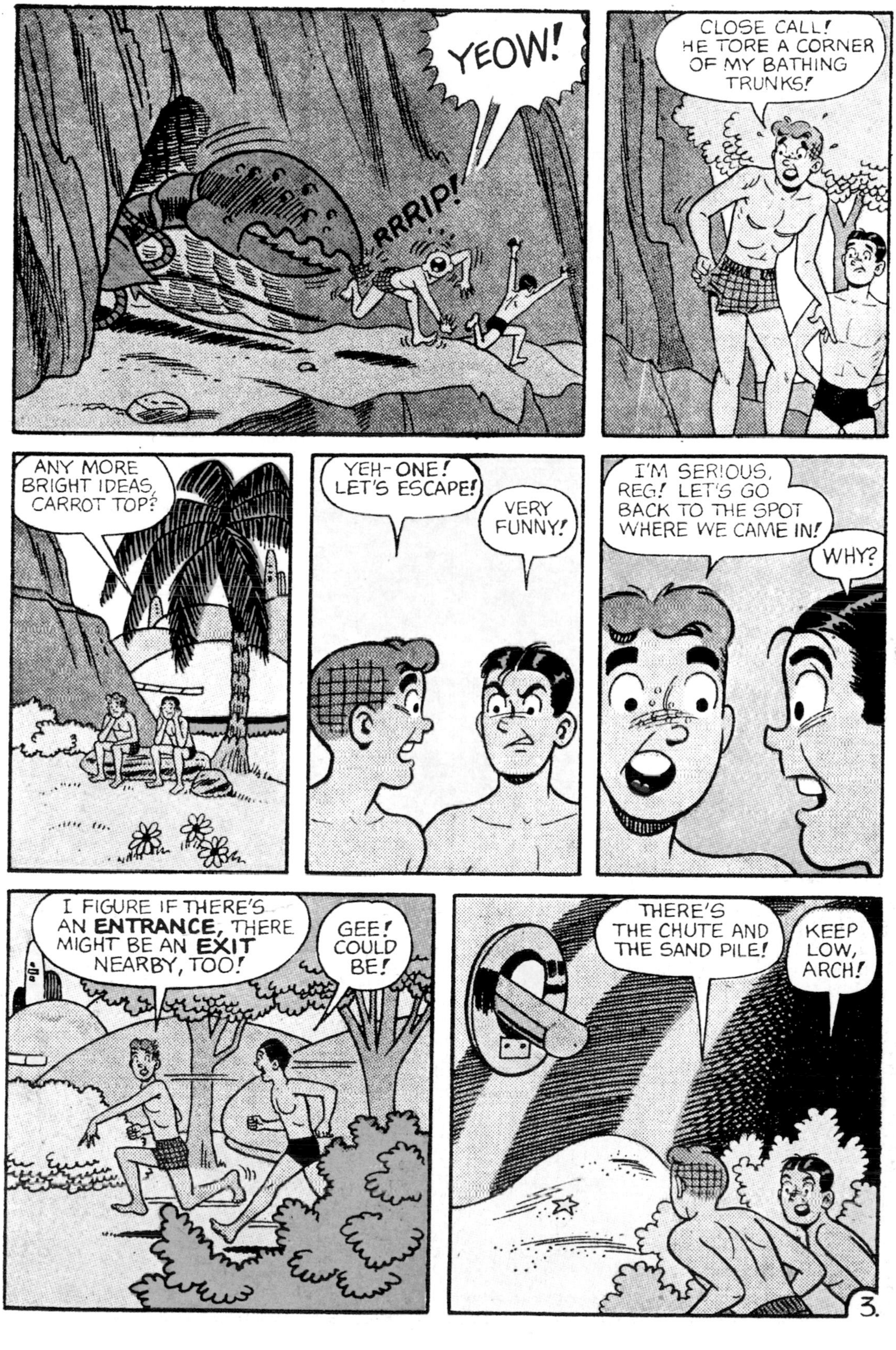
YEOW!
RRRIP!
CLOSE CALL! HE TORE A CORNER OF MY BATHING TRUNKS!
ANY MORE BRIGHT IDEAS, CARROT TOP?
YEH- ONE! LET'S ESCAPE!
VERY FUNNY!
I'M SERIOUS, REG! LET'S GO BACK TO THE SPOT WHERE WE CAME IN!
WHY?
I FIGURE IF THERE'S AN **ENTRANCE**, THERE MIGHT BE AN **EXIT** NEARBY, TOO!
GEE! COULD BE!
THERE'S THE CHUTE AND THE SAND PILE!
KEEP LOW, ARCH!
3.

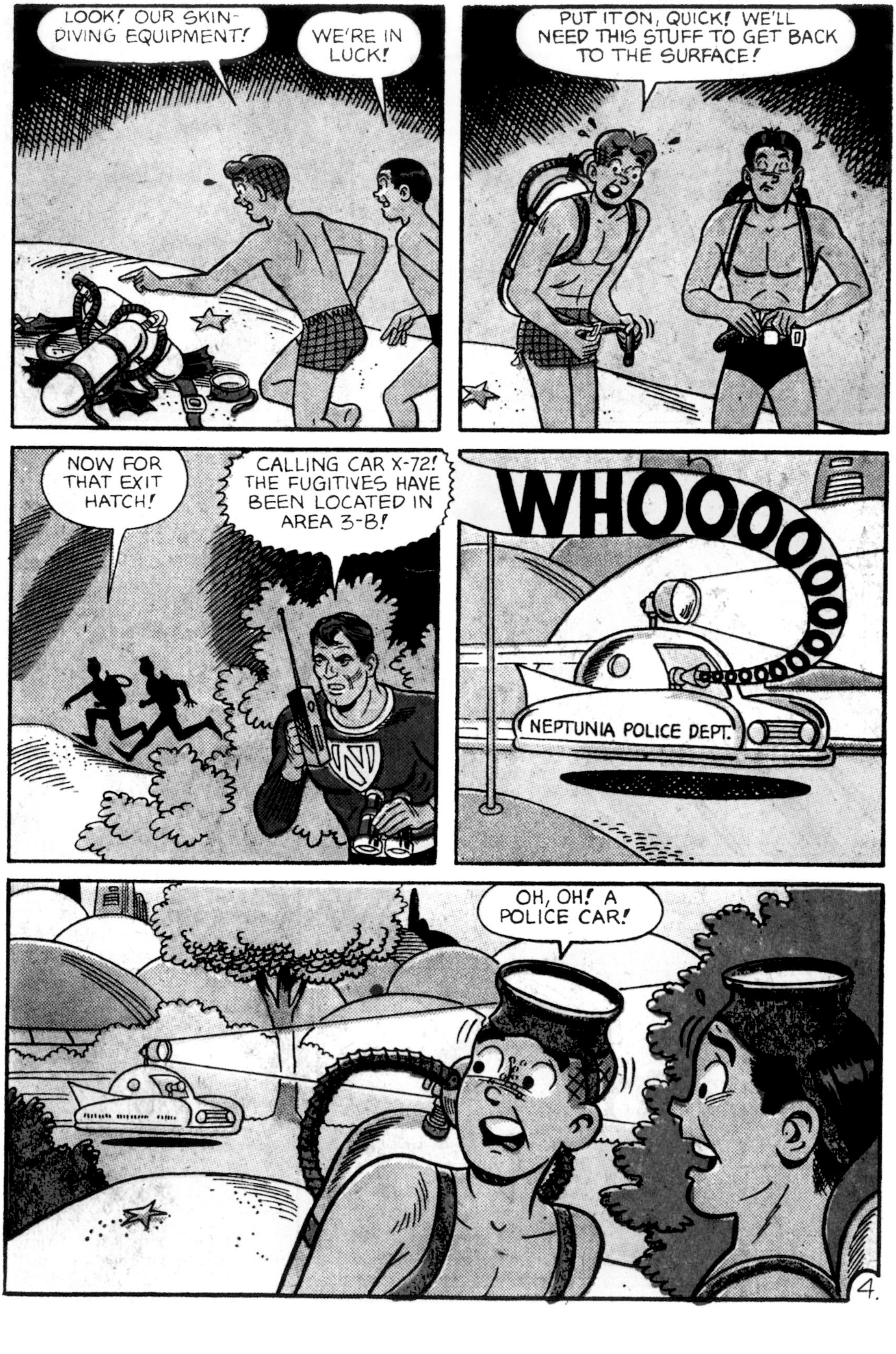
LOOK! OUR SKIN-DIVING EQUIPMENT!
WE'RE IN LUCK!
PUT IT ON, QUICK! WE'LL NEED THIS STUFF TO GET BACK TO THE SURFACE!
NOW FOR THAT EXIT HATCH!
CALLING CAR X-72! THE FUGITIVES HAVE BEEN LOCATED IN AREA 3-B!
WHOOOOOOOOOOOOOOOOO
NEPTUNIA POLICE DEPT.
OH, OH! A POLICE CAR!
4.

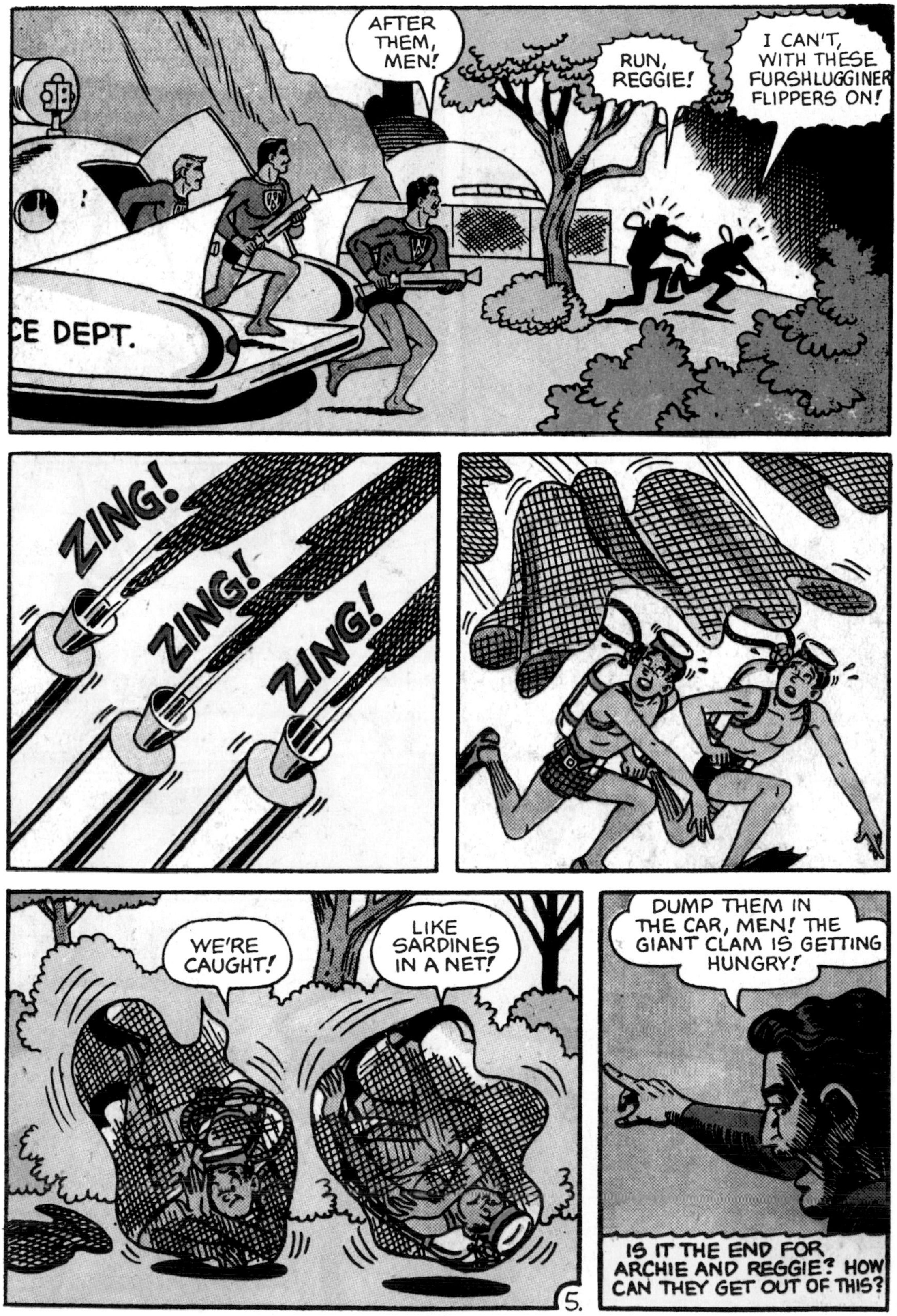

AFTER THEM, MEN!
RUN, REGGIE!
I CAN'T, WITH THESE FURSHLUGGINER FLIPPERS ON!
CE DEPT.
ZING!
ZING!
ZING!
WE'RE CAUGHT!
LIKE SARDINES IN A NET!
5.
DUMP THEM IN THE CAR, MEN! THE GIANT CLAM IS GETTING HUNGRY!
IS IT THE END FOR ARCHIE AND REGGIE? HOW CAN THEY GET OUT OF THIS?

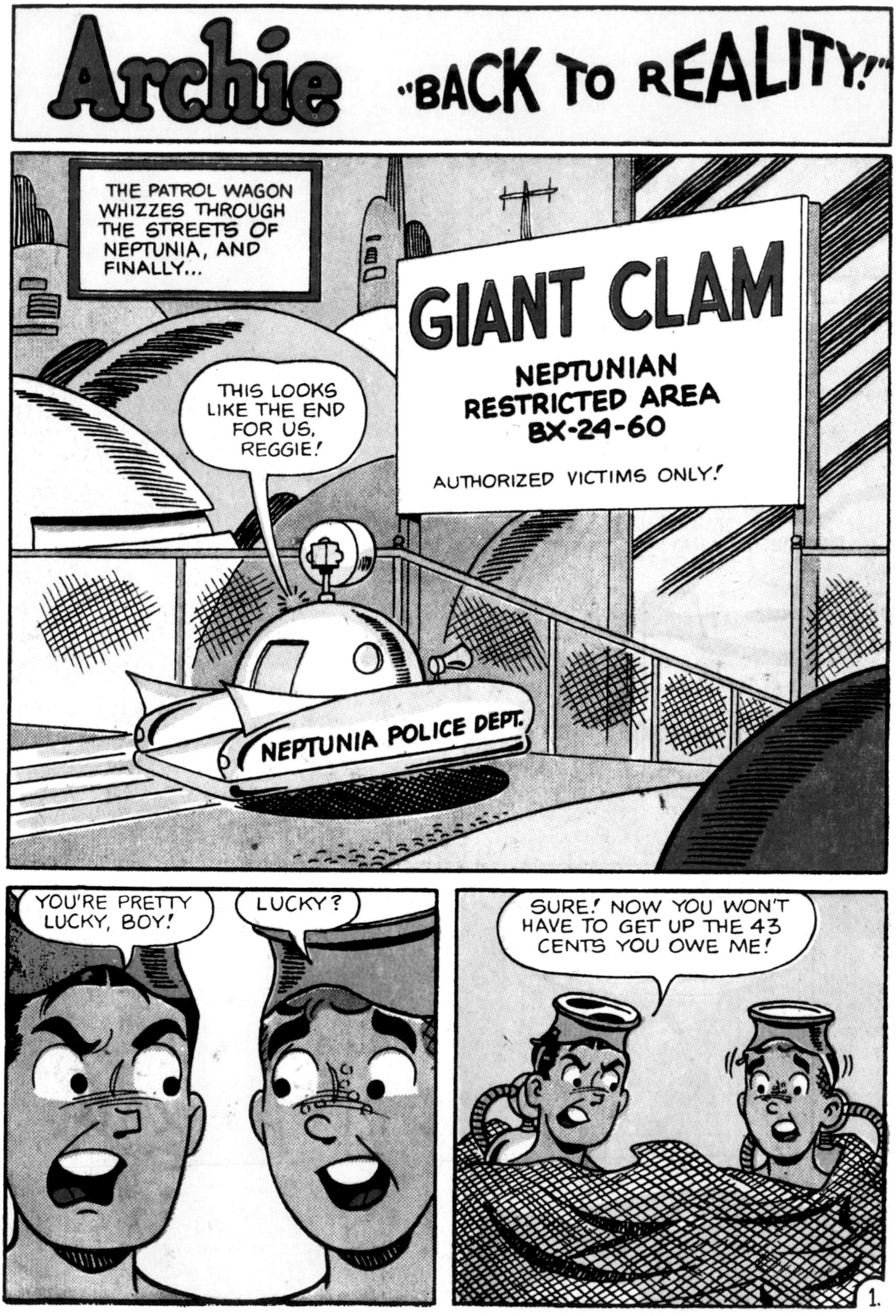
Archie
"BACK TO REALITY!"
THE PATROL WAGON WHIZZES THROUGH THE STREETS OF NEPTUNIA, AND FINALLY...
GIANT CLAM
NEPTUNIAN RESTRICTED AREA BX-24-60
AUTHORIZED VICTIMS ONLY!
THIS LOOKS LIKE THE END FOR US, REGGIE!
NEPTUNIA POLICE DEPT.
YOU'RE PRETTY LUCKY, BOY!
LUCKY?
SURE! NOW YOU WON'T HAVE TO GET UP THE 43 CENTS YOU OWE ME!
1.

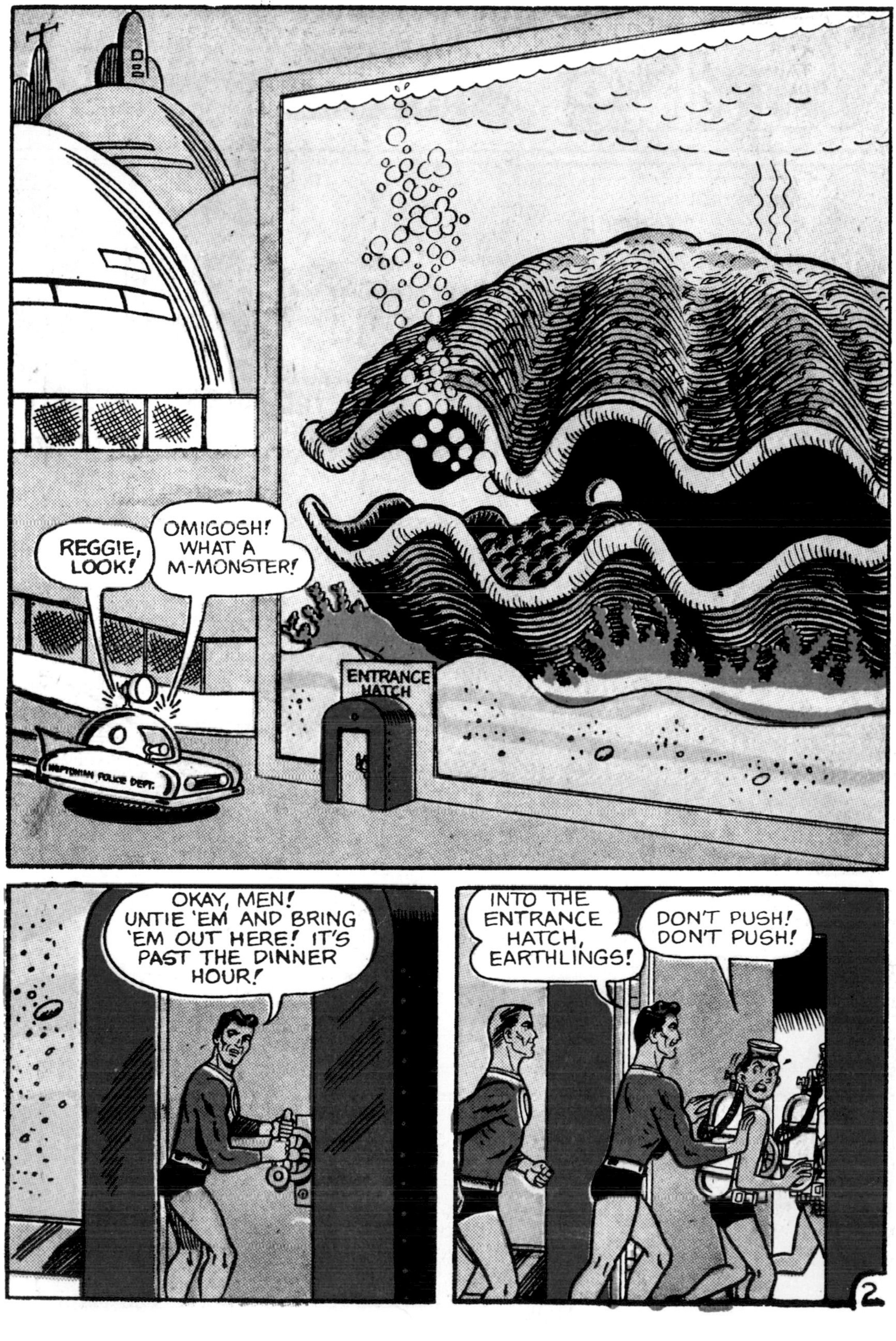
REGGIE, LOOK!
OMIGOSH! WHAT A M-MONSTER!
ENTRANCE HATCH
OKAY, MEN! UNTIE 'EM AND BRING 'EM OUT HERE! IT'S PAST THE DINNER HOUR!
INTO THE ENTRANCE HATCH, EARTHLINGS!
DON'T PUSH! DON'T PUSH!
2

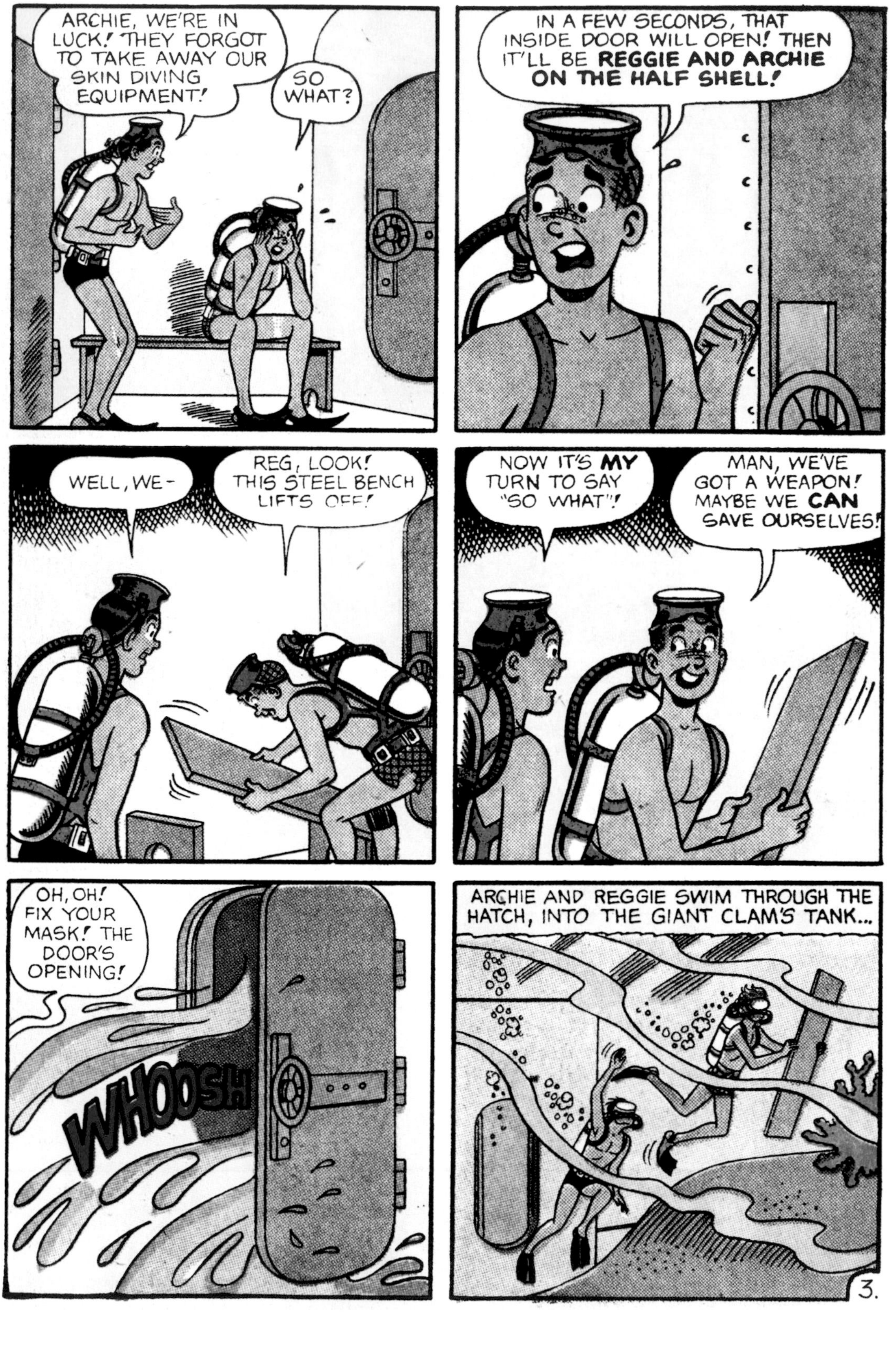
ARCHIE, WE'RE IN LUCK! THEY FORGOT TO TAKE AWAY OUR SKIN DIVING EQUIPMENT!
SO WHAT?
IN A FEW SECONDS, THAT INSIDE DOOR WILL OPEN! THEN IT'LL BE REGGIE AND ARCHIE ON THE HALF SHELL!
WELL, WE-
REG, LOOK! THIS STEEL BENCH LIFTS OFF!
NOW IT'S MY TURN TO SAY "SO WHAT"!
MAN, WE'VE GOT A WEAPON! MAYBE WE CAN SAVE OURSELVES!
OH, OH! FIX YOUR MASK! THE DOOR'S OPENING!
WHOOSH
ARCHIE AND REGGIE SWIM THROUGH THE HATCH, INTO THE GIANT CLAM'S TANK...
3.

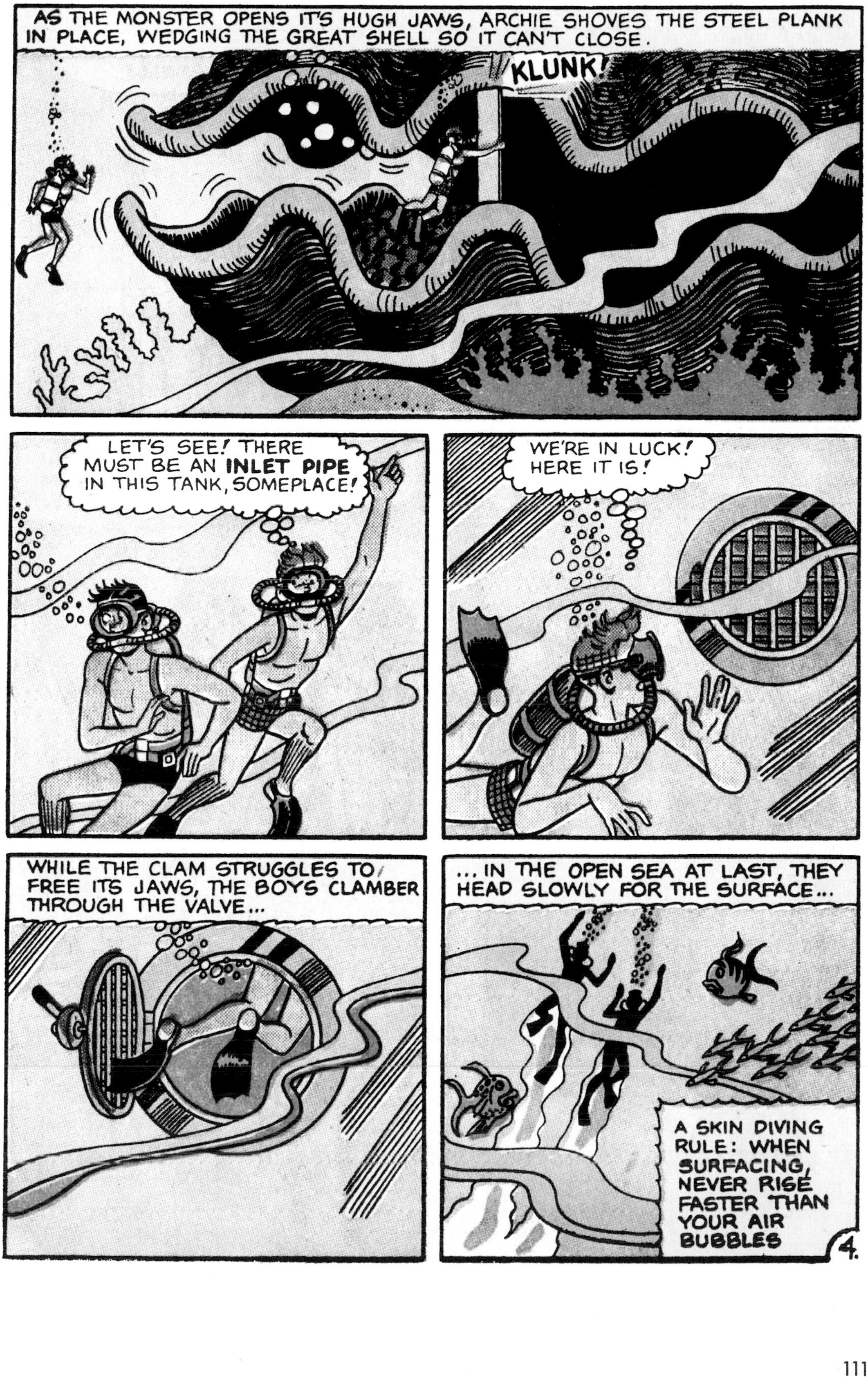
AS THE MONSTER OPENS IT'S HUGH JAWS, ARCHIE SHOVES THE STEEL PLANK IN PLACE, WEDGING THE GREAT SHELL SO IT CAN'T CLOSE.
KLUNK!
LET'S SEE! THERE MUST BE AN INLET PIPE IN THIS TANK, SOMEPLACE!
WE'RE IN LUCK! HERE IT IS!
WHILE THE CLAM STRUGGLES TO FREE ITS JAWS, THE BOYS CLAMBER THROUGH THE VALVE...
... IN THE OPEN SEA AT LAST, THEY HEAD SLOWLY FOR THE SURFACE...
A SKIN DIVING RULE: WHEN SURFACING, NEVER RISE FASTER THAN YOUR AIR BUBBLES
4.

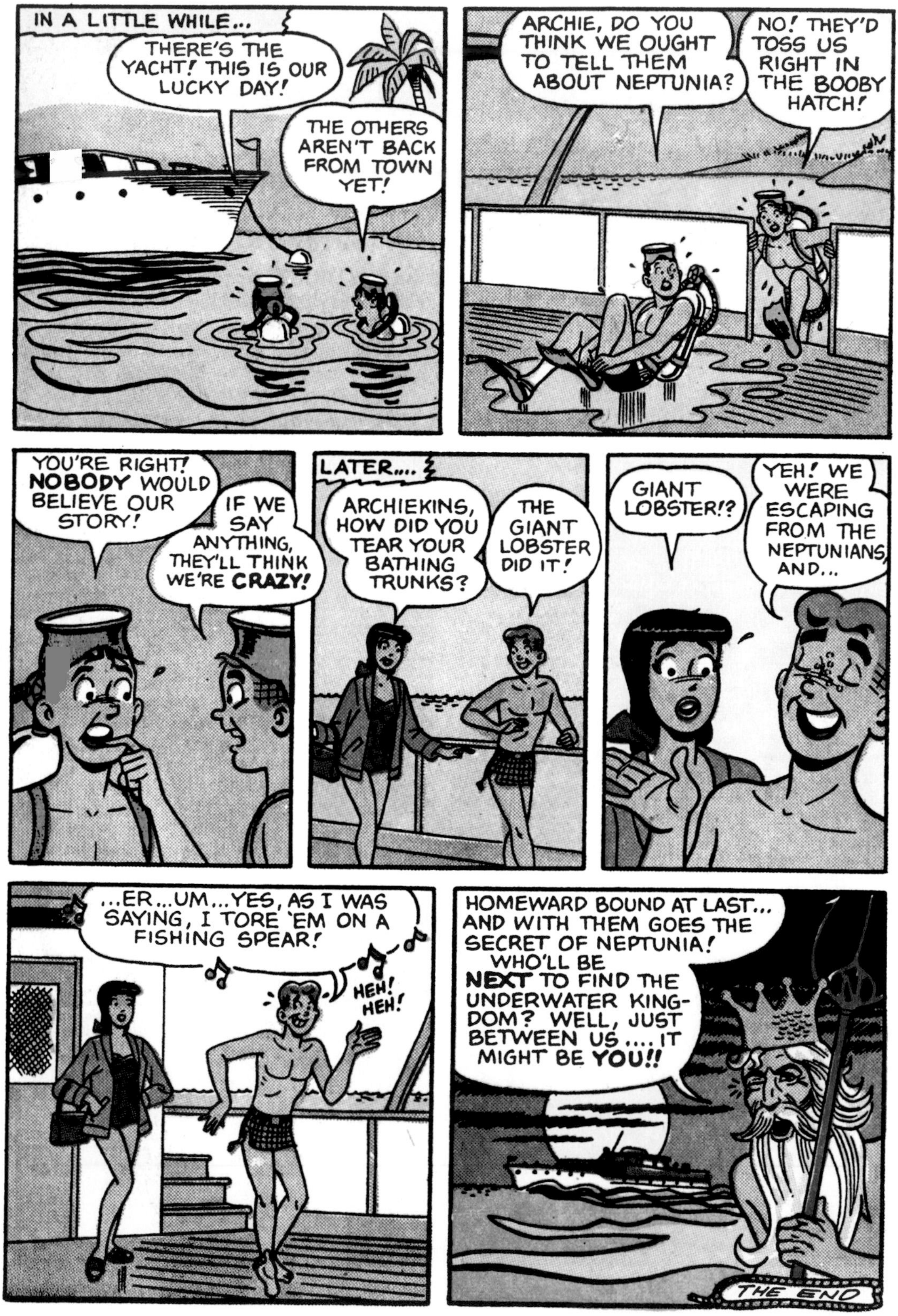

IN A LITTLE WHILE...
THERE'S THE YACHT! THIS IS OUR LUCKY DAY!
THE OTHERS AREN'T BACK FROM TOWN YET!
ARCHIE, DO YOU THINK WE OUGHT TO TELL THEM ABOUT NEPTUNIA?
NO! THEY'D TOSS US RIGHT IN THE BOOBY HATCH!
YOU'RE RIGHT! NOBODY WOULD BELIEVE OUR STORY!
IF WE SAY ANYTHING, THEY'LL THINK WE'RE CRAZY!
LATER....
ARCHIEKINS, HOW DID YOU TEAR YOUR BATHING TRUNKS?
THE GIANT LOBSTER DID IT!
GIANT LOBSTER!?
YEH! WE WERE ESCAPING FROM THE NEPTUNIANS, AND...
...ER...UM...YES, AS I WAS SAYING, I TORE 'EM ON A FISHING SPEAR!
HEH! HEH!
HOMEWARD BOUND AT LAST... AND WITH THEM GOES THE SECRET OF NEPTUNIA! WHO'LL BE NEXT TO FIND THE UNDERWATER KINGDOM? WELL, JUST BETWEEN US.... IT MIGHT BE YOU!!
THE END

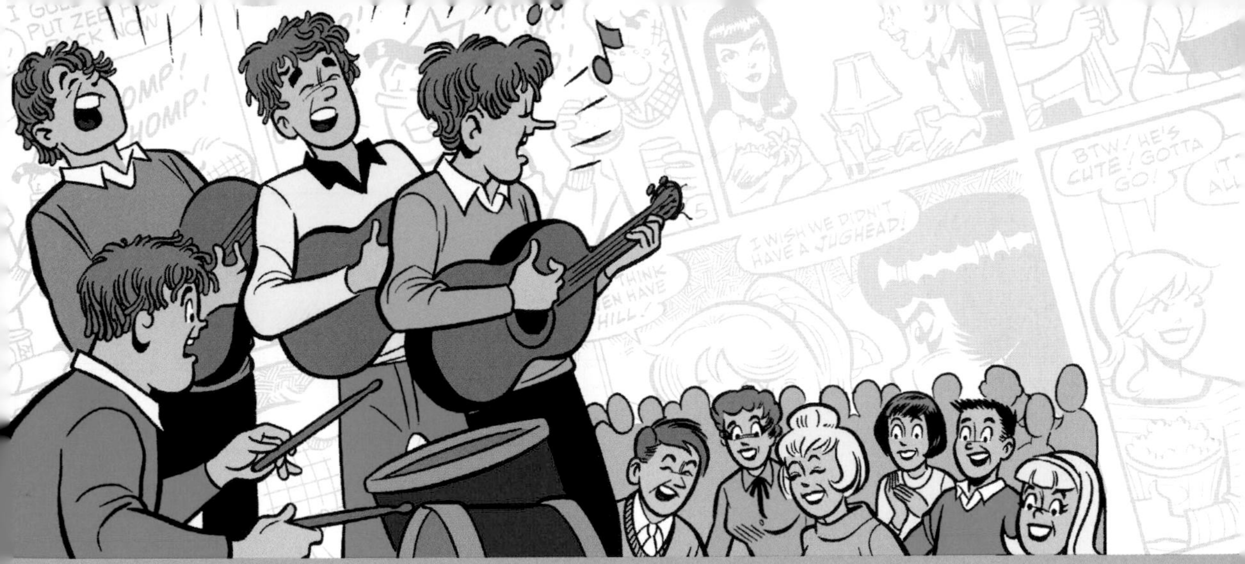
I WISH WE DIDN'T HAVE A JUGHEAD!
BTW! HE'S CUTE! GOTTA GO!

BEETLEMANIA
PALS & GALS #29, 1964
BY FRANK DOYLE, SAMM SCHWARTZ & MARTY EPP

I didn't have a subscription to Archie comics or buy them at the newsstands like most kids. I found Archie in a different way, through neighborhood "yard sales" where you could sometimes find a stack of 20 or 30 Archie, DC, and Marvel comics for a few dollars. Archie seemed to be about the promise of interaction between men and women. I know, I know, Archie was actually a high school student, however, when I was a ten year old boy, I figured, once you could drive, date girls and afford to go out to eat, you were a man. Archie laid it all out like a catalog of things to look forward to and offered up these scintillating coming attractions in brief, colorful, easy to absorb, and fun to read pictographs. I don't think Archie comics made me any less nervous around girls that reminded me of Betty and Veronica, but it did show me how they might behave if I had the presence of mind to treat them right.

—Joel Hodgson
Creator,
Mystery Science Theater 3000

Archie Beetlemania
GET AWAY FROM THAT SET! I'LL DIE! I'LL ABSOLUTELY EXPIRE IF I'M DENIED THE SIGHT AND SOUND OF THOSE DARLING BOYS!
OH, NO YOU'RE NOT! NOT IN MY HOUSE! YOU'RE NOT ABOUT TO WATCH THOSE SHAGGY HAIRED INSECTS! NOT ON MY TV!
YOU TELL 'EM, ARCH!

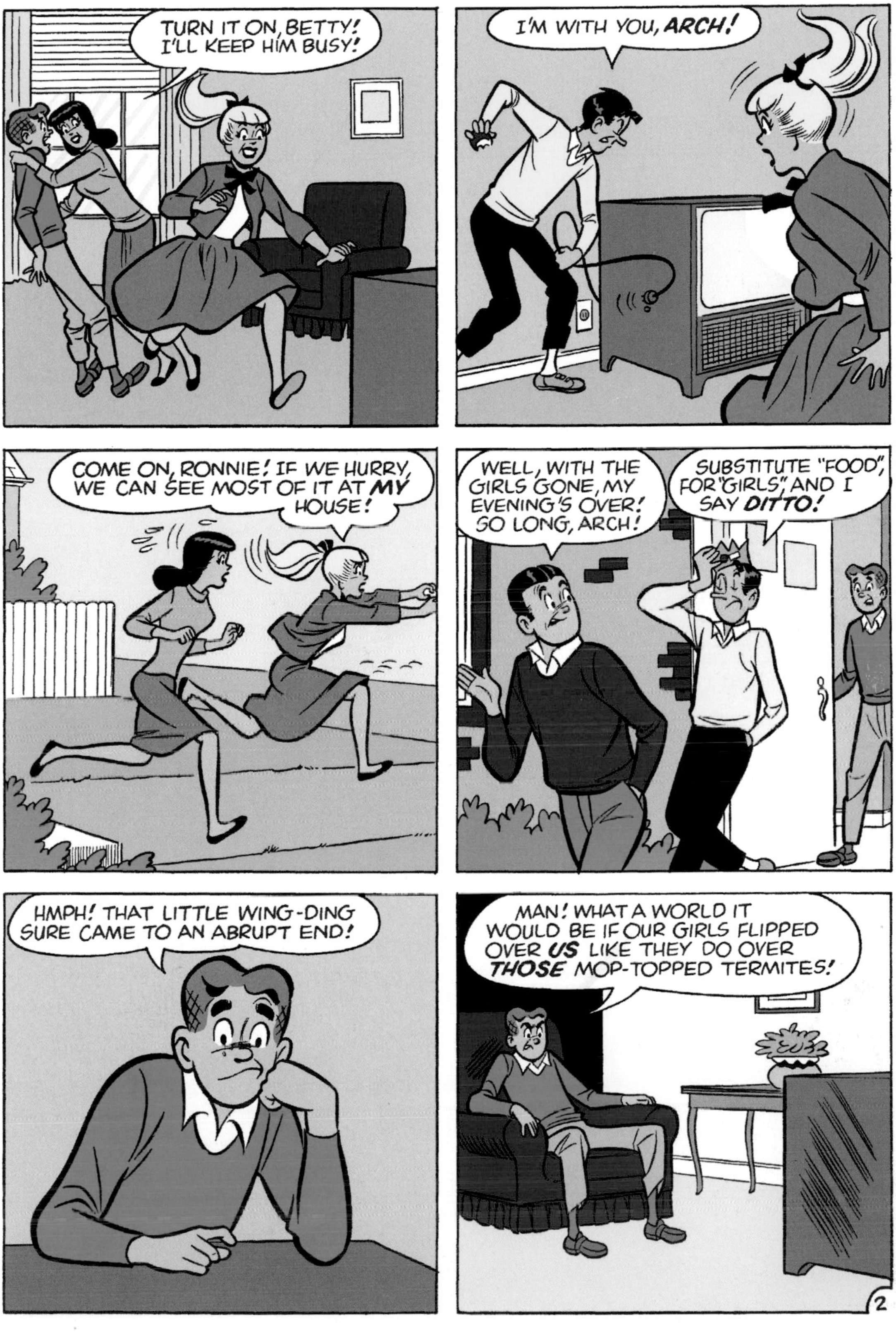
TURN IT ON, BETTY! I'LL KEEP HIM BUSY!
I'M WITH YOU, ARCH!
COME ON, RONNIE! IF WE HURRY, WE CAN SEE MOST OF IT AT MY HOUSE!
WELL, WITH THE GIRLS GONE, MY EVENING'S OVER! SO LONG, ARCH!
SUBSTITUTE "FOOD" FOR "GIRLS" AND I SAY DITTO!
HMPH! THAT LITTLE WING-DING SURE CAME TO AN ABRUPT END!
MAN! WHAT A WORLD IT WOULD BE IF OUR GIRLS FLIPPED OVER US LIKE THEY DO OVER THOSE MOP-TOPPED TERMITES!
2

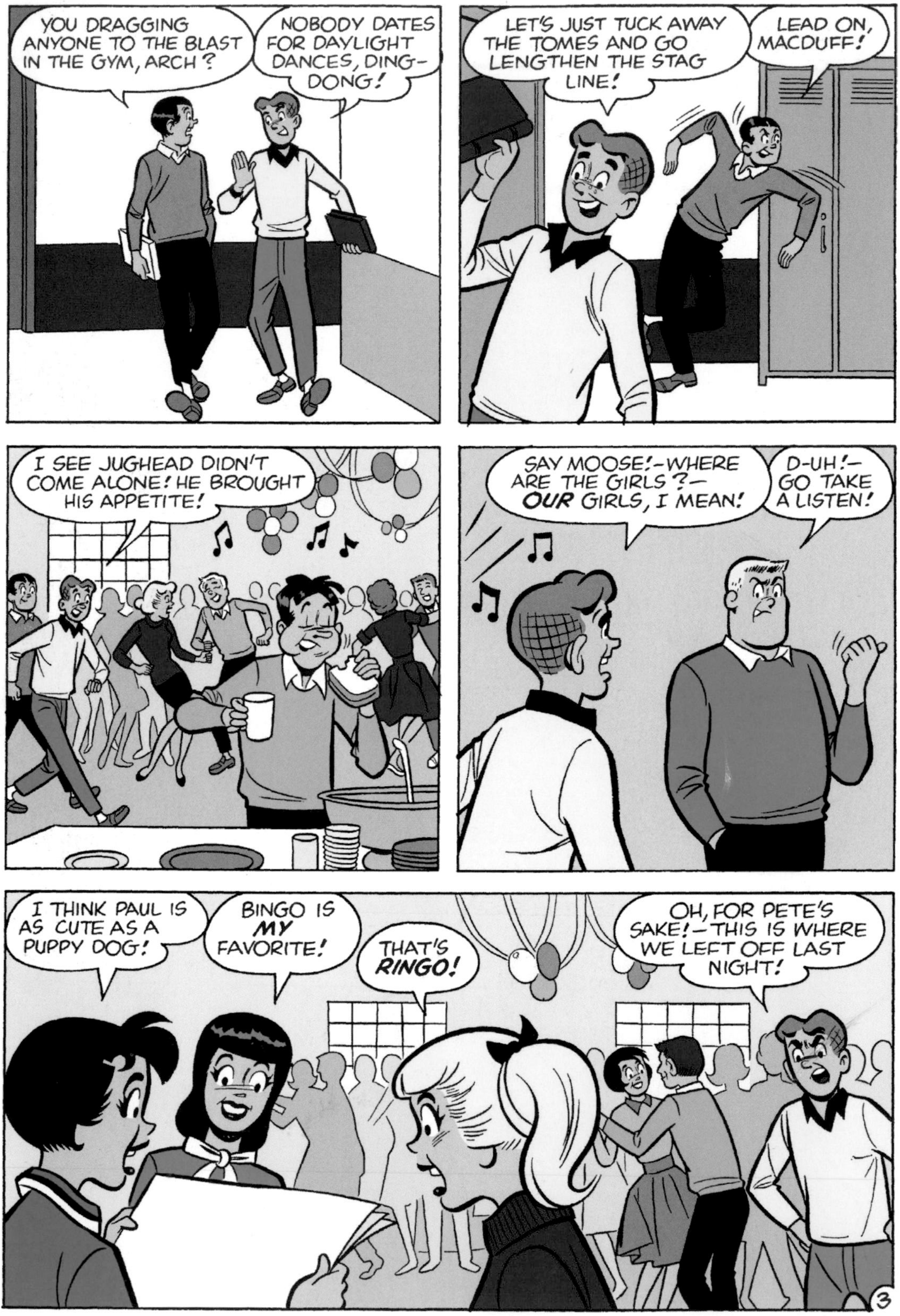
YOU DRAGGING ANYONE TO THE BLAST IN THE GYM, ARCH?
NOBODY DATES FOR DAYLIGHT DANCES, DING-DONG!
LET'S JUST TUCK AWAY THE TOMES AND GO LENGTHEN THE STAG LINE!
LEAD ON, MACDUFF!
I SEE JUGHEAD DIDN'T COME ALONE! HE BROUGHT HIS APPETITE!
SAY MOOSE!-WHERE ARE THE GIRLS?- **OUR** GIRLS, I MEAN!
D-UH!- GO TAKE A LISTEN!
I THINK PAUL IS AS CUTE AS A PUPPY DOG!
BINGO IS **MY** FAVORITE!
THAT'S **RINGO!**
OH, FOR PETE'S SAKE!-THIS IS WHERE WE LEFT OFF LAST NIGHT!
3

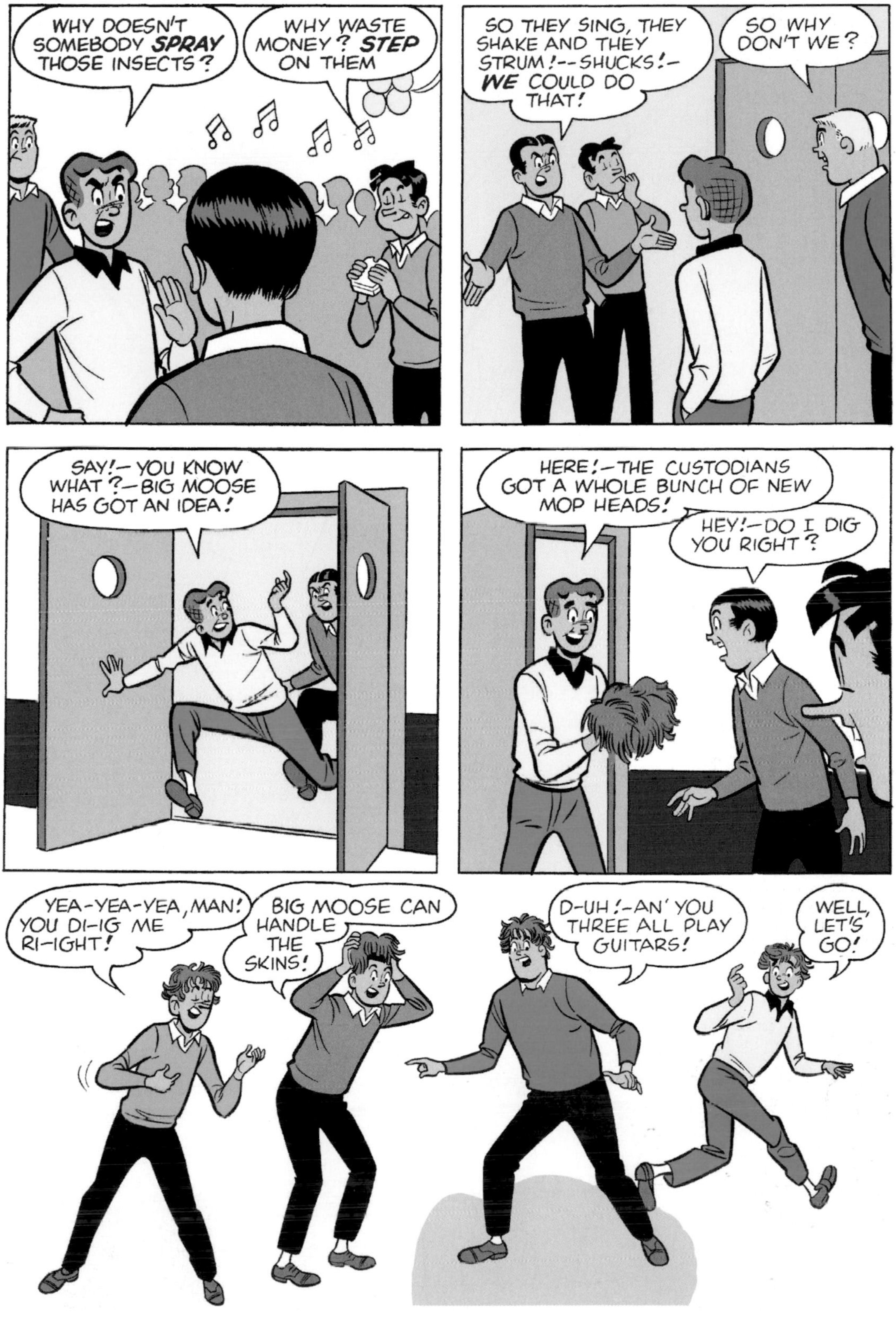
WHY DOESN'T SOMEBODY SPRAY THOSE INSECTS?
WHY WASTE MONEY? STEP ON THEM
SO THEY SING, THEY SHAKE AND THEY STRUM!--SHUCKS!- WE COULD DO THAT!
SO WHY DON'T WE?
SAY!- YOU KNOW WHAT?- BIG MOOSE HAS GOT AN IDEA!
HERE!-THE CUSTODIANS GOT A WHOLE BUNCH OF NEW MOP HEADS!
HEY!-DO I DIG YOU RIGHT?
YEA-YEA-YEA, MAN! YOU DI-IG ME RI-IGHT!
BIG MOOSE CAN HANDLE THE SKINS!
D-UH!-AN' YOU THREE ALL PLAY GUITARS!
WELL, LET'S GO!

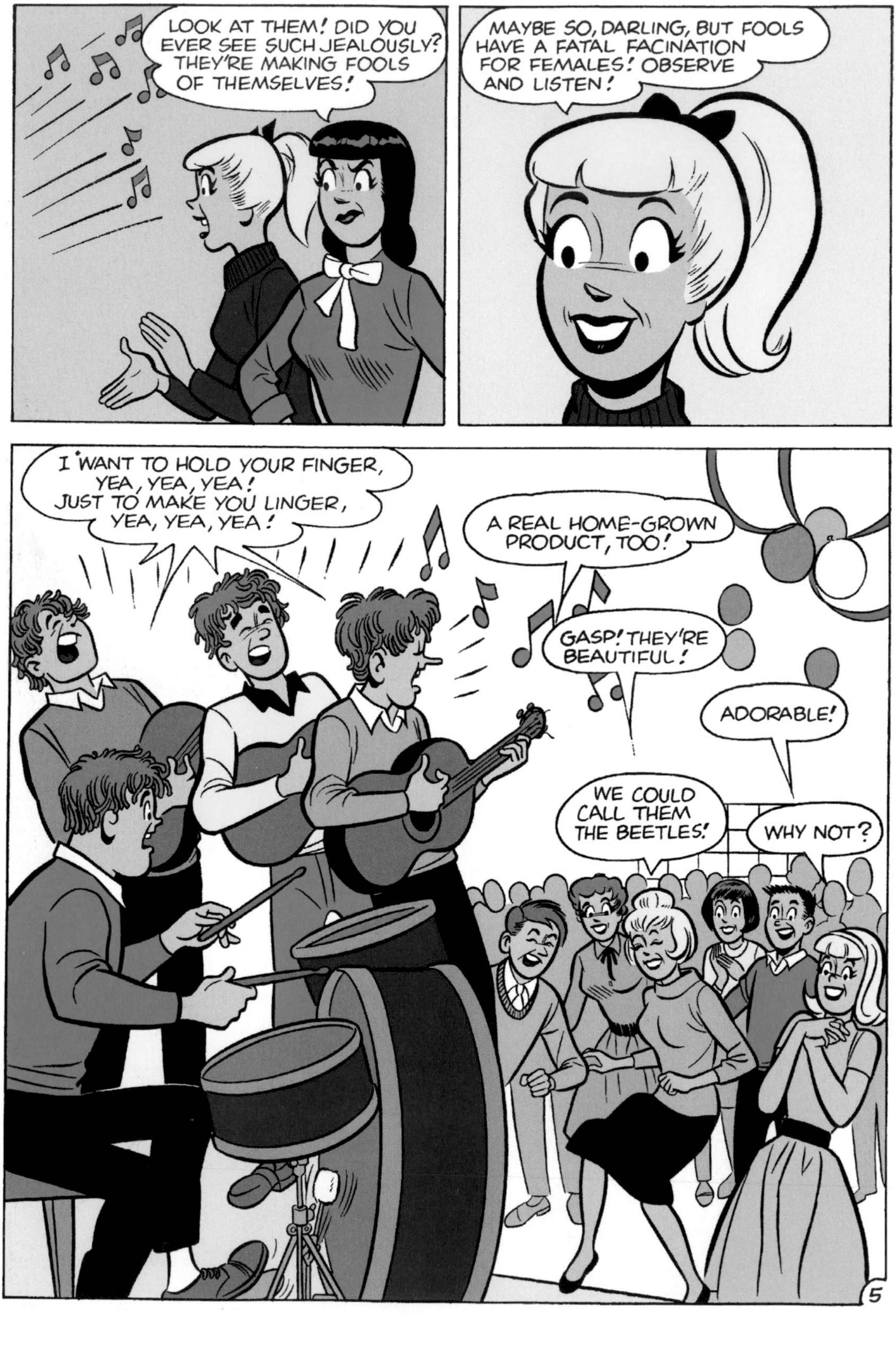
LOOK AT THEM! DID YOU EVER SEE SUCH JEALOUSLY? THEY'RE MAKING FOOLS OF THEMSELVES!
MAYBE SO, DARLING, BUT FOOLS HAVE A FATAL FACINATION FOR FEMALES! OBSERVE AND LISTEN!
I WANT TO HOLD YOUR FINGER, YEA, YEA, YEA! JUST TO MAKE YOU LINGER, YEA, YEA, YEA!
A REAL HOME-GROWN PRODUCT, TOO!
GASP! THEY'RE BEAUTIFUL!
ADORABLE!
WE COULD CALL THEM THE BEETLES!
WHY NOT?
5

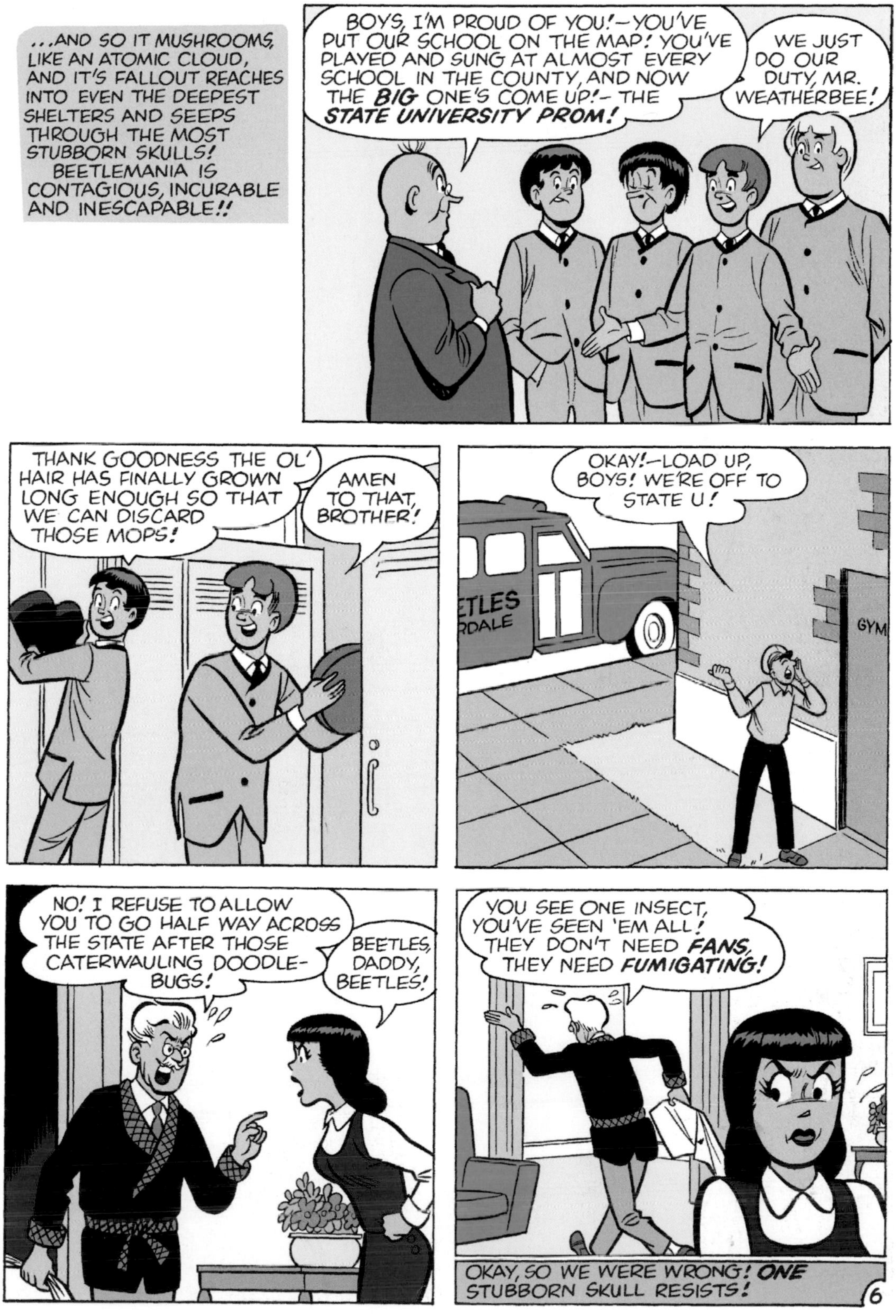
...AND SO IT MUSHROOMS, LIKE AN ATOMIC CLOUD, AND IT'S FALLOUT REACHES INTO EVEN THE DEEPEST SHELTERS AND SEEPS THROUGH THE MOST STUBBORN SKULLS! BEETLEMANIA IS CONTAGIOUS, INCURABLE AND INESCAPABLE!!
BOYS, I'M PROUD OF YOU!—YOU'VE PUT OUR SCHOOL ON THE MAP! YOU'VE PLAYED AND SUNG AT ALMOST EVERY SCHOOL IN THE COUNTY, AND NOW THE BIG ONE'S COME UP!— THE STATE UNIVERSITY PROM!
WE JUST DO OUR DUTY, MR. WEATHERBEE!
THANK GOODNESS THE OL' HAIR HAS FINALLY GROWN LONG ENOUGH SO THAT WE CAN DISCARD THOSE MOPS!
AMEN TO THAT, BROTHER!
OKAY!—LOAD UP, BOYS! WE'RE OFF TO STATE U!
ETLES
RDALE
GYM
NO! I REFUSE TO ALLOW YOU TO GO HALF WAY ACROSS THE STATE AFTER THOSE CATERWAULING DOODLE-BUGS!
BEETLES, DADDY, BEETLES!
YOU SEE ONE INSECT, YOU'VE SEEN 'EM ALL! THEY DON'T NEED FANS, THEY NEED FUMIGATING!
OKAY, SO WE WERE WRONG! ONE STUBBORN SKULL RESISTS!
6

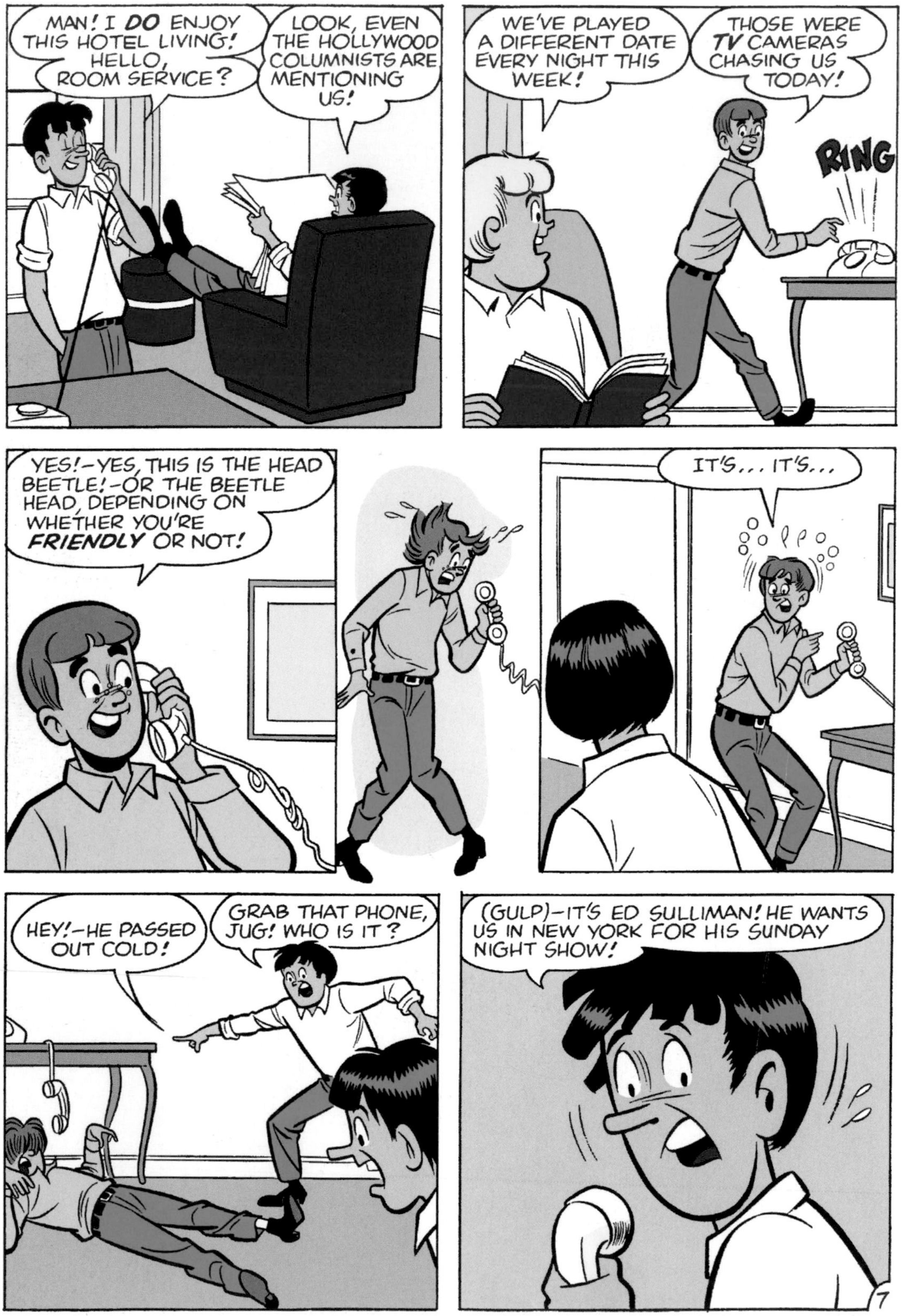
MAN! I DO ENJOY THIS HOTEL LIVING! HELLO, ROOM SERVICE?
LOOK, EVEN THE HOLLYWOOD COLUMNISTS ARE MENTIONING US!
WE'VE PLAYED A DIFFERENT DATE EVERY NIGHT THIS WEEK!
THOSE WERE TV CAMERAS CHASING US TODAY!
RING
YES!—YES, THIS IS THE HEAD BEETLE!—OR THE BEETLE HEAD, DEPENDING ON WHETHER YOU'RE FRIENDLY OR NOT!
IT'S... IT'S...
HEY!—HE PASSED OUT COLD!
GRAB THAT PHONE, JUG! WHO IS IT?
(GULP)—IT'S ED SULLIMAN! HE WANTS US IN NEW YORK FOR HIS SUNDAY NIGHT SHOW!
7

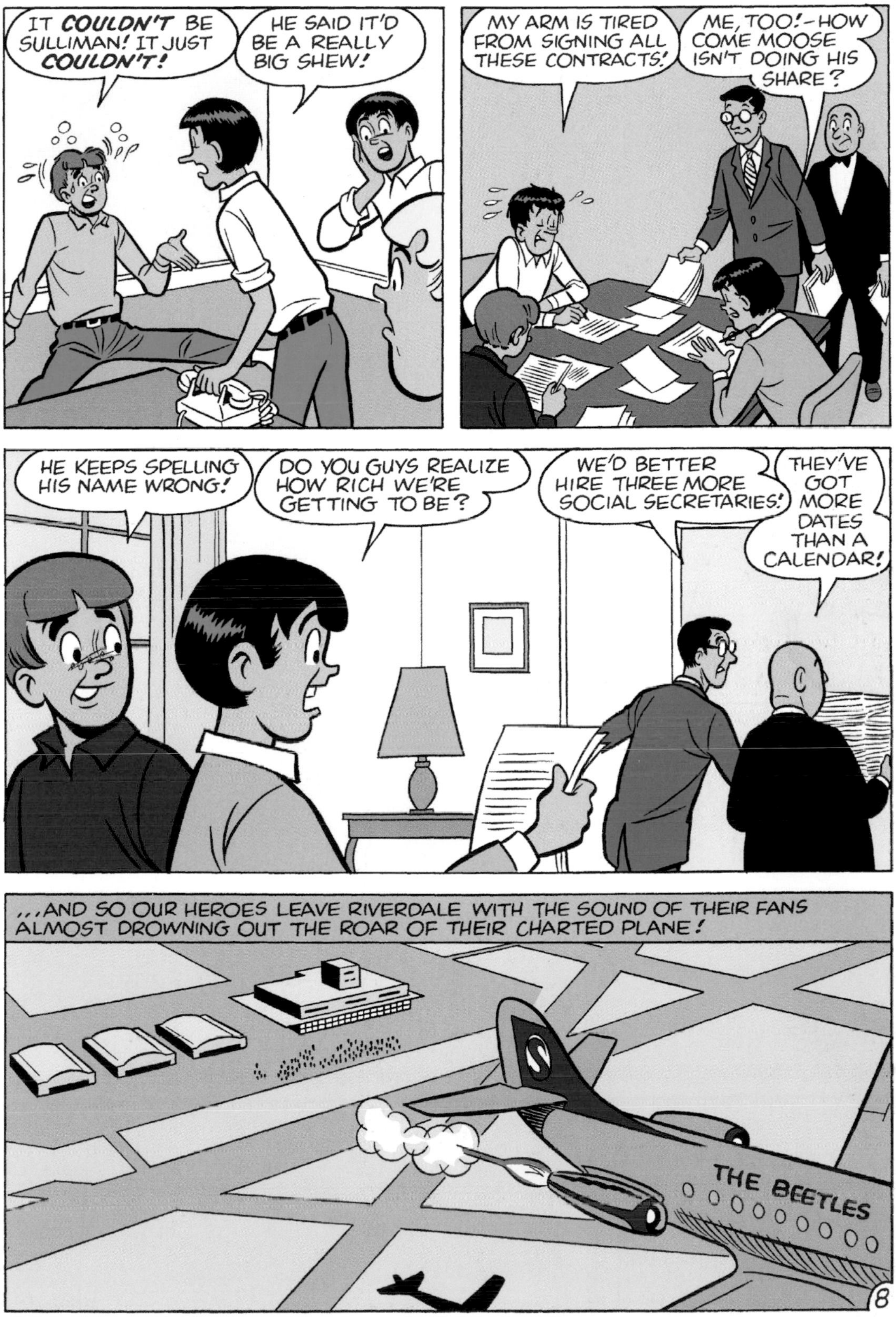
IT COULDN'T BE SULLIMAN! IT JUST COULDN'T!
HE SAID IT'D BE A REALLY BIG SHEW!
MY ARM IS TIRED FROM SIGNING ALL THESE CONTRACTS!
ME, TOO!-HOW COME MOOSE ISN'T DOING HIS SHARE?
HE KEEPS SPELLING HIS NAME WRONG!
DO YOU GUYS REALIZE HOW RICH WE'RE GETTING TO BE?
WE'D BETTER HIRE THREE MORE SOCIAL SECRETARIES!
THEY'VE GOT MORE DATES THAN A CALENDAR!
...AND SO OUR HEROES LEAVE RIVERDALE WITH THE SOUND OF THEIR FANS ALMOST DROWNING OUT THE ROAR OF THEIR CHARTED PLANE!
THE BEETLES
8

THE BIG TOWN PULLS OUT ALL THE STOPS...

WE LOVE THE BEETLES

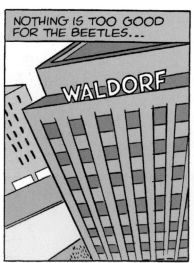

NOTHING IS TOO GOOD FOR THE BEETLES...

WALDORF

YOU KNOW, THIS IS NOT HARD TO GET USED TO!

9

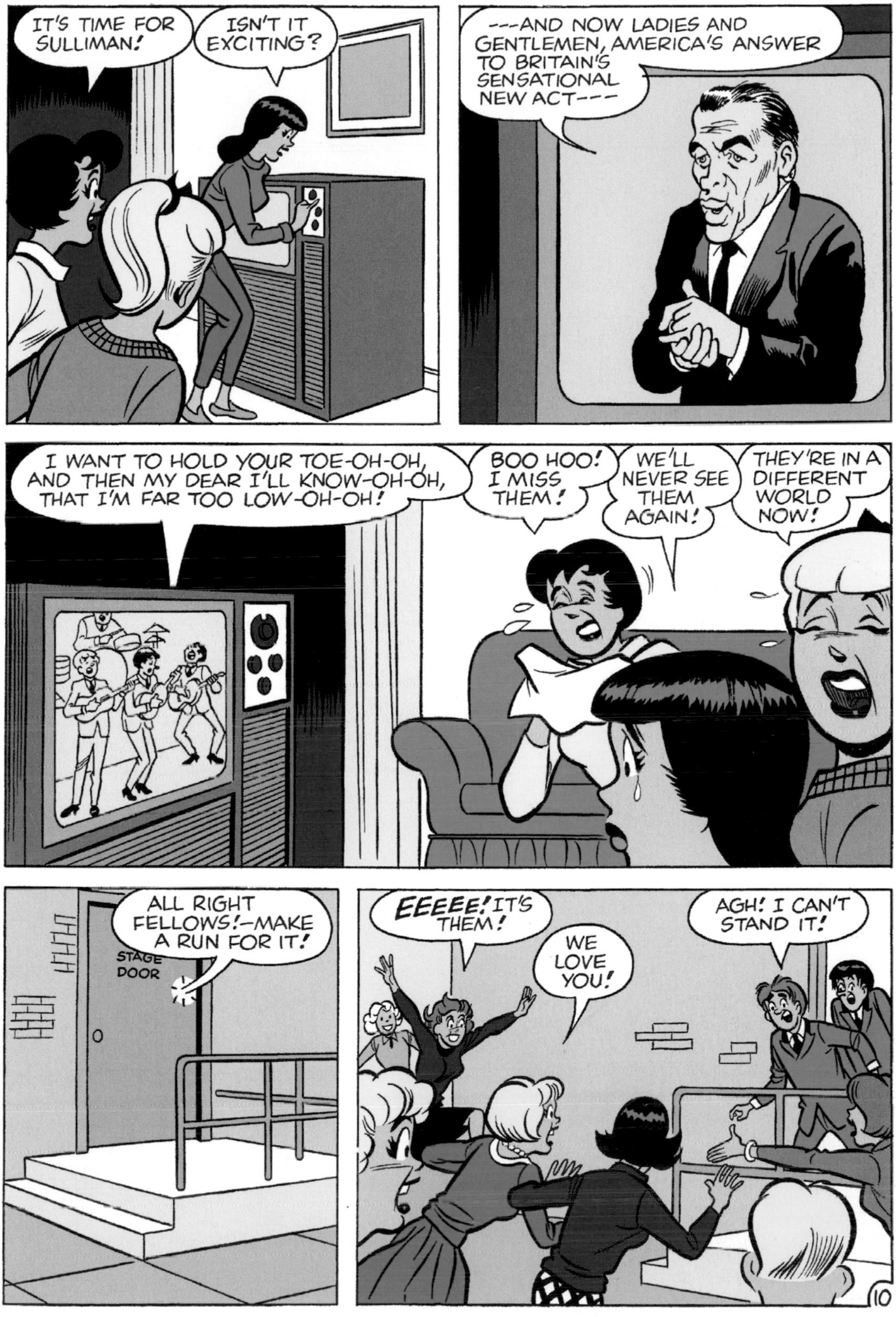
IT'S TIME FOR SULLIMAN!
ISN'T IT EXCITING?
---AND NOW LADIES AND GENTLEMEN, AMERICA'S ANSWER TO BRITAIN'S SENSATIONAL NEW ACT---
I WANT TO HOLD YOUR TOE-OH-OH, AND THEN MY DEAR I'LL KNOW-OH-OH, THAT I'M FAR TOO LOW-OH-OH!
BOO HOO! I MISS THEM!
WE'LL NEVER SEE THEM AGAIN!
THEY'RE IN A DIFFERENT WORLD NOW!
STAGE DOOR
ALL RIGHT FELLOWS!—MAKE A RUN FOR IT!
EEEEE! IT'S THEM!
WE LOVE YOU!
AGH! I CAN'T STAND IT!
10

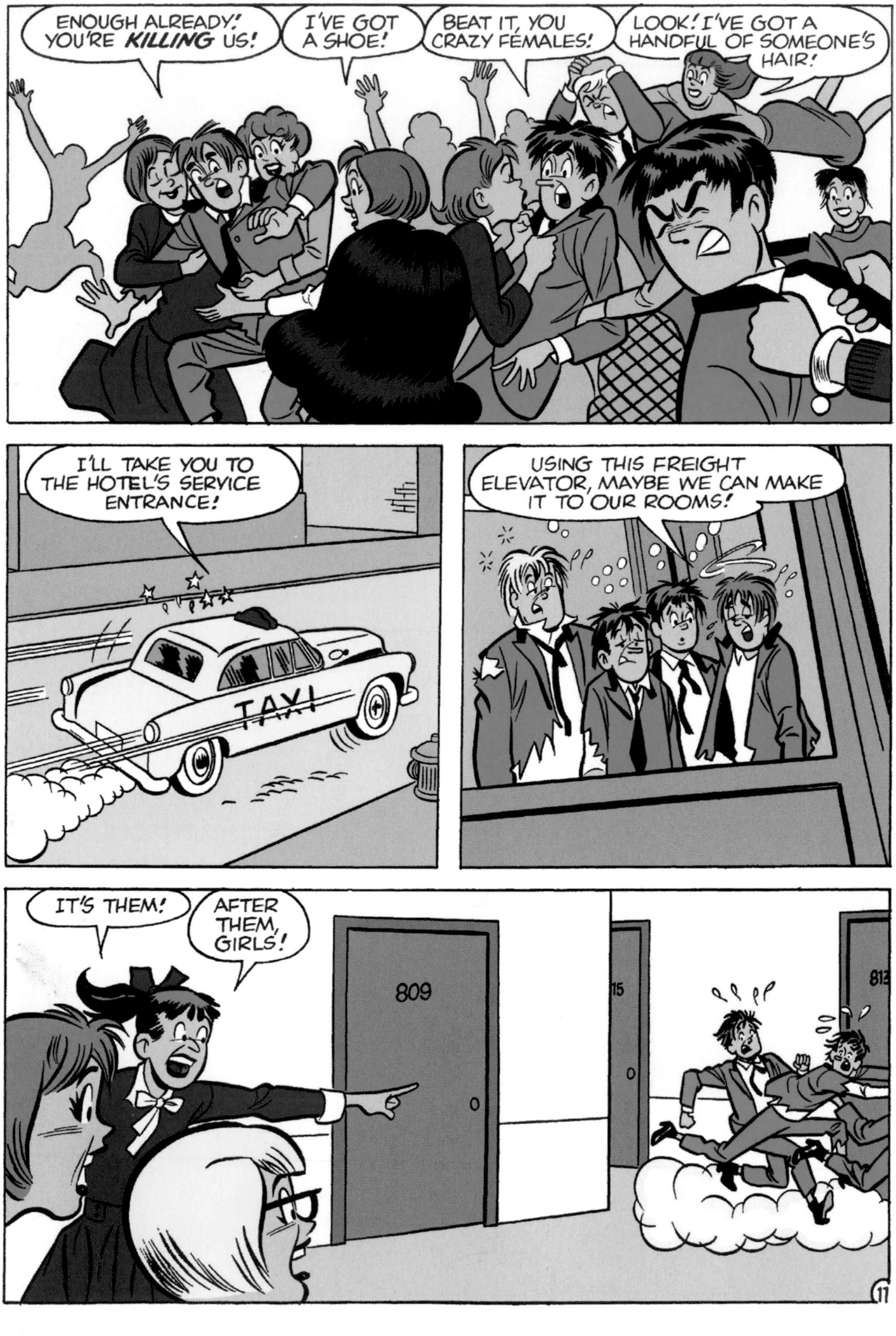

ENOUGH ALREADY! YOU'RE KILLING US!
I'VE GOT A SHOE!
BEAT IT, YOU CRAZY FEMALES!
LOOK! I'VE GOT A HANDFUL OF SOMEONE'S HAIR!
I'LL TAKE YOU TO THE HOTEL'S SERVICE ENTRANCE!
TAXI
USING THIS FREIGHT ELEVATOR, MAYBE WE CAN MAKE IT TO OUR ROOMS!
IT'S THEM!
AFTER THEM, GIRLS!
809
15
813
11

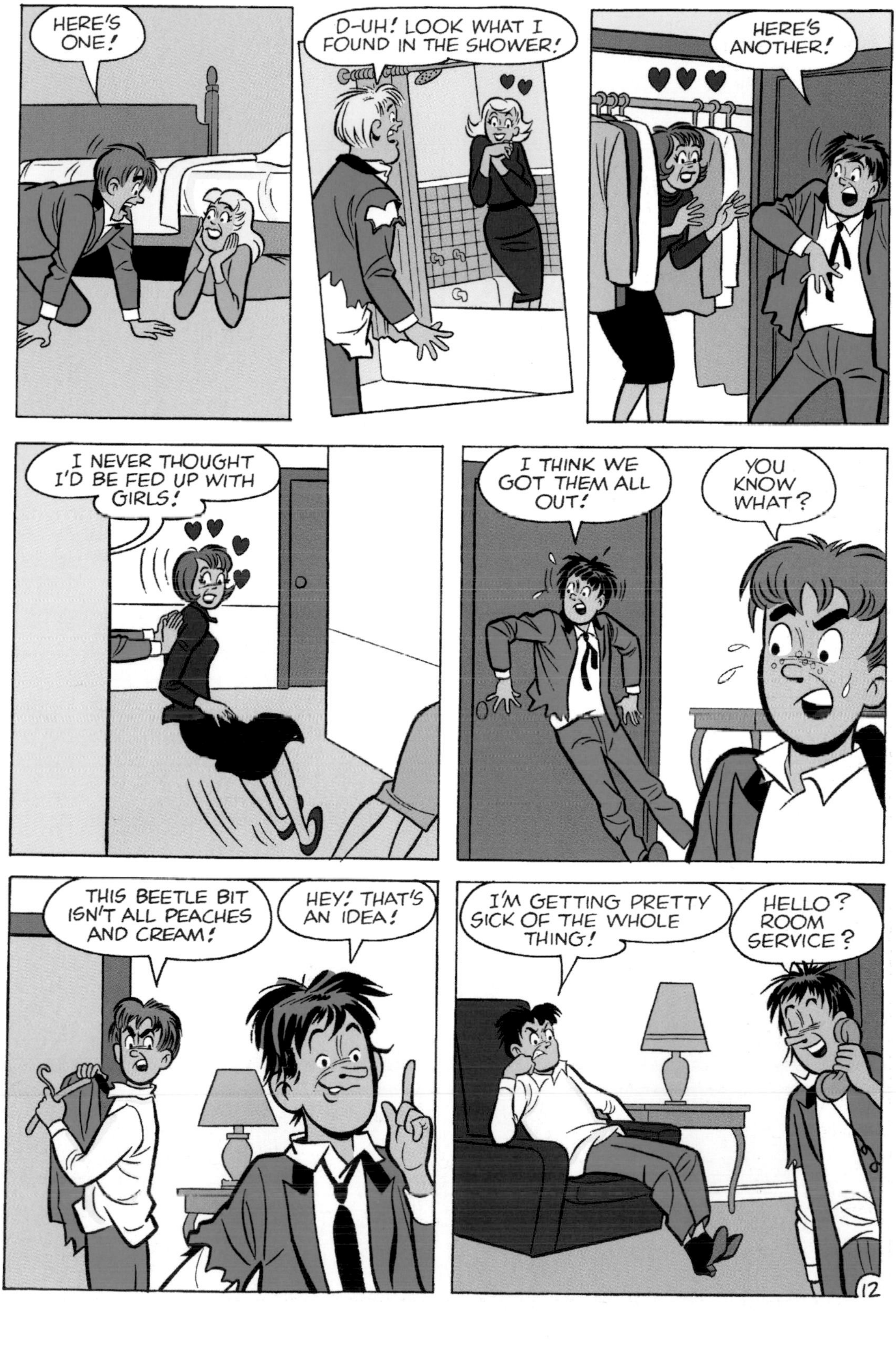
HERE'S ONE!
D-UH! LOOK WHAT I FOUND IN THE SHOWER!
HERE'S ANOTHER!
I NEVER THOUGHT I'D BE FED UP WITH GIRLS!
I THINK WE GOT THEM ALL OUT!
YOU KNOW WHAT?
THIS BEETLE BIT ISN'T ALL PEACHES AND CREAM!
HEY! THAT'S AN IDEA!
I'M GETTING PRETTY SICK OF THE WHOLE THING!
HELLO? ROOM SERVICE?
12

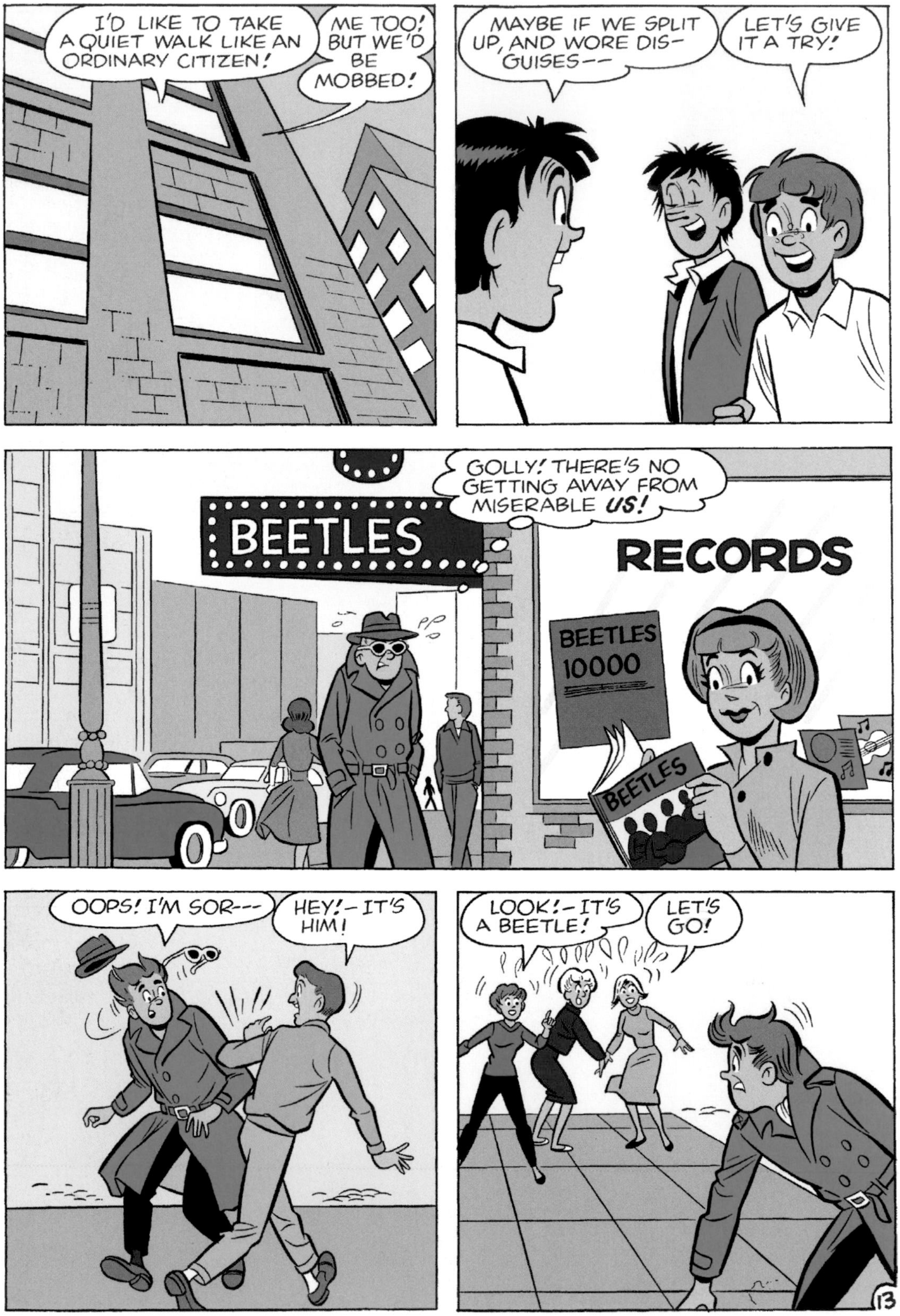
I'D LIKE TO TAKE A QUIET WALK LIKE AN ORDINARY CITIZEN!
ME TOO! BUT WE'D BE MOBBED!
MAYBE IF WE SPLIT UP, AND WORE DIS-GUISES--
LET'S GIVE IT A TRY!
GOLLY! THERE'S NO GETTING AWAY FROM MISERABLE US!
BEETLES
RECORDS
BEETLES 10000
BEETLES
OOPS! I'M SOR---
HEY!- IT'S HIM!
LOOK!- IT'S A BEETLE!
LET'S GO!
13

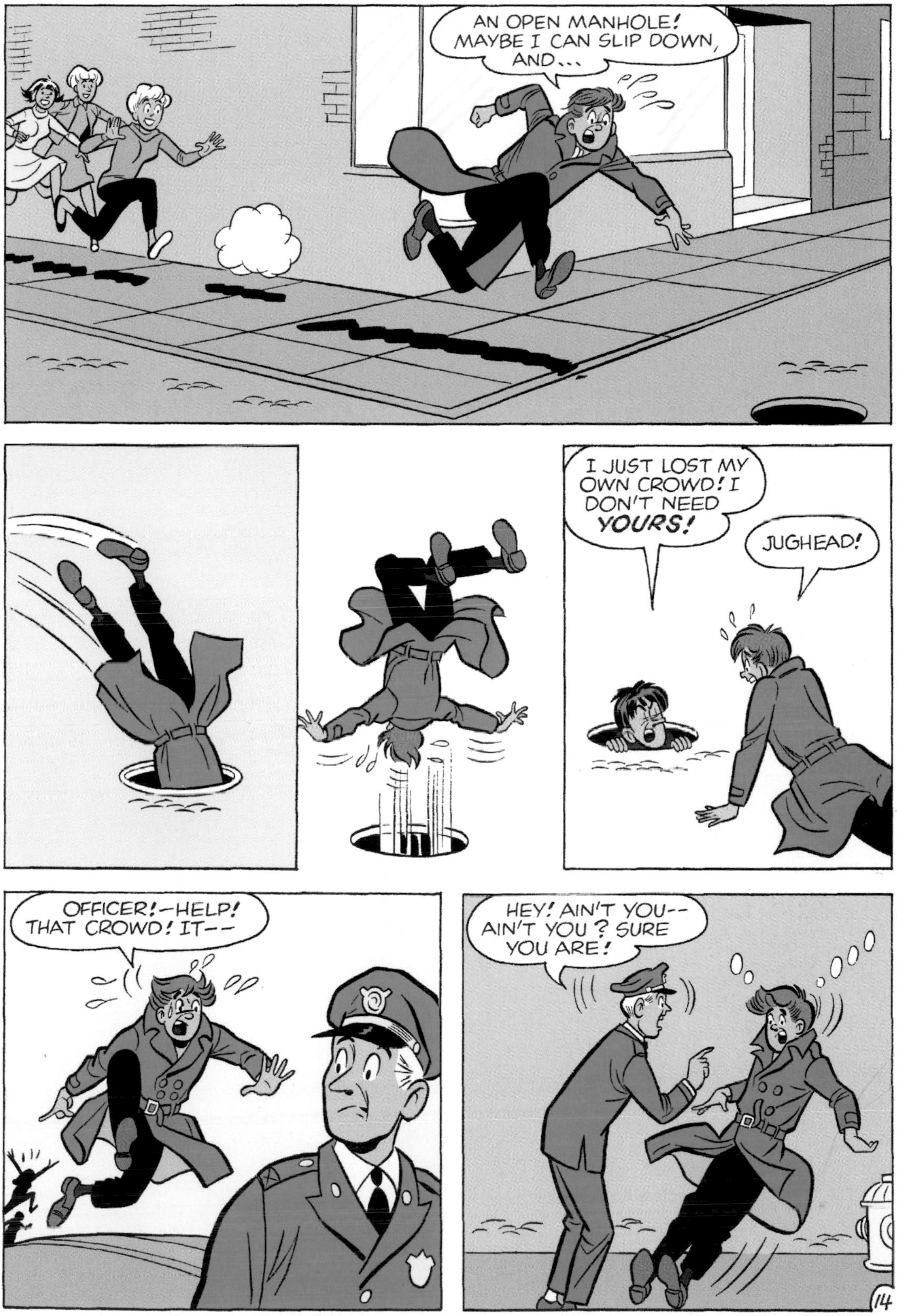
AN OPEN MANHOLE! MAYBE I CAN SLIP DOWN, AND...
I JUST LOST MY OWN CROWD! I DON'T NEED YOURS!
JUGHEAD!
OFFICER!--HELP! THAT CROWD! IT--
HEY! AIN'T YOU-- AIN'T YOU? SURE YOU ARE!
14

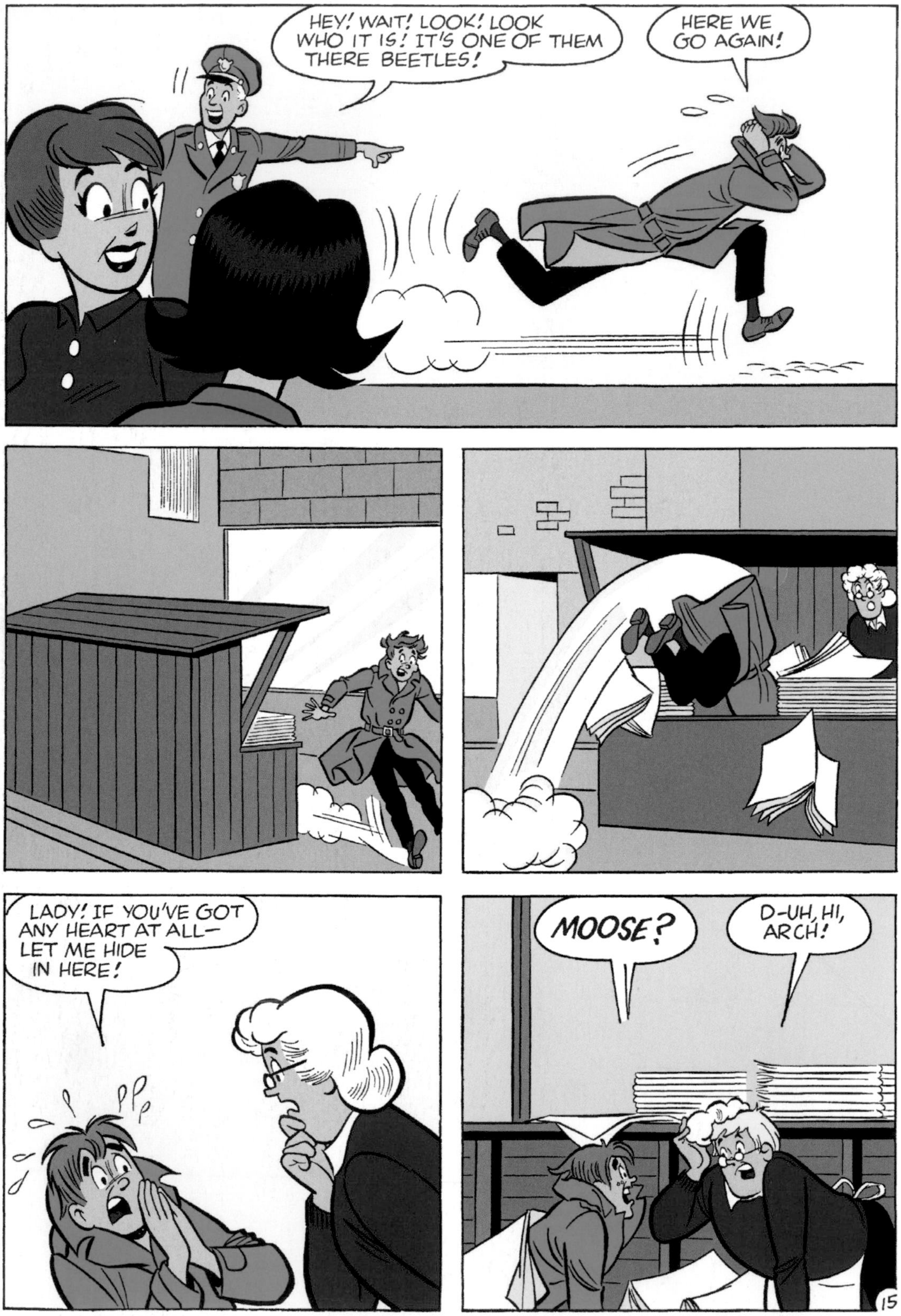
HEY! WAIT! LOOK! LOOK WHO IT IS! IT'S ONE OF THEM THERE BEETLES!
HERE WE GO AGAIN!
LADY! IF YOU'VE GOT ANY HEART AT ALL— LET ME HIDE IN HERE!
MOOSE?
D-UH, HI, ARCH!
15

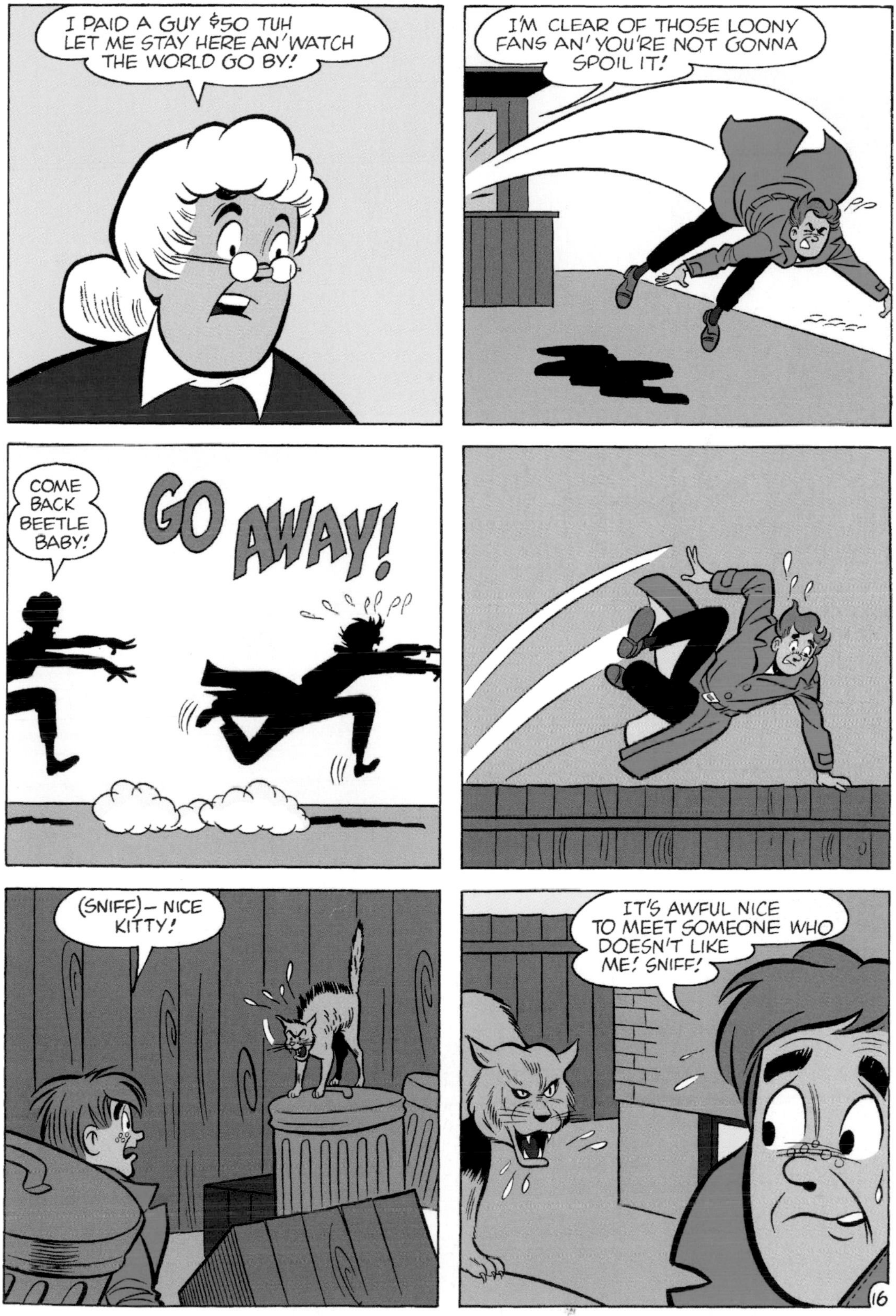

I PAID A GUY $50 TUH LET ME STAY HERE AN' WATCH THE WORLD GO BY!
I'M CLEAR OF THOSE LOONY FANS AN' YOU'RE NOT GONNA SPOIL IT!
COME BACK BEETLE BABY!
GO AWAY!
(SNIFF)— NICE KITTY!
IT'S AWFUL NICE TO MEET SOMEONE WHO DOESN'T LIKE ME! SNIFF!
16

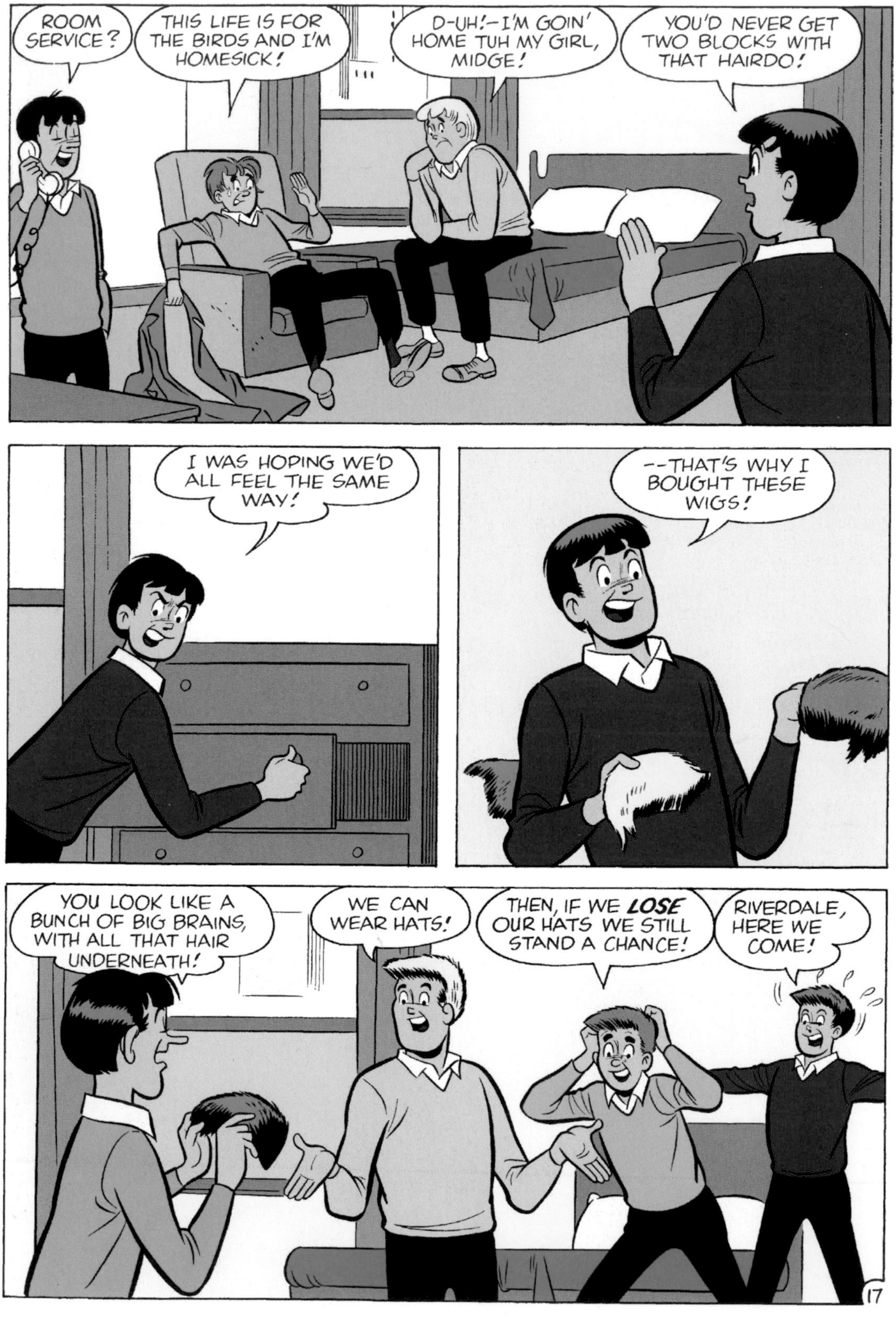

ROOM SERVICE?
THIS LIFE IS FOR THE BIRDS AND I'M HOMESICK!
D-UH!—I'M GOIN' HOME TUH MY GIRL, MIDGE!
YOU'D NEVER GET TWO BLOCKS WITH THAT HAIRDO!
I WAS HOPING WE'D ALL FEEL THE SAME WAY!
--THAT'S WHY I BOUGHT THESE WIGS!
YOU LOOK LIKE A BUNCH OF BIG BRAINS, WITH ALL THAT HAIR UNDERNEATH!
WE CAN WEAR HATS!
THEN, IF WE LOSE OUR HATS WE STILL STAND A CHANCE!
RIVERDALE, HERE WE COME!
17

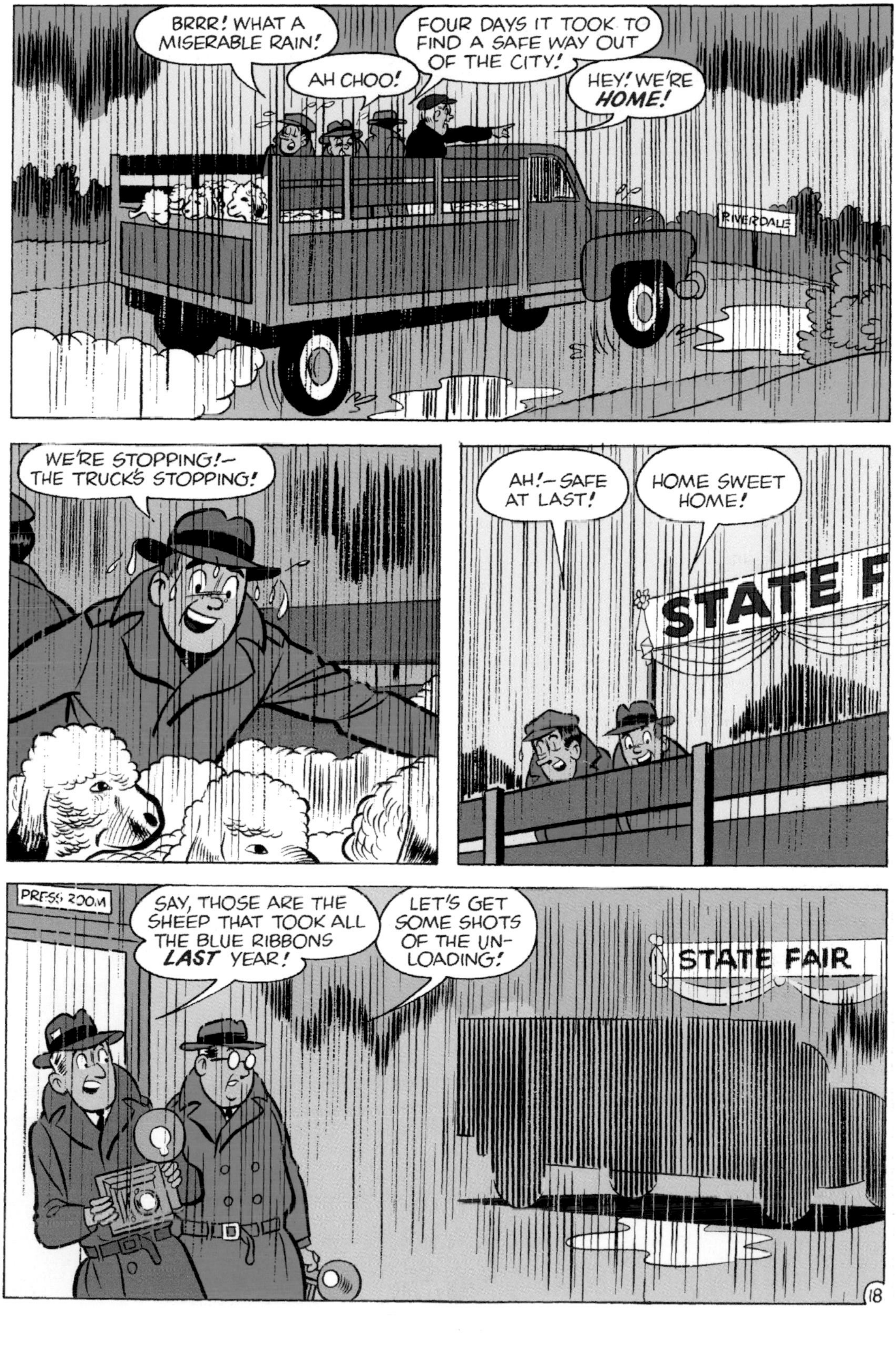
BRRR! WHAT A MISERABLE RAIN!
AH CHOO!
FOUR DAYS IT TOOK TO FIND A SAFE WAY OUT OF THE CITY!
HEY! WE'RE HOME!
RIVERDALE
WE'RE STOPPING!— THE TRUCK'S STOPPING!
AH!—SAFE AT LAST!
HOME SWEET HOME!
STATE F
PRESS ROOM
SAY, THOSE ARE THE SHEEP THAT TOOK ALL THE BLUE RIBBONS LAST YEAR!
LET'S GET SOME SHOTS OF THE UN-LOADING!
STATE FAIR
18

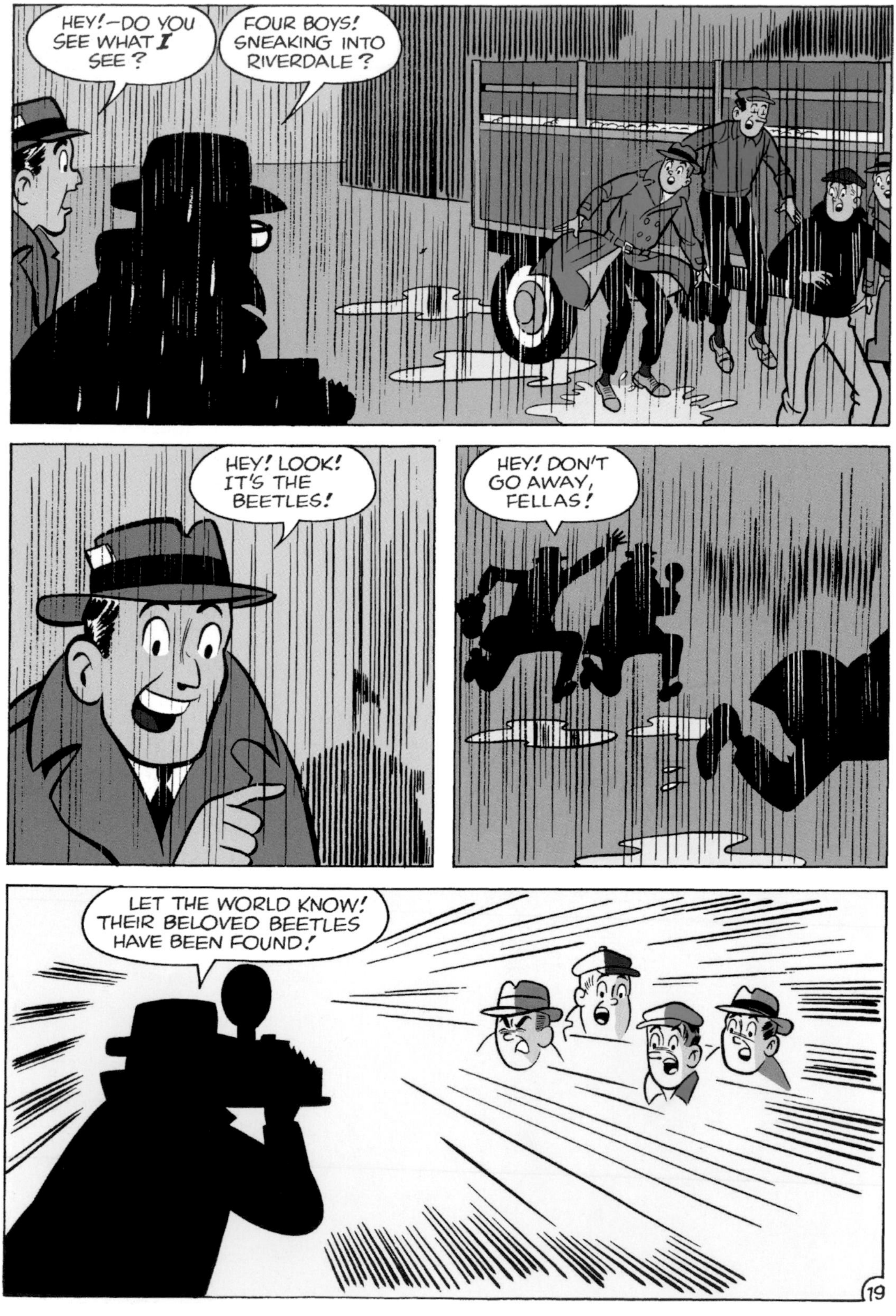
HEY!—DO YOU SEE WHAT I SEE?
FOUR BOYS! SNEAKING INTO RIVERDALE?
HEY! LOOK! IT'S THE BEETLES!
HEY! DON'T GO AWAY, FELLAS!
LET THE WORLD KNOW! THEIR BELOVED BEETLES HAVE BEEN FOUND!
19

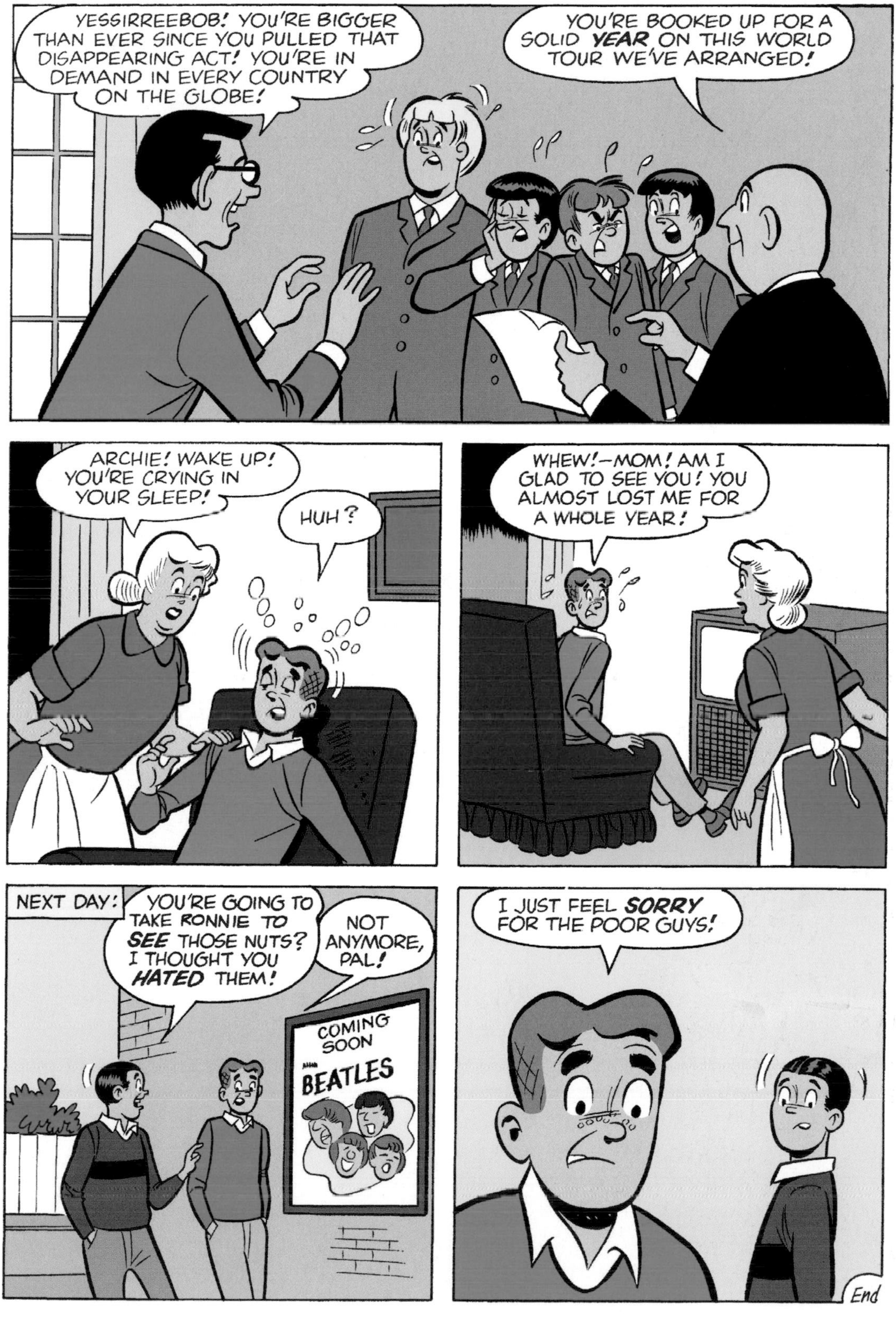
YESSIRREEBOB! YOU'RE BIGGER THAN EVER SINCE YOU PULLED THAT DISAPPEARING ACT! YOU'RE IN DEMAND IN EVERY COUNTRY ON THE GLOBE!
YOU'RE BOOKED UP FOR A SOLID YEAR, ON THIS WORLD TOUR WE'VE ARRANGED!
ARCHIE! WAKE UP! YOU'RE CRYING IN YOUR SLEEP!
HUH?
WHEW!–MOM! AM I GLAD TO SEE YOU! YOU ALMOST LOST ME FOR A WHOLE YEAR!
NEXT DAY:
YOU'RE GOING TO TAKE RONNIE TO SEE THOSE NUTS? I THOUGHT YOU HATED THEM!
NOT ANYMORE, PAL!
COMING SOON
BEATLES
I JUST FEEL SORRY FOR THE POOR GUYS!
End

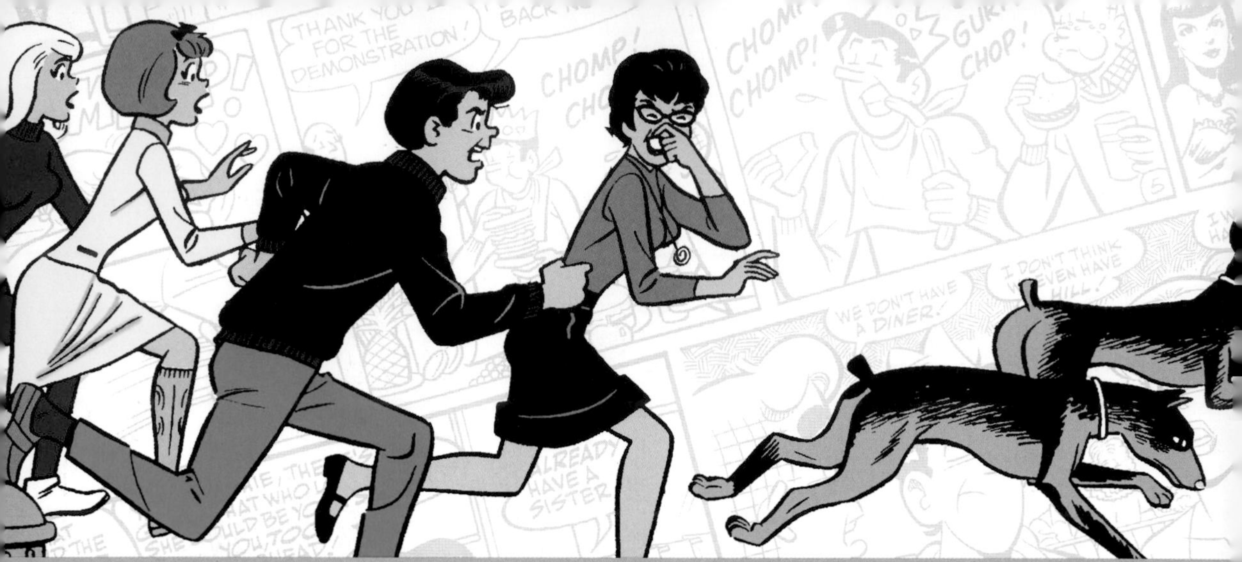
THANK YOU FOR THE DEMONSTRATION!
CHOMP! CHOMP!
WE DON'T HAVE A DINER.
ALREADY HAVE A SISTER

THE HOLD UP

JOSIE #19, 1966

BY FRANK DOYLE, DAN DECARLO, RUDY LAPICK & VINCE DECARLO

As this story further reiterates, Josie and her friends don't require the assistance of any men to help them solve their problems. They are strong, independent women whose bonds of friendship and sisterhood are unbreakable despite outside forces trying to complicate their journey.

From a historical view, however, there are two men in the Josieverse whose interactions with our girls have led to one madcap situation after another: Alan M. and Alexander Cabot III.

Let's begin with Alan M, AKA Alan Mayberry. Ruggedly handsome, down to Earth and nice to a fault, he has been Josie's most consistent love interest since she made her debut in 1963. Alan is always looking to help Josie and company in whatever way possible.

As for Alexander Cabot III. Well, he tries. Sometimes. Looking like the lost twin brother of *That Wilkin Boy*'s Tough Teddy Tambourine, Alexander is most often portrayed as a spoiled rich brat whose wealth has made him completely out of touch with the needs and problems of his working class peers. Despite his often selfish nature, he regularly utilizes his vast resources as The Pussycats' tour manager. Given the fact that he himself is already rolling in the dough, his financial motivations for helping the group are overshadowed by his genuine belief in their musical abilities. His being absolutely smitten for Josie helps dictate his actions as well. It seems behind all that smugness there lies a genuinely nice guy. Who would've guessed?

—Chris Cummins
Writer, Archie Comics

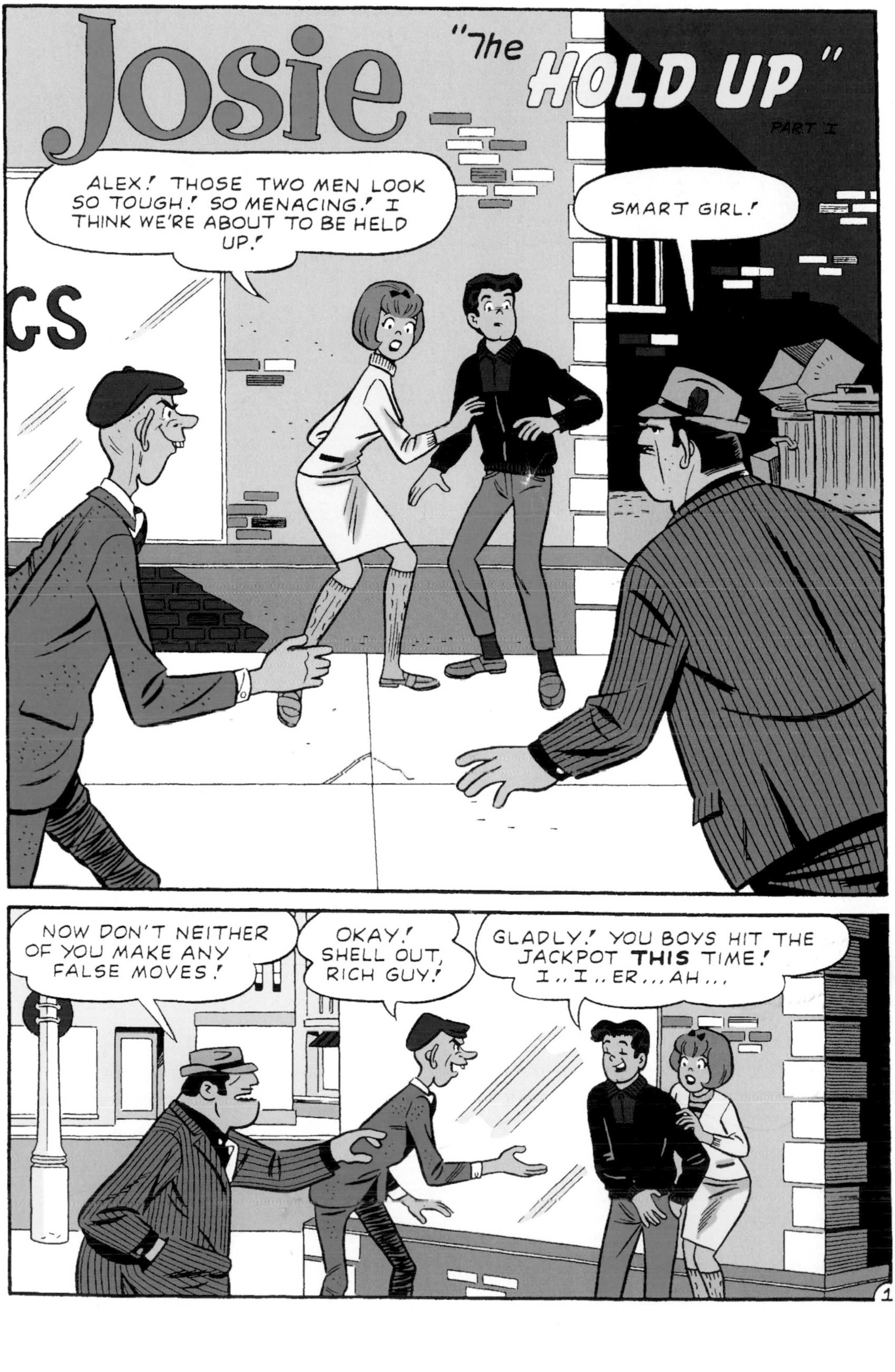
Josie
"The HOLD UP"
PART I
ALEX! THOSE TWO MEN LOOK SO TOUGH! SO MENACING! I THINK WE'RE ABOUT TO BE HELD UP!
SMART GIRL!
GS
NOW DON'T NEITHER OF YOU MAKE ANY FALSE MOVES!
OKAY! SHELL OUT, RICH GUY!
GLADLY! YOU BOYS HIT THE JACKPOT **THIS** TIME! I.. I.. ER... AH...
1

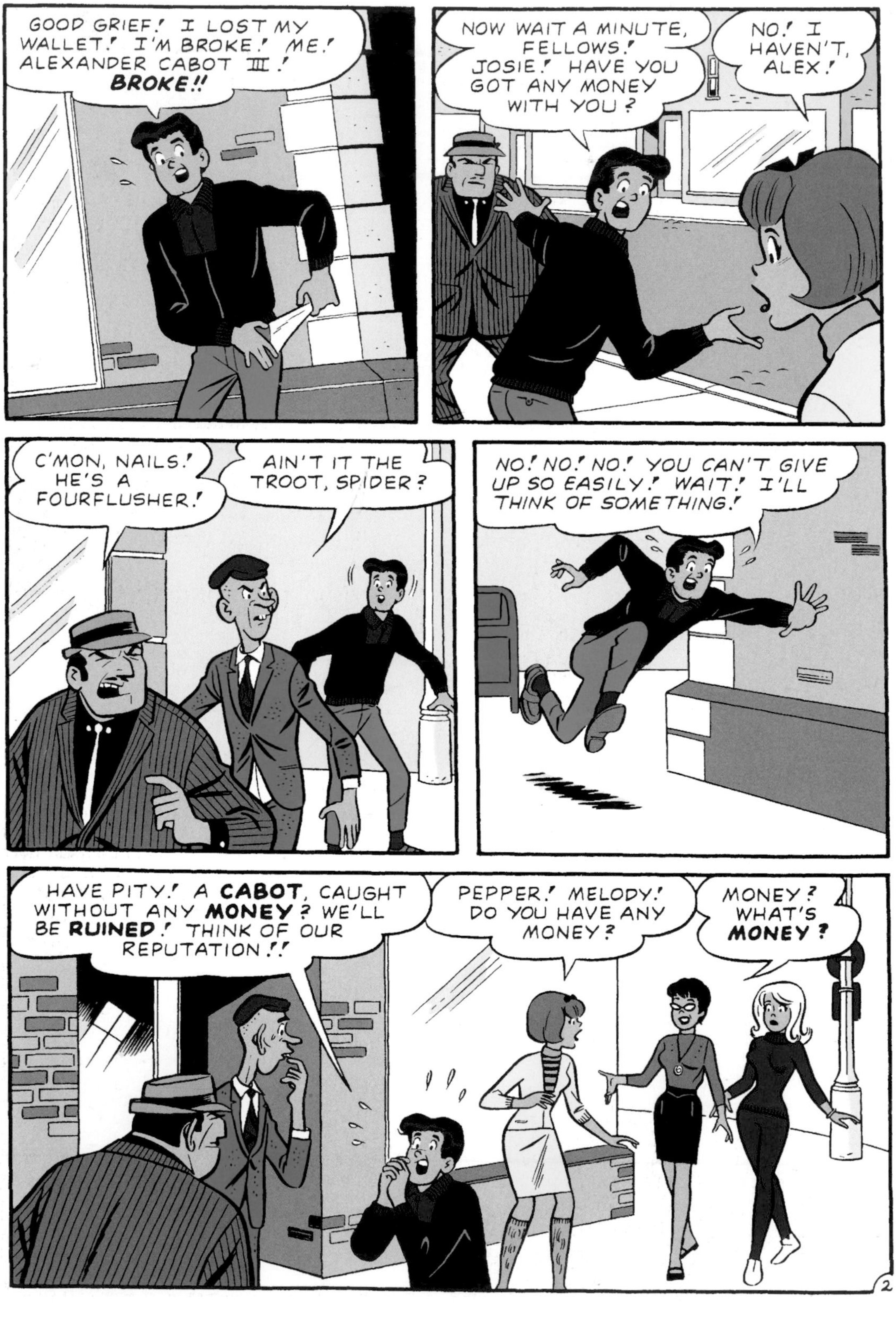
GOOD GRIEF! I LOST MY WALLET! I'M BROKE! ME! ALEXANDER CABOT III! BROKE!!
NOW WAIT A MINUTE, FELLOWS! JOSIE! HAVE YOU GOT ANY MONEY WITH YOU?
NO! I HAVEN'T, ALEX!
C'MON, NAILS! HE'S A FOURFLUSHER!
AIN'T IT THE TROOT, SPIDER?
NO! NO! NO! YOU CAN'T GIVE UP SO EASILY! WAIT! I'LL THINK OF SOMETHING!
HAVE PITY! A CABOT, CAUGHT WITHOUT ANY MONEY? WE'LL BE RUINED! THINK OF OUR REPUTATION!!
PEPPER! MELODY! DO YOU HAVE ANY MONEY?
MONEY? WHAT'S MONEY?
2

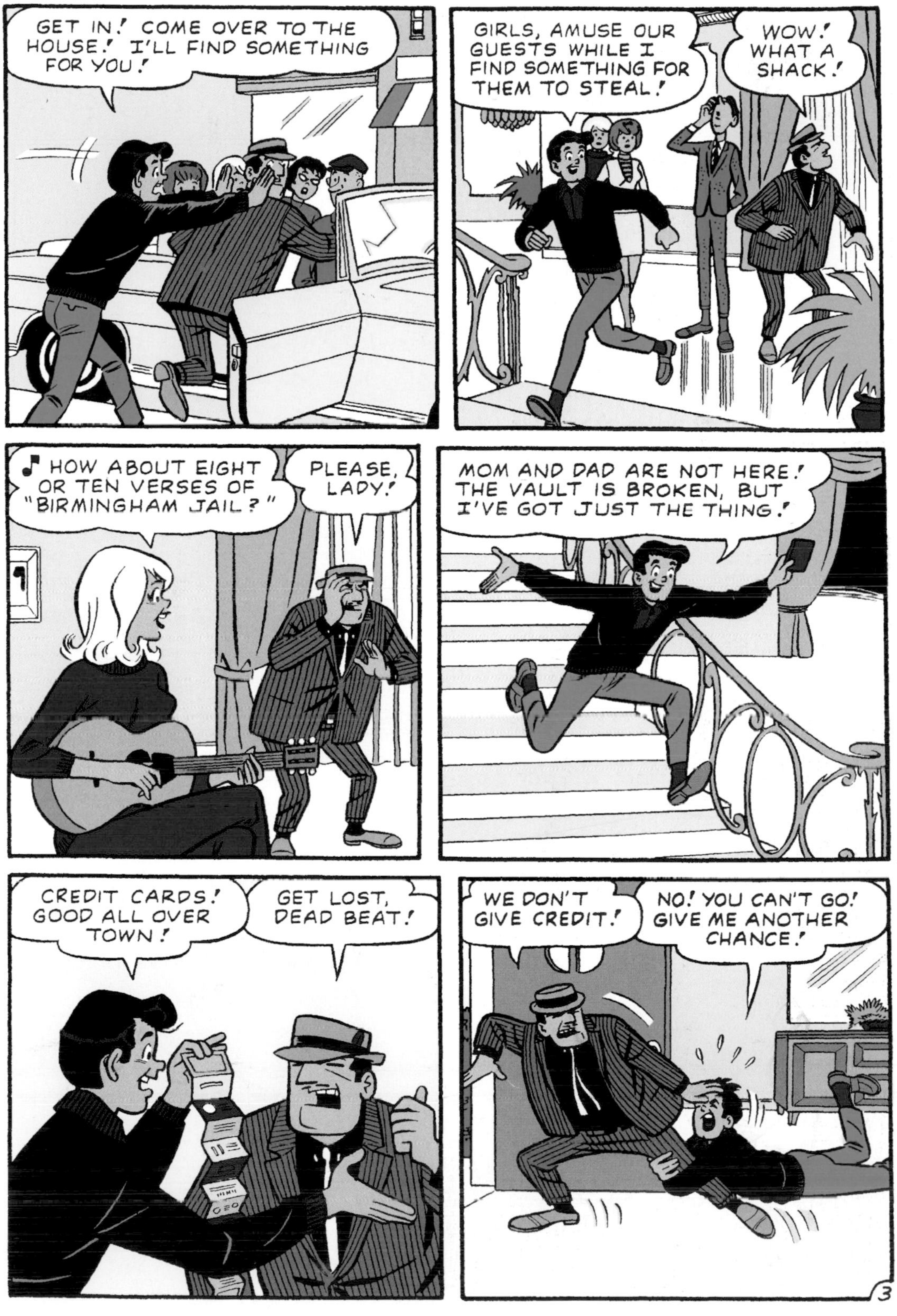
GET IN! COME OVER TO THE HOUSE! I'LL FIND SOMETHING FOR YOU!
GIRLS, AMUSE OUR GUESTS WHILE I FIND SOMETHING FOR THEM TO STEAL!
WOW! WHAT A SHACK!
HOW ABOUT EIGHT OR TEN VERSES OF "BIRMINGHAM JAIL?"
PLEASE, LADY!
MOM AND DAD ARE NOT HERE! THE VAULT IS BROKEN, BUT I'VE GOT JUST THE THING!
CREDIT CARDS! GOOD ALL OVER TOWN!
GET LOST, DEAD BEAT!
WE DON'T GIVE CREDIT!
NO! YOU CAN'T GO! GIVE ME ANOTHER CHANCE!
3

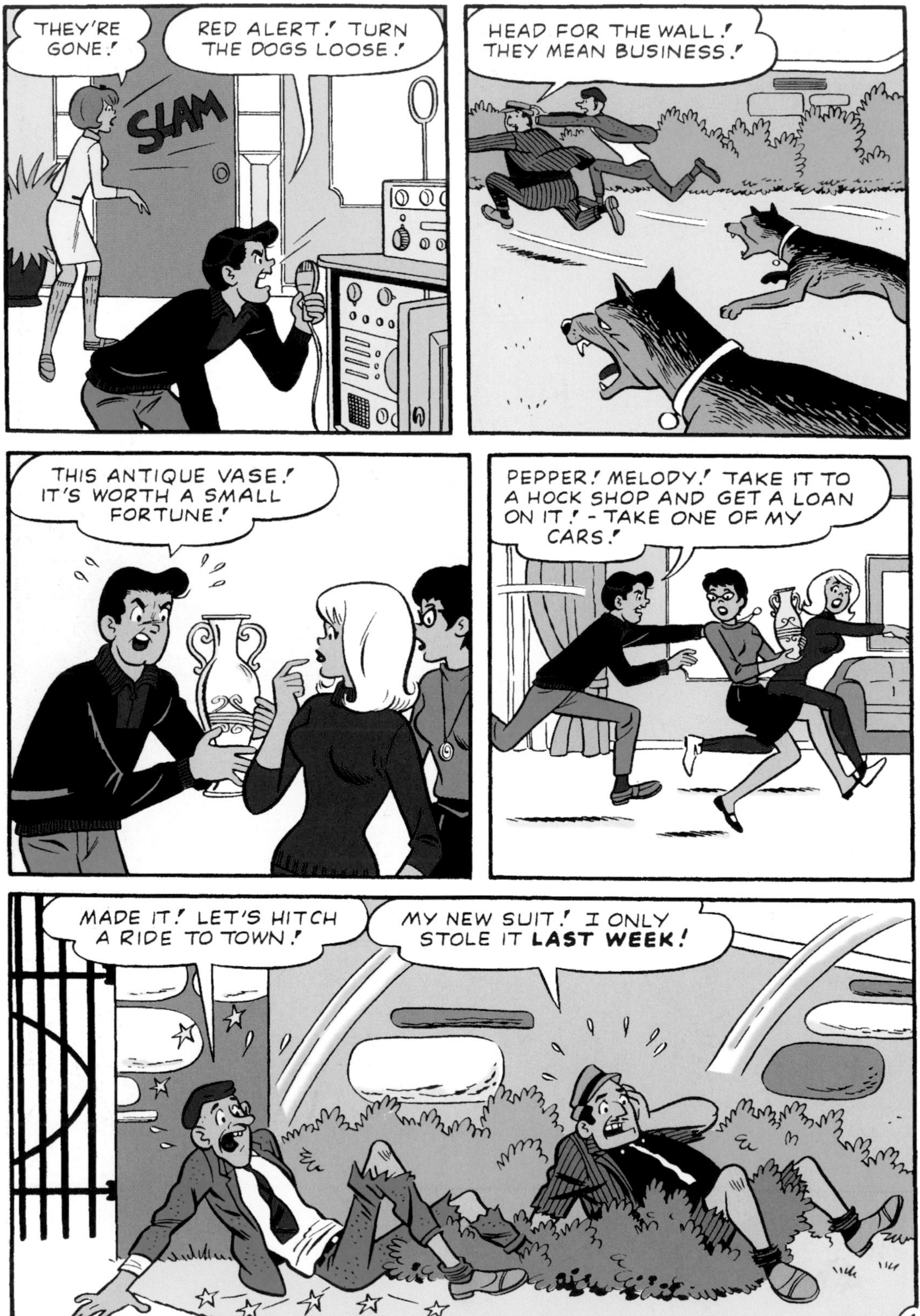
THEY'RE GONE!
RED ALERT! TURN THE DOGS LOOSE!
SLAM
HEAD FOR THE WALL! THEY MEAN BUSINESS!
THIS ANTIQUE VASE! IT'S WORTH A SMALL FORTUNE!
PEPPER! MELODY! TAKE IT TO A HOCK SHOP AND GET A LOAN ON IT! - TAKE ONE OF MY CARS!
MADE IT! LET'S HITCH A RIDE TO TOWN!
MY NEW SUIT! I ONLY STOLE IT **LAST WEEK!**
4

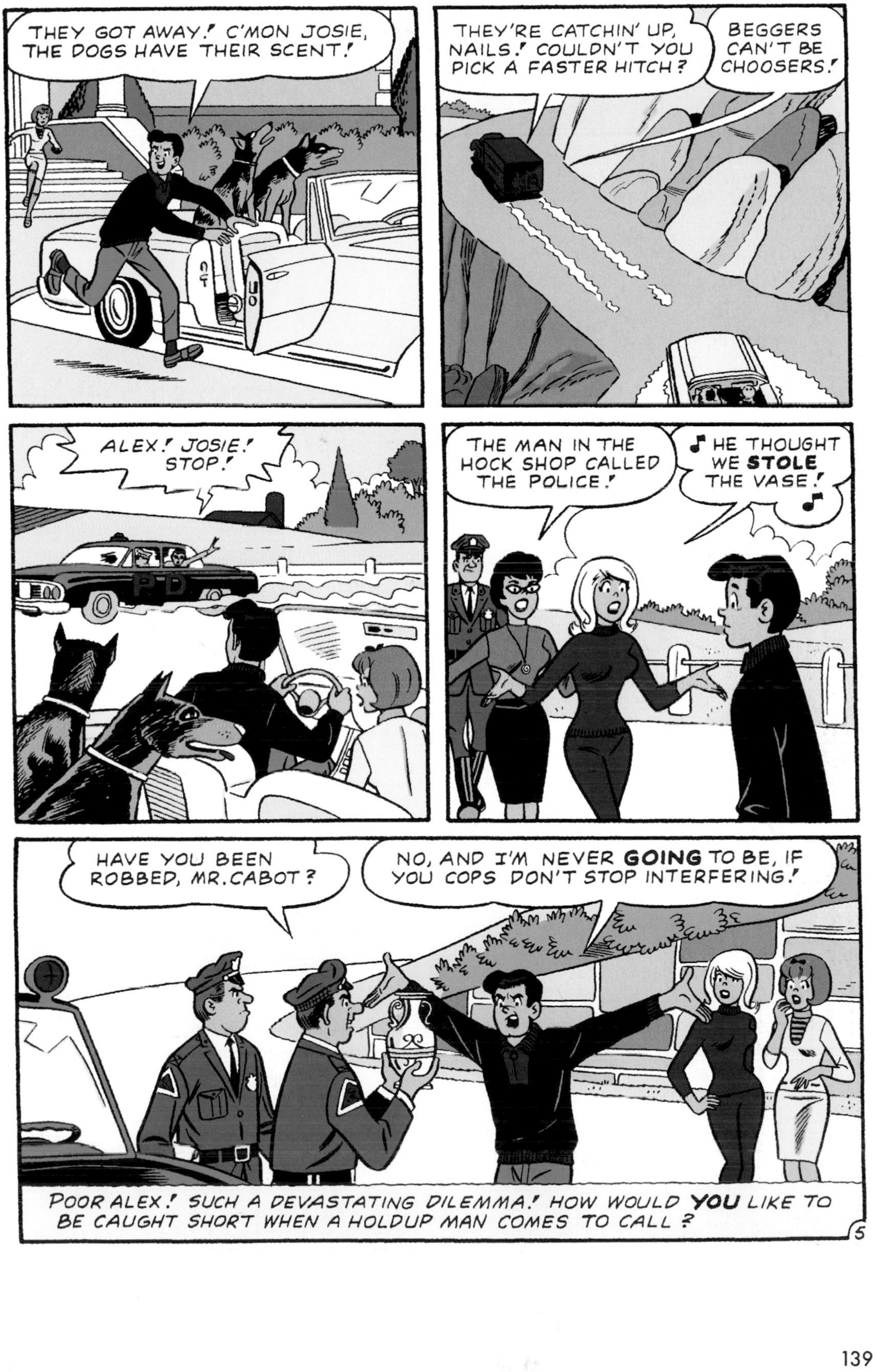

THEY GOT AWAY! C'MON JOSIE, THE DOGS HAVE THEIR SCENT!
THEY'RE CATCHIN' UP, NAILS! COULDN'T YOU PICK A FASTER HITCH?
BEGGERS CAN'T BE CHOOSERS!
ALEX! JOSIE! STOP!
THE MAN IN THE HOCK SHOP CALLED THE POLICE!
HE THOUGHT WE **STOLE** THE VASE!
HAVE YOU BEEN ROBBED, MR. CABOT?
NO, AND I'M NEVER **GOING** TO BE, IF YOU COPS DON'T STOP INTERFERING!
POOR ALEX! SUCH A DEVASTATING DILEMMA! HOW WOULD **YOU** LIKE TO BE CAUGHT SHORT WHEN A HOLDUP MAN COMES TO CALL?
5

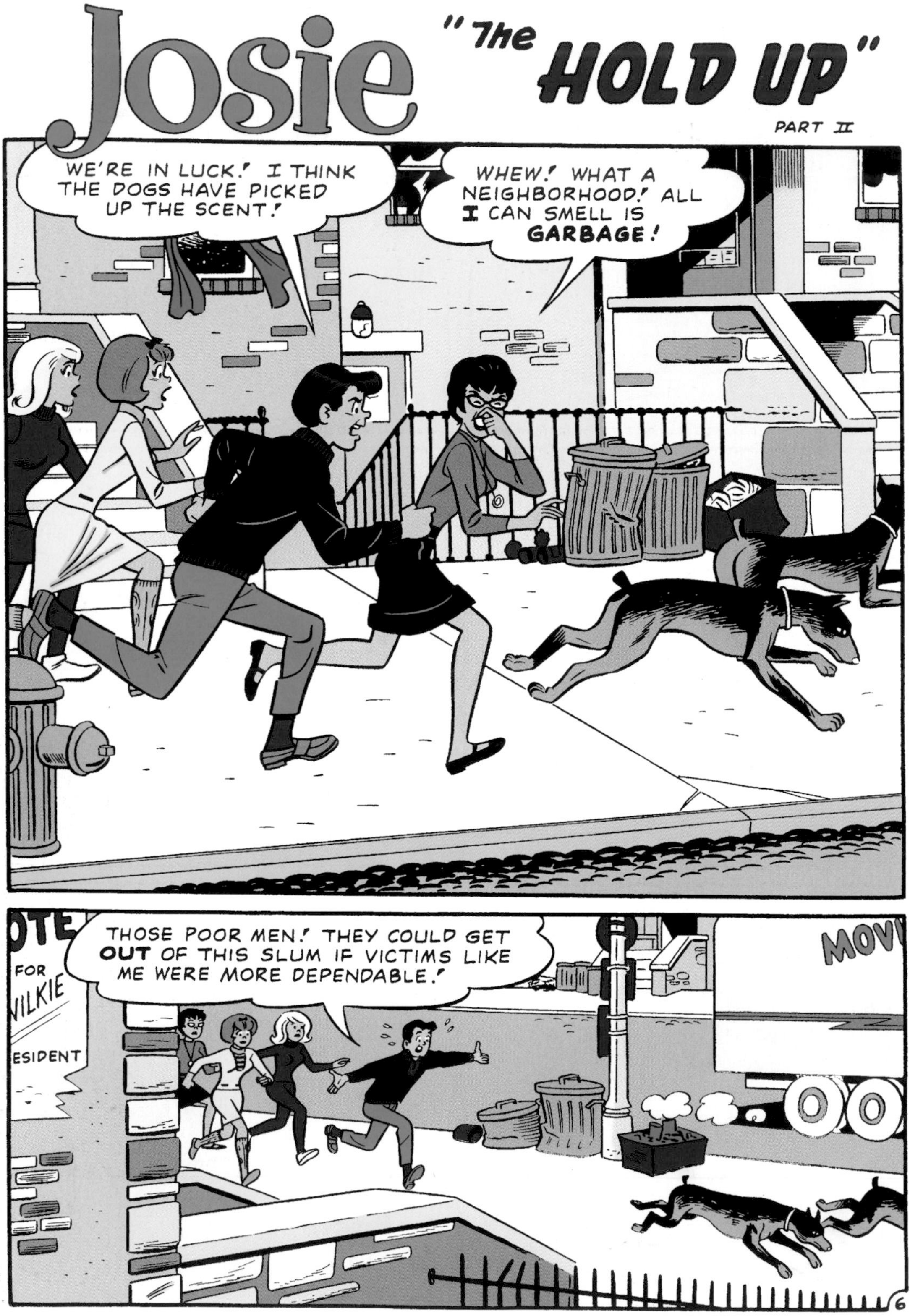
Josie
"The HOLD UP"
PART II
WE'RE IN LUCK! I THINK THE DOGS HAVE PICKED UP THE SCENT!
WHEW! WHAT A NEIGHBORHOOD! ALL I CAN SMELL IS GARBAGE!
THOSE POOR MEN! THEY COULD GET OUT OF THIS SLUM IF VICTIMS LIKE ME WERE MORE DEPENDABLE!
OTE
FOR
VILKIE
ESIDENT
MOV
6

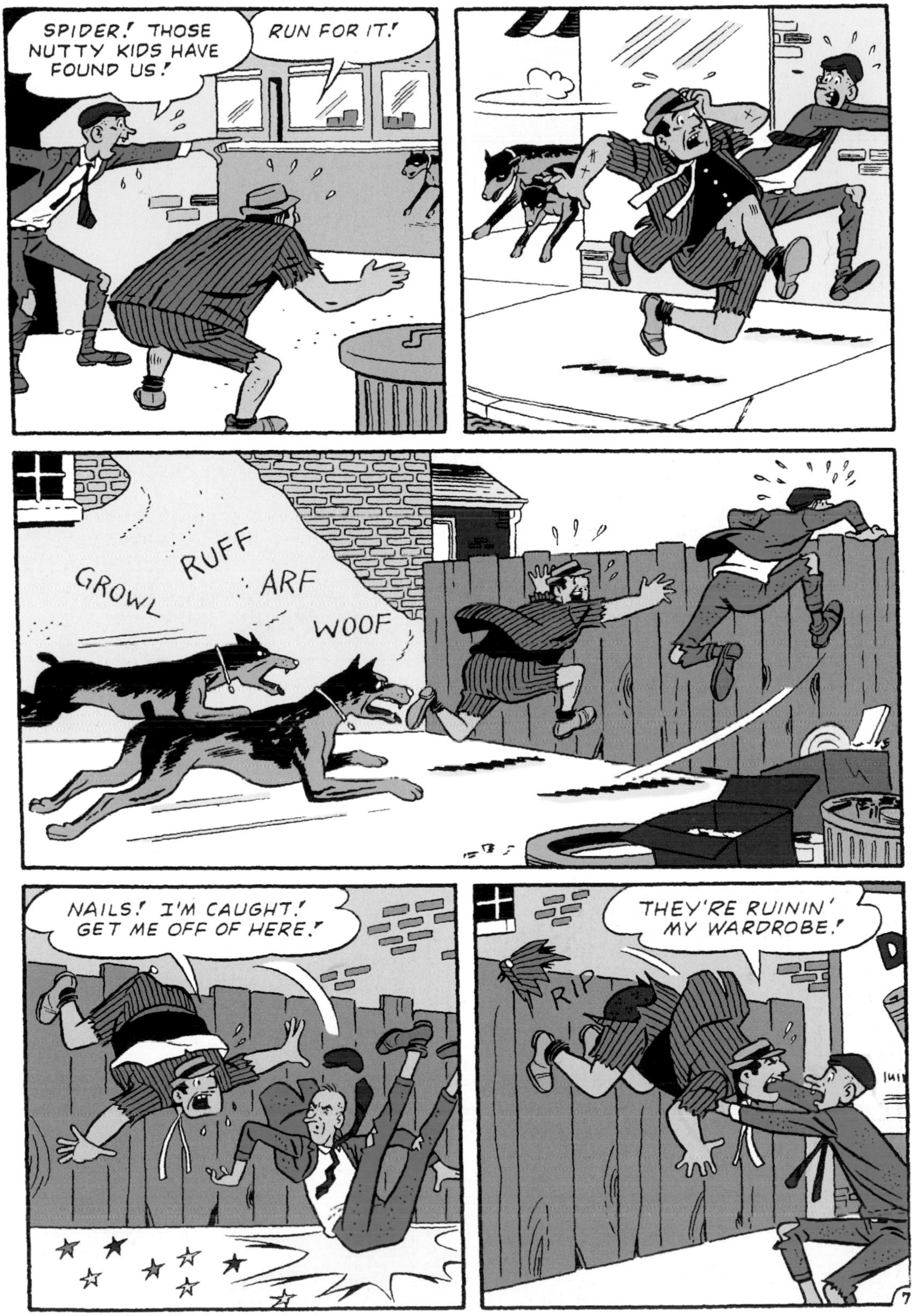
SPIDER! THOSE NUTTY KIDS HAVE FOUND US!
RUN FOR IT!
GROWL
RUFF
ARF
WOOF
NAILS! I'M CAUGHT! GET ME OFF OF HERE!
THEY'RE RUININ' MY WARDROBE!
RIP
7

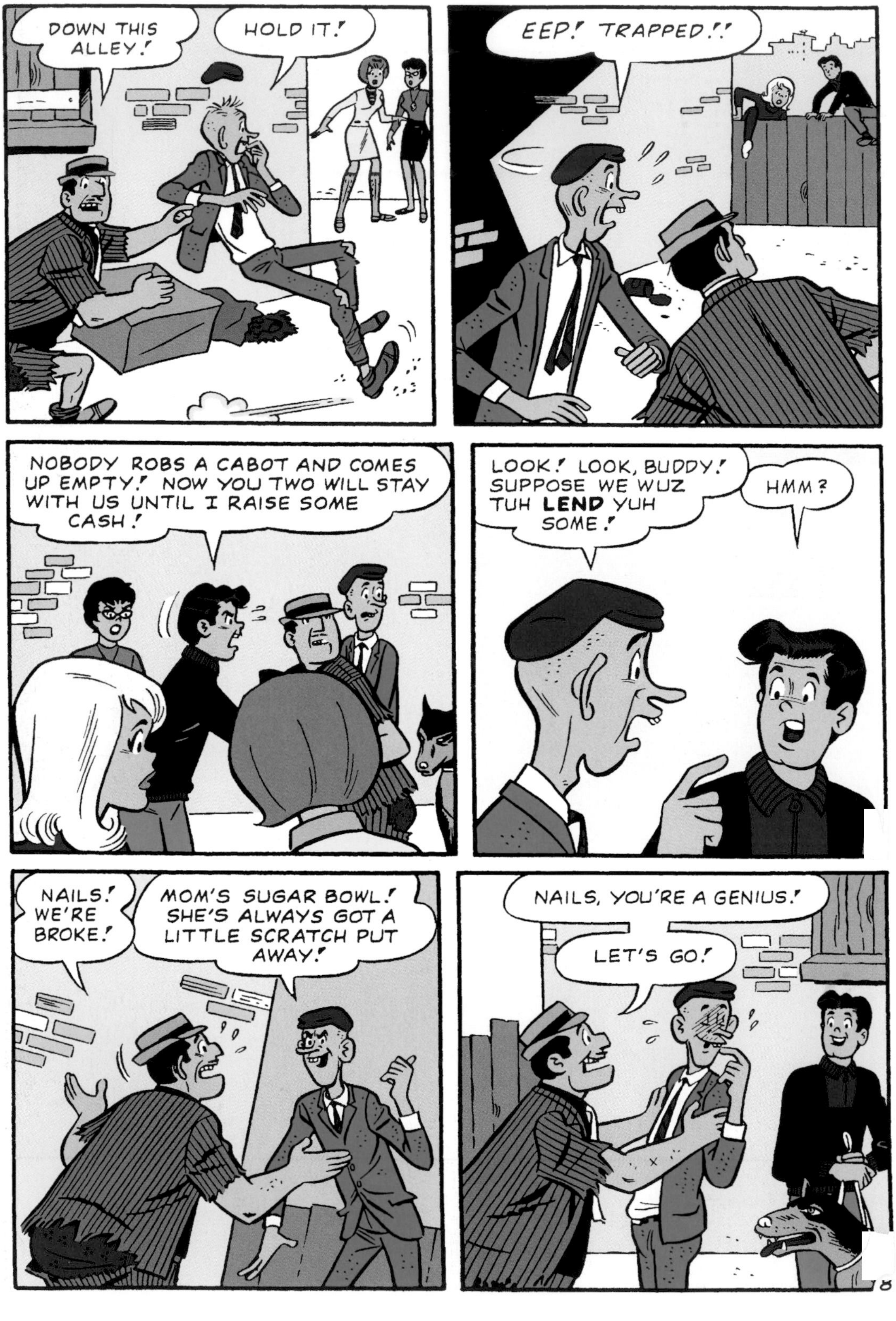
DOWN THIS ALLEY!
HOLD IT!
EEP! TRAPPED!!
NOBODY ROBS A CABOT AND COMES UP EMPTY! NOW YOU TWO WILL STAY WITH US UNTIL I RAISE SOME CASH!
LOOK! LOOK, BUDDY! SUPPOSE WE WUZ TUH LEND YUH SOME!
HMM?
NAILS! WE'RE BROKE!
MOM'S SUGAR BOWL! SHE'S ALWAYS GOT A LITTLE SCRATCH PUT AWAY!
NAILS, YOU'RE A GENIUS!
LET'S GO!

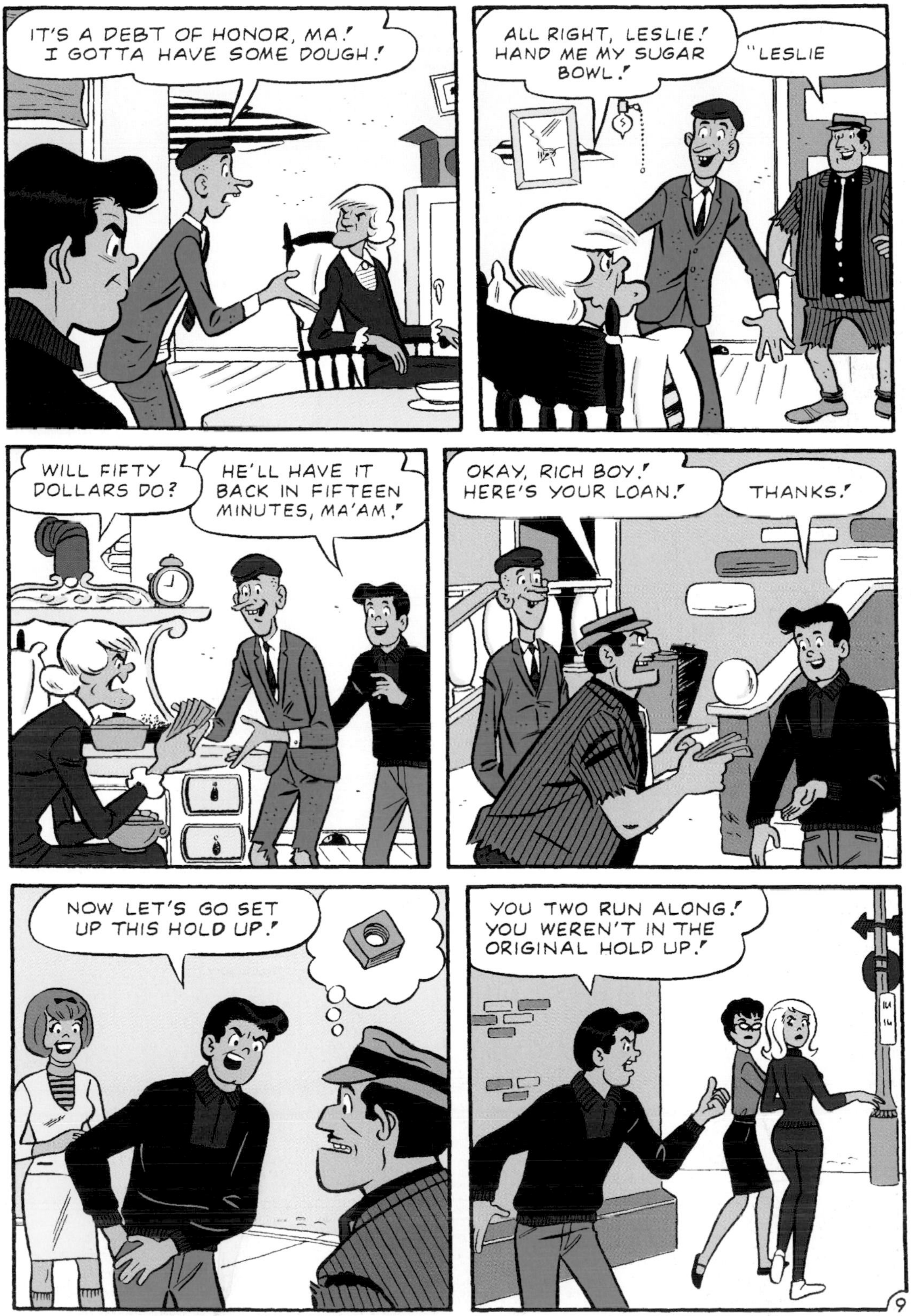
IT'S A DEBT OF HONOR, MA! I GOTTA HAVE SOME DOUGH!
ALL RIGHT, LESLIE! HAND ME MY SUGAR BOWL!
"LESLIE
WILL FIFTY DOLLARS DO?
HE'LL HAVE IT BACK IN FIFTEEN MINUTES, MA'AM!
OKAY, RICH BOY! HERE'S YOUR LOAN!
THANKS!
NOW LET'S GO SET UP THIS HOLD UP!
YOU TWO RUN ALONG! YOU WEREN'T IN THE ORIGINAL HOLD UP!
9

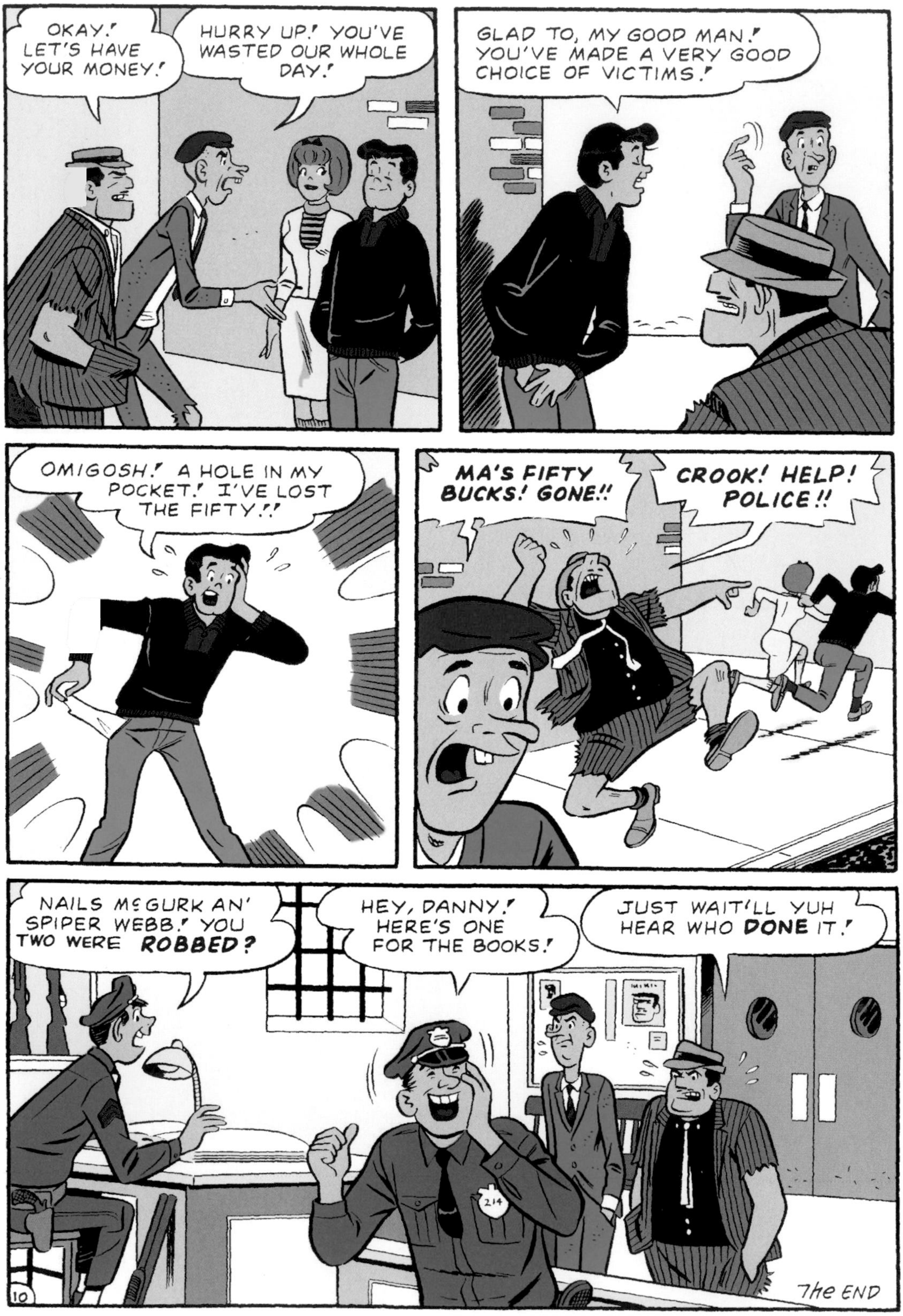
OKAY! LET'S HAVE YOUR MONEY!
HURRY UP! YOU'VE WASTED OUR WHOLE DAY!
GLAD TO, MY GOOD MAN! YOU'VE MADE A VERY GOOD CHOICE OF VICTIMS!
OMIGOSH! A HOLE IN MY POCKET! I'VE LOST THE FIFTY!!
MA'S FIFTY BUCKS! GONE!!
CROOK! HELP! POLICE!!
NAILS McGURK AN' SPIDER WEBB! YOU TWO WERE ROBBED?
HEY, DANNY! HERE'S ONE FOR THE BOOKS!
JUST WAIT'LL YUH HEAR WHO DONE IT!
10
The END

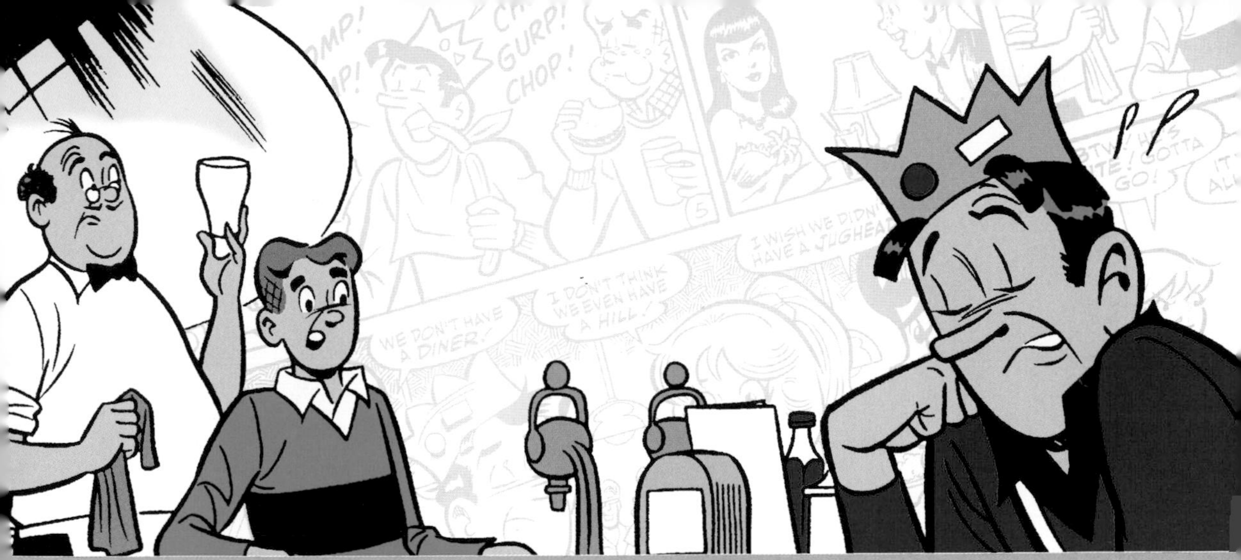
GURP!
CHOP!
WE DON'T HAVE A DINER!
I DON'T THINK WE EVEN HAVE A HILL!

PARDON MY COMPUTER

JUGHEAD #119, 1966

BY GEORGE GLADIR, SAMM SCHWARTZ & MARTY EPP

Ever get the feeling you're being watched? Or that something bad is going to happen? Jughead knows. So what happens when a group of young ladies form a United Girls Against Jughead group?! His sixth sense kicks into high gear and he starts freaking out!

This may be the best of Archie Comics, but the gray crowned king of foods has some of his own best moments too, and this is one of them! Today, we turn to our top-of-the-line computers, tablets, and phones to solve our daily problems and we often get the answers we seek. However, even with the help of modern computer science, the U.G.A.J. still couldn't get the best of Jughead!

—Victor Gorelick
Co-President/Editor-in-Chief,
Archie Comics

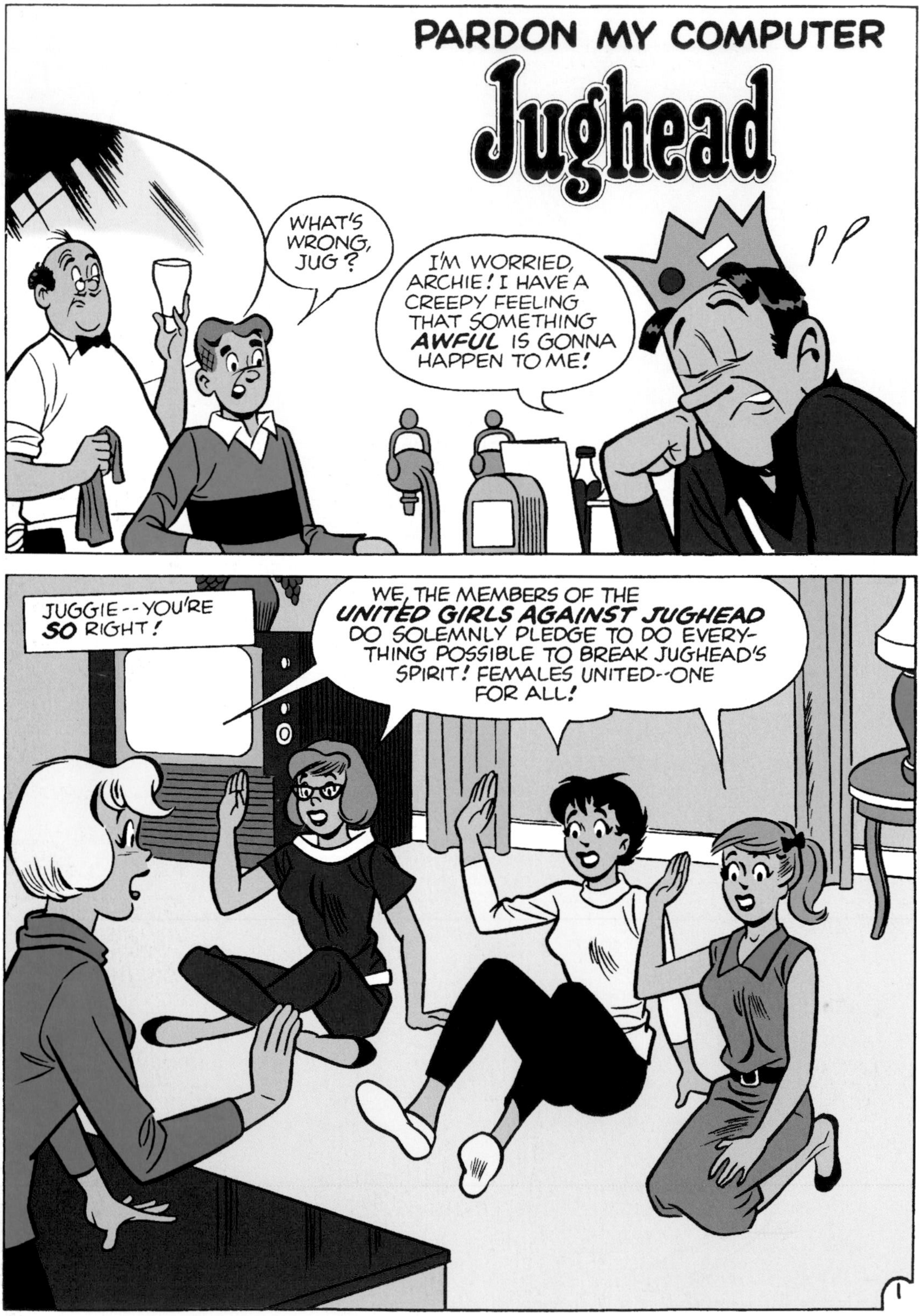
PARDON MY COMPUTER
Jughead
WHAT'S WRONG, JUG?
I'M WORRIED, ARCHIE! I HAVE A CREEPY FEELING THAT SOMETHING AWFUL IS GONNA HAPPEN TO ME!
JUGGIE--YOU'RE SO RIGHT!
WE, THE MEMBERS OF THE UNITED GIRLS AGAINST JUGHEAD DO SOLEMNLY PLEDGE TO DO EVERYTHING POSSIBLE TO BREAK JUGHEAD'S SPIRIT! FEMALES UNITED--ONE FOR ALL!
1

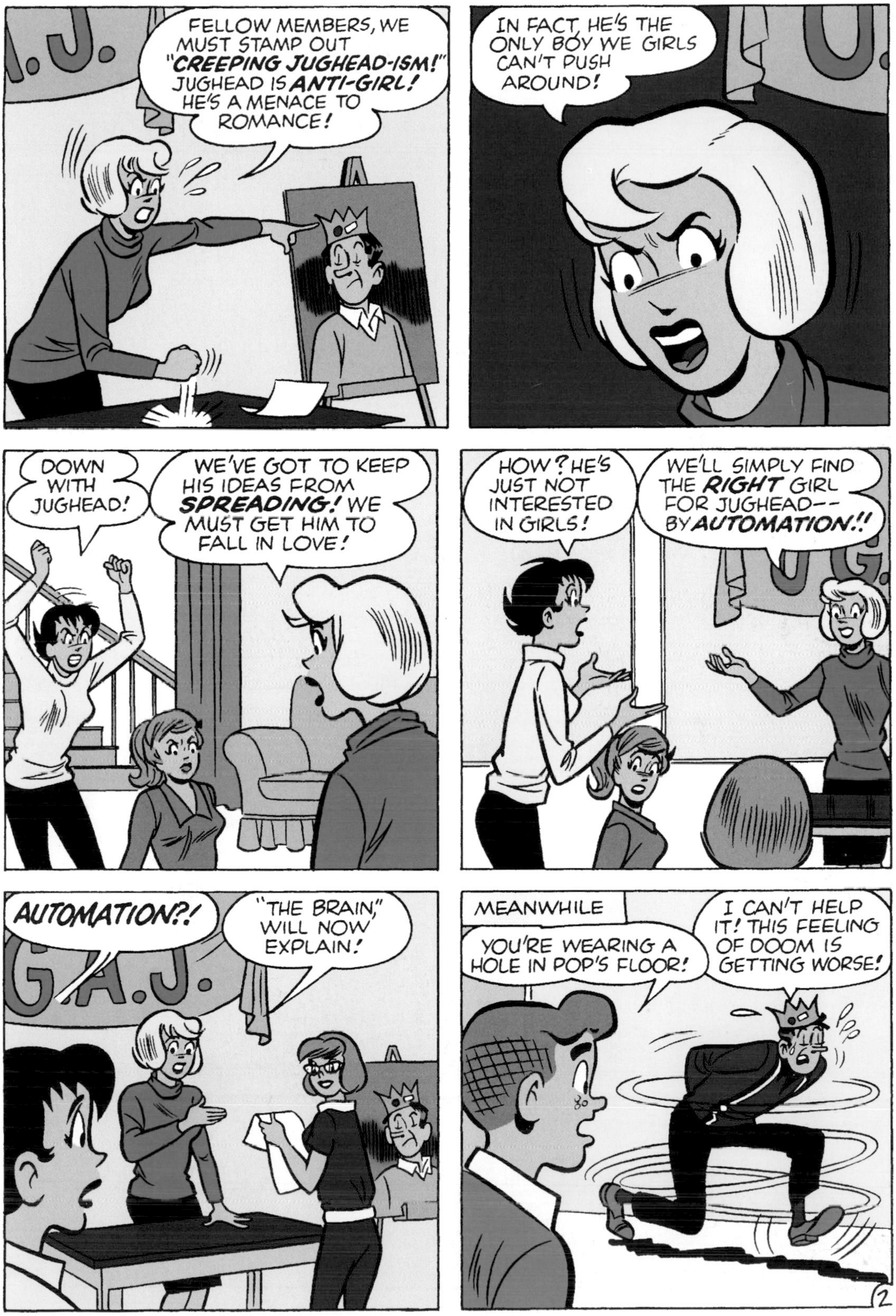
FELLOW MEMBERS, WE MUST STAMP OUT "CREEPING JUGHEAD-ISM!" JUGHEAD IS ANTI-GIRL! HE'S A MENACE TO ROMANCE!
IN FACT, HE'S THE ONLY BOY WE GIRLS CAN'T PUSH AROUND!
DOWN WITH JUGHEAD!
WE'VE GOT TO KEEP HIS IDEAS FROM SPREADING! WE MUST GET HIM TO FALL IN LOVE!
HOW? HE'S JUST NOT INTERESTED IN GIRLS!
WE'LL SIMPLY FIND THE RIGHT GIRL FOR JUGHEAD-- BY AUTOMATION!!
AUTOMATION?!
"THE BRAIN," WILL NOW EXPLAIN!
MEANWHILE
YOU'RE WEARING A HOLE IN POP'S FLOOR!
I CAN'T HELP IT! THIS FEELING OF DOOM IS GETTING WORSE!
2

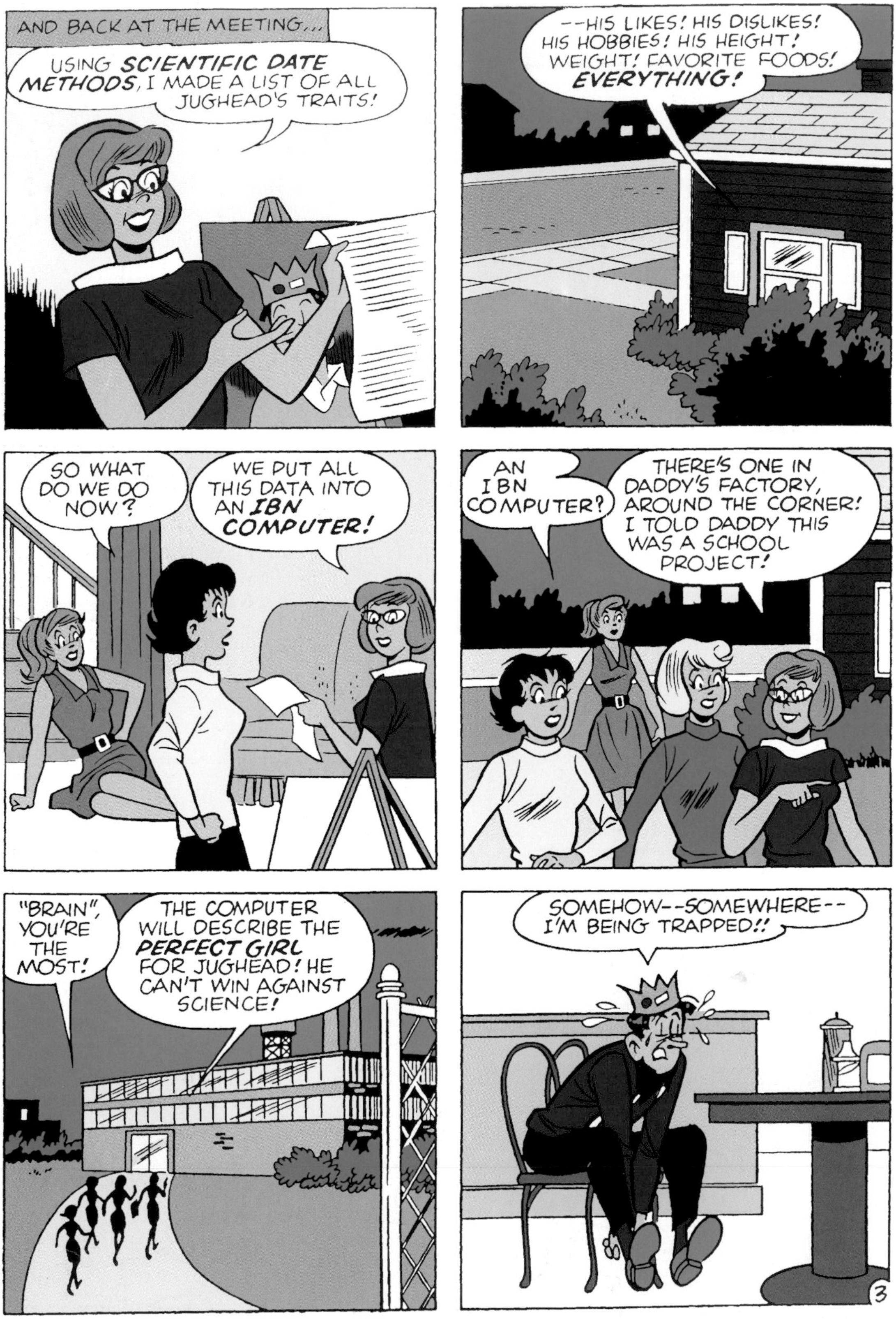
AND BACK AT THE MEETING...
USING SCIENTIFIC DATE METHODS, I MADE A LIST OF ALL JUGHEAD'S TRAITS!
--HIS LIKES! HIS DISLIKES! HIS HOBBIES! HIS HEIGHT! WEIGHT! FAVORITE FOODS! EVERYTHING!
SO WHAT DO WE DO NOW?
WE PUT ALL THIS DATA INTO AN IBN COMPUTER!
AN IBN COMPUTER?
THERE'S ONE IN DADDY'S FACTORY, AROUND THE CORNER! I TOLD DADDY THIS WAS A SCHOOL PROJECT!
"BRAIN", YOU'RE THE MOST!
THE COMPUTER WILL DESCRIBE THE PERFECT GIRL FOR JUGHEAD! HE CAN'T WIN AGAINST SCIENCE!
SOMEHOW--SOMEWHERE-- I'M BEING TRAPPED!!
3

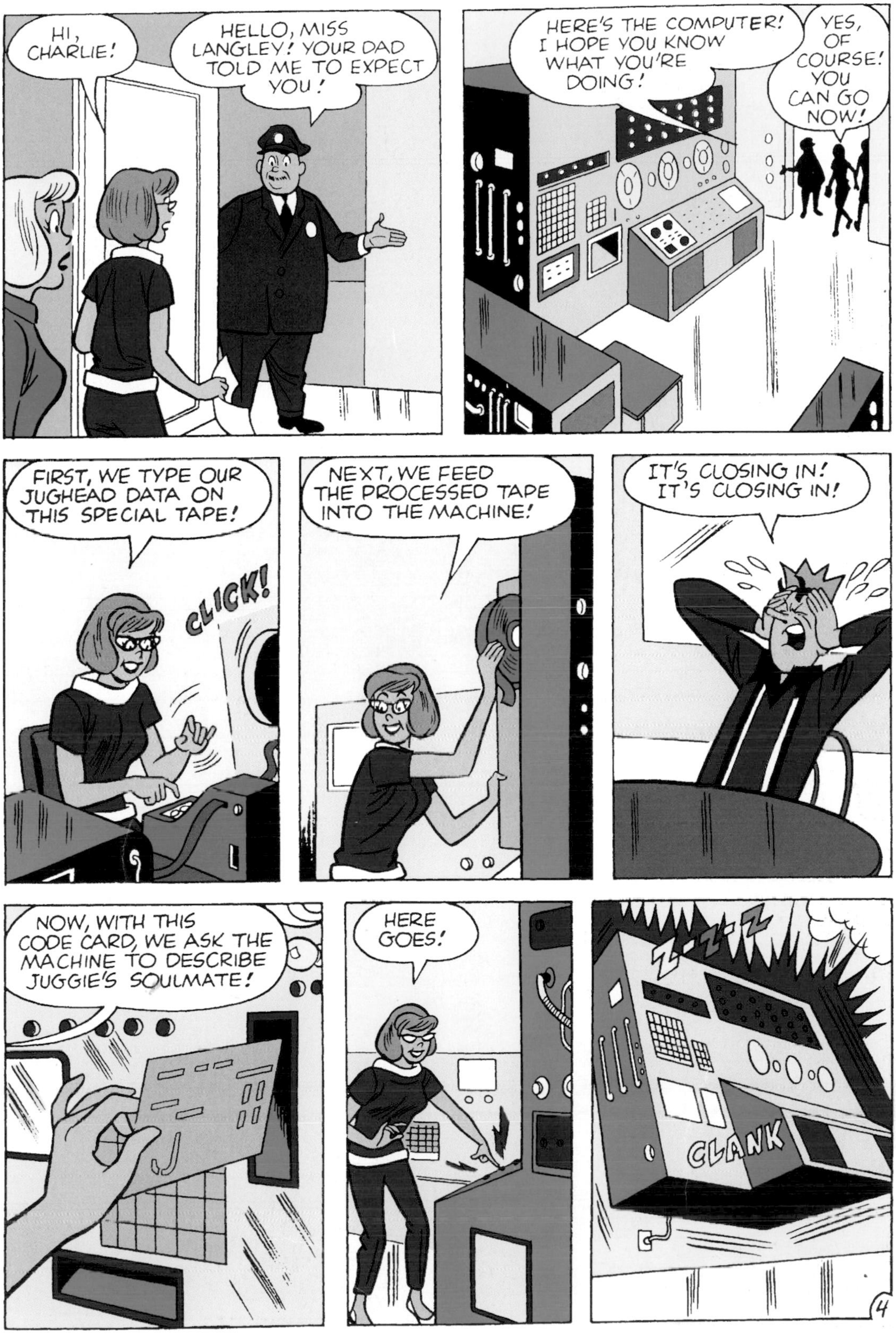
HI, CHARLIE!
HELLO, MISS LANGLEY! YOUR DAD TOLD ME TO EXPECT YOU!
HERE'S THE COMPUTER! I HOPE YOU KNOW WHAT YOU'RE DOING!
YES, OF COURSE! YOU CAN GO NOW!
FIRST, WE TYPE OUR JUGHEAD DATA ON THIS SPECIAL TAPE!
CLICK!
NEXT, WE FEED THE PROCESSED TAPE INTO THE MACHINE!
IT'S CLOSING IN! IT'S CLOSING IN!
NOW, WITH THIS CODE CARD, WE ASK THE MACHINE TO DESCRIBE JUGGIE'S SOULMATE!
HERE GOES!
Z-Z-Z-Z
CLANK
4

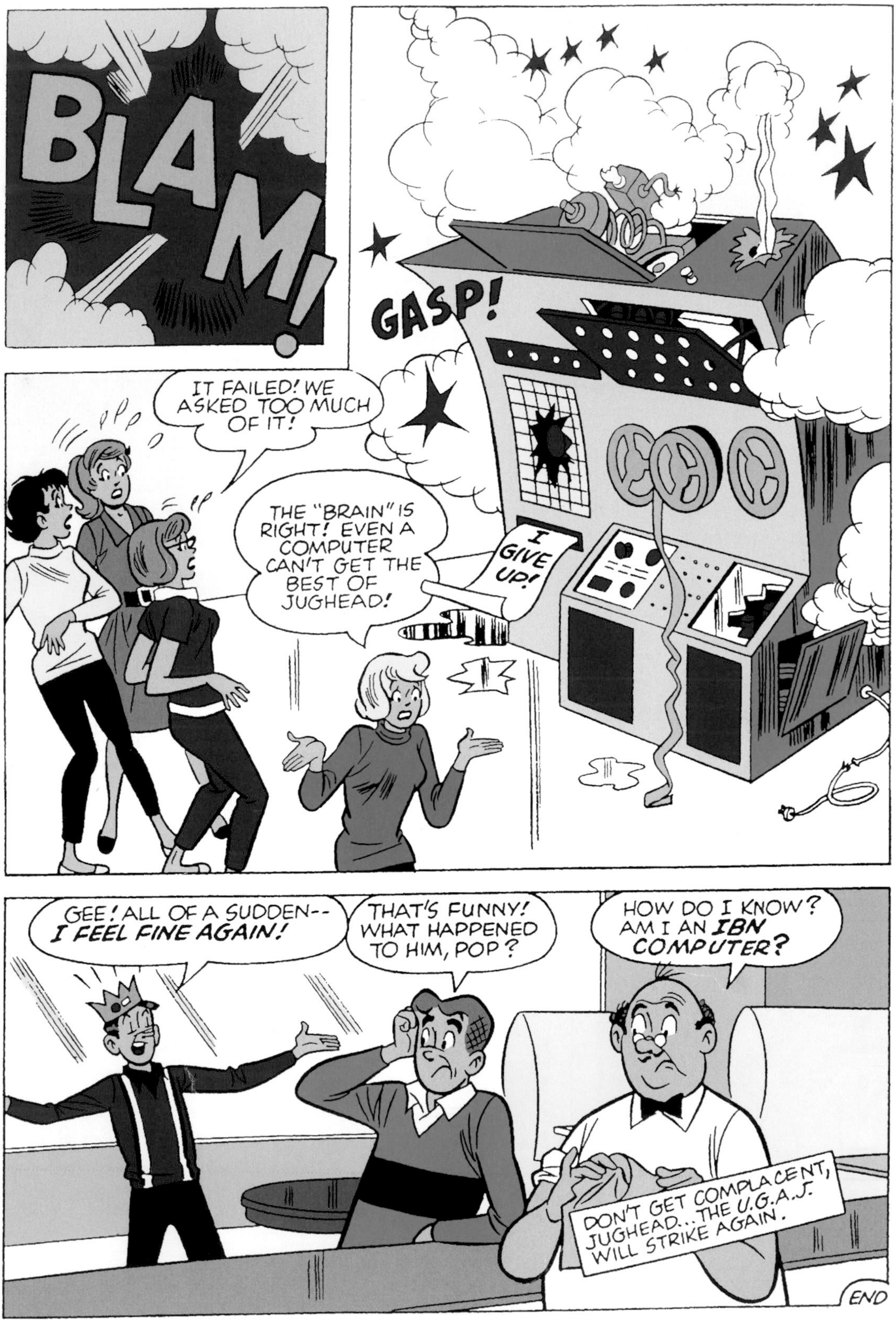

BLAM!
GASP!
IT FAILED! WE ASKED TOO MUCH OF IT!
THE "BRAIN" IS RIGHT! EVEN A COMPUTER CAN'T GET THE BEST OF JUGHEAD!
I GIVE UP!
GEE! ALL OF A SUDDEN-- I FEEL FINE AGAIN!
THAT'S FUNNY! WHAT HAPPENED TO HIM, POP?
HOW DO I KNOW? AM I AN IBN COMPUTER?
DON'T GET COMPLACENT, JUGHEAD... THE U.G.A.J. WILL STRIKE AGAIN.
END

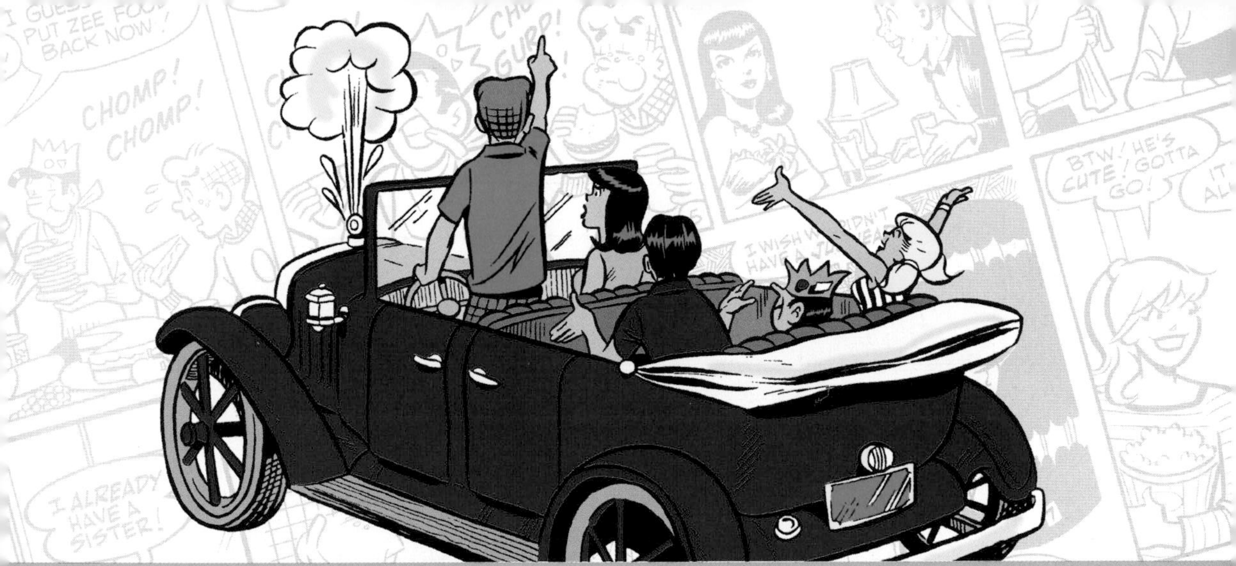
CHOMP!
CHOMP!
I ALREADY HAVE A SISTER!
BTW! HE'S CUTE! GOTTA GO!

VISIT TO A SMALL PANIC

EVERYTHING'S ARCHIE #1, 1969

BY GEORGE GLADIR, HARRY LUCEY, MARTY EPP & BILL YOSHIDA

The Archie animated cartoon was really my first brush with Archie and the gang. I could see parts of myself—and perhaps, who I wanted to be—displayed between Archie, Reggie, and Jughead. Even now if I happen to spot an old Archie comic, I am transported for an instant back to the happy child I was.

—*Kyle Gass*
Actor / Musician,
Tenacious D

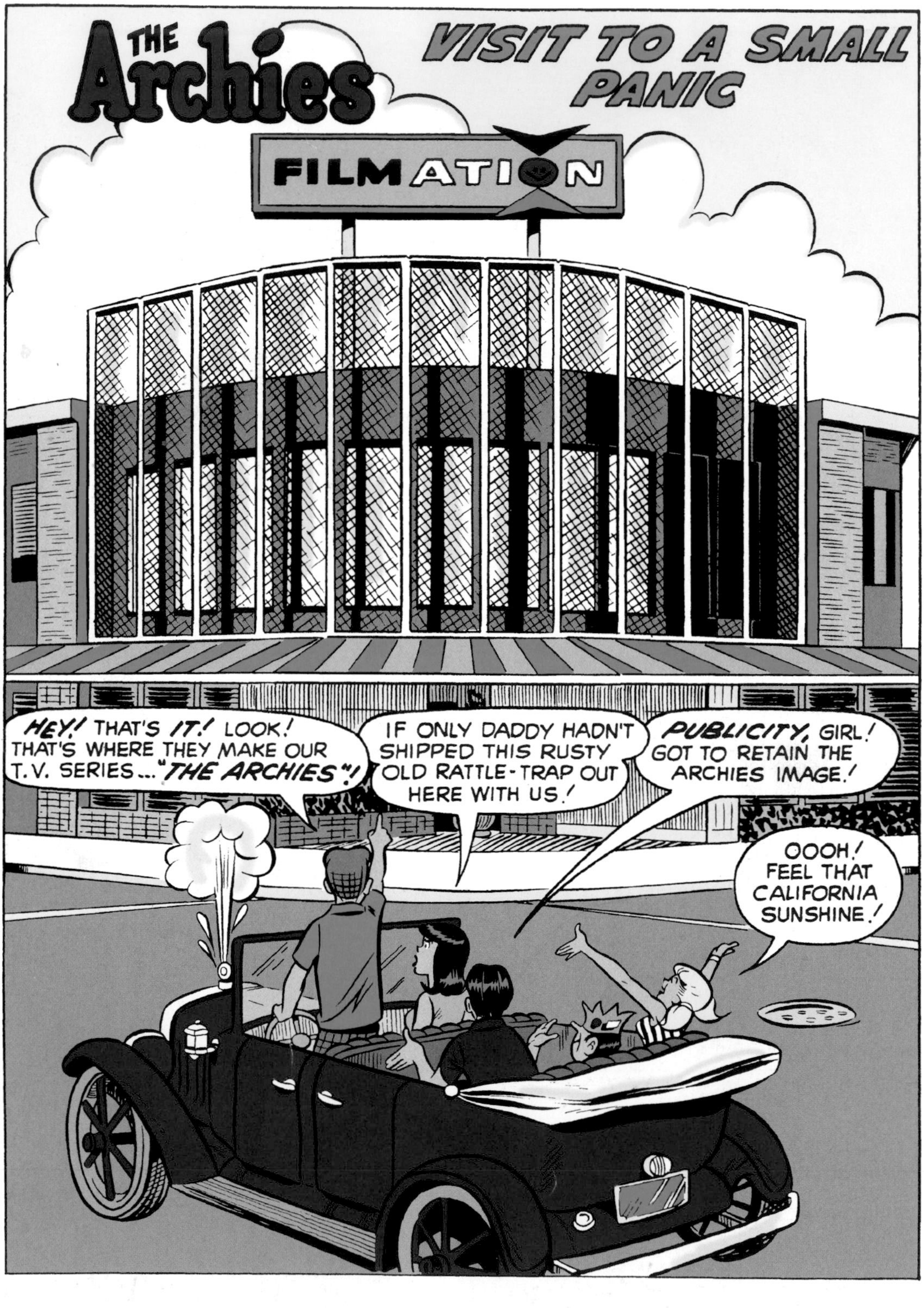
THE Archies
VISIT TO A SMALL PANIC
FILMATION
HEY! THAT'S IT! LOOK! THAT'S WHERE THEY MAKE OUR T.V. SERIES..."THE ARCHIES"!
IF ONLY DADDY HADN'T SHIPPED THIS RUSTY OLD RATTLE-TRAP OUT HERE WITH US!
PUBLICITY, GIRL! GOT TO RETAIN THE ARCHIES IMAGE!
OOOH! FEEL THAT CALIFORNIA SUNSHINE!

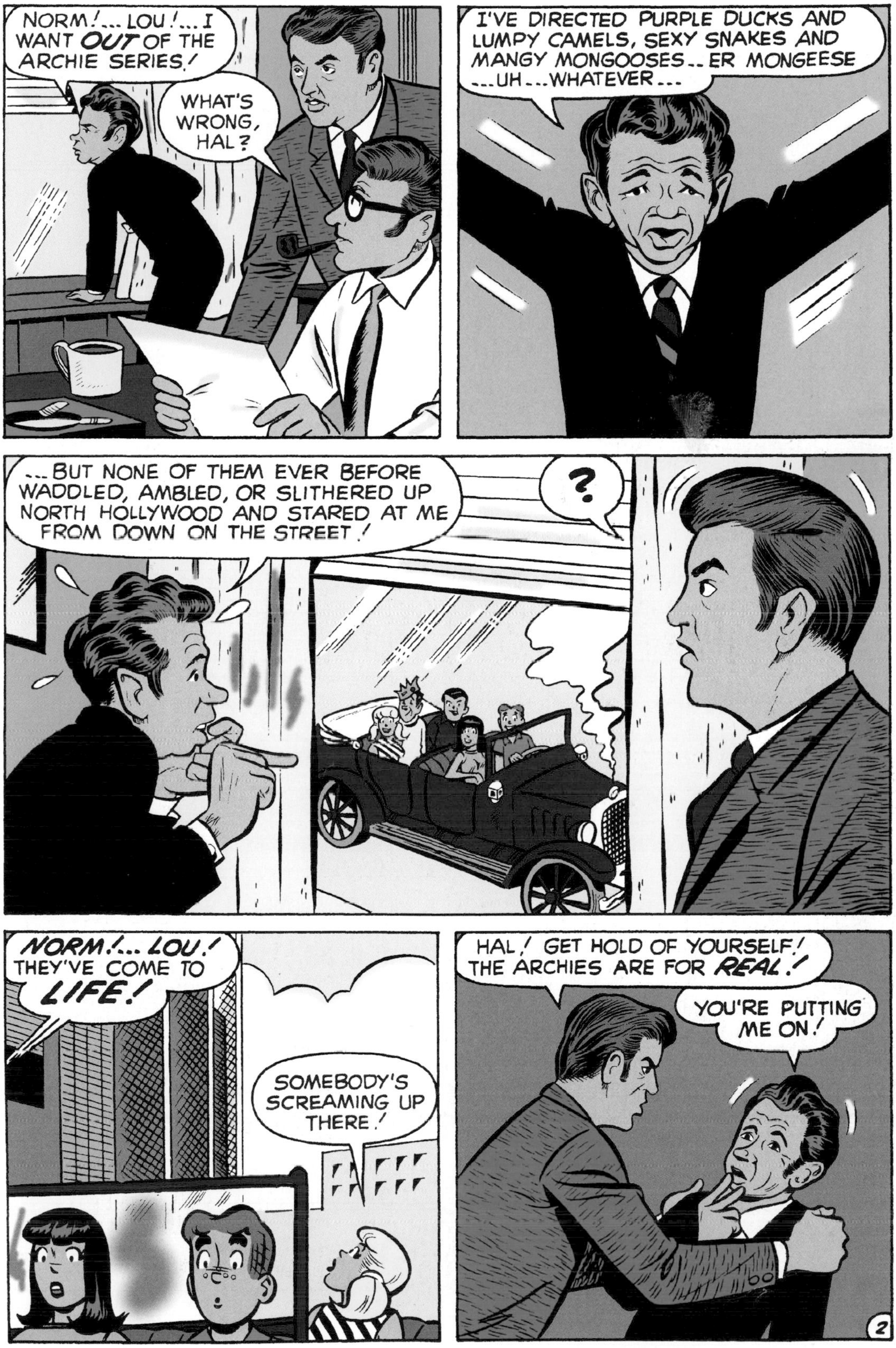
NORM!... LOU!... I WANT OUT OF THE ARCHIE SERIES!
WHAT'S WRONG, HAL?
I'VE DIRECTED PURPLE DUCKS AND LUMPY CAMELS, SEXY SNAKES AND MANGY MONGOOSES.. ER MONGEESE ...UH...WHATEVER...
...BUT NONE OF THEM EVER BEFORE WADDLED, AMBLED, OR SLITHERED UP NORTH HOLLYWOOD AND STARED AT ME FROM DOWN ON THE STREET!
?
NORM!... LOU! THEY'VE COME TO LIFE!
SOMEBODY'S SCREAMING UP THERE!
HAL! GET HOLD OF YOURSELF! THE ARCHIES ARE FOR REAL!
YOU'RE PUTTING ME ON!
2

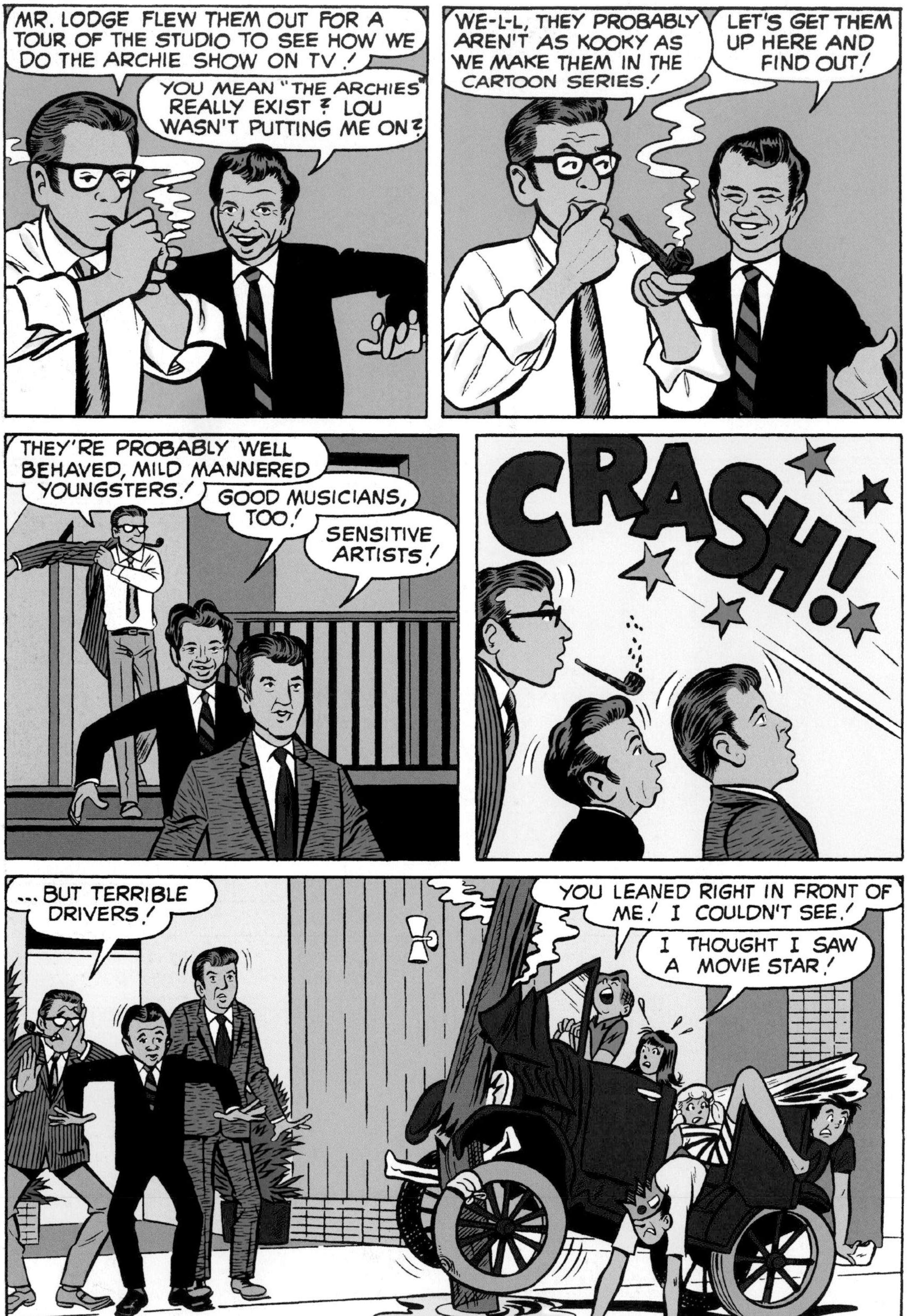
MR. LODGE FLEW THEM OUT FOR A TOUR OF THE STUDIO TO SEE HOW WE DO THE ARCHIE SHOW ON TV!
YOU MEAN "THE ARCHIES" REALLY EXIST? LOU WASN'T PUTTING ME ON?
WE-L-L, THEY PROBABLY AREN'T AS KOOKY AS WE MAKE THEM IN THE CARTOON SERIES!
LET'S GET THEM UP HERE AND FIND OUT!
THEY'RE PROBABLY WELL BEHAVED, MILD MANNERED YOUNGSTERS!
GOOD MUSICIANS, TOO!
SENSITIVE ARTISTS!
CRASH!!
...BUT TERRIBLE DRIVERS!
YOU LEANED RIGHT IN FRONT OF ME! I COULDN'T SEE!
I THOUGHT I SAW A MOVIE STAR!
3

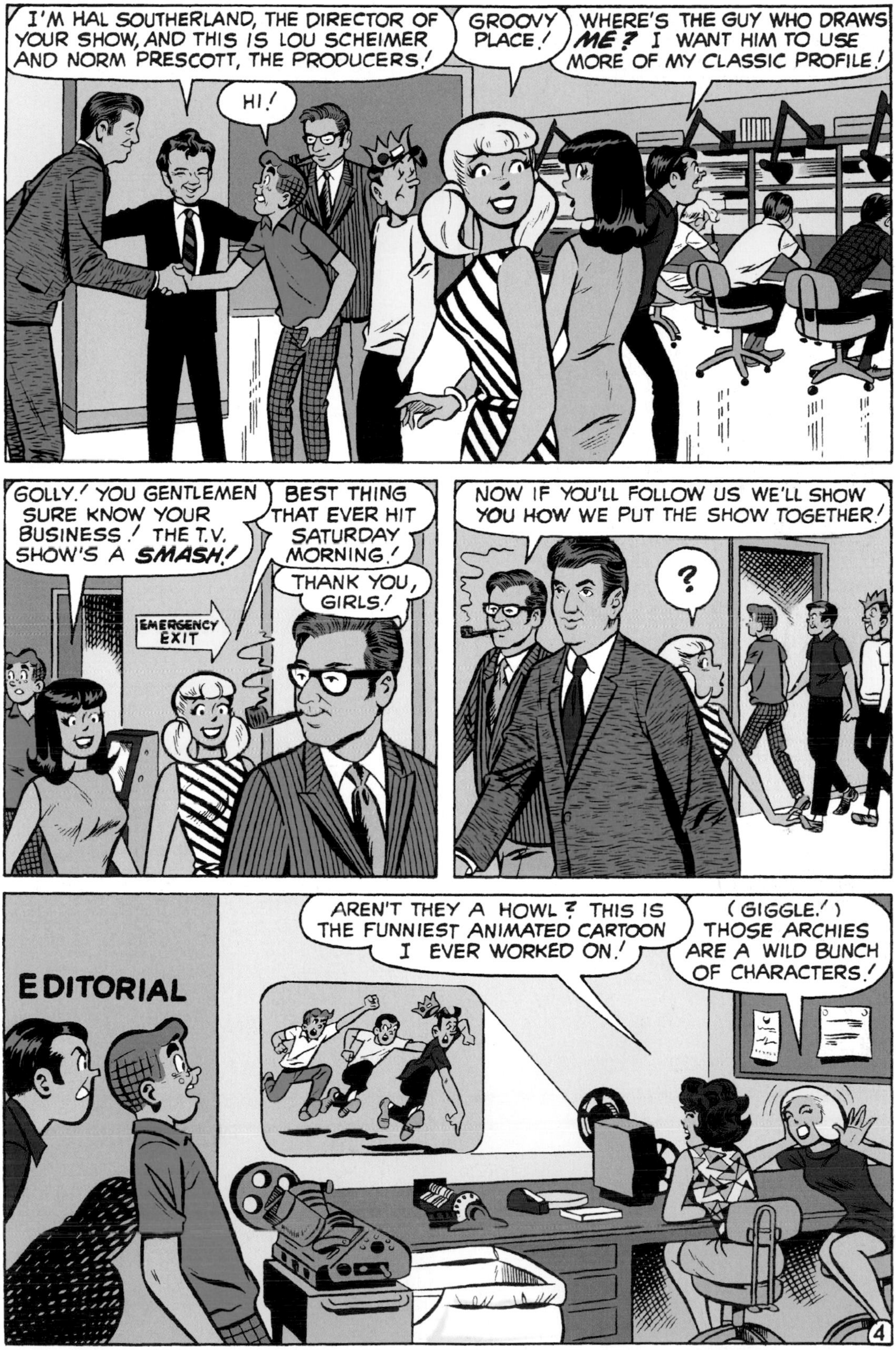
I'M HAL SOUTHERLAND, THE DIRECTOR OF YOUR SHOW, AND THIS IS LOU SCHEIMER AND NORM PRESCOTT, THE PRODUCERS!
HI!
GROOVY PLACE!
WHERE'S THE GUY WHO DRAWS ME? I WANT HIM TO USE MORE OF MY CLASSIC PROFILE!
GOLLY! YOU GENTLEMEN SURE KNOW YOUR BUSINESS! THE T.V. SHOW'S A SMASH!
BEST THING THAT EVER HIT SATURDAY MORNING!
THANK YOU, GIRLS!
EMERGENCY EXIT
NOW IF YOU'LL FOLLOW US WE'LL SHOW YOU HOW WE PUT THE SHOW TOGETHER!
?
EDITORIAL
AREN'T THEY A HOWL? THIS IS THE FUNNIEST ANIMATED CARTOON I EVER WORKED ON!
(GIGGLE!) THOSE ARCHIES ARE A WILD BUNCH OF CHARACTERS!
4

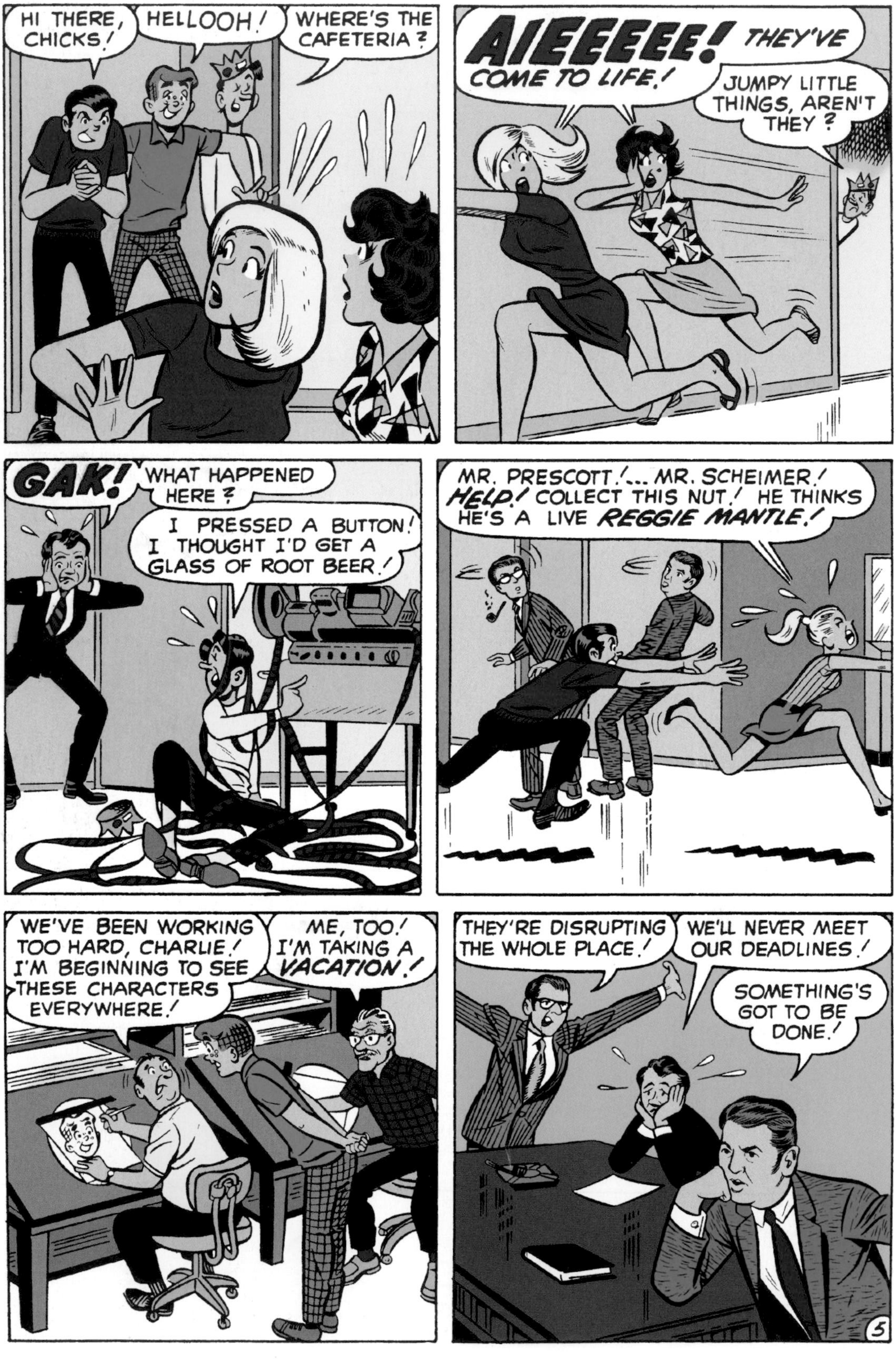

HI THERE, CHICKS!
HELLOOH!
WHERE'S THE CAFETERIA?
AIEEEEE! THEY'VE COME TO LIFE!
JUMPY LITTLE THINGS, AREN'T THEY?
GAK!
WHAT HAPPENED HERE?
I PRESSED A BUTTON! I THOUGHT I'D GET A GLASS OF ROOT BEER!
MR. PRESCOTT!... MR. SCHEIMER! HELP! COLLECT THIS NUT! HE THINKS HE'S A LIVE REGGIE MANTLE!
WE'VE BEEN WORKING TOO HARD, CHARLIE! I'M BEGINNING TO SEE THESE CHARACTERS EVERYWHERE!
ME, TOO! I'M TAKING A VACATION!
THEY'RE DISRUPTING THE WHOLE PLACE!
WE'LL NEVER MEET OUR DEADLINES!
SOMETHING'S GOT TO BE DONE!
5

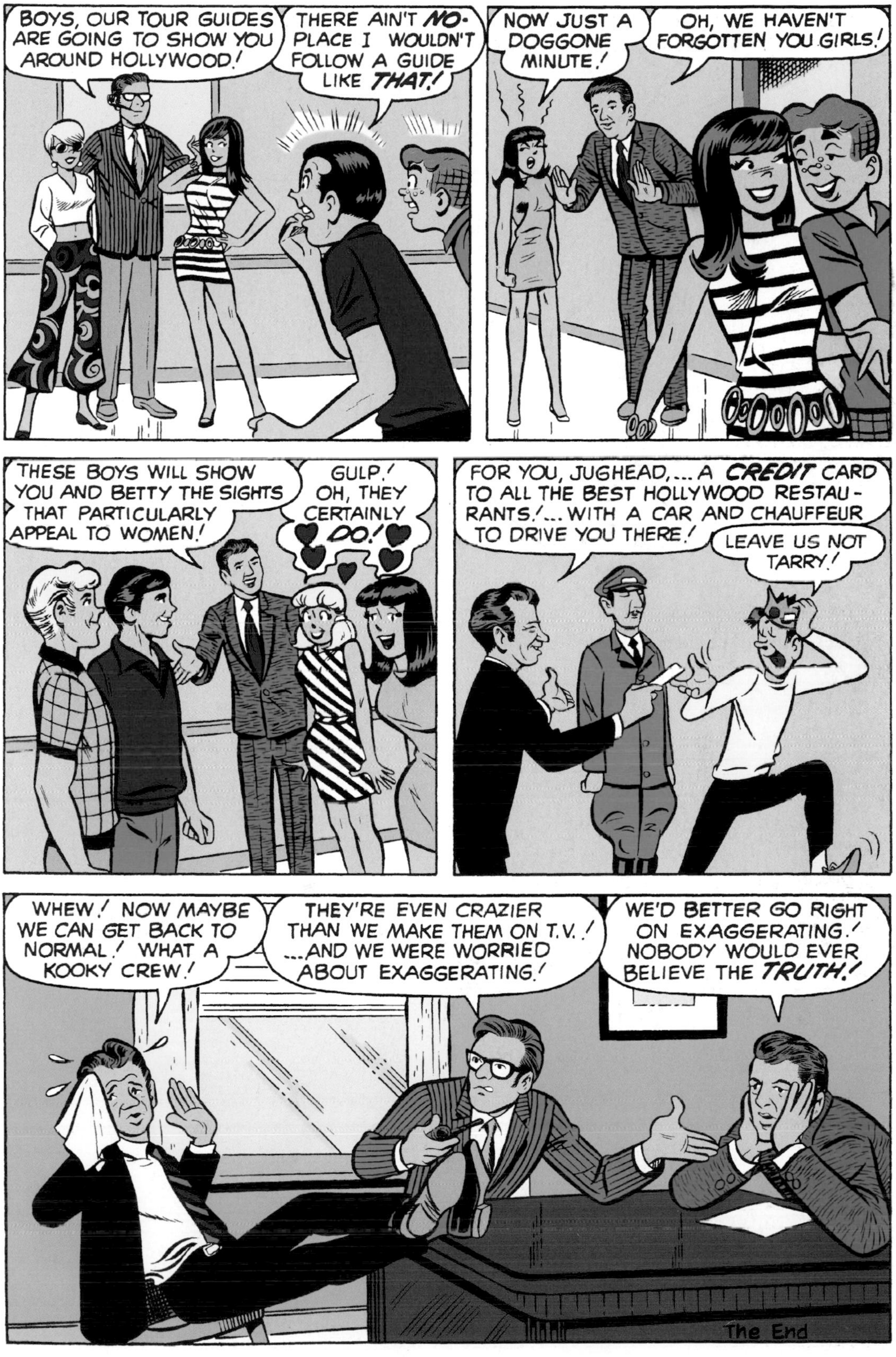

BOYS, OUR TOUR GUIDES ARE GOING TO SHOW YOU AROUND HOLLYWOOD!
THERE AIN'T NO-PLACE I WOULDN'T FOLLOW A GUIDE LIKE THAT!
NOW JUST A DOGGONE MINUTE!
OH, WE HAVEN'T FORGOTTEN YOU GIRLS!
THESE BOYS WILL SHOW YOU AND BETTY THE SIGHTS THAT PARTICULARLY APPEAL TO WOMEN!
GULP! OH, THEY CERTAINLY DO!
FOR YOU, JUGHEAD, ... A CREDIT CARD TO ALL THE BEST HOLLYWOOD RESTAU-RANTS! ... WITH A CAR AND CHAUFFEUR TO DRIVE YOU THERE!
LEAVE US NOT TARRY!
WHEW! NOW MAYBE WE CAN GET BACK TO NORMAL! WHAT A KOOKY CREW!
THEY'RE EVEN CRAZIER THAN WE MAKE THEM ON T.V.! ...AND WE WERE WORRIED ABOUT EXAGGERATING!
WE'D BETTER GO RIGHT ON EXAGGERATING! NOBODY WOULD EVER BELIEVE THE TRUTH!
The End

The BEST of Archie COMICS

1970s

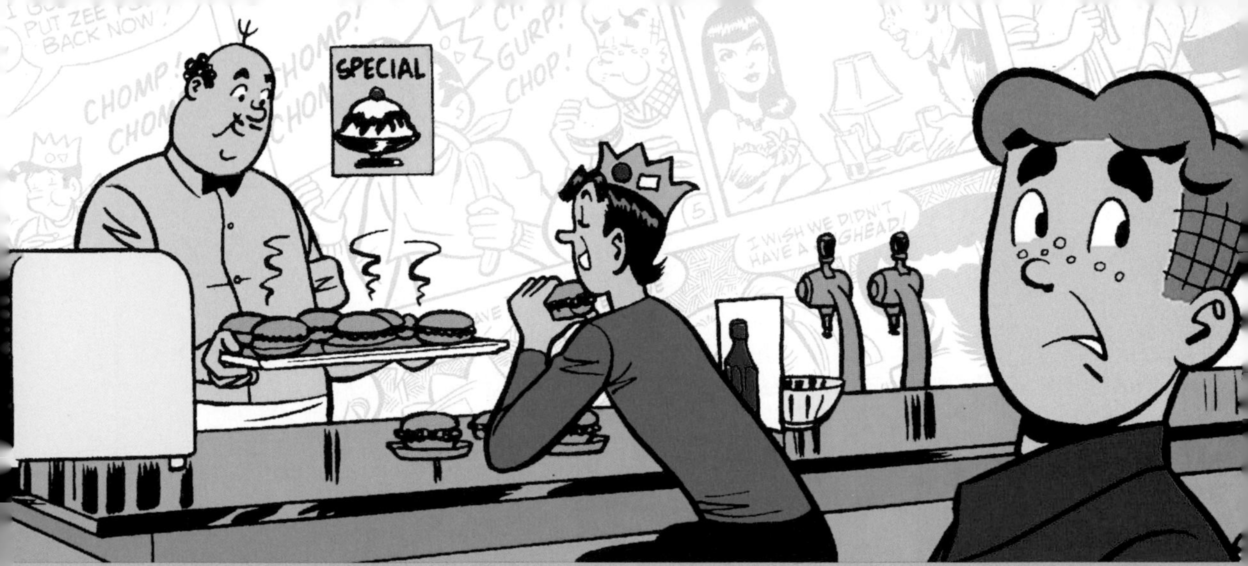
SPECIAL

THE BYE BYE BLUES
LAUGH #276, 1974
BY FRANK DOYLE, HARRY LUCEY, BILL YOSHIDA & BARRY GROSSMAN

The '70s were a time where philosophical thought was breaking new grounds. An attitude of counter-culture ideals left over from the '60s bled into this new decade, and everyone was looking for ways to achieve or realize their true selves. Existentialism peaked during this time. French existentialist writer Jean-Paul Sartre's slogan was that "existence precedes essence," and that what it means to be human is decided in existence itself. What you are is what you make of yourself and what you become of it. Archie's philosophy is a simple one, "live each day like it's your last," but is it not existentialist in nature? Would Sartre approve of it?

I think he would. But then again, Sartre's never been punched in the face by Moose Mason. I like this story. It's funny.

—Jamie Lee Rotante
Writer/Editor,
Archie Comics

KONG PHOO
ARCHIE AT RIVERDALE HIGH #18, 1974
BY FRANK DOYLE & HARRY LUCEY

As a HUGE fan of the Kung Fu tv series at the time I remember getting a big kick out of this one. And I always liked any stories where Reggie was made the fool.

—Rich Koslowski
Artist / Inker,
Archie Comics

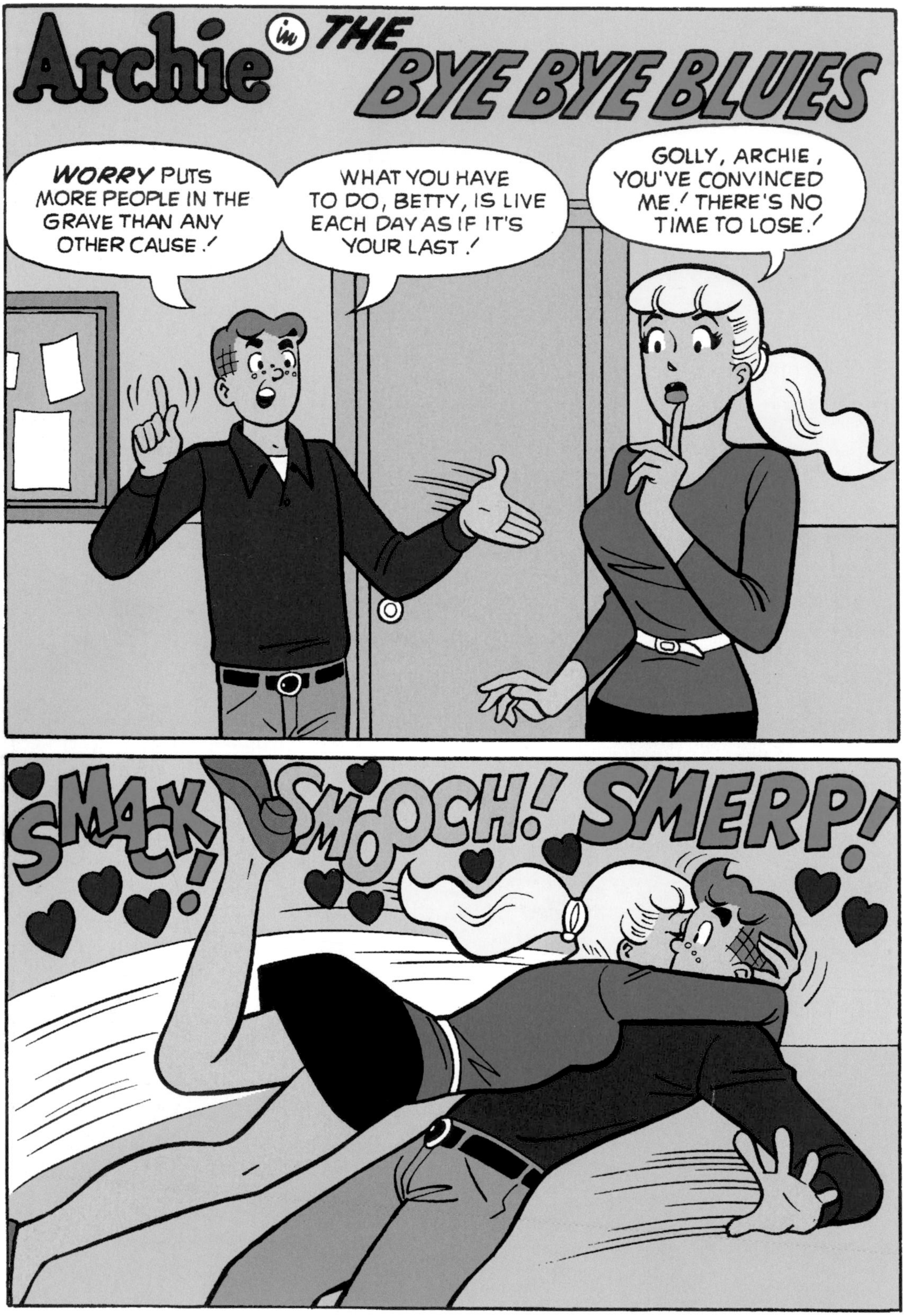
Archie in THE BYE BYE BLUES
WORRY PUTS MORE PEOPLE IN THE GRAVE THAN ANY OTHER CAUSE.!
WHAT YOU HAVE TO DO, BETTY, IS LIVE EACH DAY AS IF IT'S YOUR LAST.!
GOLLY, ARCHIE, YOU'VE CONVINCED ME.! THERE'S NO TIME TO LOSE.!
SMACK! SMOOCH! SMERP!

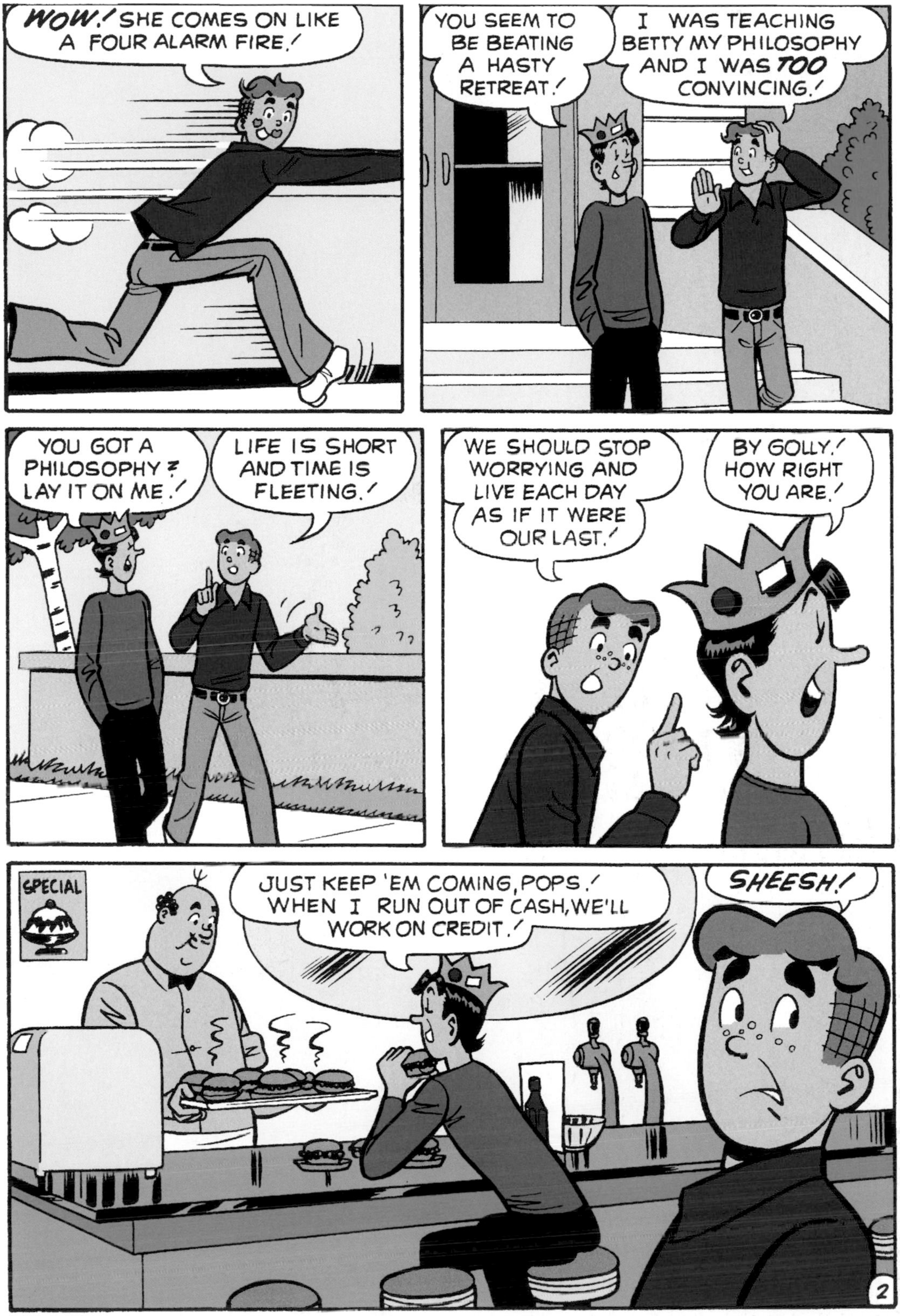
WOW! SHE COMES ON LIKE A FOUR ALARM FIRE!
YOU SEEM TO BE BEATING A HASTY RETREAT!
I WAS TEACHING BETTY MY PHILOSOPHY AND I WAS TOO CONVINCING!
YOU GOT A PHILOSOPHY? LAY IT ON ME!
LIFE IS SHORT AND TIME IS FLEETING!
WE SHOULD STOP WORRYING AND LIVE EACH DAY AS IF IT WERE OUR LAST!
BY GOLLY! HOW RIGHT YOU ARE!
SPECIAL
JUST KEEP 'EM COMING, POPS! WHEN I RUN OUT OF CASH, WE'LL WORK ON CREDIT!
SHEESH!
2

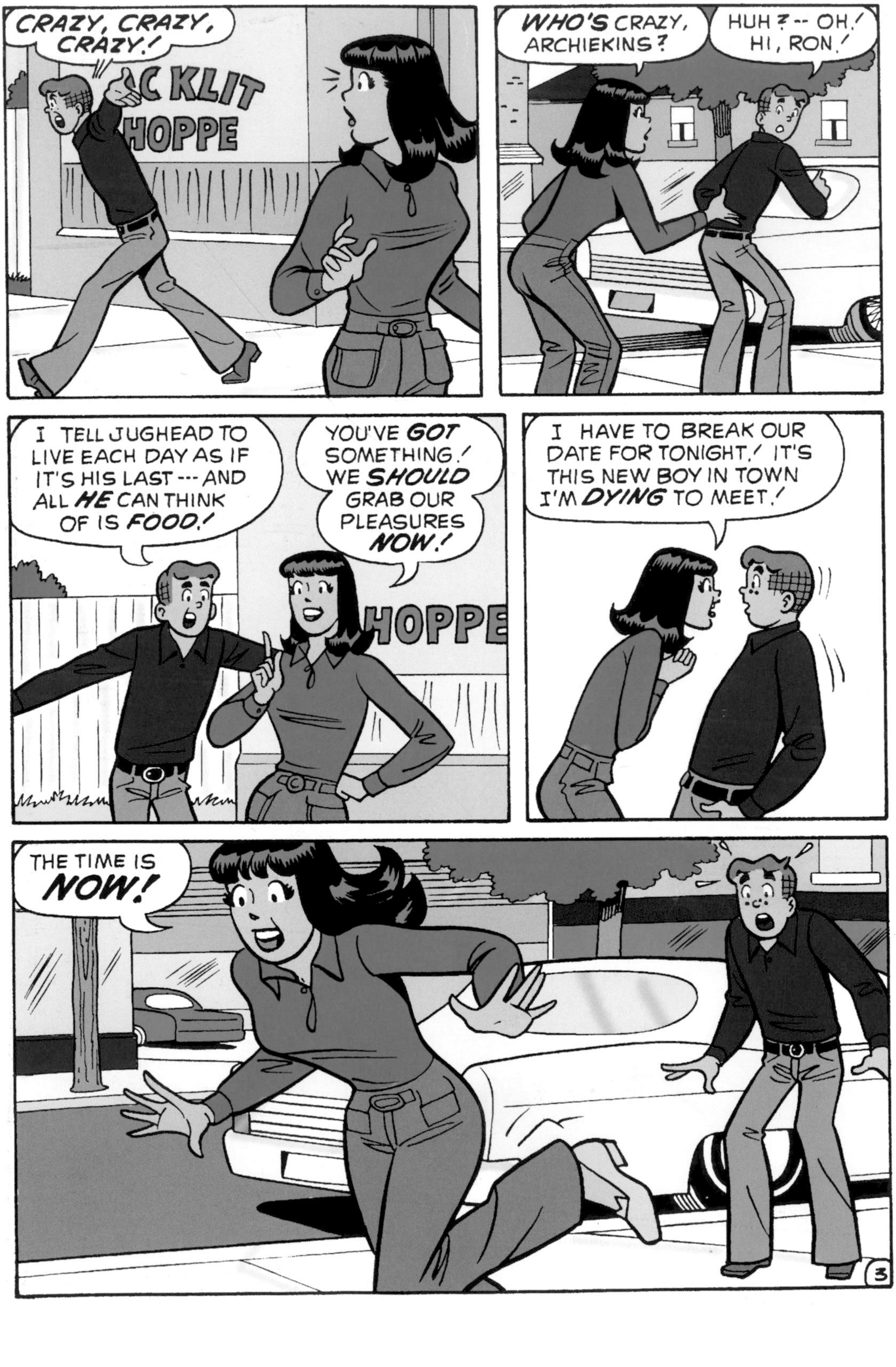
CRAZY, CRAZY, CRAZY!
C KLIT HOPPE
WHO'S CRAZY, ARCHIEKINS?
HUH? -- OH! HI, RON!
I TELL JUGHEAD TO LIVE EACH DAY AS IF IT'S HIS LAST --- AND ALL HE CAN THINK OF IS FOOD!
YOU'VE GOT SOMETHING! WE SHOULD GRAB OUR PLEASURES NOW!
HOPPE
I HAVE TO BREAK OUR DATE FOR TONIGHT! IT'S THIS NEW BOY IN TOWN I'M DYING TO MEET!
THE TIME IS NOW!
3

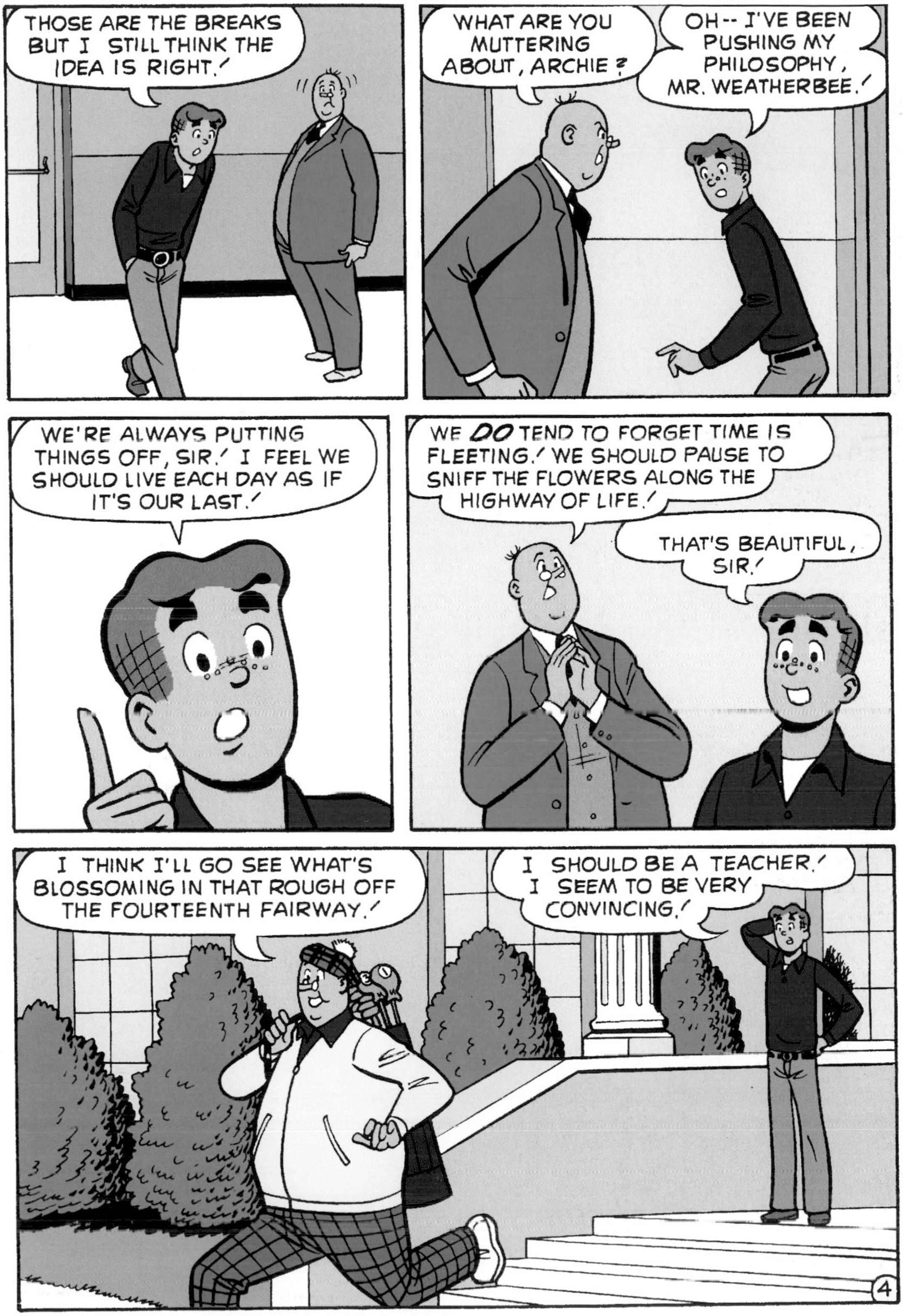
THOSE ARE THE BREAKS BUT I STILL THINK THE IDEA IS RIGHT!
WHAT ARE YOU MUTTERING ABOUT, ARCHIE?
OH-- I'VE BEEN PUSHING MY PHILOSOPHY, MR. WEATHERBEE!
WE'RE ALWAYS PUTTING THINGS OFF, SIR! I FEEL WE SHOULD LIVE EACH DAY AS IF IT'S OUR LAST!
WE DO TEND TO FORGET TIME IS FLEETING! WE SHOULD PAUSE TO SNIFF THE FLOWERS ALONG THE HIGHWAY OF LIFE!
THAT'S BEAUTIFUL, SIR!
I THINK I'LL GO SEE WHAT'S BLOSSOMING IN THAT ROUGH OFF THE FOURTEENTH FAIRWAY!
I SHOULD BE A TEACHER! I SEEM TO BE VERY CONVINCING!
4

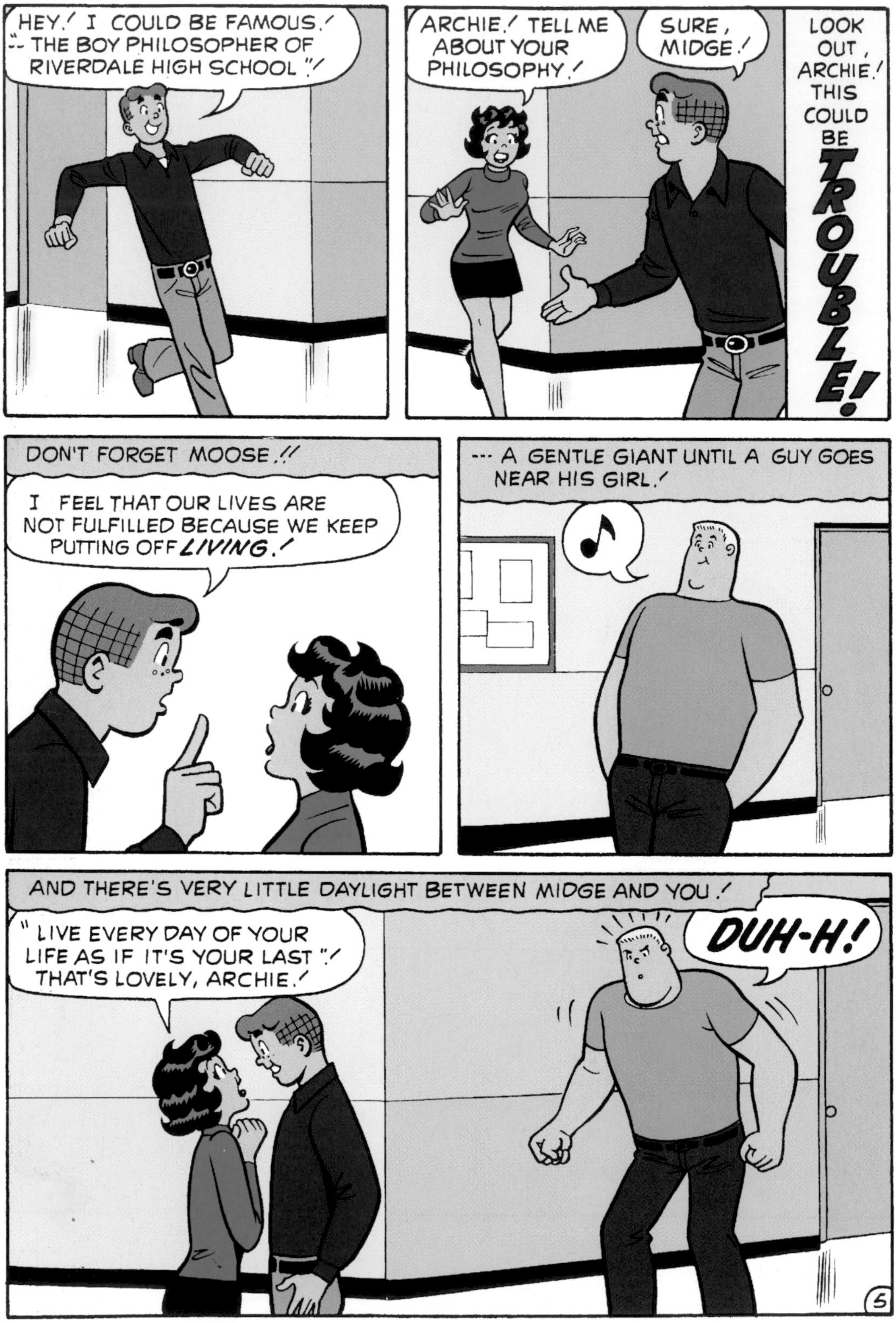
HEY! I COULD BE FAMOUS! -- THE BOY PHILOSOPHER OF RIVERDALE HIGH SCHOOL"!
ARCHIE! TELL ME ABOUT YOUR PHILOSOPHY!
SURE, MIDGE!
LOOK OUT, ARCHIE! THIS COULD BE TROUBLE!
DON'T FORGET MOOSE!!
I FEEL THAT OUR LIVES ARE NOT FULFILLED BECAUSE WE KEEP PUTTING OFF LIVING!
--- A GENTLE GIANT UNTIL A GUY GOES NEAR HIS GIRL!
AND THERE'S VERY LITTLE DAYLIGHT BETWEEN MIDGE AND YOU!
" LIVE EVERY DAY OF YOUR LIFE AS IF IT'S YOUR LAST "! THAT'S LOVELY, ARCHIE!
DUH-H!
5

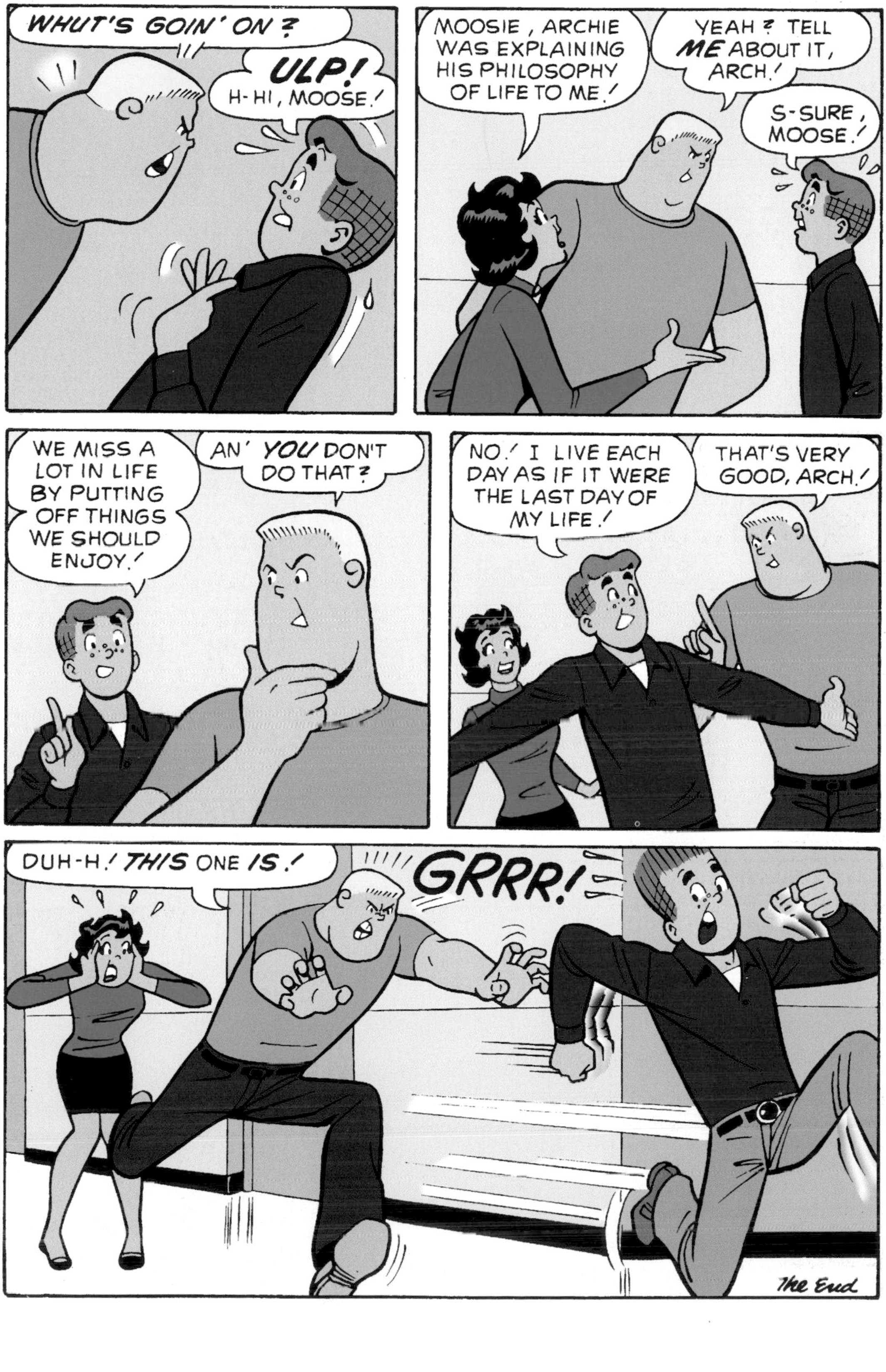
WHUT'S GOIN' ON ?
ULP! H-HI, MOOSE.!
MOOSIE, ARCHIE WAS EXPLAINING HIS PHILOSOPHY OF LIFE TO ME.!
YEAH ? TELL ME ABOUT IT, ARCH.!
S-SURE, MOOSE.!
WE MISS A LOT IN LIFE BY PUTTING OFF THINGS WE SHOULD ENJOY.!
AN' YOU DON'T DO THAT ?
NO.! I LIVE EACH DAY AS IF IT WERE THE LAST DAY OF MY LIFE.!
THAT'S VERY GOOD, ARCH.!
DUH-H.! THIS ONE IS.!
GRRR!
The End

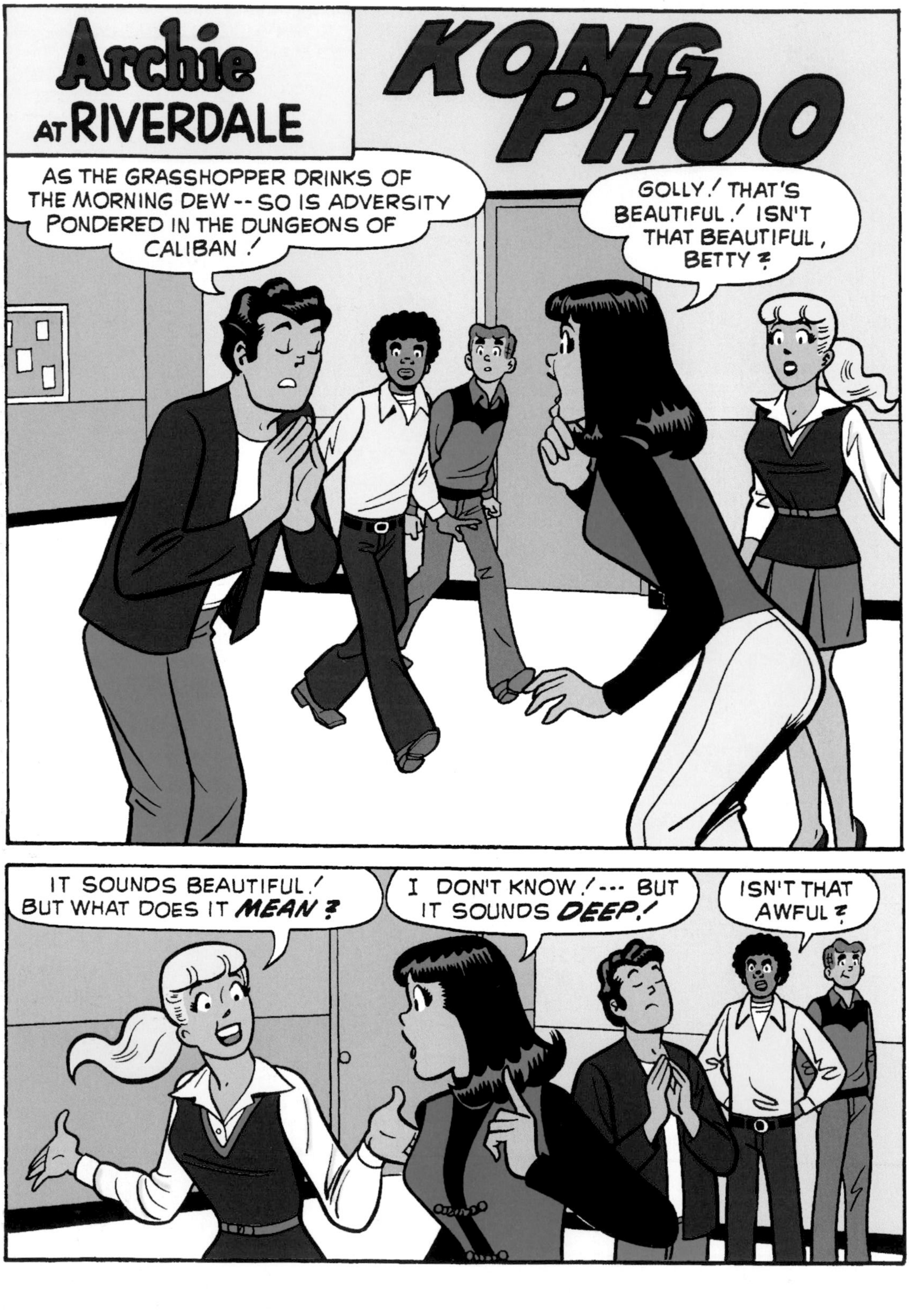
Archie AT RIVERDALE
KONG PHOO
AS THE GRASSHOPPER DRINKS OF THE MORNING DEW -- SO IS ADVERSITY PONDERED IN THE DUNGEONS OF CALIBAN!
GOLLY! THAT'S BEAUTIFUL! ISN'T THAT BEAUTIFUL, BETTY?
IT SOUNDS BEAUTIFUL! BUT WHAT DOES IT MEAN?
I DON'T KNOW! --- BUT IT SOUNDS DEEP!
ISN'T THAT AWFUL?

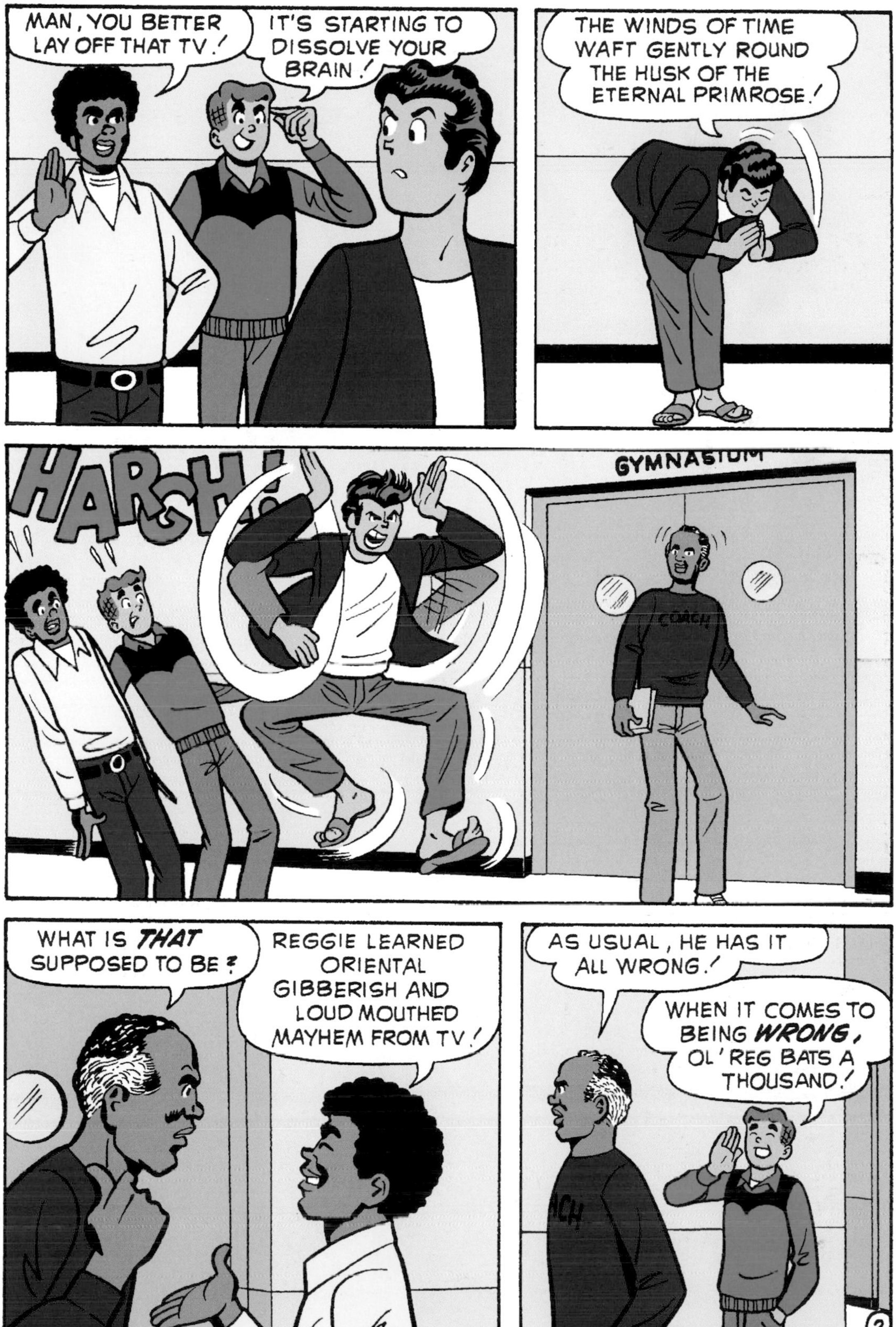
MAN, YOU BETTER LAY OFF THAT TV!
IT'S STARTING TO DISSOLVE YOUR BRAIN!
THE WINDS OF TIME WAFT GENTLY ROUND THE HUSK OF THE ETERNAL PRIMROSE!
HARGH!
GYMNASIUM
COACH
WHAT IS THAT SUPPOSED TO BE?
REGGIE LEARNED ORIENTAL GIBBERISH AND LOUD MOUTHED MAYHEM FROM TV!
AS USUAL, HE HAS IT ALL WRONG!
WHEN IT COMES TO BEING WRONG, OL' REG BATS A THOUSAND!
2

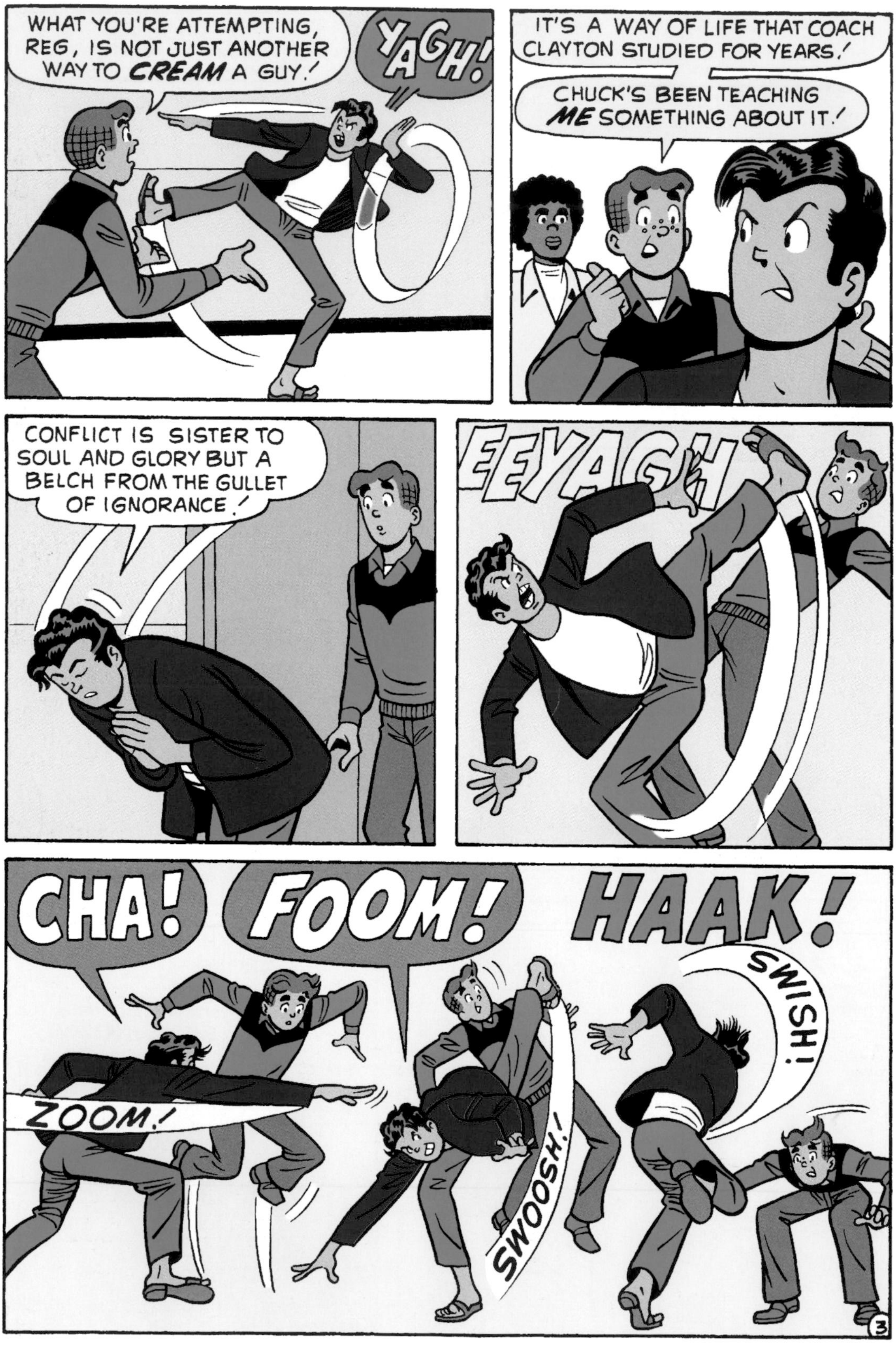
WHAT YOU'RE ATTEMPTING, REG, IS NOT JUST ANOTHER WAY TO CREAM A GUY!
YAGH!
IT'S A WAY OF LIFE THAT COACH CLAYTON STUDIED FOR YEARS!
CHUCK'S BEEN TEACHING ME SOMETHING ABOUT IT!
CONFLICT IS SISTER TO SOUL AND GLORY BUT A BELCH FROM THE GULLET OF IGNORANCE!
EEYAGH
CHA!
FOOM!
HAAK!
ZOOM!
SWOOSH!
SWISH!
3

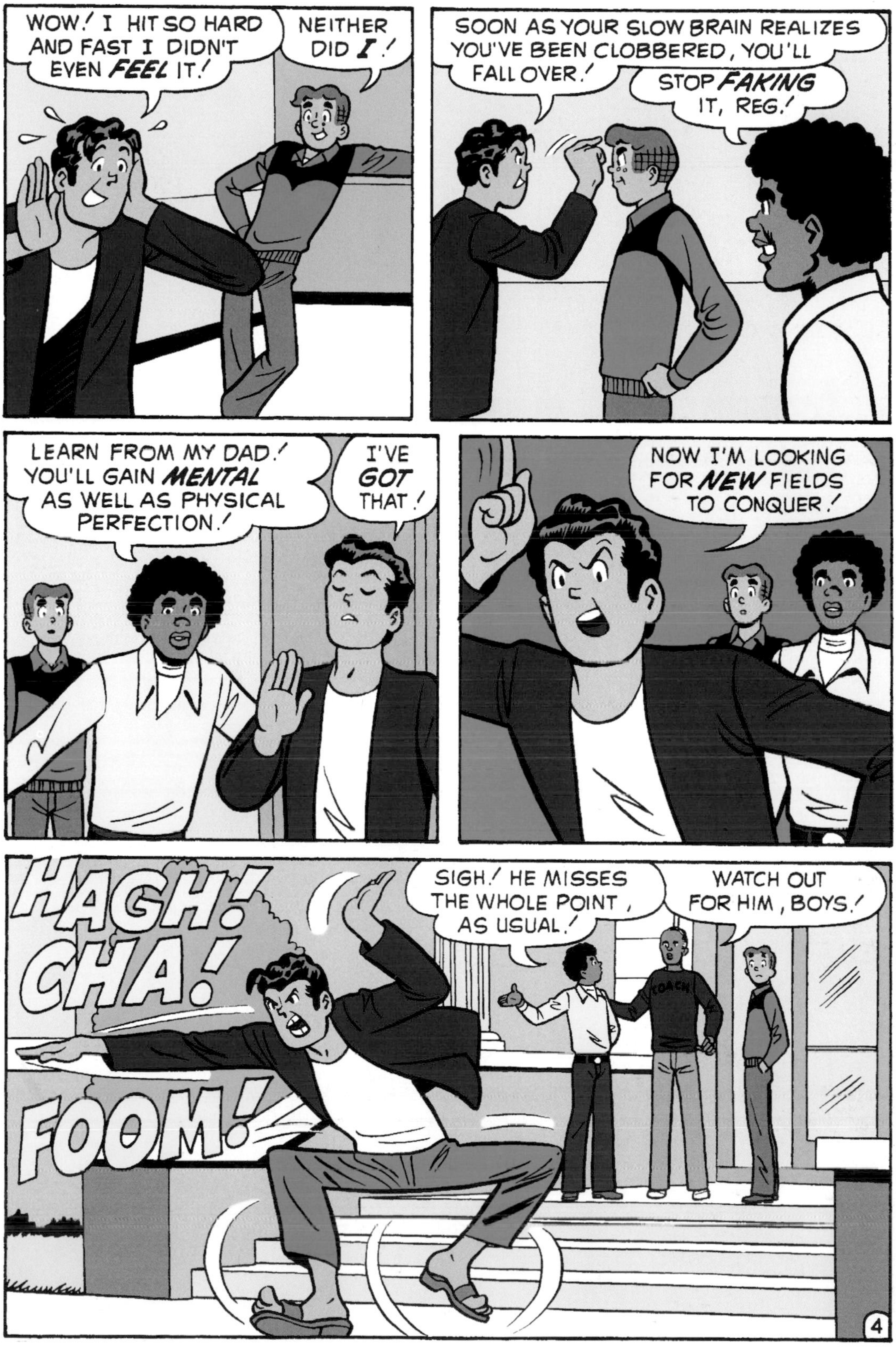
WOW! I HIT SO HARD AND FAST I DIDN'T EVEN FEEL IT!
NEITHER DID I!
SOON AS YOUR SLOW BRAIN REALIZES YOU'VE BEEN CLOBBERED, YOU'LL FALL OVER!
STOP FAKING IT, REG!
LEARN FROM MY DAD! YOU'LL GAIN MENTAL AS WELL AS PHYSICAL PERFECTION!
I'VE GOT THAT!
NOW I'M LOOKING FOR NEW FIELDS TO CONQUER!
HAGH! CHA!
FOOM!
SIGH! HE MISSES THE WHOLE POINT, AS USUAL!
WATCH OUT FOR HIM, BOYS!
COACH
4

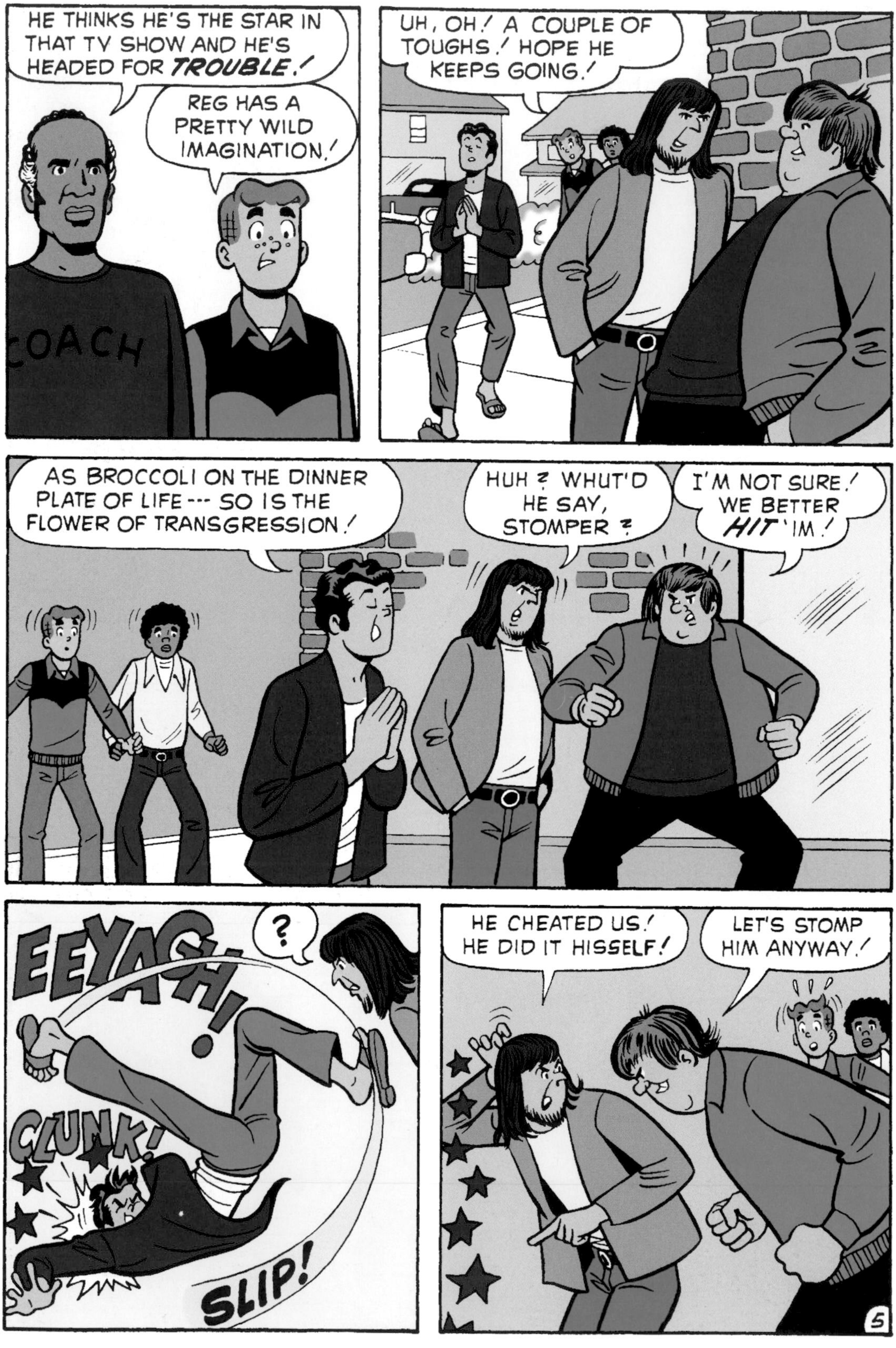

HE THINKS HE'S THE STAR IN THAT TV SHOW AND HE'S HEADED FOR TROUBLE!
REG HAS A PRETTY WILD IMAGINATION!
COACH
UH, OH! A COUPLE OF TOUGHS! HOPE HE KEEPS GOING!
AS BROCCOLI ON THE DINNER PLATE OF LIFE --- SO IS THE FLOWER OF TRANSGRESSION!
HUH? WHUT'D HE SAY, STOMPER?
I'M NOT SURE! WE BETTER HIT 'IM!
EEYAGH!
?
CLUNK!
SLIP!
HE CHEATED US! HE DID IT HISSELF!
LET'S STOMP HIM ANYWAY!
5

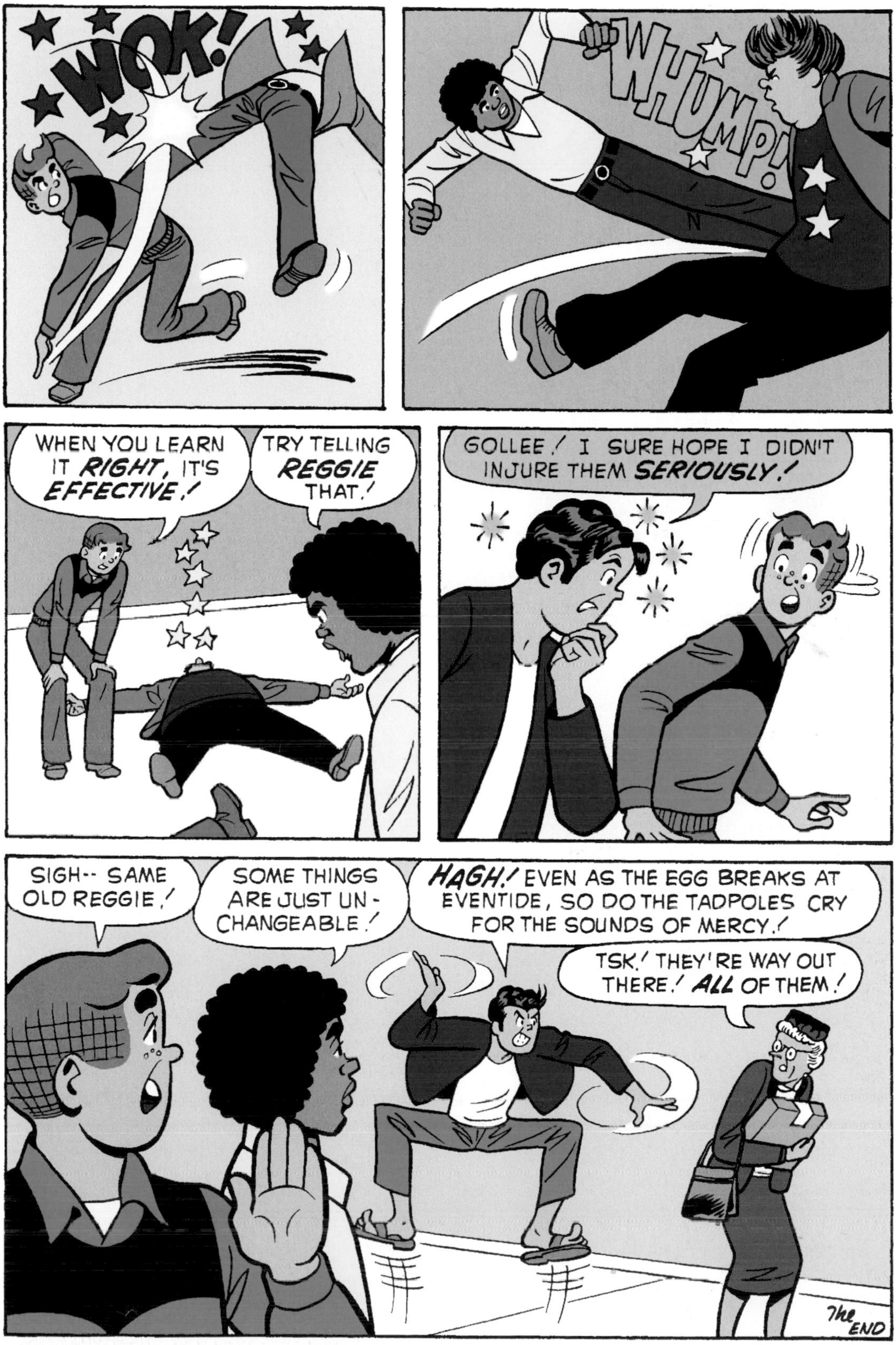
WOK!
WHUMP!
WHEN YOU LEARN IT RIGHT, IT'S EFFECTIVE!
TRY TELLING REGGIE THAT!
GOLLEE! I SURE HOPE I DIDN'T INJURE THEM SERIOUSLY!
SIGH-- SAME OLD REGGIE!
SOME THINGS ARE JUST UN-CHANGEABLE!
HAGH! EVEN AS THE EGG BREAKS AT EVENTIDE, SO DO THE TADPOLES CRY FOR THE SOUNDS OF MERCY!
TSK! THEY'RE WAY OUT THERE! ALL OF THEM!
The END

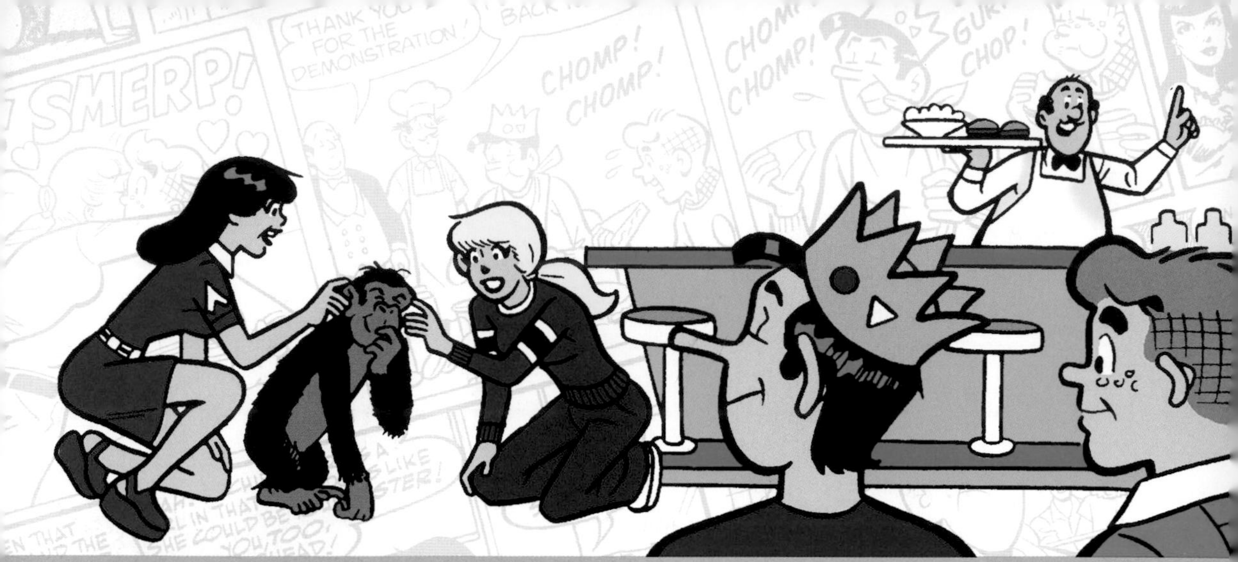
THANK YOU FOR THE DEMONSTRATION!
CHOMP! CHOMP!
CHOMP! CHOMP!

MINDING A STAR
ARCHIE #264, 1977
BY FRANK DOYLE, DAN DECARLO, JIM DECARLO & BARRY GROSSMAN

Much like the classic combination of peanut butter and banana, gorillas and comics are forever a perfect pair. However, Archie isn't exactly battling an agitated ape in the jungle. Zappy the Gorilla is a famous TV animal with enough adoring fans to make Reggie jealous! The gang is tasked with watching over the star simian, but this King of Kongs is smarter than they realize. He's bigger, faster and stronger too.

—Jonathan Betancourt
Director of Book Sales & Operations,
Archie Comics

COSTUME CAPER
REGGIE AND ME #104, 1978
BY FRANK DOYLE, DAN DECARLO JR., JIM DECARLO, BILL YOSHIDA, & BARRY GROSSMAN

I've been a *Star Wars* and Archie fan for a long time and it was really neat to see a *Star Wars*-based story. One of my favorite characters in the *Star Wars* universe is Darth Vader and it was cool to see Reggie in the costume. I'm hoping that they get the chance to make some more of this type of story.

—Robert Lisanti
Accounting,
Archie Comics

Archie in "MINDING A STAR"

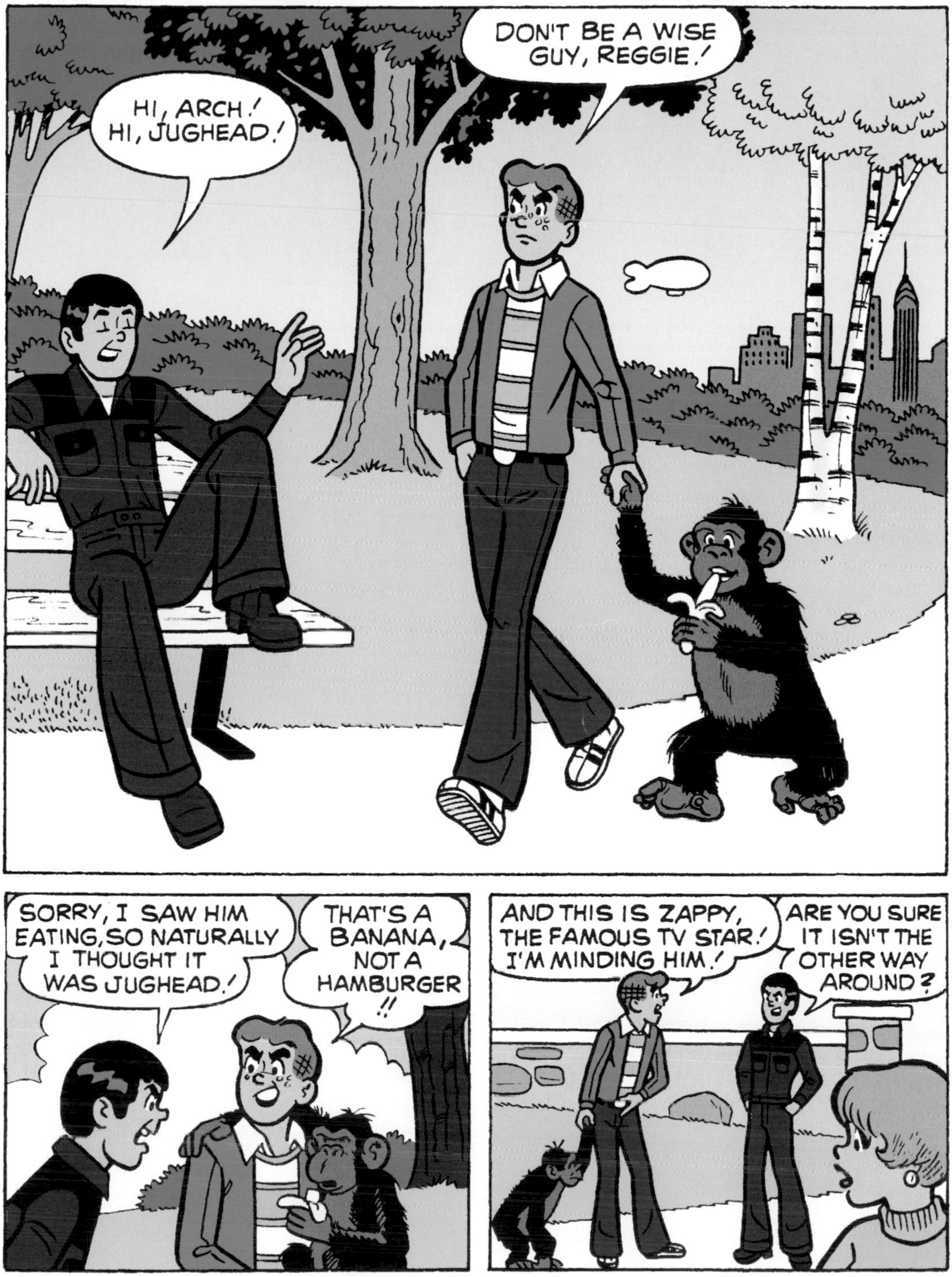
HI, ARCH! HI, JUGHEAD!
DON'T BE A WISE GUY, REGGIE!
SORRY, I SAW HIM EATING, SO NATURALLY I THOUGHT IT WAS JUGHEAD!
THAT'S A BANANA, NOT A HAMBURGER!!
AND THIS IS ZAPPY, THE FAMOUS TV STAR! I'M MINDING HIM!
ARE YOU SURE IT ISN'T THE OTHER WAY AROUND?

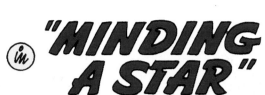

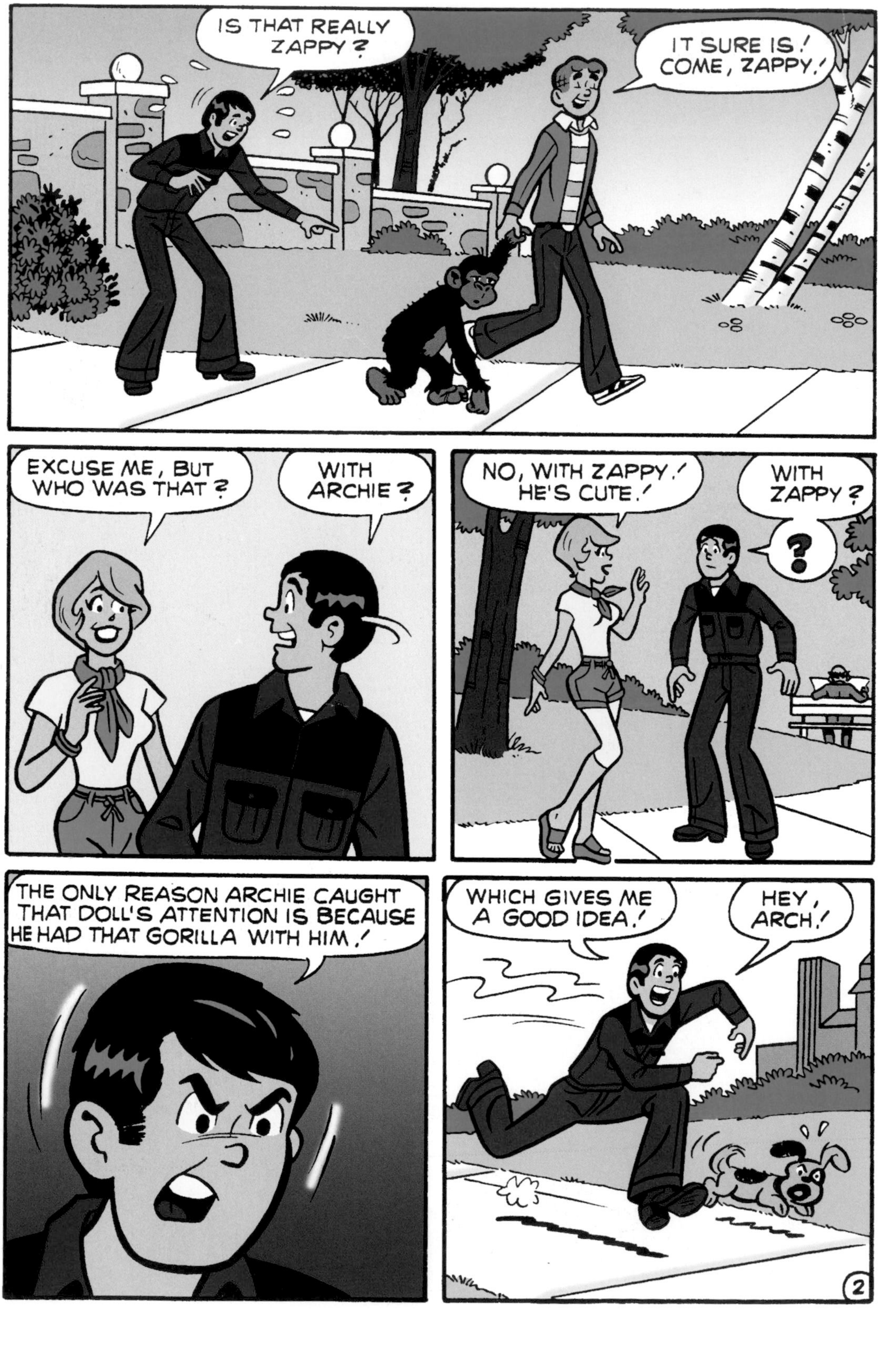
IS THAT REALLY ZAPPY ?
IT SURE IS ! COME, ZAPPY !
EXCUSE ME, BUT WHO WAS THAT ?
WITH ARCHIE ?
NO, WITH ZAPPY ! HE'S CUTE !
WITH ZAPPY ?
?
THE ONLY REASON ARCHIE CAUGHT THAT DOLL'S ATTENTION IS BECAUSE HE HAD THAT GORILLA WITH HIM !
WHICH GIVES ME A GOOD IDEA !
HEY, ARCH !
2

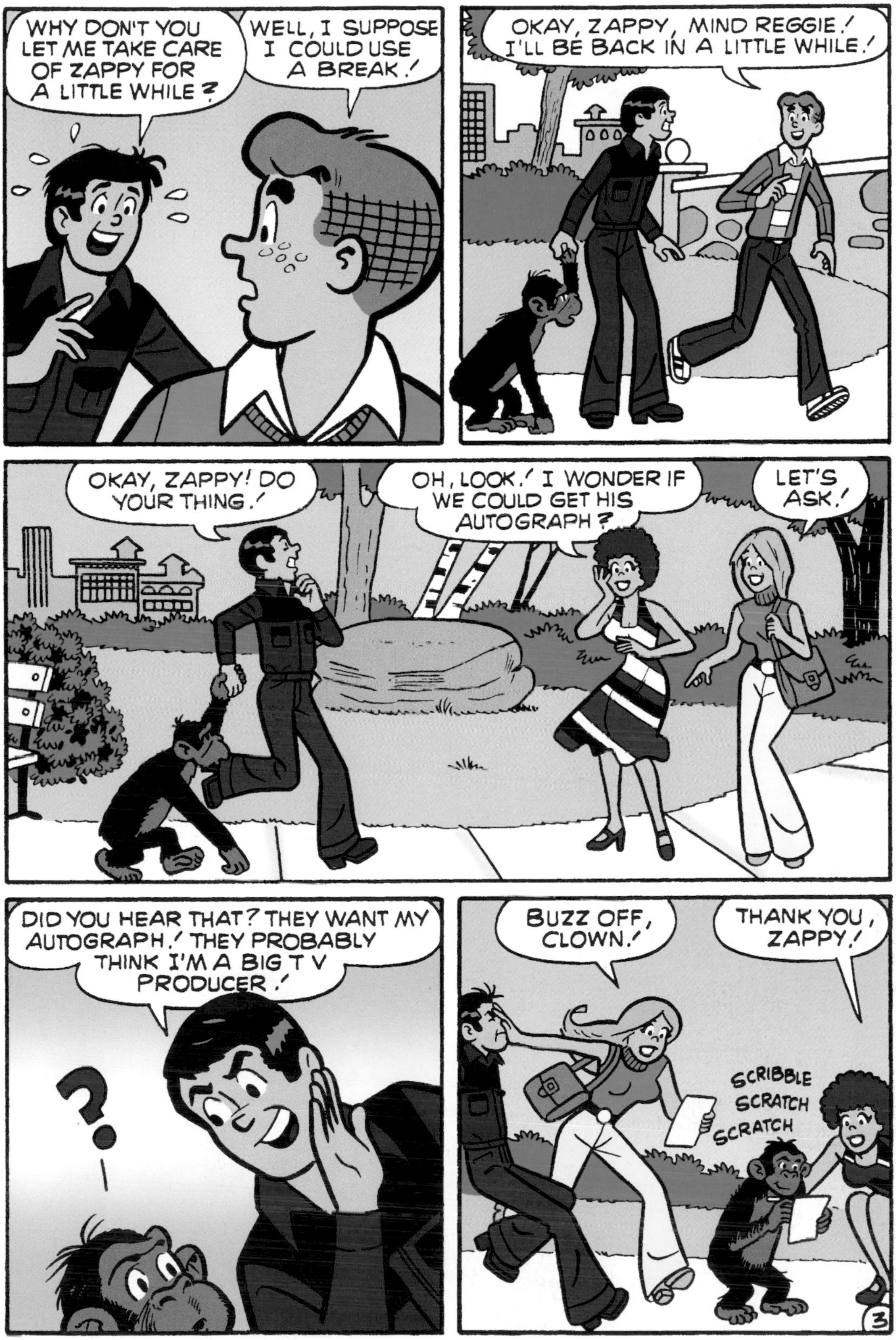
WHY DON'T YOU LET ME TAKE CARE OF ZAPPY FOR A LITTLE WHILE?
WELL, I SUPPOSE I COULD USE A BREAK!
OKAY, ZAPPY, MIND REGGIE! I'LL BE BACK IN A LITTLE WHILE!
OKAY, ZAPPY! DO YOUR THING!
OH, LOOK! I WONDER IF WE COULD GET HIS AUTOGRAPH?
LET'S ASK!
DID YOU HEAR THAT? THEY WANT MY AUTOGRAPH! THEY PROBABLY THINK I'M A BIG T V PRODUCER!
BUZZ OFF, CLOWN!
THANK YOU, ZAPPY!
SCRIBBLE
SCRATCH
SCRATCH
3

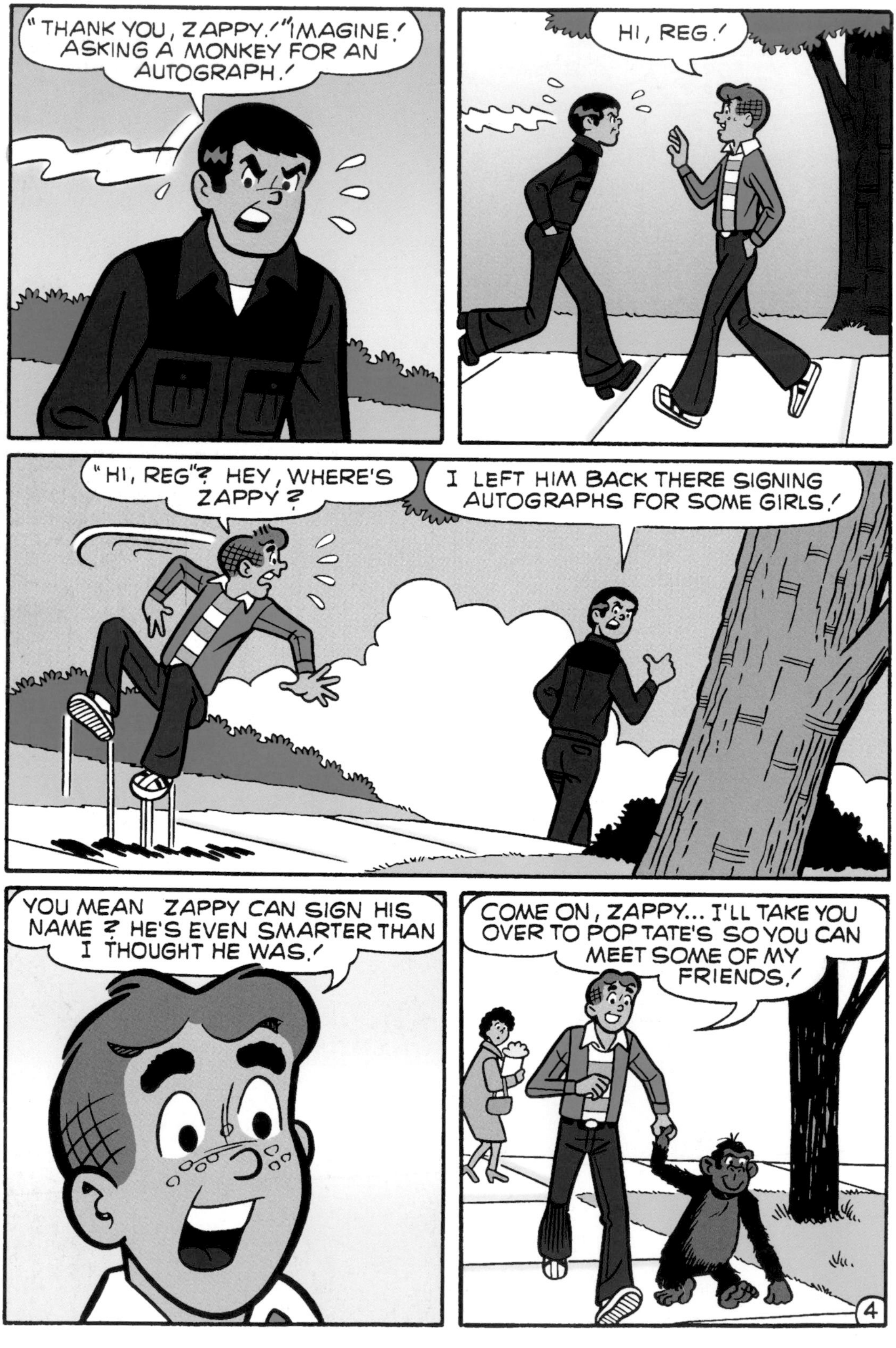
"THANK YOU, ZAPPY!" "IMAGINE! ASKING A MONKEY FOR AN AUTOGRAPH!"
HI, REG!
"HI, REG"? HEY, WHERE'S ZAPPY?
I LEFT HIM BACK THERE SIGNING AUTOGRAPHS FOR SOME GIRLS!
YOU MEAN ZAPPY CAN SIGN HIS NAME? HE'S EVEN SMARTER THAN I THOUGHT HE WAS!
COME ON, ZAPPY... I'LL TAKE YOU OVER TO POP TATE'S SO YOU CAN MEET SOME OF MY FRIENDS!
4

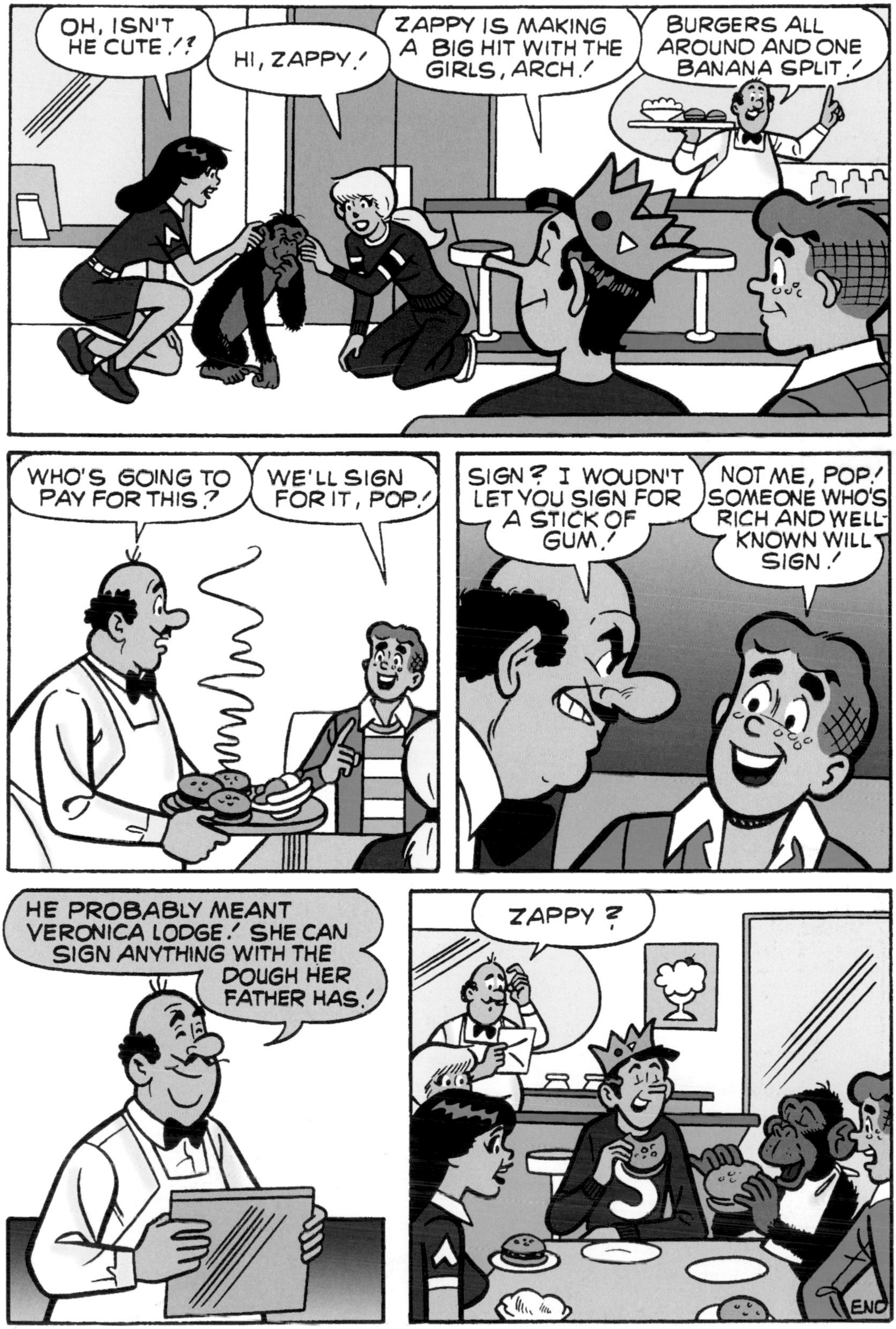
OH, ISN'T HE CUTE!?
HI, ZAPPY!
ZAPPY IS MAKING A BIG HIT WITH THE GIRLS, ARCH!
BURGERS ALL AROUND AND ONE BANANA SPLIT!
WHO'S GOING TO PAY FOR THIS?
WE'LL SIGN FOR IT, POP!
SIGN? I WOUDN'T LET YOU SIGN FOR A STICK OF GUM!
NOT ME, POP! SOMEONE WHO'S RICH AND WELL-KNOWN WILL SIGN!
HE PROBABLY MEANT VERONICA LODGE! SHE CAN SIGN ANYTHING WITH THE DOUGH HER FATHER HAS!
ZAPPY?
END

Reggie and Me in "COSTUME CAPER"

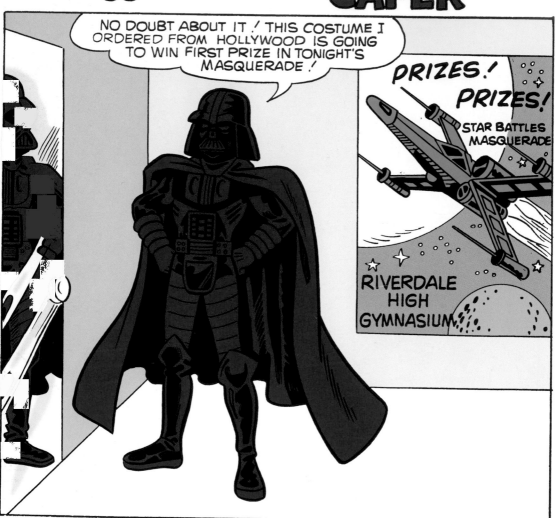

NO DOUBT ABOUT IT! THIS COSTUME I ORDERED FROM HOLLYWOOD IS GOING TO WIN FIRST PRIZE IN TONIGHT'S MASQUERADE!

PRIZES! PRIZES! STAR BATTLES MASQUERADE

RIVERDALE HIGH GYMNASIUM

---BUT I STILL BETTER CHECK OUT THE COMPETITION!

JUST AS I THOUGHT! NO ONE EVEN COMES CLOSE TO MY COSTUME!

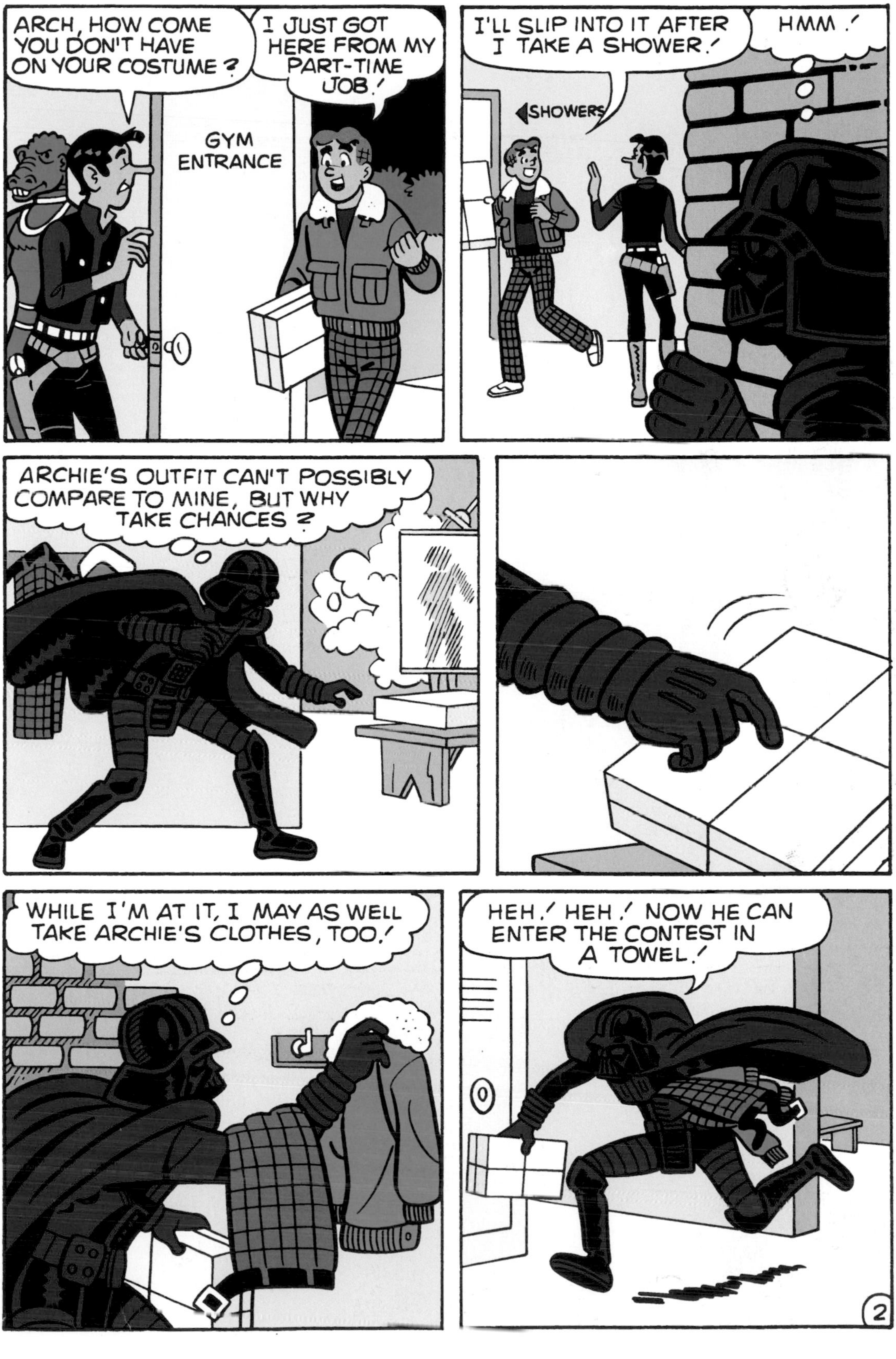
ARCH, HOW COME YOU DON'T HAVE ON YOUR COSTUME ?
I JUST GOT HERE FROM MY PART-TIME JOB!
GYM ENTRANCE
I'LL SLIP INTO IT AFTER I TAKE A SHOWER!
SHOWERS
HMM!
ARCHIE'S OUTFIT CAN'T POSSIBLY COMPARE TO MINE, BUT WHY TAKE CHANCES ?
WHILE I'M AT IT, I MAY AS WELL TAKE ARCHIE'S CLOTHES, TOO!
HEH! HEH! NOW HE CAN ENTER THE CONTEST IN A TOWEL!
2

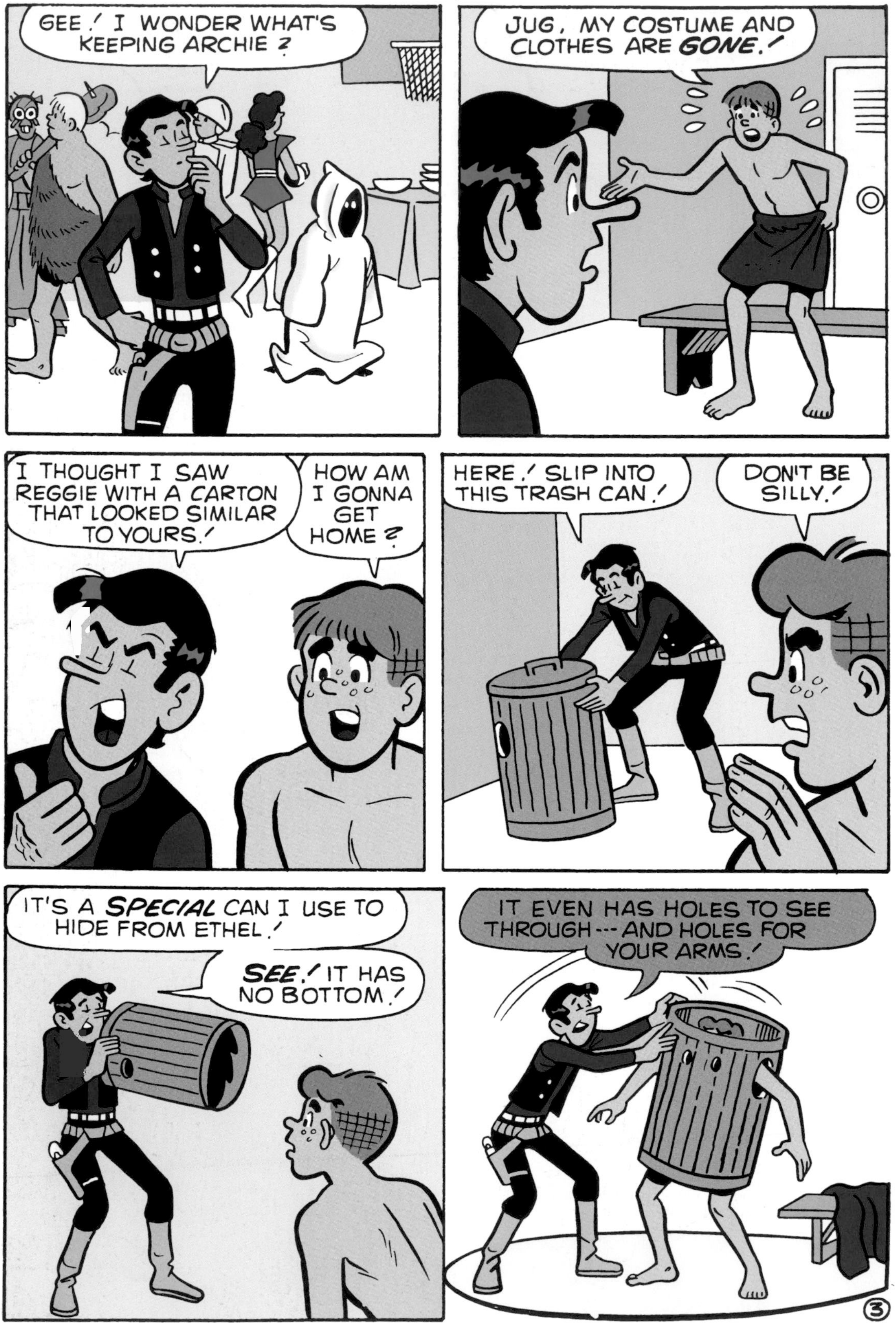
GEE! I WONDER WHAT'S KEEPING ARCHIE?
JUG, MY COSTUME AND CLOTHES ARE GONE!
I THOUGHT I SAW REGGIE WITH A CARTON THAT LOOKED SIMILAR TO YOURS!
HOW AM I GONNA GET HOME?
HERE! SLIP INTO THIS TRASH CAN!
DON'T BE SILLY!
IT'S A SPECIAL CAN I USE TO HIDE FROM ETHEL!
SEE! IT HAS NO BOTTOM!
IT EVEN HAS HOLES TO SEE THROUGH --- AND HOLES FOR YOUR ARMS!
3

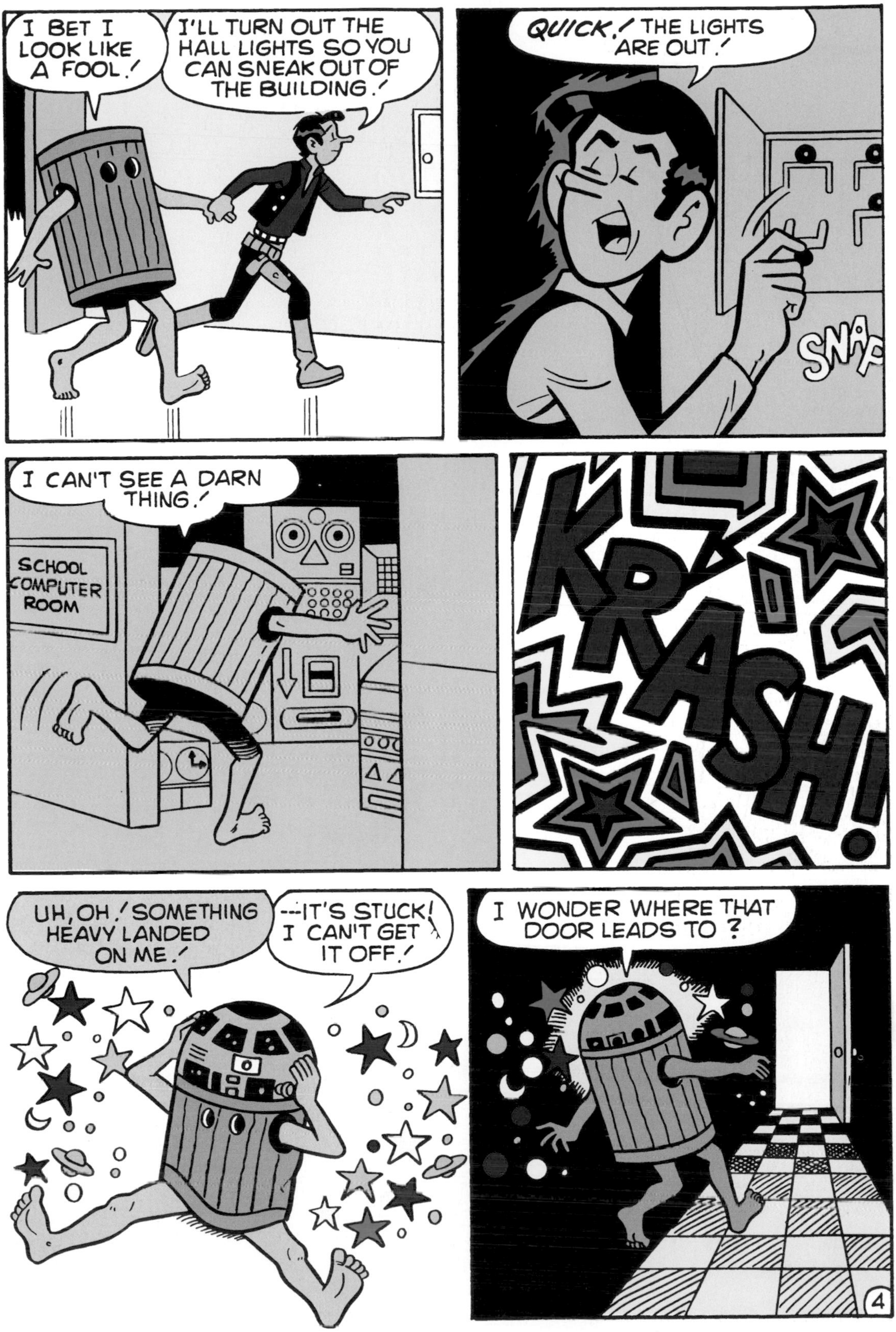
I BET I LOOK LIKE A FOOL!
I'LL TURN OUT THE HALL LIGHTS SO YOU CAN SNEAK OUT OF THE BUILDING!
QUICK! THE LIGHTS ARE OUT!
SNAP
I CAN'T SEE A DARN THING!
SCHOOL COMPUTER ROOM
KRASH!
UH, OH! SOMETHING HEAVY LANDED ON ME!
--IT'S STUCK! I CAN'T GET IT OFF!
I WONDER WHERE THAT DOOR LEADS TO?
4

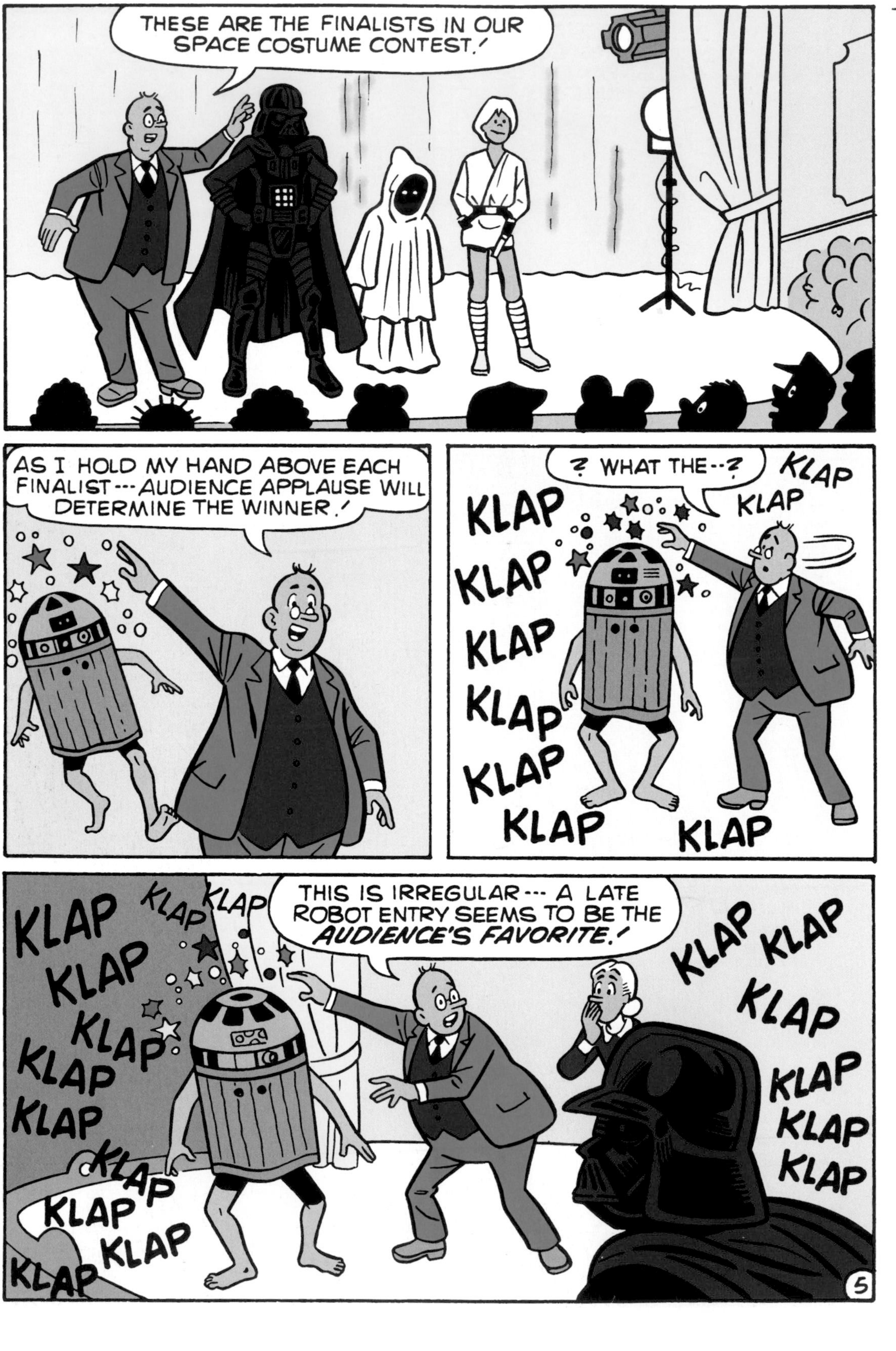
THESE ARE THE FINALISTS IN OUR SPACE COSTUME CONTEST.!
AS I HOLD MY HAND ABOVE EACH FINALIST --- AUDIENCE APPLAUSE WILL DETERMINE THE WINNER.!
? WHAT THE--?
KLAP KLAP KLAP KLAP KLAP KLAP KLAP KLAP KLAP
THIS IS IRREGULAR --- A LATE ROBOT ENTRY SEEMS TO BE THE *AUDIENCE'S FAVORITE*.!
KLAP KLAP KLAP KLAP KLAP KLAP KLAP KLAP KLAP KLAP KLAP KLAP KLAP KLAP KLAP KLAP KLAP KLAP
5

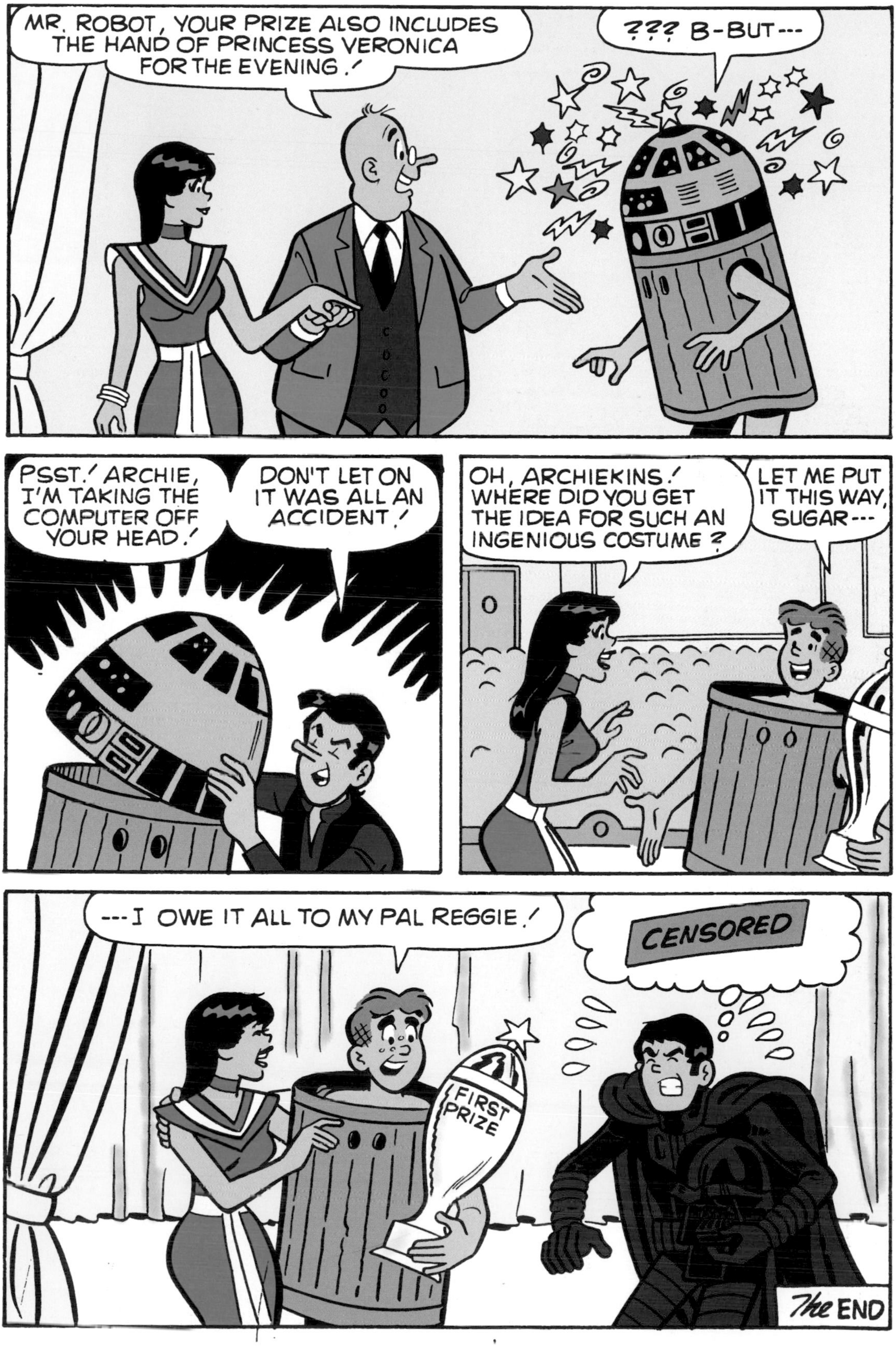
MR. ROBOT, YOUR PRIZE ALSO INCLUDES THE HAND OF PRINCESS VERONICA FOR THE EVENING!
??? B-BUT---
PSST! ARCHIE, I'M TAKING THE COMPUTER OFF YOUR HEAD!
DON'T LET ON IT WAS ALL AN ACCIDENT!
OH, ARCHIEKINS! WHERE DID YOU GET THE IDEA FOR SUCH AN INGENIOUS COSTUME?
LET ME PUT IT THIS WAY, SUGAR---
---I OWE IT ALL TO MY PAL REGGIE!
CENSORED
FIRST PRIZE
The END

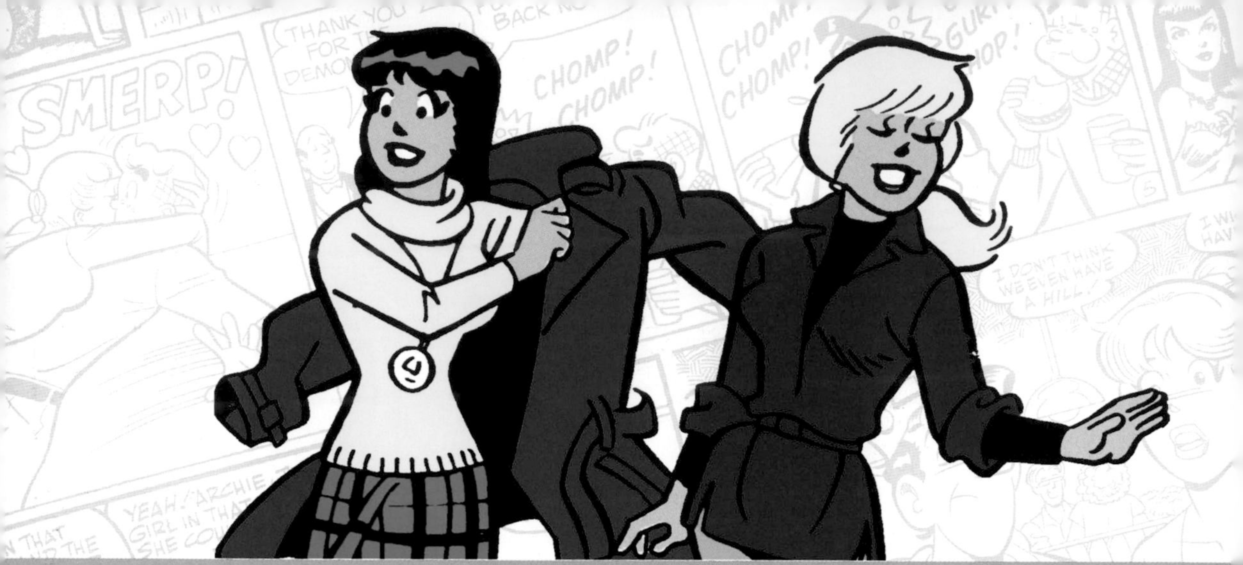
SMERP!
CHOMP! CHOMP!
CHOMP! CHOMP!
I DON'T THINK WE EVEN HAVE A HILL!

MELVIN'S ANGELS

BETTY & VERONICA #277, 1979

BY FRANK DOYLE, DAN DECARLO, JIM DECARLO, BILL YOSHIDA & BARRY GROSSMAN

Betty and Veronica play the roles of two glamorous detectives in a story that was undoubtedly influenced by the "Angels in Springtime" episode of *Charlie's Angels,* right down to the matronly, overbearing Ilsa character in the comic being nearly identical to the Zora character in the episode. Not only does Archie pay homage to what was popular at the time, but it also pokes fun at some of the more ridiculous aspects of the decade. *Charlie's Angels* was often criticized as having no substance but instead garnering ratings by flaunting the bodies of the often scantily-clad lead actresses. This story turns that concept on its ear by instead having the girls don unflattering sweat suits for a majority of the story. This is an example of my favorite kind of Archie story—it's not only humorous, but also gives an introspective view of society as a whole.

—Jamie Lee Rotante
Writer/Editor,
Archie Comics

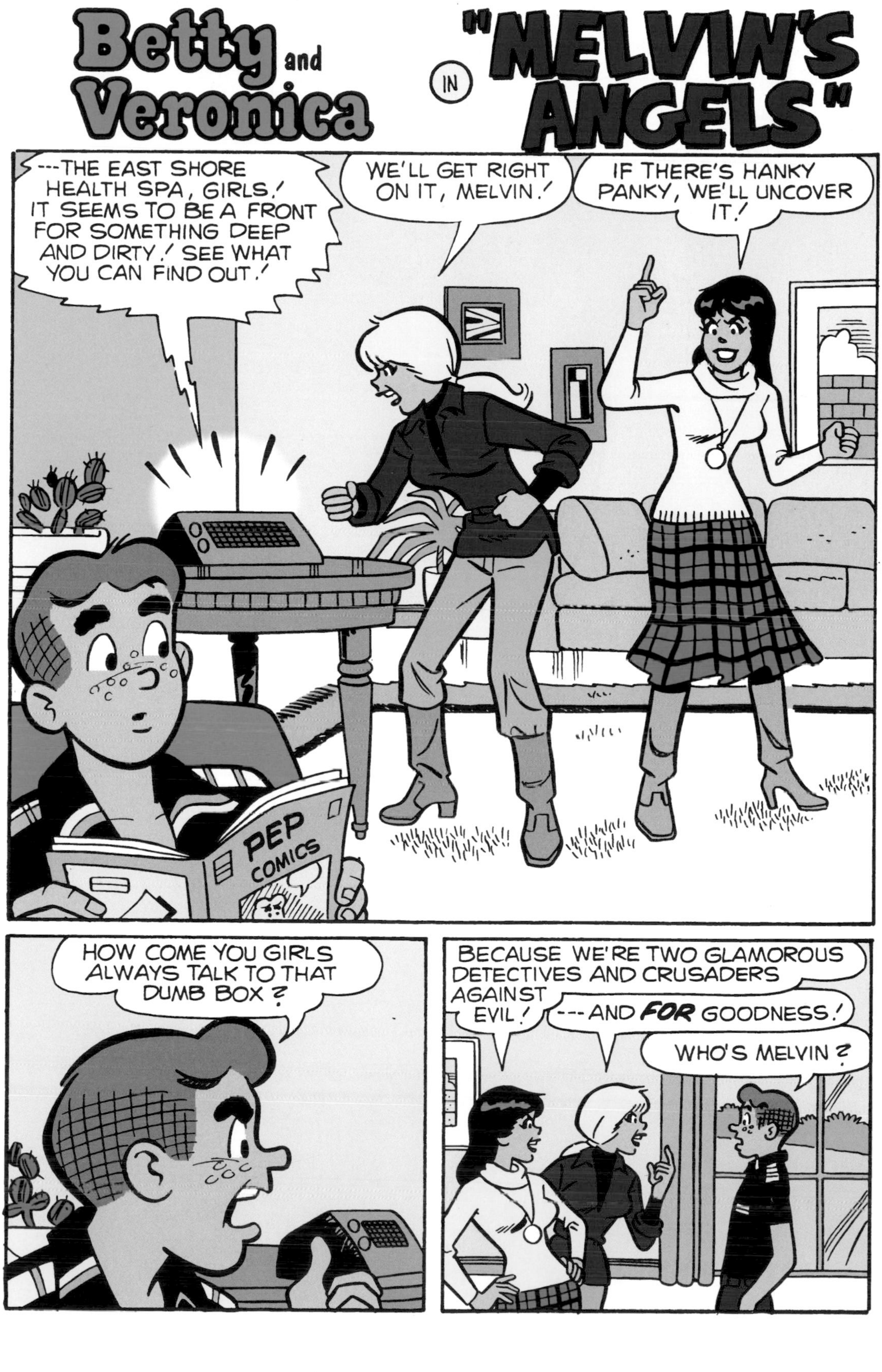
Betty and Veronica
IN
"MELVIN'S ANGELS"
---THE EAST SHORE HEALTH SPA, GIRLS! IT SEEMS TO BE A FRONT FOR SOMETHING DEEP AND DIRTY! SEE WHAT YOU CAN FIND OUT!
WE'LL GET RIGHT ON IT, MELVIN!
IF THERE'S HANKY PANKY, WE'LL UNCOVER IT!
PEP COMICS
HOW COME YOU GIRLS ALWAYS TALK TO THAT DUMB BOX?
BECAUSE WE'RE TWO GLAMOROUS DETECTIVES AND CRUSADERS AGAINST EVIL!
---AND FOR GOODNESS!
WHO'S MELVIN?

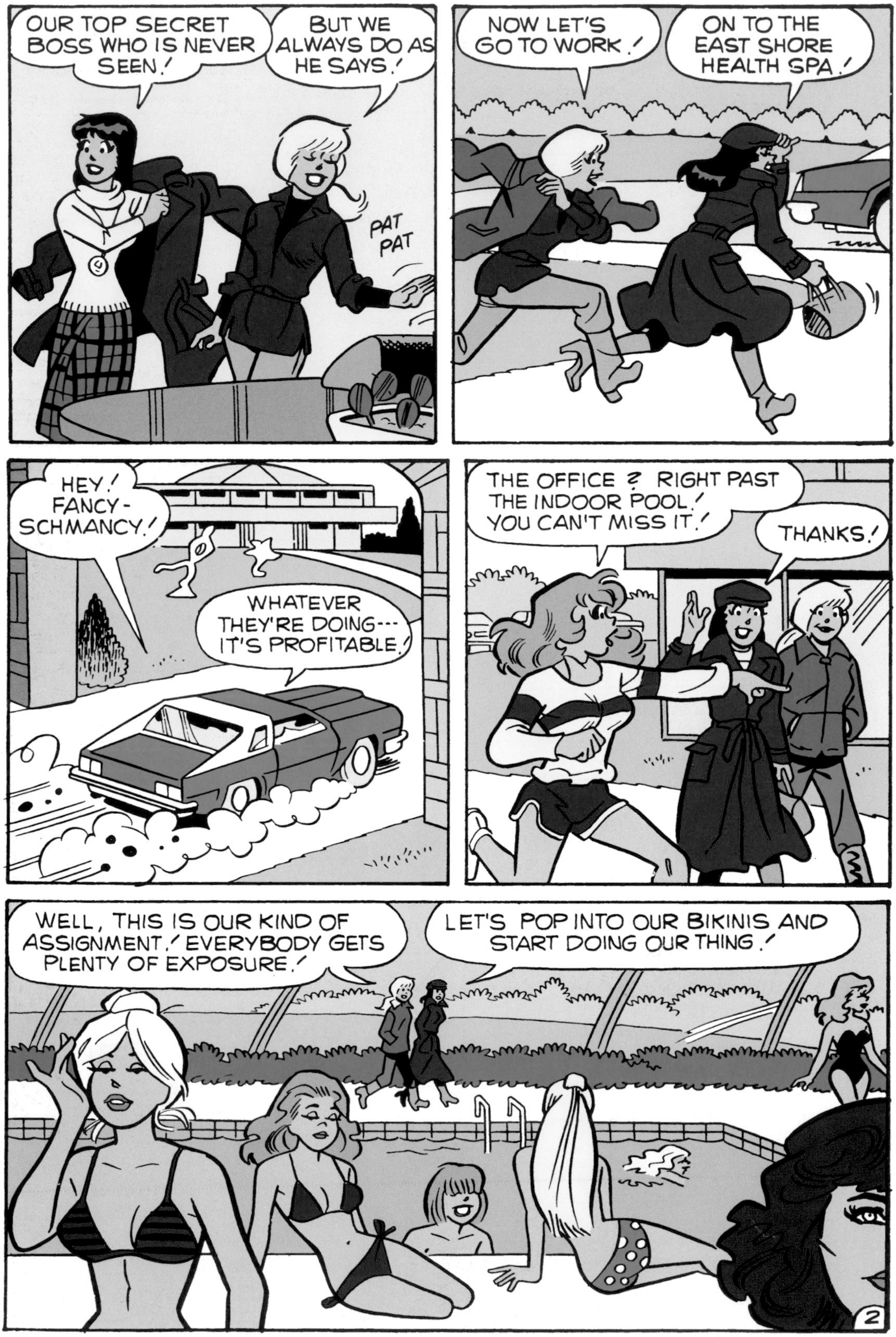
OUR TOP SECRET BOSS WHO IS NEVER SEEN!
BUT WE ALWAYS DO AS HE SAYS!
PAT PAT
NOW LET'S GO TO WORK!
ON TO THE EAST SHORE HEALTH SPA!
HEY! FANCY-SCHMANCY!
WHATEVER THEY'RE DOING--- IT'S PROFITABLE!
THE OFFICE? RIGHT PAST THE INDOOR POOL! YOU CAN'T MISS IT!
THANKS!
WELL, THIS IS OUR KIND OF ASSIGNMENT! EVERYBODY GETS PLENTY OF EXPOSURE!
LET'S POP INTO OUR BIKINIS AND START DOING OUR THING!
2

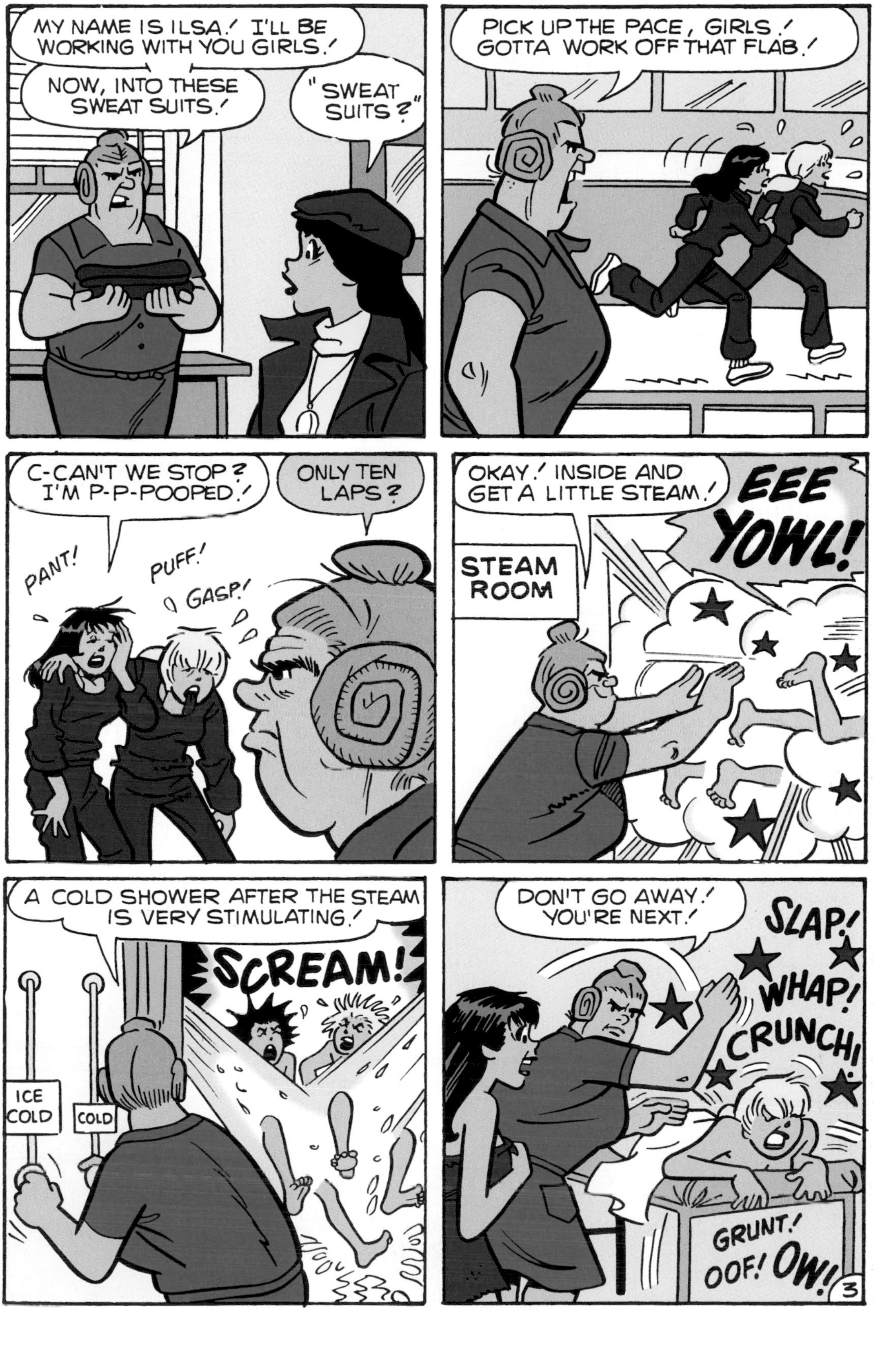

MY NAME IS ILSA! I'LL BE WORKING WITH YOU GIRLS!
NOW, INTO THESE SWEAT SUITS!
"SWEAT SUITS?"
PICK UP THE PACE, GIRLS! GOTTA WORK OFF THAT FLAB!
C-CAN'T WE STOP? I'M P-P-POOPED!
ONLY TEN LAPS?
PANT!
PUFF!
GASP!
OKAY! INSIDE AND GET A LITTLE STEAM!
STEAM ROOM
EEE YOWL!
A COLD SHOWER AFTER THE STEAM IS VERY STIMULATING!
SCREAM!
ICE COLD
COLD
DON'T GO AWAY! YOU'RE NEXT!
SLAP!
WHAP!
CRUNCH!
GRUNT!
OOF! OW!
3

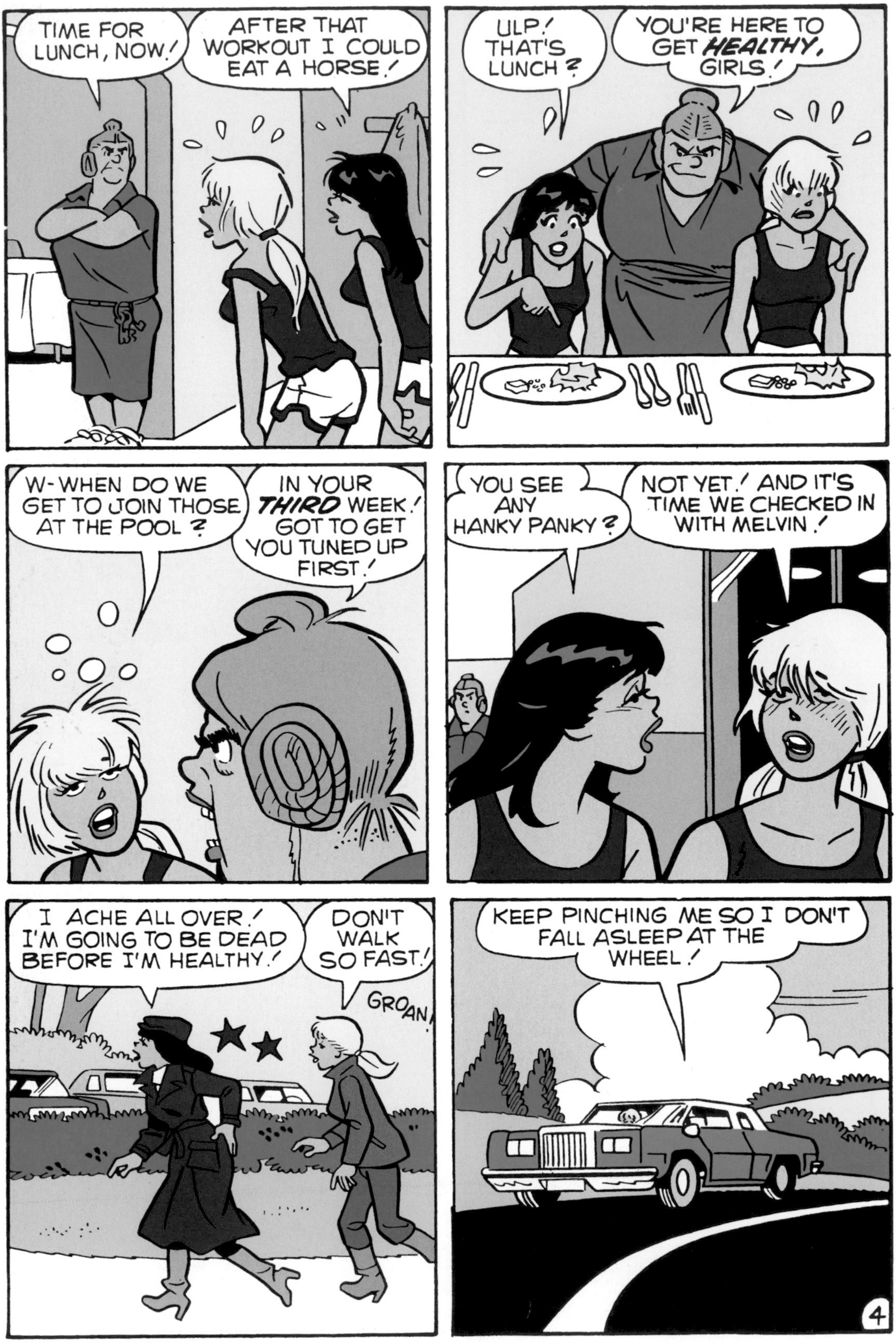
TIME FOR LUNCH, NOW!
AFTER THAT WORKOUT I COULD EAT A HORSE!
ULP! THAT'S LUNCH?
YOU'RE HERE TO GET HEALTHY, GIRLS!
W-WHEN DO WE GET TO JOIN THOSE AT THE POOL?
IN YOUR THIRD WEEK! GOT TO GET YOU TUNED UP FIRST!
YOU SEE ANY HANKY PANKY?
NOT YET! AND IT'S TIME WE CHECKED IN WITH MELVIN!
I ACHE ALL OVER! I'M GOING TO BE DEAD BEFORE I'M HEALTHY!
DON'T WALK SO FAST!
GROAN!
KEEP PINCHING ME SO I DON'T FALL ASLEEP AT THE WHEEL!
4

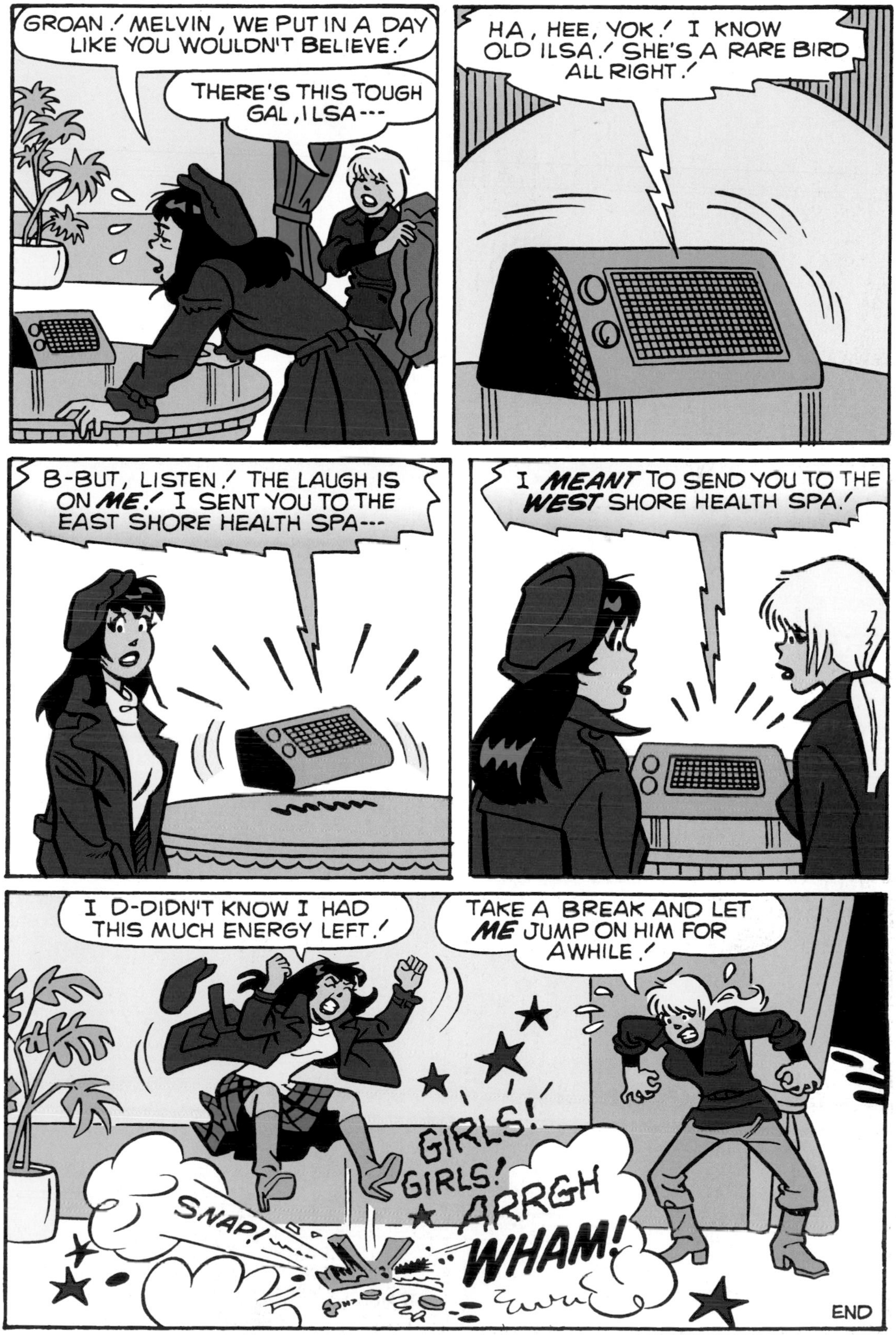
GROAN! MELVIN, WE PUT IN A DAY LIKE YOU WOULDN'T BELIEVE!
THERE'S THIS TOUGH GAL, ILSA---
HA, HEE, YOK! I KNOW OLD ILSA! SHE'S A RARE BIRD ALL RIGHT!
B-BUT, LISTEN! THE LAUGH IS ON ME! I SENT YOU TO THE EAST SHORE HEALTH SPA---
I MEANT TO SEND YOU TO THE WEST SHORE HEALTH SPA!
I D-DIDN'T KNOW I HAD THIS MUCH ENERGY LEFT!
TAKE A BREAK AND LET ME JUMP ON HIM FOR AWHILE!
GIRLS!
GIRLS!
ARRGH
SNAP!
WHAM!
END

The BEST of Archie COMICS

1980s

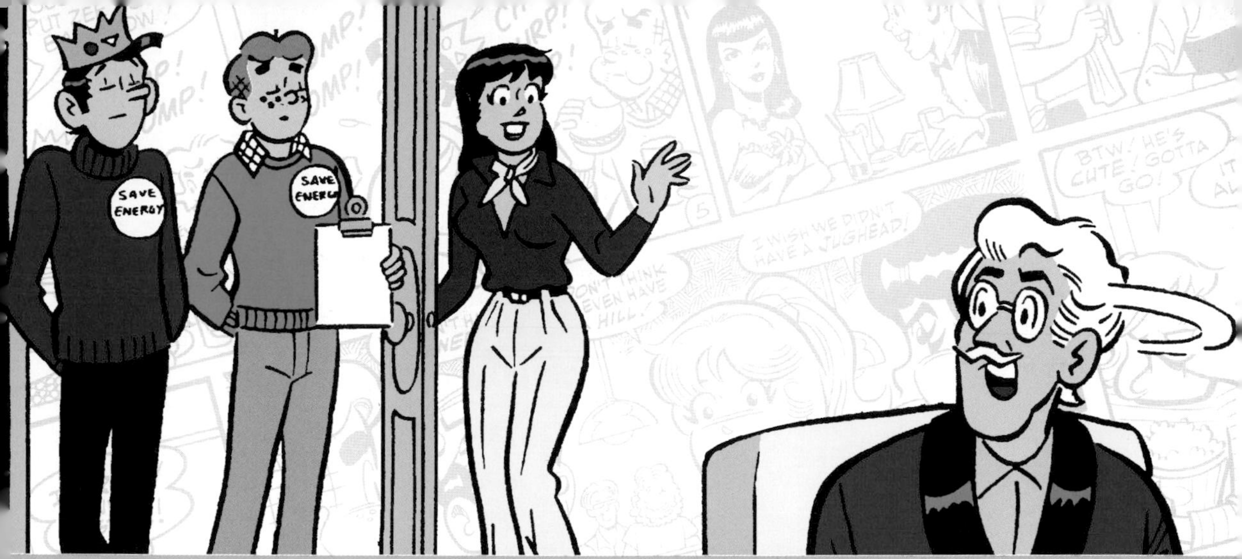
SAVE ENERGY
SAVE ENERGY
I WISH WE DIDN'T HAVE A JUGHEAD!
BTW! HE'S CUTE! GOTTA GO!

VERVE TO CONSERVE
ARCHIE #292, 1980
BY GEORGE GLADIR, DAN DECARLO JR., RUDY LAPICK & BILL YOSHIDA

Okay, maybe I'm known mostly for superhero yarns, but I've always had a warm spot in my heart for Archie, Jughead and the ever-lovely Betty and Veronica. Youthful stories of humor and romance, handled with a light touch, have always been popular and always will be as long as the Archie series is here to entertain us.

—Stan Lee
Creator of Spider-Man

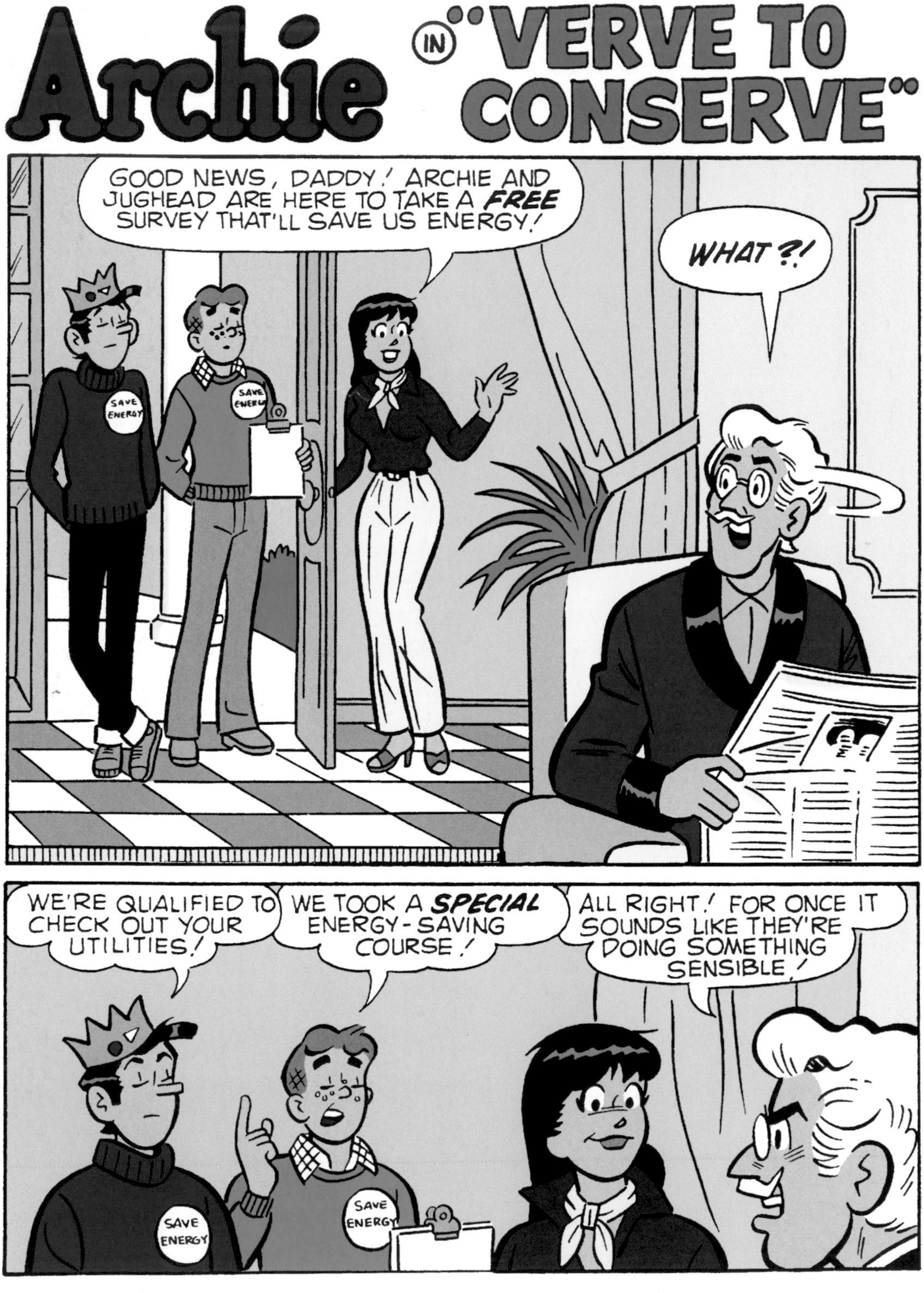
Archie IN "VERVE TO CONSERVE"
GOOD NEWS, DADDY! ARCHIE AND JUGHEAD ARE HERE TO TAKE A FREE SURVEY THAT'LL SAVE US ENERGY!
WHAT?!
SAVE ENERGY
WE'RE QUALIFIED TO CHECK OUT YOUR UTILITIES!
WE TOOK A SPECIAL ENERGY-SAVING COURSE!
ALL RIGHT! FOR ONCE IT SOUNDS LIKE THEY'RE DOING SOMETHING SENSIBLE!
SAVE ENERGY

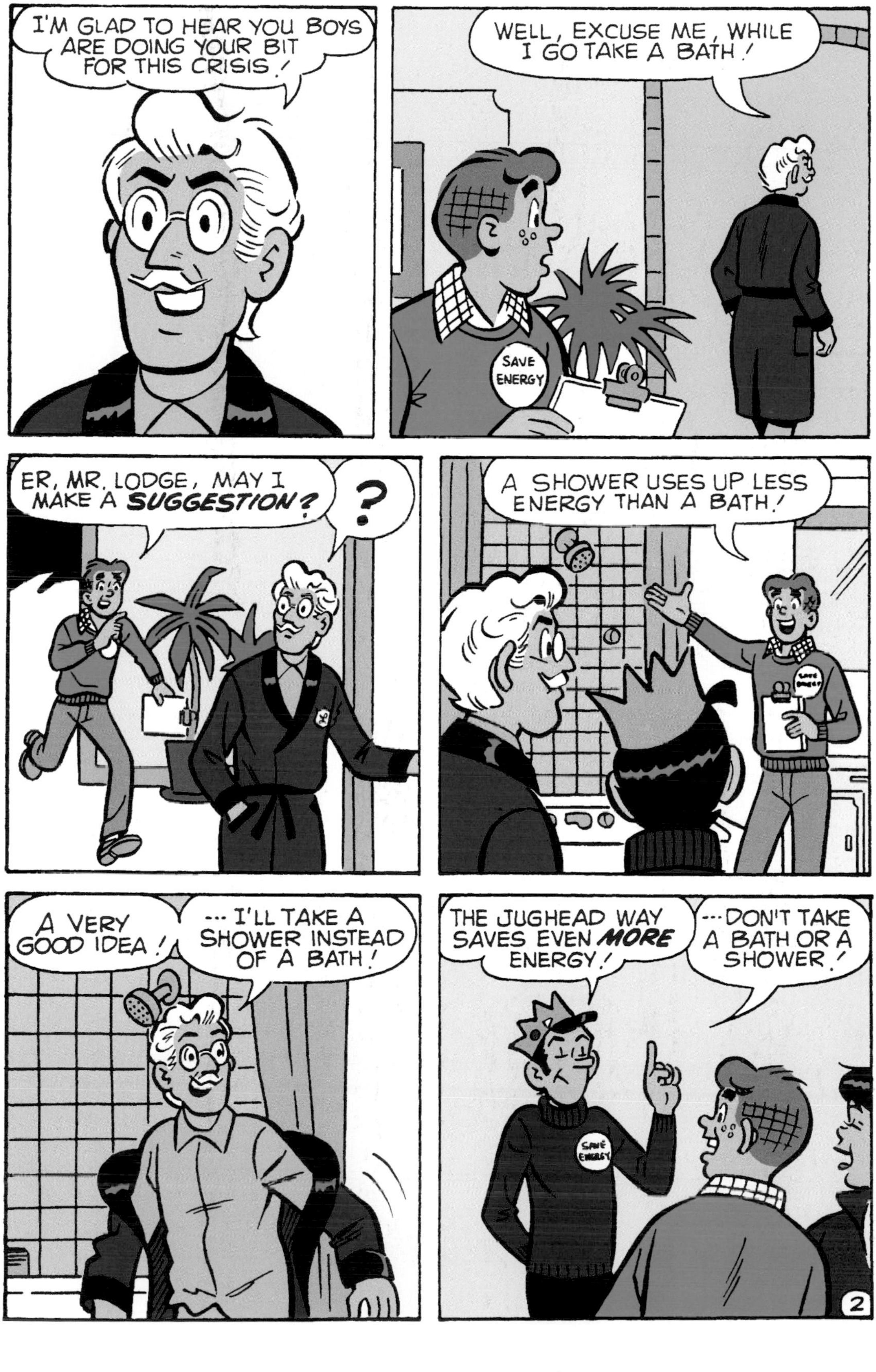
I'M GLAD TO HEAR YOU BOYS ARE DOING YOUR BIT FOR THIS CRISIS!
WELL, EXCUSE ME, WHILE I GO TAKE A BATH!
SAVE ENERGY
ER, MR. LODGE, MAY I MAKE A SUGGESTION?
?
A SHOWER USES UP LESS ENERGY THAN A BATH!
A VERY GOOD IDEA!
--- I'LL TAKE A SHOWER INSTEAD OF A BATH!
THE JUGHEAD WAY SAVES EVEN MORE ENERGY!
---DON'T TAKE A BATH OR A SHOWER!
SAVE ENERGY
2

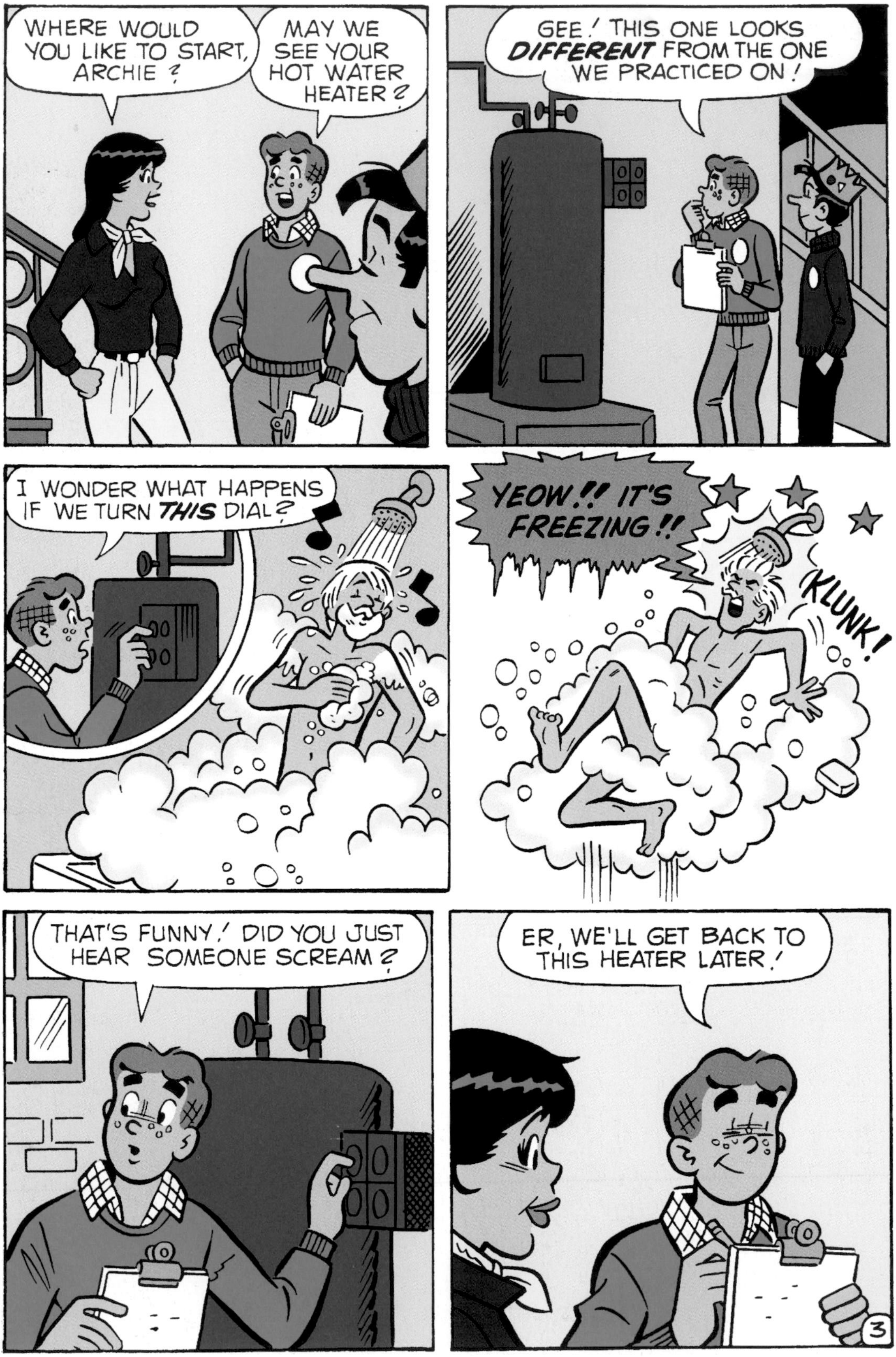
WHERE WOULD YOU LIKE TO START, ARCHIE ?
MAY WE SEE YOUR HOT WATER HEATER ?
GEE! THIS ONE LOOKS DIFFERENT FROM THE ONE WE PRACTICED ON!
I WONDER WHAT HAPPENS IF WE TURN THIS DIAL?
YEOW!! IT'S FREEZING!!
KLUNK!
THAT'S FUNNY! DID YOU JUST HEAR SOMEONE SCREAM?
ER, WE'LL GET BACK TO THIS HEATER LATER!
3

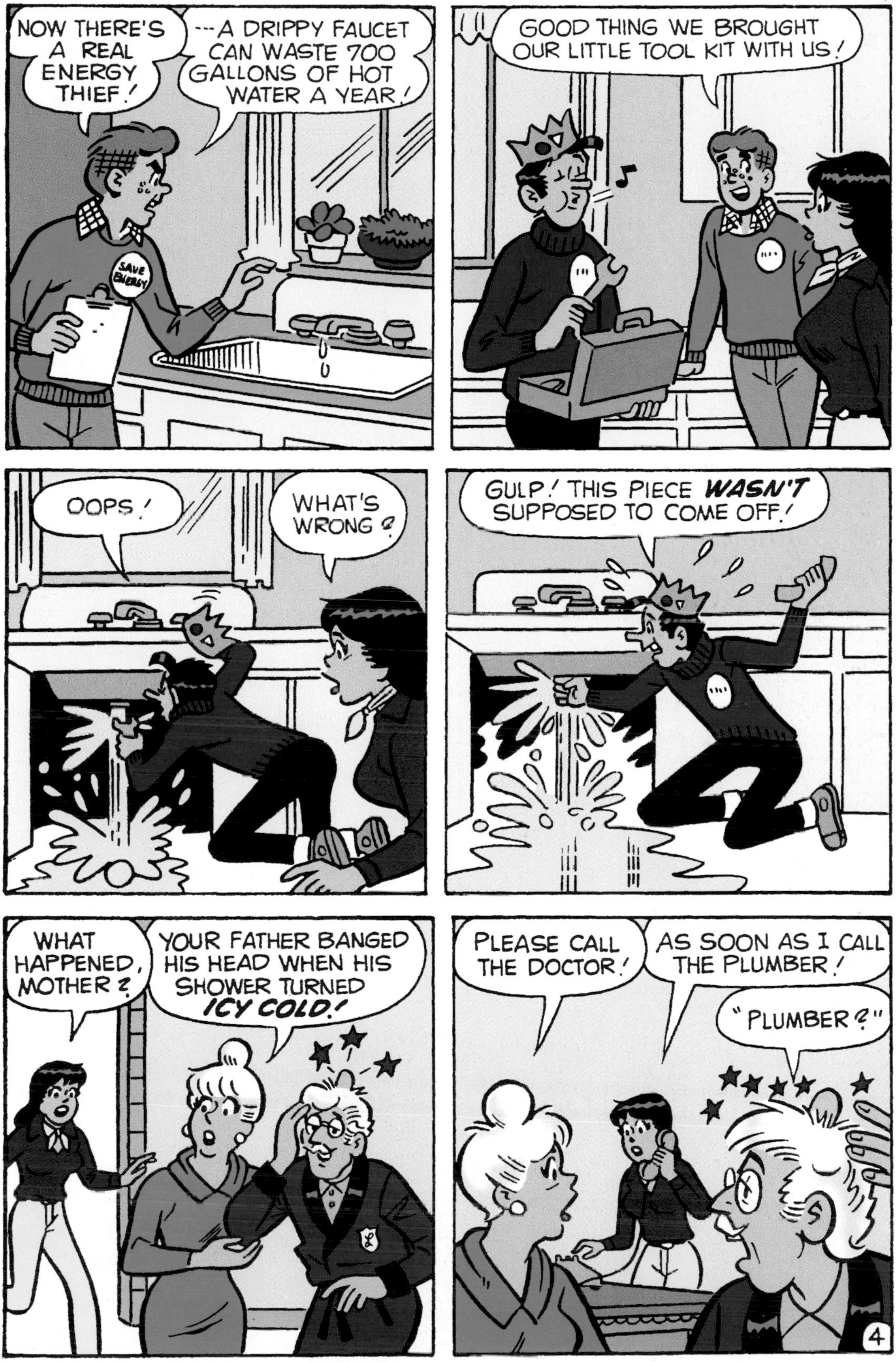
NOW THERE'S A REAL ENERGY THIEF!
---A DRIPPY FAUCET CAN WASTE 700 GALLONS OF HOT WATER A YEAR!
SAVE ENERGY
GOOD THING WE BROUGHT OUR LITTLE TOOL KIT WITH US!
OOPS!
WHAT'S WRONG?
GULP! THIS PIECE **WASN'T** SUPPOSED TO COME OFF!
WHAT HAPPENED, MOTHER?
YOUR FATHER BANGED HIS HEAD WHEN HIS SHOWER TURNED ***ICY COLD!***
PLEASE CALL THE DOCTOR!
AS SOON AS I CALL THE PLUMBER!
"PLUMBER?"
4

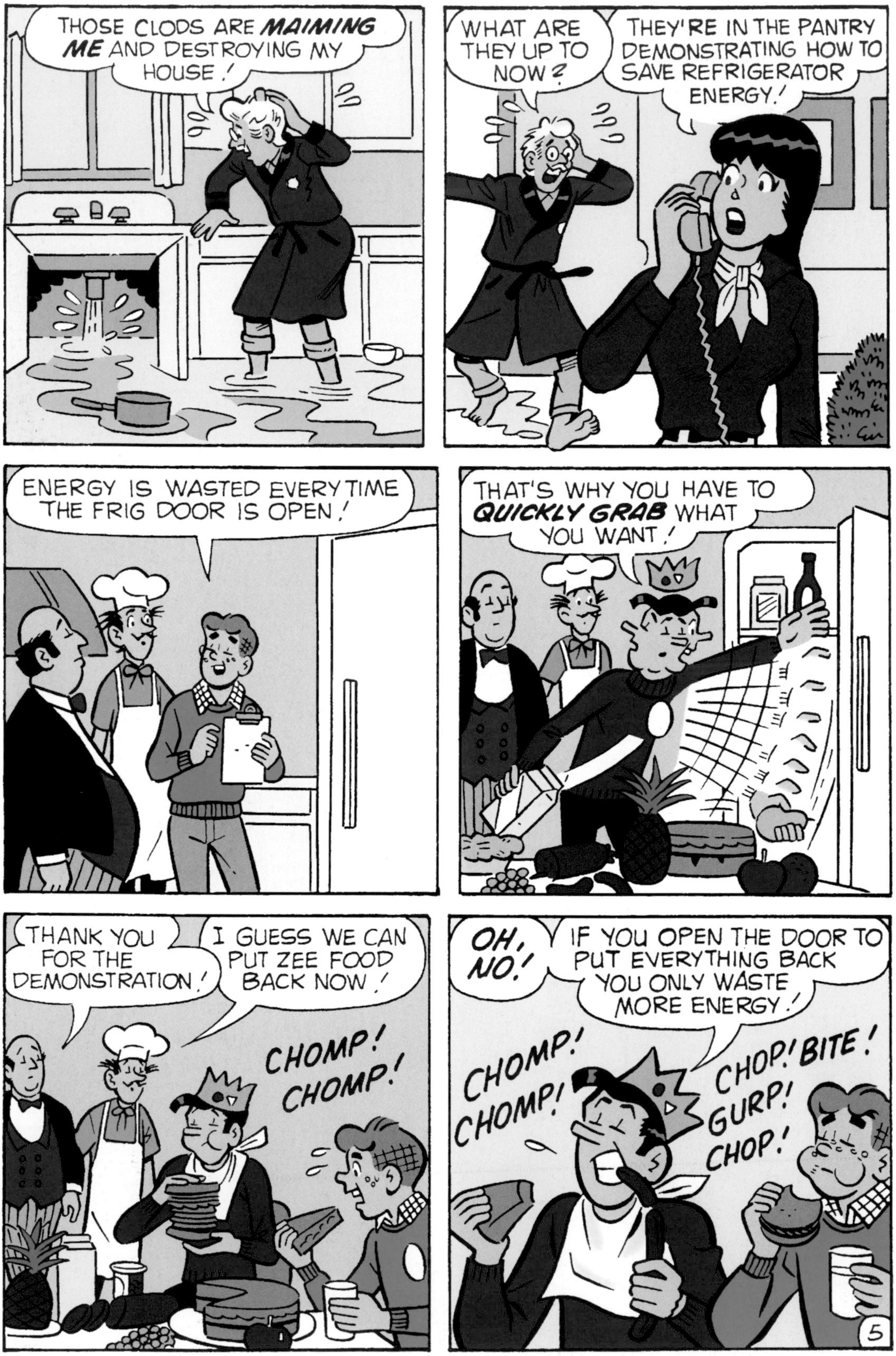
THOSE CLODS ARE MAIMING ME AND DESTROYING MY HOUSE!
WHAT ARE THEY UP TO NOW?
THEY'RE IN THE PANTRY DEMONSTRATING HOW TO SAVE REFRIGERATOR ENERGY!
ENERGY IS WASTED EVERYTIME THE FRIG DOOR IS OPEN!
THAT'S WHY YOU HAVE TO QUICKLY GRAB WHAT YOU WANT!
THANK YOU FOR THE DEMONSTRATION!
I GUESS WE CAN PUT ZEE FOOD BACK NOW!
CHOMP! CHOMP!
OH, NO!
IF YOU OPEN THE DOOR TO PUT EVERYTHING BACK YOU ONLY WASTE MORE ENERGY!
CHOMP! CHOMP!
CHOP! BITE! GURP! CHOP!
5

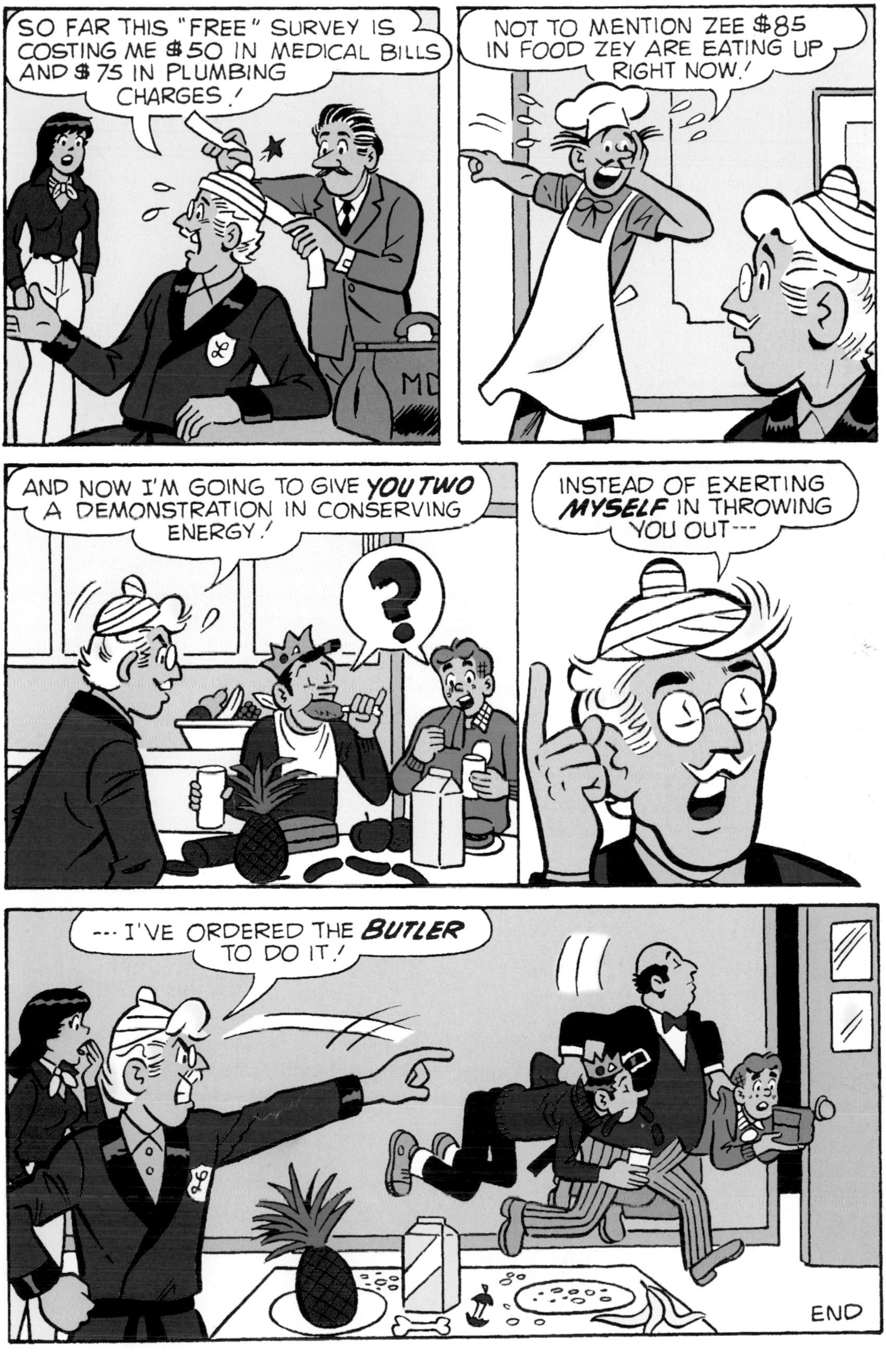
SO FAR THIS "FREE" SURVEY IS COSTING ME $50 IN MEDICAL BILLS AND $75 IN PLUMBING CHARGES!
MD
NOT TO MENTION ZEE $85 IN FOOD ZEY ARE EATING UP RIGHT NOW!
AND NOW I'M GOING TO GIVE YOU TWO A DEMONSTRATION IN CONSERVING ENERGY!
?
INSTEAD OF EXERTING MYSELF IN THROWING YOU OUT---
--- I'VE ORDERED THE BUTLER TO DO IT!
END

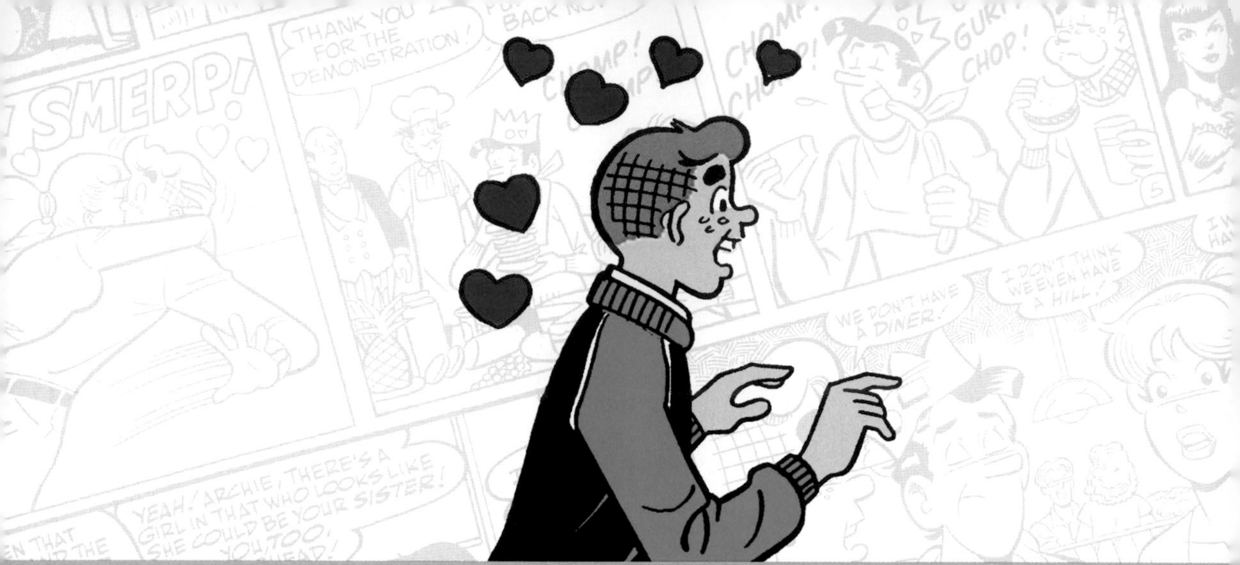
SMERP!
THANK YOU FOR THE DEMONSTRATION!
WE DON'T HAVE A DINER!
I DON'T THINK WE EVEN HAVE A HILL!

SATURDAY'S CHILD

ARCHIE #331, 1984

BY FRANK DOYLE, DAN DECARLO JR. & JIM DECARLO

Weekends are of utmost importance to most American teens, where kids aren't bound by the shackles of homework and the ever-dreaded detention! Archie plans to make the most of his weekend, but ends up realizing that sometimes work is just plain unavoidable—just wait until Archie becomes an adult, he'll wish he really cherished those Saturdays of his youth! What is really great about this story beyond the generational aspects of the story page, is the generational aspects behind the story. This story is by the great Frank Doyle, one of the best and longest tenured writers in Archie history. He really made a career working with the equally great artist Dan DeCarlo. Here, however the art is handled by the sons of DeCarlo; Dan Jr. pencilling and Jimmy inking. You can see so much of their father's way of doing things work, but so much of their own voice as well.

—Mike Pellerito
Co-President,
Archie Comics

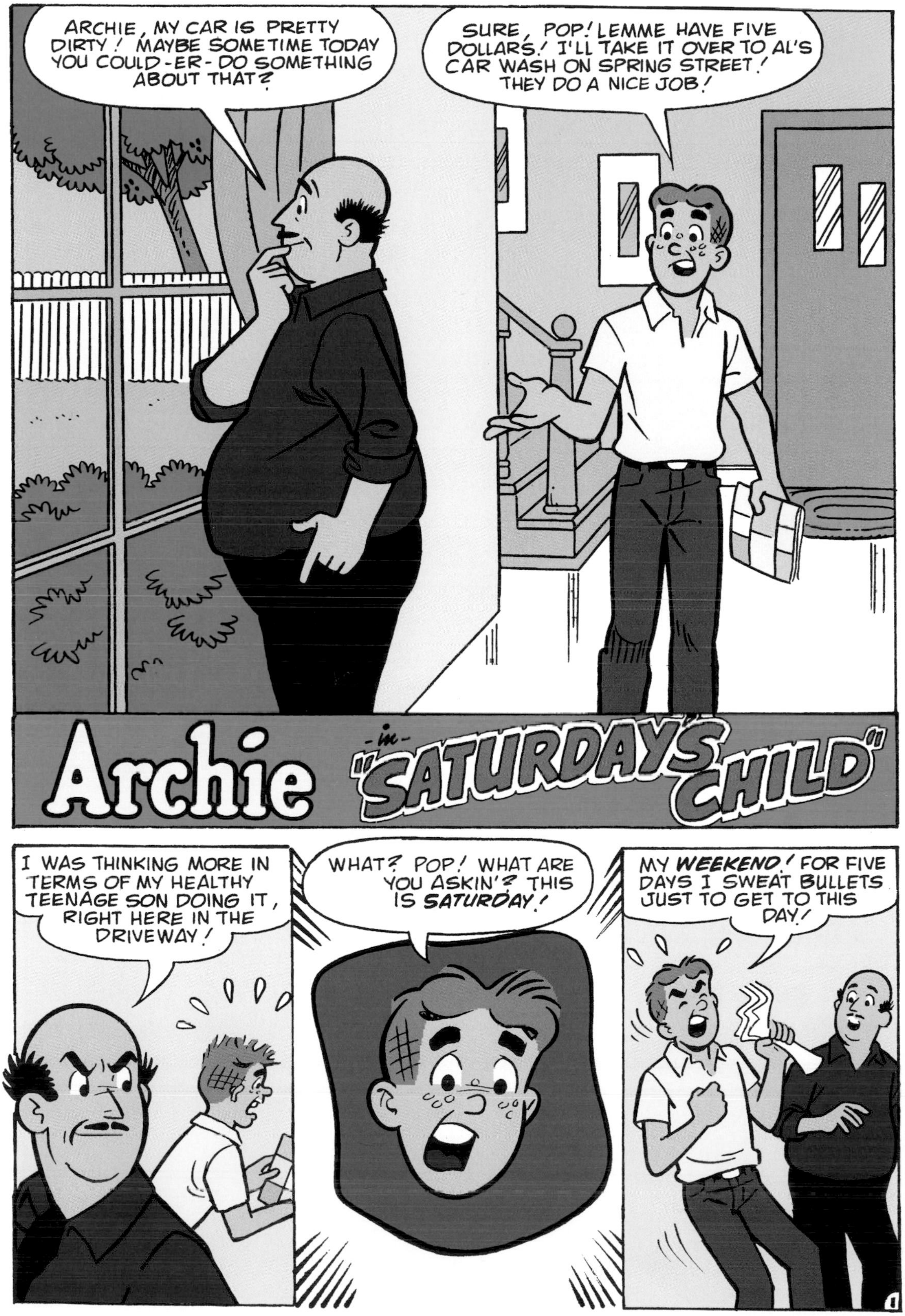
ARCHIE, MY CAR IS PRETTY DIRTY! MAYBE SOMETIME TODAY YOU COULD-ER-DO SOMETHING ABOUT THAT?
SURE, POP! LEMME HAVE FIVE DOLLARS! I'LL TAKE IT OVER TO AL'S CAR WASH ON SPRING STREET! THEY DO A NICE JOB!
Archie -in- "SATURDAY'S CHILD"
I WAS THINKING MORE IN TERMS OF MY HEALTHY TEENAGE SON DOING IT, RIGHT HERE IN THE DRIVEWAY!
WHAT? POP! WHAT ARE YOU ASKIN'? THIS IS SATURDAY!
MY WEEKEND! FOR FIVE DAYS I SWEAT BULLETS JUST TO GET TO THIS DAY!
1

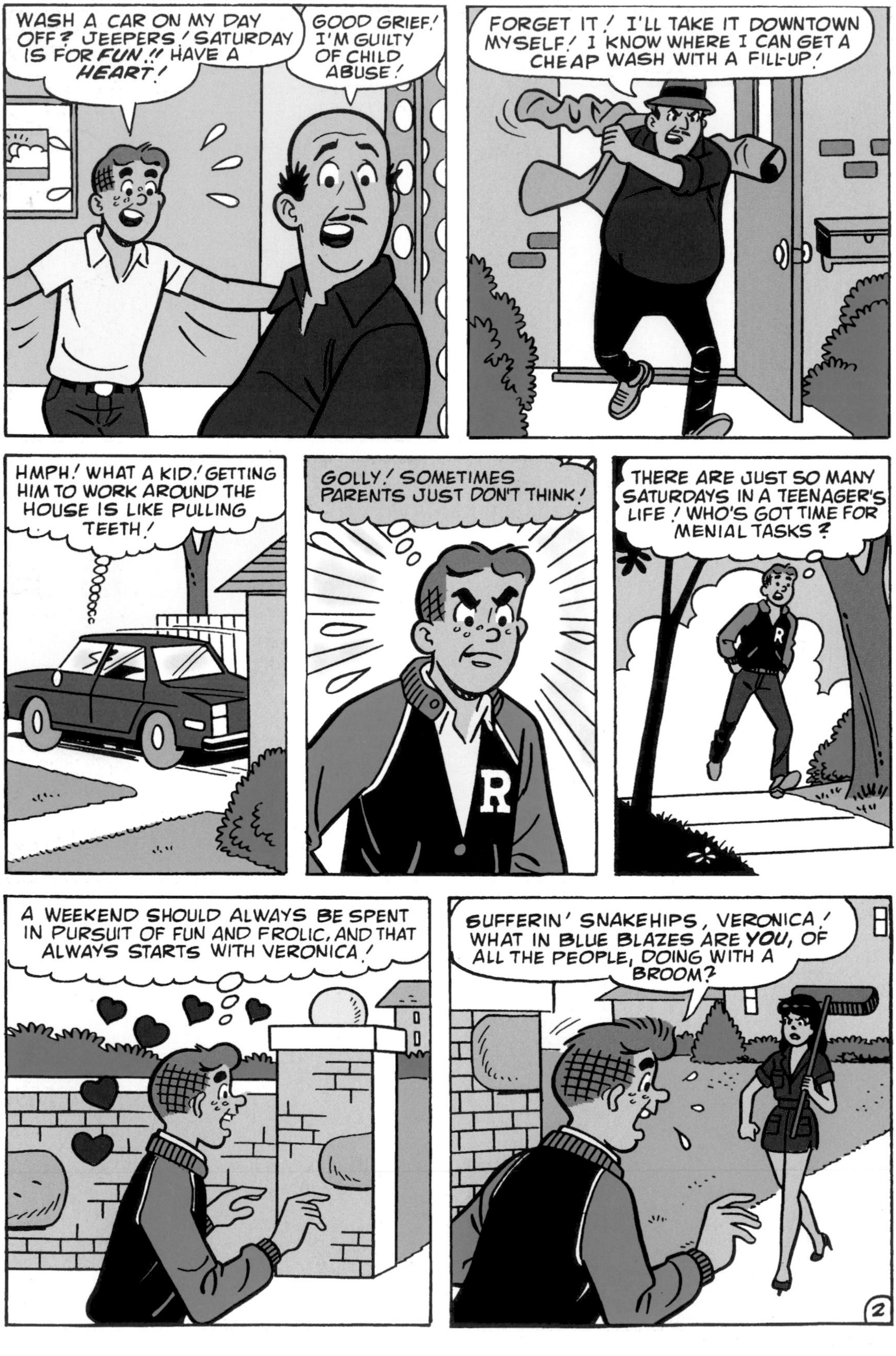
WASH A CAR ON MY DAY OFF? JEEPERS! SATURDAY IS FOR FUN!! HAVE A HEART!
GOOD GRIEF! I'M GUILTY OF CHILD ABUSE!
FORGET IT! I'LL TAKE IT DOWNTOWN MYSELF! I KNOW WHERE I CAN GET A CHEAP WASH WITH A FILL-UP!
HMPH! WHAT A KID! GETTING HIM TO WORK AROUND THE HOUSE IS LIKE PULLING TEETH!
GOLLY! SOMETIMES PARENTS JUST DON'T THINK!
R
THERE ARE JUST SO MANY SATURDAYS IN A TEENAGER'S LIFE! WHO'S GOT TIME FOR MENIAL TASKS?
R
A WEEKEND SHOULD ALWAYS BE SPENT IN PURSUIT OF FUN AND FROLIC, AND THAT ALWAYS STARTS WITH VERONICA!
SUFFERIN' SNAKEHIPS, VERONICA! WHAT IN BLUE BLAZES ARE YOU, OF ALL THE PEOPLE, DOING WITH A BROOM?
2

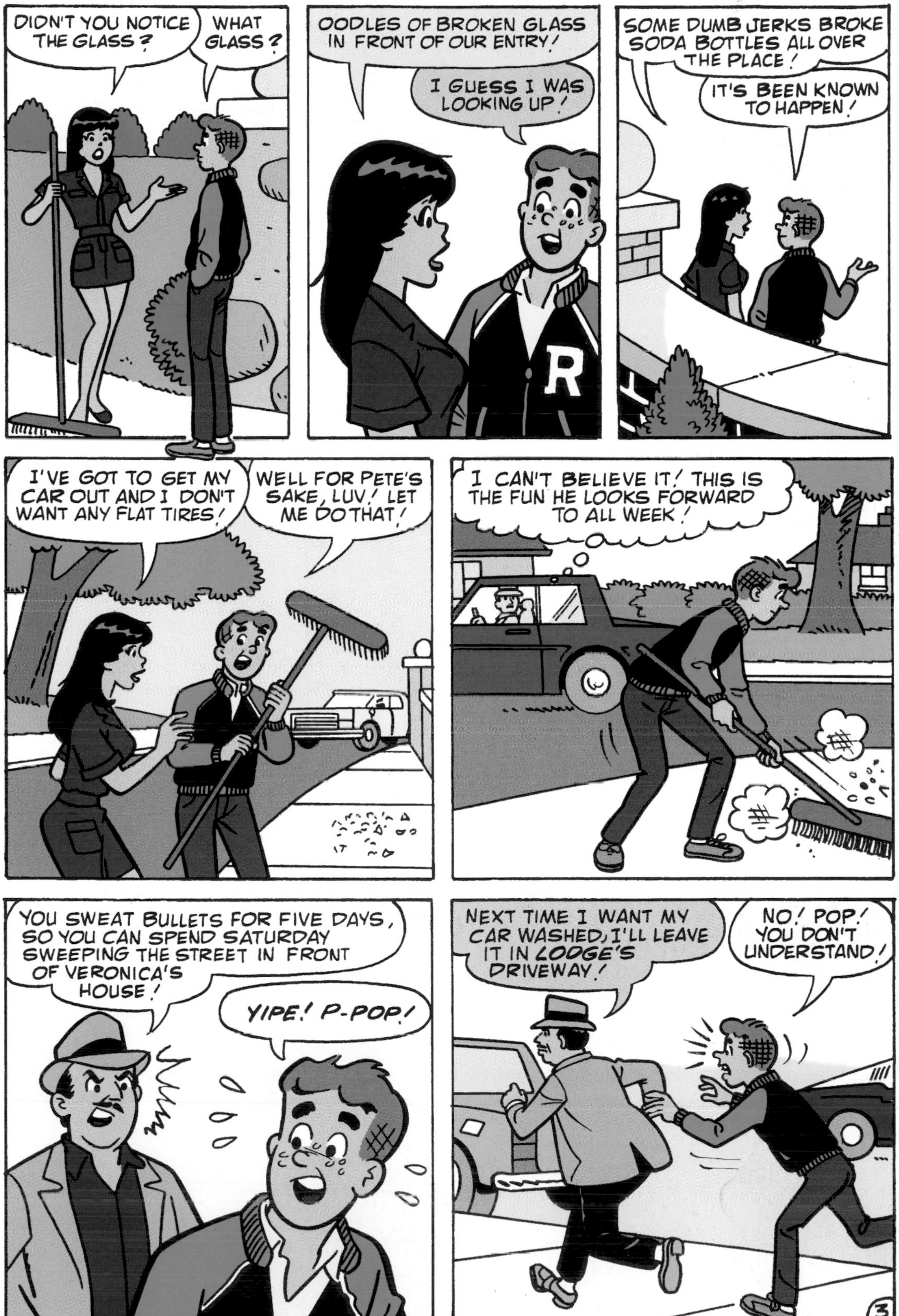
DIDN'T YOU NOTICE THE GLASS?
WHAT GLASS?
OODLES OF BROKEN GLASS IN FRONT OF OUR ENTRY!
I GUESS I WAS LOOKING UP!
SOME DUMB JERKS BROKE SODA BOTTLES ALL OVER THE PLACE!
IT'S BEEN KNOWN TO HAPPEN!
I'VE GOT TO GET MY CAR OUT AND I DON'T WANT ANY FLAT TIRES!
WELL FOR PETE'S SAKE, LUV! LET ME DO THAT!
I CAN'T BELIEVE IT! THIS IS THE FUN HE LOOKS FORWARD TO ALL WEEK!
YOU SWEAT BULLETS FOR FIVE DAYS, SO YOU CAN SPEND SATURDAY SWEEPING THE STREET IN FRONT OF VERONICA'S HOUSE!
YIPE! P-POP!
NEXT TIME I WANT MY CAR WASHED, I'LL LEAVE IT IN LODGE'S DRIVEWAY!
NO! POP! YOU DON'T UNDERSTAND!
3

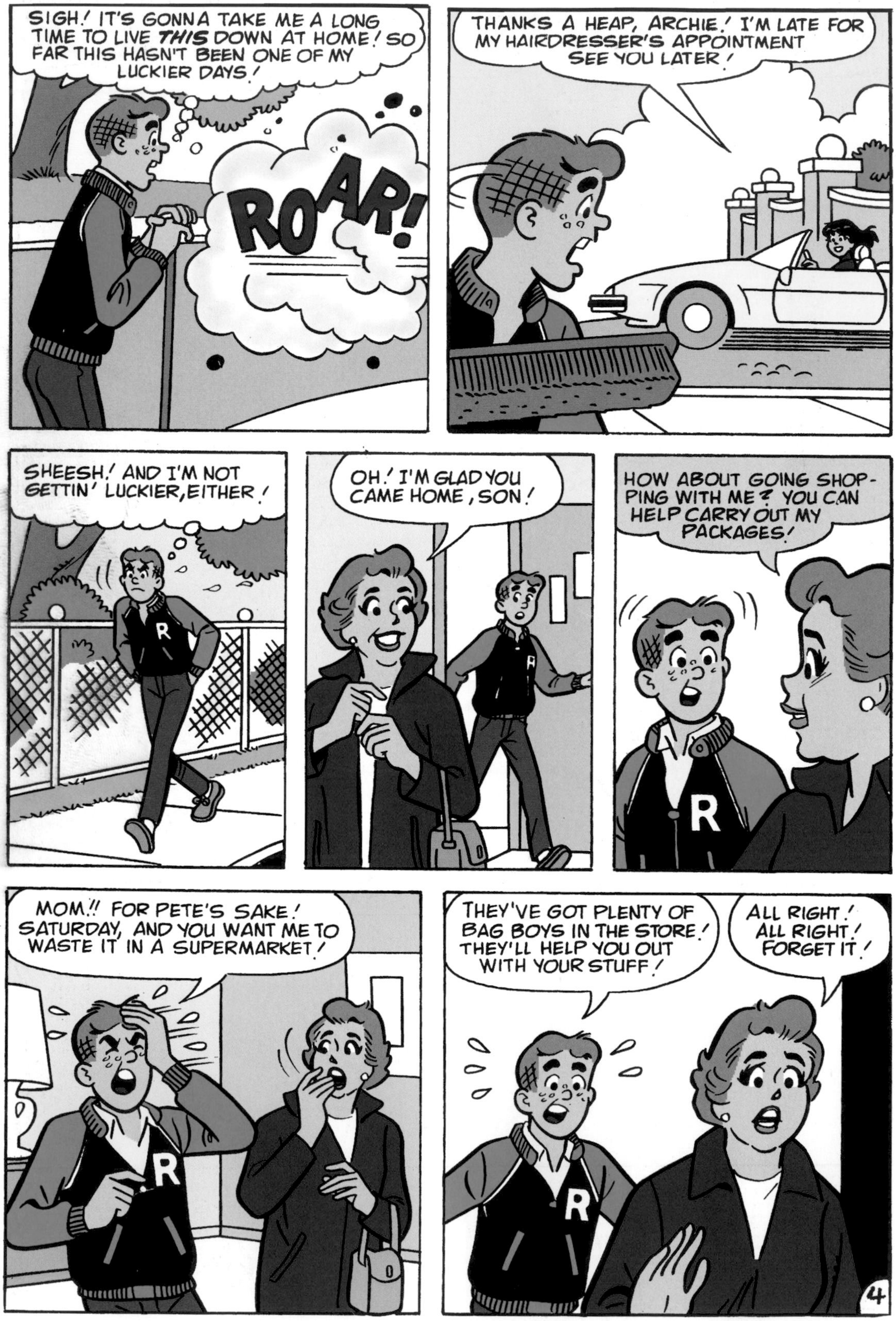
SIGH! IT'S GONNA TAKE ME A LONG TIME TO LIVE THIS DOWN AT HOME! SO FAR THIS HASN'T BEEN ONE OF MY LUCKIER DAYS!
ROAR!
THANKS A HEAP, ARCHIE! I'M LATE FOR MY HAIRDRESSER'S APPOINTMENT SEE YOU LATER!
SHEESH! AND I'M NOT GETTIN' LUCKIER, EITHER!
OH! I'M GLAD YOU CAME HOME, SON!
HOW ABOUT GOING SHOPPING WITH ME? YOU CAN HELP CARRY OUT MY PACKAGES!
MOM!! FOR PETE'S SAKE! SATURDAY, AND YOU WANT ME TO WASTE IT IN A SUPERMARKET!
THEY'VE GOT PLENTY OF BAG BOYS IN THE STORE! THEY'LL HELP YOU OUT WITH YOUR STUFF!
ALL RIGHT! ALL RIGHT! FORGET IT!
4

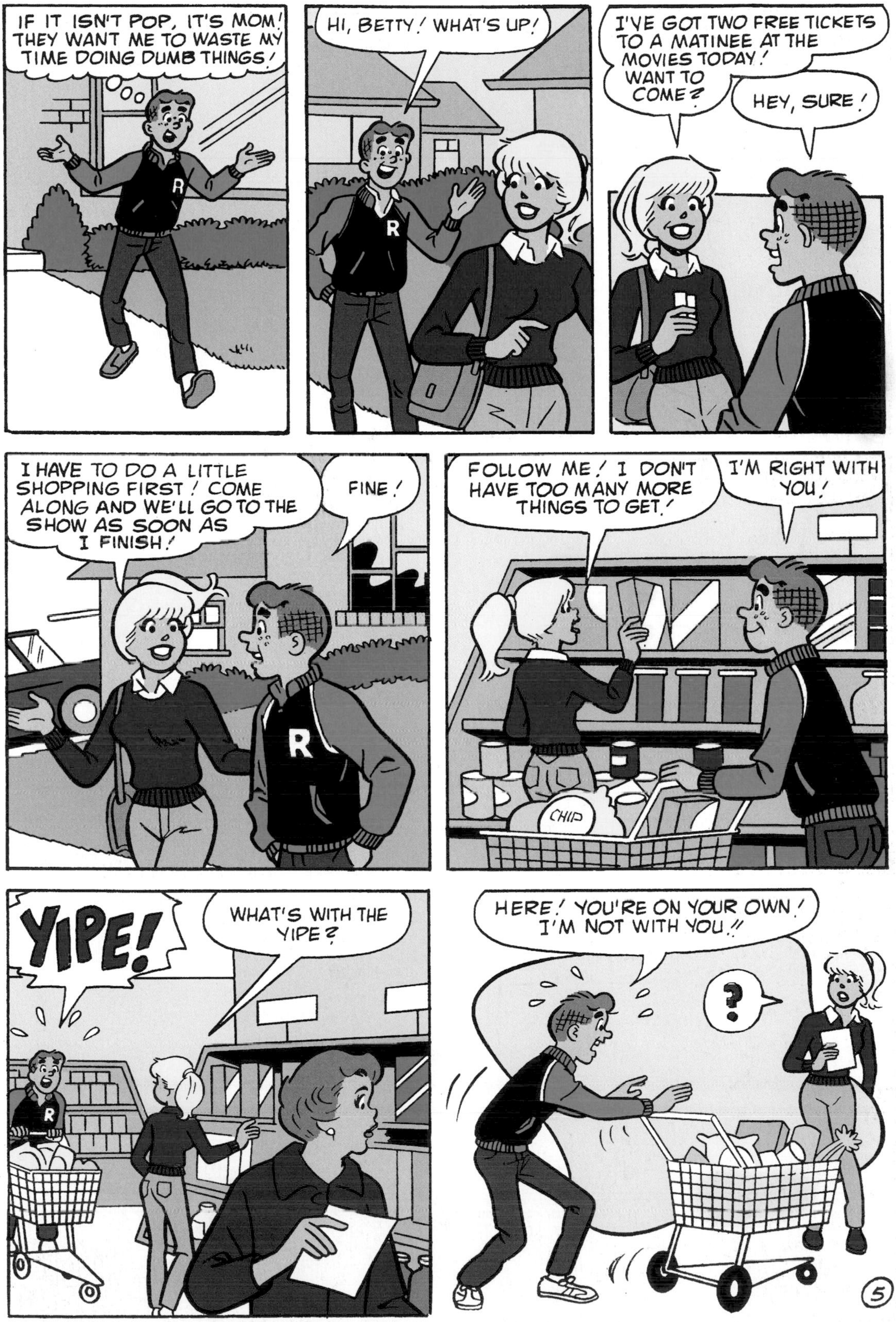
IF IT ISN'T POP, IT'S MOM! THEY WANT ME TO WASTE MY TIME DOING DUMB THINGS!
HI, BETTY! WHAT'S UP!
I'VE GOT TWO FREE TICKETS TO A MATINEE AT THE MOVIES TODAY! WANT TO COME?
HEY, SURE!
I HAVE TO DO A LITTLE SHOPPING FIRST! COME ALONG AND WE'LL GO TO THE SHOW AS SOON AS I FINISH!
FINE!
FOLLOW ME! I DON'T HAVE TOO MANY MORE THINGS TO GET!
I'M RIGHT WITH YOU!
CHIP
YIPE!
WHAT'S WITH THE YIPE?
HERE! YOU'RE ON YOUR OWN! I'M NOT WITH YOU!!
?
5

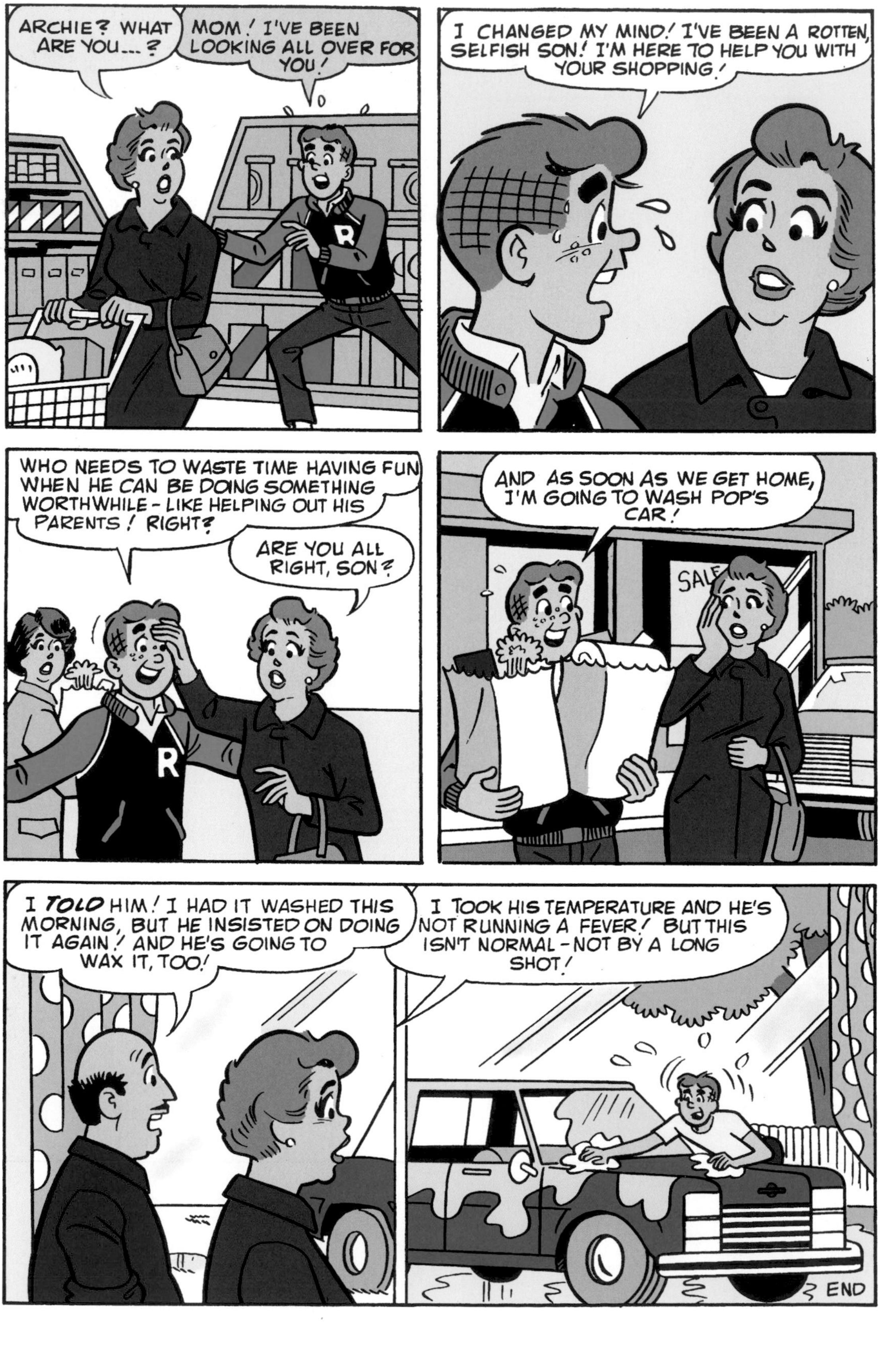
ARCHIE? WHAT ARE YOU...?
MOM! I'VE BEEN LOOKING ALL OVER FOR YOU!
I CHANGED MY MIND! I'VE BEEN A ROTTEN, SELFISH SON! I'M HERE TO HELP YOU WITH YOUR SHOPPING!
WHO NEEDS TO WASTE TIME HAVING FUN WHEN HE CAN BE DOING SOMETHING WORTHWHILE - LIKE HELPING OUT HIS PARENTS! RIGHT?
ARE YOU ALL RIGHT, SON?
AND AS SOON AS WE GET HOME, I'M GOING TO WASH POP'S CAR!
SALE
I TOLD HIM! I HAD IT WASHED THIS MORNING, BUT HE INSISTED ON DOING IT AGAIN! AND HE'S GOING TO WAX IT, TOO!
I TOOK HIS TEMPERATURE AND HE'S NOT RUNNING A FEVER! BUT THIS ISN'T NORMAL - NOT BY A LONG SHOT!
END

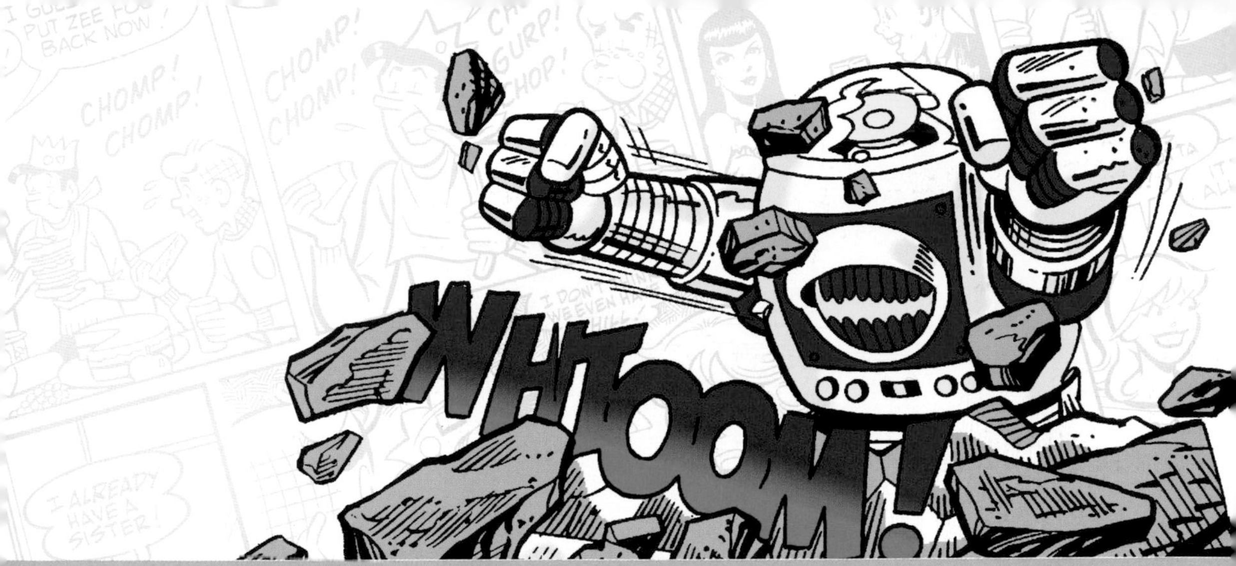
CHOMP! CHOMP!
CHOMP! CHOMP!
I ALREADY HAVE A SISTER!
WHTOOM!

THE ART LESSON
BETTY'S DIARY #1, 1987
BY KATHLEEN WEBB, DAN DECARLO, JIM DECARLO & BILL YOSHIDA

As a kid, I've spent many lazy summer afternoons devouring an Archie Digest Magazine—and some recent afternoons as well! But when I was asked to recommend a story for this collection, I knew I wanted to recommend a story from *Betty's Diary*. While Betty and Veronica are famous for fighting over Archie, *Betty's Diary* is where we learned more about Betty Cooper's life outside of romance. This very first story "The Art Lesson" is a great example as it not only shows how Betty is the most well-rounded character in the Archie-verse, but shows the reader how important it is to be true to yourself—ESPECIALLY in the face of peer pressure. And as someone who covers movies and comics where there are plenty of opinions and peer pressure from fellow fans, I think this is a great message! Enjoy!

—Grace Randolph
Host / Writer,
Beyond the Trailer

BACK FROM THE FUTURE
ARCHIE GIANT SERIES #590, 1988
BY RICH MARGOPOULOS, REX LINDSEY, JON D'AGOSTINO, BILL YOSHIDA & BARRY GROSSMAN

If The New Archies are the peanut butter sandwich of my world, then *Jughead's Time Police* is the White Castle crave case! You just can't get better than Jughead, food and time travel all wrapped up into one!

Up until this point in my life reading Archie comics was only good for belly laughs and rolling on the floor in hysterics, but now, now we're talking action and adventure too! What young boy could resist? I could just imagine visiting all those red letter dates in history, like when the first slider came off the grill or when Nathan Handwerker told Feltman to cut his own buns! Ah yes, history you can taste is the best kind. I mean where would we be without food? Luckily "Back From the Future" is a fulfilling and gluttonous treat with its amazing art and script, you may not have room left for dessert.

—Stephen Oswald
Production Manager/Associate Editor,
Archie Comics

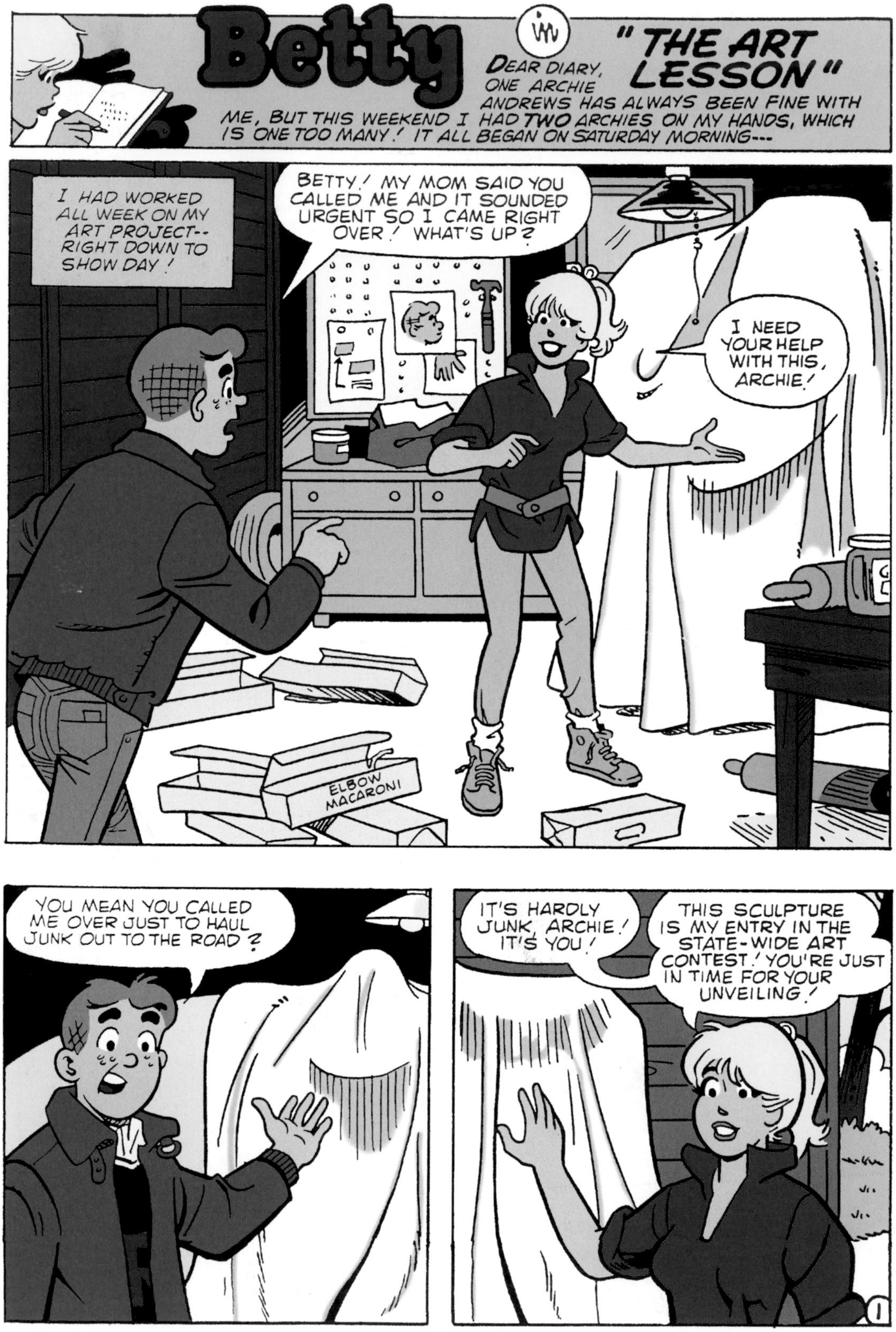
Betty in "THE ART LESSON"
DEAR DIARY, ONE ARCHIE ANDREWS HAS ALWAYS BEEN FINE WITH ME, BUT THIS WEEKEND I HAD TWO ARCHIES ON MY HANDS, WHICH IS ONE TOO MANY! IT ALL BEGAN ON SATURDAY MORNING---
I HAD WORKED ALL WEEK ON MY ART PROJECT-- RIGHT DOWN TO SHOW DAY!
BETTY! MY MOM SAID YOU CALLED ME AND IT SOUNDED URGENT SO I CAME RIGHT OVER! WHAT'S UP?
I NEED YOUR HELP WITH THIS, ARCHIE!
ELBOW MACARONI
YOU MEAN YOU CALLED ME OVER JUST TO HAUL JUNK OUT TO THE ROAD?
IT'S HARDLY JUNK, ARCHIE! IT'S YOU!
THIS SCULPTURE IS MY ENTRY IN THE STATE-WIDE ART CONTEST! YOU'RE JUST IN TIME FOR YOUR UNVEILING!
1

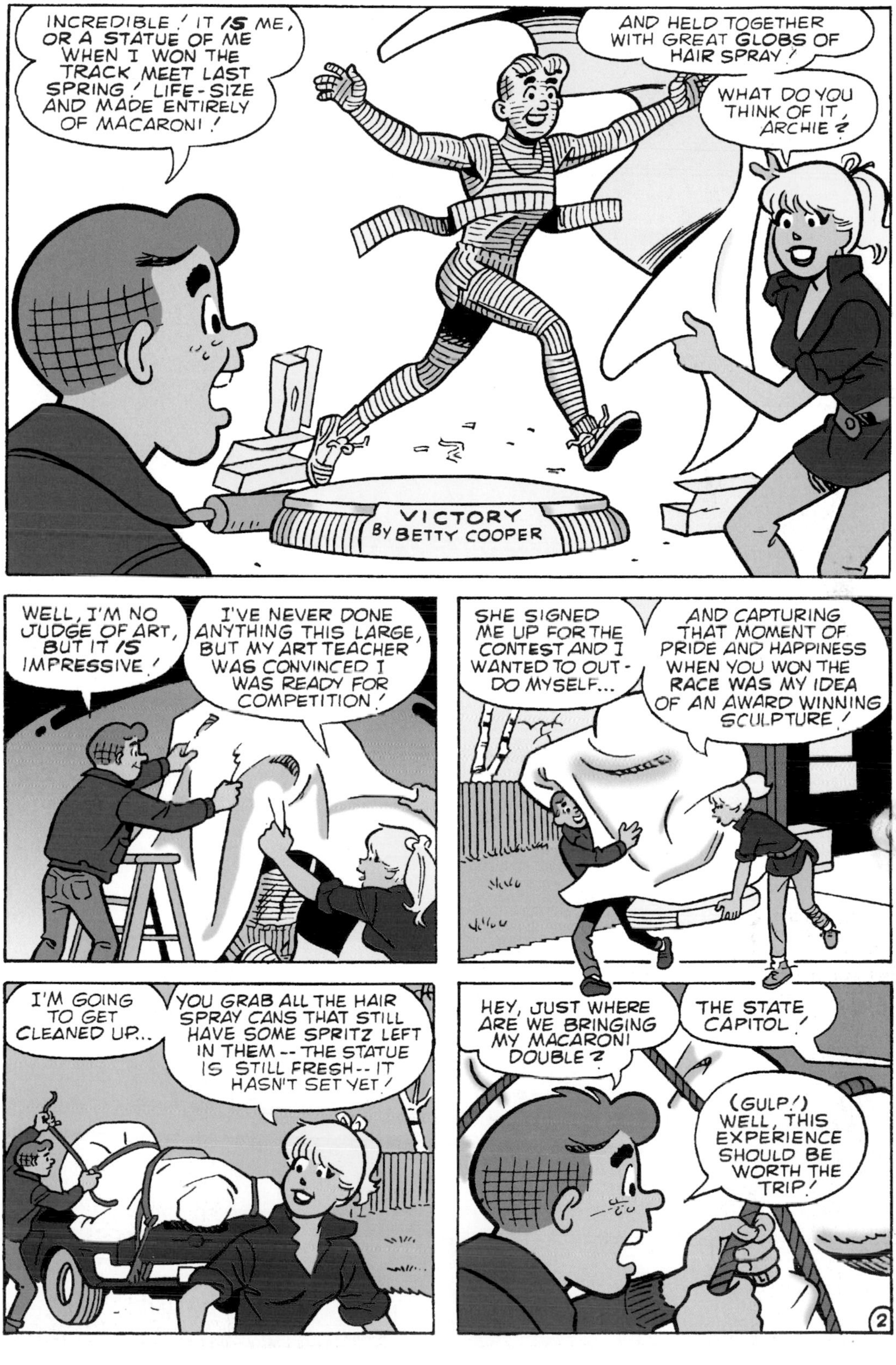

INCREDIBLE! IT IS ME, OR A STATUE OF ME WHEN I WON THE TRACK MEET LAST SPRING! LIFE-SIZE AND MADE ENTIRELY OF MACARONI!
AND HELD TOGETHER WITH GREAT GLOBS OF HAIR SPRAY!
WHAT DO YOU THINK OF IT, ARCHIE?
VICTORY BY BETTY COOPER
WELL, I'M NO JUDGE OF ART, BUT IT IS IMPRESSIVE!
I'VE NEVER DONE ANYTHING THIS LARGE, BUT MY ART TEACHER WAS CONVINCED I WAS READY FOR COMPETITION!
SHE SIGNED ME UP FOR THE CONTEST AND I WANTED TO OUT-DO MYSELF...
AND CAPTURING THAT MOMENT OF PRIDE AND HAPPINESS WHEN YOU WON THE RACE WAS MY IDEA OF AN AWARD WINNING SCULPTURE!
I'M GOING TO GET CLEANED UP...
YOU GRAB ALL THE HAIR SPRAY CANS THAT STILL HAVE SOME SPRITZ LEFT IN THEM -- THE STATUE IS STILL FRESH -- IT HASN'T SET YET!
HEY, JUST WHERE ARE WE BRINGING MY MACARONI DOUBLE?
THE STATE CAPITOL!
(GULP!) WELL, THIS EXPERIENCE SHOULD BE WORTH THE TRIP!
2

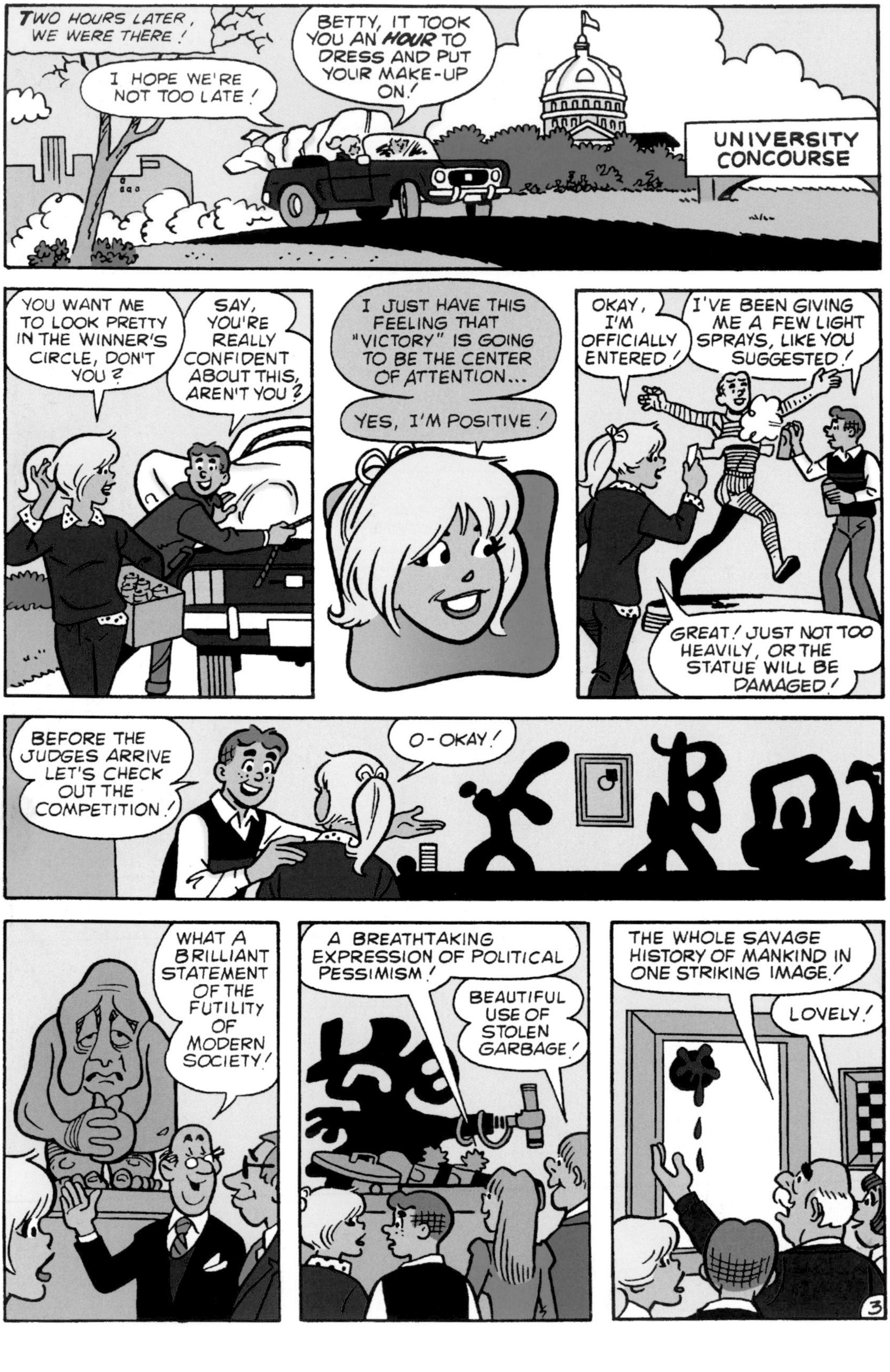
TWO HOURS LATER, WE WERE THERE!
I HOPE WE'RE NOT TOO LATE!
BETTY, IT TOOK YOU AN HOUR TO DRESS AND PUT YOUR MAKE-UP ON!
UNIVERSITY CONCOURSE
YOU WANT ME TO LOOK PRETTY IN THE WINNER'S CIRCLE, DON'T YOU?
SAY, YOU'RE REALLY CONFIDENT ABOUT THIS, AREN'T YOU?
I JUST HAVE THIS FEELING THAT "VICTORY" IS GOING TO BE THE CENTER OF ATTENTION...
YES, I'M POSITIVE!
OKAY, I'M OFFICIALLY ENTERED!
I'VE BEEN GIVING ME A FEW LIGHT SPRAYS, LIKE YOU SUGGESTED!
GREAT! JUST NOT TOO HEAVILY, OR THE STATUE WILL BE DAMAGED!
BEFORE THE JUDGES ARRIVE LET'S CHECK OUT THE COMPETITION!
O-OKAY!
WHAT A BRILLIANT STATEMENT OF THE FUTILITY OF MODERN SOCIETY!
A BREATHTAKING EXPRESSION OF POLITICAL PESSIMISM!
BEAUTIFUL USE OF STOLEN GARBAGE!
THE WHOLE SAVAGE HISTORY OF MANKIND IN ONE STRIKING IMAGE!
LOVELY!
3

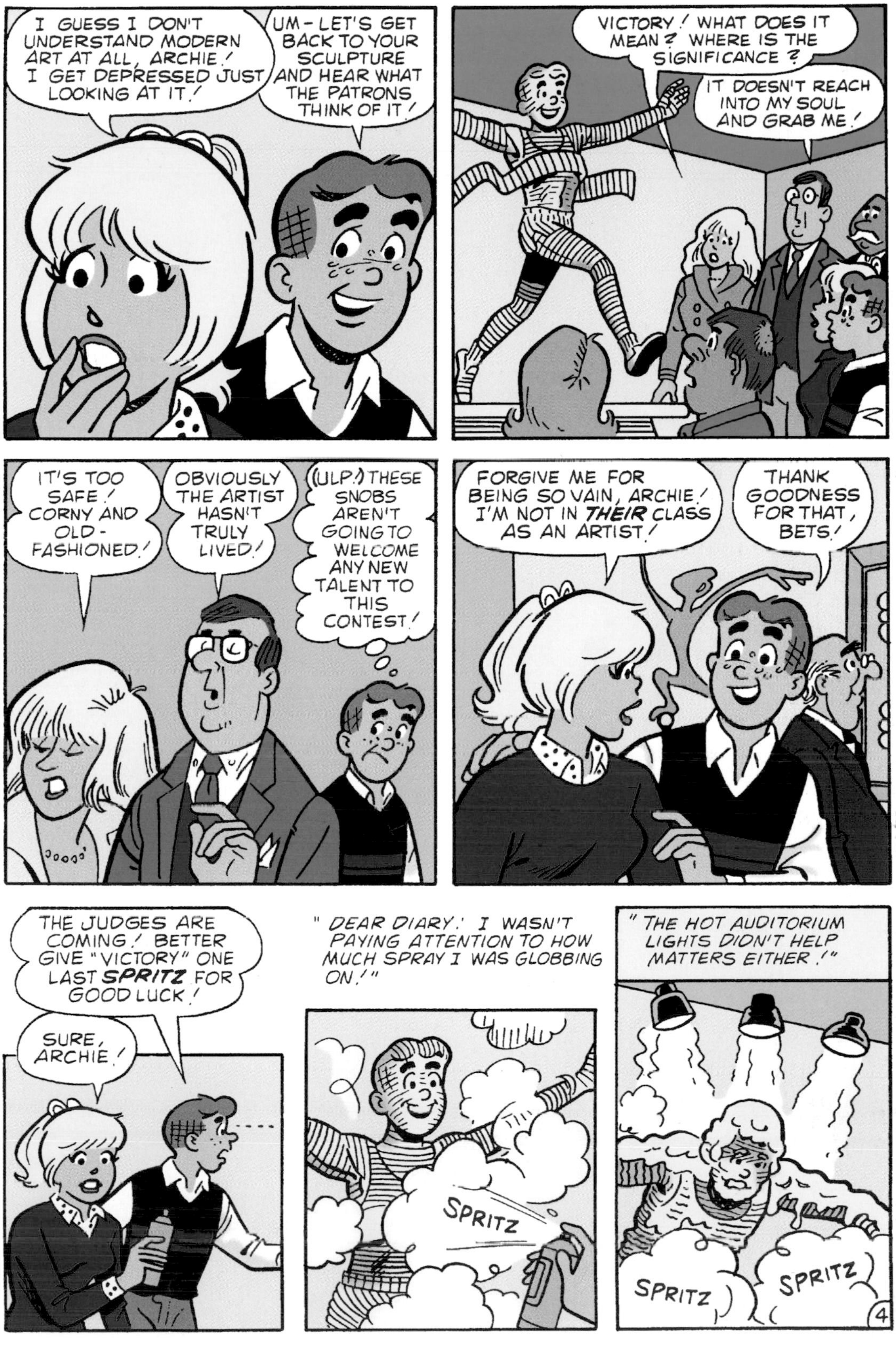
I GUESS I DON'T UNDERSTAND MODERN ART AT ALL, ARCHIE! I GET DEPRESSED JUST LOOKING AT IT!
UM - LET'S GET BACK TO YOUR SCULPTURE AND HEAR WHAT THE PATRONS THINK OF IT!
VICTORY! WHAT DOES IT MEAN? WHERE IS THE SIGNIFICANCE?
IT DOESN'T REACH INTO MY SOUL AND GRAB ME!
IT'S TOO SAFE! CORNY AND OLD-FASHIONED!
OBVIOUSLY THE ARTIST HASN'T TRULY LIVED!
(ULP!) THESE SNOBS AREN'T GOING TO WELCOME ANY NEW TALENT TO THIS CONTEST!
FORGIVE ME FOR BEING SO VAIN, ARCHIE! I'M NOT IN THEIR CLASS AS AN ARTIST!
THANK GOODNESS FOR THAT, BETS!
THE JUDGES ARE COMING! BETTER GIVE "VICTORY" ONE LAST SPRITZ FOR GOOD LUCK!
SURE, ARCHIE!
"DEAR DIARY: I WASN'T PAYING ATTENTION TO HOW MUCH SPRAY I WAS GLOBBING ON!"
SPRITZ
"THE HOT AUDITORIUM LIGHTS DIDN'T HELP MATTERS EITHER!"
SPRITZ
SPRITZ
4

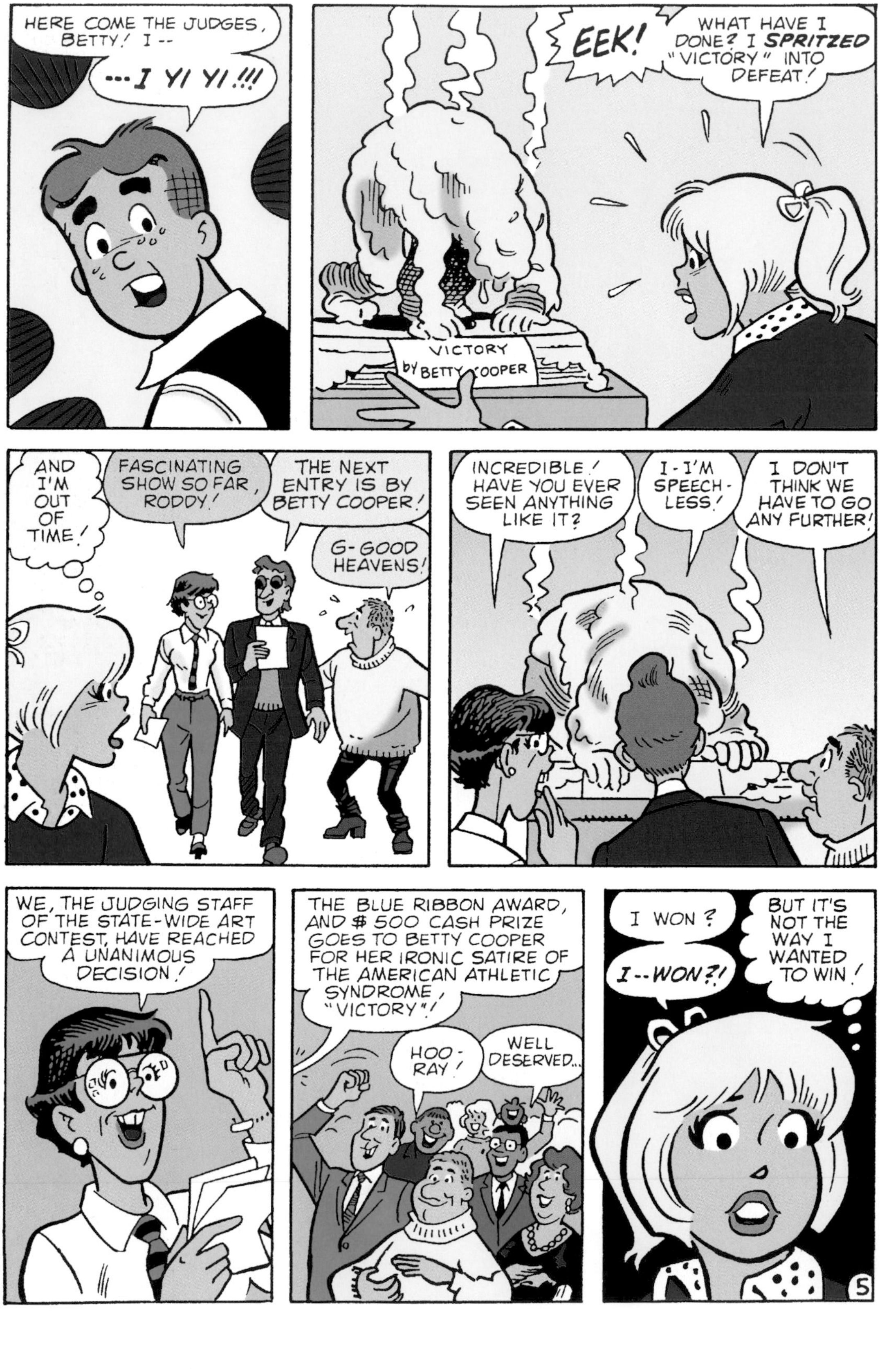
HERE COME THE JUDGES, BETTY! I --
---I YI YI!!!
EEK!
WHAT HAVE I DONE? I SPRITZED "VICTORY" INTO DEFEAT!
VICTORY by BETTY COOPER
AND I'M OUT OF TIME!
FASCINATING SHOW SO FAR, RODDY!
THE NEXT ENTRY IS BY BETTY COOPER!
G-GOOD HEAVENS!
INCREDIBLE! HAVE YOU EVER SEEN ANYTHING LIKE IT?
I-I'M SPEECH-LESS!
I DON'T THINK WE HAVE TO GO ANY FURTHER!
WE, THE JUDGING STAFF OF THE STATE-WIDE ART CONTEST, HAVE REACHED A UNANIMOUS DECISION!
THE BLUE RIBBON AWARD, AND $ 500 CASH PRIZE GOES TO BETTY COOPER FOR HER IRONIC SATIRE OF THE AMERICAN ATHLETIC SYNDROME, "VICTORY"!
HOO-RAY!
WELL DESERVED...
I WON?
I--WON?!
BUT IT'S NOT THE WAY I WANTED TO WIN!
5

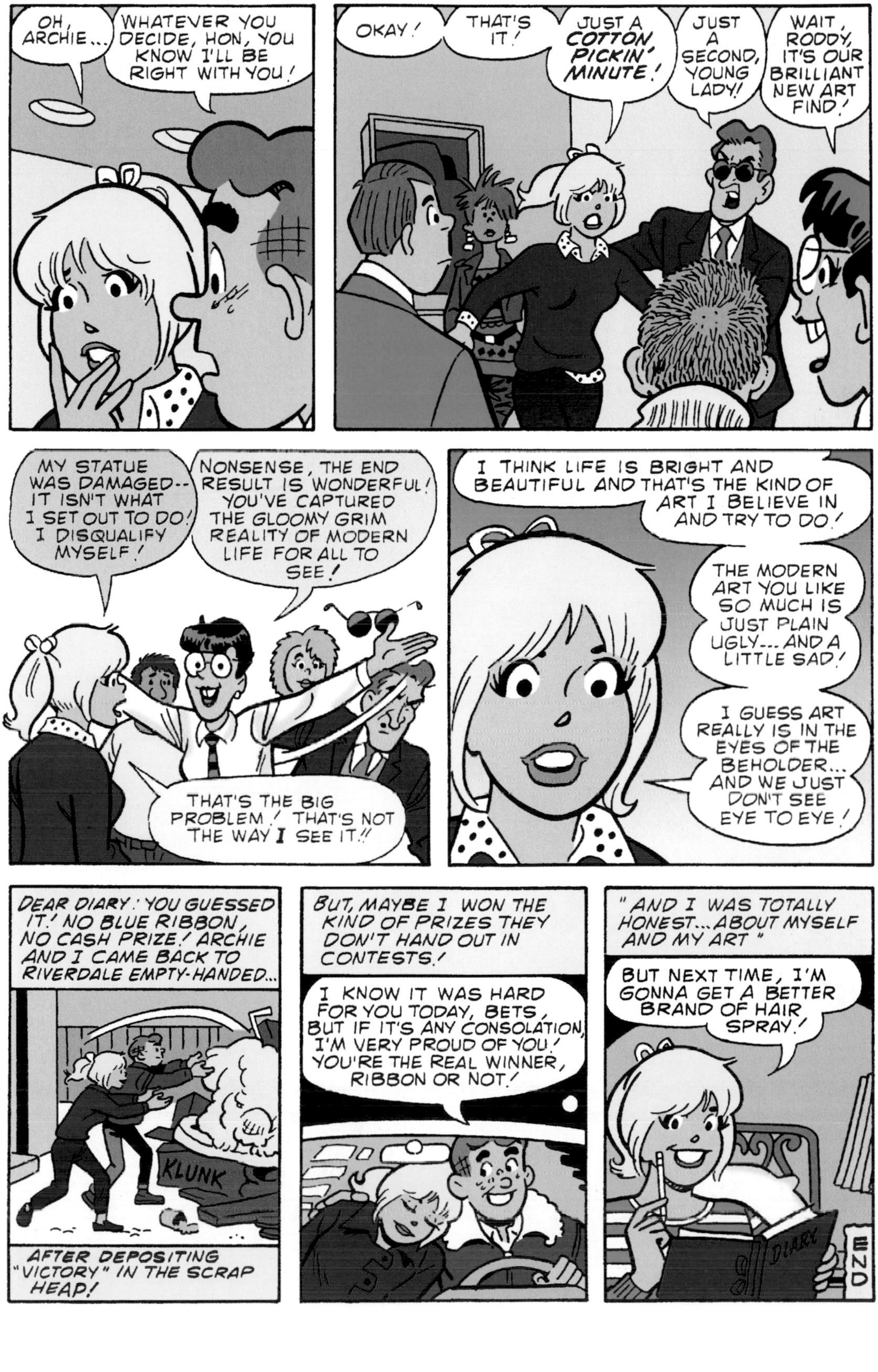
OH, ARCHIE...
WHATEVER YOU DECIDE, HON, YOU KNOW I'LL BE RIGHT WITH YOU!
OKAY!
THAT'S IT!
JUST A COTTON PICKIN' MINUTE!
JUST A SECOND, YOUNG LADY!
WAIT, RODDY, IT'S OUR BRILLIANT NEW ART FIND!
MY STATUE WAS DAMAGED-- IT ISN'T WHAT I SET OUT TO DO! I DISQUALIFY MYSELF!
NONSENSE, THE END RESULT IS WONDERFUL! YOU'VE CAPTURED THE GLOOMY GRIM REALITY OF MODERN LIFE FOR ALL TO SEE!
THAT'S THE BIG PROBLEM! THAT'S NOT THE WAY I SEE IT!!
I THINK LIFE IS BRIGHT AND BEAUTIFUL AND THAT'S THE KIND OF ART I BELIEVE IN AND TRY TO DO!
THE MODERN ART YOU LIKE SO MUCH IS JUST PLAIN UGLY... AND A LITTLE SAD!
I GUESS ART REALLY IS IN THE EYES OF THE BEHOLDER... AND WE JUST DON'T SEE EYE TO EYE!
DEAR DIARY: YOU GUESSED IT! NO BLUE RIBBON, NO CASH PRIZE! ARCHIE AND I CAME BACK TO RIVERDALE EMPTY-HANDED...
KLUNK
AFTER DEPOSITING "VICTORY" IN THE SCRAP HEAP!
BUT, MAYBE I WON THE KIND OF PRIZES THEY DON'T HAND OUT IN CONTESTS!
I KNOW IT WAS HARD FOR YOU TODAY, BETS, BUT IF IT'S ANY CONSOLATION, I'M VERY PROUD OF YOU! YOU'RE THE REAL WINNER, RIBBON OR NOT!
"AND I WAS TOTALLY HONEST... ABOUT MYSELF AND MY ART"
BUT NEXT TIME, I'M GONNA GET A BETTER BRAND OF HAIR SPRAY!
DIARY
END

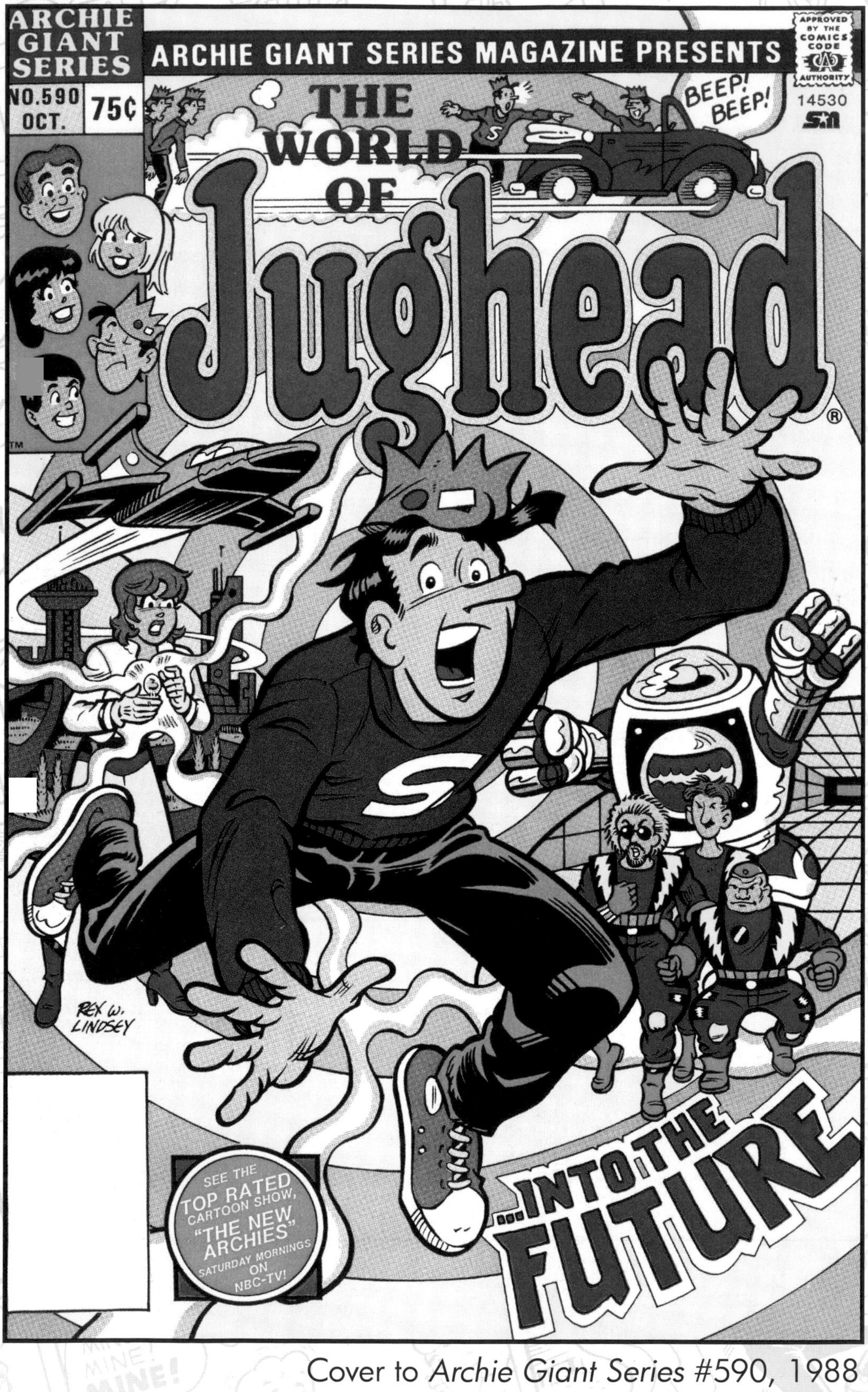
ARCHIE GIANT SERIES
NO.590 OCT.
75¢
ARCHIE GIANT SERIES MAGAZINE PRESENTS
APPROVED BY THE COMICS CODE AUTHORITY
14530
THE WORLD OF Jughead
BEEP! BEEP!
REX W. LINDSEY
SEE THE TOP RATED CARTOON SHOW, "THE NEW ARCHIES" SATURDAY MORNINGS ON NBC-TV!
...INTO THE FUTURE

Cover to *Archie Giant Series* #590, 1988
art by Rex Lindsey

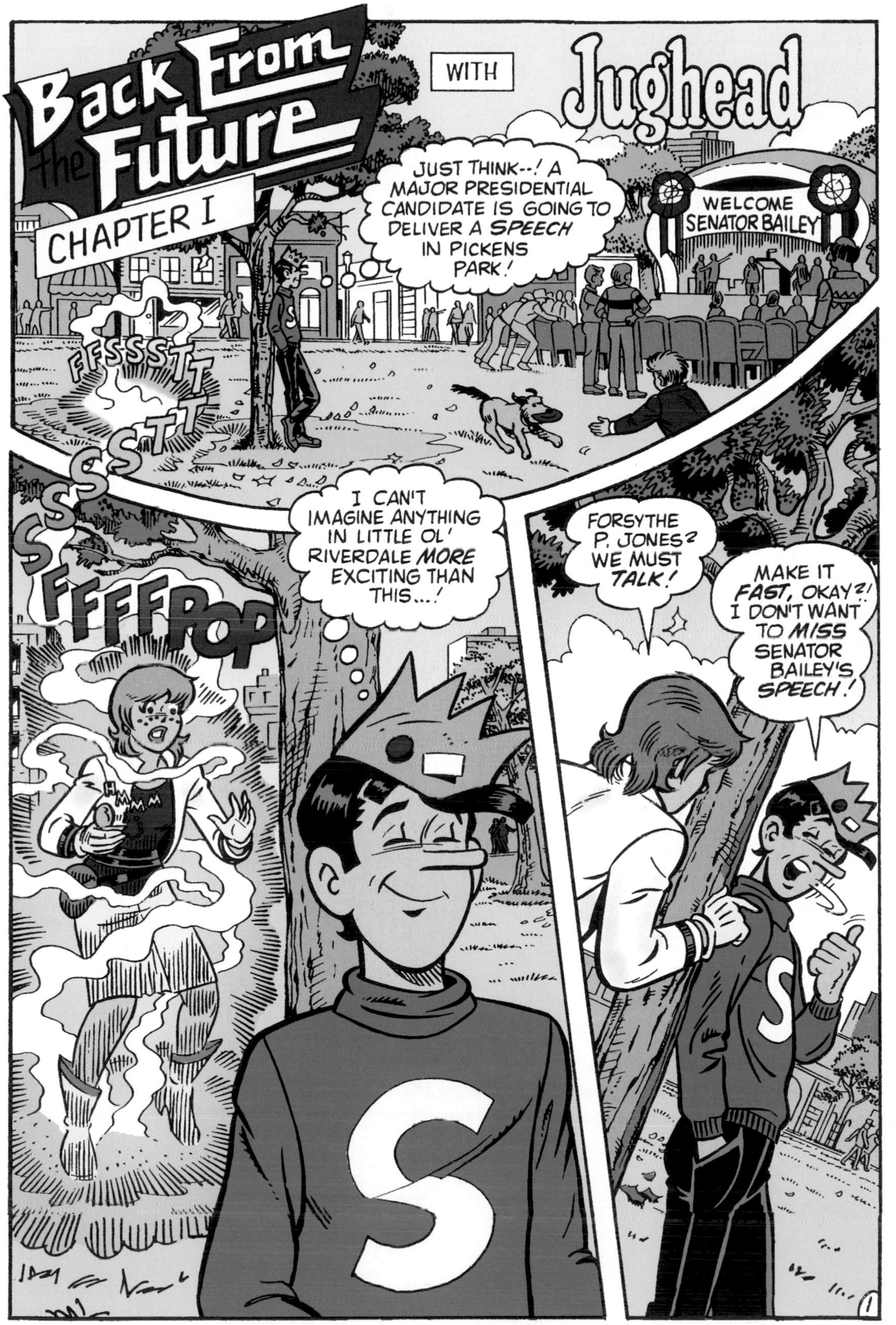

Back From the Future
WITH
Jughead
CHAPTER I
JUST THINK--! A MAJOR PRESIDENTIAL CANDIDATE IS GOING TO DELIVER A SPEECH IN PICKENS PARK!
WELCOME SENATOR BAILEY
FFSSSTTT
SSSTTT
SSSFFFFPOP
I CAN'T IMAGINE ANYTHING IN LITTLE OL' RIVERDALE MORE EXCITING THAN THIS...!
FORSYTHE P. JONES? WE MUST TALK!
MAKE IT FAST, OKAY?! I DON'T WANT TO MISS SENATOR BAILEY'S SPEECH!
1

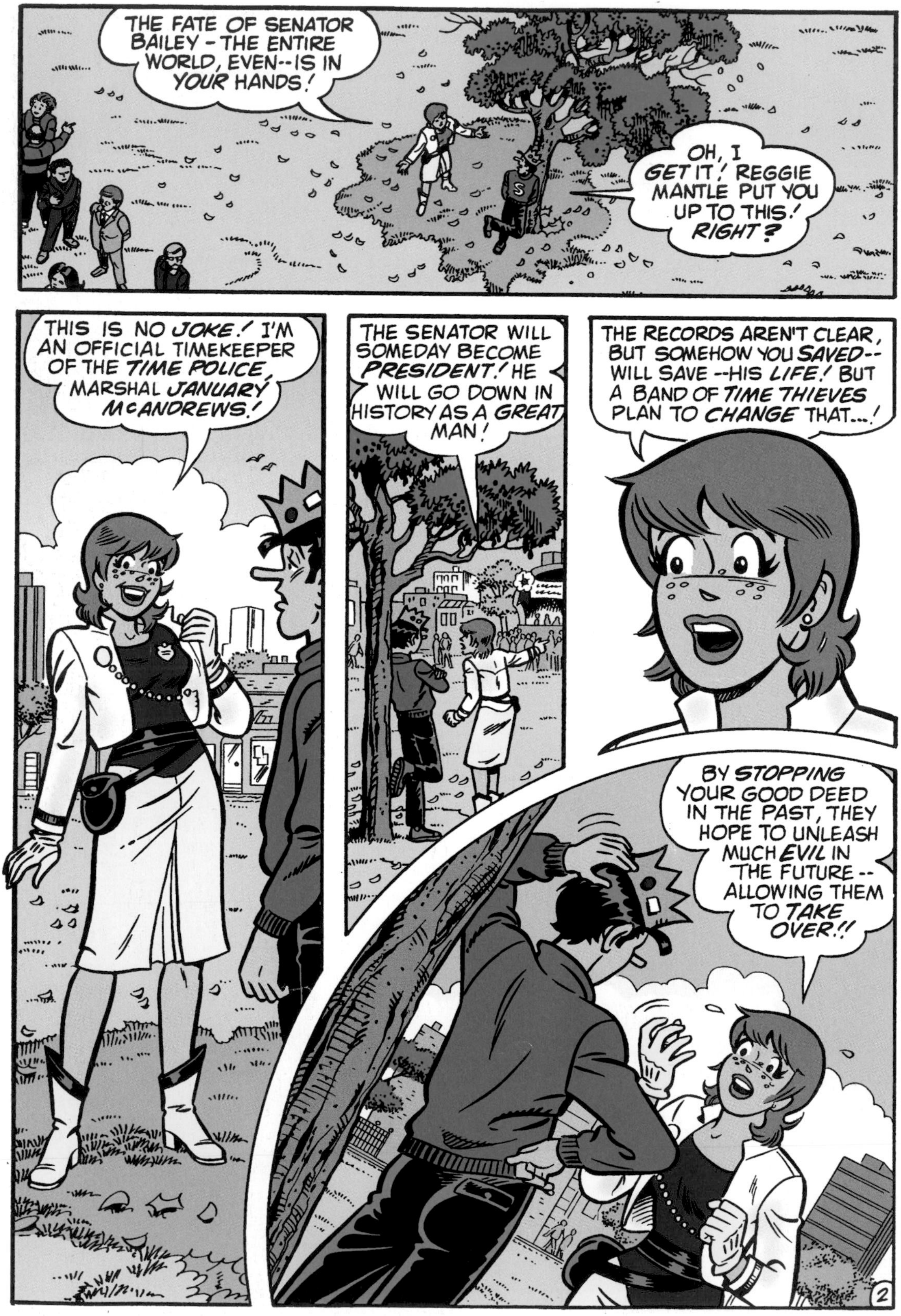
THE FATE OF SENATOR BAILEY - THE ENTIRE WORLD, EVEN--IS IN YOUR HANDS!
OH, I GET IT! REGGIE MANTLE PUT YOU UP TO THIS! RIGHT?
THIS IS NO JOKE! I'M AN OFFICIAL TIMEKEEPER OF THE TIME POLICE, MARSHAL JANUARY McANDREWS!
THE SENATOR WILL SOMEDAY BECOME PRESIDENT! HE WILL GO DOWN IN HISTORY AS A GREAT MAN!
THE RECORDS AREN'T CLEAR, BUT SOMEHOW YOU SAVED-- WILL SAVE --HIS LIFE! BUT A BAND OF TIME THIEVES PLAN TO CHANGE THAT...!
BY STOPPING YOUR GOOD DEED IN THE PAST, THEY HOPE TO UNLEASH MUCH EVIL IN THE FUTURE -- ALLOWING THEM TO TAKE OVER!!
2

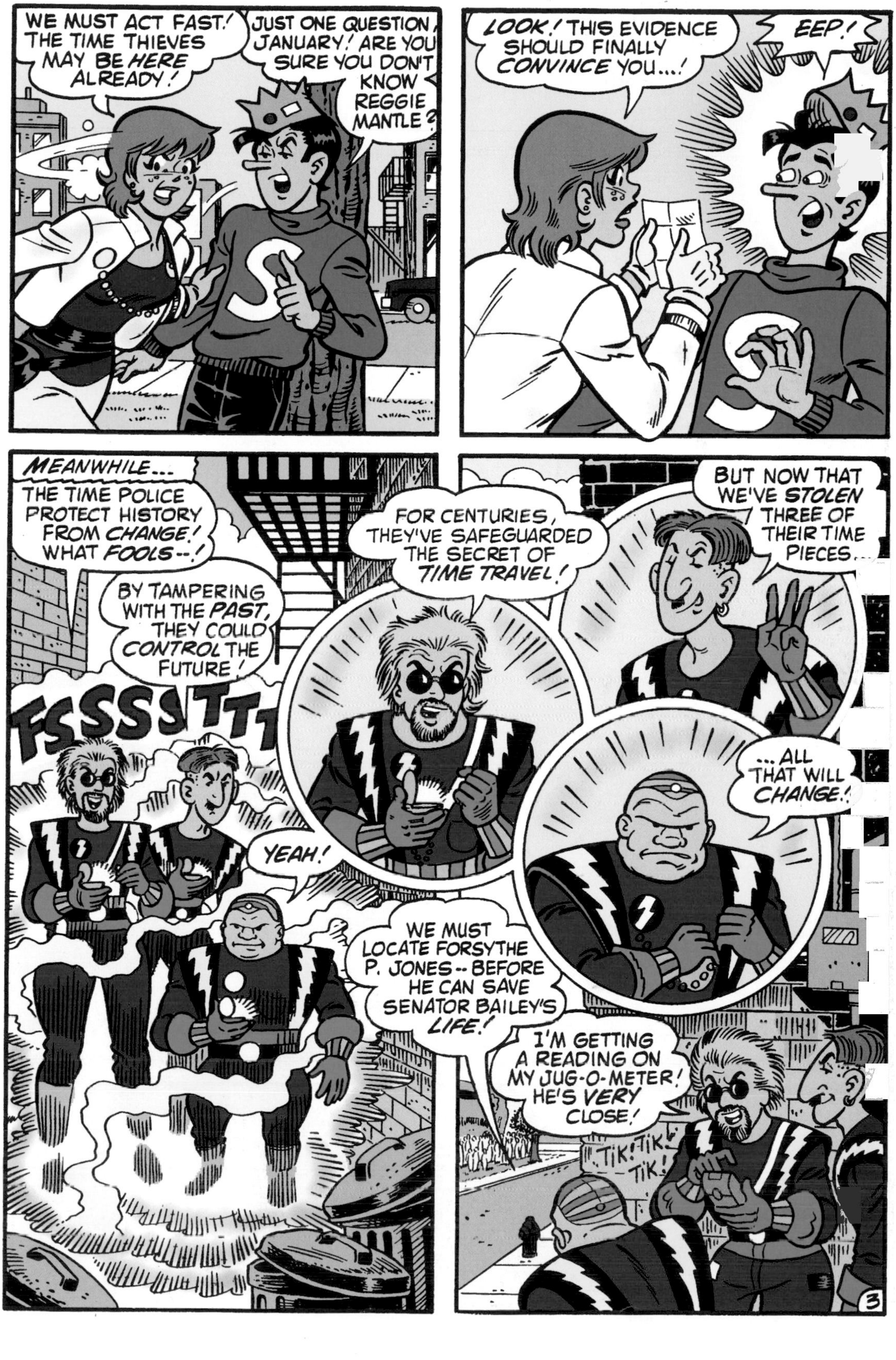
WE MUST ACT FAST! THE TIME THIEVES MAY BE HERE ALREADY!
JUST ONE QUESTION, JANUARY! ARE YOU SURE YOU DON'T KNOW REGGIE MANTLE?
LOOK! THIS EVIDENCE SHOULD FINALLY CONVINCE YOU...!
EEP!
MEANWHILE...
THE TIME POLICE PROTECT HISTORY FROM CHANGE! WHAT FOOLS--!
BY TAMPERING WITH THE PAST, THEY COULD CONTROL THE FUTURE!
FSSSSTTT
FOR CENTURIES, THEY'VE SAFEGUARDED THE SECRET OF TIME TRAVEL!
BUT NOW THAT WE'VE STOLEN THREE OF THEIR TIME PIECES...
...ALL THAT WILL CHANGE!
YEAH!
WE MUST LOCATE FORSYTHE P. JONES-- BEFORE HE CAN SAVE SENATOR BAILEY'S LIFE!
I'M GETTING A READING ON MY JUG-O-METER! HE'S VERY CLOSE!
TIK! TIK! TIK!
3

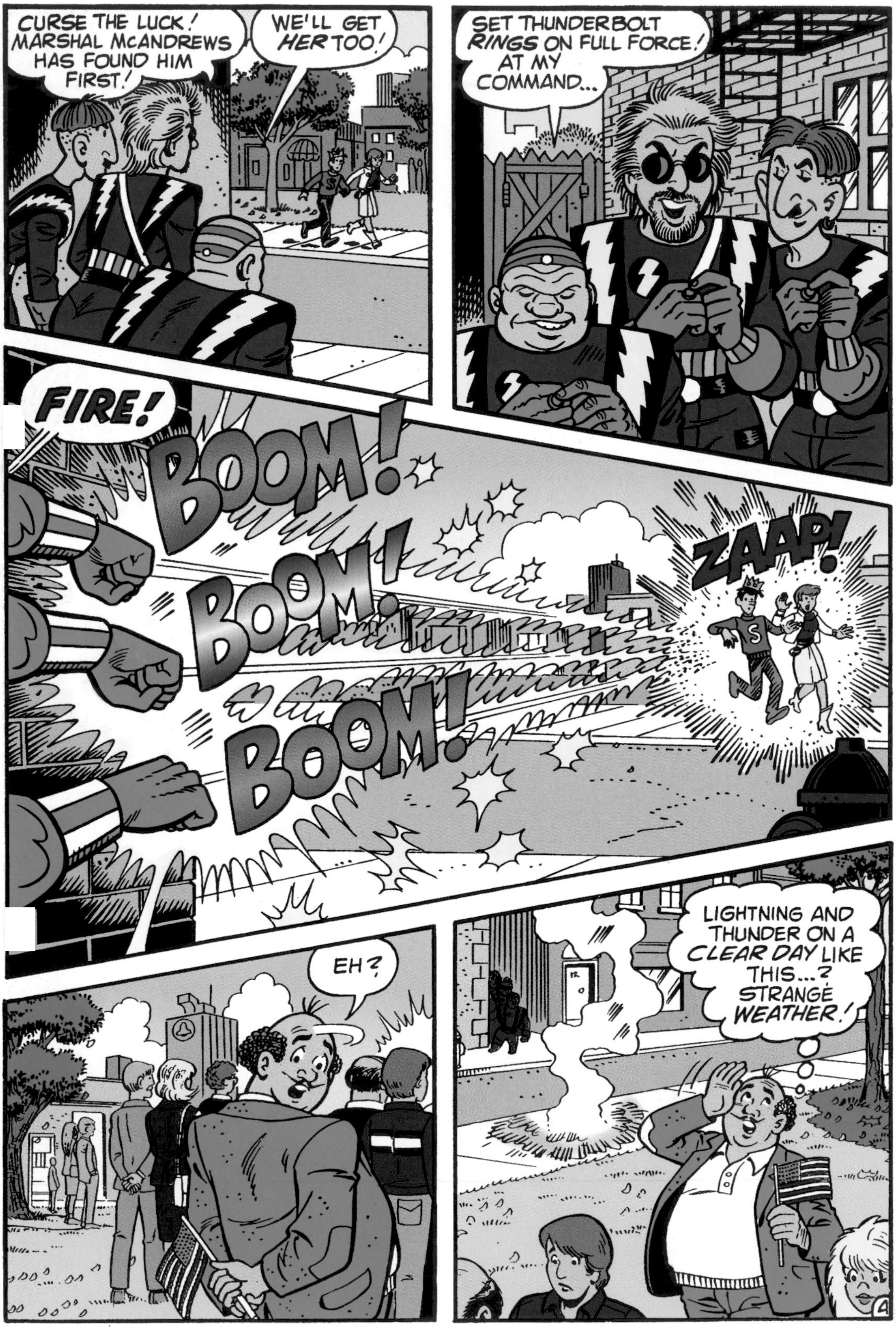
CURSE THE LUCK! MARSHAL McANDREWS HAS FOUND HIM FIRST!
WE'LL GET HER TOO!
SET THUNDERBOLT RINGS ON FULL FORCE! AT MY COMMAND...
FIRE!
BOOM!
BOOM!
BOOM!
ZAAP!
EH?
LIGHTNING AND THUNDER ON A CLEAR DAY LIKE THIS...? STRANGE WEATHER!
4

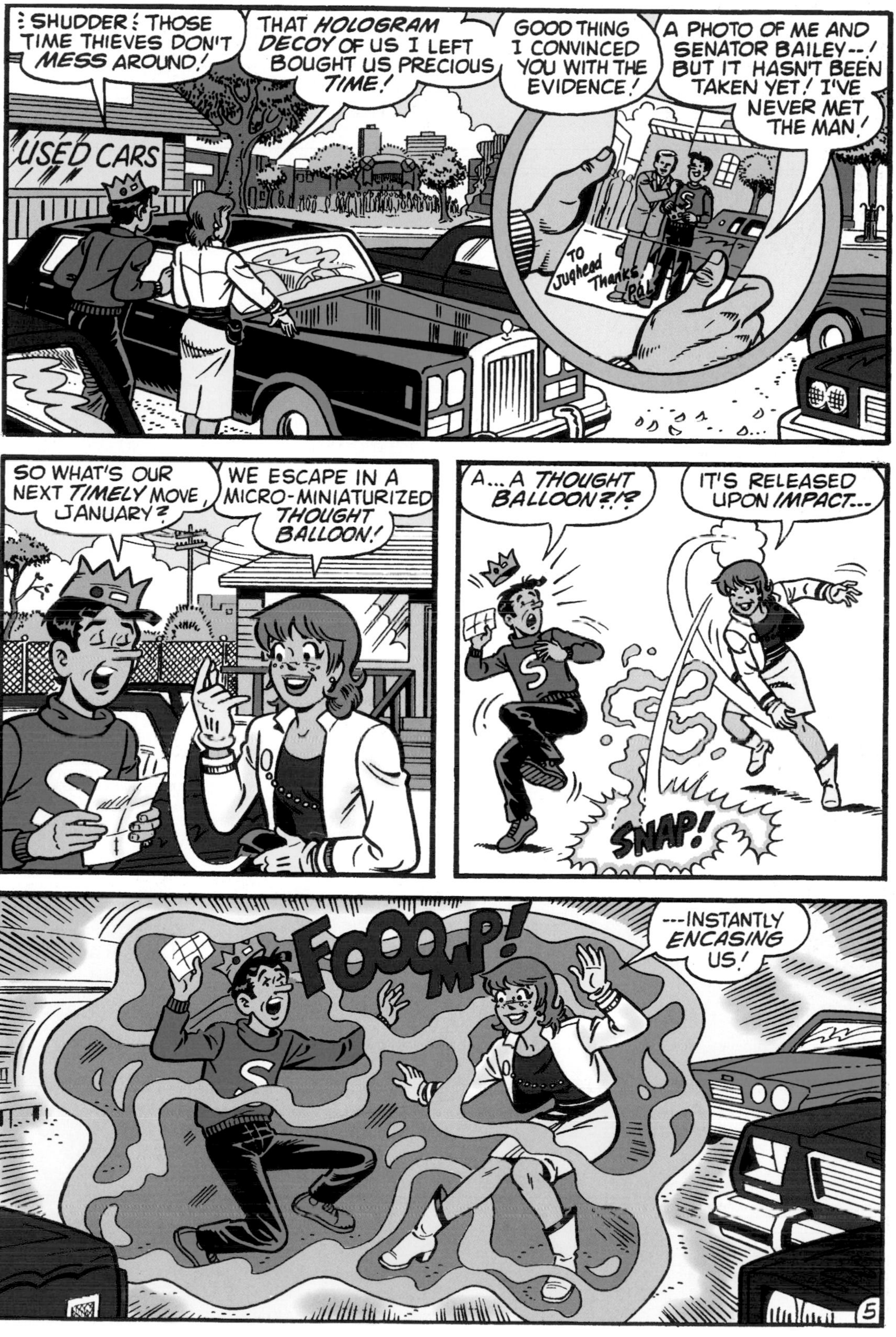

:SHUDDER: THOSE TIME THIEVES DON'T MESS AROUND!
THAT HOLOGRAM DECOY OF US I LEFT BOUGHT US PRECIOUS TIME!
GOOD THING I CONVINCED YOU WITH THE EVIDENCE!
A PHOTO OF ME AND SENATOR BAILEY--! BUT IT HASN'T BEEN TAKEN YET! I'VE NEVER MET THE MAN!
USED CARS
TO Jughead Thanks, Pal
SO WHAT'S OUR NEXT TIMELY MOVE, JANUARY?
WE ESCAPE IN A MICRO-MINIATURIZED THOUGHT BALLOON!
A... A THOUGHT BALLOON?!?
IT'S RELEASED UPON IMPACT...
SNAP!
FOOOMP!
---INSTANTLY ENCASING US!
5

THINK OF WHERE YOU WANT TO GO - AND THE BALLOON RESPONDS TO YOUR THOUGHTS!
JUST SO LONG AS IT ISN'T HOBOKEN!
WAYNE & ENID'S
USED CARS
THE FAMOUS FORSYTHE P. JONES WIT--! EVEN IN THE FACE OF DANGER!
PLEASE! CALL ME JUG! EVERYONE ELSE DOES!
ALL RIGHT! I SHALL, FORSYTHE! I-I MEAN JUG!
AND I'LL CALL YOU JAN! ISN'T THAT BETTER?
ELSEWHERE...
I'M STILL GETTING A LIFE-SIGN ON MY JUG-O-METER!
TIK TIK TIK
LOOK! WE'VE BEEN TRICKED! THEY'RE ESCAPING IN A THOUGHT BALLOON!
ADJUST T-BOLT RINGS FOR MAXIMUM RANGE! ON MY COMMAND--- FIRE!!
K-K-RACK
KRAZ
CONTINUED 6

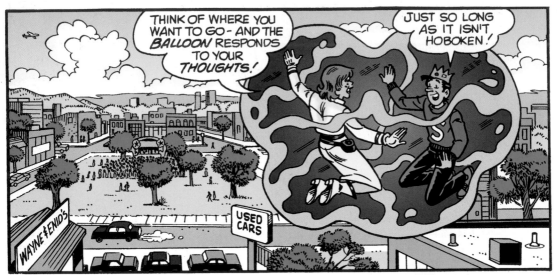

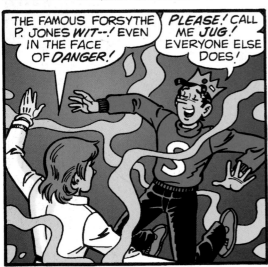

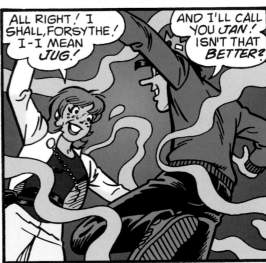

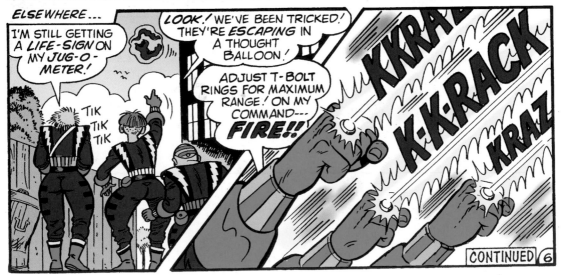

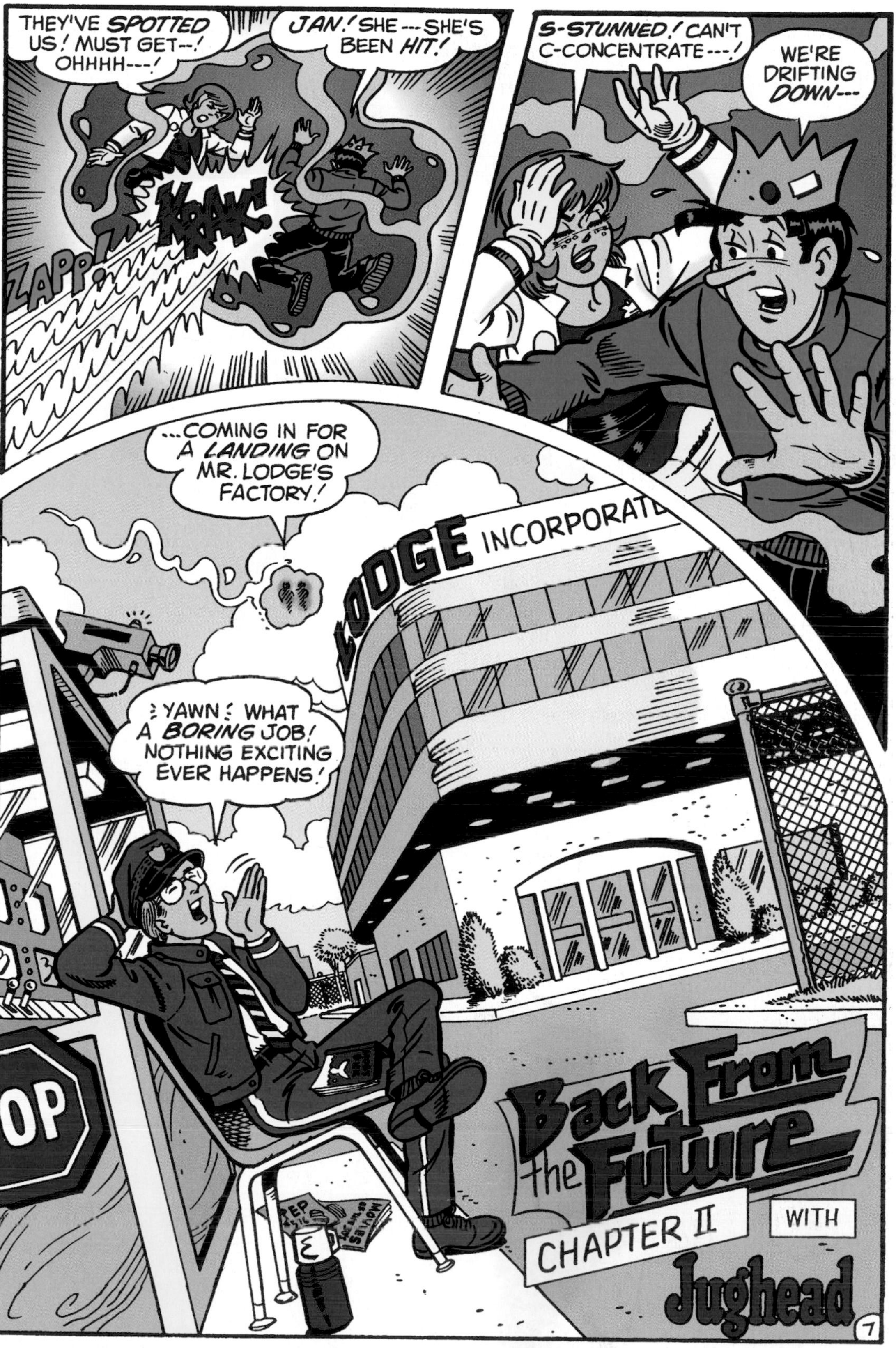
THEY'VE SPOTTED US! MUST GET--! OHHHH---!
JAN! SHE---SHE'S BEEN HIT!
ZAPP!
KRAK!
S-STUNNED! CAN'T C-CONCENTRATE---!
WE'RE DRIFTING DOWN---
...COMING IN FOR A LANDING ON MR. LODGE'S FACTORY!
LODGE INCORPORATE
YAWN WHAT A BORING JOB! NOTHING EXCITING EVER HAPPENS!
OP
Back From the Future
CHAPTER II
WITH
Jughead
7

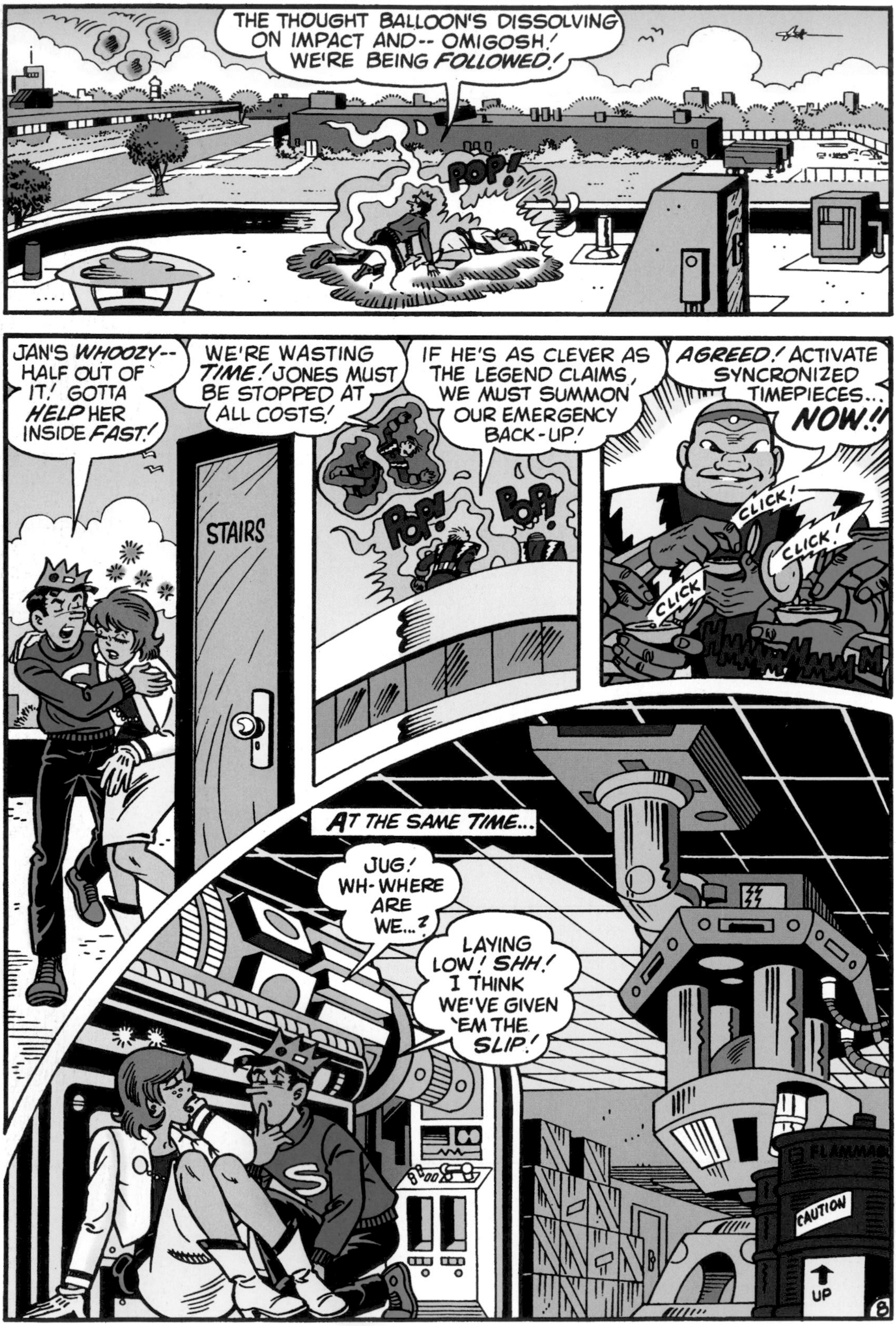
THE THOUGHT BALLOON'S DISSOLVING ON IMPACT AND-- OMIGOSH! WE'RE BEING FOLLOWED!
POP!
JAN'S WHOOZY-- HALF OUT OF IT! GOTTA HELP HER INSIDE FAST!
STAIRS
WE'RE WASTING TIME! JONES MUST BE STOPPED AT ALL COSTS!
IF HE'S AS CLEVER AS THE LEGEND CLAIMS, WE MUST SUMMON OUR EMERGENCY BACK-UP!
POP!
POP!
AGREED! ACTIVATE SYNCRONIZED TIMEPIECES... NOW!!
CLICK!
CLICK!
CLICK
AT THE SAME TIME...
JUG! WH-WHERE ARE WE...?
LAYING LOW! SHH! I THINK WE'VE GIVEN 'EM THE SLIP!
CAUTION
UP
8

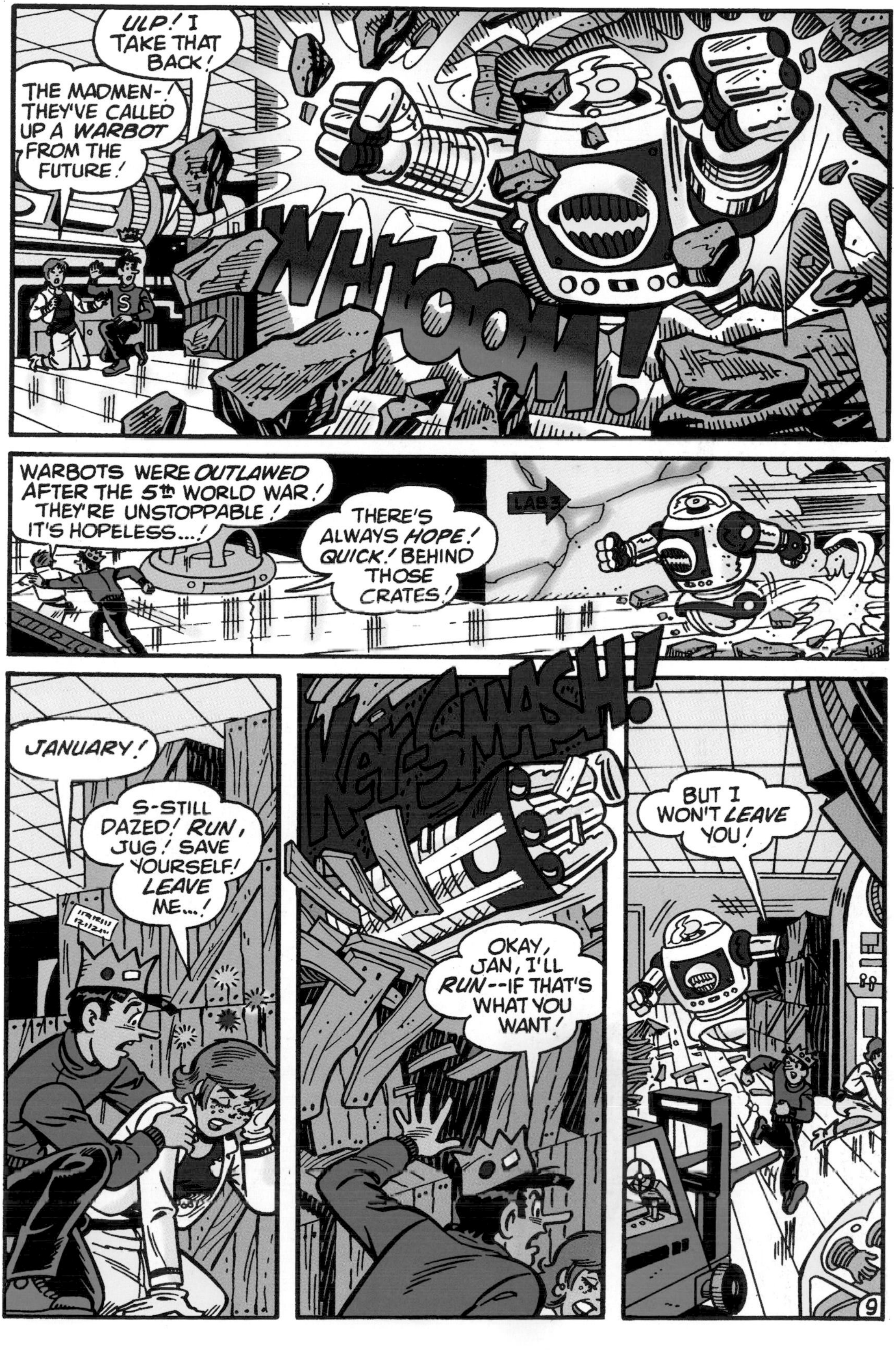
ULP! I TAKE THAT BACK!
THE MADMEN-! THEY'VE CALLED UP A WARBOT FROM THE FUTURE!
WHOOM!
WARBOTS WERE OUTLAWED AFTER THE 5th WORLD WAR! THEY'RE UNSTOPPABLE! IT'S HOPELESS...!
THERE'S ALWAYS HOPE! QUICK! BEHIND THOSE CRATES!
LAB 3
JANUARY!
S-STILL DAZED! RUN, JUG! SAVE YOURSELF! LEAVE ME...!
KAT-SMASH!
OKAY, JAN, I'LL RUN--IF THAT'S WHAT YOU WANT!
BUT I WON'T LEAVE YOU!
9

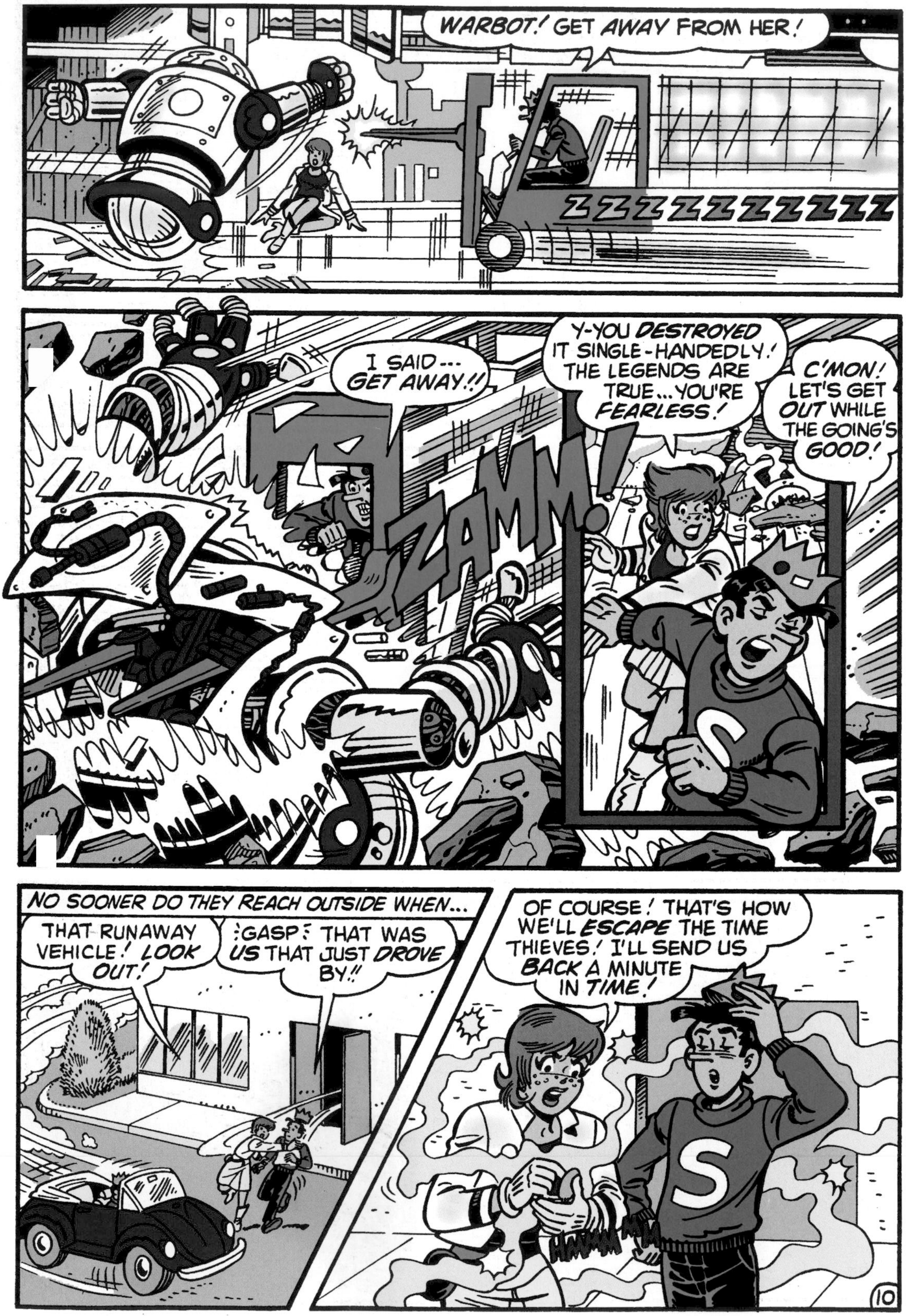
WARBOT! GET AWAY FROM HER!
ZZZZZZZZZZZ
I SAID... GET AWAY!!
ZAMM!
Y-YOU DESTROYED IT SINGLE-HANDEDLY! THE LEGENDS ARE TRUE... YOU'RE FEARLESS!
C'MON! LET'S GET OUT WHILE THE GOING'S GOOD!
NO SOONER DO THEY REACH OUTSIDE WHEN...
THAT RUNAWAY VEHICLE! LOOK OUT!
GASP THAT WAS US THAT JUST DROVE BY!!
OF COURSE! THAT'S HOW WE'LL ESCAPE THE TIME THIEVES! I'LL SEND US BACK A MINUTE IN TIME!
10

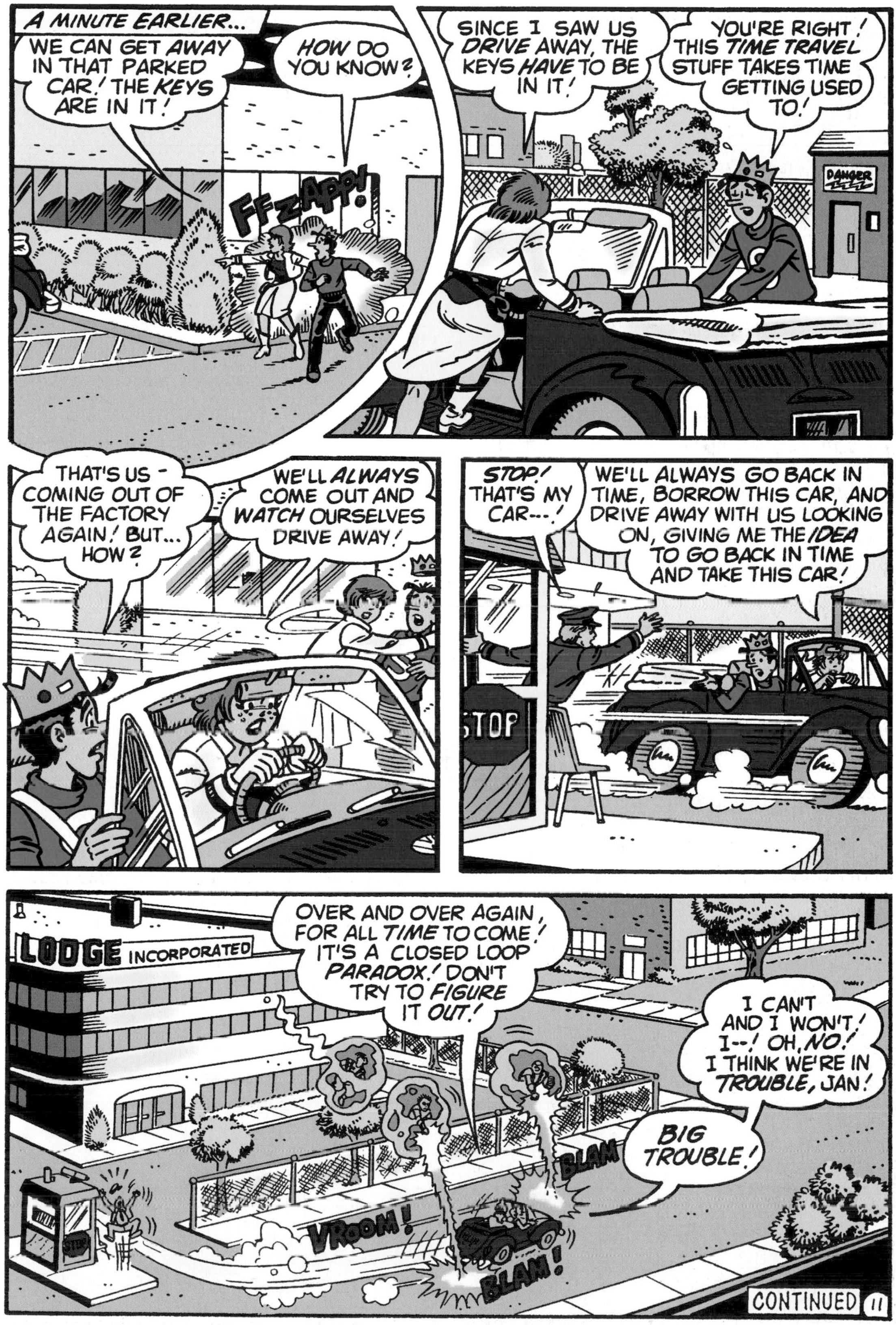
A MINUTE EARLIER...
WE CAN GET AWAY IN THAT PARKED CAR! THE KEYS ARE IN IT!
HOW DO YOU KNOW?
FFZAPP!
SINCE I SAW US DRIVE AWAY, THE KEYS HAVE TO BE IN IT!
YOU'RE RIGHT! THIS TIME TRAVEL STUFF TAKES TIME GETTING USED TO!
DANGER
THAT'S US - COMING OUT OF THE FACTORY AGAIN! BUT... HOW?
WE'LL ALWAYS COME OUT AND WATCH OURSELVES DRIVE AWAY!
STOP! THAT'S MY CAR--!
WE'LL ALWAYS GO BACK IN TIME, BORROW THIS CAR, AND DRIVE AWAY WITH US LOOKING ON, GIVING ME THE IDEA TO GO BACK IN TIME AND TAKE THIS CAR!
STOP
LODGE INCORPORATED
OVER AND OVER AGAIN, FOR ALL TIME TO COME! IT'S A CLOSED LOOP PARADOX! DON'T TRY TO FIGURE IT OUT!
I CAN'T AND I WON'T! I--! OH, NO! I THINK WE'RE IN TROUBLE, JAN!
BIG TROUBLE!
BLAM
VROOM!
BLAM!
CONTINUED 11

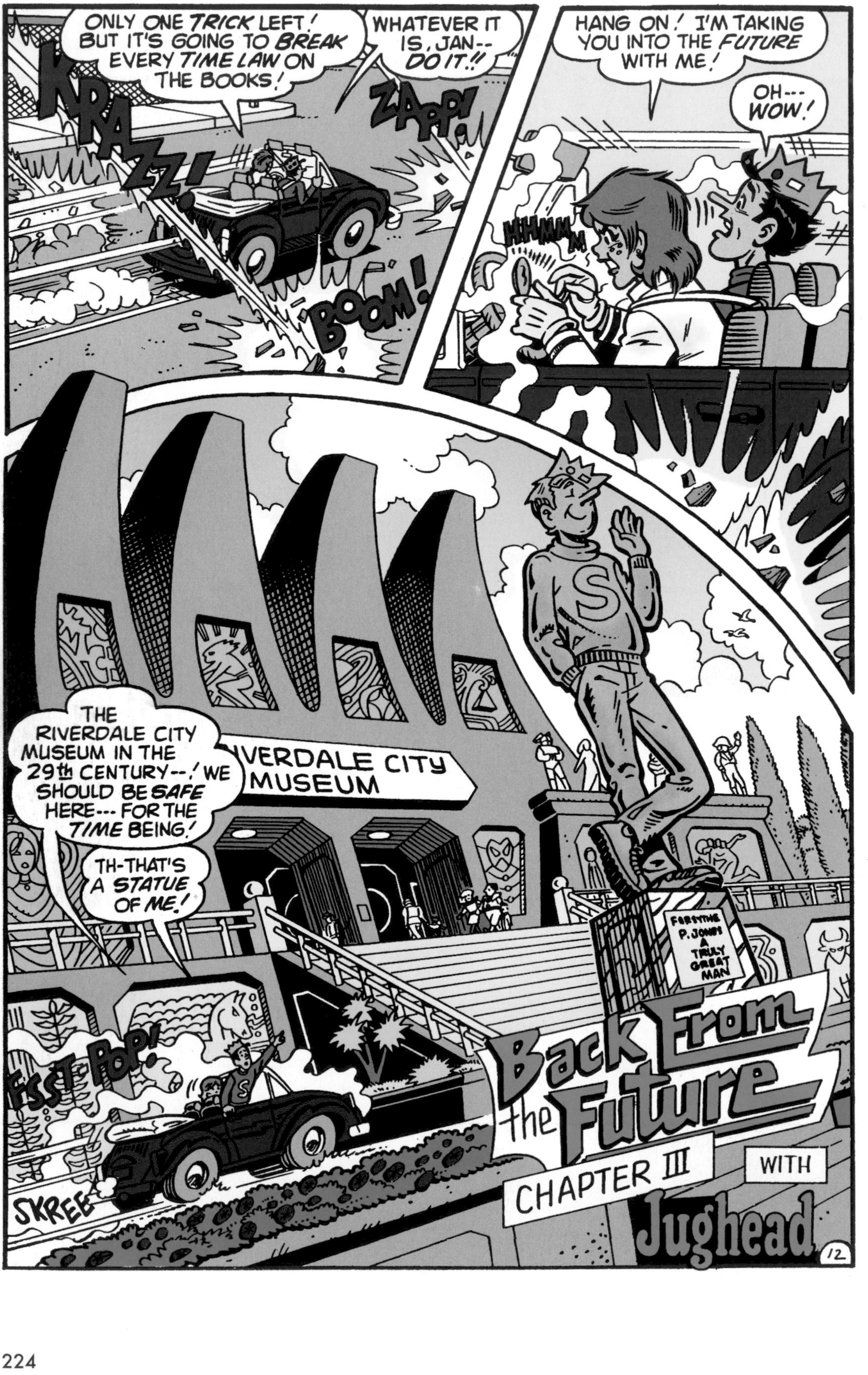
ONLY ONE TRICK LEFT! BUT IT'S GOING TO BREAK EVERY TIME LAW ON THE BOOKS!
WHATEVER IT IS, JAN-- DO IT!!
KRAZZZ!
ZAPP!
BOOM!
HANG ON! I'M TAKING YOU INTO THE FUTURE WITH ME!
OH--- WOW!
HHMMM
THE RIVERDALE CITY MUSEUM IN THE 29th CENTURY--! WE SHOULD BE SAFE HERE--- FOR THE TIME BEING!
TH-THAT'S A STATUE OF ME!
VERDALE CITY MUSEUM
FORSYTHE P. JONES A TRULY GREAT MAN
FSST-POP!
SKREE
Back From the Future
CHAPTER III
WITH
Jughead
12

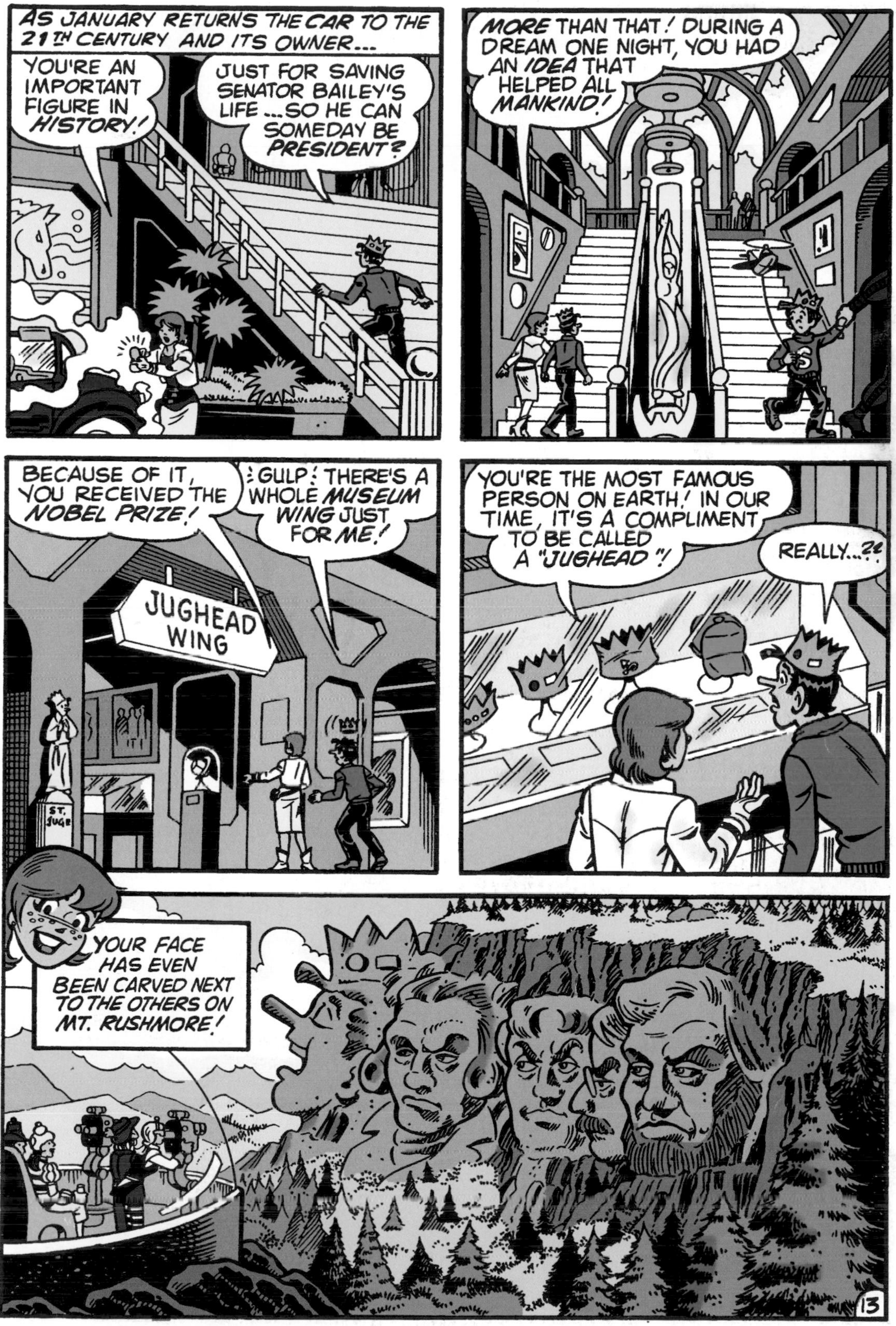

AS JANUARY RETURNS THE CAR TO THE 21TH CENTURY AND ITS OWNER...
YOU'RE AN IMPORTANT FIGURE IN HISTORY!
JUST FOR SAVING SENATOR BAILEY'S LIFE ...SO HE CAN SOMEDAY BE PRESIDENT?
MORE THAN THAT! DURING A DREAM ONE NIGHT, YOU HAD AN IDEA THAT HELPED ALL MANKIND!
BECAUSE OF IT, YOU RECEIVED THE NOBEL PRIZE!
GULP! THERE'S A WHOLE MUSEUM WING JUST FOR ME!
JUGHEAD WING
ST. JUGE
YOU'RE THE MOST FAMOUS PERSON ON EARTH! IN OUR TIME, IT'S A COMPLIMENT TO BE CALLED A "JUGHEAD"!
REALLY...??
YOUR FACE HAS EVEN BEEN CARVED NEXT TO THE OTHERS ON MT. RUSHMORE!
13

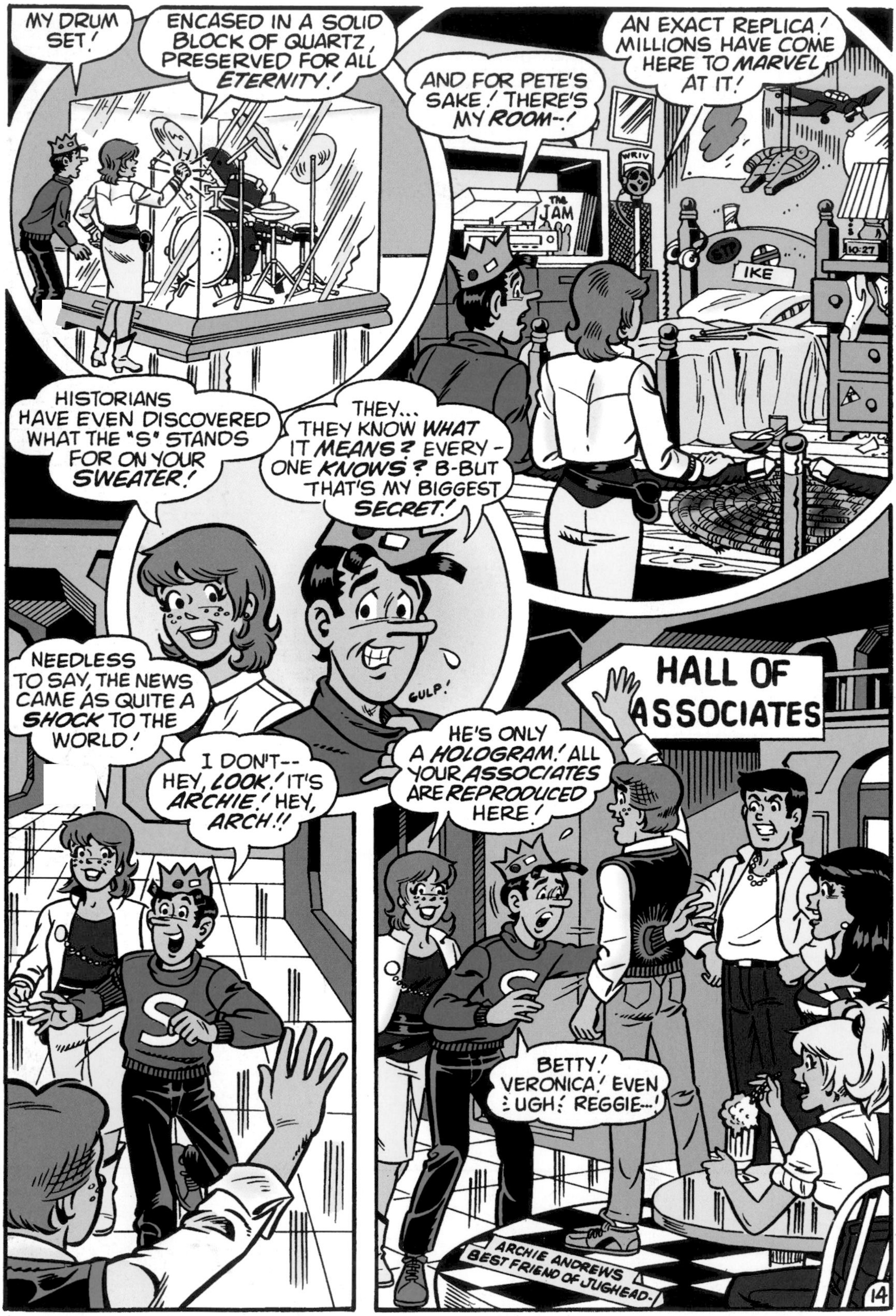
MY DRUM SET!
ENCASED IN A SOLID BLOCK OF QUARTZ, PRESERVED FOR ALL ETERNITY!
AN EXACT REPLICA! MILLIONS HAVE COME HERE TO MARVEL AT IT!
AND FOR PETE'S SAKE! THERE'S MY ROOM--!
THE JAM
WRIV
IKE
10:27
HISTORIANS HAVE EVEN DISCOVERED WHAT THE "S" STANDS FOR ON YOUR SWEATER!
THEY... THEY KNOW WHAT IT MEANS? EVERY-ONE KNOWS? B-BUT THAT'S MY BIGGEST SECRET!
GULP!
NEEDLESS TO SAY, THE NEWS CAME AS QUITE A SHOCK TO THE WORLD!
I DON'T-- HEY, LOOK! IT'S ARCHIE! HEY, ARCH!!
HALL OF ASSOCIATES
HE'S ONLY A HOLOGRAM! ALL YOUR ASSOCIATES ARE REPRODUCED HERE!
BETTY! VERONICA! EVEN UGH! REGGIE--!
ARCHIE ANDREWS BEST FRIEND OF JUGHEAD.
14

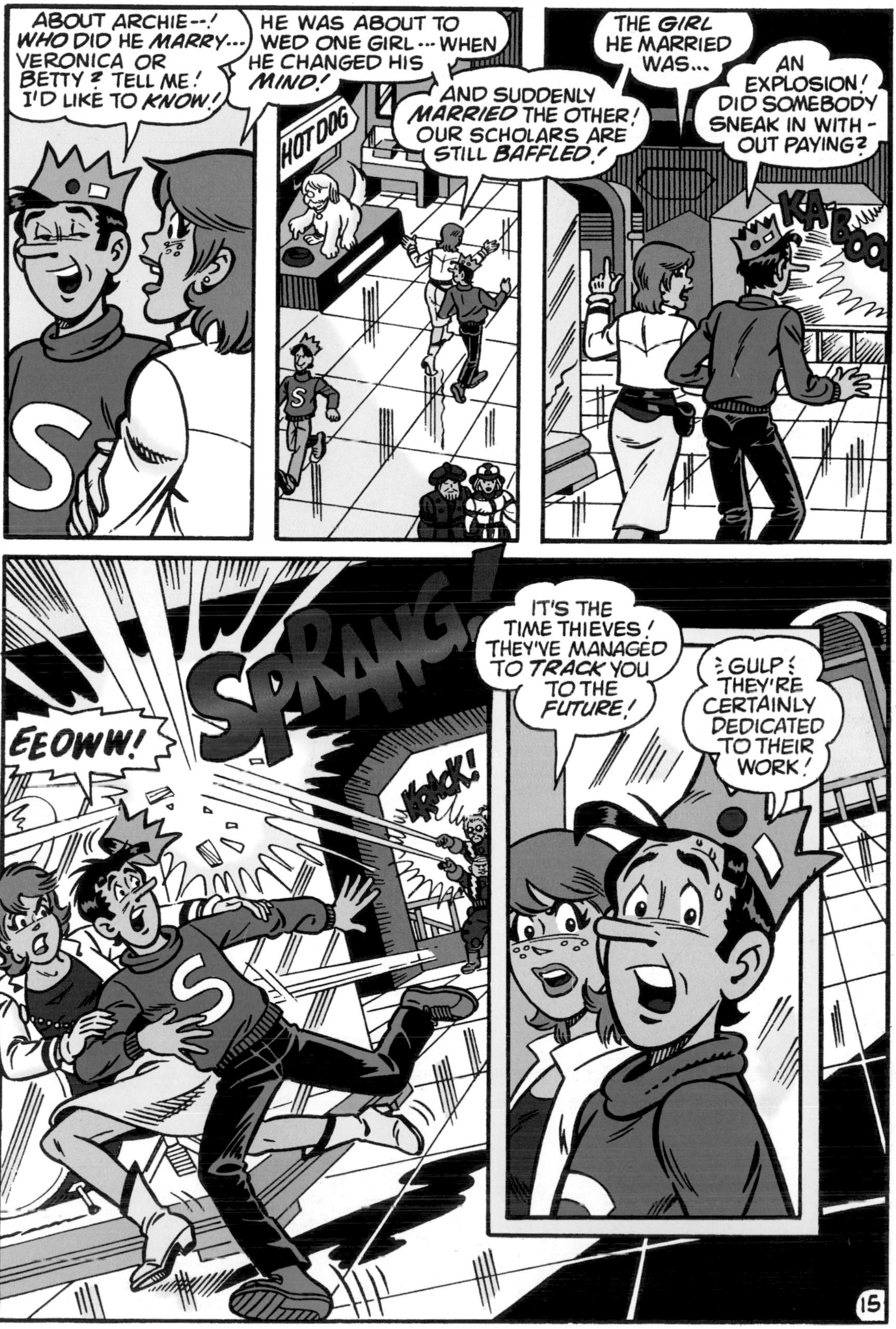
ABOUT ARCHIE--! WHO DID HE MARRY... VERONICA OR BETTY? TELL ME! I'D LIKE TO KNOW!
HE WAS ABOUT TO WED ONE GIRL... WHEN HE CHANGED HIS MIND!
HOT DOG
AND SUDDENLY MARRIED THE OTHER! OUR SCHOLARS ARE STILL BAFFLED!
THE GIRL HE MARRIED WAS...
AN EXPLOSION! DID SOMEBODY SNEAK IN WITH-OUT PAYING?
KA BOOM
SPRANG!
EEOWW!
KRACK!
IT'S THE TIME THIEVES! THEY'VE MANAGED TO TRACK YOU TO THE FUTURE!
GULP THEY'RE CERTAINLY DEDICATED TO THEIR WORK!
15

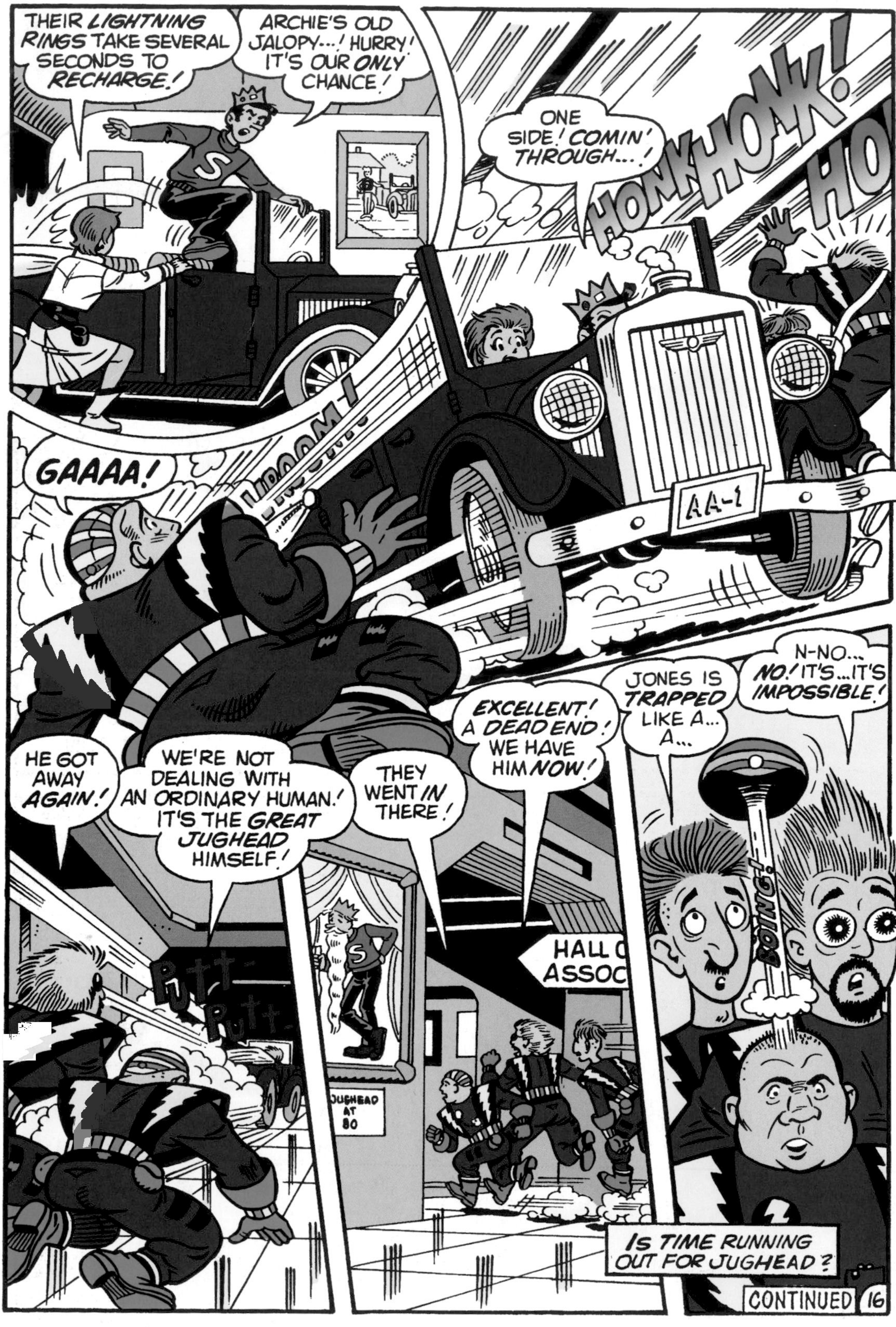
THEIR LIGHTNING RINGS TAKE SEVERAL SECONDS TO RECHARGE!
ARCHIE'S OLD JALOPY...! HURRY! IT'S OUR ONLY CHANCE!
ONE SIDE! COMIN' THROUGH...!
HONK HONK! HO
VROOM!
GAAAA!
AA-1
HE GOT AWAY AGAIN!
WE'RE NOT DEALING WITH AN ORDINARY HUMAN! IT'S THE GREAT JUGHEAD HIMSELF!
PUTT-PUTT-PUTT-
THEY WENT IN THERE!
EXCELLENT! A DEAD END! WE HAVE HIM NOW!
HALL O
ASSOC
JUGHEAD AT 80
JONES IS TRAPPED LIKE A... A...
N-NO... NO! IT'S...IT'S IMPOSSIBLE!
BOING!
IS TIME RUNNING OUT FOR JUGHEAD?
CONTINUED 16

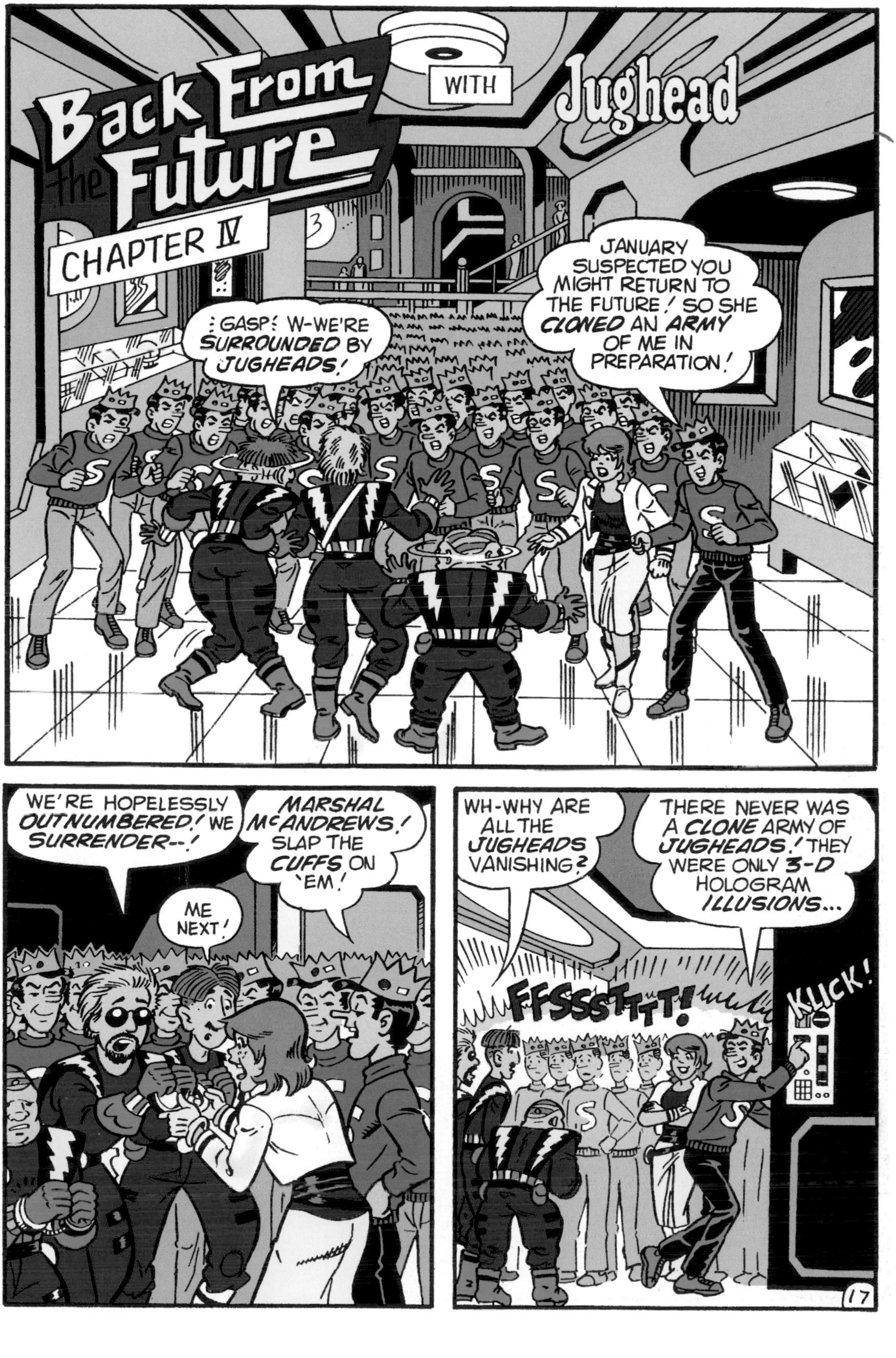
Back From the Future
WITH
Jughead
CHAPTER IV
:GASP: W-WE'RE SURROUNDED BY JUGHEADS!
JANUARY SUSPECTED YOU MIGHT RETURN TO THE FUTURE! SO SHE CLONED AN ARMY OF ME IN PREPARATION!
WE'RE HOPELESSLY OUTNUMBERED! WE SURRENDER--!
MARSHAL McANDREWS! SLAP THE CUFFS ON 'EM!
ME NEXT!
WH-WHY ARE ALL THE JUGHEADS VANISHING?
THERE NEVER WAS A CLONE ARMY OF JUGHEADS! THEY WERE ONLY 3-D HOLOGRAM ILLUSIONS...
FFSSSTTTT!
KLICK!
17

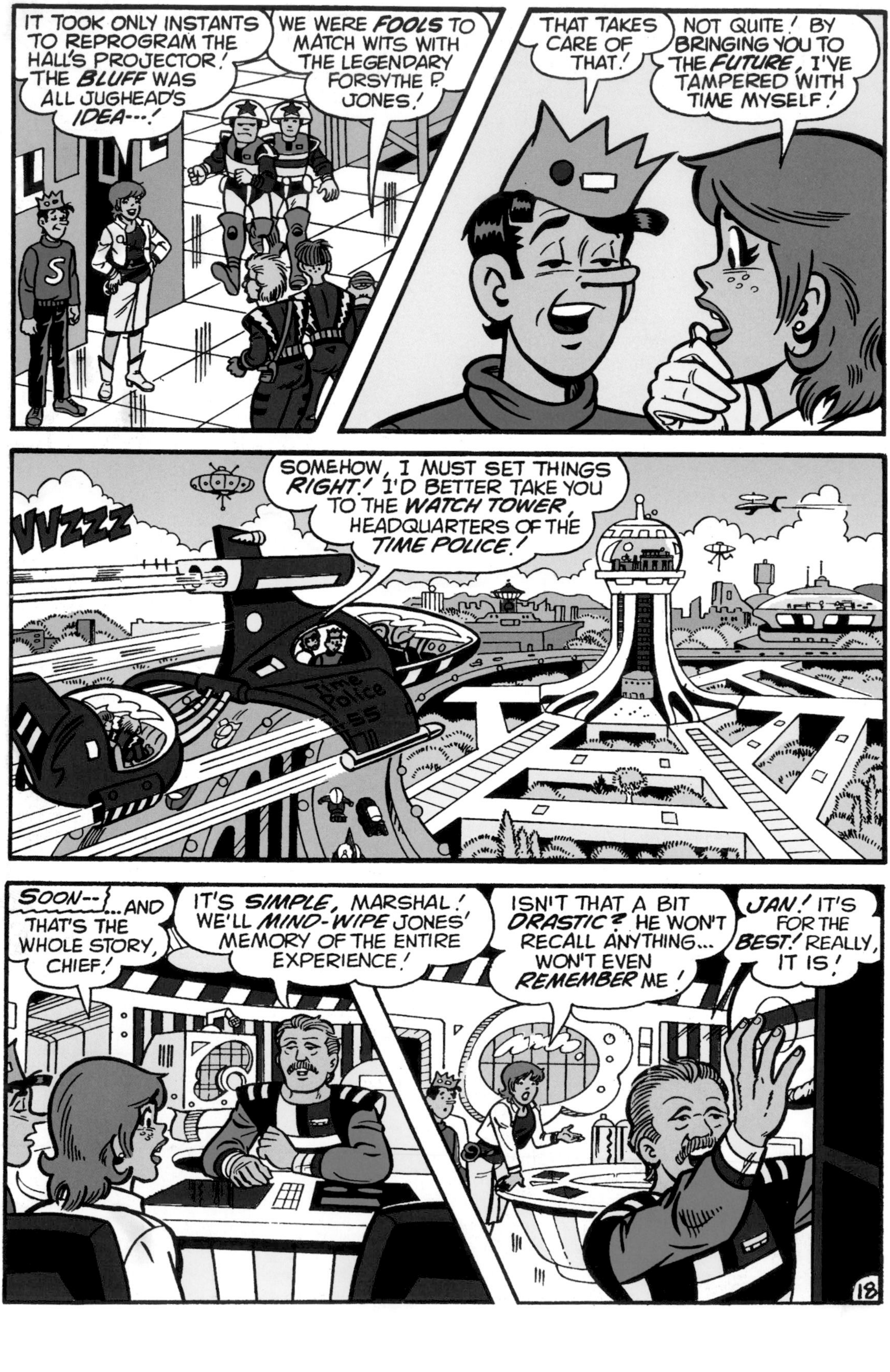
IT TOOK ONLY INSTANTS TO REPROGRAM THE HALL'S PROJECTOR! THE BLUFF WAS ALL JUGHEAD'S IDEA---!
WE WERE FOOLS TO MATCH WITS WITH THE LEGENDARY FORSYTHE P. JONES!
THAT TAKES CARE OF THAT!
NOT QUITE! BY BRINGING YOU TO THE FUTURE, I'VE TAMPERED WITH TIME MYSELF!
SOMEHOW, I MUST SET THINGS RIGHT! I'D BETTER TAKE YOU TO THE WATCH TOWER, HEADQUARTERS OF THE TIME POLICE!
VVZZZ
Time Police
55
SOON--
...AND THAT'S THE WHOLE STORY, CHIEF!
IT'S SIMPLE, MARSHAL! WE'LL MIND-WIPE JONES' MEMORY OF THE ENTIRE EXPERIENCE!
ISN'T THAT A BIT DRASTIC? HE WON'T RECALL ANYTHING... WON'T EVEN REMEMBER ME!
JAN! IT'S FOR THE BEST! REALLY, IT IS!
18

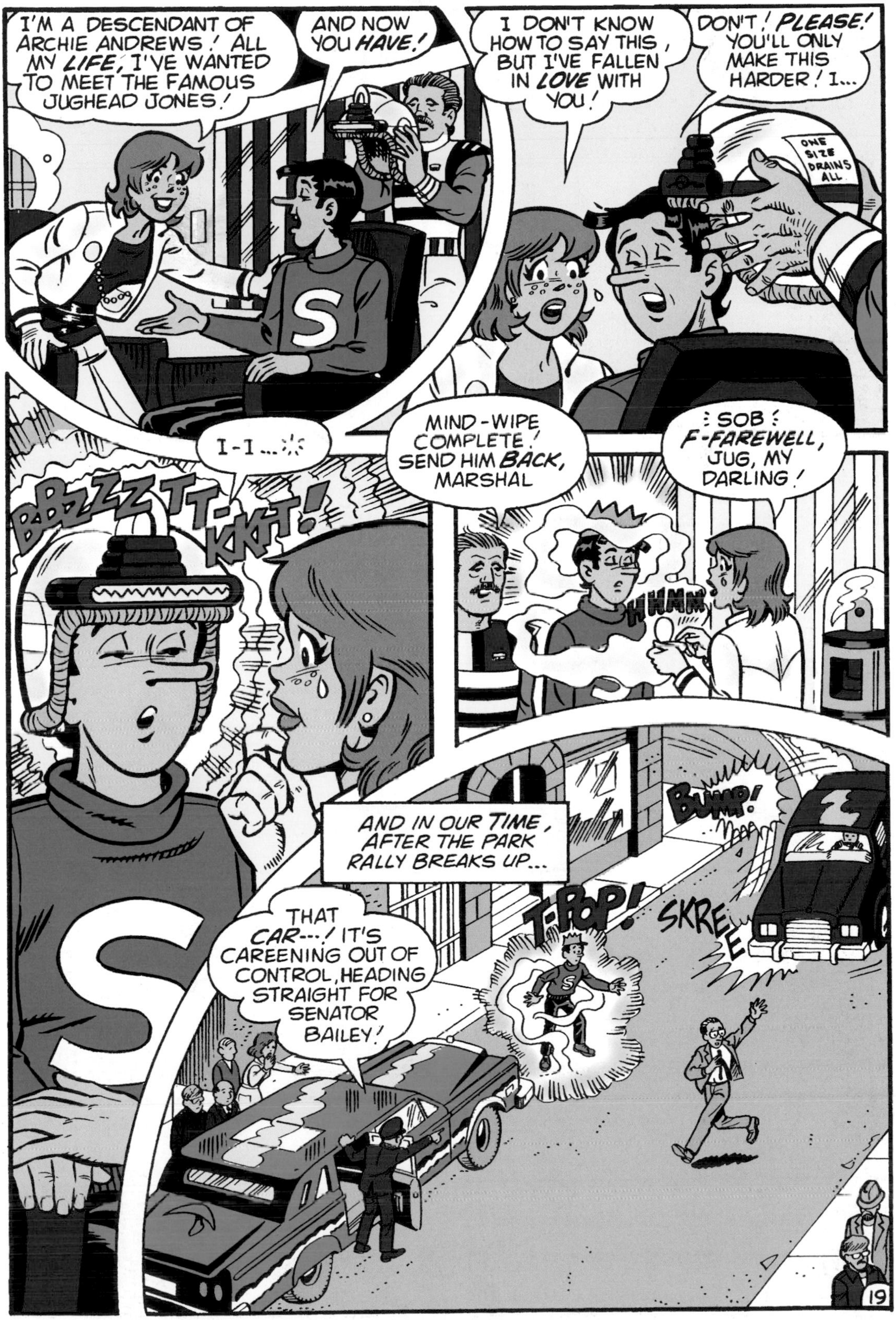
I'M A DESCENDANT OF ARCHIE ANDREWS! ALL MY LIFE, I'VE WANTED TO MEET THE FAMOUS JUGHEAD JONES!
AND NOW YOU HAVE!
I DON'T KNOW HOW TO SAY THIS, BUT I'VE FALLEN IN LOVE WITH YOU!
DON'T! PLEASE! YOU'LL ONLY MAKE THIS HARDER! I...
ONE SIZE DRAINS ALL
I-I...
BBZZZ TT-KKKT!
MIND-WIPE COMPLETE! SEND HIM BACK, MARSHAL
SOB F-FAREWELL, JUG, MY DARLING!
HMMM
AND IN OUR TIME, AFTER THE PARK RALLY BREAKS UP...
BUMP!
T-POP!
SKREE
THAT CAR---! IT'S CAREENING OUT OF CONTROL, HEADING STRAIGHT FOR SENATOR BAILEY!
19

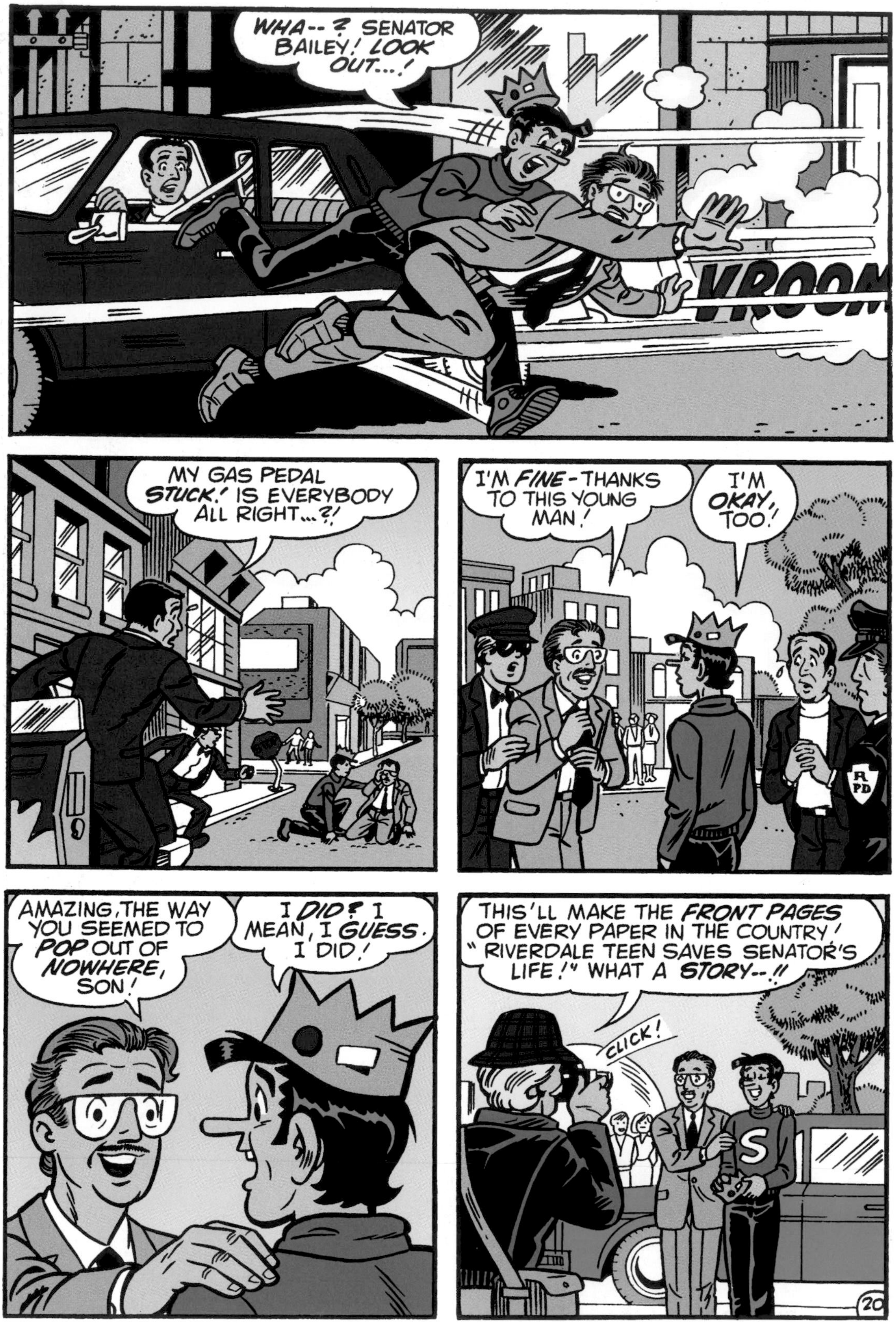
WHA--? SENATOR BAILEY! LOOK OUT...!
VROOM
MY GAS PEDAL STUCK! IS EVERYBODY ALL RIGHT...?!
I'M FINE - THANKS TO THIS YOUNG MAN!
I'M OKAY, TOO!
AMAZING, THE WAY YOU SEEMED TO POP OUT OF NOWHERE, SON!
I DID? I MEAN, I GUESS. I DID!
THIS'LL MAKE THE FRONT PAGES OF EVERY PAPER IN THE COUNTRY! "RIVERDALE TEEN SAVES SENATOR'S LIFE!" WHAT A STORY--!!
CLICK!
20

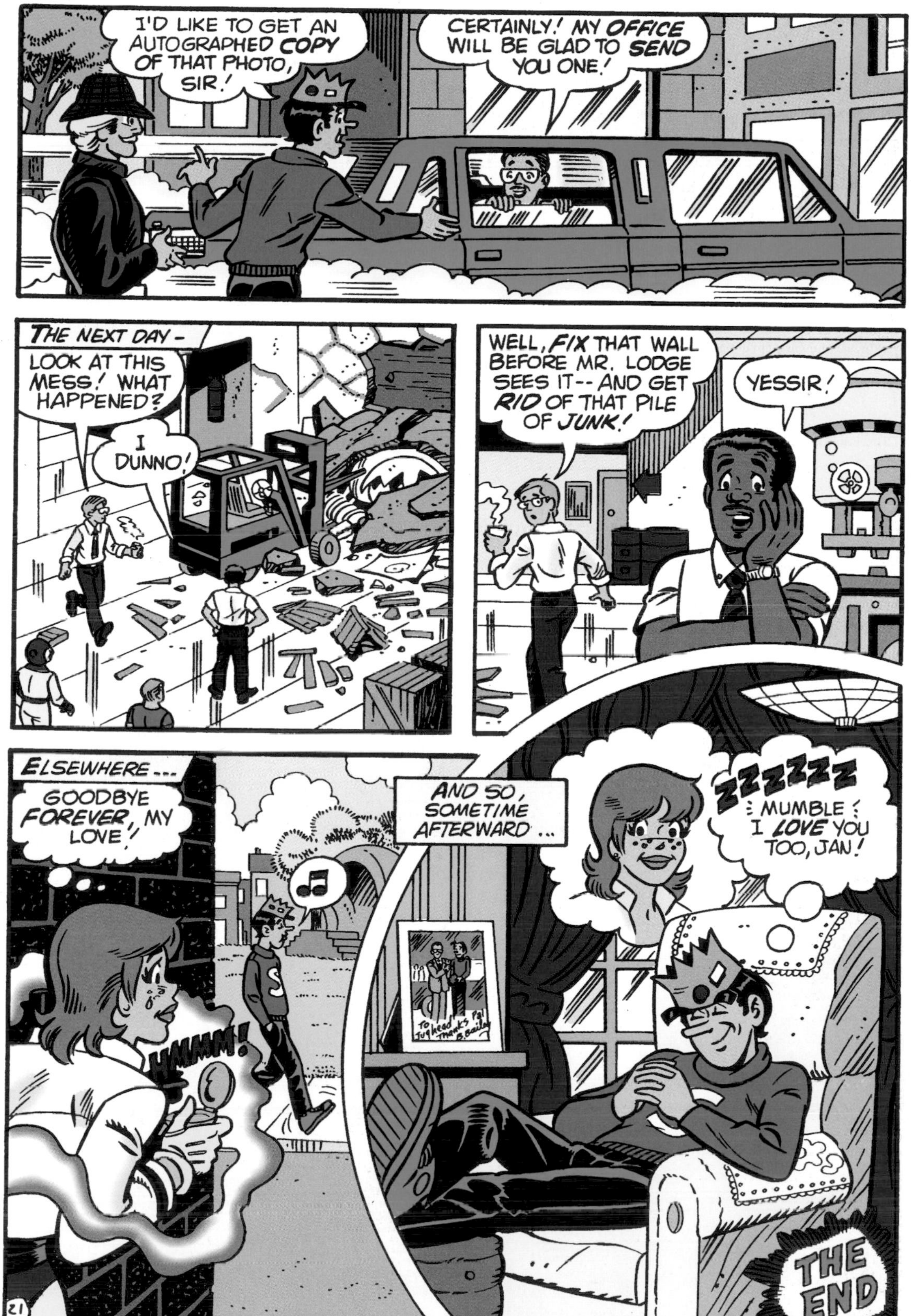
I'D LIKE TO GET AN AUTOGRAPHED COPY OF THAT PHOTO, SIR!
CERTAINLY! MY OFFICE WILL BE GLAD TO SEND YOU ONE!
THE NEXT DAY -
LOOK AT THIS MESS! WHAT HAPPENED?
I DUNNO!
WELL, FIX THAT WALL BEFORE MR. LODGE SEES IT-- AND GET RID OF THAT PILE OF JUNK!
YESSIR!
ELSEWHERE...
GOODBYE FOREVER, MY LOVE!
HMMM!
AND SO, SOMETIME AFTERWARD...
ZZZZZZ
MUMBLE I LOVE YOU TOO, JAN!
To Jughead Thanks Pal B.Bailey
THE END
21

The BEST of Archie® COMICS

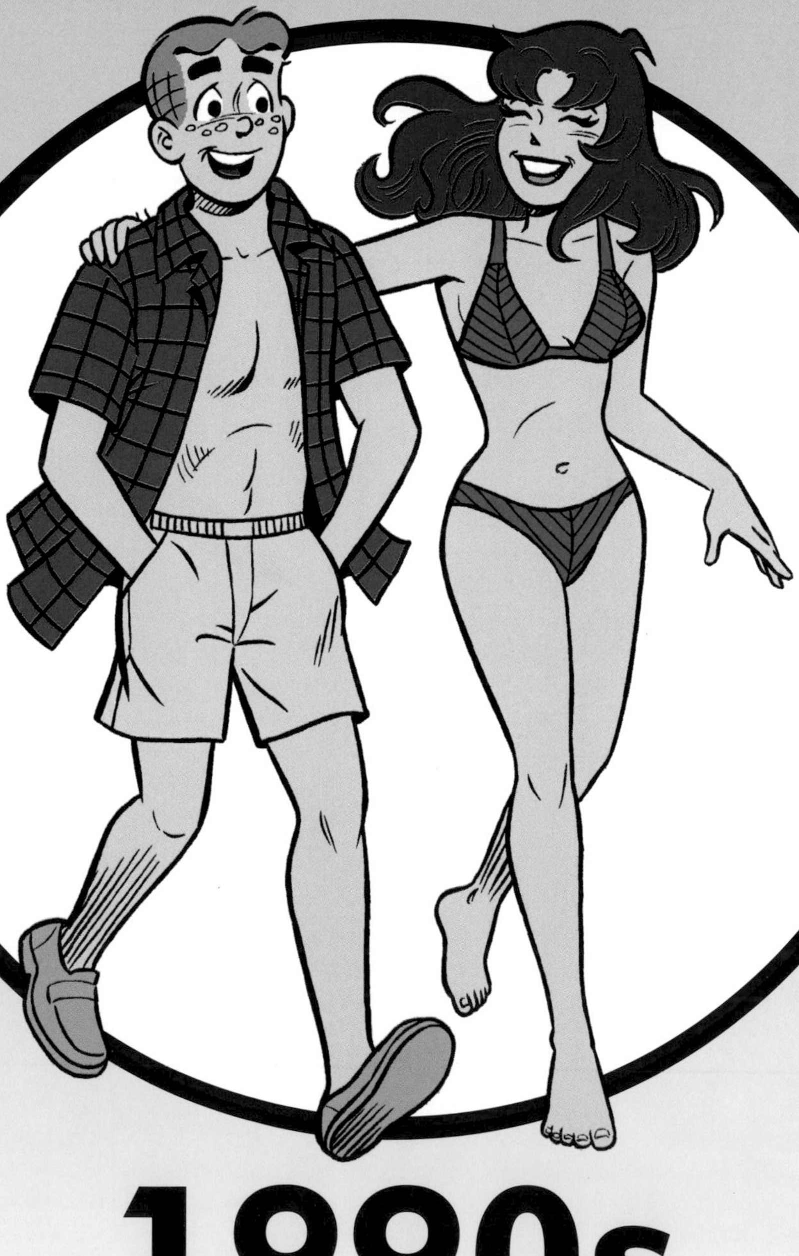

1990s

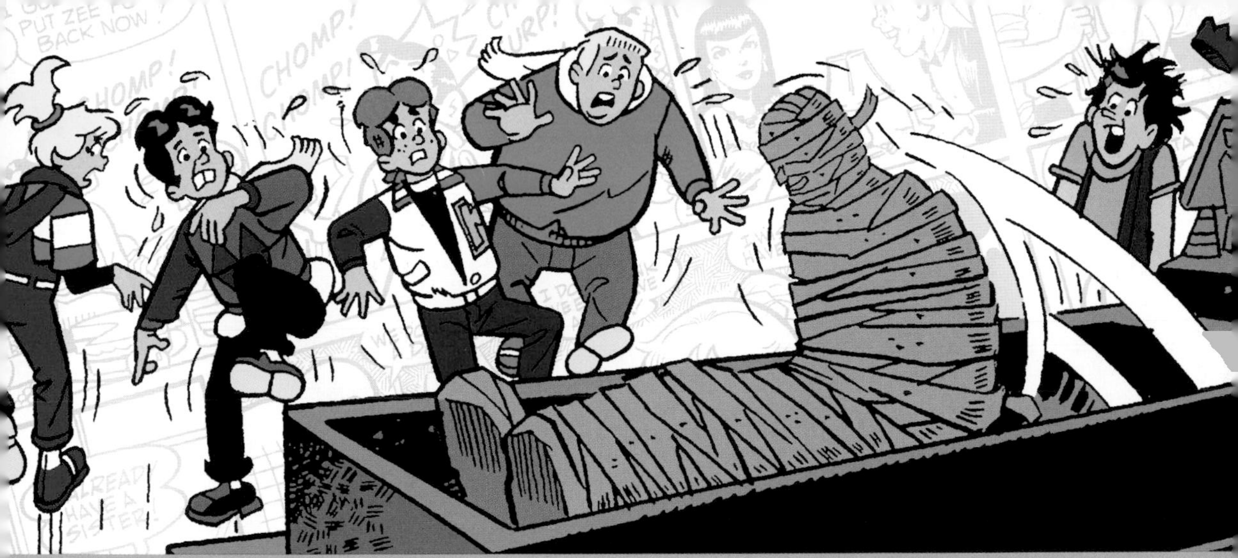
BACK NOW
CHOMP!

MYSTERY OF THE MUMMY'S CURSE

NEW ARCHIES DIGEST #10, 1990

BY MIKE PELLOWSKI, HENRY SCARPELLI, BILL YOSHIDA, BARRY GROSSMAN, NANCI TSETSEKAS & GREGG SUCHOW

This story is a smorgasbord of hilarious hi-jinks and silly situations. After reading this you'll be asking—where's my *New Archies* deluxe hardcover collection with all the trimmings? That's right, I put it out there, now start writing and demanding this collection!

As you can tell these are some of my favorite stories. What else can I say about *The New Archies* that I haven't already said? Without its influence my life would have been far different. Without that red haired mullet wearing kid I may have had my peanut butter sandwiches cut diagonally with the crust left on!

—Stephen Oswald
Production Manager/Associate Editor, Archie Comics

CHERYL'S BEACH BASH

CHERYL BLOSSOM #15, 1995

BY DAN PARENT, JON D'AGOSTINO, BILL YOSHIDA & BARRY GROSSMAN

I can't believe so many years have passed since I wrote and drew "Cheryl's Beach Bash"! It was a fun three-parter where Cheryl has her own MTV-style show set in a beach house. For all you kids out there, there was a time when MTV showed videos, and they had a beach house show during the summer where they would show various videos, do celebrity interviews, etc.

At this point in Cheryl's solo series, we had established her as a real media attention-grabber. She was getting known for being famous for just being famous. And this was pre-Kardashian!

What I love most about these stories was poking fun at pop culture and what a great character Cheryl is. I think a reality show with Cheryl would've been perfect. Hmmmm, sounds like an idea for a new storyline.

—Dan Parent
Writer and Artist, Archie Comics

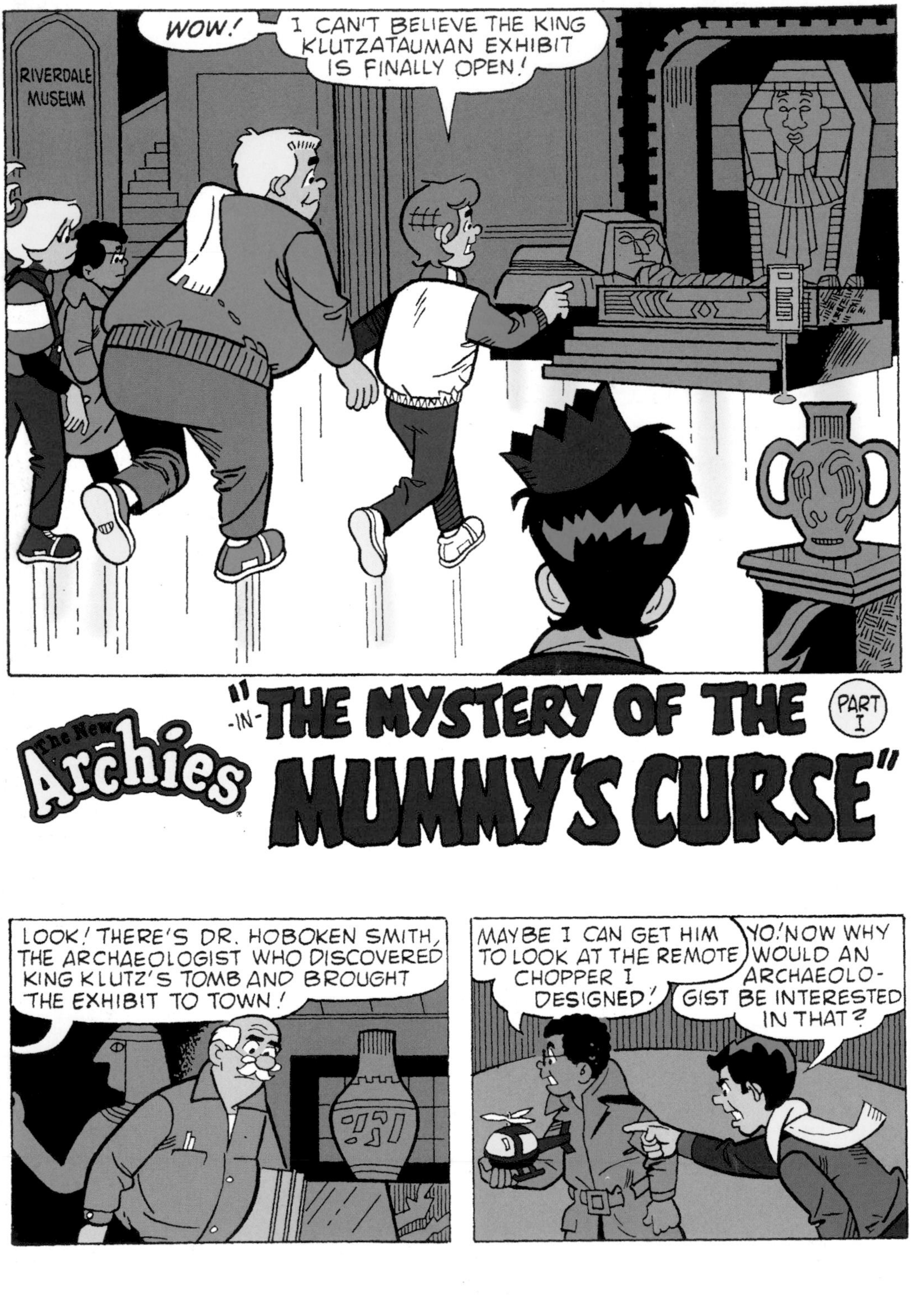
RIVERDALE MUSEUM
WOW!
I CAN'T BELIEVE THE KING KLUTZATAUMAN EXHIBIT IS FINALLY OPEN!
The New Archies
-IN- "THE MYSTERY OF THE MUMMY'S CURSE" PART I
LOOK! THERE'S DR. HOBOKEN SMITH, THE ARCHAEOLOGIST WHO DISCOVERED KING KLUTZ'S TOMB AND BROUGHT THE EXHIBIT TO TOWN!
MAYBE I CAN GET HIM TO LOOK AT THE REMOTE CHOPPER I DESIGNED!
YO! NOW WHY WOULD AN ARCHAEOLO-GIST BE INTERESTED IN THAT?

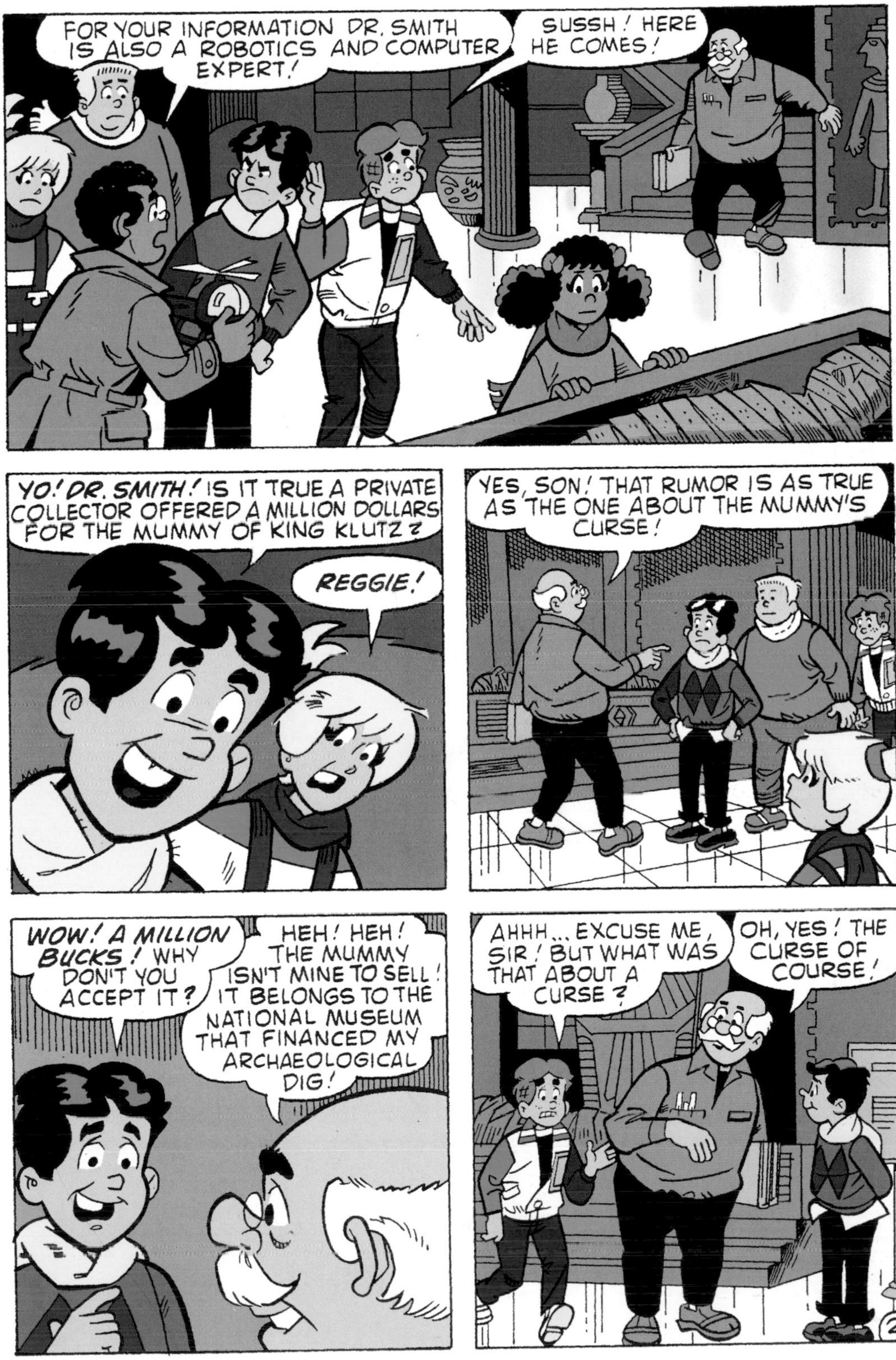
FOR YOUR INFORMATION DR. SMITH IS ALSO A ROBOTICS AND COMPUTER EXPERT!
SUSSH! HERE HE COMES!
YO! DR. SMITH! IS IT TRUE A PRIVATE COLLECTOR OFFERED A MILLION DOLLARS FOR THE MUMMY OF KING KLUTZ?
REGGIE!
YES, SON! THAT RUMOR IS AS TRUE AS THE ONE ABOUT THE MUMMY'S CURSE!
WOW! A MILLION BUCKS! WHY DON'T YOU ACCEPT IT?
HEH! HEH! THE MUMMY ISN'T MINE TO SELL! IT BELONGS TO THE NATIONAL MUSEUM THAT FINANCED MY ARCHAEOLOGICAL DIG!
AHHH... EXCUSE ME, SIR! BUT WHAT WAS THAT ABOUT A CURSE?
OH, YES! THE CURSE OF COURSE!
2

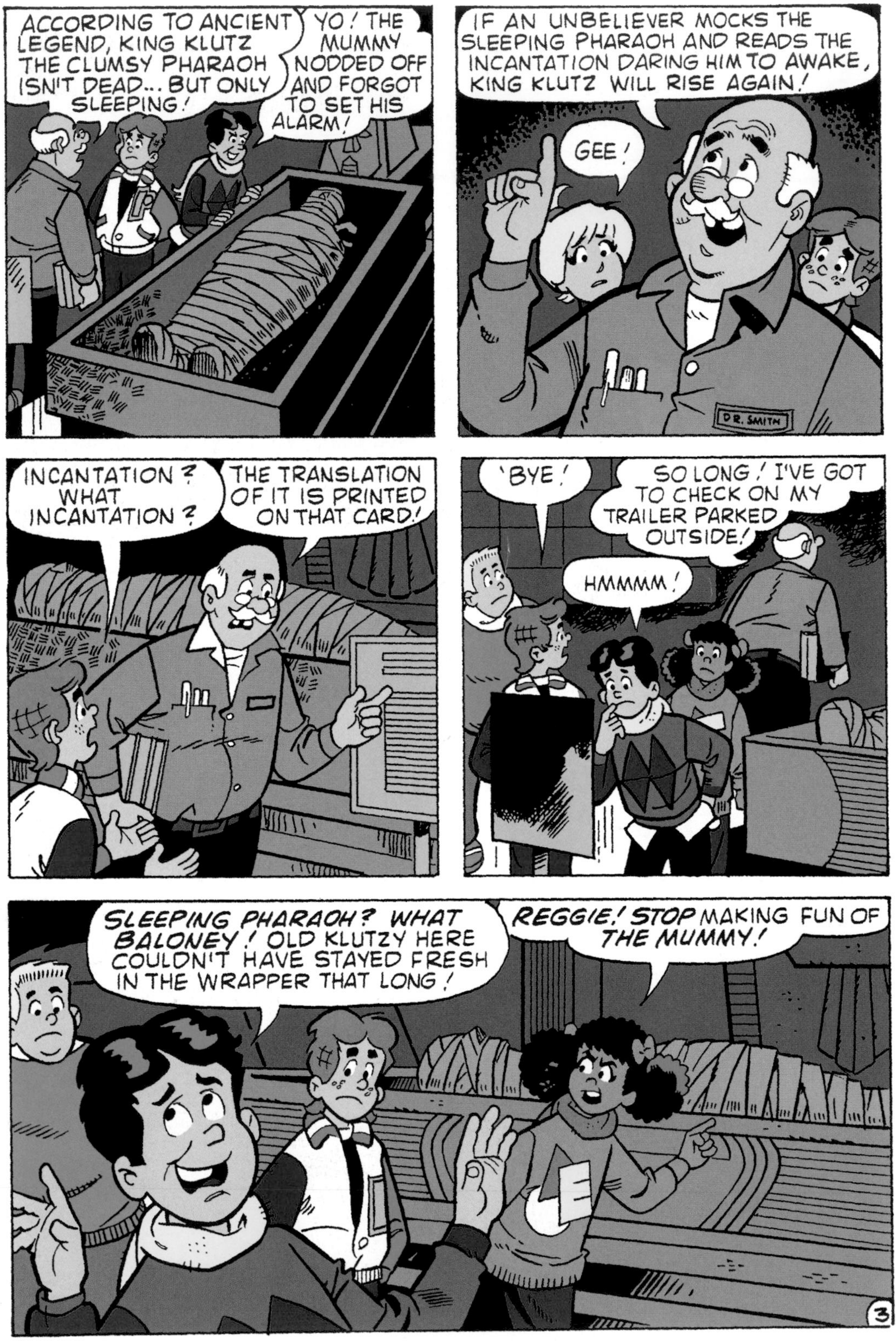
ACCORDING TO ANCIENT LEGEND, KING KLUTZ THE CLUMSY PHARAOH ISN'T DEAD... BUT ONLY SLEEPING!
YO! THE MUMMY NODDED OFF AND FORGOT TO SET HIS ALARM!
IF AN UNBELIEVER MOCKS THE SLEEPING PHARAOH AND READS THE INCANTATION DARING HIM TO AWAKE, KING KLUTZ WILL RISE AGAIN!
GEE!
DR. SMITH
INCANTATION? WHAT INCANTATION?
THE TRANSLATION OF IT IS PRINTED ON THAT CARD!
'BYE!
SO LONG! I'VE GOT TO CHECK ON MY TRAILER PARKED OUTSIDE!
HMMMM!
SLEEPING PHARAOH? WHAT BALONEY! OLD KLUTZY HERE COULDN'T HAVE STAYED FRESH IN THE WRAPPER THAT LONG!
REGGIE! STOP MAKING FUN OF THE MUMMY!
3

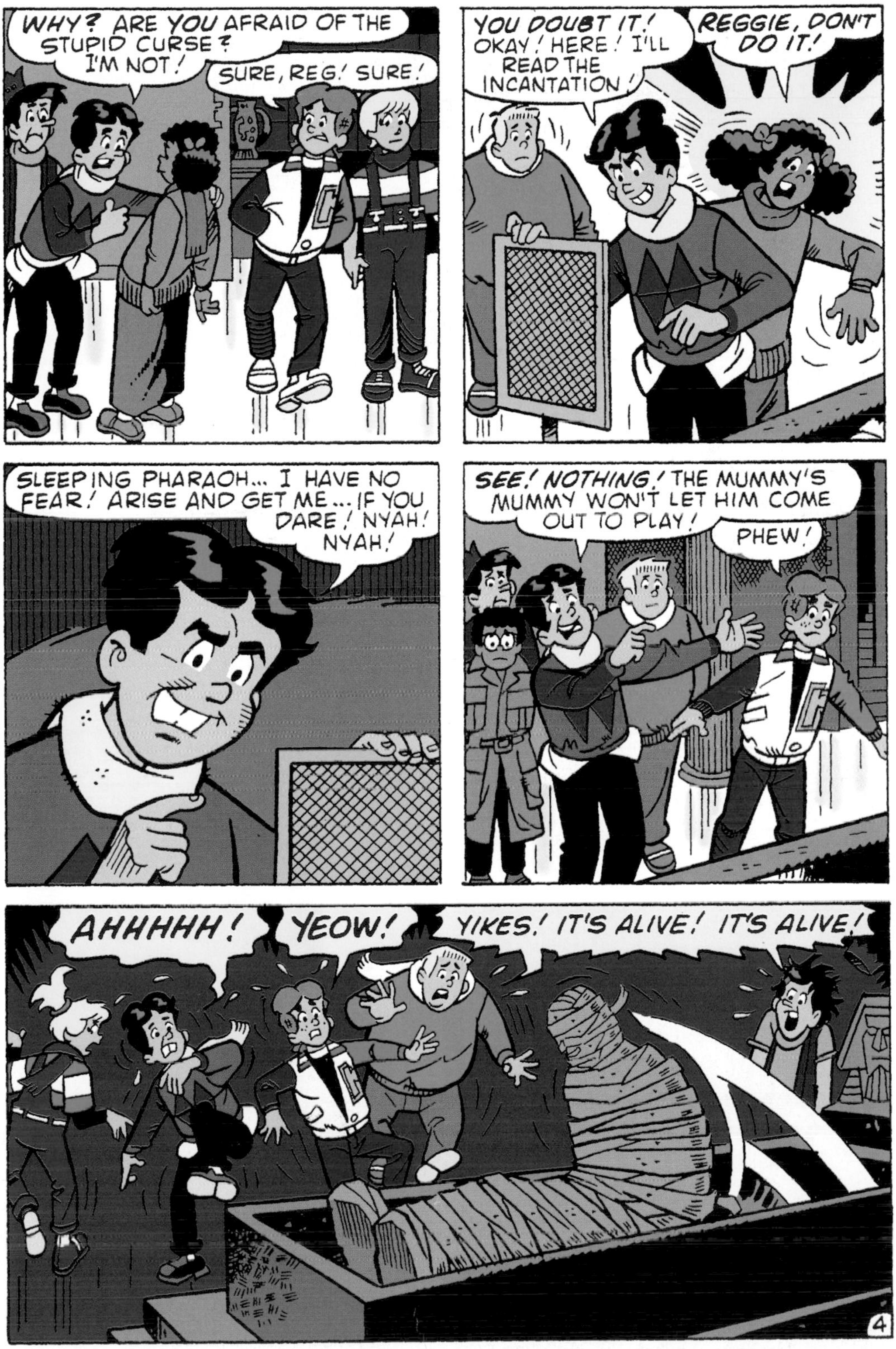

WHY? ARE YOU AFRAID OF THE STUPID CURSE? I'M NOT!
SURE, REG! SURE!
YOU DOUBT IT! OKAY! HERE! I'LL READ THE INCANTATION!
REGGIE, DON'T DO IT!
SLEEPING PHARAOH... I HAVE NO FEAR! ARISE AND GET ME... IF YOU DARE! NYAH! NYAH!
SEE! NOTHING! THE MUMMY'S MUMMY WON'T LET HIM COME OUT TO PLAY!
PHEW!
AHHHHH!
YEOW!
YIKES! IT'S ALIVE! IT'S ALIVE!
4

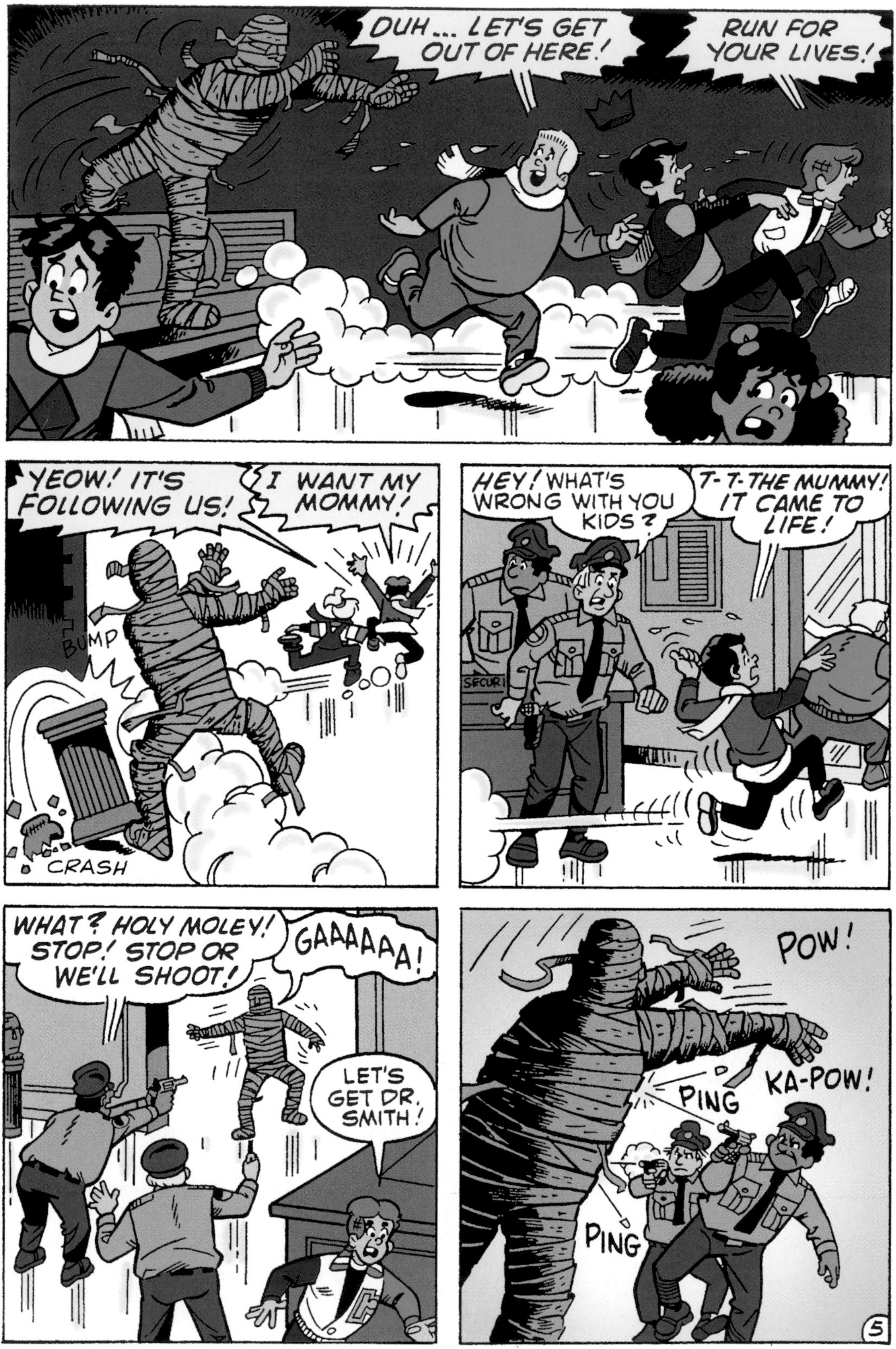
DUH ... LET'S GET OUT OF HERE!
RUN FOR YOUR LIVES!
YEOW! IT'S FOLLOWING US!
I WANT MY MOMMY!
BUMP
CRASH
HEY! WHAT'S WRONG WITH YOU KIDS?
T-T-THE MUMMY! IT CAME TO LIFE!
WHAT? HOLY MOLEY! STOP! STOP OR WE'LL SHOOT!
GAAAAAAA!
LET'S GET DR. SMITH!
POW!
KA-POW!
PING
PING
5

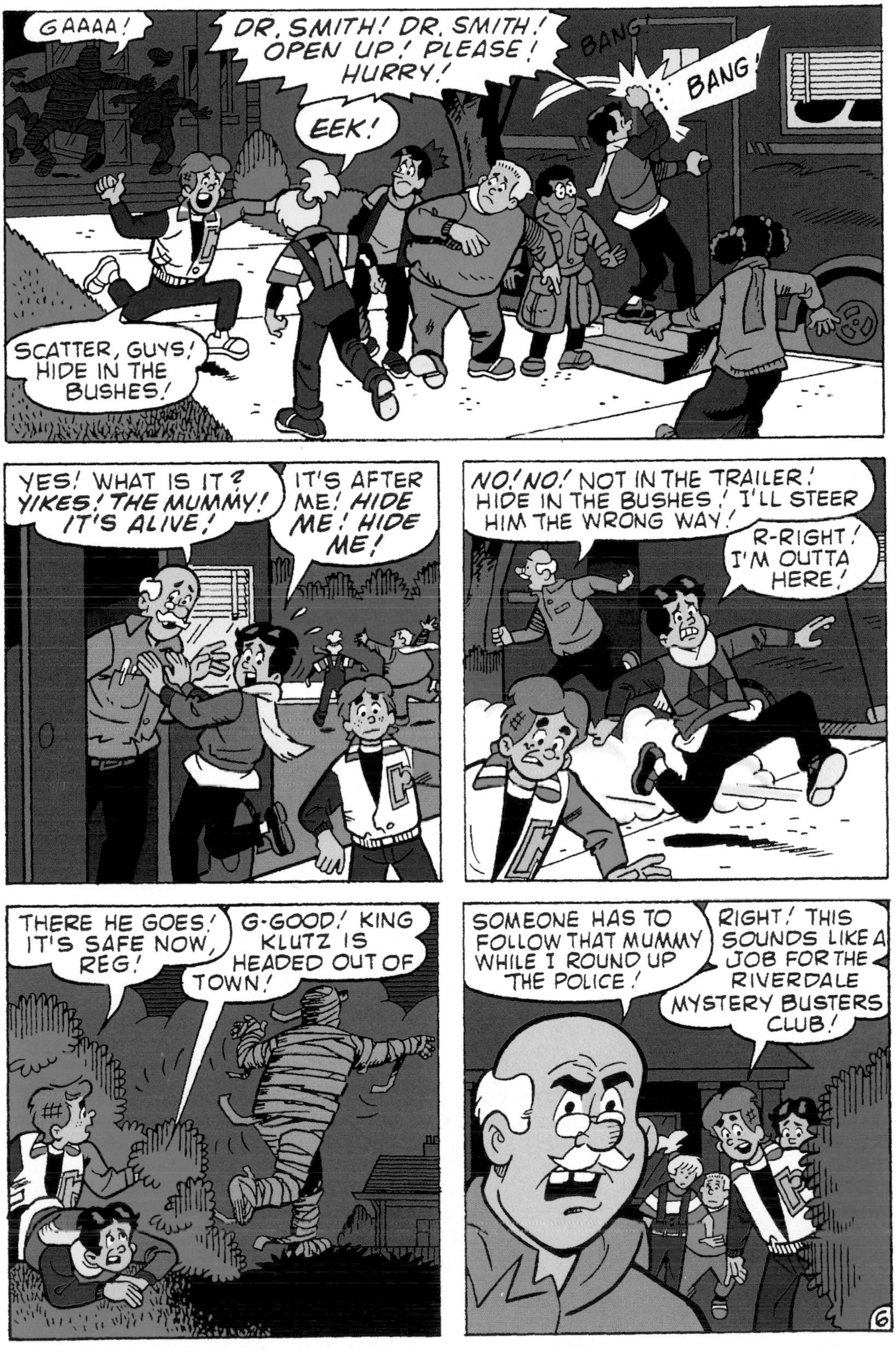
GAAAA!
DR. SMITH! DR. SMITH! OPEN UP! PLEASE! HURRY!
BANG!
BANG!
EEK!
SCATTER, GUYS! HIDE IN THE BUSHES!
YES! WHAT IS IT? YIKES! THE MUMMY! IT'S ALIVE!
IT'S AFTER ME! HIDE ME! HIDE ME!
NO! NO! NOT IN THE TRAILER! HIDE IN THE BUSHES! I'LL STEER HIM THE WRONG WAY!
R-RIGHT! I'M OUTTA HERE!
THERE HE GOES! IT'S SAFE NOW, REG!
G-GOOD! KING KLUTZ IS HEADED OUT OF TOWN!
SOMEONE HAS TO FOLLOW THAT MUMMY WHILE I ROUND UP THE POLICE!
RIGHT! THIS SOUNDS LIKE A JOB FOR THE RIVERDALE MYSTERY BUSTERS CLUB!
6

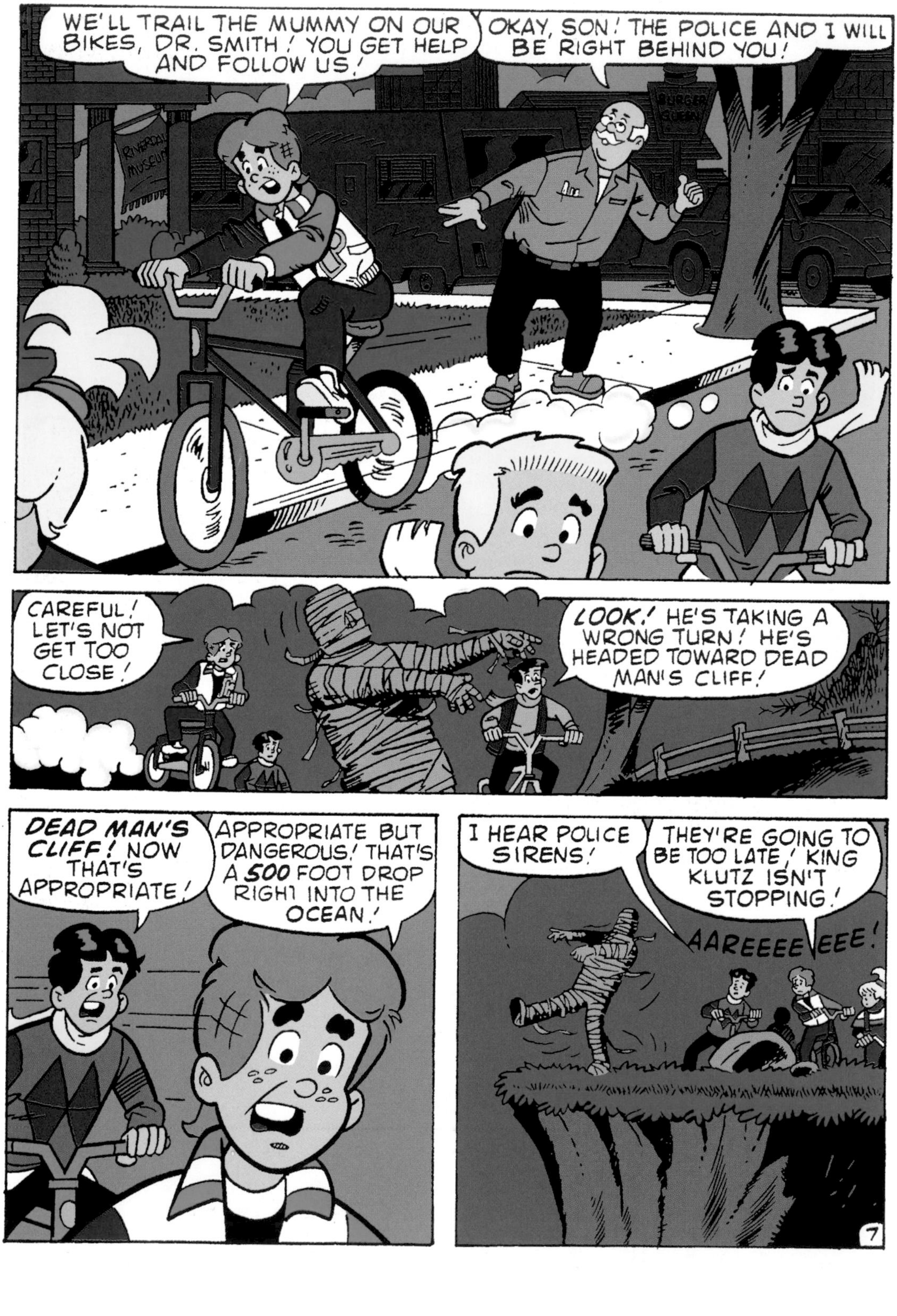
WE'LL TRAIL THE MUMMY ON OUR BIKES, DR. SMITH! YOU GET HELP AND FOLLOW US!
OKAY, SON! THE POLICE AND I WILL BE RIGHT BEHIND YOU!
RIVERDALE MUSEUM
BURGER QUEEN
CAREFUL! LET'S NOT GET TOO CLOSE!
LOOK! HE'S TAKING A WRONG TURN! HE'S HEADED TOWARD DEAD MAN'S CLIFF!
DEAD MAN'S CLIFF! NOW THAT'S APPROPRIATE!
APPROPRIATE BUT DANGEROUS! THAT'S A 500 FOOT DROP RIGHT INTO THE OCEAN!
I HEAR POLICE SIRENS!
THEY'RE GOING TO BE TOO LATE! KING KLUTZ ISN'T STOPPING!
AAREEEEEEEE!
7

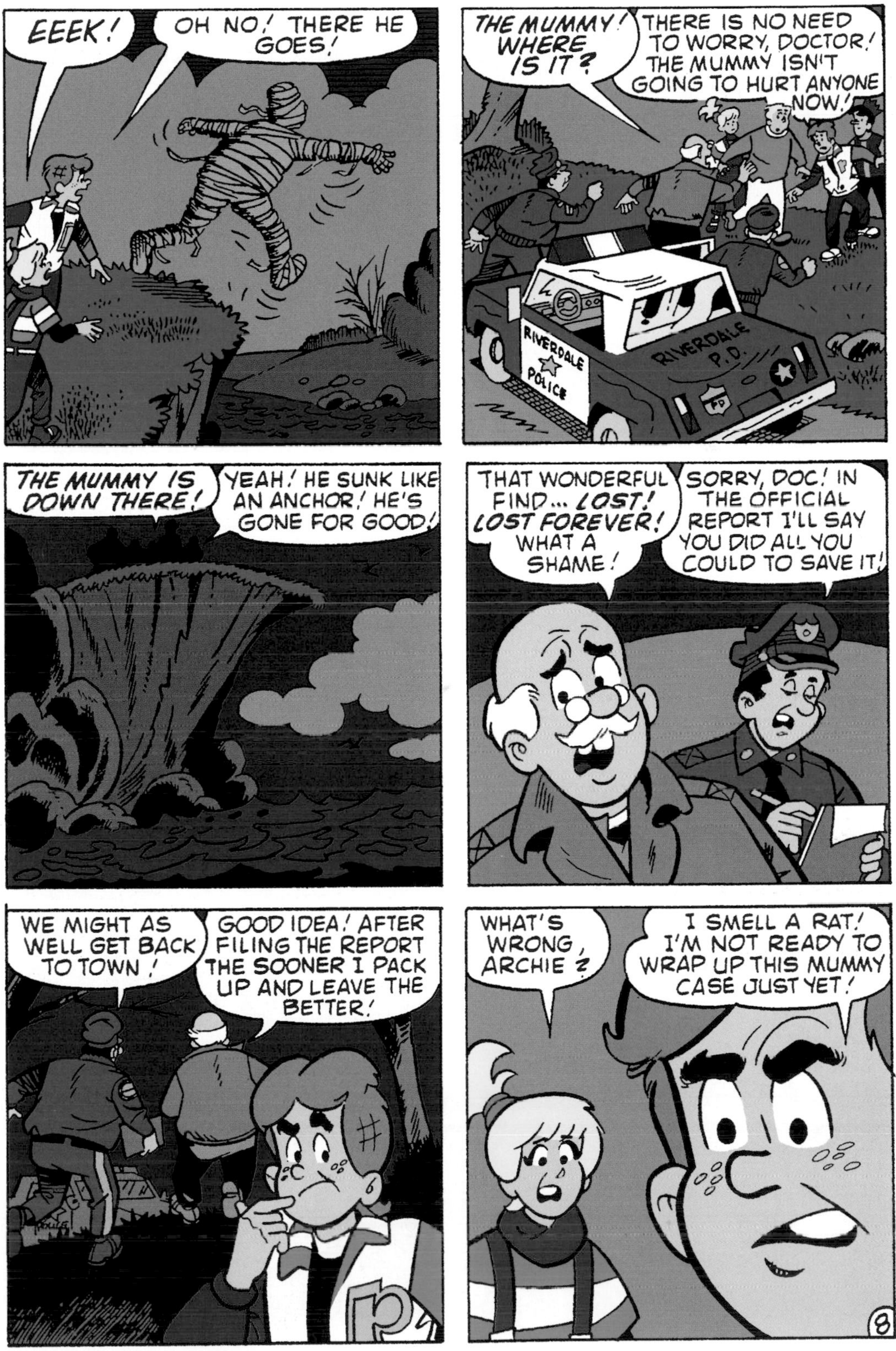
EEEK!
OH NO! THERE HE GOES!
THE MUMMY! WHERE IS IT?
THERE IS NO NEED TO WORRY, DOCTOR! THE MUMMY ISN'T GOING TO HURT ANYONE NOW!
RIVERDALE POLICE
RIVERDALE P.D.
THE MUMMY IS DOWN THERE!
YEAH! HE SUNK LIKE AN ANCHOR! HE'S GONE FOR GOOD!
THAT WONDERFUL FIND... LOST! LOST FOREVER! WHAT A SHAME!
SORRY, DOC! IN THE OFFICIAL REPORT I'LL SAY YOU DID ALL YOU COULD TO SAVE IT!
WE MIGHT AS WELL GET BACK TO TOWN!
GOOD IDEA! AFTER FILING THE REPORT THE SOONER I PACK UP AND LEAVE THE BETTER!
WHAT'S WRONG, ARCHIE?
I SMELL A RAT! I'M NOT READY TO WRAP UP THIS MUMMY CASE JUST YET!
8

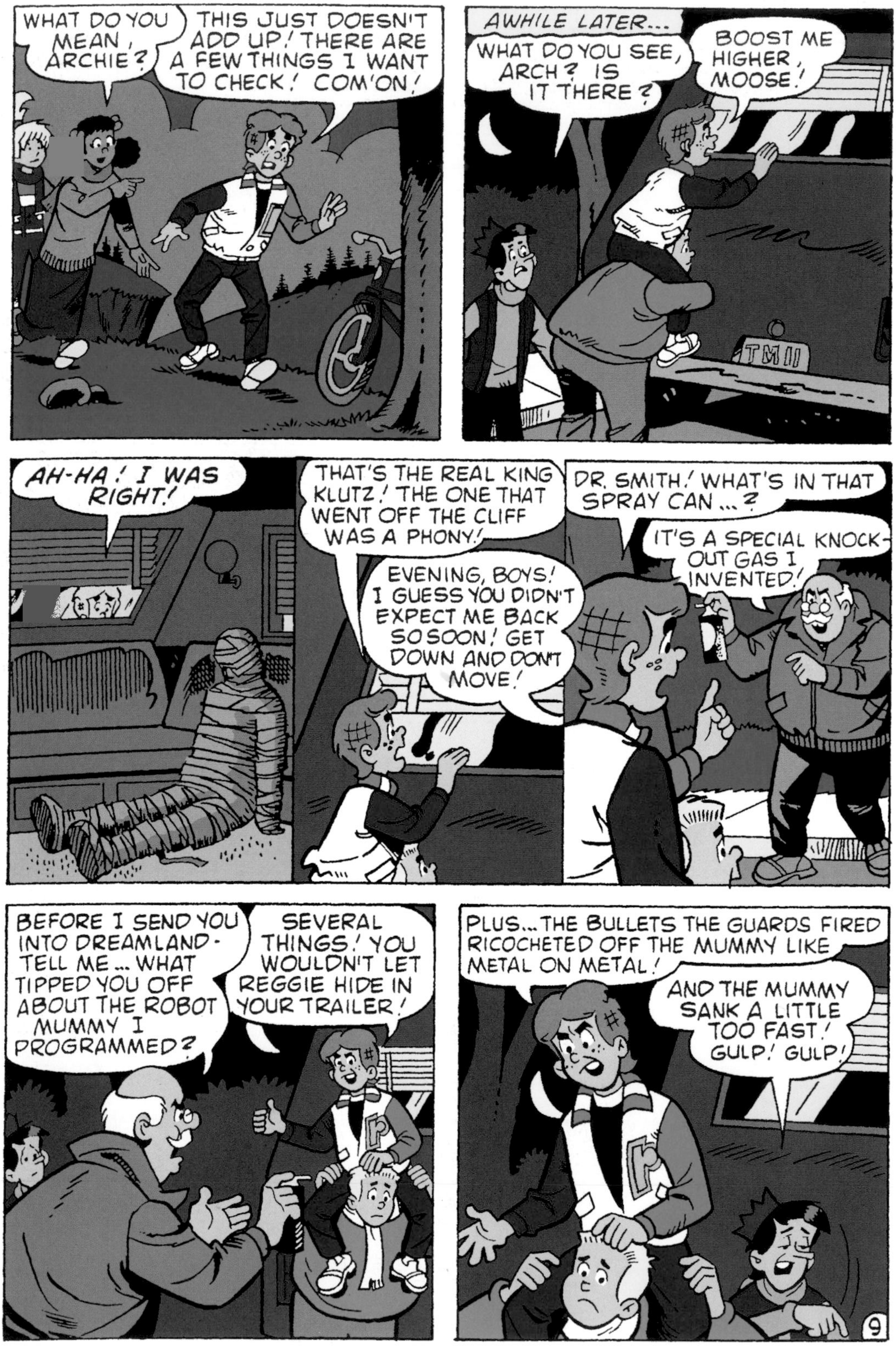
WHAT DO YOU MEAN, ARCHIE?
THIS JUST DOESN'T ADD UP! THERE ARE A FEW THINGS I WANT TO CHECK! COM'ON!
AWHILE LATER...
WHAT DO YOU SEE, ARCH? IS IT THERE?
BOOST ME HIGHER, MOOSE!
TM II
AH-HA! I WAS RIGHT!
THAT'S THE REAL KING KLUTZ! THE ONE THAT WENT OFF THE CLIFF WAS A PHONY!
EVENING, BOYS! I GUESS YOU DIDN'T EXPECT ME BACK SO SOON! GET DOWN AND DON'T MOVE!
DR. SMITH! WHAT'S IN THAT SPRAY CAN ...?
IT'S A SPECIAL KNOCK-OUT GAS I INVENTED!
BEFORE I SEND YOU INTO DREAMLAND - TELL ME ... WHAT TIPPED YOU OFF ABOUT THE ROBOT MUMMY I PROGRAMMED?
SEVERAL THINGS! YOU WOULDN'T LET REGGIE HIDE IN YOUR TRAILER!
PLUS... THE BULLETS THE GUARDS FIRED RICOCHETED OFF THE MUMMY LIKE METAL ON METAL!
AND THE MUMMY SANK A LITTLE TOO FAST! GULP! GULP!
9

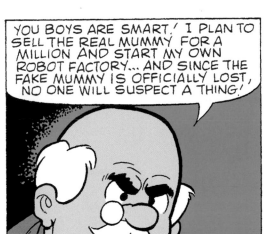

YOU BOYS ARE SMART! I PLAN TO SELL THE REAL MUMMY FOR A MILLION AND START MY OWN ROBOT FACTORY... AND SINCE THE FAKE MUMMY IS OFFICIALLY LOST, NO ONE WILL SUSPECT A THING!

I'VE WAITED FOR JUST THE RIGHT HICK TOWN TO PULL THIS STUNT! I THOUGHT RIVERDALE WAS IT! I WAS MISTAKEN!

YOU'VE MADE A LOT OF MISTAKES, DR. SMITH! DON'T MAKE ANYMORE! PUT DOWN THAT CAN!

DON'T WORRY! I WON'T MAKE ANYMORE MISTAKES! BY THE TIME YOU WAKE UP I'LL BE LONG GONE!

GULP!

DO SOMETHING, EUGENE! ARCHIE TOLD US TO HIDE HERE AS HIS BACKUP!

OKAY, BETTY! I HOPE THIS WORKS!

WHIRRRRR

HERE GOES!

YEOW! MY HAND!

WACK!

WHIRR

RRRRR

QUICK! GRAB THE KNOCKOUT GAS, MOOSE!

245

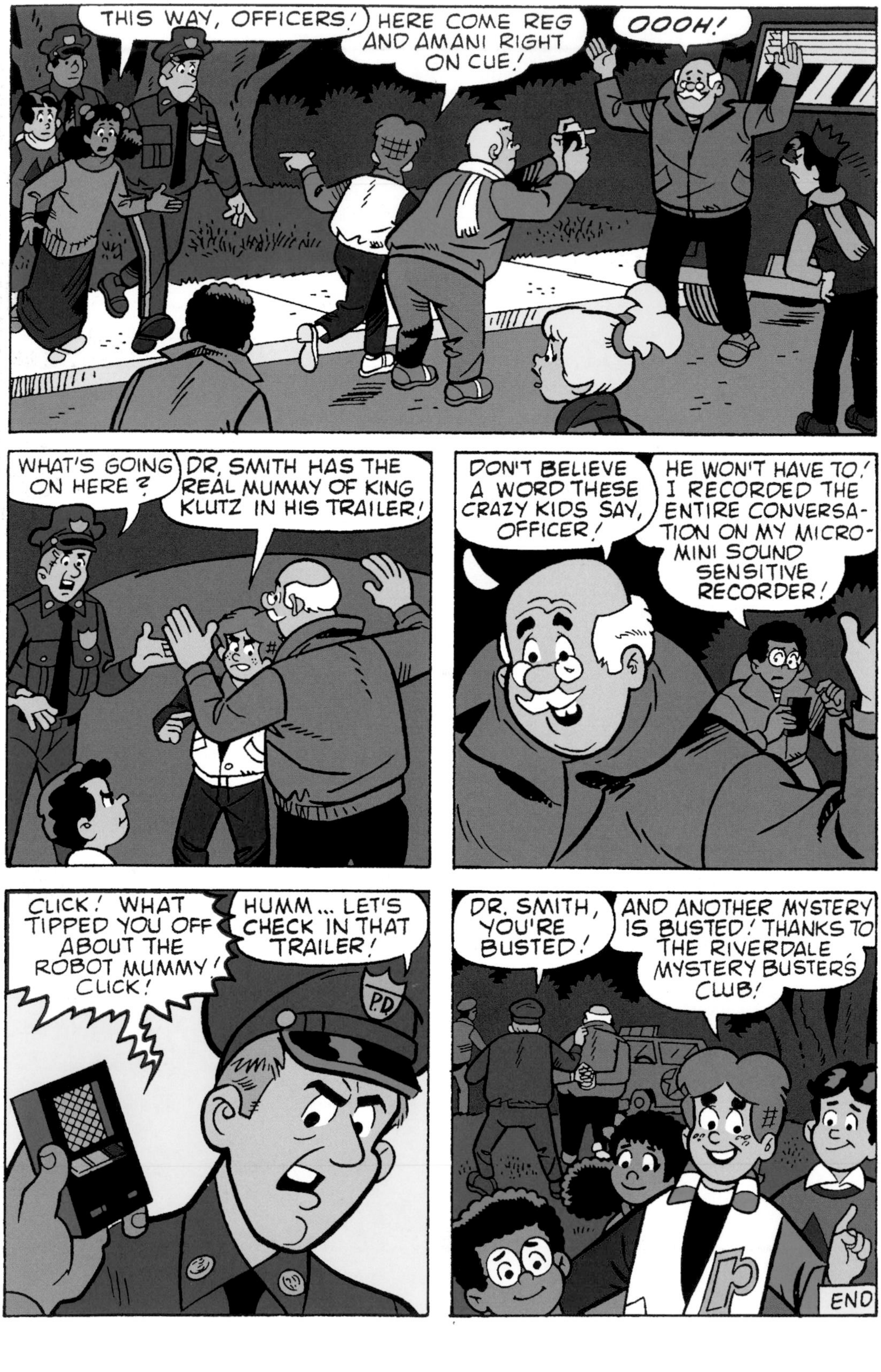
THIS WAY, OFFICERS!
HERE COME REG AND AMANI RIGHT ON CUE!
OOOH!
WHAT'S GOING ON HERE?
DR. SMITH HAS THE REAL MUMMY OF KING KLUTZ IN HIS TRAILER!
DON'T BELIEVE A WORD THESE CRAZY KIDS SAY, OFFICER!
HE WON'T HAVE TO! I RECORDED THE ENTIRE CONVERSATION ON MY MICRO-MINI SOUND SENSITIVE RECORDER!
CLICK! WHAT TIPPED YOU OFF ABOUT THE ROBOT MUMMY! CLICK!
HUMM... LET'S CHECK IN THAT TRAILER!
P.D.
DR. SMITH, YOU'RE BUSTED!
AND ANOTHER MYSTERY IS BUSTED! THANKS TO THE RIVERDALE MYSTERY BUSTERS CLUB!
END

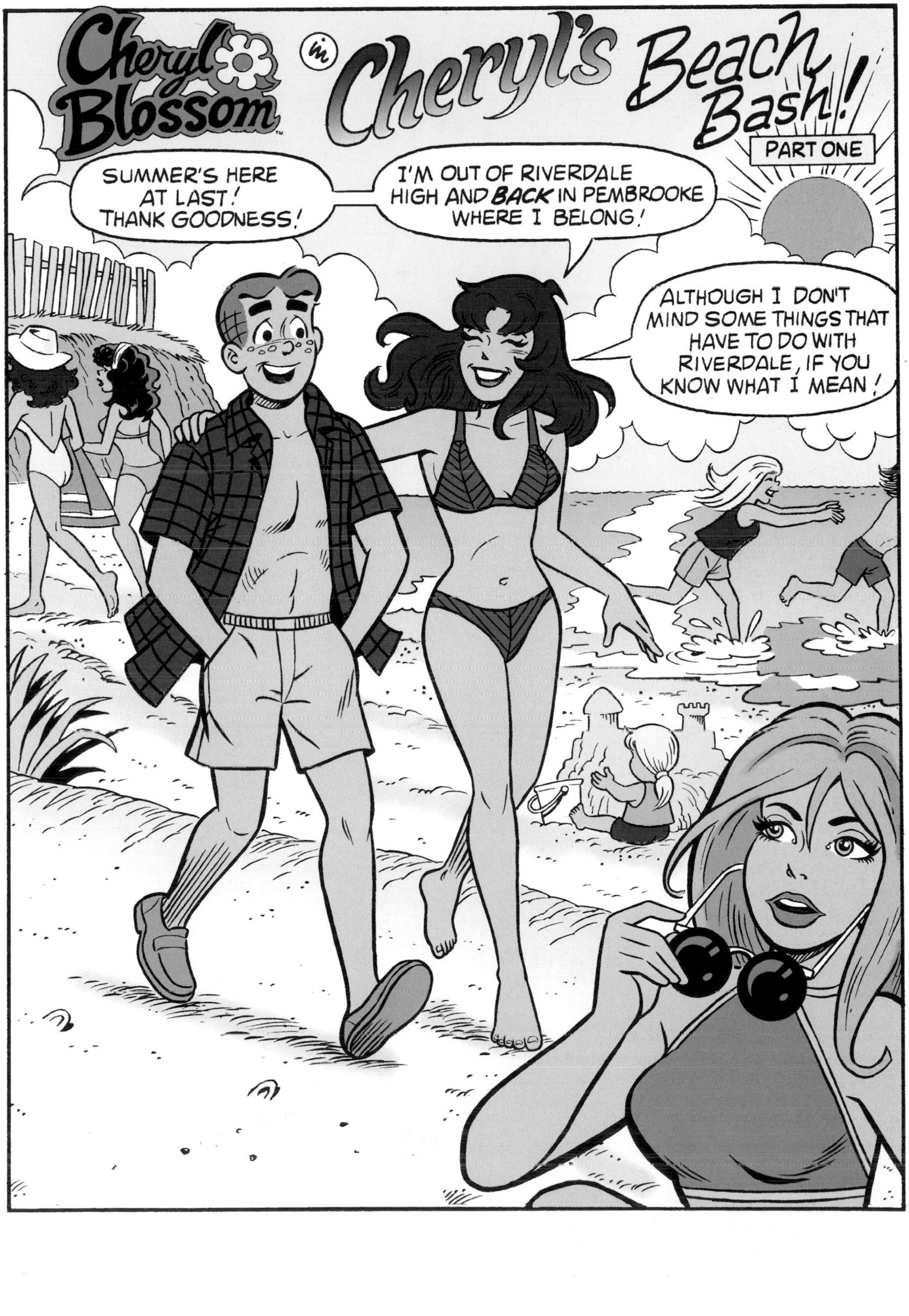
Cheryl Blossom
in
Cheryl's Beach Bash!
PART ONE
SUMMER'S HERE AT LAST! THANK GOODNESS!
I'M OUT OF RIVERDALE HIGH AND BACK IN PEMBROOKE WHERE I BELONG!
ALTHOUGH I DON'T MIND SOME THINGS THAT HAVE TO DO WITH RIVERDALE, IF YOU KNOW WHAT I MEAN!

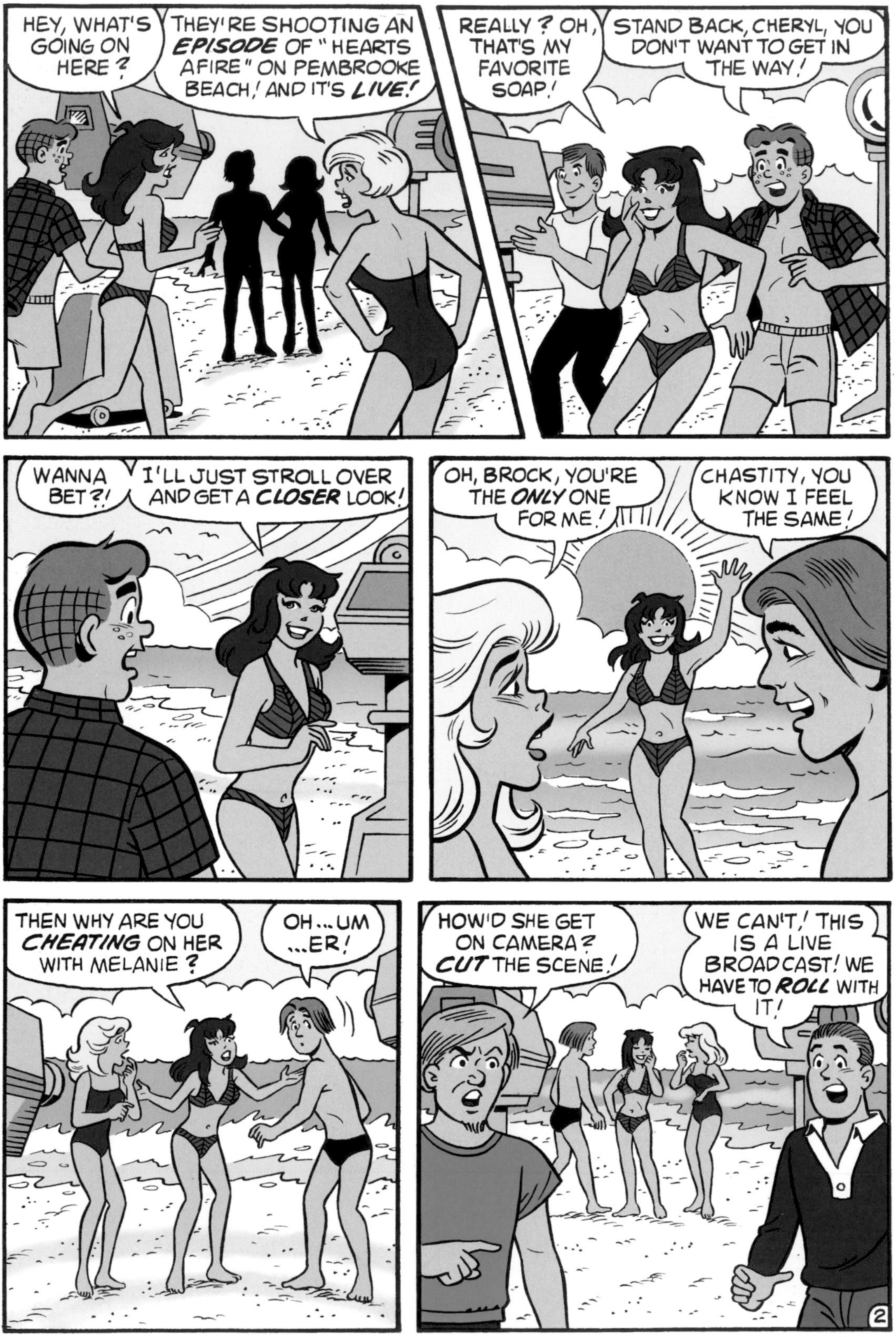
HEY, WHAT'S GOING ON HERE?
THEY'RE SHOOTING AN EPISODE OF "HEARTS AFIRE" ON PEMBROOKE BEACH! AND IT'S LIVE!
REALLY? OH, THAT'S MY FAVORITE SOAP!
STAND BACK, CHERYL, YOU DON'T WANT TO GET IN THE WAY!
WANNA BET?!
I'LL JUST STROLL OVER AND GET A CLOSER LOOK!
OH, BROCK, YOU'RE THE ONLY ONE FOR ME!
CHASTITY, YOU KNOW I FEEL THE SAME!
THEN WHY ARE YOU CHEATING ON HER WITH MELANIE?
OH...UM ...ER!
HOW'D SHE GET ON CAMERA? CUT THE SCENE!
WE CAN'T! THIS IS A LIVE BROADCAST! WE HAVE TO ROLL WITH IT!
2

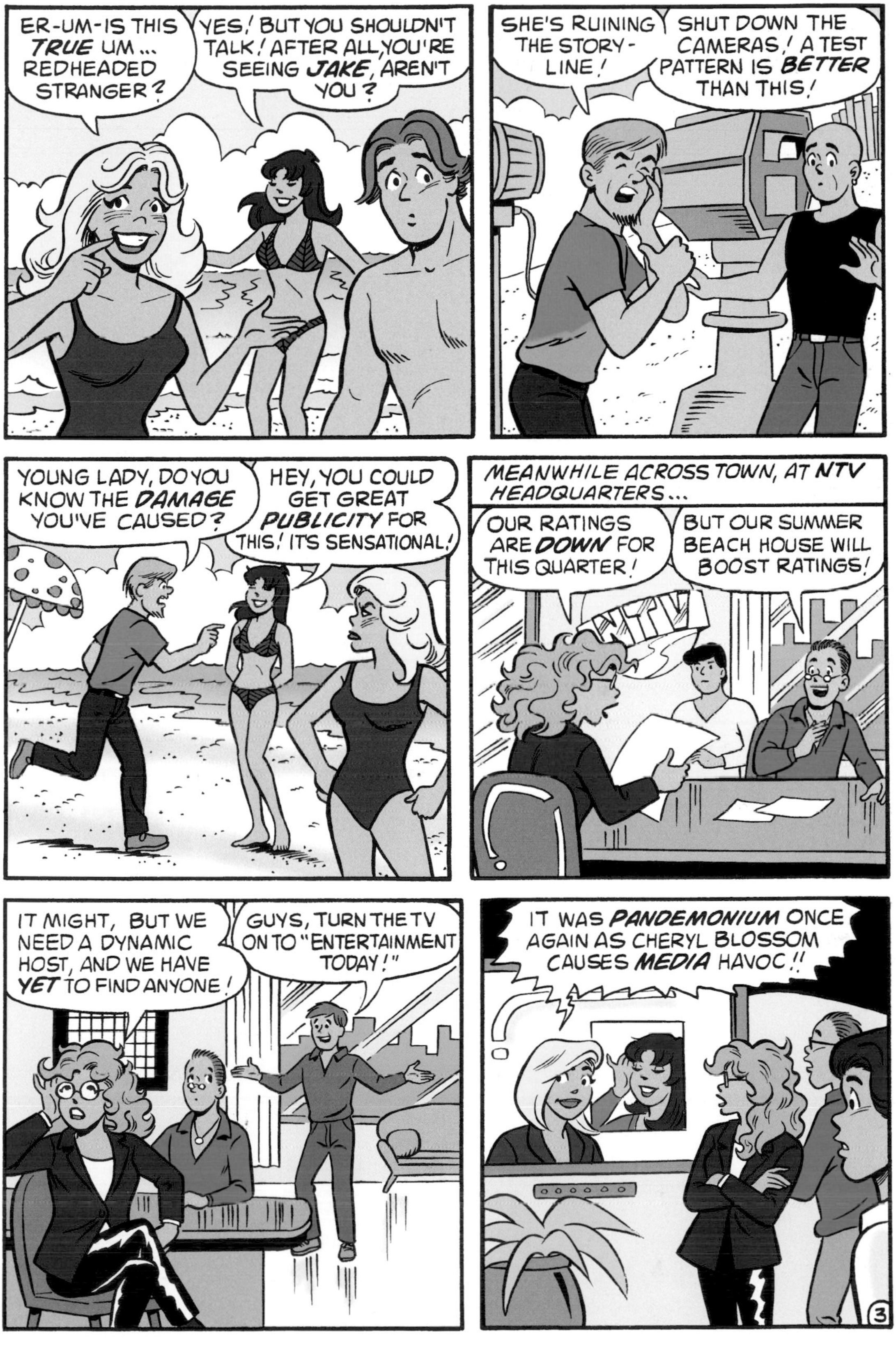
ER-UM-IS THIS TRUE UM... REDHEADED STRANGER?
YES! BUT YOU SHOULDN'T TALK! AFTER ALL, YOU'RE SEEING JAKE, AREN'T YOU?
SHE'S RUINING THE STORY-LINE!
SHUT DOWN THE CAMERAS! A TEST PATTERN IS BETTER THAN THIS!
YOUNG LADY, DO YOU KNOW THE DAMAGE YOU'VE CAUSED?
HEY, YOU COULD GET GREAT PUBLICITY FOR THIS! IT'S SENSATIONAL!
MEANWHILE ACROSS TOWN, AT NTV HEADQUARTERS...
OUR RATINGS ARE DOWN FOR THIS QUARTER!
BUT OUR SUMMER BEACH HOUSE WILL BOOST RATINGS!
NTV
IT MIGHT, BUT WE NEED A DYNAMIC HOST, AND WE HAVE YET TO FIND ANYONE!
GUYS, TURN THE TV ON TO "ENTERTAINMENT TODAY!"
IT WAS PANDEMONIUM ONCE AGAIN AS CHERYL BLOSSOM CAUSES MEDIA HAVOC!!
3

THIS TIME IT WAS DURING THE *LIVE* BROADCAST OF "HEARTS AFIRE"!

CHERYL BLOSSOM! HMM!

SHE'S YOUNG, PRETTY AND *OUTRAGEOUS*!

PLUS SHE'S WELL KNOWN FOR HER WILD *PUBLICITY* STUNTS!

ARE YOU THINKING WHAT I'M *THINKING*?

LET'S GO!

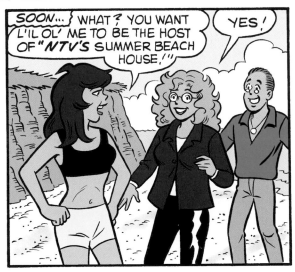

SOON... WHAT? YOU WANT L'IL OL' ME TO BE THE HOST OF "*NTV'S* SUMMER BEACH HOUSE,'"

YES!

WELL, I DON'T KNOW! I'M SORT OF *BUSY* THIS SUMMER!

IT'S EASY! YOU JUST HAVE TO INTRODUCE MUSIC VIDEOS AND INTERVIEW ROCK STARS!

WELL, IT SOUNDS *INTERESTING*, BUT COULD I HAVE MY AGENT PROPOSE A FEW CHANGES ALSO?

CERTAINLY!

④

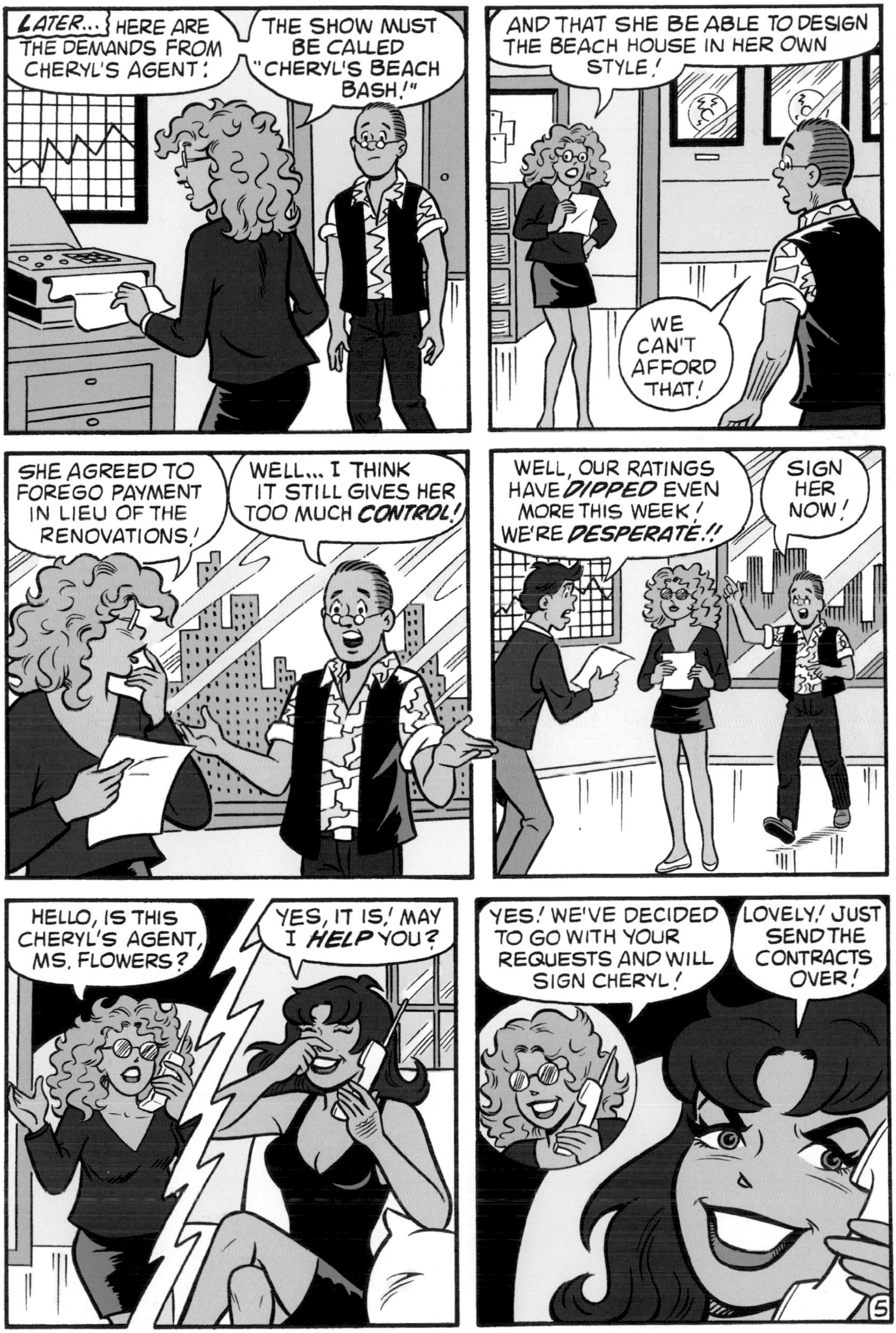
LATER...
HERE ARE THE DEMANDS FROM CHERYL'S AGENT!
THE SHOW MUST BE CALLED "CHERYL'S BEACH BASH!"
AND THAT SHE BE ABLE TO DESIGN THE BEACH HOUSE IN HER OWN STYLE!
WE CAN'T AFFORD THAT!
SHE AGREED TO FOREGO PAYMENT IN LIEU OF THE RENOVATIONS!
WELL... I THINK IT STILL GIVES HER TOO MUCH CONTROL!
WELL, OUR RATINGS HAVE DIPPED EVEN MORE THIS WEEK! WE'RE DESPERATE!!
SIGN HER NOW!
HELLO, IS THIS CHERYL'S AGENT, MS. FLOWERS?
YES, IT IS! MAY I HELP YOU?
YES! WE'VE DECIDED TO GO WITH YOUR REQUESTS AND WILL SIGN CHERYL!
LOVELY! JUST SEND THE CONTRACTS OVER!
5

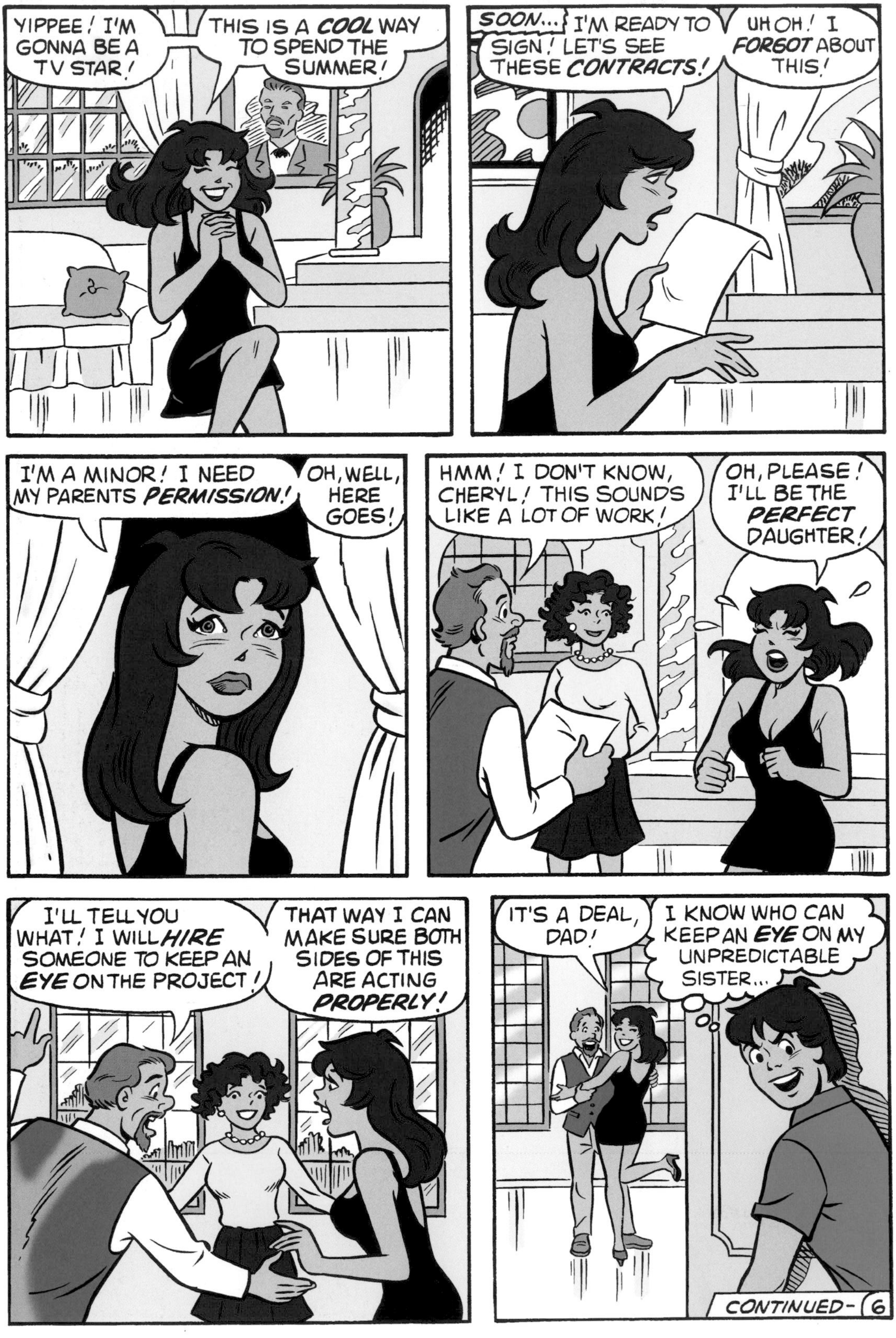
YIPPEE! I'M GONNA BE A TV STAR!
THIS IS A COOL WAY TO SPEND THE SUMMER!
SOON...
I'M READY TO SIGN! LET'S SEE THESE CONTRACTS!
UH OH! I FORGOT ABOUT THIS!
I'M A MINOR! I NEED MY PARENTS PERMISSION!
OH, WELL, HERE GOES!
HMM! I DON'T KNOW, CHERYL! THIS SOUNDS LIKE A LOT OF WORK!
OH, PLEASE! I'LL BE THE PERFECT DAUGHTER!
I'LL TELL YOU WHAT! I WILL HIRE SOMEONE TO KEEP AN EYE ON THE PROJECT!
THAT WAY I CAN MAKE SURE BOTH SIDES OF THIS ARE ACTING PROPERLY!
IT'S A DEAL, DAD!
I KNOW WHO CAN KEEP AN EYE ON MY UNPREDICTABLE SISTER...
CONTINUED- 6

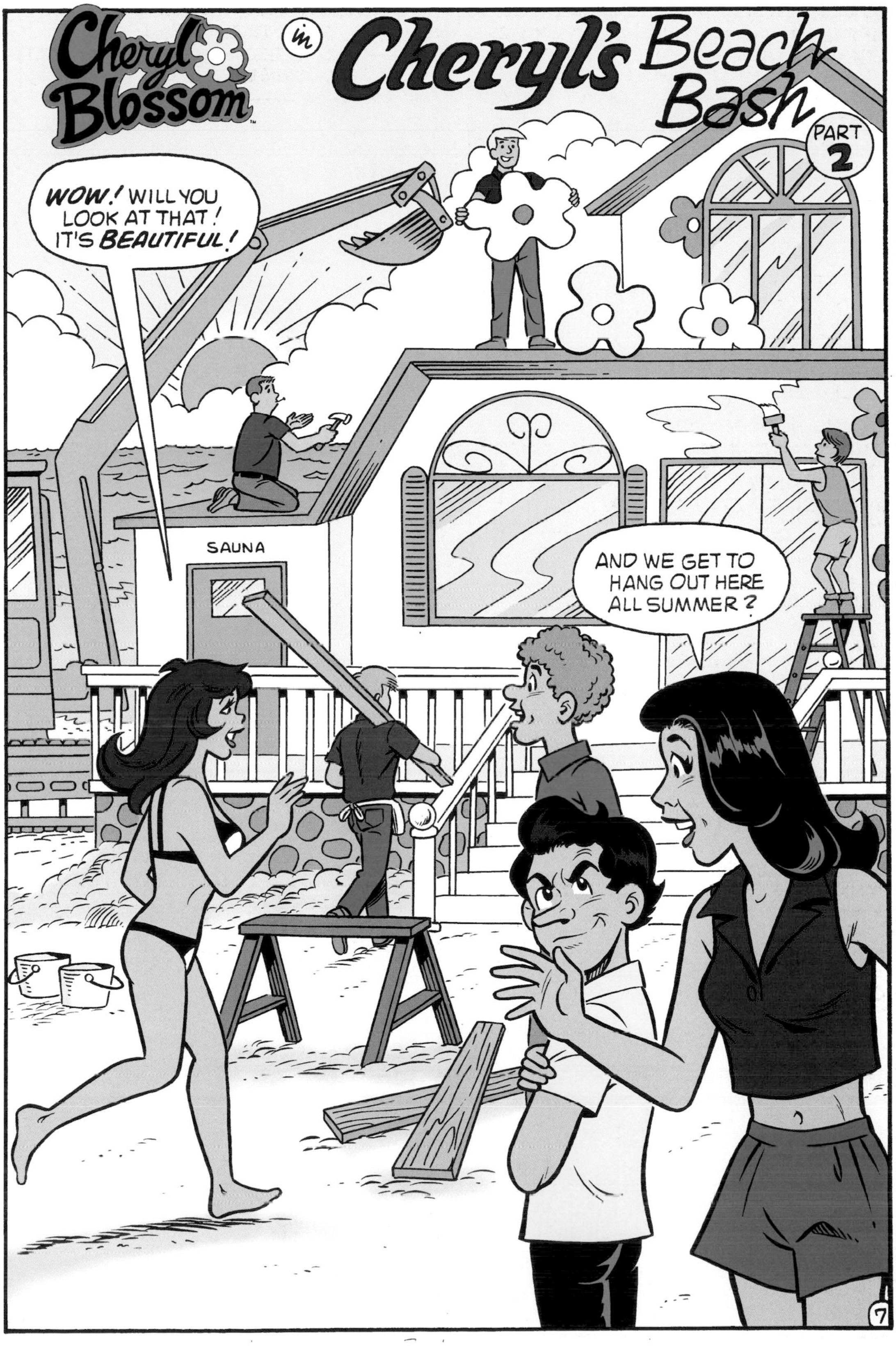
Cheryl Blossom
in
Cheryl's Beach Bash
PART 2
WOW! WILL YOU LOOK AT THAT! IT'S BEAUTIFUL!
SAUNA
AND WE GET TO HANG OUT HERE ALL SUMMER?
7

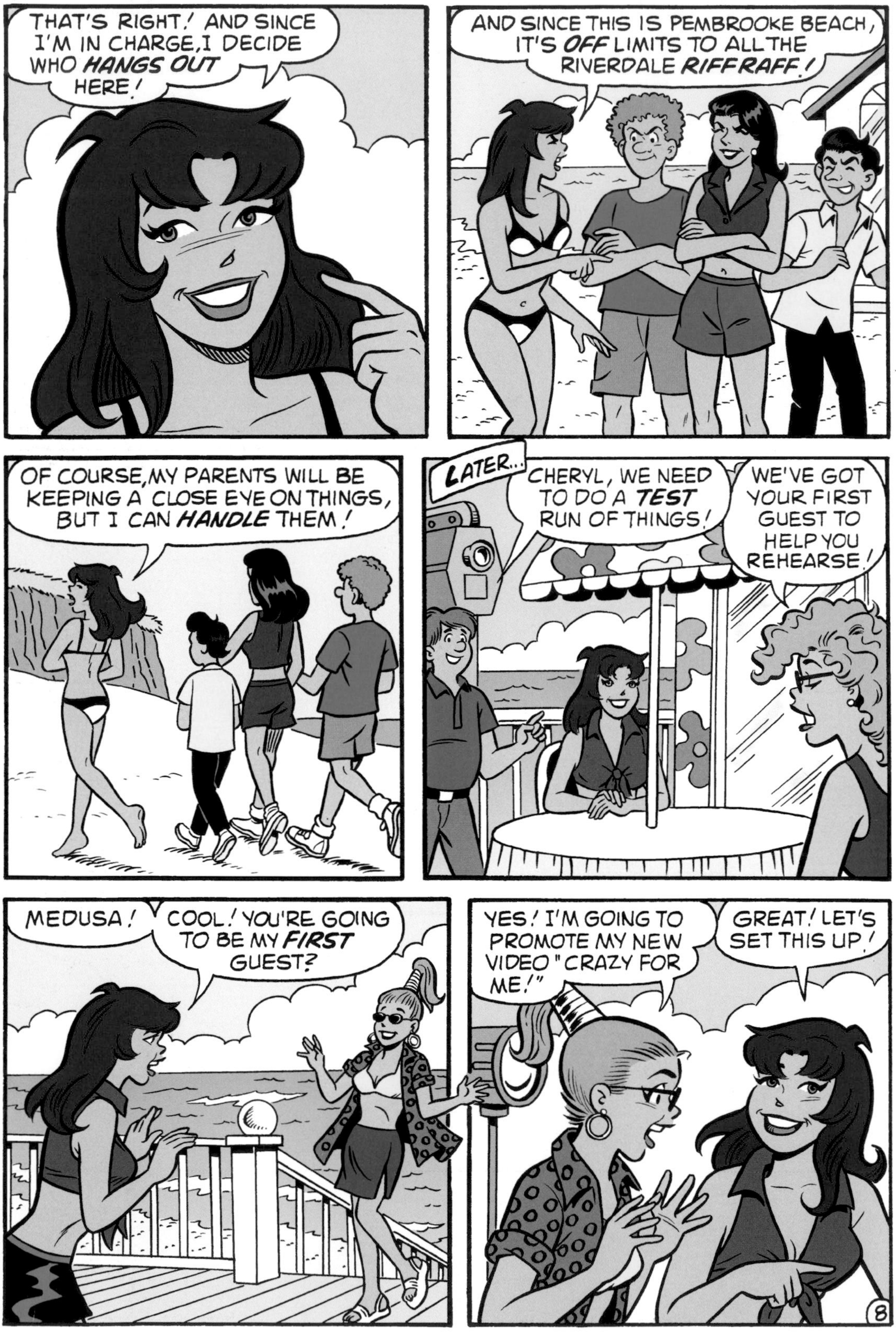
THAT'S RIGHT! AND SINCE I'M IN CHARGE, I DECIDE WHO HANGS OUT HERE!
AND SINCE THIS IS PEMBROOKE BEACH, IT'S OFF LIMITS TO ALL THE RIVERDALE RIFFRAFF!
OF COURSE, MY PARENTS WILL BE KEEPING A CLOSE EYE ON THINGS, BUT I CAN HANDLE THEM!
LATER...
CHERYL, WE NEED TO DO A TEST RUN OF THINGS!
WE'VE GOT YOUR FIRST GUEST TO HELP YOU REHEARSE!
MEDUSA!
COOL! YOU'RE GOING TO BE MY FIRST GUEST?
YES! I'M GOING TO PROMOTE MY NEW VIDEO "CRAZY FOR ME!"
GREAT! LET'S SET THIS UP!
8

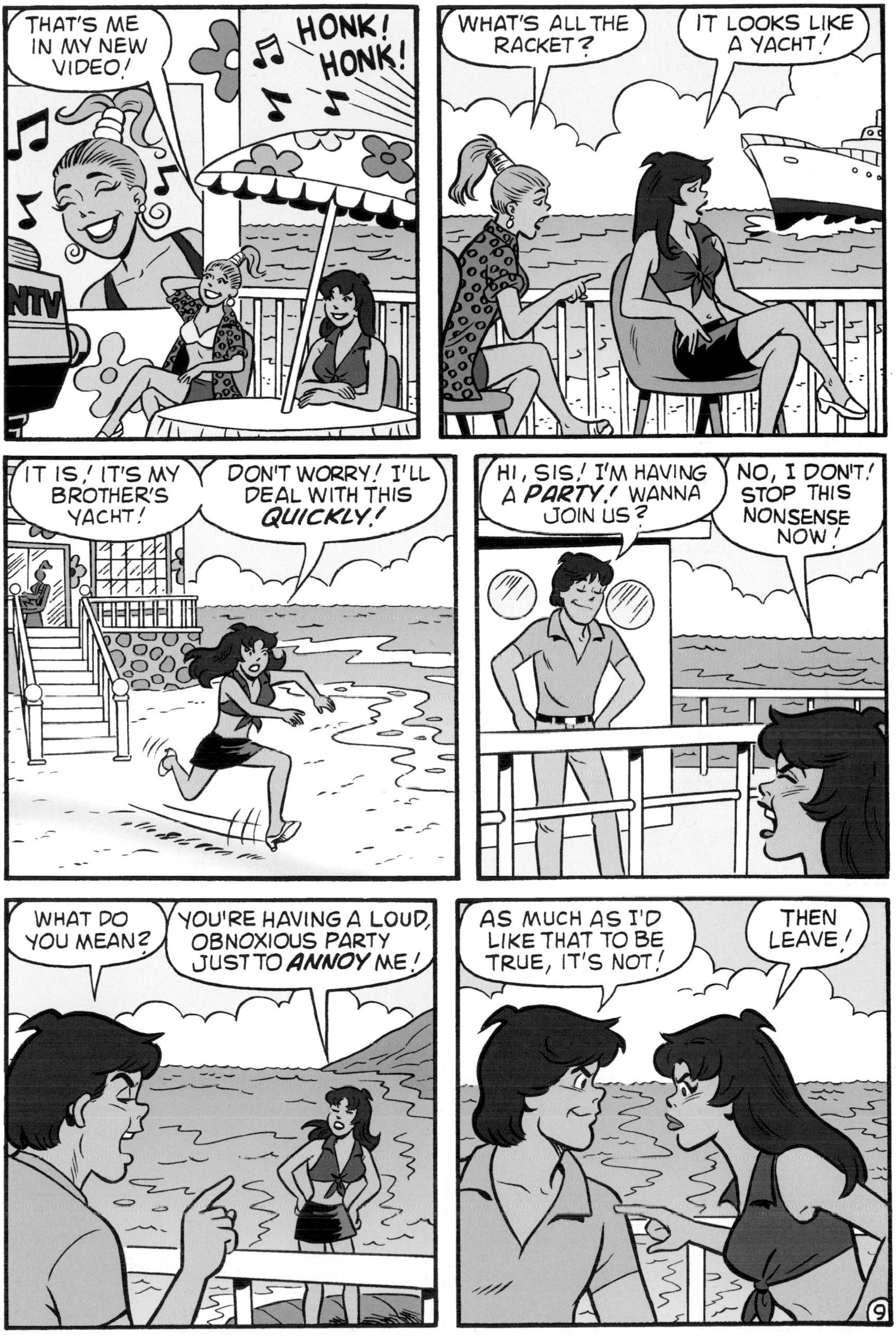
THAT'S ME IN MY NEW VIDEO!
HONK! HONK!
NTV
WHAT'S ALL THE RACKET?
IT LOOKS LIKE A YACHT!
IT IS! IT'S MY BROTHER'S YACHT!
DON'T WORRY! I'LL DEAL WITH THIS QUICKLY!
HI, SIS! I'M HAVING A PARTY! WANNA JOIN US?
NO, I DON'T! STOP THIS NONSENSE NOW!
WHAT DO YOU MEAN?
YOU'RE HAVING A LOUD, OBNOXIOUS PARTY JUST TO ANNOY ME!
AS MUCH AS I'D LIKE THAT TO BE TRUE, IT'S NOT!
THEN LEAVE!
9

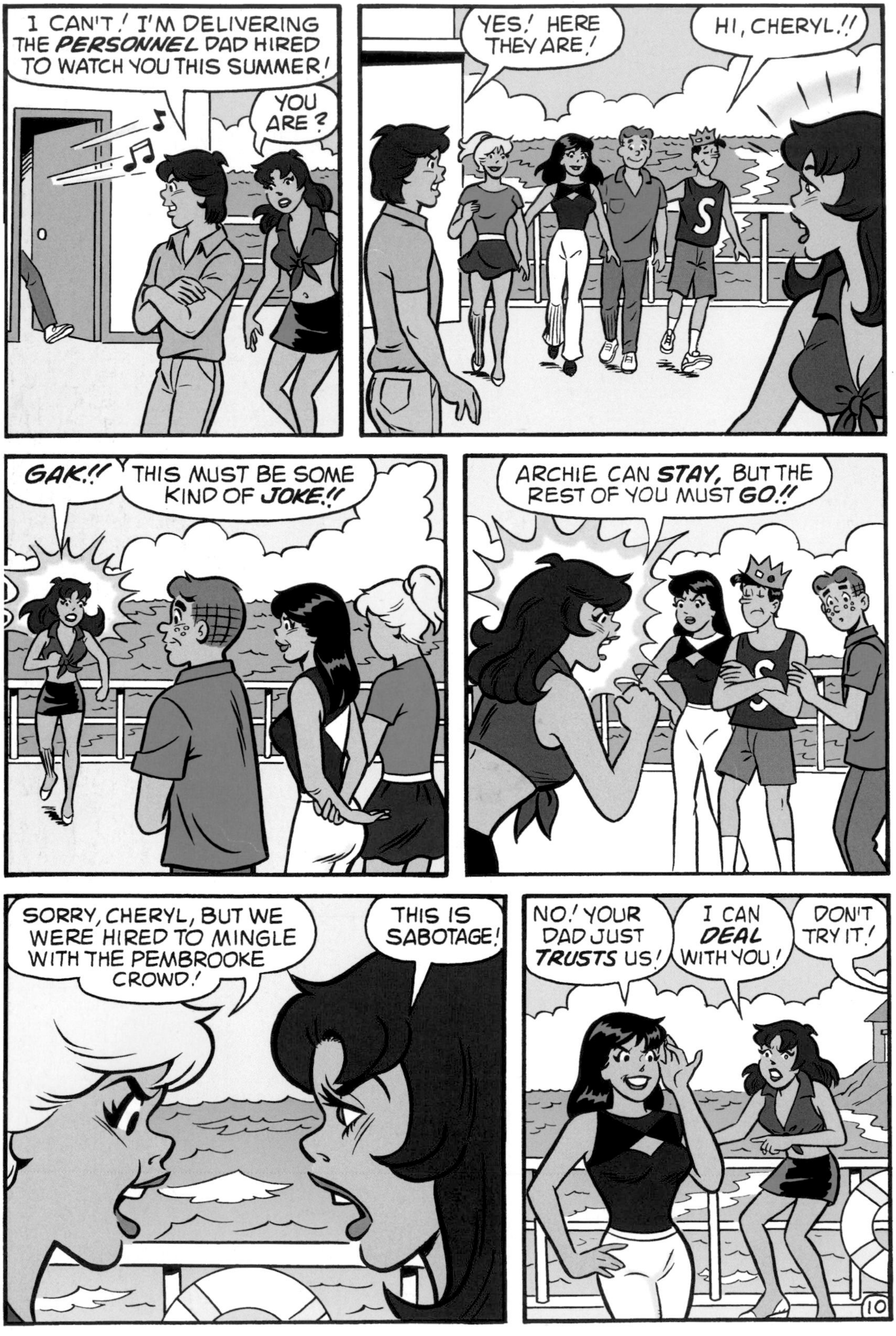
I CAN'T! I'M DELIVERING THE PERSONNEL DAD HIRED TO WATCH YOU THIS SUMMER!
YOU ARE?
YES! HERE THEY ARE!
HI, CHERYL!!
GAK!!
THIS MUST BE SOME KIND OF JOKE!!
ARCHIE CAN STAY, BUT THE REST OF YOU MUST GO!!
SORRY, CHERYL, BUT WE WERE HIRED TO MINGLE WITH THE PEMBROOKE CROWD!
THIS IS SABOTAGE!
NO! YOUR DAD JUST TRUSTS US!
I CAN DEAL WITH YOU!
DON'T TRY IT!
10

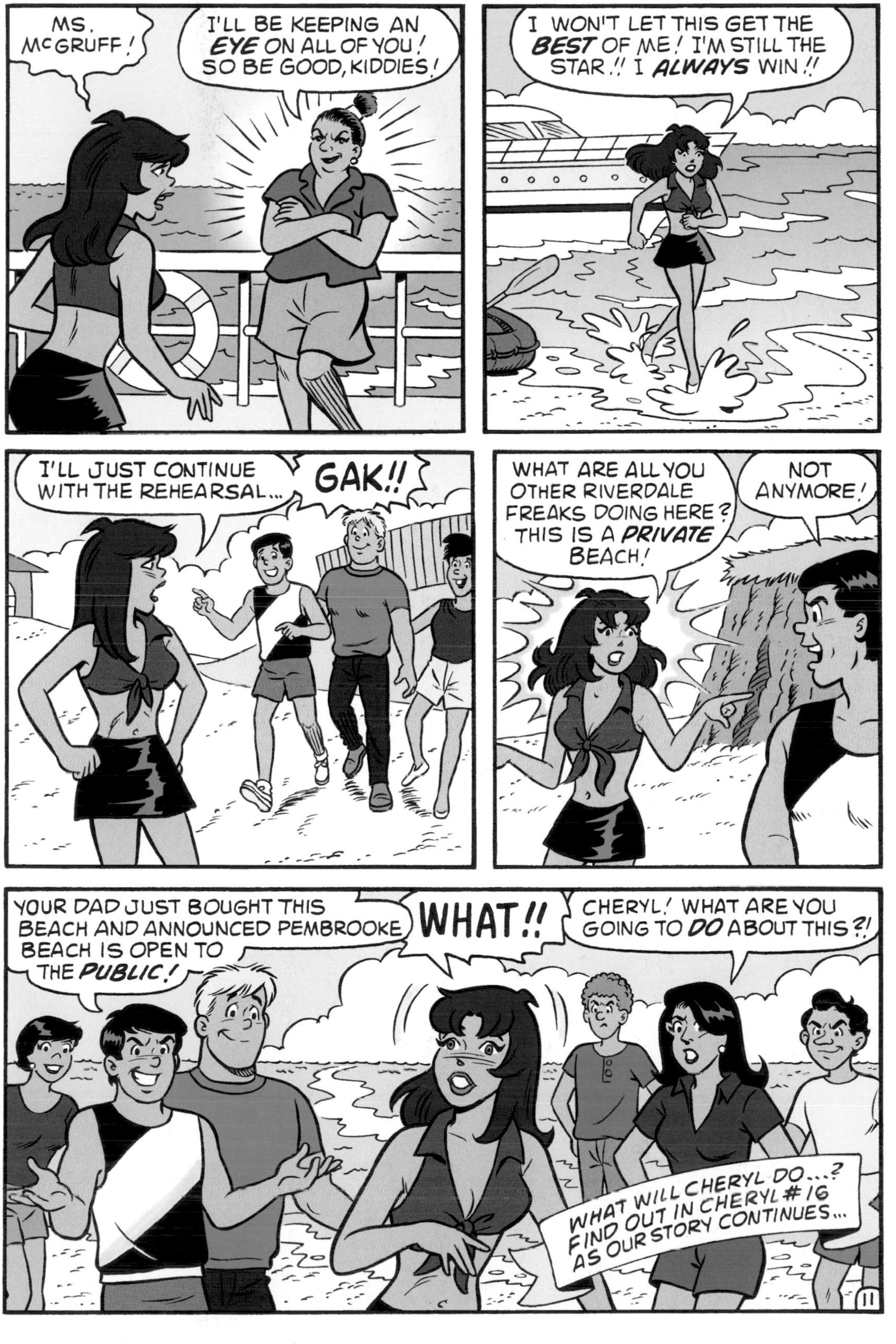

MS. McGRUFF!
I'LL BE KEEPING AN EYE ON ALL OF YOU! SO BE GOOD, KIDDIES!
I WON'T LET THIS GET THE BEST OF ME! I'M STILL THE STAR!! I ALWAYS WIN!!
I'LL JUST CONTINUE WITH THE REHEARSAL...
GAK!!
WHAT ARE ALL YOU OTHER RIVERDALE FREAKS DOING HERE? THIS IS A PRIVATE BEACH!
NOT ANYMORE!
YOUR DAD JUST BOUGHT THIS BEACH AND ANNOUNCED PEMBROOKE BEACH IS OPEN TO THE PUBLIC!
WHAT!!
CHERYL! WHAT ARE YOU GOING TO DO ABOUT THIS?!
WHAT WILL CHERYL DO...? FIND OUT IN CHERYL #16 AS OUR STORY CONTINUES...
11

The BEST of Archie® COMICS

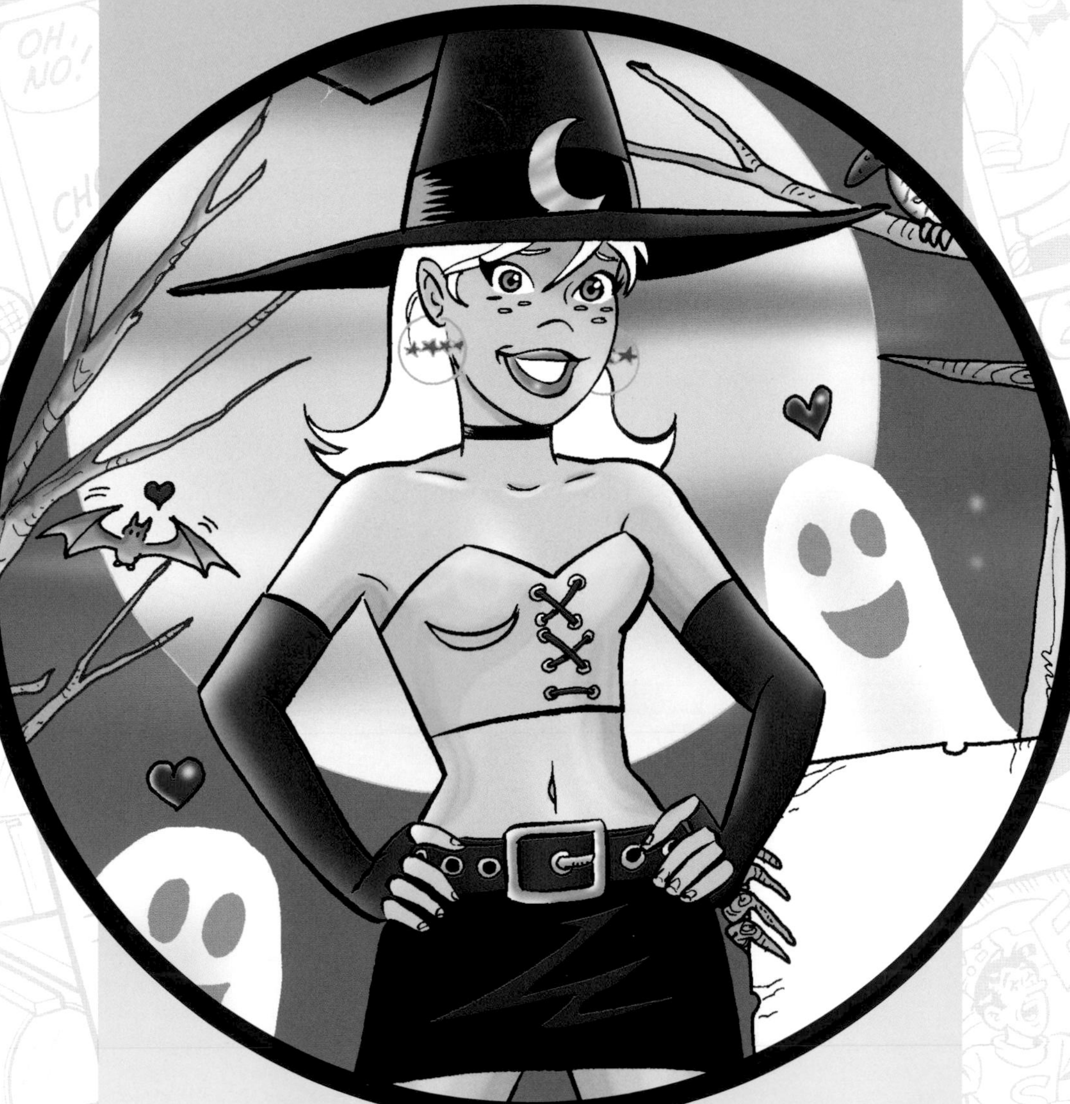

2000s

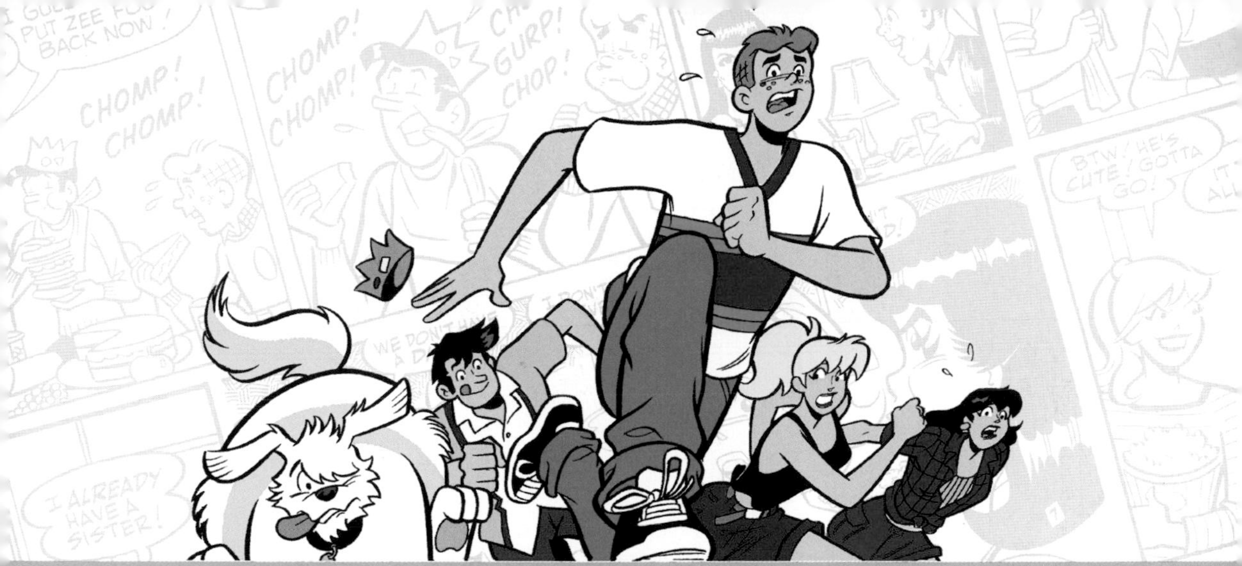
CHOMP! CHOMP!
CHOMP! CHOMP!
GURP! CHOP!
BTW! HE'S CUTE! GOTTA GO!
I ALREADY HAVE A SISTER!

A FAMILIAR OLD HAUNT

ARCHIE'S WEIRD MYSTERIES #6, 2000

BY PAUL CASTIGLIA, FERNANDO RUIZ, RICH KOSLOWSKI, VICKIE WILLIAMS & RICK TAYLOR

The animated series *Archie's Weird Mysteries* was in development while I was still working on staff at Archie. I was involved from the standpoint of reviewing the pre-production materials and some early scripts to ensure they stayed true to the Archie characters. As a long-time fan of horror-comedy films I had a great desire to work on a comic book adaptation of *Archie's Weird Mysteries*. I pushed the publishers to move forward with the comic… and to let me write it. I had a good relationship with one of the show's story editors and one of its chief writers. They were pretty much open to anything I wanted to do story-wise in the comic. They enjoyed the fact that I stretched past the monsters and aliens of the show to offer some thrills and chills the regular readers of Archie Comics could appreciate, which is why I made an effort to incorporate some of the more familiar elements of the comics mythology—like the love triangle.

With the continued popularity of horror and sci-fi, plus franchises that put teens and young adults right in the middle of the action, mixing romance and adventure, I can't think of a better time for an *Archie's Weird Mysteries* comeback!

—Paul Castiglia
Writer & Archivist,
Archie Comics

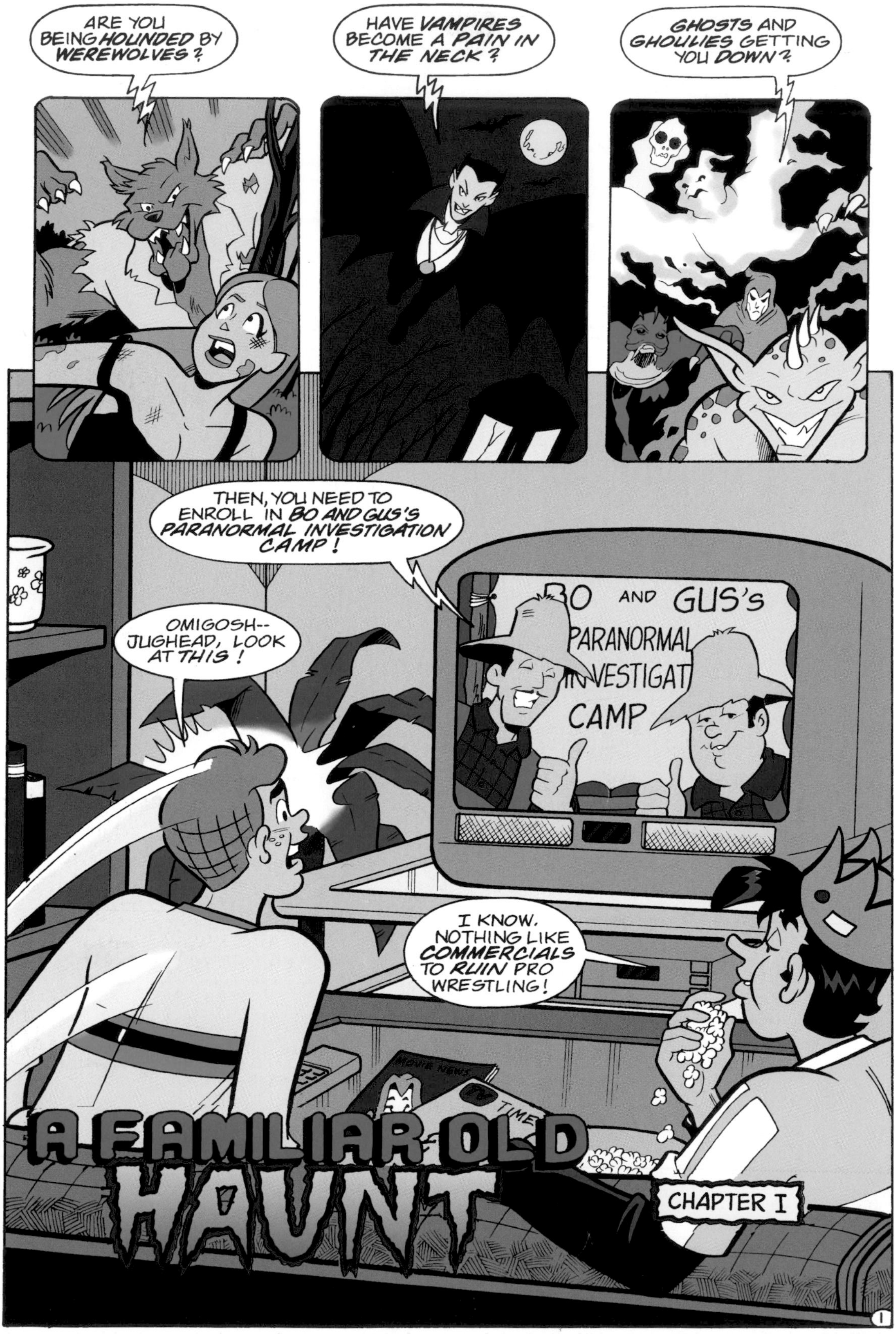

ARE YOU BEING HOUNDED BY WEREWOLVES?
HAVE VAMPIRES BECOME A PAIN IN THE NECK?
GHOSTS AND GHOULIES GETTING YOU DOWN?
THEN, YOU NEED TO ENROLL IN BO AND GUS'S PARANORMAL INVESTIGATION CAMP!
BO AND GUS's PARANORMAL INVESTIGAT CAMP
OMIGOSH-- JUGHEAD, LOOK AT THIS!
I KNOW. NOTHING LIKE COMMERCIALS TO RUIN PRO WRESTLING!
MOVIE NEWS
TV TIMES
A FAMILIAR OLD HAUNT
CHAPTER I
1

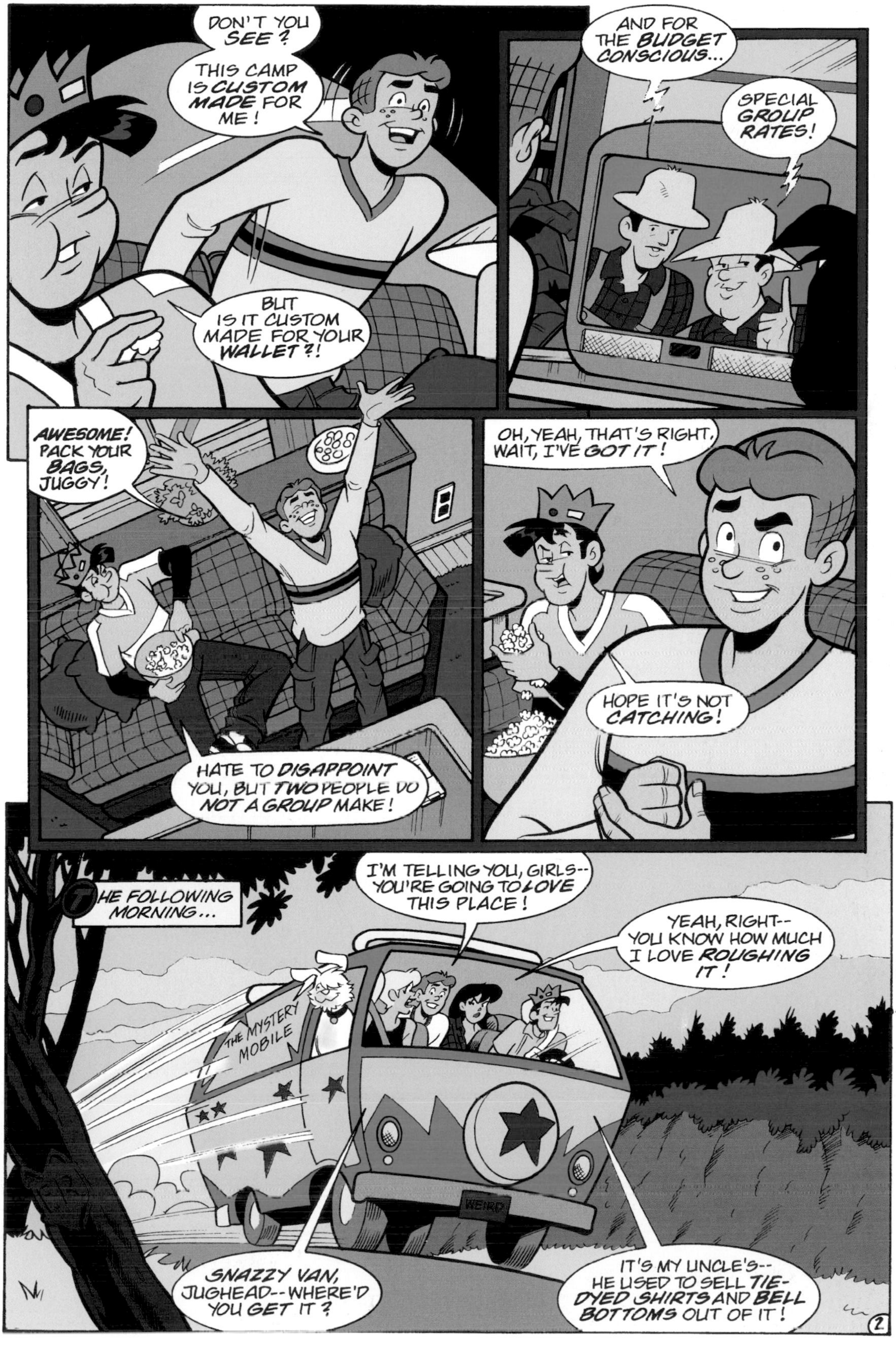

DON'T YOU SEE?
THIS CAMP IS CUSTOM MADE FOR ME!
BUT IS IT CUSTOM MADE FOR YOUR WALLET?!
AND FOR THE BUDGET CONSCIOUS...
SPECIAL GROUP RATES!
AWESOME! PACK YOUR BAGS, JUGGY!
HATE TO DISAPPOINT YOU, BUT TWO PEOPLE DO NOT A GROUP MAKE!
OH, YEAH, THAT'S RIGHT. WAIT, I'VE GOT IT!
HOPE IT'S NOT CATCHING!
THE FOLLOWING MORNING...
I'M TELLING YOU, GIRLS-- YOU'RE GOING TO LOVE THIS PLACE!
YEAH, RIGHT-- YOU KNOW HOW MUCH I LOVE ROUGHING IT!
THE MYSTERY MOBILE
WEIRD
SNAZZY VAN, JUGHEAD--WHERE'D YOU GET IT?
IT'S MY UNCLE'S-- HE USED TO SELL TIE-DYED SHIRTS AND BELL BOTTOMS OUT OF IT!
2

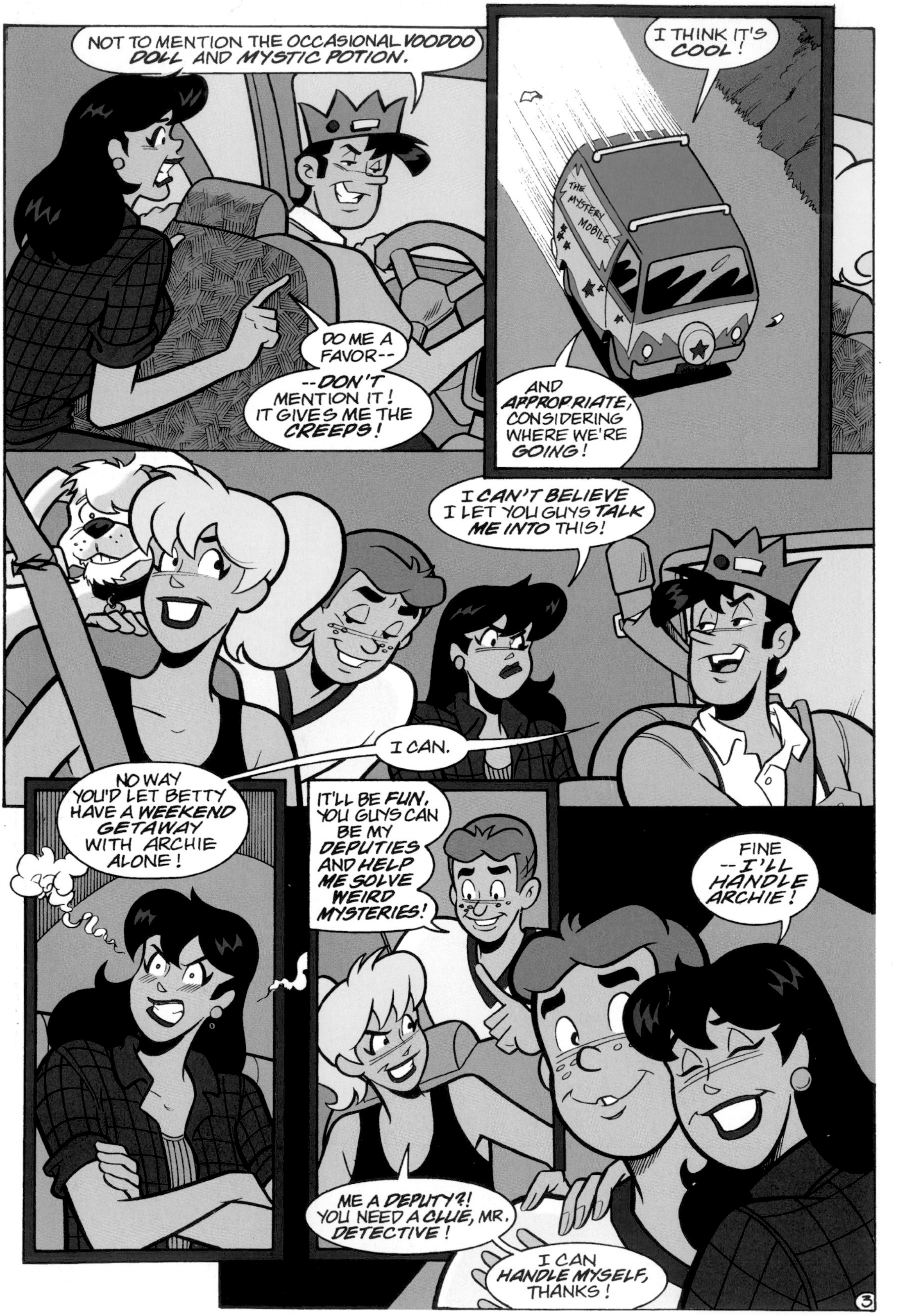
NOT TO MENTION THE OCCASIONAL VOODOO DOLL AND MYSTIC POTION.
DO ME A FAVOR--
--DON'T MENTION IT! IT GIVES ME THE CREEPS!
I THINK IT'S COOL!
THE MYSTERY MOBILE
AND APPROPRIATE, CONSIDERING WHERE WE'RE GOING!
I CAN'T BELIEVE I LET YOU GUYS TALK ME INTO THIS!
I CAN.
NO WAY YOU'D LET BETTY HAVE A WEEKEND GETAWAY WITH ARCHIE ALONE!
IT'LL BE FUN. YOU GUYS CAN BE MY DEPUTIES AND HELP ME SOLVE WEIRD MYSTERIES!
ME A DEPUTY?! YOU NEED A CLUE, MR. DETECTIVE!
FINE --I'LL HANDLE ARCHIE!
I CAN HANDLE MYSELF, THANKS!
3

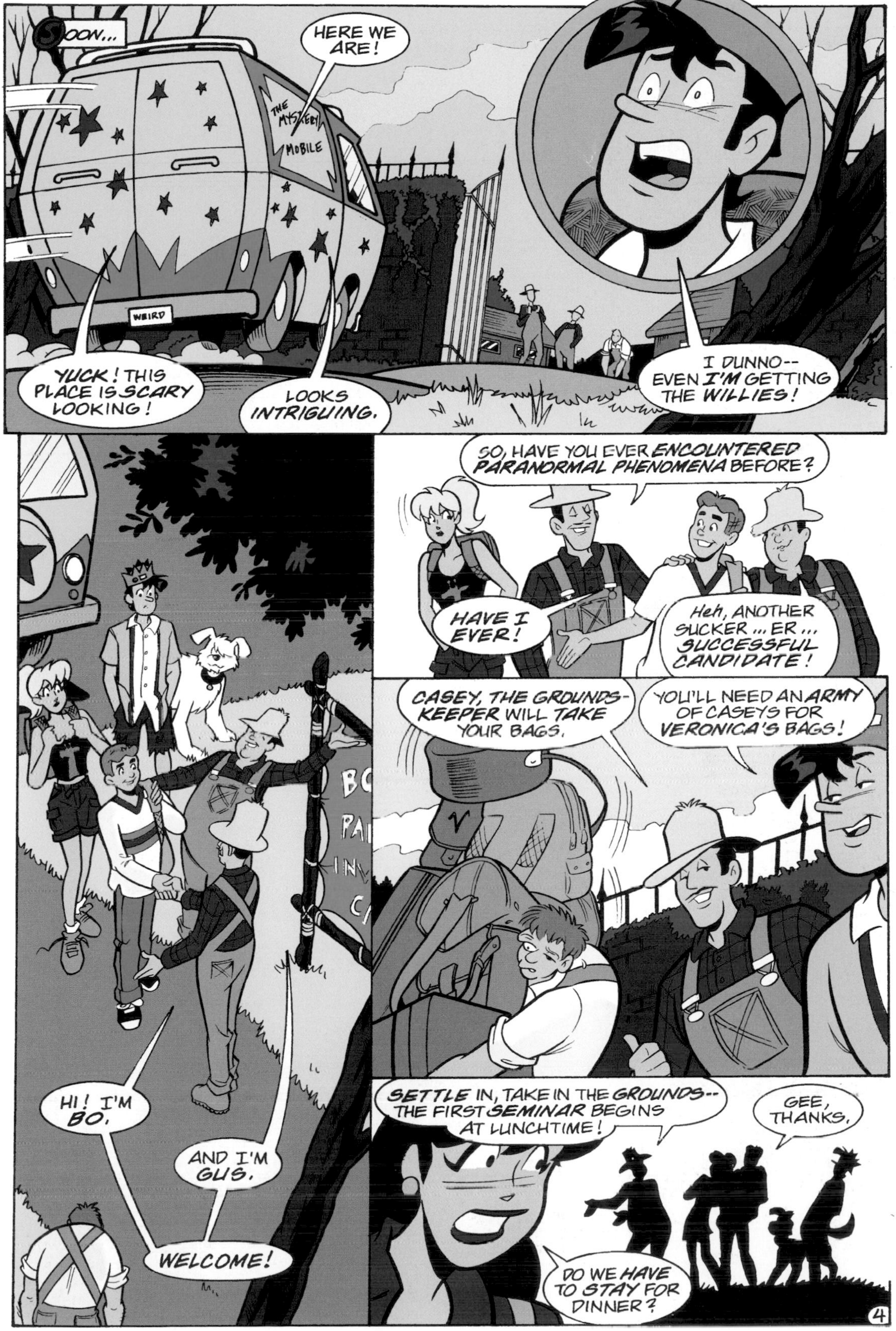
SOON...
HERE WE ARE!
THE MYSTERY MOBILE
WEIRD
YUCK! THIS PLACE IS SCARY LOOKING!
LOOKS INTRIGUING.
I DUNNO-- EVEN I'M GETTING THE WILLIES!
HI! I'M BO.
AND I'M GUS.
WELCOME!
SO, HAVE YOU EVER ENCOUNTERED PARANORMAL PHENOMENA BEFORE?
HAVE I EVER!
Heh, ANOTHER SUCKER ... ER ... SUCCESSFUL CANDIDATE!
CASEY, THE GROUNDS-KEEPER WILL TAKE YOUR BAGS.
YOU'LL NEED AN ARMY OF CASEYS FOR VERONICA'S BAGS!
SETTLE IN, TAKE IN THE GROUNDS-- THE FIRST SEMINAR BEGINS AT LUNCHTIME!
GEE, THANKS.
DO WE HAVE TO STAY FOR DINNER?
4

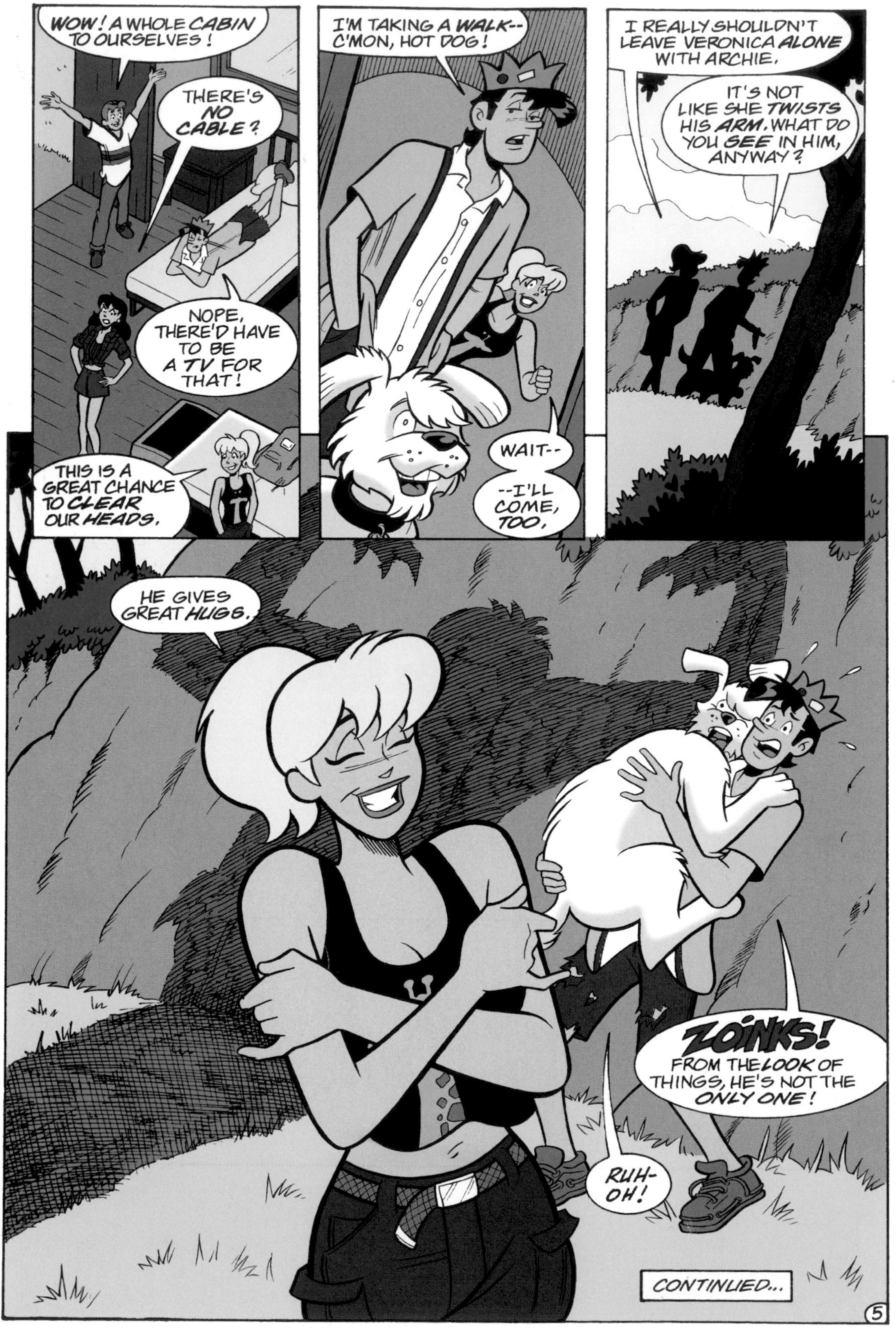
WOW! A WHOLE CABIN TO OURSELVES!
THERE'S NO CABLE?
NOPE, THERE'D HAVE TO BE A TV FOR THAT!
THIS IS A GREAT CHANCE TO CLEAR OUR HEADS.
I'M TAKING A WALK-- C'MON, HOT DOG!
WAIT--
--I'LL COME, TOO.
I REALLY SHOULDN'T LEAVE VERONICA ALONE WITH ARCHIE.
IT'S NOT LIKE SHE TWISTS HIS ARM. WHAT DO YOU SEE IN HIM, ANYWAY?
HE GIVES GREAT HUGS.
ZOINKS!
FROM THE LOOK OF THINGS, HE'S NOT THE ONLY ONE!
RUH-OH!
CONTINUED...
5

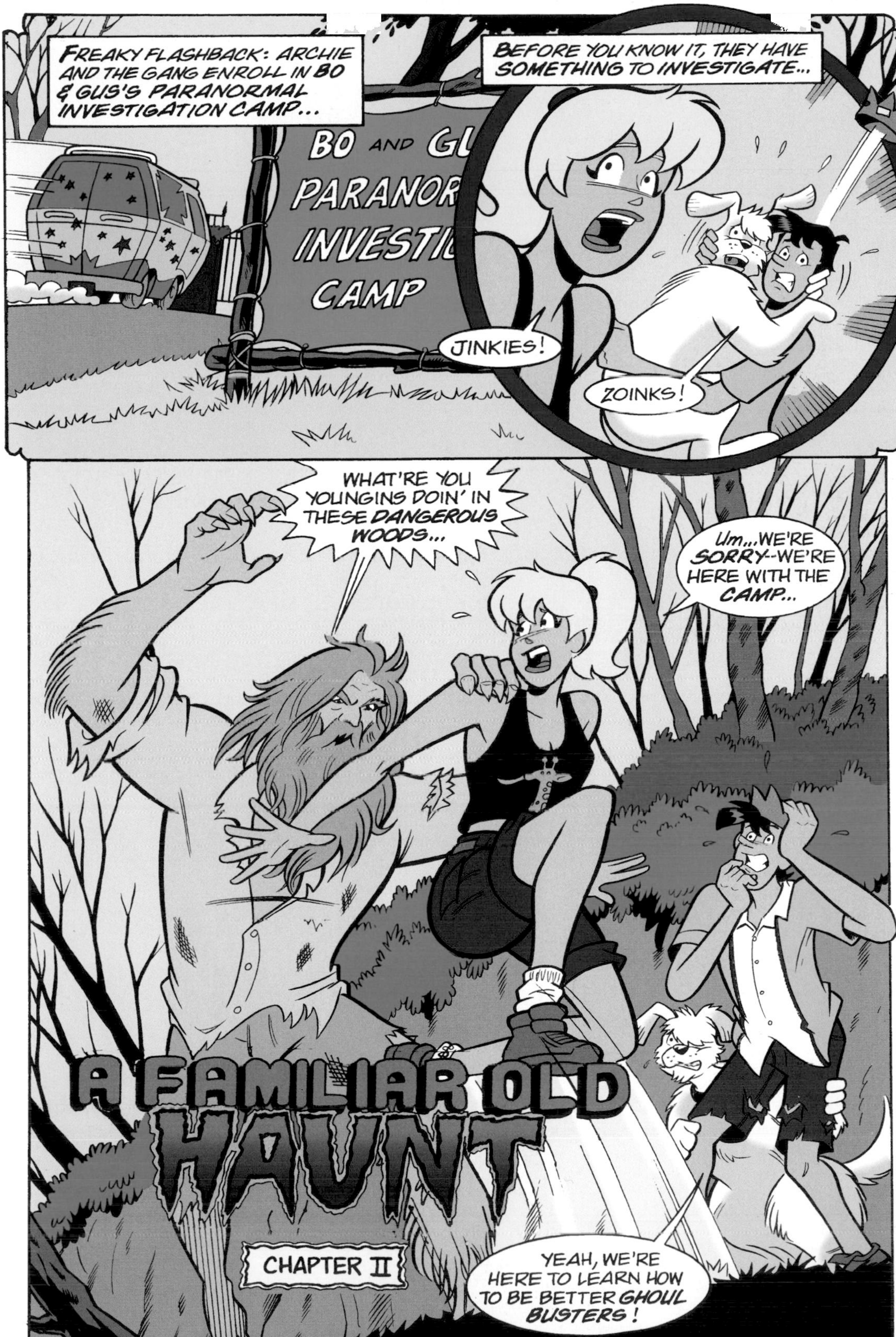
FREAKY FLASHBACK: ARCHIE AND THE GANG ENROLL IN BO & GUS'S PARANORMAL INVESTIGATION CAMP...
BO AND GU
PARANOR
INVESTIG
CAMP
BEFORE YOU KNOW IT, THEY HAVE SOMETHING TO INVESTIGATE...
JINKIES!
ZOINKS!
WHAT'RE YOU YOUNGINS DOIN' IN THESE DANGEROUS WOODS...
Um... WE'RE SORRY--WE'RE HERE WITH THE CAMP...
A FAMILIAR OLD HAUNT
CHAPTER II
YEAH, WE'RE HERE TO LEARN HOW TO BE BETTER GHOUL BUSTERS!
6

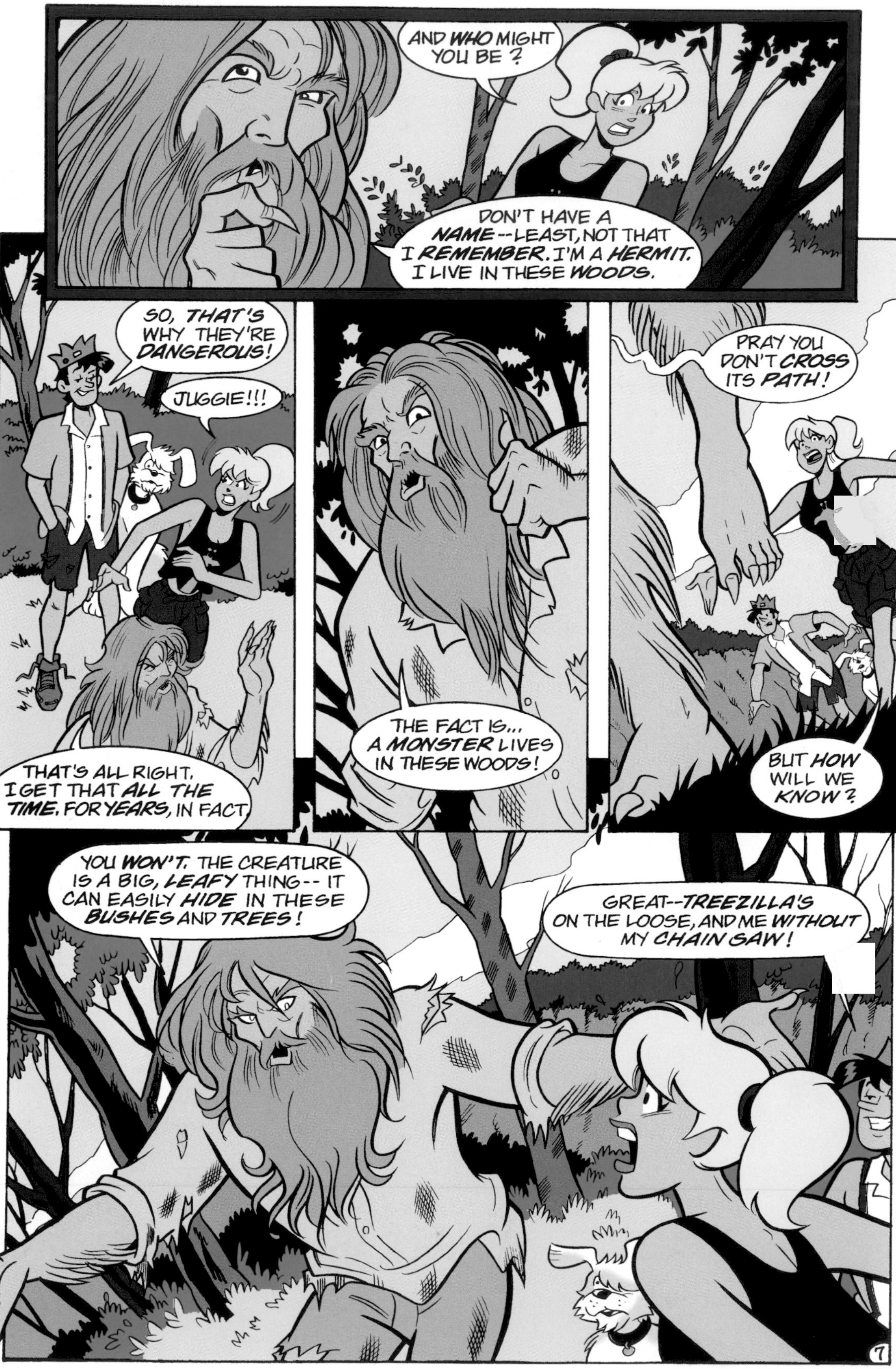
AND WHO MIGHT YOU BE?
DON'T HAVE A NAME--LEAST, NOT THAT I REMEMBER. I'M A HERMIT. I LIVE IN THESE WOODS.
SO, THAT'S WHY THEY'RE DANGEROUS!
JUGGIE!!!
THAT'S ALL RIGHT. I GET THAT ALL THE TIME. FOR YEARS, IN FACT.
THE FACT IS... A MONSTER LIVES IN THESE WOODS!
PRAY YOU DON'T CROSS ITS PATH!
BUT HOW WILL WE KNOW?
YOU WON'T. THE CREATURE IS A BIG, LEAFY THING-- IT CAN EASILY HIDE IN THESE BUSHES AND TREES!
GREAT--TREEZILLA'S ON THE LOOSE, AND ME WITHOUT MY CHAIN SAW!
7

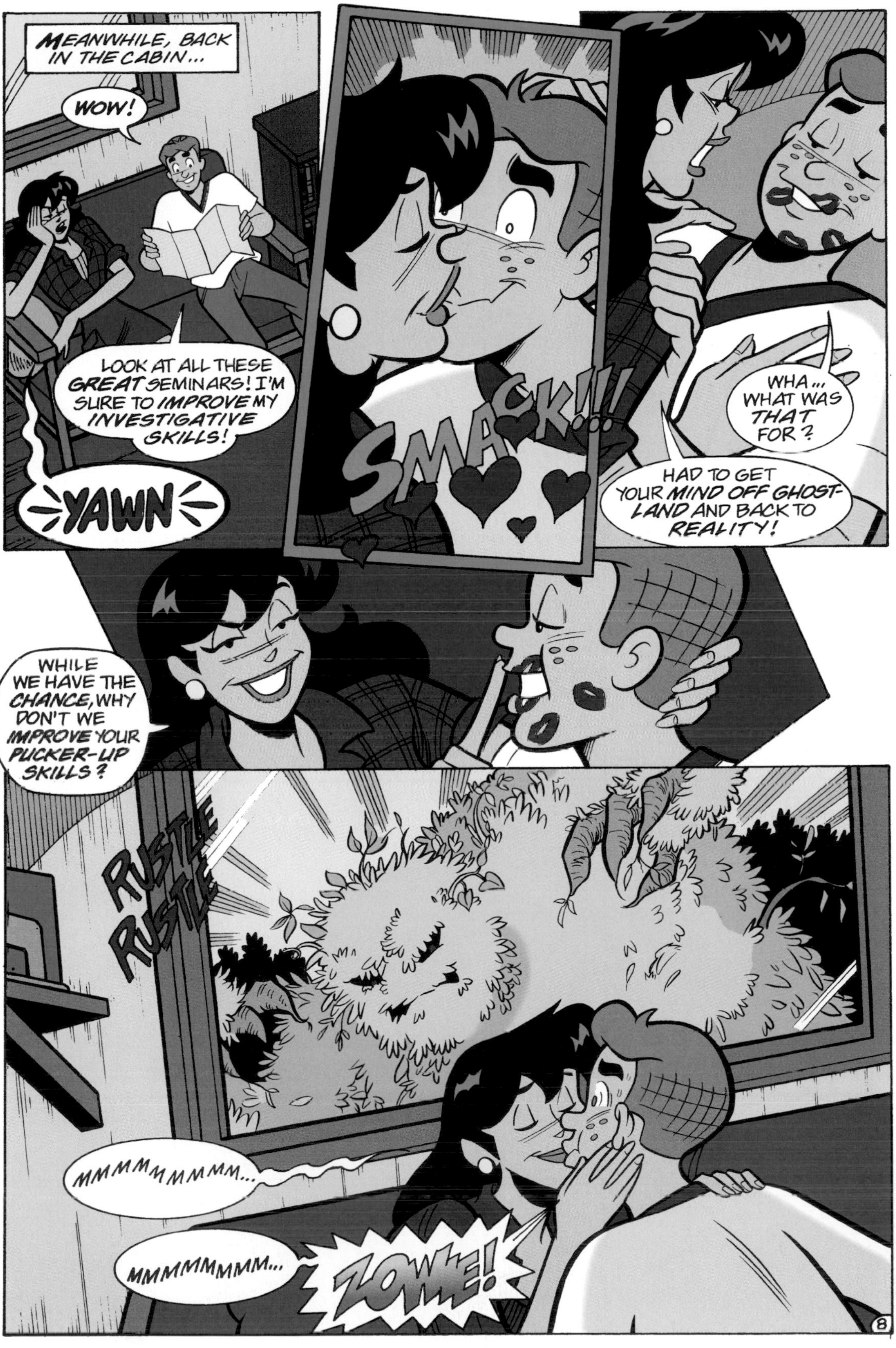
MEANWHILE, BACK IN THE CABIN...
WOW!
LOOK AT ALL THESE GREAT SEMINARS! I'M SURE TO IMPROVE MY INVESTIGATIVE SKILLS!
YAWN
SMACK!!!
WHA... WHAT WAS THAT FOR?
HAD TO GET YOUR MIND OFF GHOST-LAND AND BACK TO REALITY!
WHILE WE HAVE THE CHANCE, WHY DON'T WE IMPROVE YOUR PUCKER-UP SKILLS?
RUSTLE RUSTLE
MMMMMMMMMM...
MMMMMMMM...
ZOWIE!
8

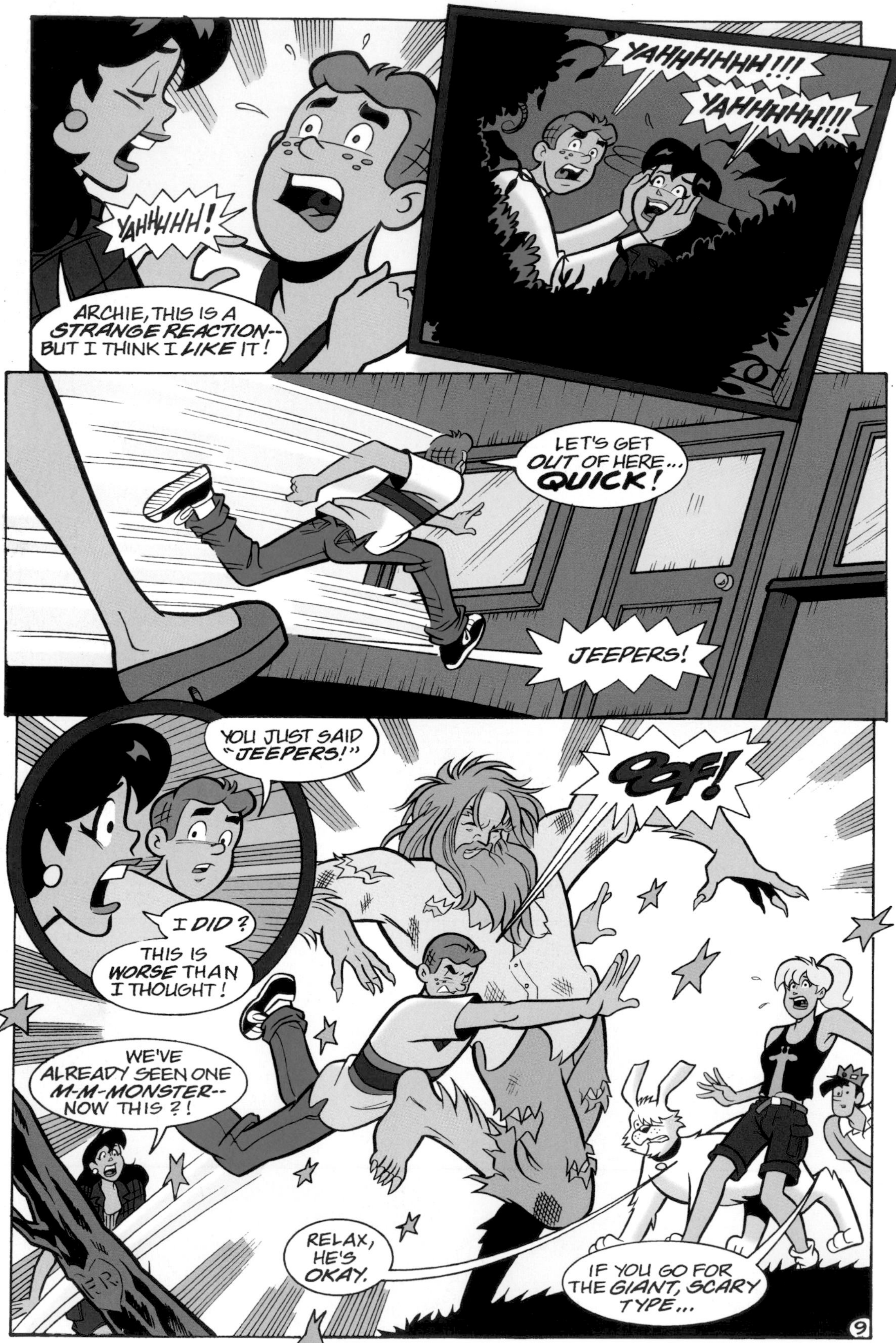
YAHHHHH!
ARCHIE, THIS IS A STRANGE REACTION-- BUT I THINK I LIKE IT!
YAHHHHHH!!!
YAHHHHH!!!
LET'S GET OUT OF HERE... QUICK!
JEEPERS!
YOU JUST SAID "JEEPERS!"
OOF!
I DID?
THIS IS WORSE THAN I THOUGHT!
WE'VE ALREADY SEEN ONE M-M-MONSTER-- NOW THIS?!
RELAX, HE'S OKAY.
IF YOU GO FOR THE GIANT, SCARY TYPE...
9

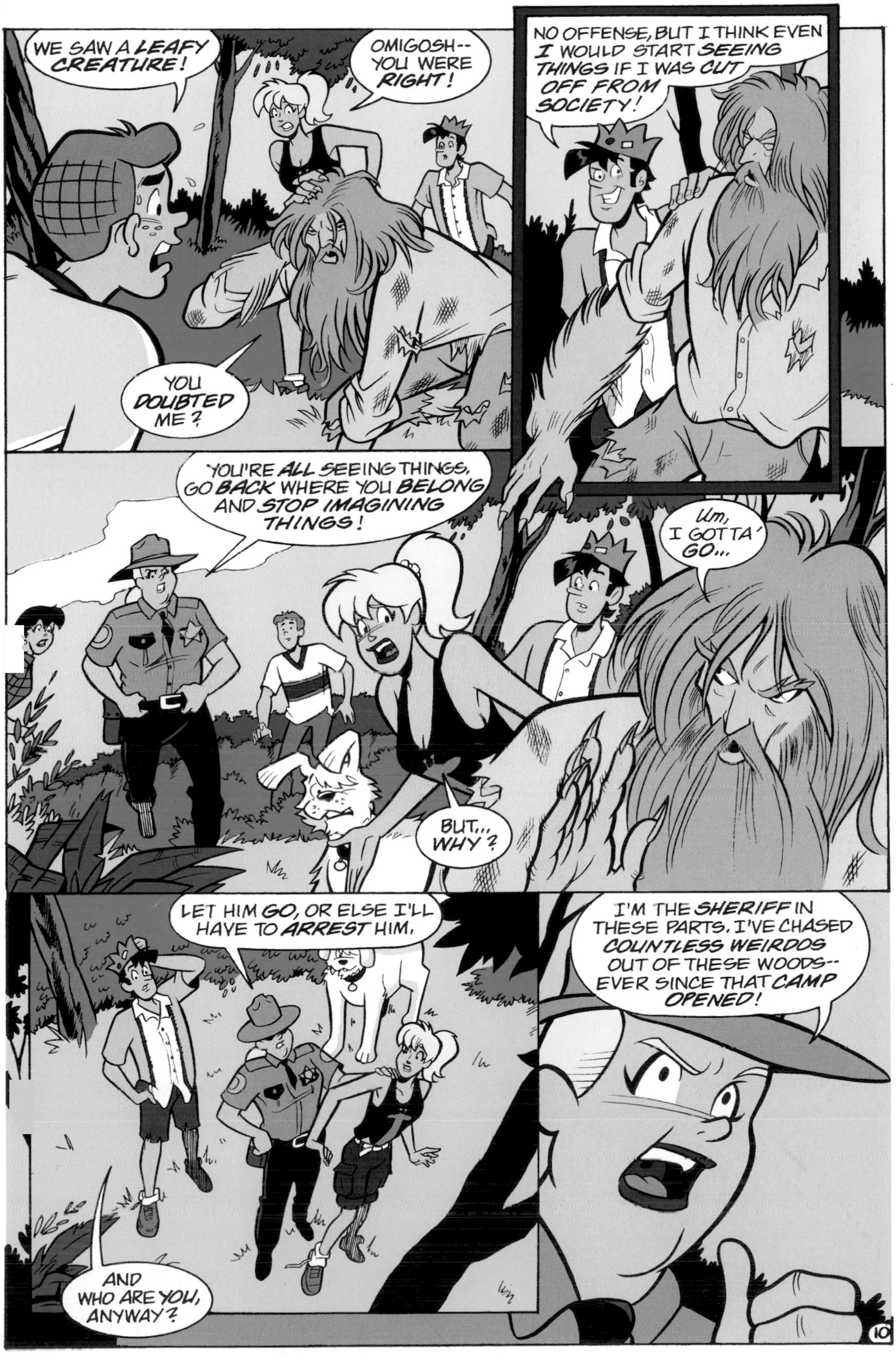

WE SAW A LEAFY CREATURE!
OMIGOSH-- YOU WERE RIGHT!
YOU DOUBTED ME?
NO OFFENSE, BUT I THINK EVEN I WOULD START SEEING THINGS IF I WAS CUT OFF FROM SOCIETY!
YOU'RE ALL SEEING THINGS, GO BACK WHERE YOU BELONG AND STOP IMAGINING THINGS!
Um, I GOTTA' GO...
BUT... WHY?
LET HIM GO, OR ELSE I'LL HAVE TO ARREST HIM.
AND WHO ARE YOU, ANYWAY?
I'M THE SHERIFF IN THESE PARTS. I'VE CHASED COUNTLESS WEIRDOS OUT OF THESE WOODS-- EVER SINCE THAT CAMP OPENED!
10

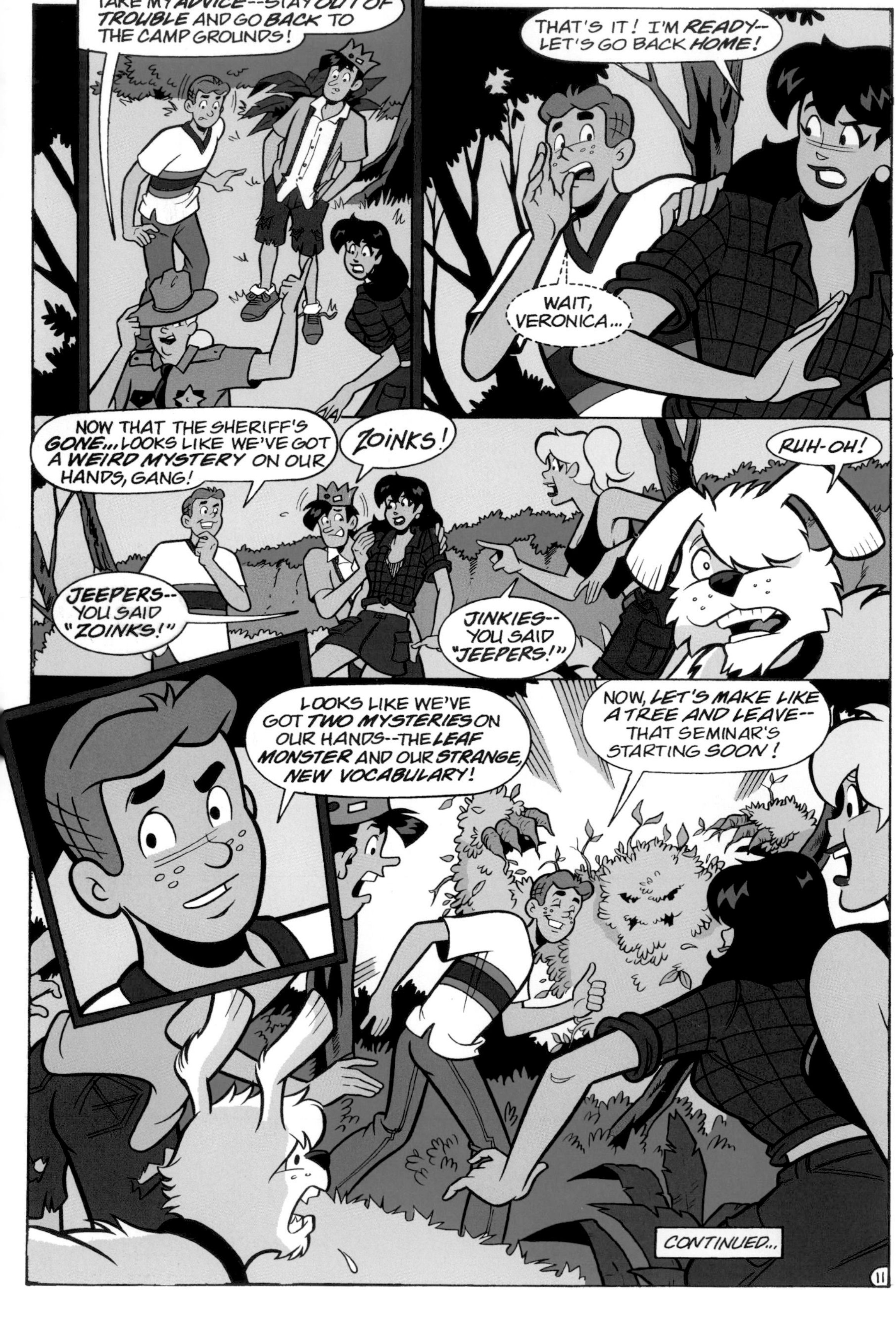
TAKE MY ADVICE--STAY OUT OF TROUBLE AND GO BACK TO THE CAMP GROUNDS!
THAT'S IT! I'M READY--LET'S GO BACK HOME!
WAIT, VERONICA...
NOW THAT THE SHERIFF'S GONE... LOOKS LIKE WE'VE GOT A WEIRD MYSTERY ON OUR HANDS, GANG!
ZOINKS!
RUH-OH!
JEEPERS--YOU SAID "ZOINKS!"
JINKIES--YOU SAID "JEEPERS!"
LOOKS LIKE WE'VE GOT TWO MYSTERIES ON OUR HANDS--THE LEAF MONSTER AND OUR STRANGE, NEW VOCABULARY!
NOW, LET'S MAKE LIKE A TREE AND LEAVE--THAT SEMINAR'S STARTING SOON!
CONTINUED...
11

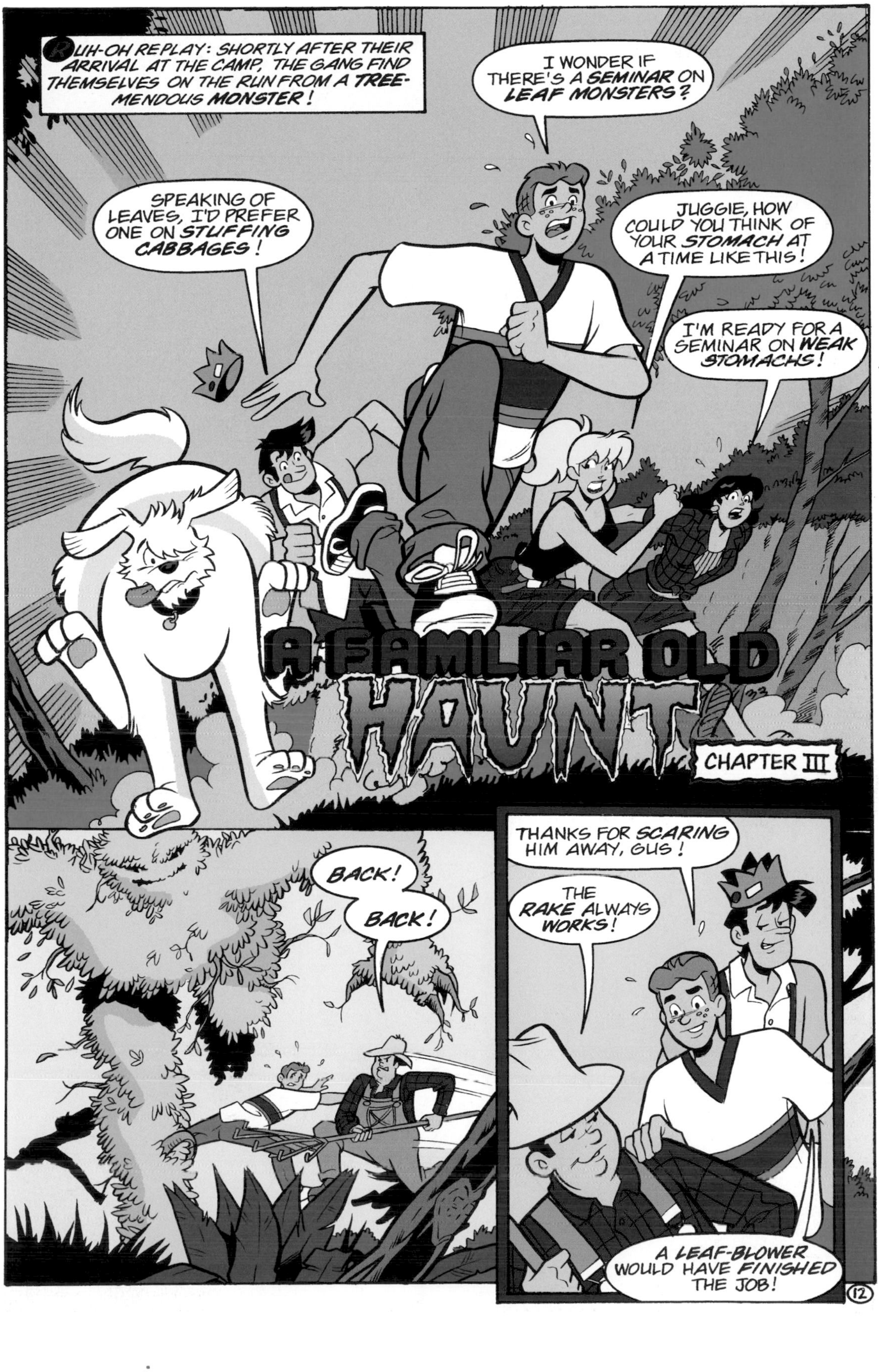
RUH-OH REPLAY: SHORTLY AFTER THEIR ARRIVAL AT THE CAMP, THE GANG FIND THEMSELVES ON THE RUN FROM A TREE-MENDOUS MONSTER!
I WONDER IF THERE'S A SEMINAR ON LEAF MONSTERS?
SPEAKING OF LEAVES, I'D PREFER ONE ON STUFFING CABBAGES!
JUGGIE, HOW COULD YOU THINK OF YOUR STOMACH AT A TIME LIKE THIS!
I'M READY FOR A SEMINAR ON WEAK STOMACHS!
A FAMILIAR OLD HAUNT
CHAPTER III
BACK!
BACK!
THANKS FOR SCARING HIM AWAY, GUS!
THE RAKE ALWAYS WORKS!
A LEAF-BLOWER WOULD HAVE FINISHED THE JOB!
12

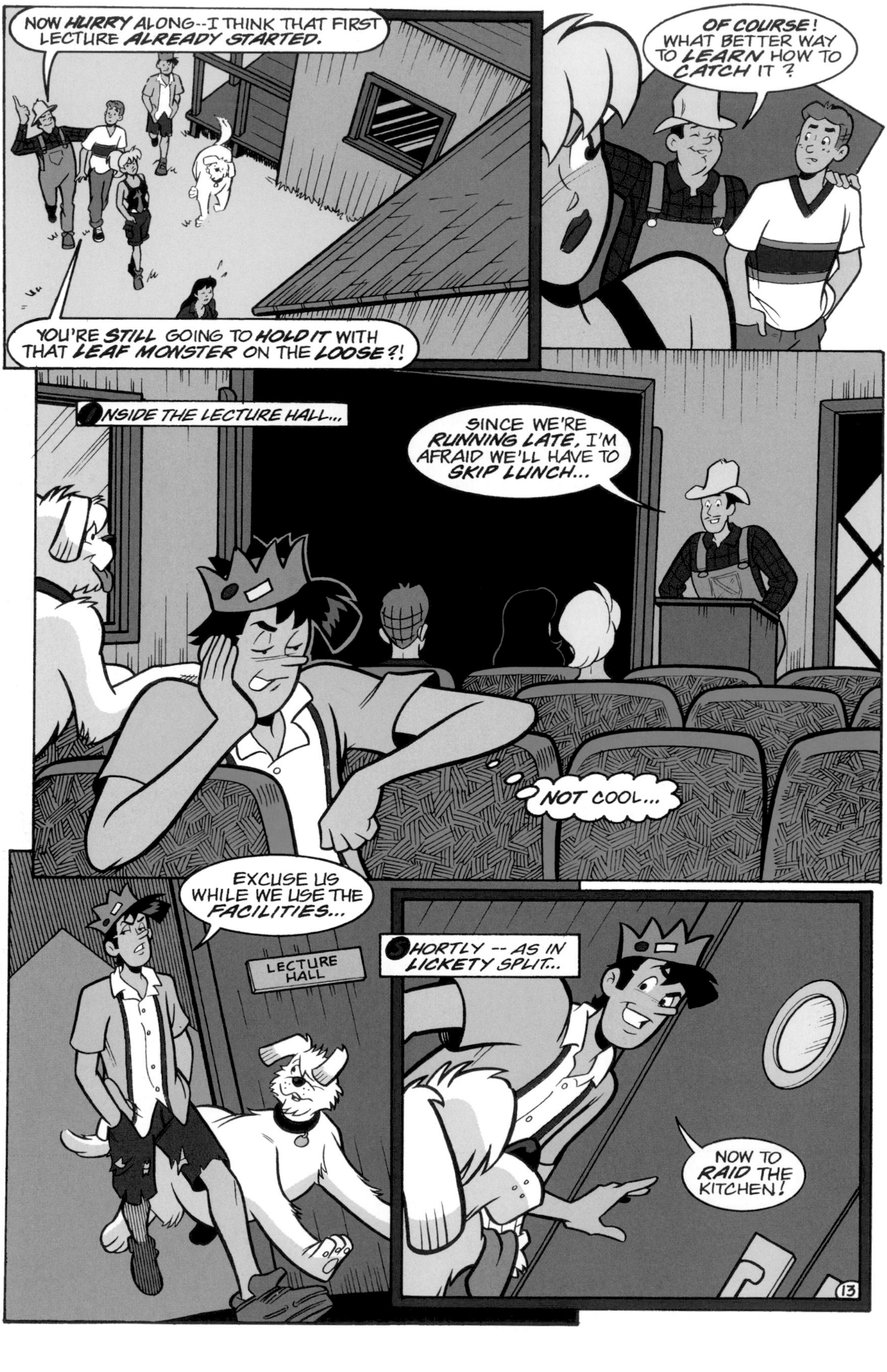

NOW HURRY ALONG--I THINK THAT FIRST LECTURE ALREADY STARTED.
YOU'RE STILL GOING TO HOLD IT WITH THAT LEAF MONSTER ON THE LOOSE?!
OF COURSE! WHAT BETTER WAY TO LEARN HOW TO CATCH IT?
INSIDE THE LECTURE HALL...
SINCE WE'RE RUNNING LATE, I'M AFRAID WE'LL HAVE TO SKIP LUNCH...
NOT COOL...
EXCUSE US WHILE WE USE THE FACILITIES...
LECTURE HALL
SHORTLY -- AS IN LICKETY SPLIT...
NOW TO RAID THE KITCHEN!
13

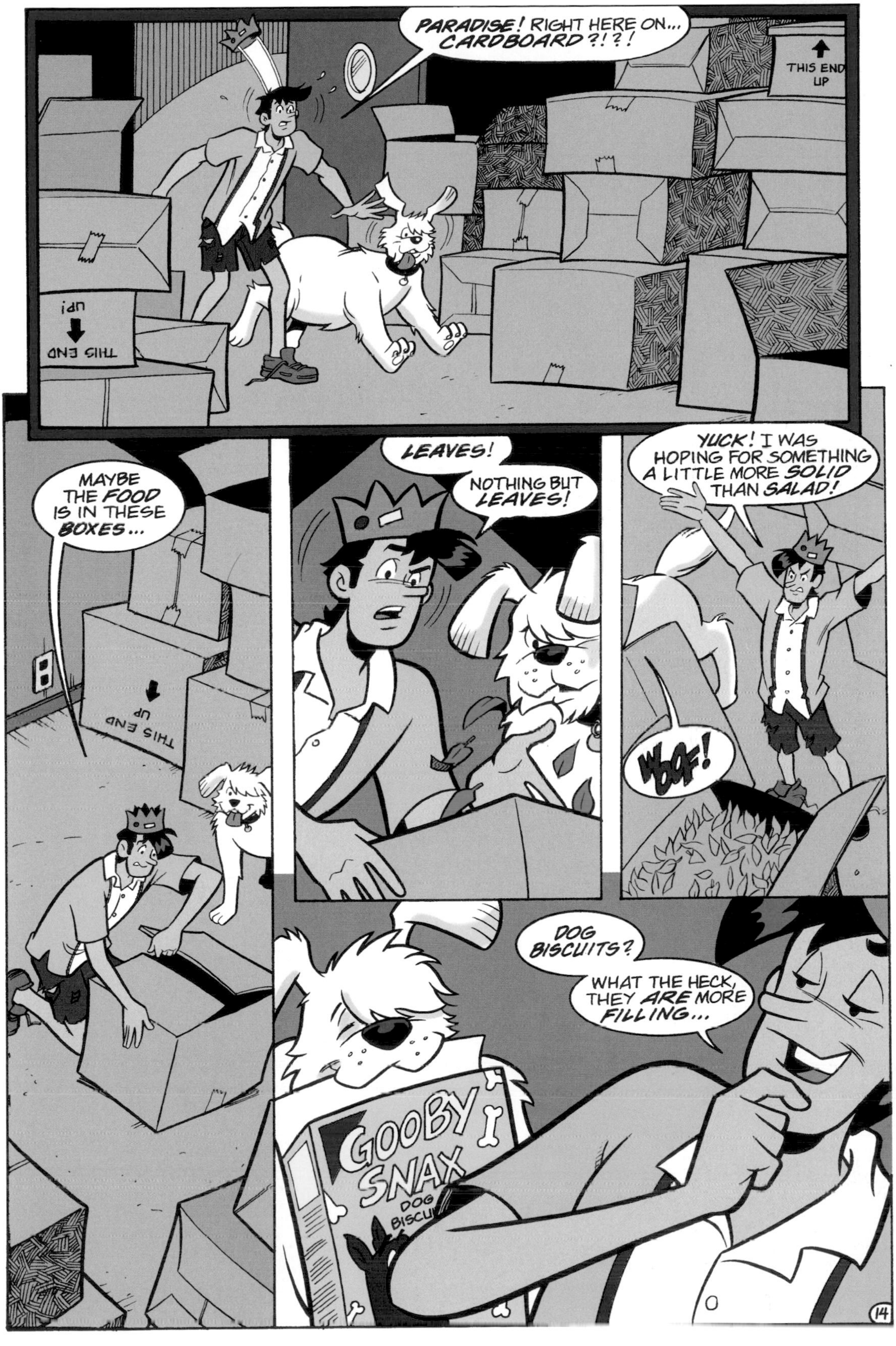
PARADISE! RIGHT HERE ON... CARDBOARD?!?!
THIS END UP
THIS END UP!
MAYBE THE FOOD IS IN THESE BOXES...
THIS END UP
LEAVES!
NOTHING BUT LEAVES!
YUCK! I WAS HOPING FOR SOMETHING A LITTLE MORE SOLID THAN SALAD!
WOOF!
DOG BISCUITS?
WHAT THE HECK, THEY ARE MORE FILLING...
GOOBY SNAX DOG BISCU
14

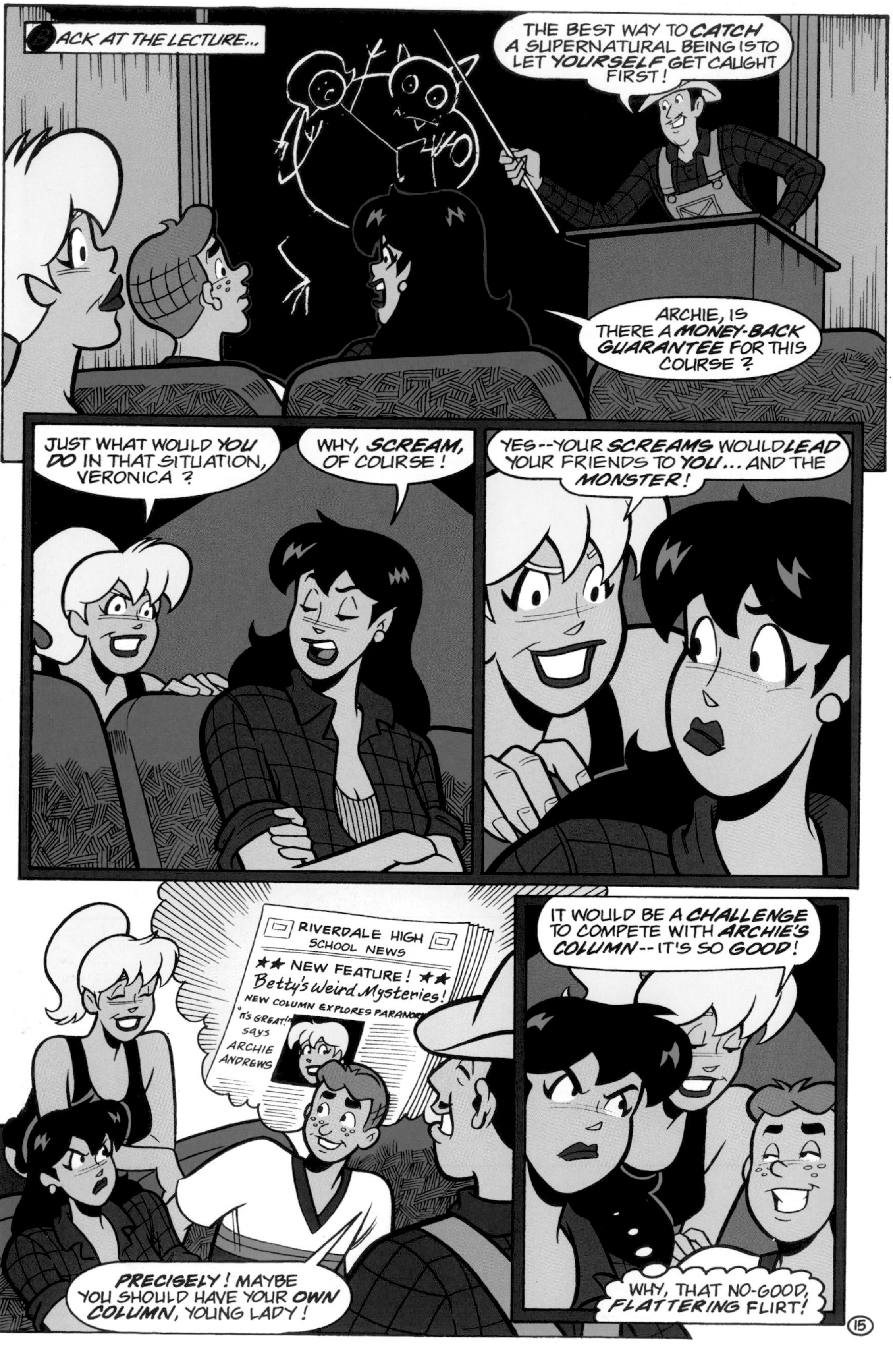

BACK AT THE LECTURE...
THE BEST WAY TO CATCH A SUPERNATURAL BEING IS TO LET YOURSELF GET CAUGHT FIRST!
ARCHIE, IS THERE A MONEY-BACK GUARANTEE FOR THIS COURSE?
JUST WHAT WOULD YOU DO IN THAT SITUATION, VERONICA?
WHY, SCREAM, OF COURSE!
YES--YOUR SCREAMS WOULD LEAD YOUR FRIENDS TO YOU... AND THE MONSTER!
RIVERDALE HIGH SCHOOL NEWS
★★ NEW FEATURE! ★★
Betty's Weird Mysteries!
NEW COLUMN EXPLORES PARANOR
"IT'S GREAT!" says ARCHIE ANDREWS
PRECISELY! MAYBE YOU SHOULD HAVE YOUR OWN COLUMN, YOUNG LADY!
IT WOULD BE A CHALLENGE TO COMPETE WITH ARCHIE'S COLUMN--IT'S SO GOOD!
WHY, THAT NO-GOOD, FLATTERING FLIRT!
15

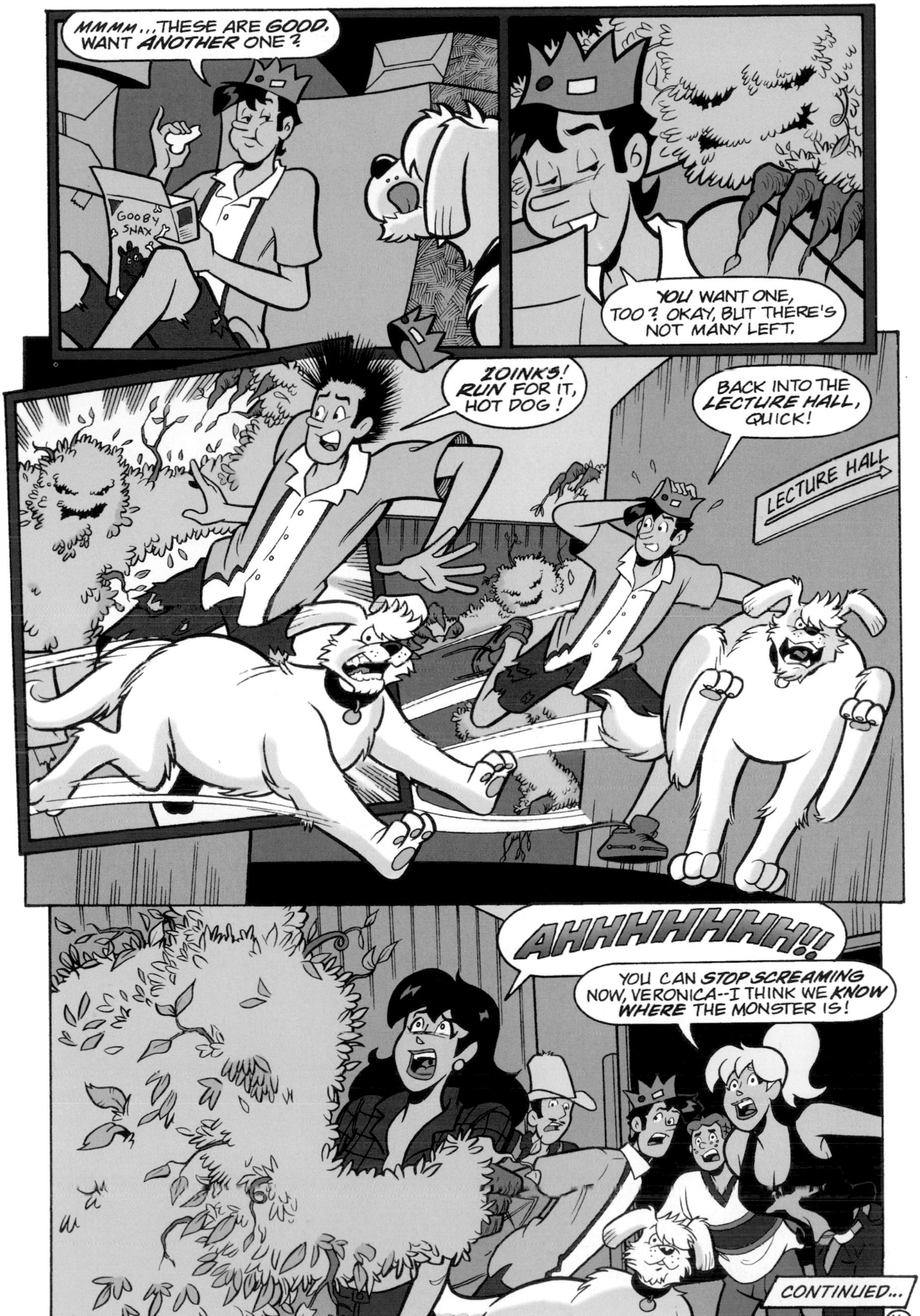
MMMM... THESE ARE GOOD. WANT ANOTHER ONE?
GOOBY SNAX
YOU WANT ONE, TOO? OKAY, BUT THERE'S NOT MANY LEFT.
ZOINKS! RUN FOR IT, HOT DOG!
BACK INTO THE LECTURE HALL, QUICK!
LECTURE HALL
AHHHHHHH!!
YOU CAN STOP SCREAMING NOW, VERONICA--I THINK WE KNOW WHERE THE MONSTER IS!
CONTINUED...
16

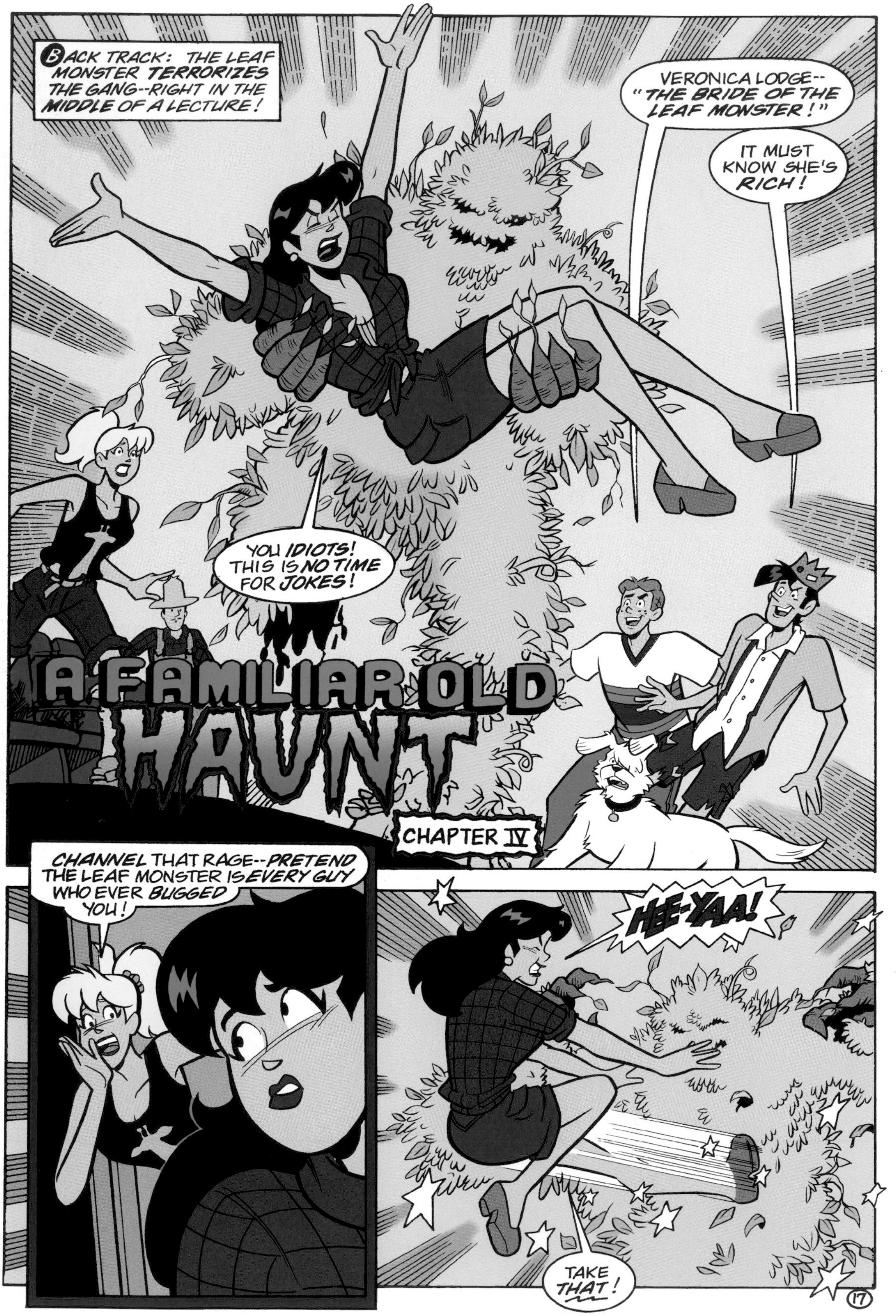
BACK TRACK: THE LEAF MONSTER TERRORIZES THE GANG--RIGHT IN THE MIDDLE OF A LECTURE!
VERONICA LODGE-- "THE BRIDE OF THE LEAF MONSTER!"
IT MUST KNOW SHE'S RICH!
YOU IDIOTS! THIS IS NO TIME FOR JOKES!
A FAMILIAR OLD HAUNT
CHAPTER IV
CHANNEL THAT RAGE--PRETEND THE LEAF MONSTER IS EVERY GUY WHO EVER BUGGED YOU!
HEE-YAA!
TAKE THAT!
17

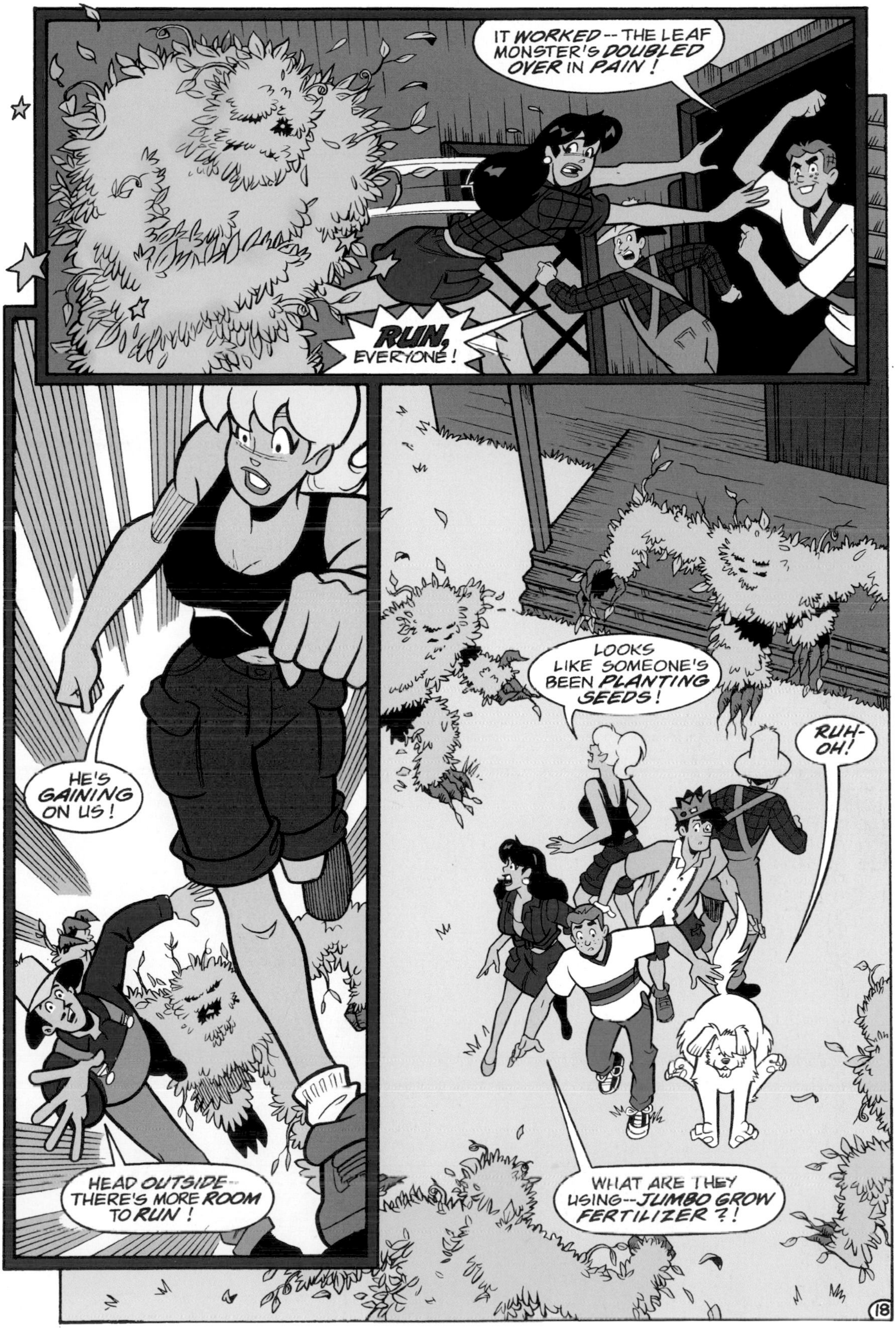

IT WORKED -- THE LEAF MONSTER'S DOUBLED OVER IN PAIN!
RUN, EVERYONE!
HE'S GAINING ON US!
HEAD OUTSIDE-- THERE'S MORE ROOM TO RUN!
LOOKS LIKE SOMEONE'S BEEN PLANTING SEEDS!
RUH-OH!
WHAT ARE THEY USING--JUMBO GROW FERTILIZER?!
18

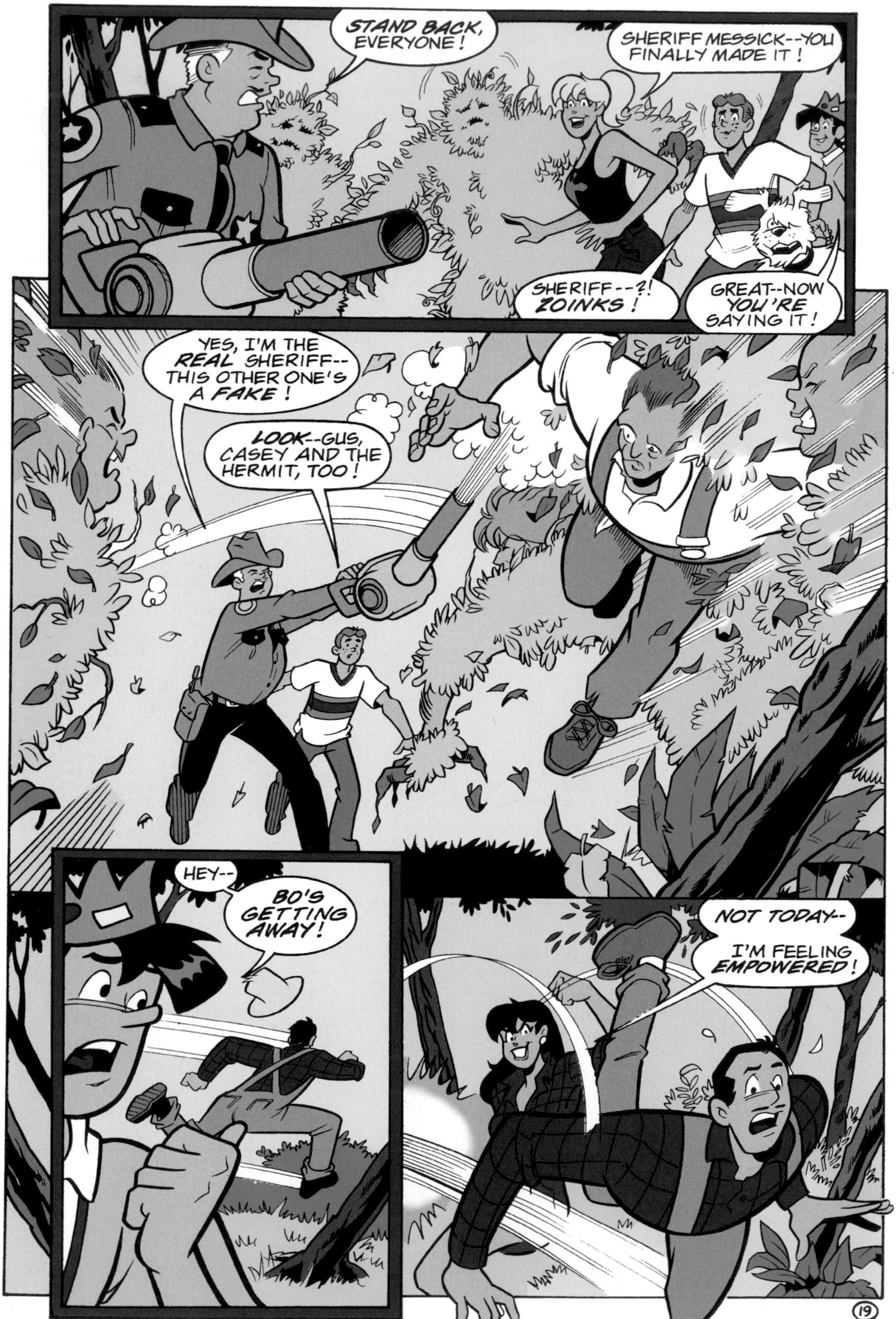
STAND BACK, EVERYONE!
SHERIFF MESSICK--YOU FINALLY MADE IT!
SHERIFF--?! ZOINKS!
GREAT--NOW YOU'RE SAYING IT!
YES, I'M THE REAL SHERIFF-- THIS OTHER ONE'S A FAKE!
LOOK--GUS, CASEY AND THE HERMIT, TOO!
HEY--
BO'S GETTING AWAY!
NOT TODAY--
I'M FEELING EMPOWERED!
19

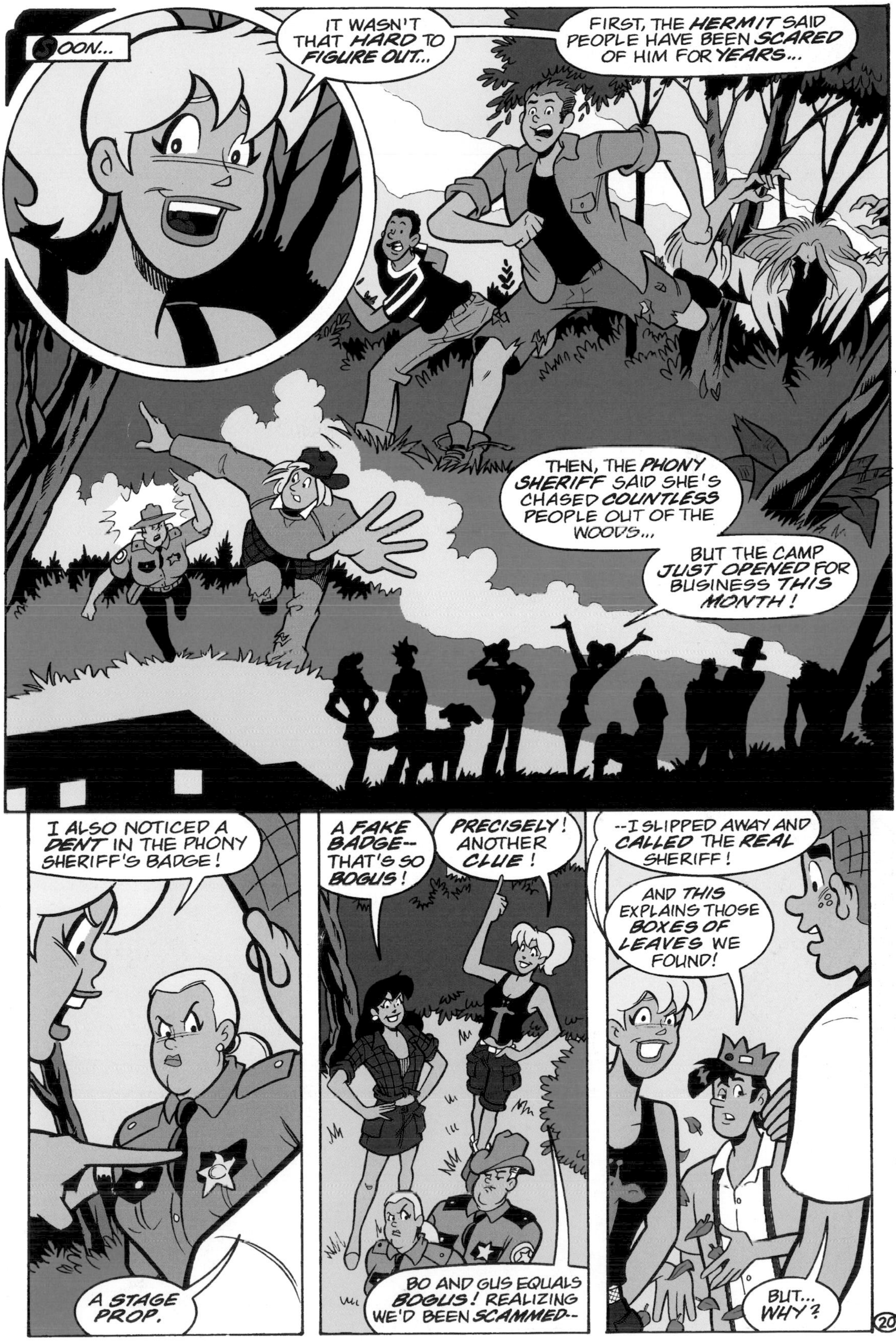
SOON...
IT WASN'T THAT HARD TO FIGURE OUT...
FIRST, THE HERMIT SAID PEOPLE HAVE BEEN SCARED OF HIM FOR YEARS...
THEN, THE PHONY SHERIFF SAID SHE'S CHASED COUNTLESS PEOPLE OUT OF THE WOODS...
BUT THE CAMP JUST OPENED FOR BUSINESS THIS MONTH!
I ALSO NOTICED A DENT IN THE PHONY SHERIFF'S BADGE!
A STAGE PROP.
A FAKE BADGE-- THAT'S SO BOGUS!
PRECISELY! ANOTHER CLUE!
BO AND GUS EQUALS BOGUS! REALIZING WE'D BEEN SCAMMED--
--I SLIPPED AWAY AND CALLED THE REAL SHERIFF!
AND THIS EXPLAINS THOSE BOXES OF LEAVES WE FOUND!
BUT... WHY?
20

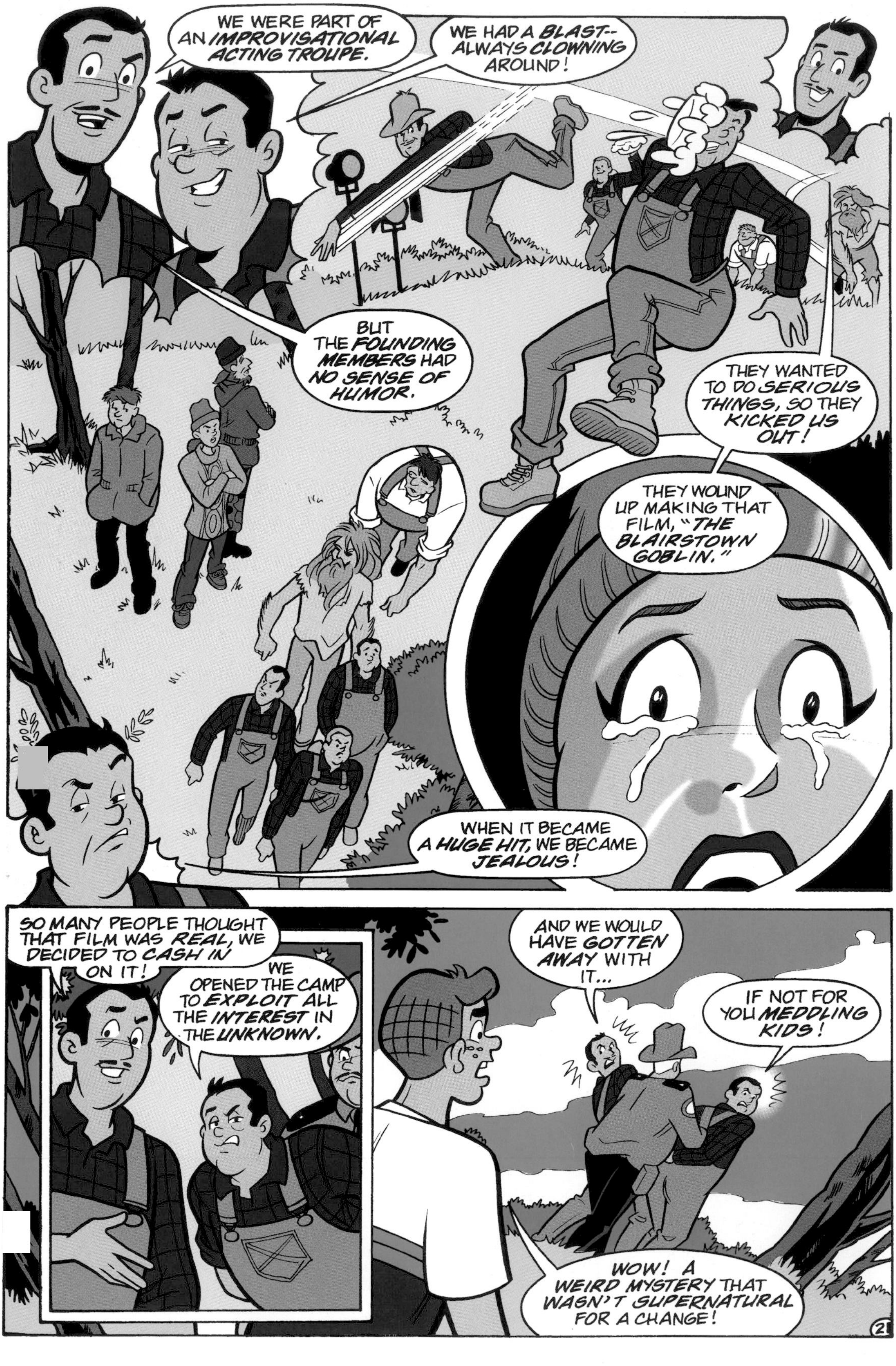
WE WERE PART OF AN IMPROVISATIONAL ACTING TROUPE.
WE HAD A BLAST-- ALWAYS CLOWNING AROUND!
BUT THE FOUNDING MEMBERS HAD NO SENSE OF HUMOR.
THEY WANTED TO DO SERIOUS THINGS, SO THEY KICKED US OUT!
THEY WOUND UP MAKING THAT FILM, "THE BLAIRSTOWN GOBLIN."
WHEN IT BECAME A HUGE HIT, WE BECAME JEALOUS!
SO MANY PEOPLE THOUGHT THAT FILM WAS REAL, WE DECIDED TO CASH IN ON IT!
WE OPENED THE CAMP TO EXPLOIT ALL THE INTEREST IN THE UNKNOWN.
AND WE WOULD HAVE GOTTEN AWAY WITH IT...
IF NOT FOR YOU MEDDLING KIDS!
WOW! A WEIRD MYSTERY THAT WASN'T SUPERNATURAL FOR A CHANGE!
21

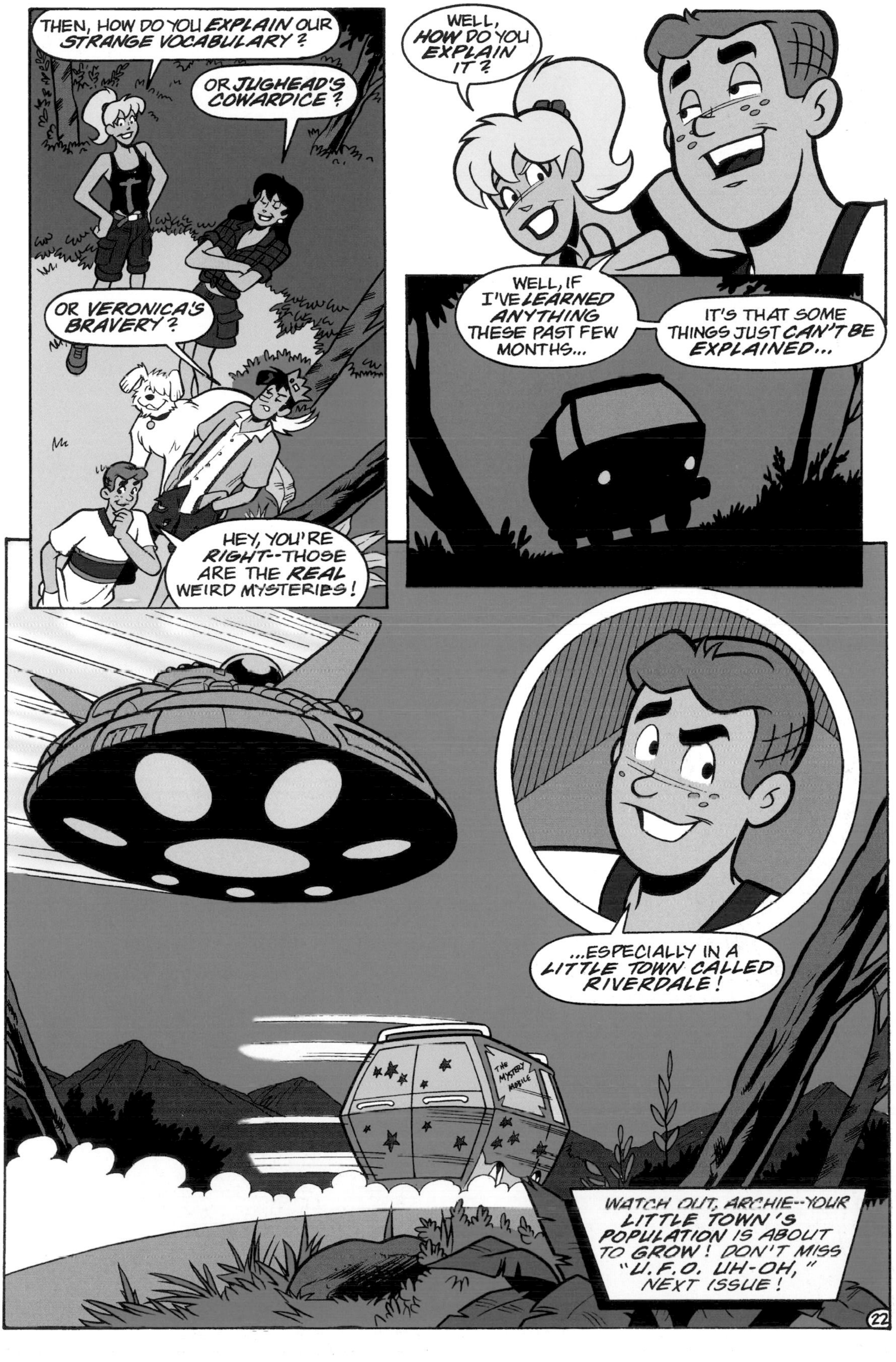
THEN, HOW DO YOU EXPLAIN OUR STRANGE VOCABULARY?
OR JUGHEAD'S COWARDICE?
OR VERONICA'S BRAVERY?
HEY, YOU'RE RIGHT--THOSE ARE THE REAL WEIRD MYSTERIES!
WELL, HOW DO YOU EXPLAIN IT?
WELL, IF I'VE LEARNED ANYTHING THESE PAST FEW MONTHS...
IT'S THAT SOME THINGS JUST CAN'T BE EXPLAINED...
...ESPECIALLY IN A LITTLE TOWN CALLED RIVERDALE!
THE MYSTERY MOBILE
WATCH OUT, ARCHIE--YOUR LITTLE TOWN'S POPULATION IS ABOUT TO GROW! DON'T MISS "U.F.O. UH-OH," NEXT ISSUE!
22

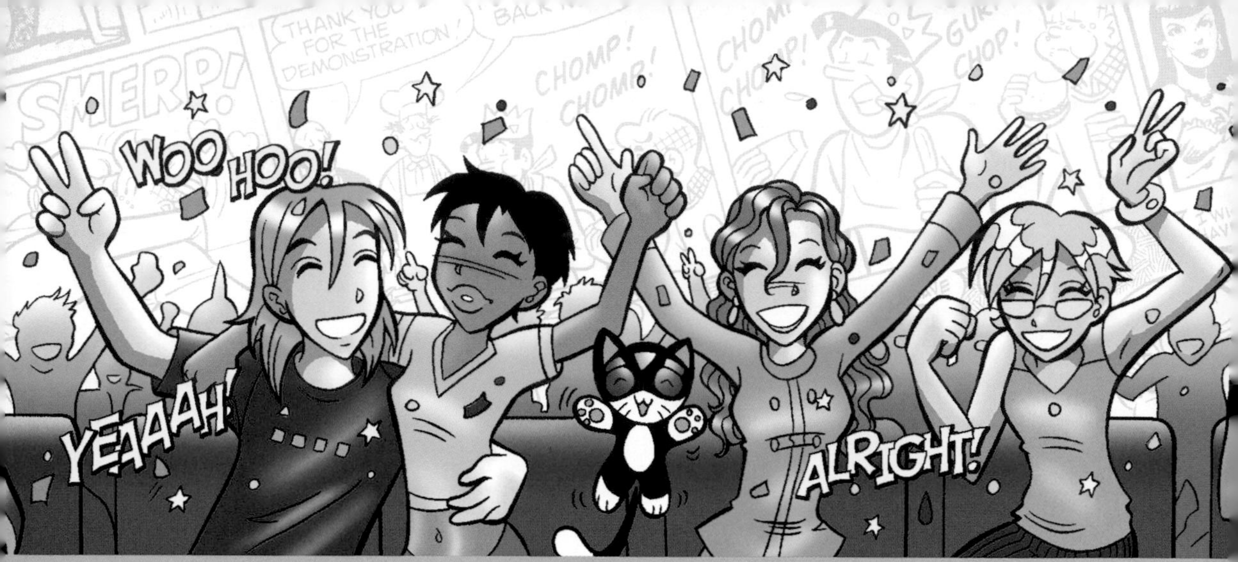
WOO HOO!
YEAAAH!
ALRIGHT!

SPELL IT OUT

SABRINA #70, 2005

BY TANIA DEL RIO, JIM AMASH, JEFF POWELL, RIDGE ROOMS & JASON JENSEN

"Spell it Out" was one of my favorite Sabrina stories to write and draw. It has it all: romantic drama surrounding a classic love triangle, a new twist on the pun behind the word "spelling" (it has a very different meaning in the Magic Realm vs. the mortal world), and intense competition with fierce rivals! Sabrina also had a chance to show off her unique magical abilities, which doubly served to advance the overall plot further by revealing more clues to the mystery behind her heightened powers.

However, what I love best about this story is that, throughout it all, Sabrina is still just an average teenage girl, getting herself into ridiculous situations in order to impress her ex-boyfriend, Harvey. I think we can all relate to that feeling of rejection and wanting to get back in the game. It doesn't matter that she's one of the most skilled witches of her time—she's more concerned about her social life than about saving the world at this point!

—*Tania del Rio*
Writer & Artist,
Archie Comics

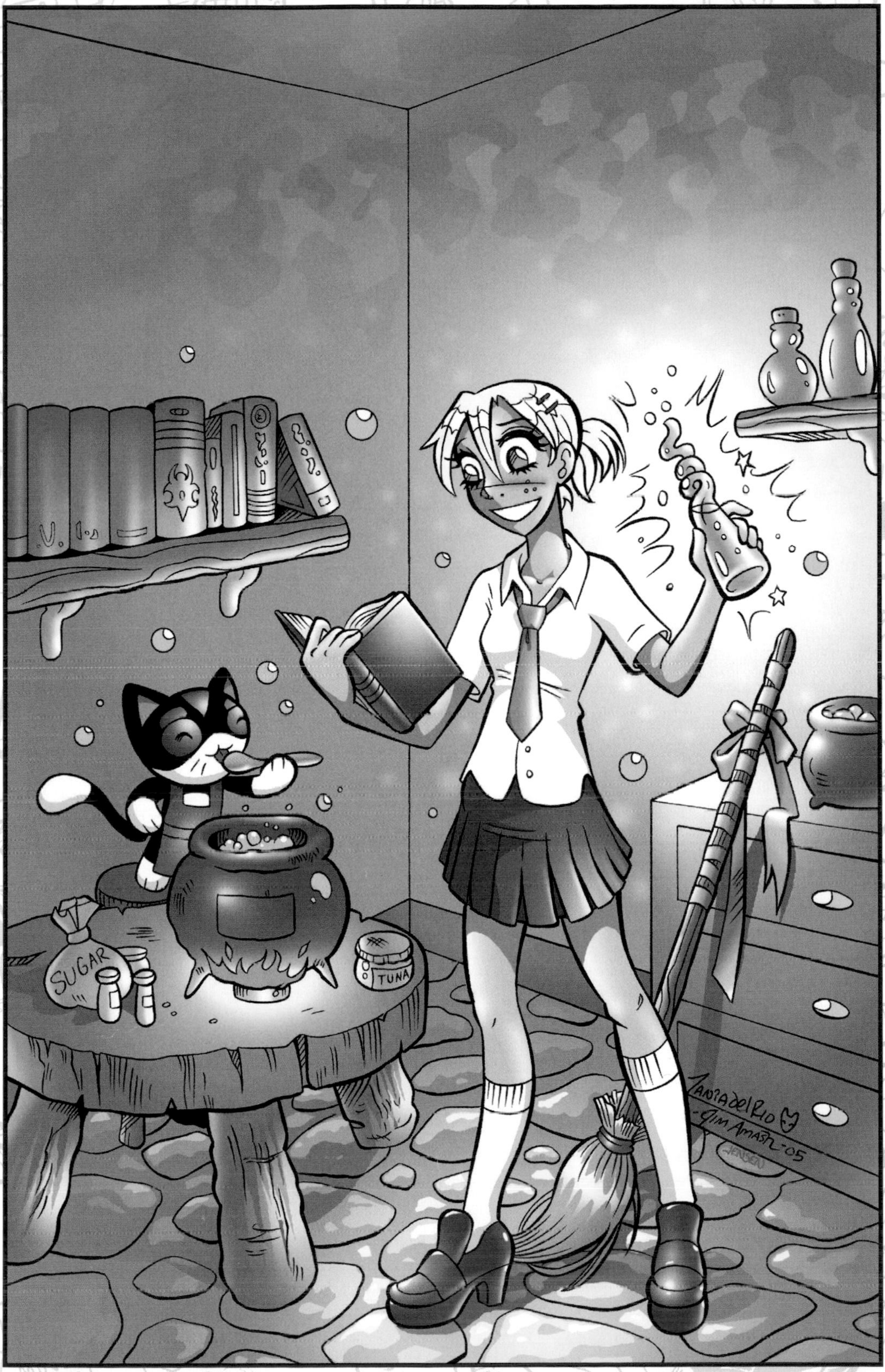
SUGAR
TUNA

Cover to *Sabrina* #70, 2005
art by Tania Del Rio

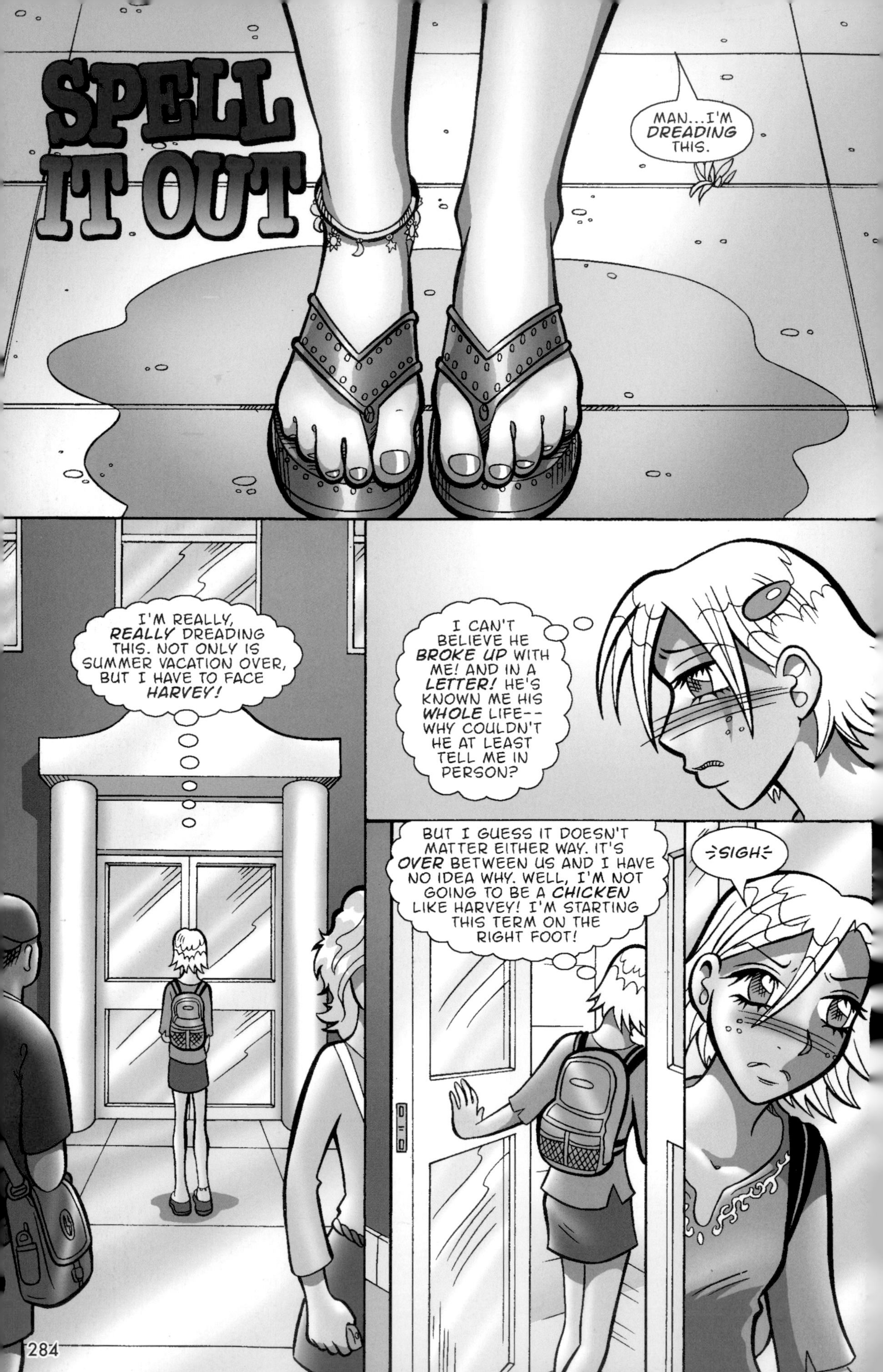
SPELL IT OUT
MAN...I'M DREADING THIS.
I'M REALLY, REALLY DREADING THIS. NOT ONLY IS SUMMER VACATION OVER, BUT I HAVE TO FACE HARVEY!
I CAN'T BELIEVE HE BROKE UP WITH ME! AND IN A LETTER! HE'S KNOWN ME HIS WHOLE LIFE--WHY COULDN'T HE AT LEAST TELL ME IN PERSON?
BUT I GUESS IT DOESN'T MATTER EITHER WAY. IT'S OVER BETWEEN US AND I HAVE NO IDEA WHY. WELL, I'M NOT GOING TO BE A CHICKEN LIKE HARVEY! I'M STARTING THIS TERM ON THE RIGHT FOOT!
SIGH

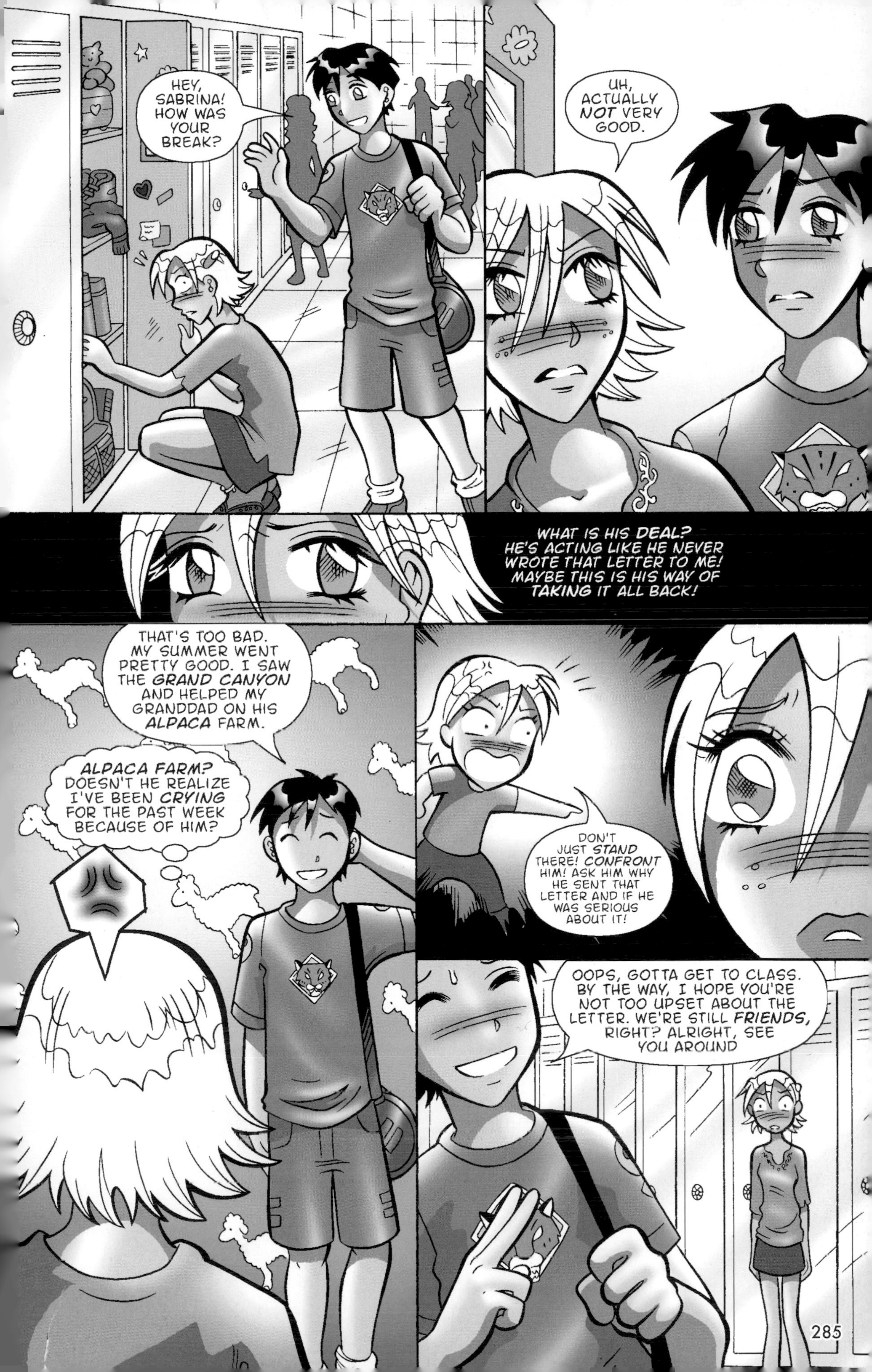
HEY, SABRINA! HOW WAS YOUR BREAK?
UH, ACTUALLY NOT VERY GOOD.
WHAT IS HIS DEAL? HE'S ACTING LIKE HE NEVER WROTE THAT LETTER TO ME! MAYBE THIS IS HIS WAY OF TAKING IT ALL BACK!
THAT'S TOO BAD. MY SUMMER WENT PRETTY GOOD. I SAW THE GRAND CANYON AND HELPED MY GRANDDAD ON HIS ALPACA FARM.
ALPACA FARM? DOESN'T HE REALIZE I'VE BEEN CRYING FOR THE PAST WEEK BECAUSE OF HIM?
DON'T JUST STAND THERE! CONFRONT HIM! ASK HIM WHY HE SENT THAT LETTER AND IF HE WAS SERIOUS ABOUT IT!
OOPS, GOTTA GET TO CLASS. BY THE WAY, I HOPE YOU'RE NOT TOO UPSET ABOUT THE LETTER. WE'RE STILL FRIENDS, RIGHT? ALRIGHT, SEE YOU AROUND

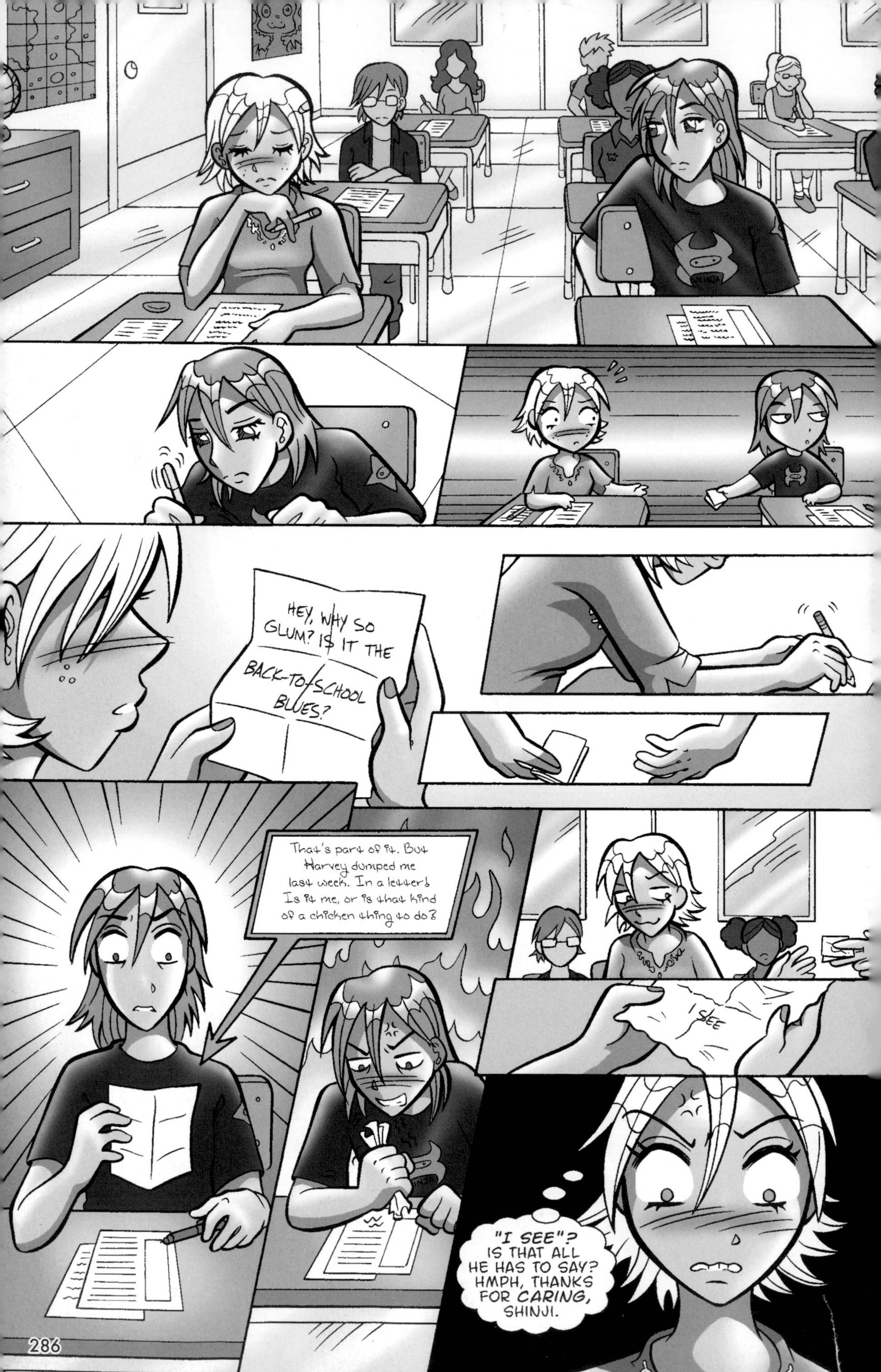

HEY, WHY SO GLUM? IS IT THE BACK-TO-SCHOOL BLUES?
That's part of it. But Harvey dumped me last week. In a letter! Is it me, or is that kind of a chicken thing to do?
I SEE
"I SEE"? IS THAT ALL HE HAS TO SAY? HMPH, THANKS FOR CARING, SHINJI.

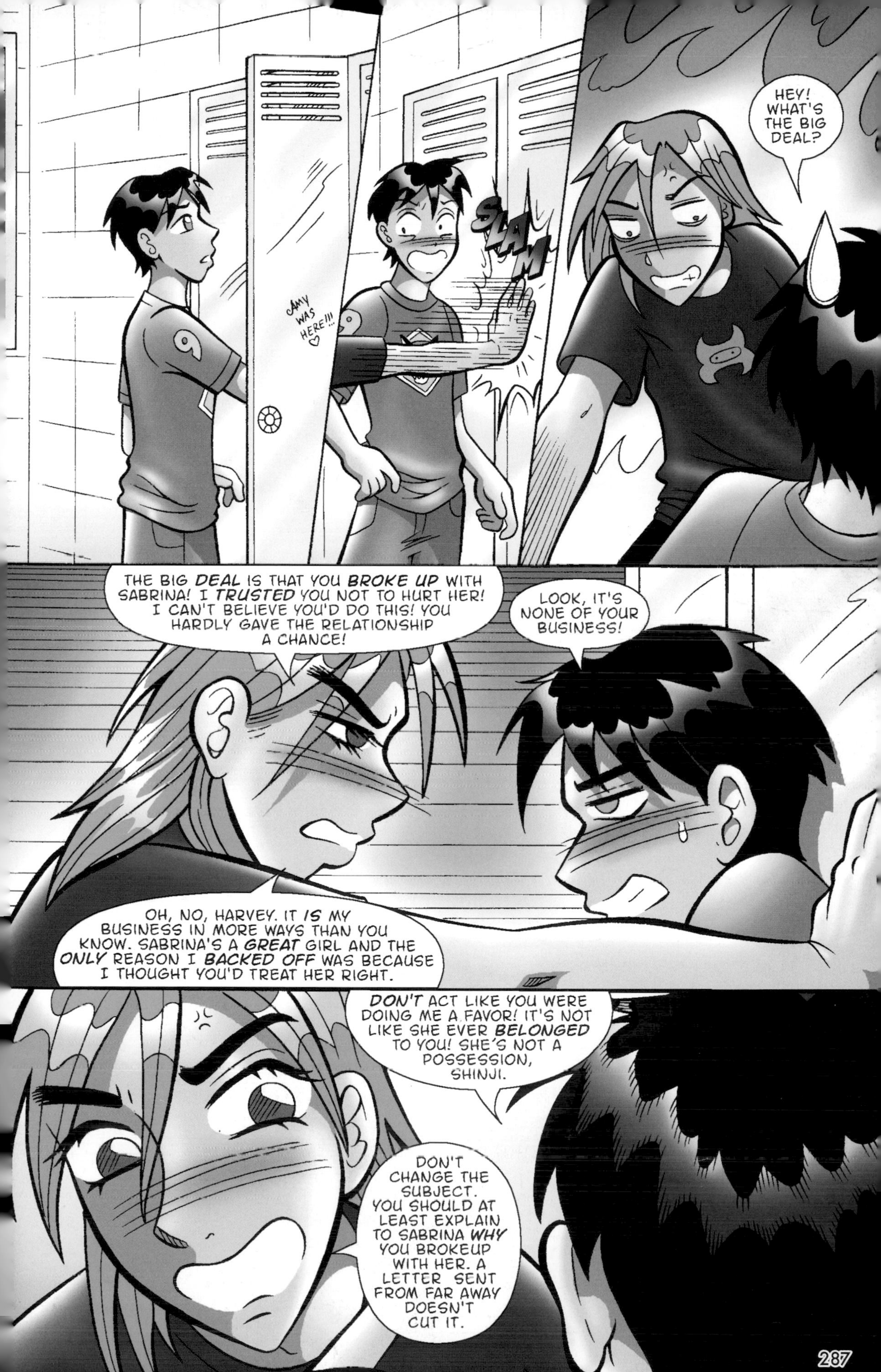

SLAM
HEY! WHAT'S THE BIG DEAL?
AMY WAS HERE!!! ♡
THE BIG DEAL IS THAT YOU BROKE UP WITH SABRINA! I TRUSTED YOU NOT TO HURT HER! I CAN'T BELIEVE YOU'D DO THIS! YOU HARDLY GAVE THE RELATIONSHIP A CHANCE!
LOOK, IT'S NONE OF YOUR BUSINESS!
OH, NO, HARVEY. IT IS MY BUSINESS IN MORE WAYS THAN YOU KNOW. SABRINA'S A GREAT GIRL AND THE ONLY REASON I BACKED OFF WAS BECAUSE I THOUGHT YOU'D TREAT HER RIGHT.
DON'T ACT LIKE YOU WERE DOING ME A FAVOR! IT'S NOT LIKE SHE EVER BELONGED TO YOU! SHE'S NOT A POSSESSION, SHINJI.
DON'T CHANGE THE SUBJECT. YOU SHOULD AT LEAST EXPLAIN TO SABRINA WHY YOU BROKEUP WITH HER. A LETTER SENT FROM FAR AWAY DOESN'T CUT IT.

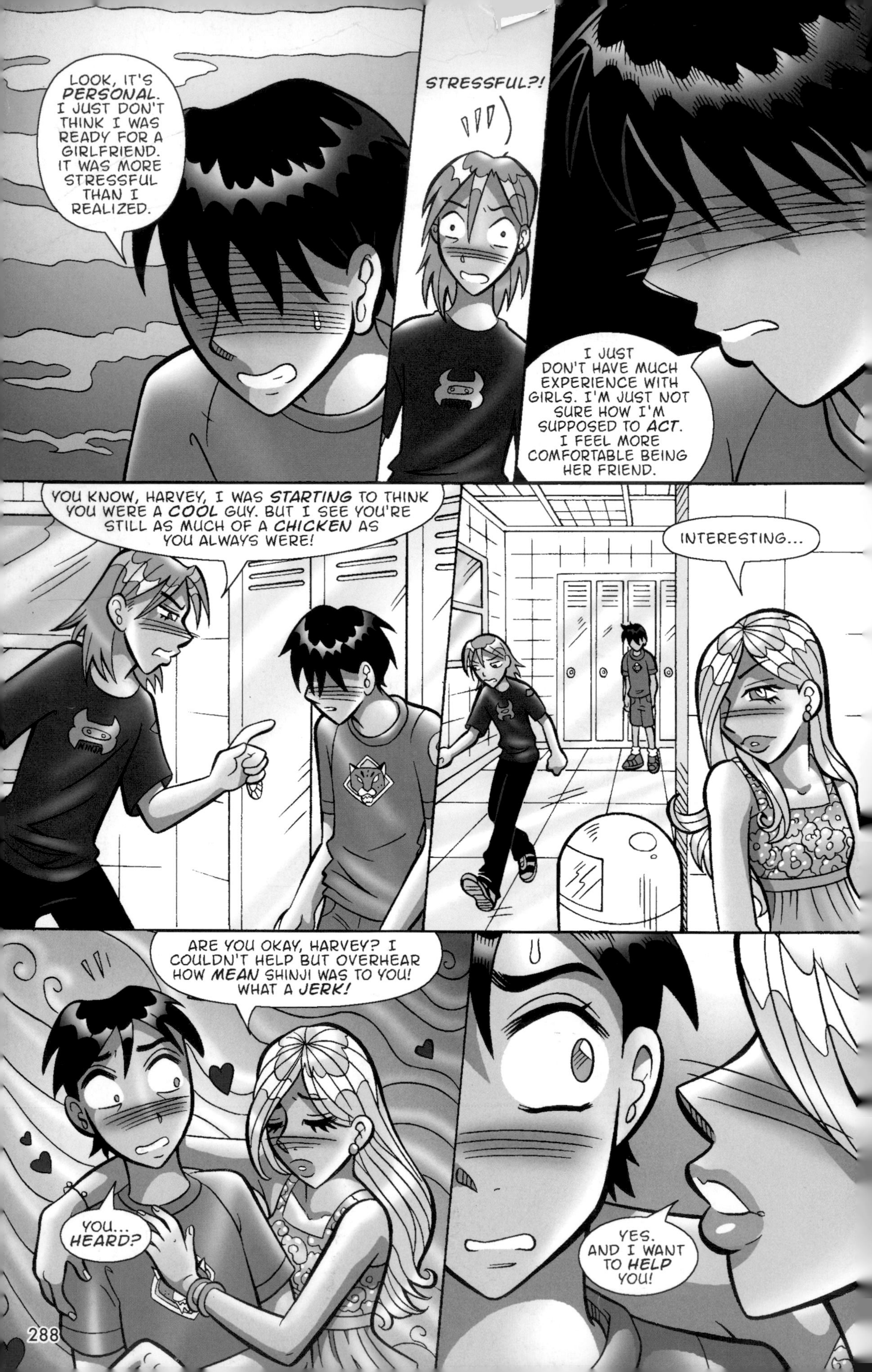

LOOK, IT'S *PERSONAL*. I JUST DON'T THINK I WAS READY FOR A GIRLFRIEND. IT WAS MORE STRESSFUL THAN I REALIZED.
STRESSFUL?!
I JUST DON'T HAVE MUCH EXPERIENCE WITH GIRLS. I'M JUST NOT SURE HOW I'M SUPPOSED TO *ACT*. I FEEL MORE COMFORTABLE BEING HER FRIEND.
YOU KNOW, HARVEY, I WAS *STARTING* TO THINK YOU WERE A *COOL* GUY. BUT I SEE YOU'RE STILL AS MUCH OF A *CHICKEN* AS YOU ALWAYS WERE!
INTERESTING...
ARE YOU OKAY, HARVEY? I COULDN'T HELP BUT OVERHEAR HOW *MEAN* SHINJI WAS TO YOU! WHAT A *JERK!*
YOU... *HEARD?*
YES. AND I WANT TO *HELP* YOU!

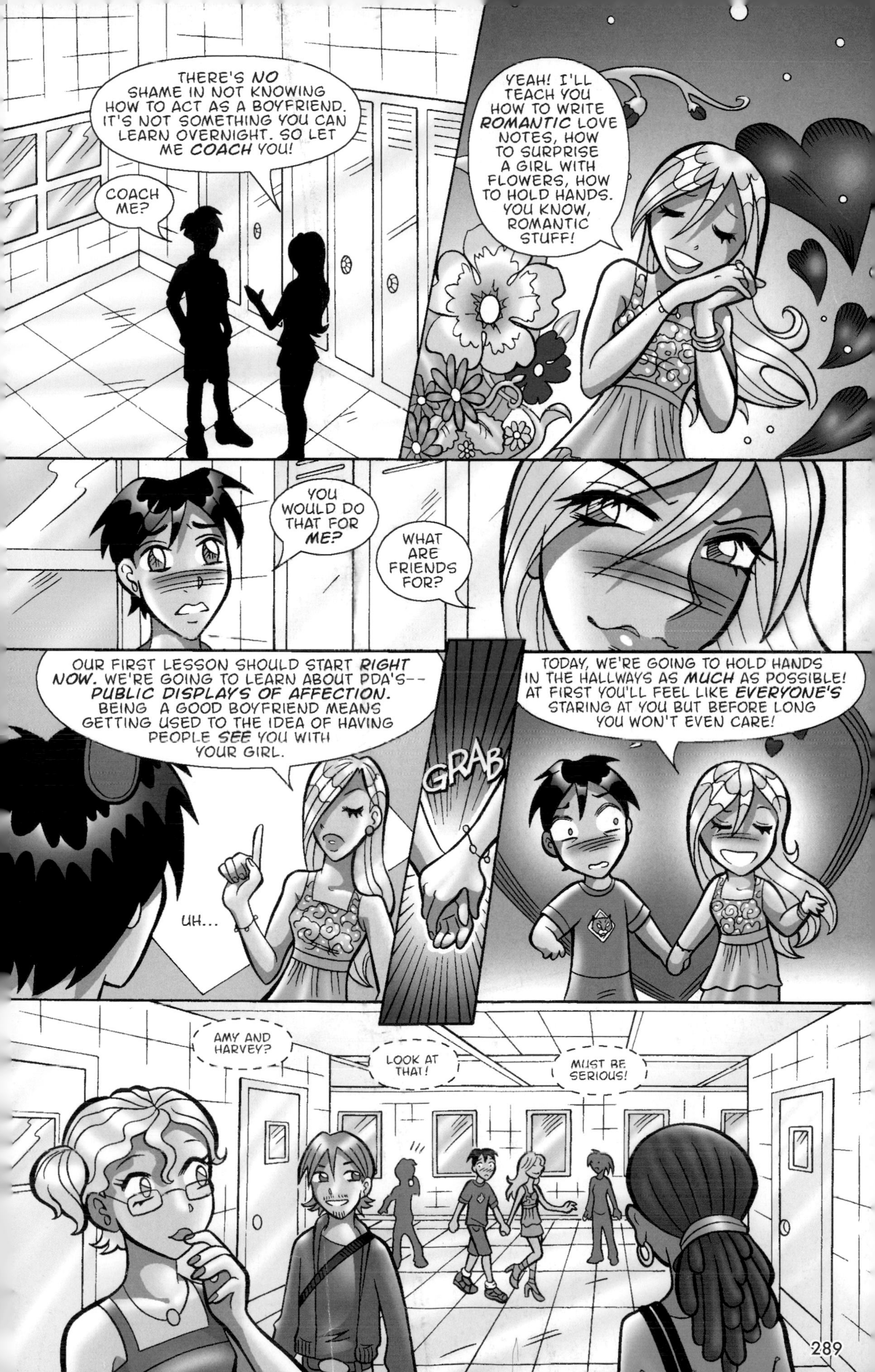
THERE'S NO SHAME IN NOT KNOWING HOW TO ACT AS A BOYFRIEND. IT'S NOT SOMETHING YOU CAN LEARN OVERNIGHT. SO LET ME COACH YOU!
COACH ME?
YEAH! I'LL TEACH YOU HOW TO WRITE ROMANTIC LOVE NOTES, HOW TO SURPRISE A GIRL WITH FLOWERS, HOW TO HOLD HANDS. YOU KNOW, ROMANTIC STUFF!
YOU WOULD DO THAT FOR ME?
WHAT ARE FRIENDS FOR?
OUR FIRST LESSON SHOULD START RIGHT NOW. WE'RE GOING TO LEARN ABOUT PDA'S-- PUBLIC DISPLAYS OF AFFECTION. BEING A GOOD BOYFRIEND MEANS GETTING USED TO THE IDEA OF HAVING PEOPLE SEE YOU WITH YOUR GIRL.
UH...
GRAB
TODAY, WE'RE GOING TO HOLD HANDS IN THE HALLWAYS AS MUCH AS POSSIBLE! AT FIRST YOU'LL FEEL LIKE EVERYONE'S STARING AT YOU BUT BEFORE LONG YOU WON'T EVEN CARE!
AMY AND HARVEY?
LOOK AT THAT!
MUST BE SERIOUS!

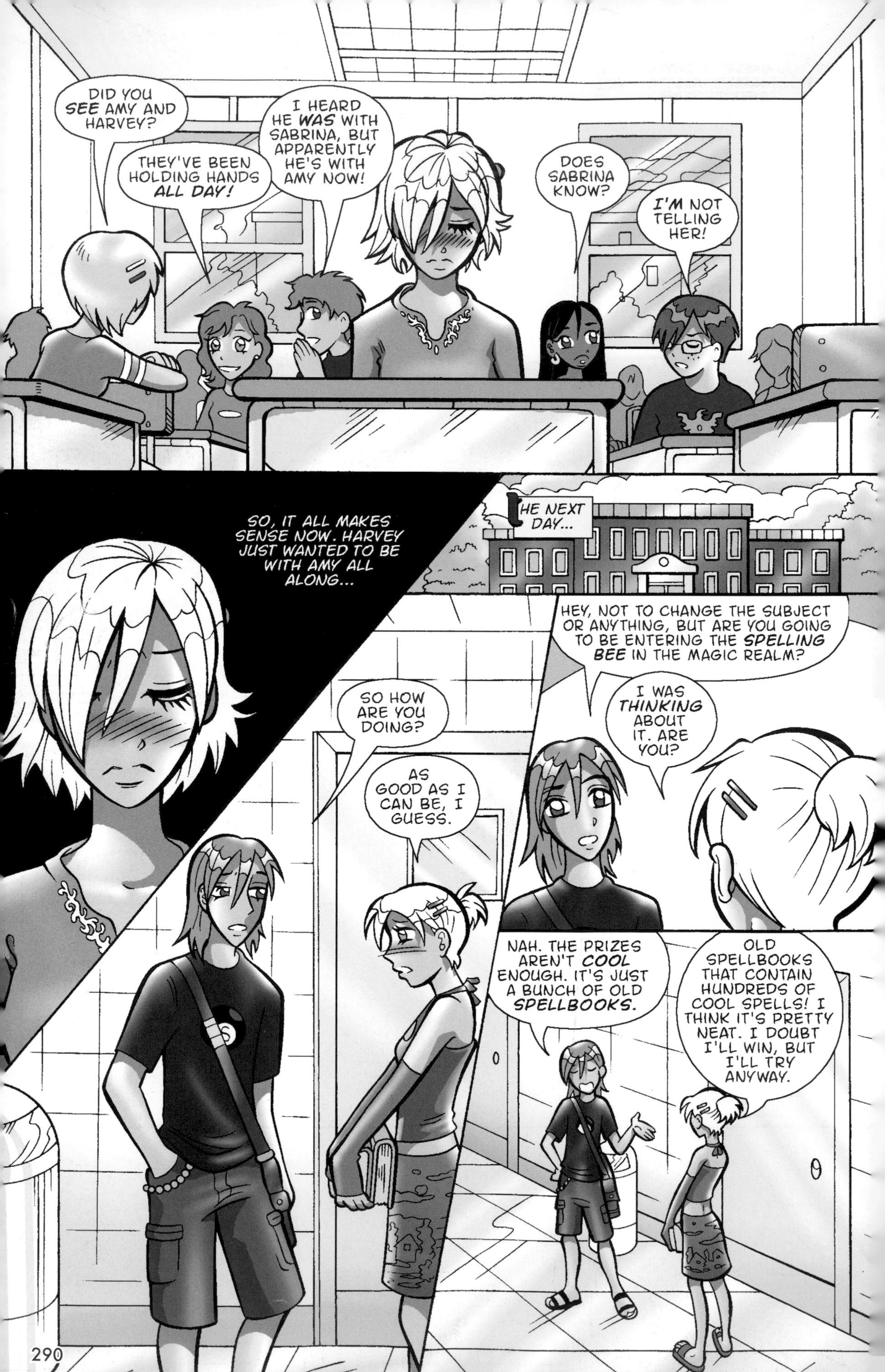
DID YOU SEE AMY AND HARVEY?
THEY'VE BEEN HOLDING HANDS ALL DAY!
I HEARD HE WAS WITH SABRINA, BUT APPARENTLY HE'S WITH AMY NOW!
DOES SABRINA KNOW?
I'M NOT TELLING HER!
SO, IT ALL MAKES SENSE NOW. HARVEY JUST WANTED TO BE WITH AMY ALL ALONG...
THE NEXT DAY...
SO HOW ARE YOU DOING?
AS GOOD AS I CAN BE, I GUESS.
HEY, NOT TO CHANGE THE SUBJECT OR ANYTHING, BUT ARE YOU GOING TO BE ENTERING THE SPELLING BEE IN THE MAGIC REALM?
I WAS THINKING ABOUT IT. ARE YOU?
NAH. THE PRIZES AREN'T COOL ENOUGH. IT'S JUST A BUNCH OF OLD SPELLBOOKS.
OLD SPELLBOOKS THAT CONTAIN HUNDREDS OF COOL SPELLS! I THINK IT'S PRETTY NEAT. I DOUBT I'LL WIN, BUT I'LL TRY ANYWAY.

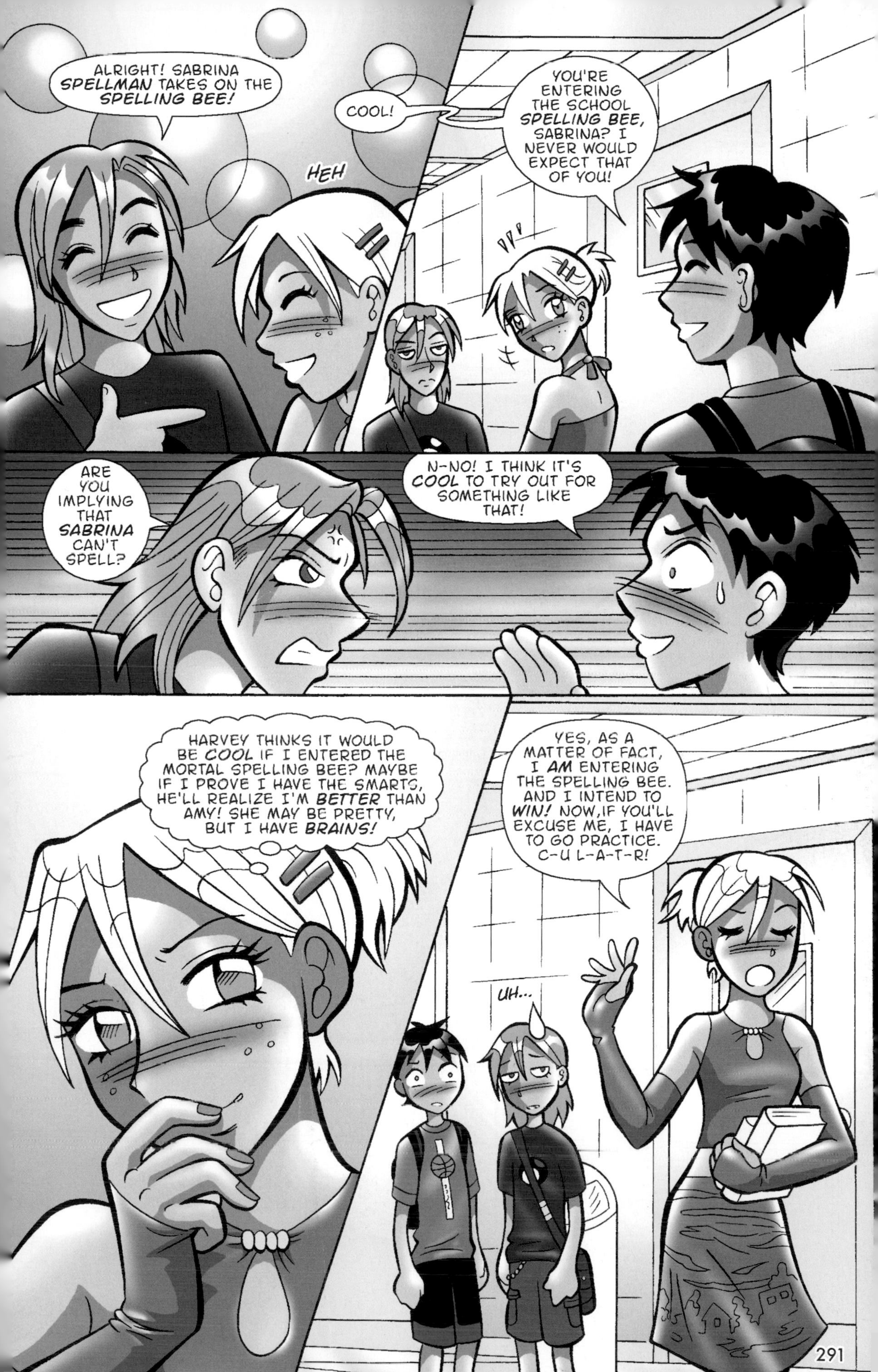
ALRIGHT! SABRINA SPELLMAN TAKES ON THE SPELLING BEE!
HEH
COOL!
YOU'RE ENTERING THE SCHOOL SPELLING BEE, SABRINA? I NEVER WOULD EXPECT THAT OF YOU!
ARE YOU IMPLYING THAT SABRINA CAN'T SPELL?
N-NO! I THINK IT'S COOL TO TRY OUT FOR SOMETHING LIKE THAT!
HARVEY THINKS IT WOULD BE COOL IF I ENTERED THE MORTAL SPELLING BEE? MAYBE IF I PROVE I HAVE THE SMARTS, HE'LL REALIZE I'M BETTER THAN AMY! SHE MAY BE PRETTY, BUT I HAVE BRAINS!
YES, AS A MATTER OF FACT, I AM ENTERING THE SPELLING BEE. AND I INTEND TO WIN! NOW, IF YOU'LL EXCUSE ME, I HAVE TO GO PRACTICE. C-U L-A-T-R!
UH...

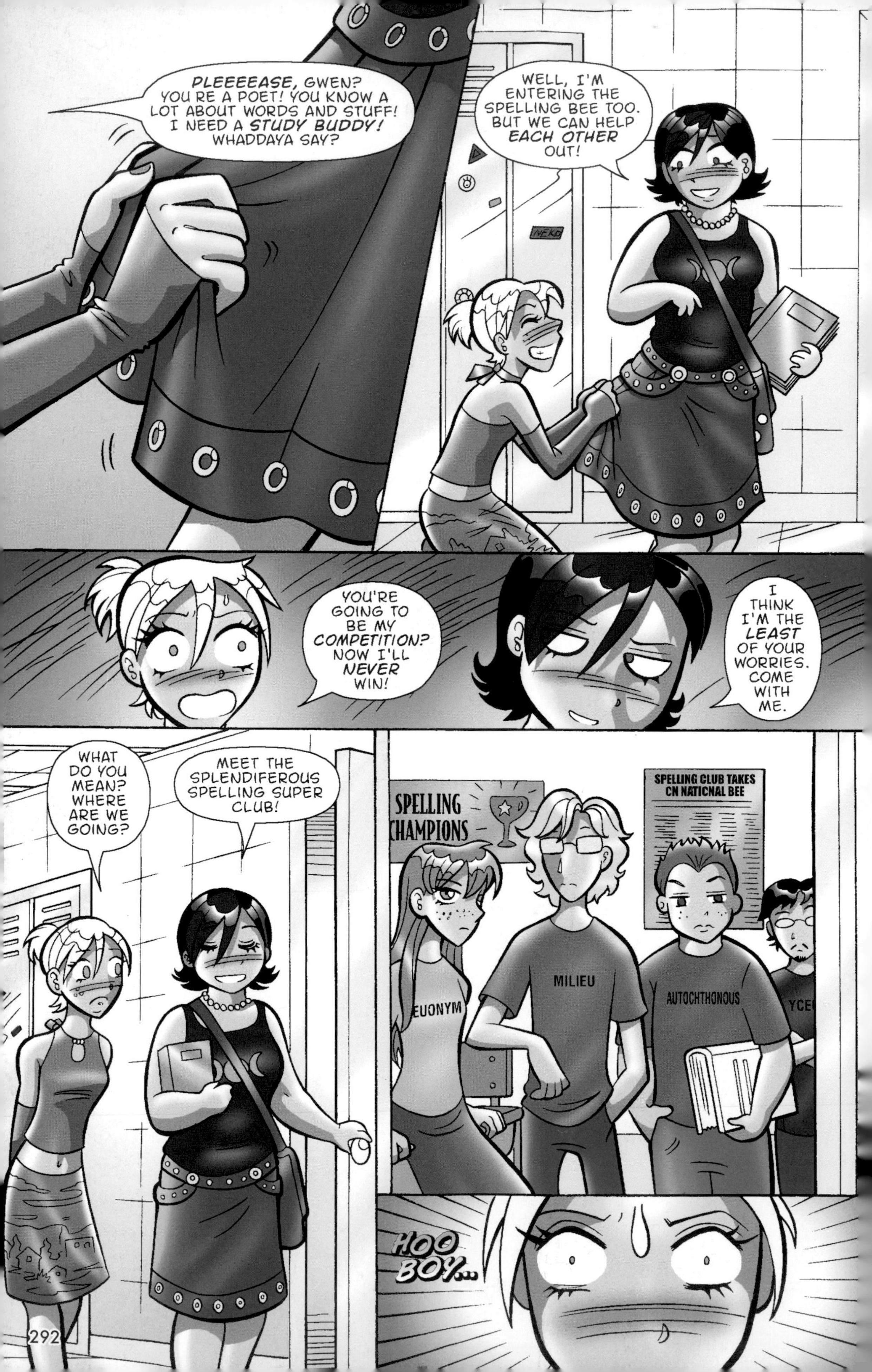
PLEEEEASE, GWEN? YOU'RE A POET! YOU KNOW A LOT ABOUT WORDS AND STUFF! I NEED A STUDY BUDDY! WHADDAYA SAY?
WELL, I'M ENTERING THE SPELLING BEE TOO. BUT WE CAN HELP EACH OTHER OUT!
NEKO
YOU'RE GOING TO BE MY COMPETITION? NOW I'LL NEVER WIN!
I THINK I'M THE LEAST OF YOUR WORRIES. COME WITH ME.
WHAT DO YOU MEAN? WHERE ARE WE GOING?
MEET THE SPLENDIFEROUS SPELLING SUPER CLUB!
SPELLING CHAMPIONS
SPELLING CLUB TAKES CN NATICNAL BEE
EUONYM
MILIEU
AUTOCHTHONOUS
YCE
HOO BOY...

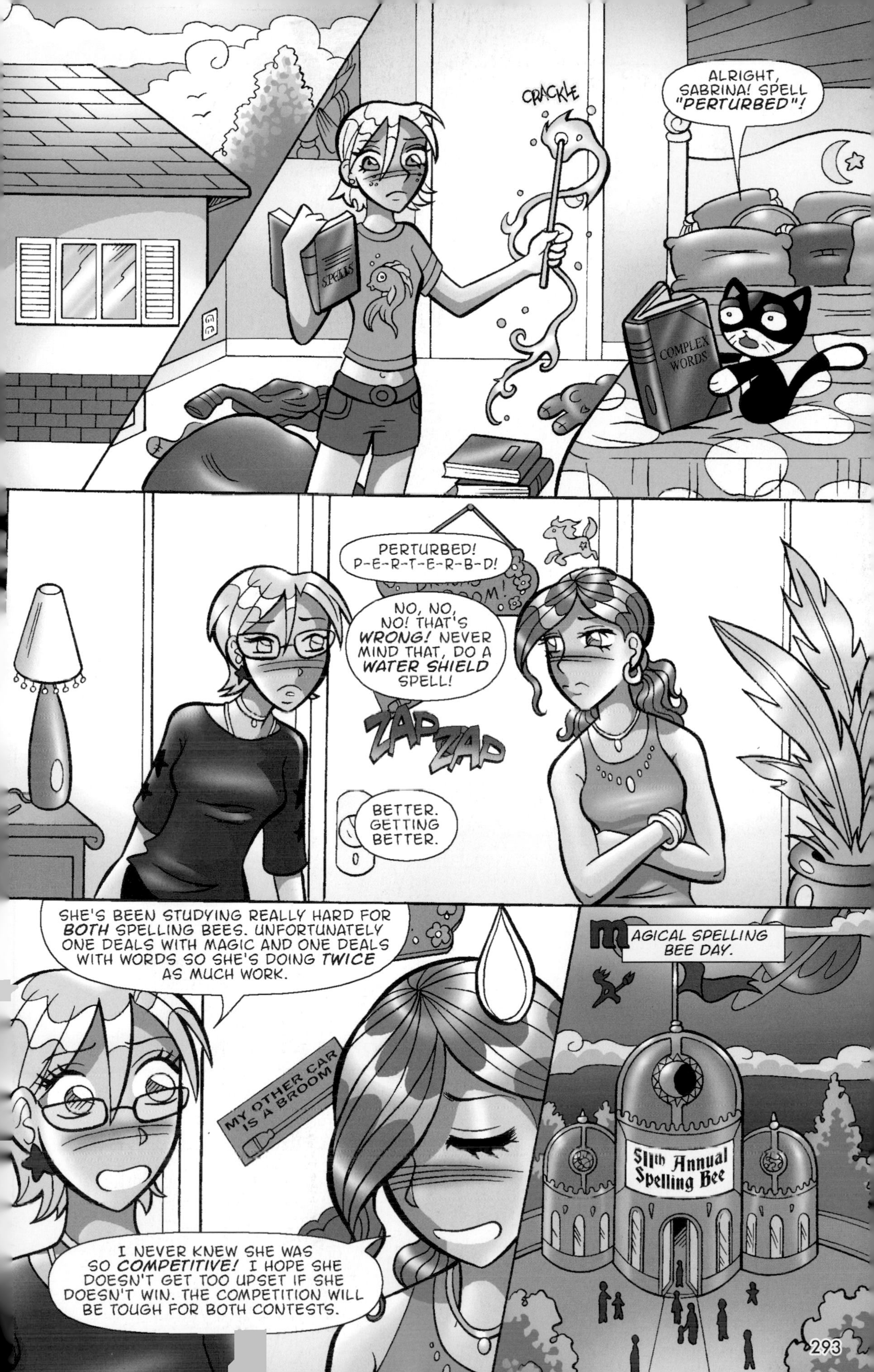
CRACKLE
ALRIGHT, SABRINA! SPELL "PERTURBED"!
SPELLS
COMPLEX WORDS
PERTURBED! P-E-R-T-E-R-B-D!
NO, NO, NO! THAT'S WRONG! NEVER MIND THAT, DO A WATER SHIELD SPELL!
ZAP ZAP
BETTER. GETTING BETTER.
SHE'S BEEN STUDYING REALLY HARD FOR BOTH SPELLING BEES. UNFORTUNATELY ONE DEALS WITH MAGIC AND ONE DEALS WITH WORDS SO SHE'S DOING TWICE AS MUCH WORK.
MY OTHER CAR IS A BROOM
I NEVER KNEW SHE WAS SO COMPETITIVE! I HOPE SHE DOESN'T GET TOO UPSET IF SHE DOESN'T WIN. THE COMPETITION WILL BE TOUGH FOR BOTH CONTESTS.
MAGICAL SPELLING BEE DAY.
511th Annual Spelling Bee

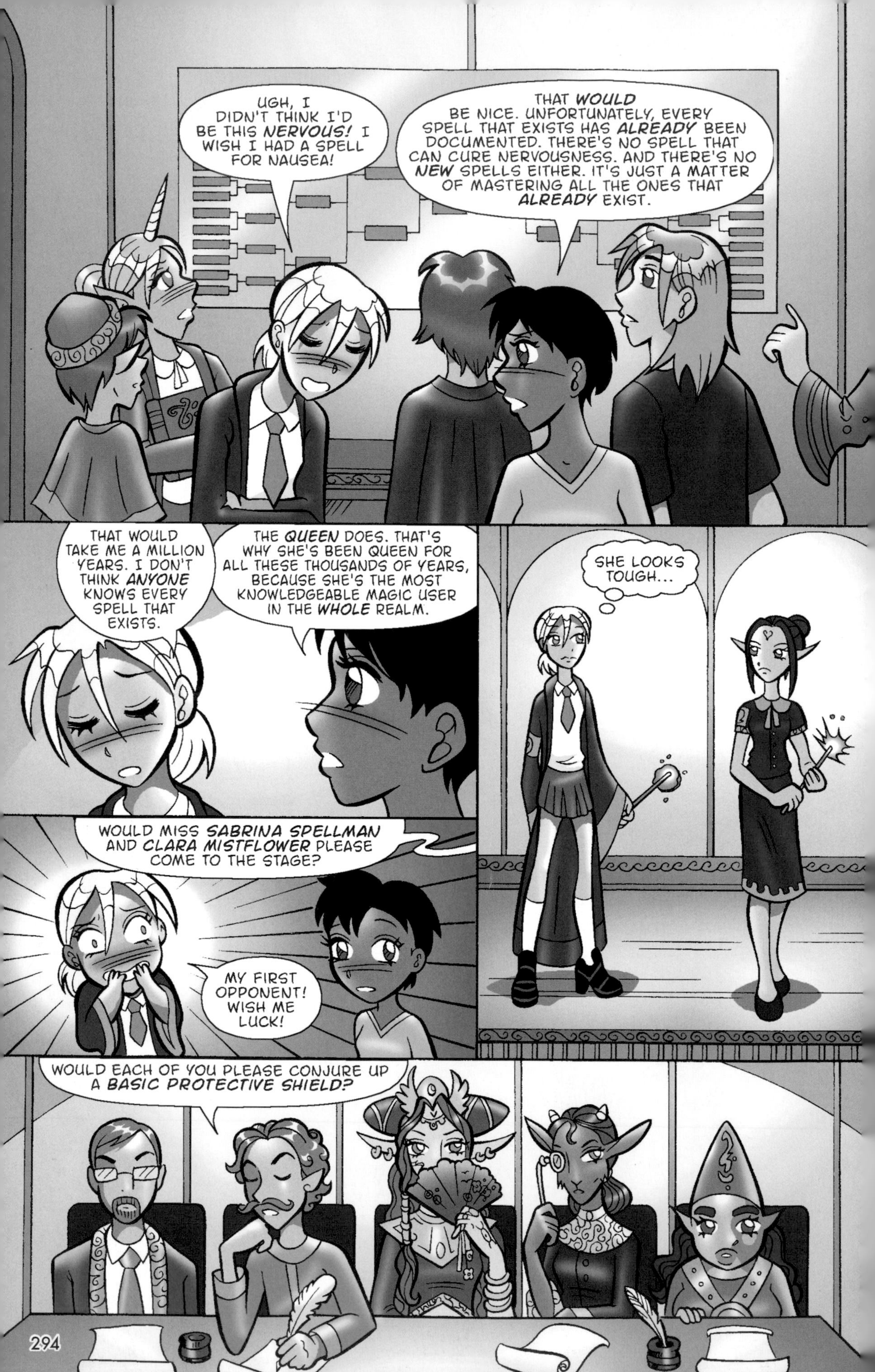
UGH, I DIDN'T THINK I'D BE THIS NERVOUS! I WISH I HAD A SPELL FOR NAUSEA!
THAT WOULD BE NICE. UNFORTUNATELY, EVERY SPELL THAT EXISTS HAS ALREADY BEEN DOCUMENTED. THERE'S NO SPELL THAT CAN CURE NERVOUSNESS. AND THERE'S NO NEW SPELLS EITHER. IT'S JUST A MATTER OF MASTERING ALL THE ONES THAT ALREADY EXIST.
THAT WOULD TAKE ME A MILLION YEARS. I DON'T THINK ANYONE KNOWS EVERY SPELL THAT EXISTS.
THE QUEEN DOES. THAT'S WHY SHE'S BEEN QUEEN FOR ALL THESE THOUSANDS OF YEARS, BECAUSE SHE'S THE MOST KNOWLEDGEABLE MAGIC USER IN THE WHOLE REALM.
WOULD MISS SABRINA SPELLMAN AND CLARA MISTFLOWER PLEASE COME TO THE STAGE?
MY FIRST OPPONENT! WISH ME LUCK!
SHE LOOKS TOUGH...
WOULD EACH OF YOU PLEASE CONJURE UP A BASIC PROTECTIVE SHIELD?

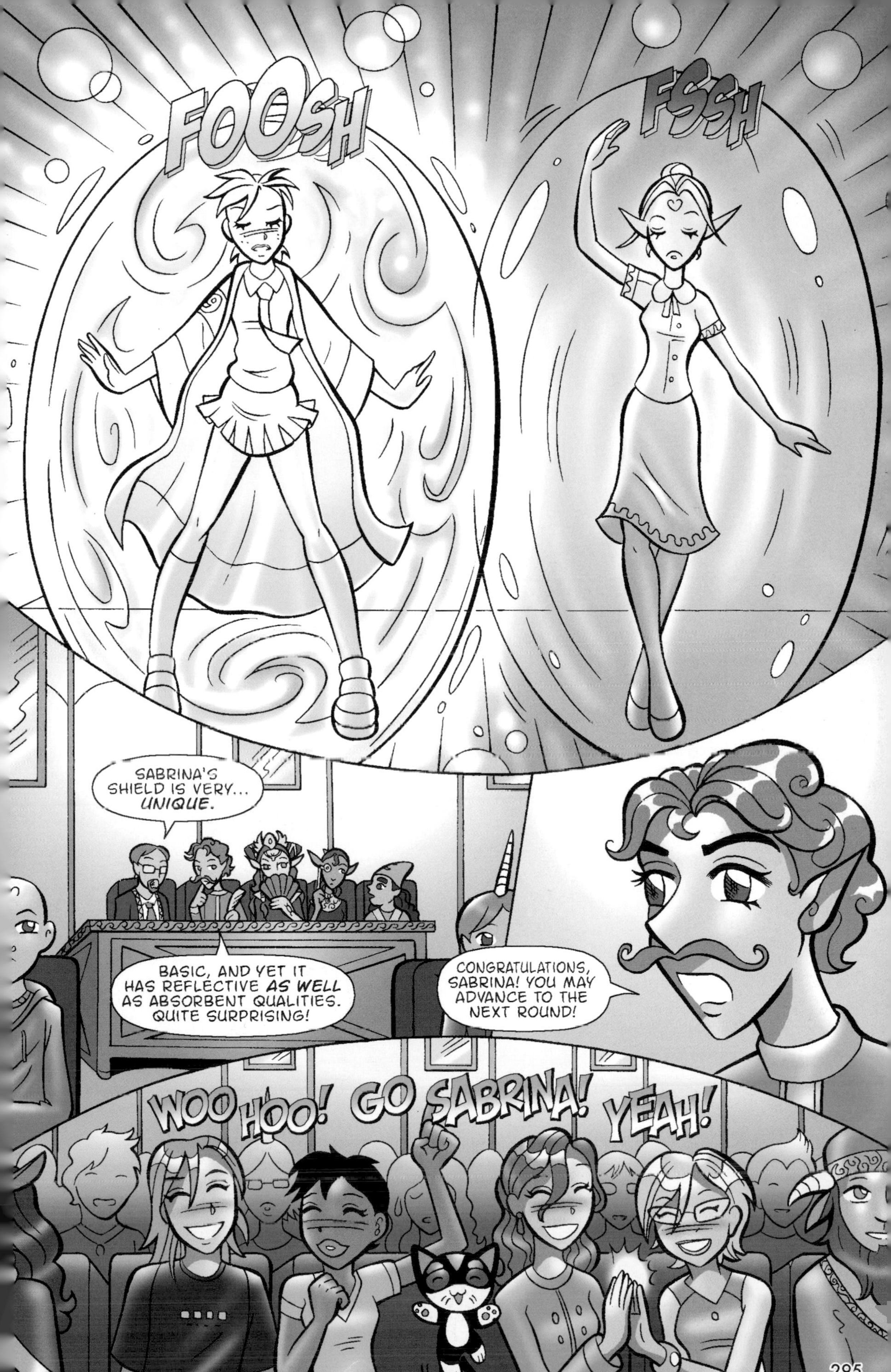
FOOSH
FSSH
SABRINA'S SHIELD IS VERY... UNIQUE.
BASIC, AND YET IT HAS REFLECTIVE AS WELL AS ABSORBENT QUALITIES. QUITE SURPRISING!
CONGRATULATIONS, SABRINA! YOU MAY ADVANCE TO THE NEXT ROUND!
WOO HOO! GO SABRINA! YEAH!

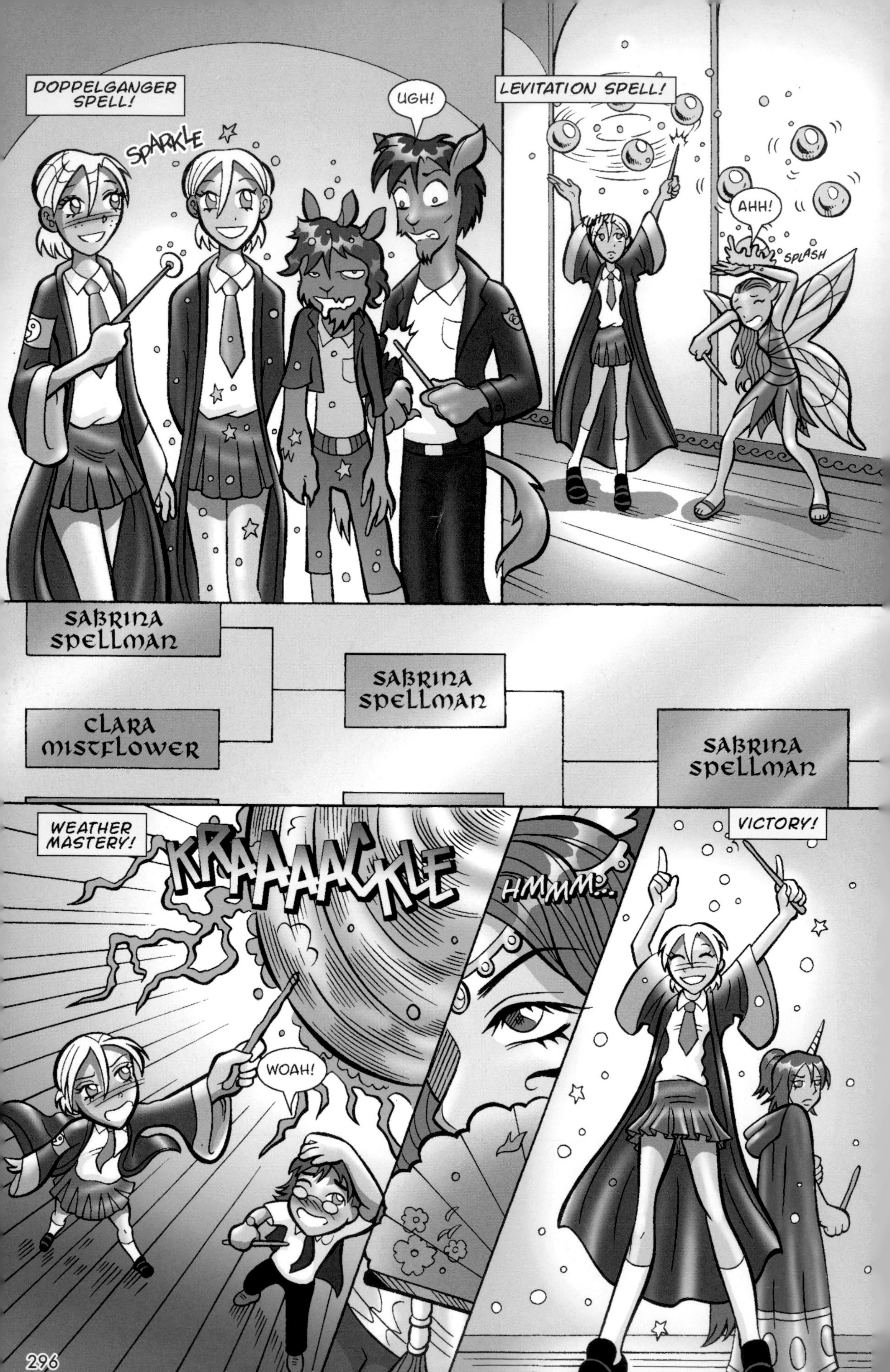
DOPPELGANGER SPELL!
SPARKLE
UGH!
LEVITATION SPELL!
AHH!
SPLASH
SABRINA SPELLMAN
CLARA MISTFLOWER
SABRINA SPELLMAN
SABRINA SPELLMAN
WEATHER MASTERY!
KRAAAACKLE
WOAH!
HMMM...
VICTORY!

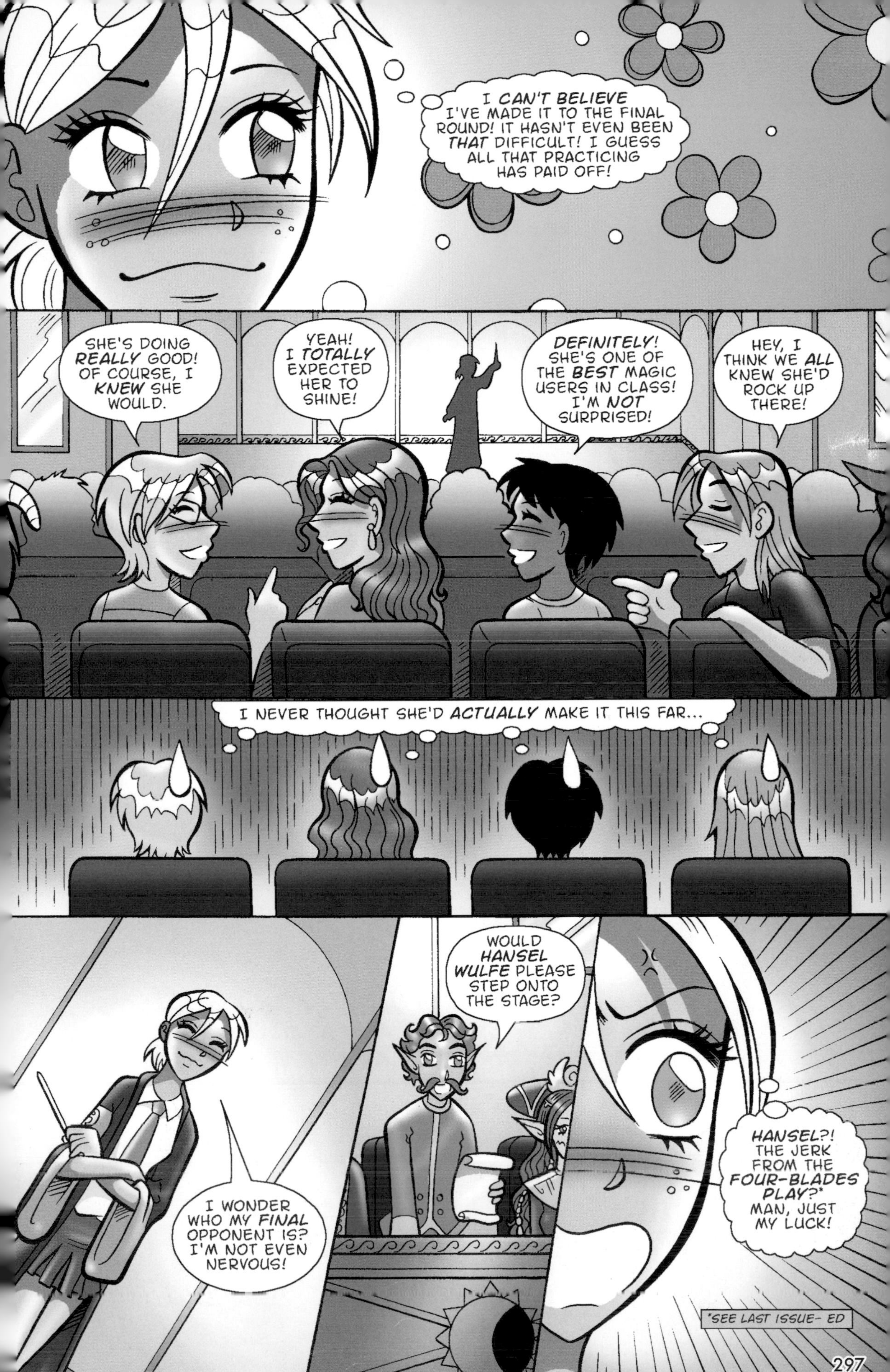
I CAN'T BELIEVE I'VE MADE IT TO THE FINAL ROUND! IT HASN'T EVEN BEEN THAT DIFFICULT! I GUESS ALL THAT PRACTICING HAS PAID OFF!
SHE'S DOING REALLY GOOD! OF COURSE, I KNEW SHE WOULD.
YEAH! I TOTALLY EXPECTED HER TO SHINE!
DEFINITELY! SHE'S ONE OF THE BEST MAGIC USERS IN CLASS! I'M NOT SURPRISED!
HEY, I THINK WE ALL KNEW SHE'D ROCK UP THERE!
I NEVER THOUGHT SHE'D ACTUALLY MAKE IT THIS FAR...
I WONDER WHO MY FINAL OPPONENT IS? I'M NOT EVEN NERVOUS!
WOULD HANSEL WULFE PLEASE STEP ONTO THE STAGE?
HANSEL?! THE JERK FROM THE FOUR-BLADES PLAY?* MAN, JUST MY LUCK!
*SEE LAST ISSUE- ED

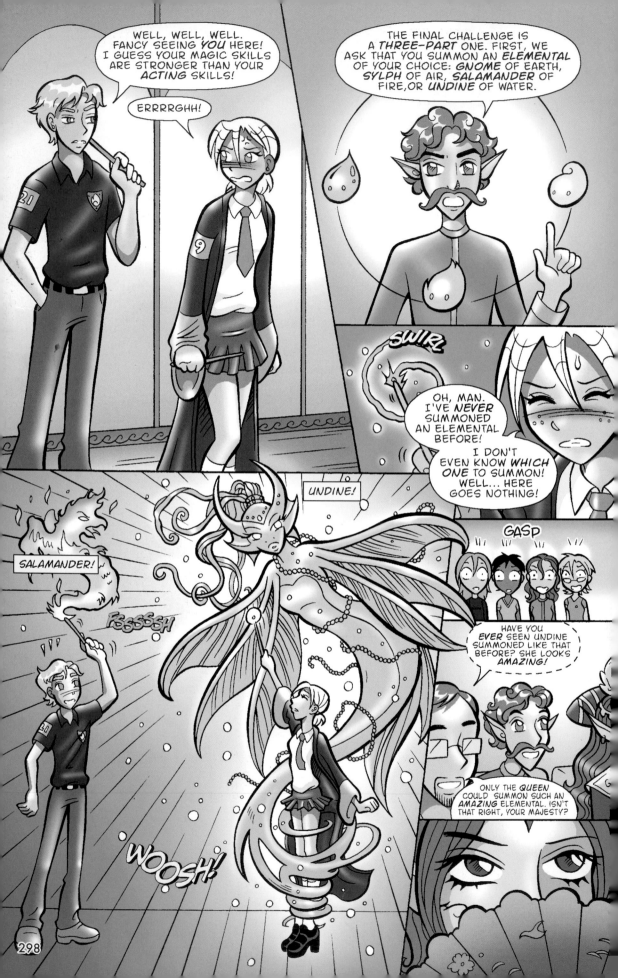

WELL, WELL, WELL. FANCY SEEING *YOU* HERE! I GUESS YOUR MAGIC SKILLS ARE STRONGER THAN YOUR *ACTING* SKILLS!

ERRRRGHH!

THE FINAL CHALLENGE IS A *THREE-PART* ONE. FIRST, WE ASK THAT YOU SUMMON AN *ELEMENTAL* OF YOUR CHOICE: *GNOME* OF EARTH, *SYLPH* OF AIR, *SALAMANDER* OF FIRE, OR *UNDINE* OF WATER.

SWIRL

OH, MAN. I'VE *NEVER* SUMMONED AN ELEMENTAL BEFORE! I DON'T EVEN KNOW *WHICH ONE* TO SUMMON! WELL... HERE GOES NOTHING!

UNDINE!

SALAMANDER!

FSSSSSH

GASP

HAVE YOU *EVER* SEEN UNDINE SUMMONED LIKE THAT BEFORE? SHE LOOKS *AMAZING!*

ONLY THE *QUEEN* COULD SUMMON SUCH AN *AMAZING* ELEMENTAL. ISN'T THAT RIGHT, YOUR MAJESTY?

WOOSH!

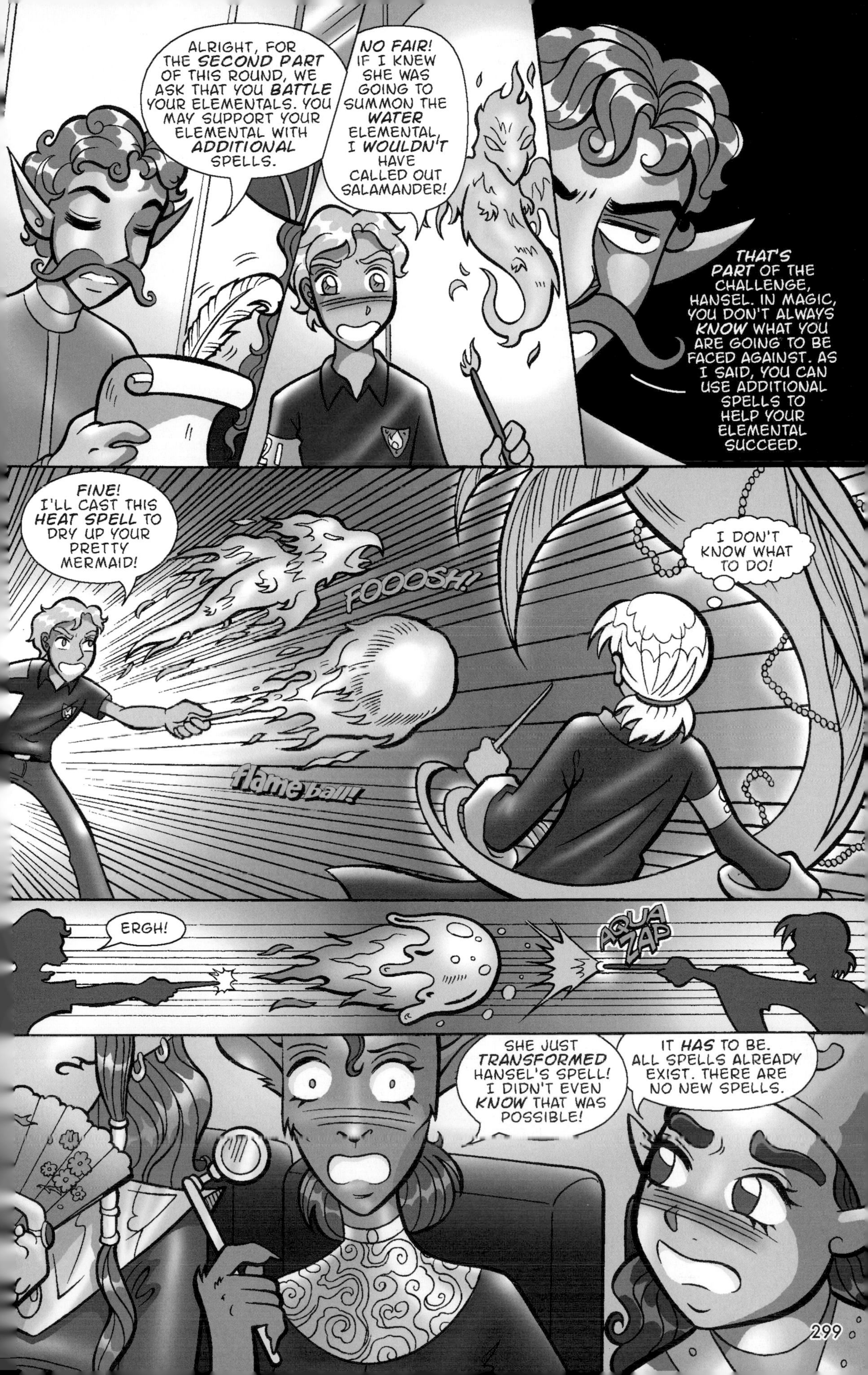
ALRIGHT, FOR THE SECOND PART OF THIS ROUND, WE ASK THAT YOU BATTLE YOUR ELEMENTALS. YOU MAY SUPPORT YOUR ELEMENTAL WITH ADDITIONAL SPELLS.
NO FAIR! IF I KNEW SHE WAS GOING TO SUMMON THE WATER ELEMENTAL, I WOULDN'T HAVE CALLED OUT SALAMANDER!
THAT'S PART OF THE CHALLENGE, HANSEL. IN MAGIC, YOU DON'T ALWAYS KNOW WHAT YOU ARE GOING TO BE FACED AGAINST. AS I SAID, YOU CAN USE ADDITIONAL SPELLS TO HELP YOUR ELEMENTAL SUCCEED.
FINE! I'LL CAST THIS HEAT SPELL TO DRY UP YOUR PRETTY MERMAID!
I DON'T KNOW WHAT TO DO!
FOOOSH!
flame ball!
ERGH!
AQUA ZAP
SHE JUST TRANSFORMED HANSEL'S SPELL! I DIDN'T EVEN KNOW THAT WAS POSSIBLE!
IT HAS TO BE. ALL SPELLS ALREADY EXIST. THERE ARE NO NEW SPELLS.

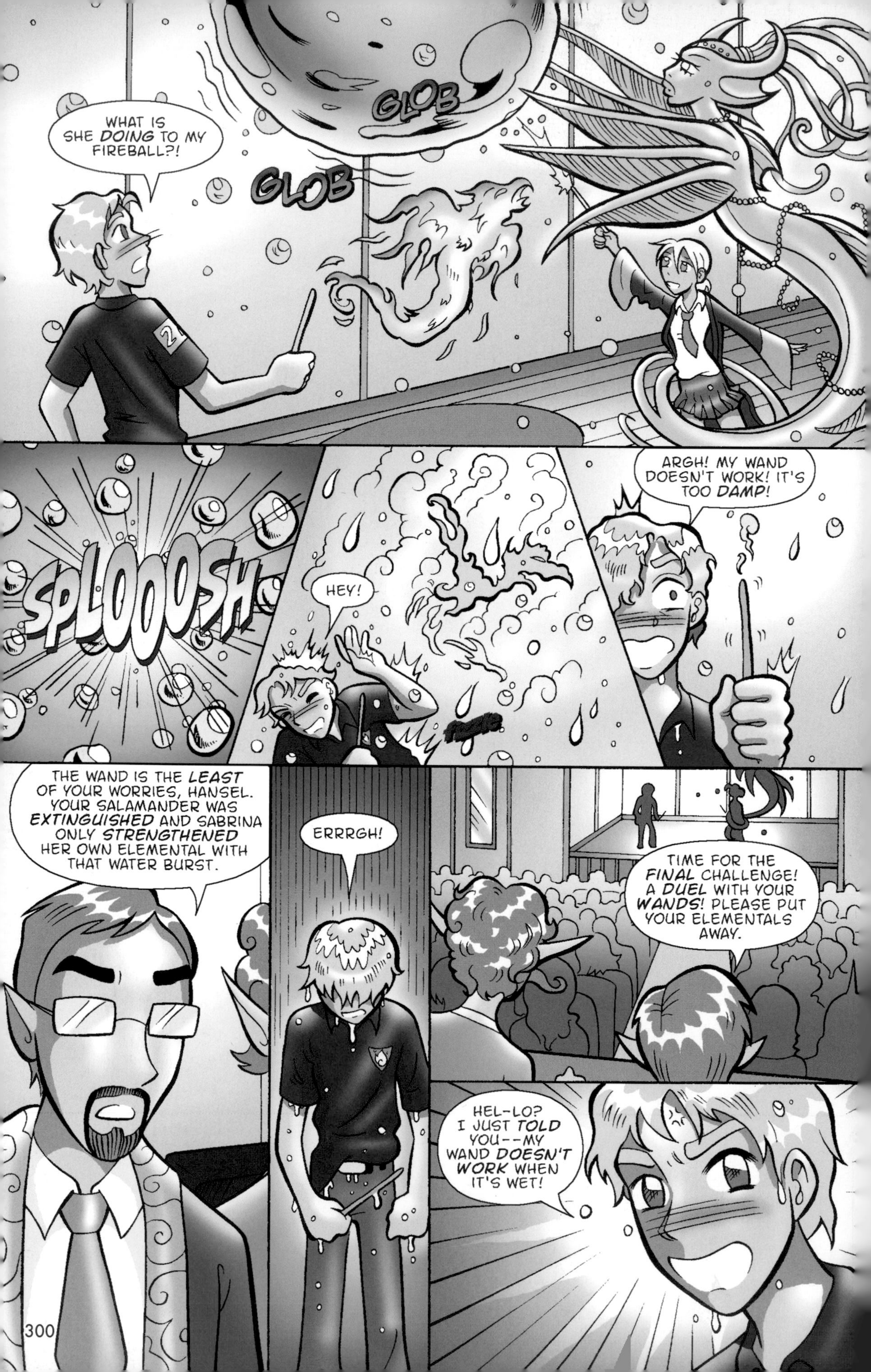
GLOB
WHAT IS SHE *DOING* TO MY FIREBALL?!
GLOB
SPLOOOSH
HEY!
ARGH! MY WAND DOESN'T WORK! IT'S TOO *DAMP*!
THE WAND IS THE *LEAST* OF YOUR WORRIES, HANSEL. YOUR SALAMANDER WAS ***EXTINGUISHED*** AND SABRINA ONLY ***STRENGTHENED*** HER OWN ELEMENTAL WITH THAT WATER BURST.
ERRRGH!
TIME FOR THE ***FINAL*** CHALLENGE! A ***DUEL*** WITH YOUR ***WANDS***! PLEASE PUT YOUR ELEMENTALS AWAY.
HEL-LO? I JUST ***TOLD*** YOU--MY WAND ***DOESN'T WORK*** WHEN IT'S WET!

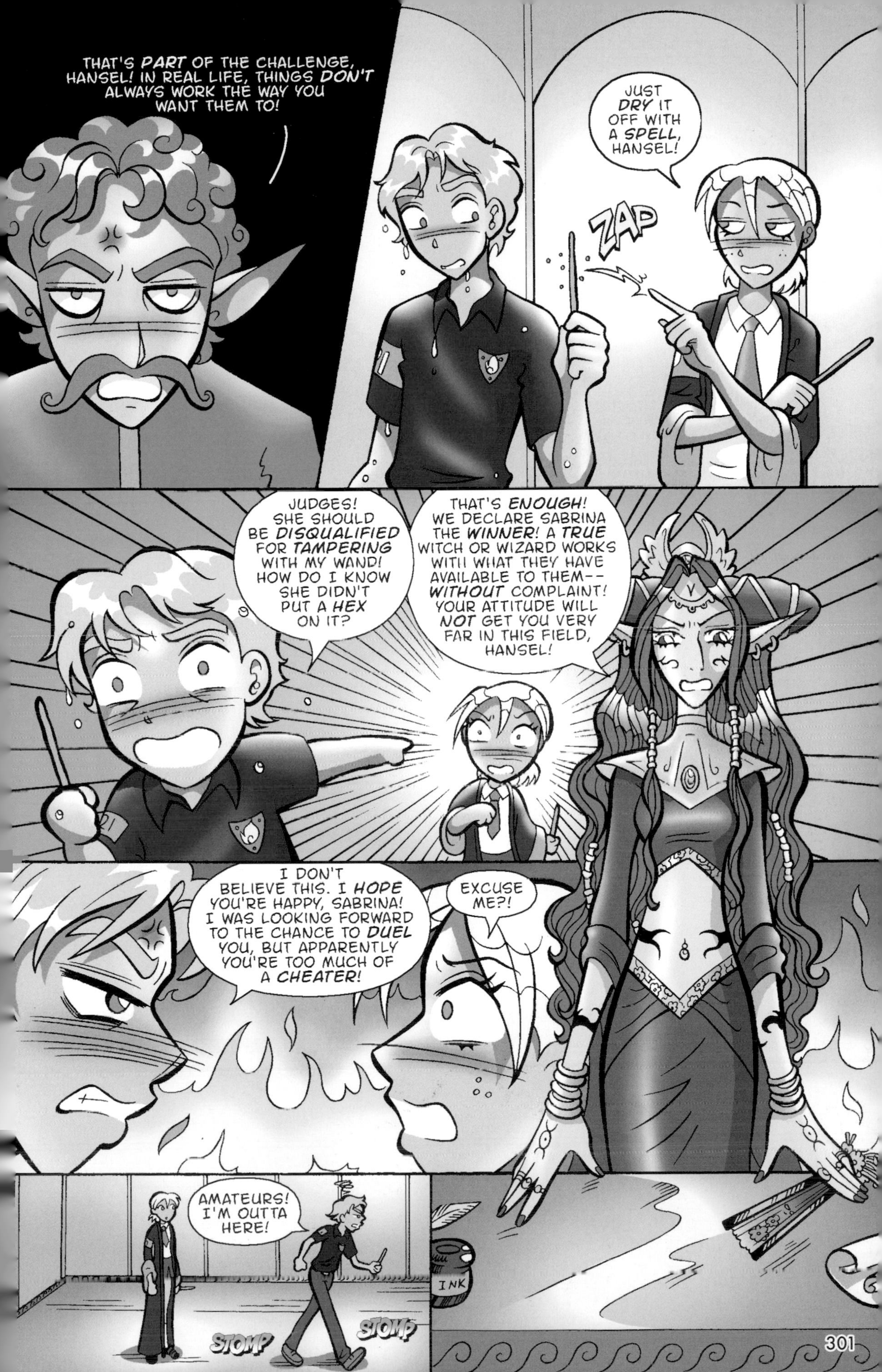
THAT'S PART OF THE CHALLENGE, HANSEL! IN REAL LIFE, THINGS DON'T ALWAYS WORK THE WAY YOU WANT THEM TO!
JUST DRY IT OFF WITH A SPELL, HANSEL!
ZAP
JUDGES! SHE SHOULD BE DISQUALIFIED FOR TAMPERING WITH MY WAND! HOW DO I KNOW SHE DIDN'T PUT A HEX ON IT?
THAT'S ENOUGH! WE DECLARE SABRINA THE WINNER! A TRUE WITCH OR WIZARD WORKS WITH WHAT THEY HAVE AVAILABLE TO THEM-- WITHOUT COMPLAINT! YOUR ATTITUDE WILL NOT GET YOU VERY FAR IN THIS FIELD, HANSEL!
I DON'T BELIEVE THIS. I HOPE YOU'RE HAPPY, SABRINA! I WAS LOOKING FORWARD TO THE CHANCE TO DUEL YOU, BUT APPARENTLY YOU'RE TOO MUCH OF A CHEATER!
EXCUSE ME?!
AMATEURS! I'M OUTTA HERE!
STOMP
STOMP
INK

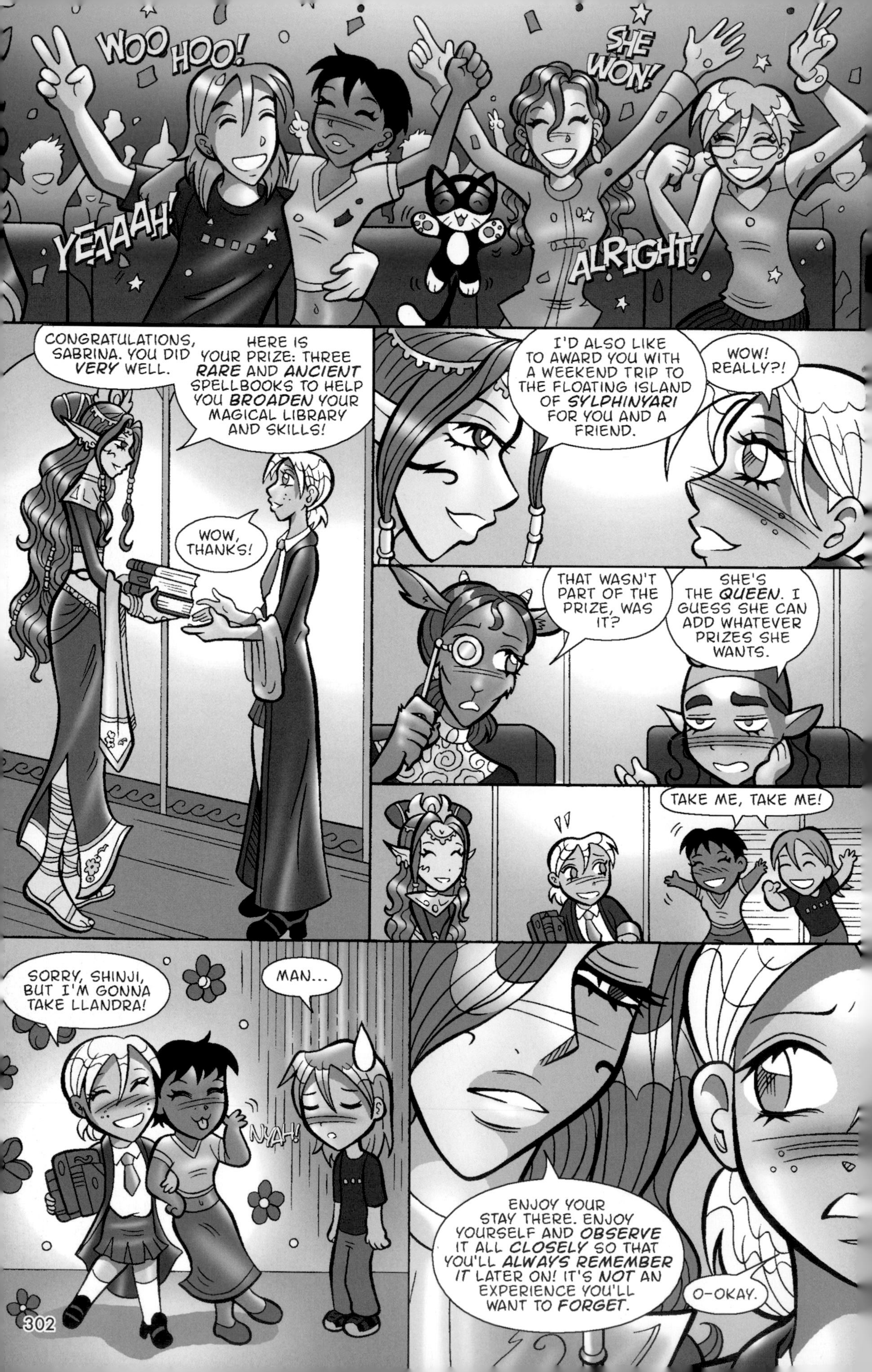
WOO HOO!
SHE WON!
YEAAAH!
ALRIGHT!
CONGRATULATIONS, SABRINA. YOU DID VERY WELL.
HERE IS YOUR PRIZE: THREE RARE AND ANCIENT SPELLBOOKS TO HELP YOU BROADEN YOUR MAGICAL LIBRARY AND SKILLS!
WOW, THANKS!
I'D ALSO LIKE TO AWARD YOU WITH A WEEKEND TRIP TO THE FLOATING ISLAND OF SYLPHINYARI FOR YOU AND A FRIEND.
WOW! REALLY?!
THAT WASN'T PART OF THE PRIZE, WAS IT?
SHE'S THE QUEEN. I GUESS SHE CAN ADD WHATEVER PRIZES SHE WANTS.
TAKE ME, TAKE ME!
SORRY, SHINJI, BUT I'M GONNA TAKE LLANDRA!
MAN...
NYAH!
ENJOY YOUR STAY THERE. ENJOY YOURSELF AND OBSERVE IT ALL CLOSELY SO THAT YOU'LL ALWAYS REMEMBER IT LATER ON! IT'S NOT AN EXPERIENCE YOU'LL WANT TO FORGET.
O-OKAY.

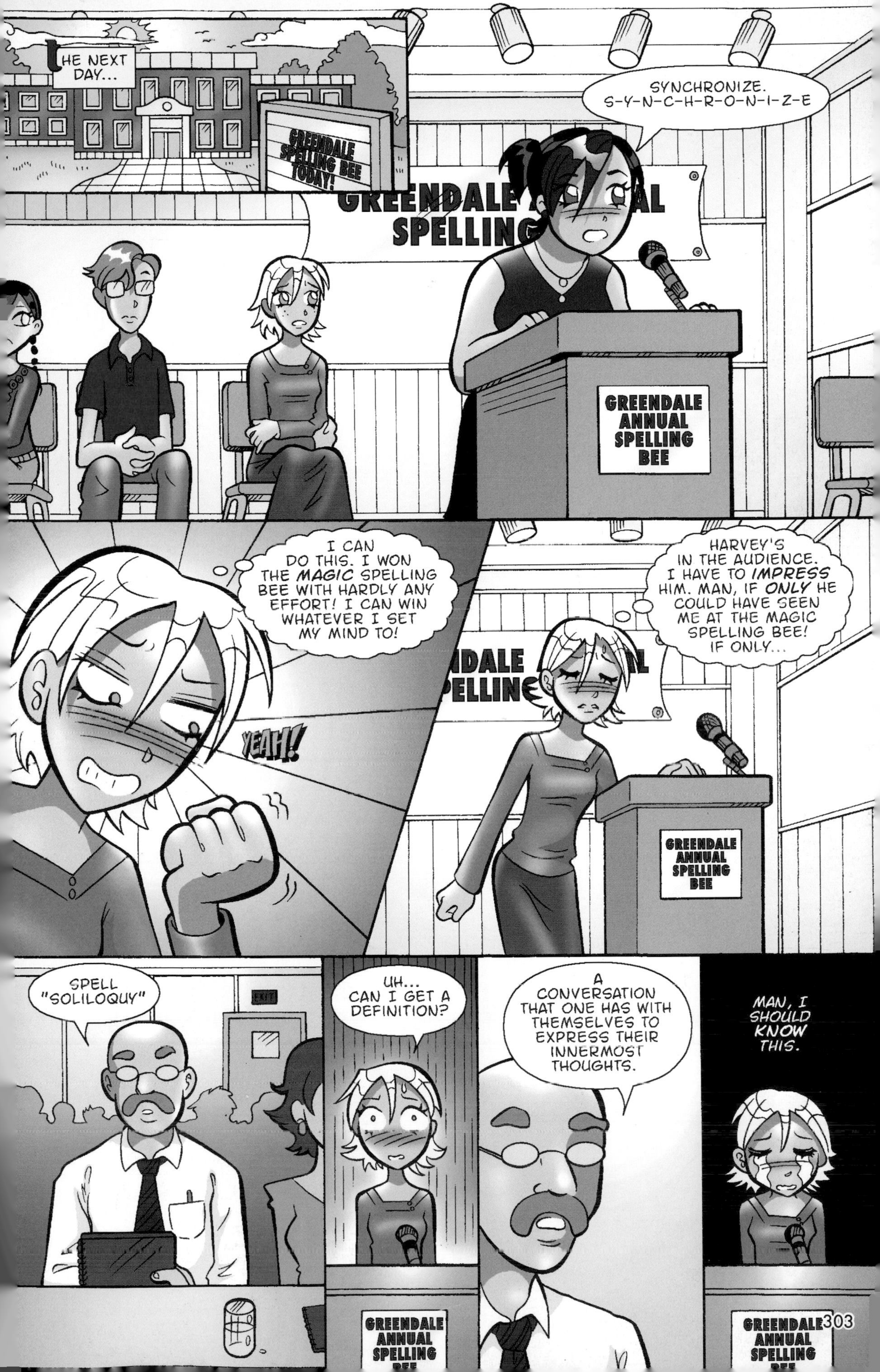
THE NEXT DAY...
GREENDALE SPELLING BEE TODAY!
SYNCHRONIZE. S-Y-N-C-H-R-O-N-I-Z-E
GREENDALE ANNUAL SPELLING
GREENDALE ANNUAL SPELLING BEE
I CAN DO THIS. I WON THE MAGIC SPELLING BEE WITH HARDLY ANY EFFORT! I CAN WIN WHATEVER I SET MY MIND TO!
YEAH!
HARVEY'S IN THE AUDIENCE. I HAVE TO IMPRESS HIM. MAN, IF ONLY HE COULD HAVE SEEN ME AT THE MAGIC SPELLING BEE! IF ONLY...
GREENDALE ANNUAL SPELLING BEE
SPELL "SOLILOQUY"
EXIT
UH... CAN I GET A DEFINITION?
A CONVERSATION THAT ONE HAS WITH THEMSELVES TO EXPRESS THEIR INNERMOST THOUGHTS.
MAN, I SHOULD KNOW THIS.
GREENDALE ANNUAL SPELLING
GREENDALE ANNUAL SPELLING

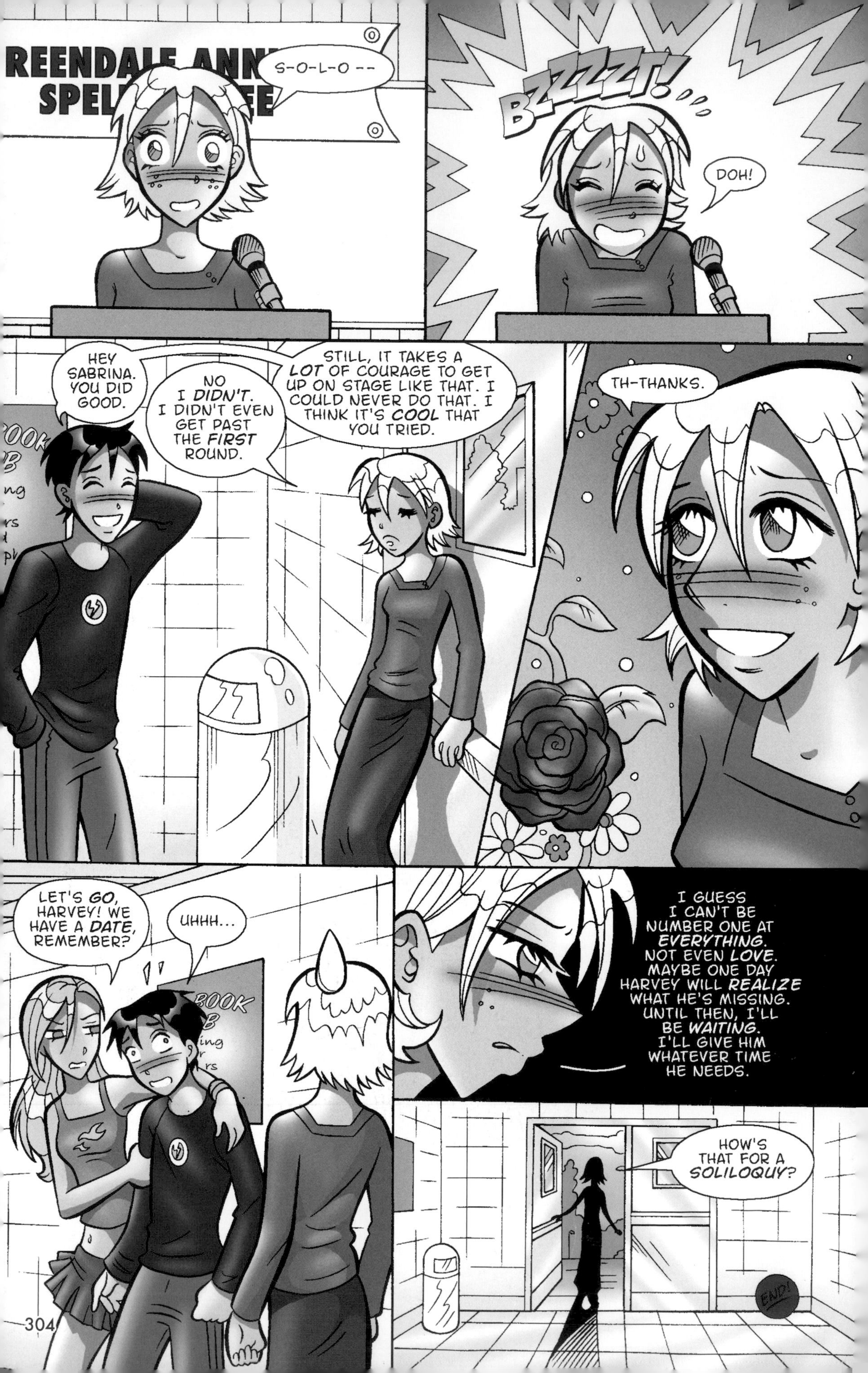
REENDALE ANN
SPEL EE
S-O-L-O --
BZZZZT!
DOH!
HEY SABRINA. YOU DID GOOD.
NO I DIDN'T. I DIDN'T EVEN GET PAST THE FIRST ROUND.
STILL, IT TAKES A LOT OF COURAGE TO GET UP ON STAGE LIKE THAT. I COULD NEVER DO THAT. I THINK IT'S COOL THAT YOU TRIED.
TH-THANKS.
LET'S GO, HARVEY! WE HAVE A DATE, REMEMBER?
UHHH...
I GUESS I CAN'T BE NUMBER ONE AT EVERYTHING. NOT EVEN LOVE. MAYBE ONE DAY HARVEY WILL REALIZE WHAT HE'S MISSING. UNTIL THEN, I'LL BE WAITING. I'LL GIVE HIM WHATEVER TIME HE NEEDS.
HOW'S THAT FOR A SOLILOQUY?
END!

The BEST of Archie COMICS

2010s

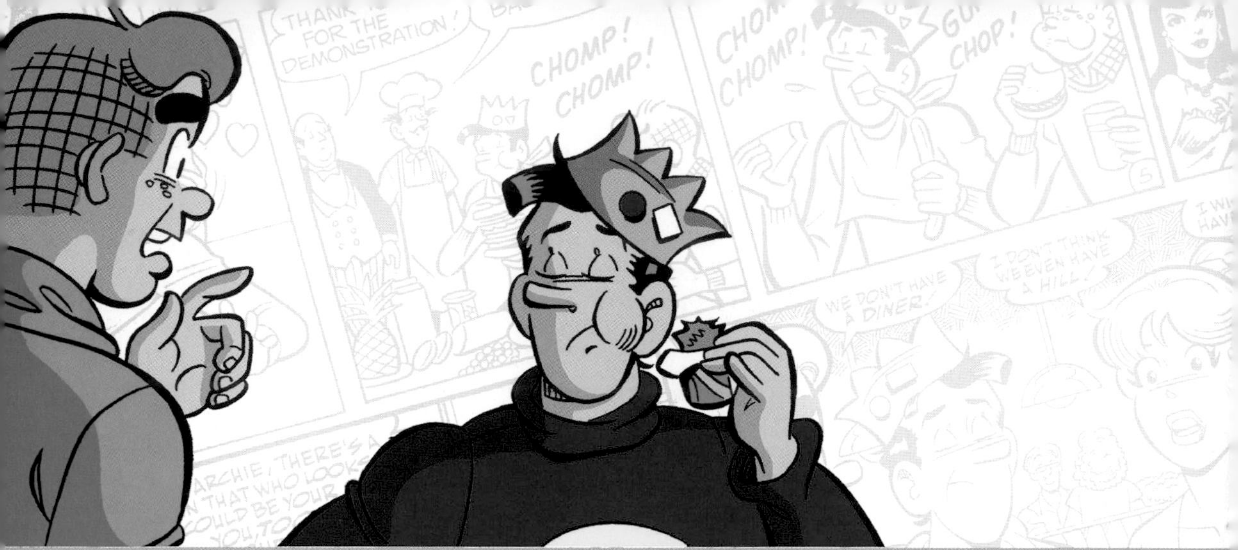
FOR THE DEMONSTRATION!
CHOMP! CHOMP!
CHOMP!
WE DON'T HAVE A DINER.
I DON'T THINK WE EVEN HAVE A HILL.

SOMETHING VENTURED, SOMETHING GAINED

JUGHEAD #200, 2010

BY TOM ROOT, REX LINDSEY, JACK MORELLI, DAN PARENT & ROSARIO "TITO" PEÑA

I'm ashamed to admit it: Jughead was my least favorite Archie character growing up. As an adult, I realize that's like saying John was your least favorite Beatle. But as a child I did not want to be friends with that lazy dude in the goofball hat. Archie, Betty, Veronica, Reggie—they knew how to have fun! Jughead just wanted to lie in a hammock and eat. Then, of course, I turned into a teenager myself. And it was like a veil had been lifted from my eyes: Jughead had it all figured out! He was sarcastic—I was sarcastic! He thought he was smarter than everyone else—so did I! Lazing around, devouring junk food—I was really digging what this Jughead was laying down.

I met Archie Comics Co-CEO Jon Goldwater at San Diego Comic-Con in 2009. He was familiar with Robot Chicken; we'd used the Archie characters in a parody of the "Final Destination" movies. When he asked me about writing *Jughead* #200, I said yes immediately. Archie Comics' best character? In a big anniversary issue? How could I refuse?

What does Jughead treasure most of all? Food. I had to hit him where it hurt —right in the breadbasket, so to speak. And rather than starve the poor kid, I'd accomplish it by giving him a very grown-up problem: the loss of the ol' teenage metabolism. Just for fun, it became a supernatural story. And somehow, through some beautiful accident, the plot I chose—that witch and her Faustian bargains —offered a perfect window into not just Jughead's soul, but the souls of all his friends, as well. In the end, that "lazy dude in the goofball hat" I so reviled in childhood had delivered me one of my most rewarding professional experiences. Sorry, Jughead! I was wrong to ever doubt you, buddy.

—Tom Root
Writer/Producer/Director/Voice Actor,
Robot Chicken

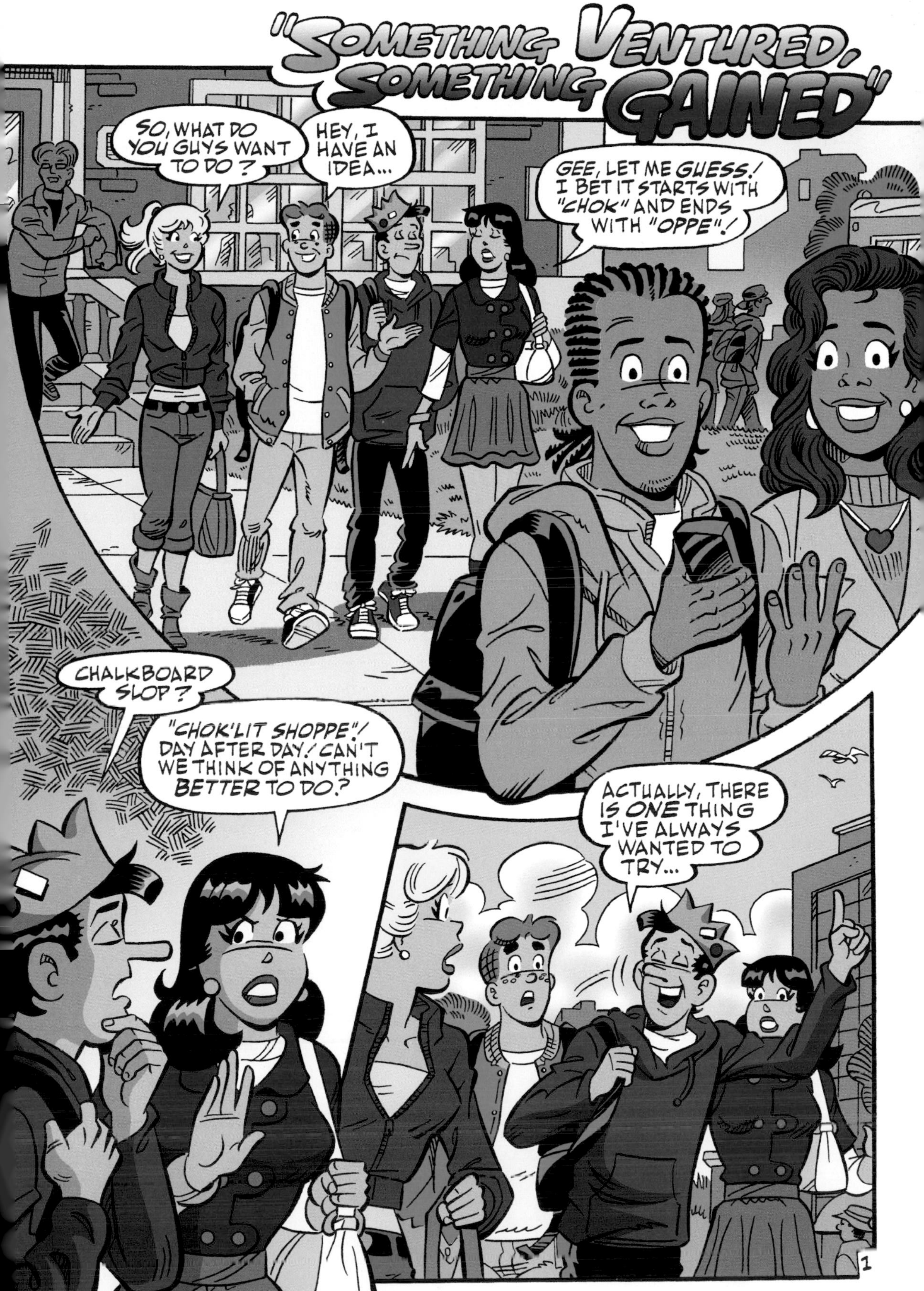
"SOMETHING VENTURED, SOMETHING GAINED"
SO, WHAT DO YOU GUYS WANT TO DO?
HEY, I HAVE AN IDEA...
GEE, LET ME GUESS! I BET IT STARTS WITH "CHOK" AND ENDS WITH "OPPE"!
CHALKBOARD SLOP?
"CHOK'LIT SHOPPE"! DAY AFTER DAY! CAN'T WE THINK OF ANYTHING BETTER TO DO?
ACTUALLY, THERE IS ONE THING I'VE ALWAYS WANTED TO TRY...
1

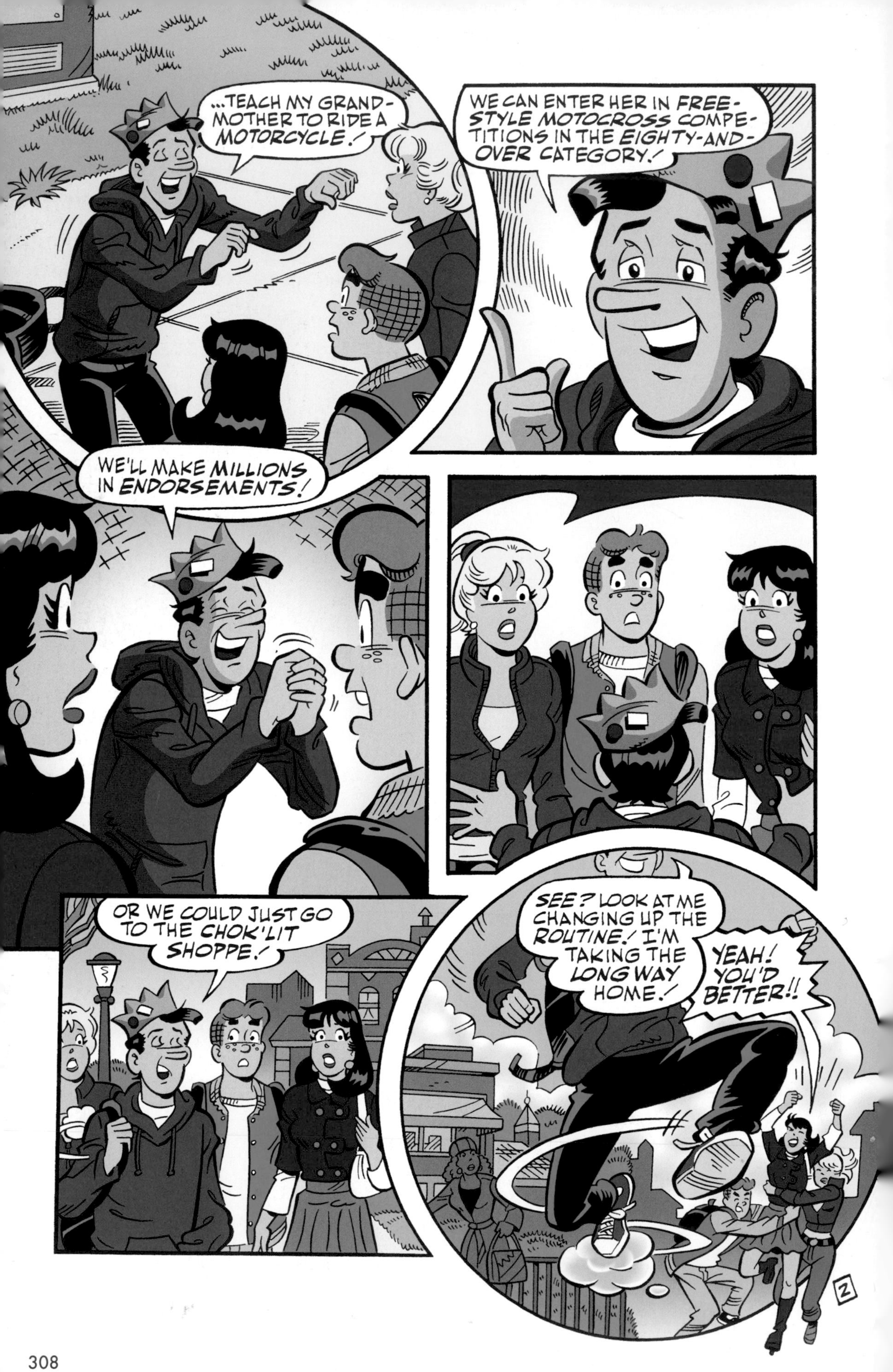
...TEACH MY GRANDMOTHER TO RIDE A MOTORCYCLE!
WE CAN ENTER HER IN FREESTYLE MOTOCROSS COMPETITIONS IN THE EIGHTY-AND-OVER CATEGORY!
WE'LL MAKE MILLIONS IN ENDORSEMENTS!
OR WE COULD JUST GO TO THE CHOK'LIT SHOPPE!
SEE? LOOK AT ME CHANGING UP THE ROUTINE! I'M TAKING THE LONG WAY HOME!
YEAH! YOU'D BETTER!!
2

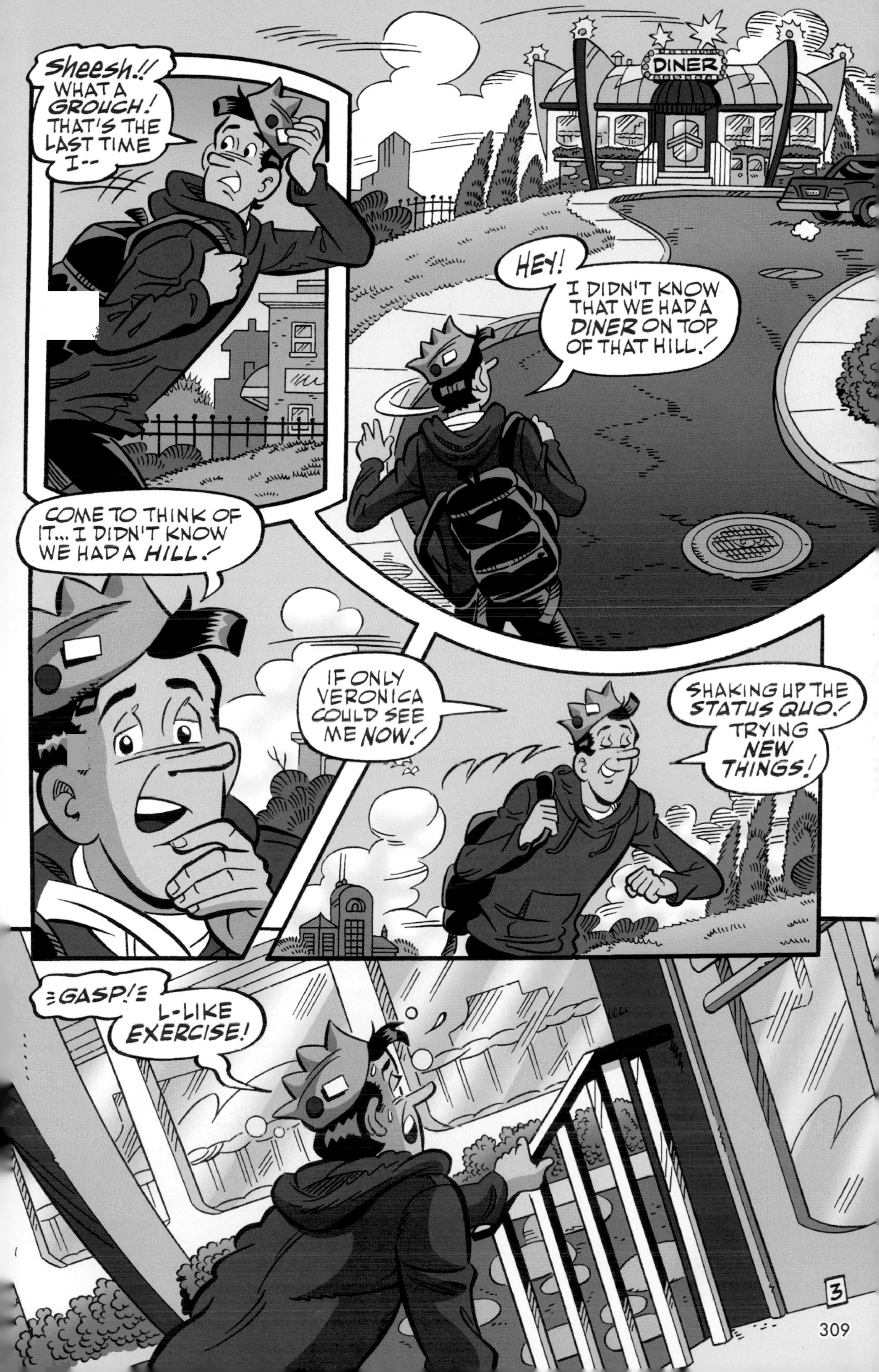
Sheesh!! WHAT A GROUCH! THAT'S THE LAST TIME I--
HEY!
I DIDN'T KNOW THAT WE HAD A DINER ON TOP OF THAT HILL.
DINER
COME TO THINK OF IT... I DIDN'T KNOW WE HAD A HILL.
IF ONLY VERONICA COULD SEE ME NOW.
SHAKING UP THE STATUS QUO. TRYING NEW THINGS!
GASP!
L-LIKE EXERCISE!
3

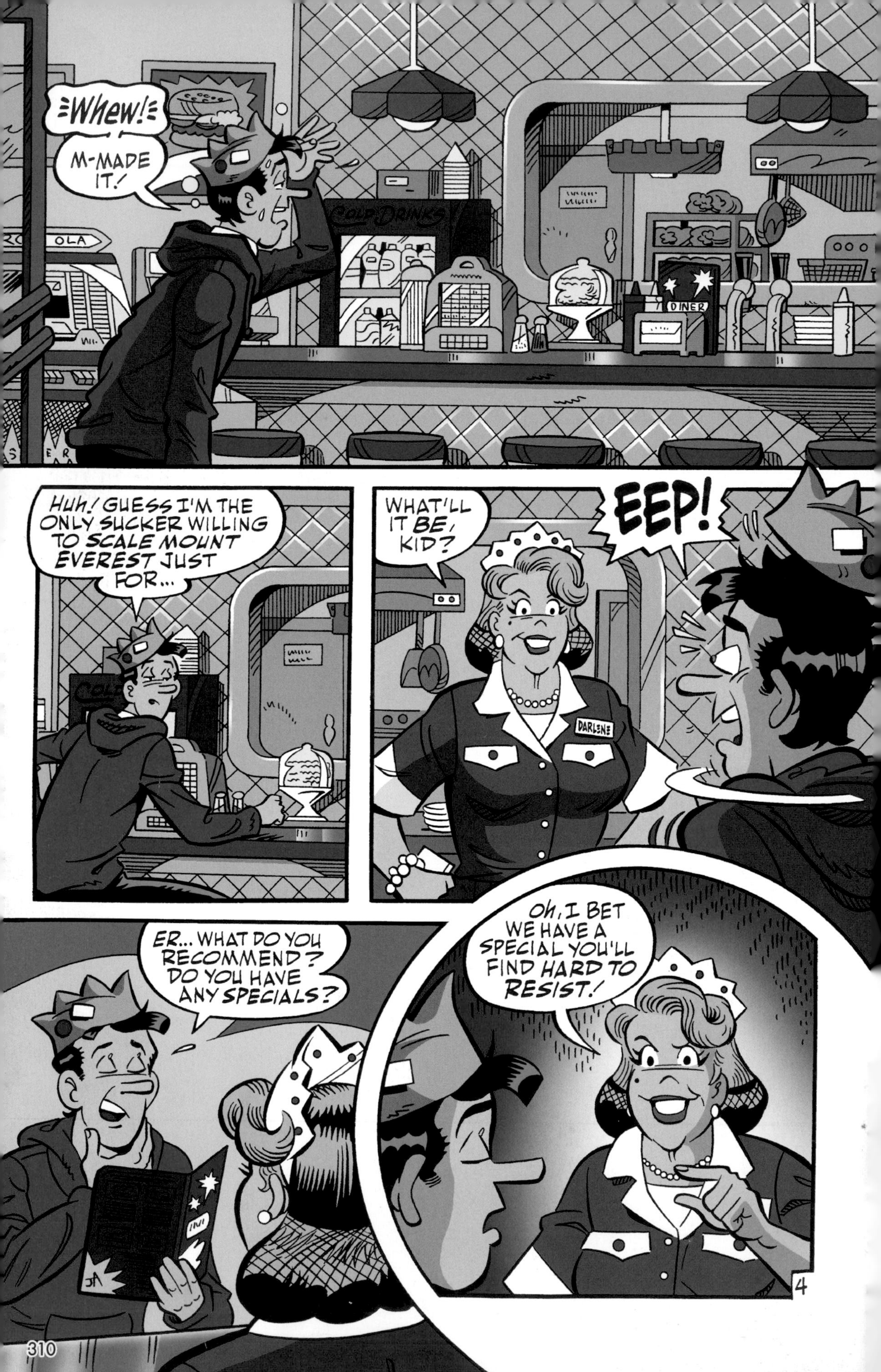
WHEW!
M-MADE IT!
DINER
HUH! GUESS I'M THE ONLY SUCKER WILLING TO SCALE MOUNT EVEREST JUST FOR...
WHAT'LL IT BE, KID?
EEP!
DARLENE
ER... WHAT DO YOU RECOMMEND? DO YOU HAVE ANY SPECIALS?
OH, I BET WE HAVE A SPECIAL YOU'LL FIND HARD TO RESIST!
4

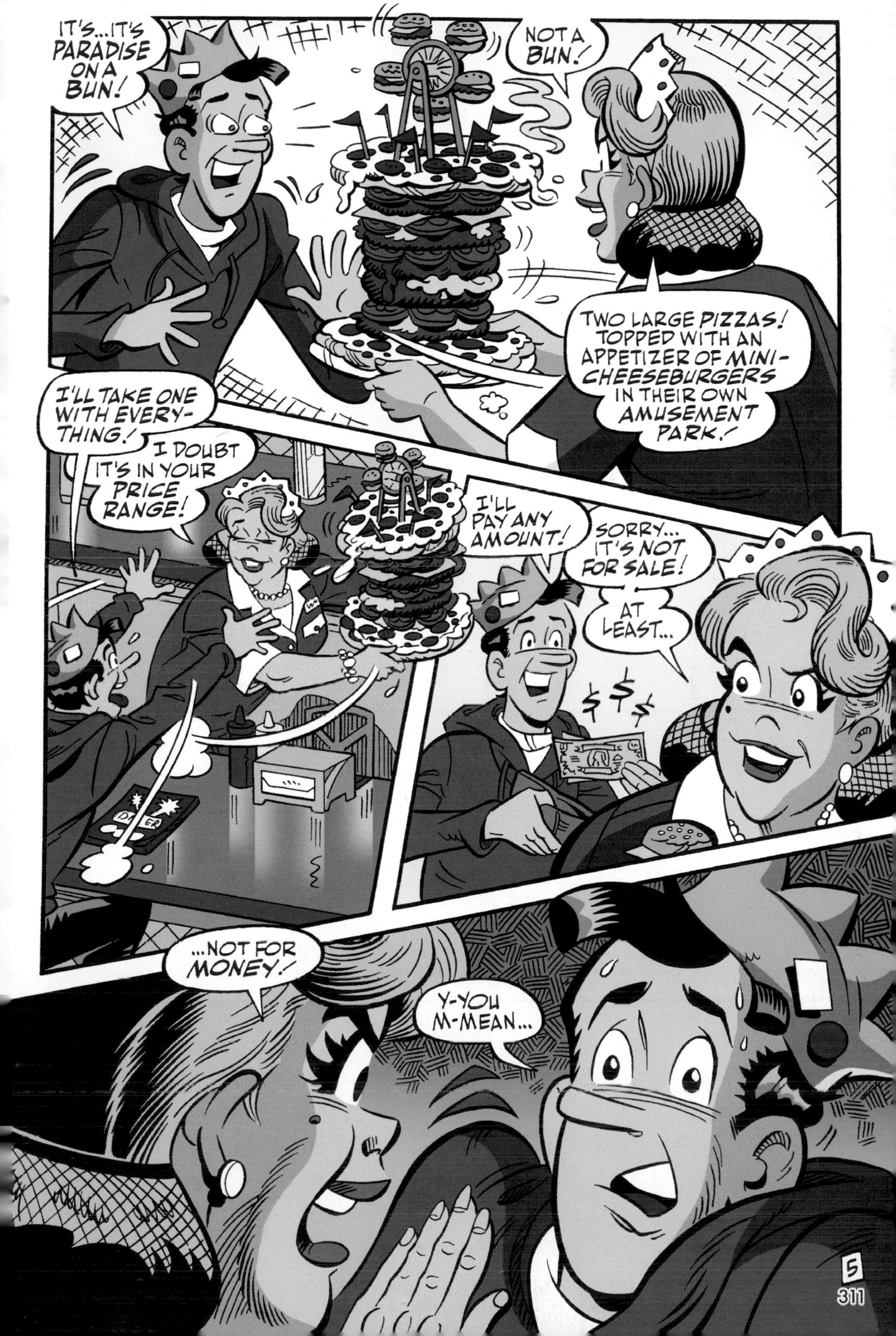
IT'S...IT'S PARADISE ON A BUN!
NOT A BUN!
TWO LARGE PIZZAS! TOPPED WITH AN APPETIZER OF MINI-CHEESEBURGERS IN THEIR OWN AMUSEMENT PARK!
I'LL TAKE ONE WITH EVERY-THING!
I DOUBT IT'S IN YOUR PRICE RANGE!
I'LL PAY ANY AMOUNT!
SORRY... IT'S NOT FOR SALE!
AT LEAST...
...NOT FOR MONEY!
Y-YOU M-MEAN...

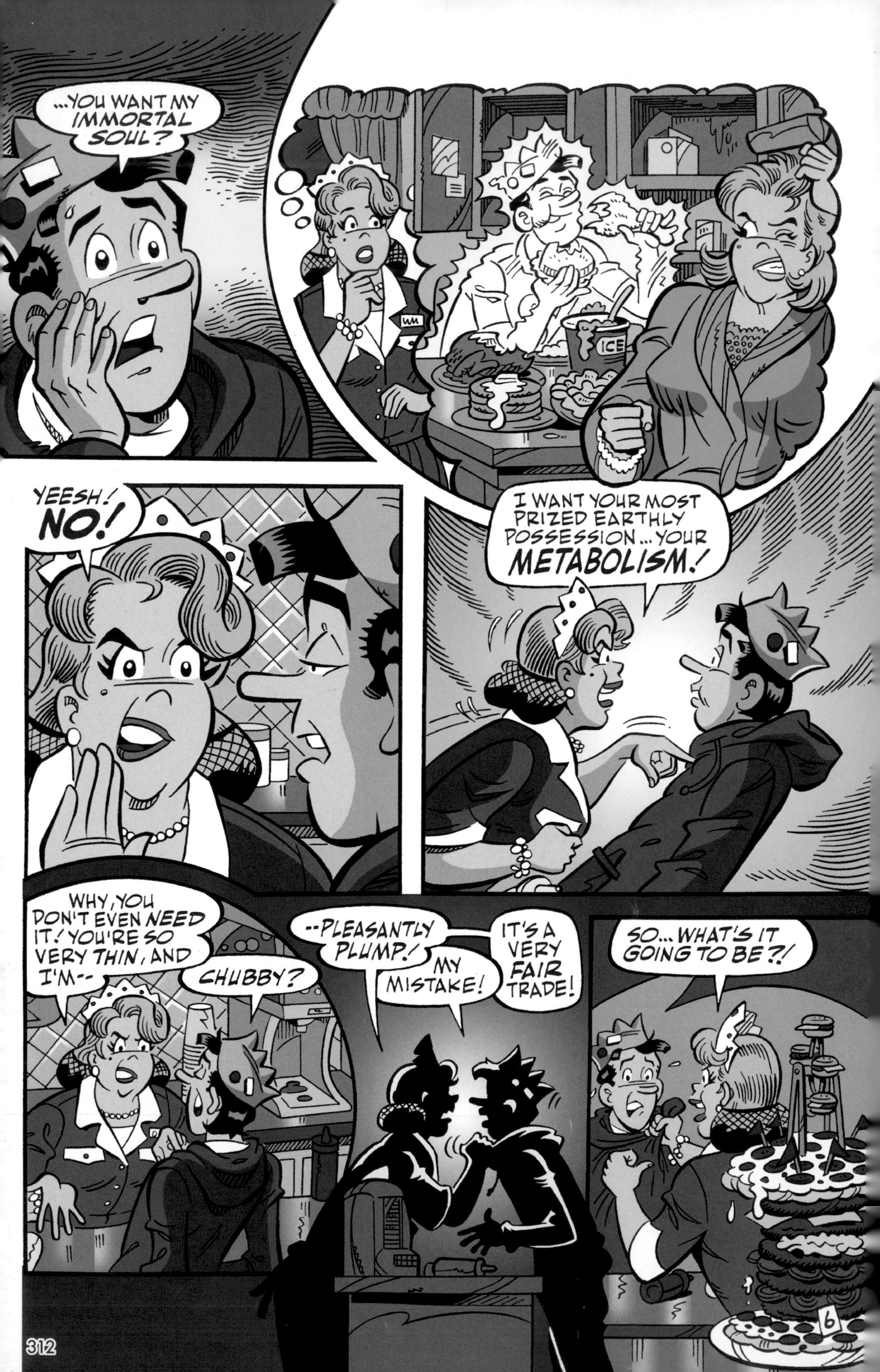
...YOU WANT MY IMMORTAL SOUL?
YEESH! NO!
I WANT YOUR MOST PRIZED EARTHLY POSSESSION ... YOUR METABOLISM!
WHY, YOU DON'T EVEN NEED IT! YOU'RE SO VERY THIN, AND I'M--
CHUBBY?
--PLEASANTLY PLUMP!
MY MISTAKE!
IT'S A VERY FAIR TRADE!
SO... WHAT'S IT GOING TO BE?!
6

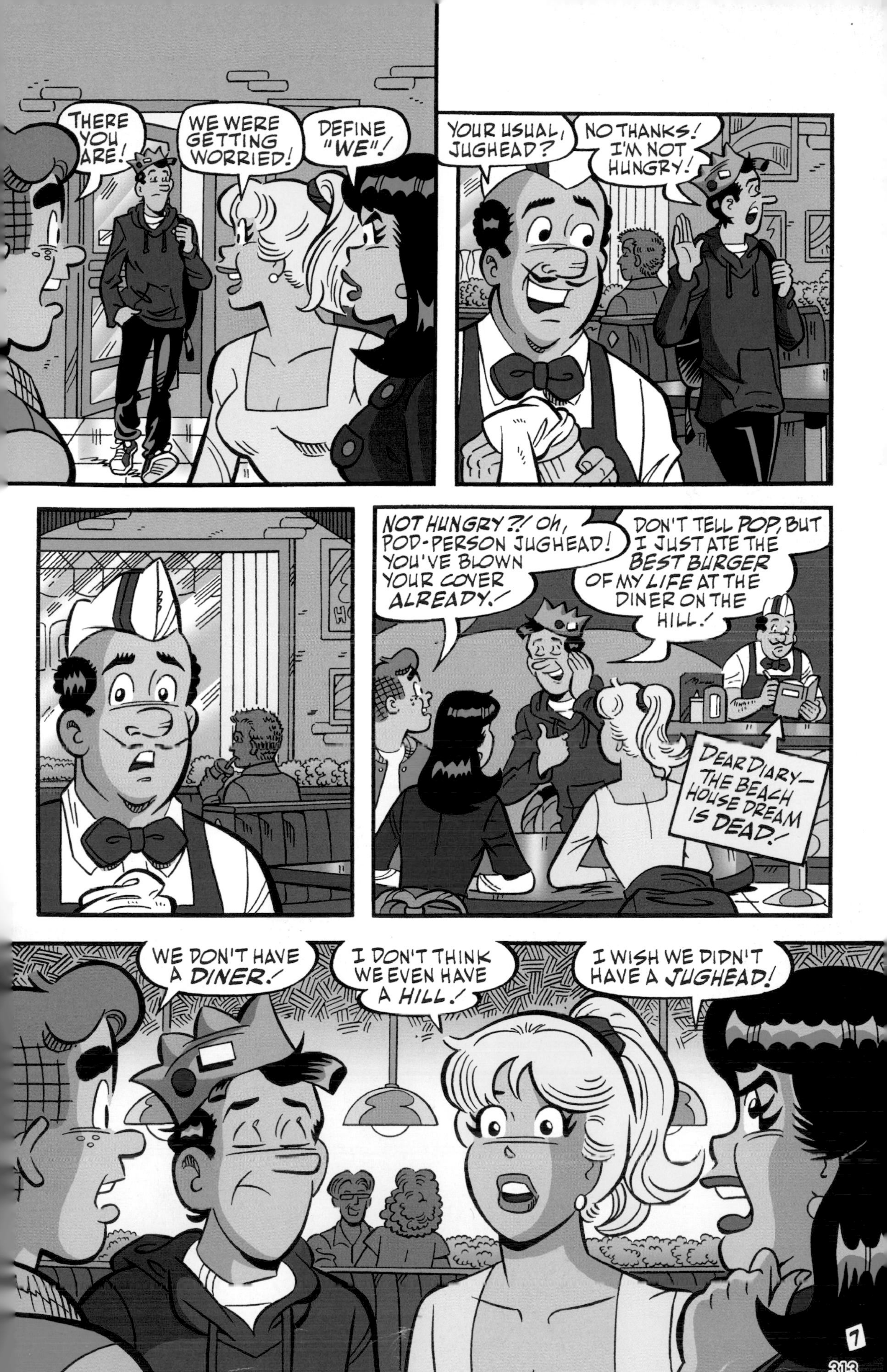
THERE YOU ARE!
WE WERE GETTING WORRIED!
DEFINE "WE"!
YOUR USUAL, JUGHEAD?
NO THANKS! I'M NOT HUNGRY!
NOT HUNGRY?! OH, POD-PERSON JUGHEAD! YOU'VE BLOWN YOUR COVER ALREADY!
DON'T TELL POP, BUT I JUST ATE THE BEST BURGER OF MY LIFE AT THE DINER ON THE HILL!
DEAR DIARY— THE BEACH HOUSE DREAM IS DEAD!
WE DON'T HAVE A DINER!
I DON'T THINK WE EVEN HAVE A HILL!
I WISH WE DIDN'T HAVE A JUGHEAD!
7

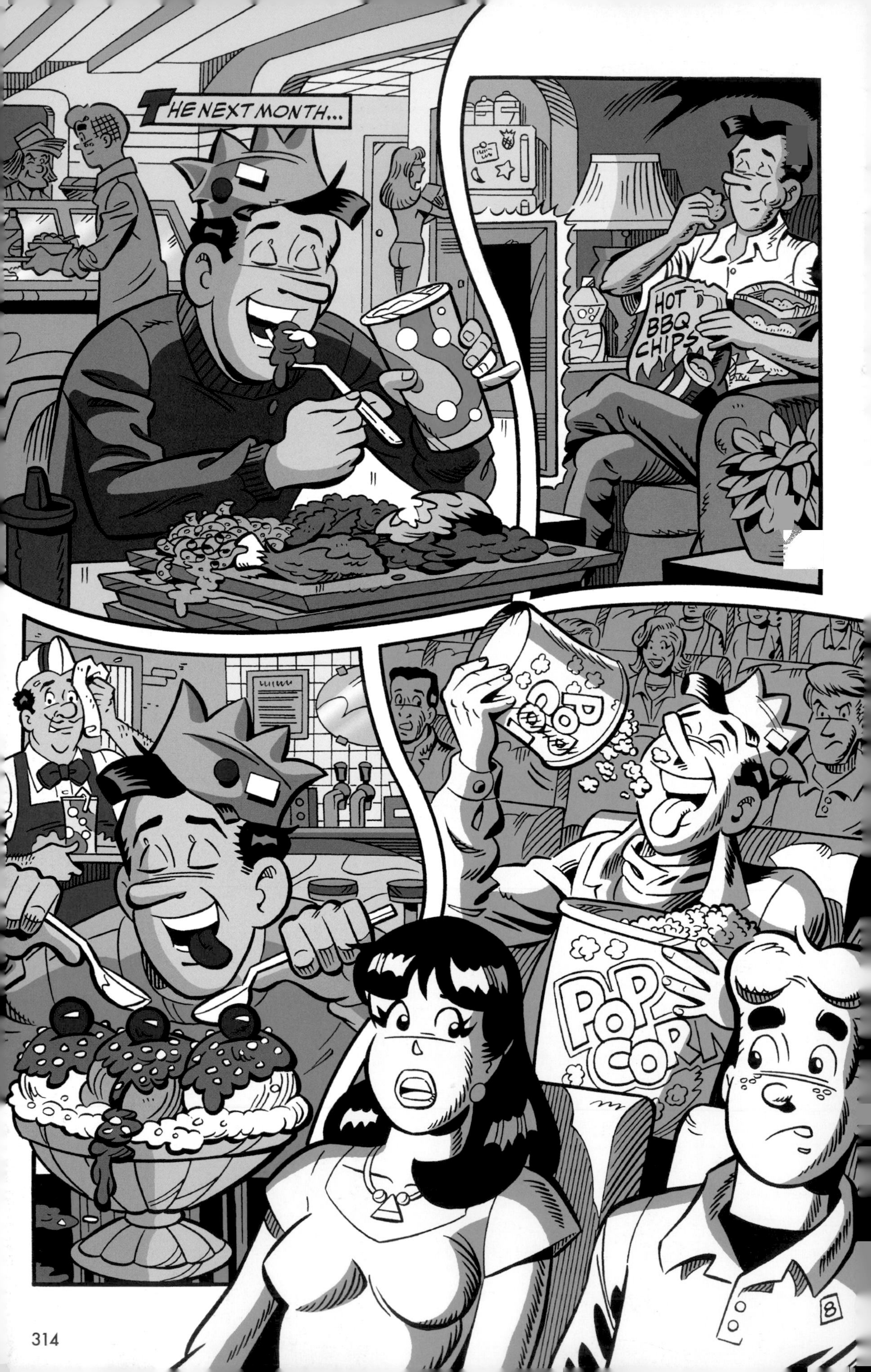
THE NEXT MONTH...
HOT BBQ CHIPS
POP CORN
POP CORN
8

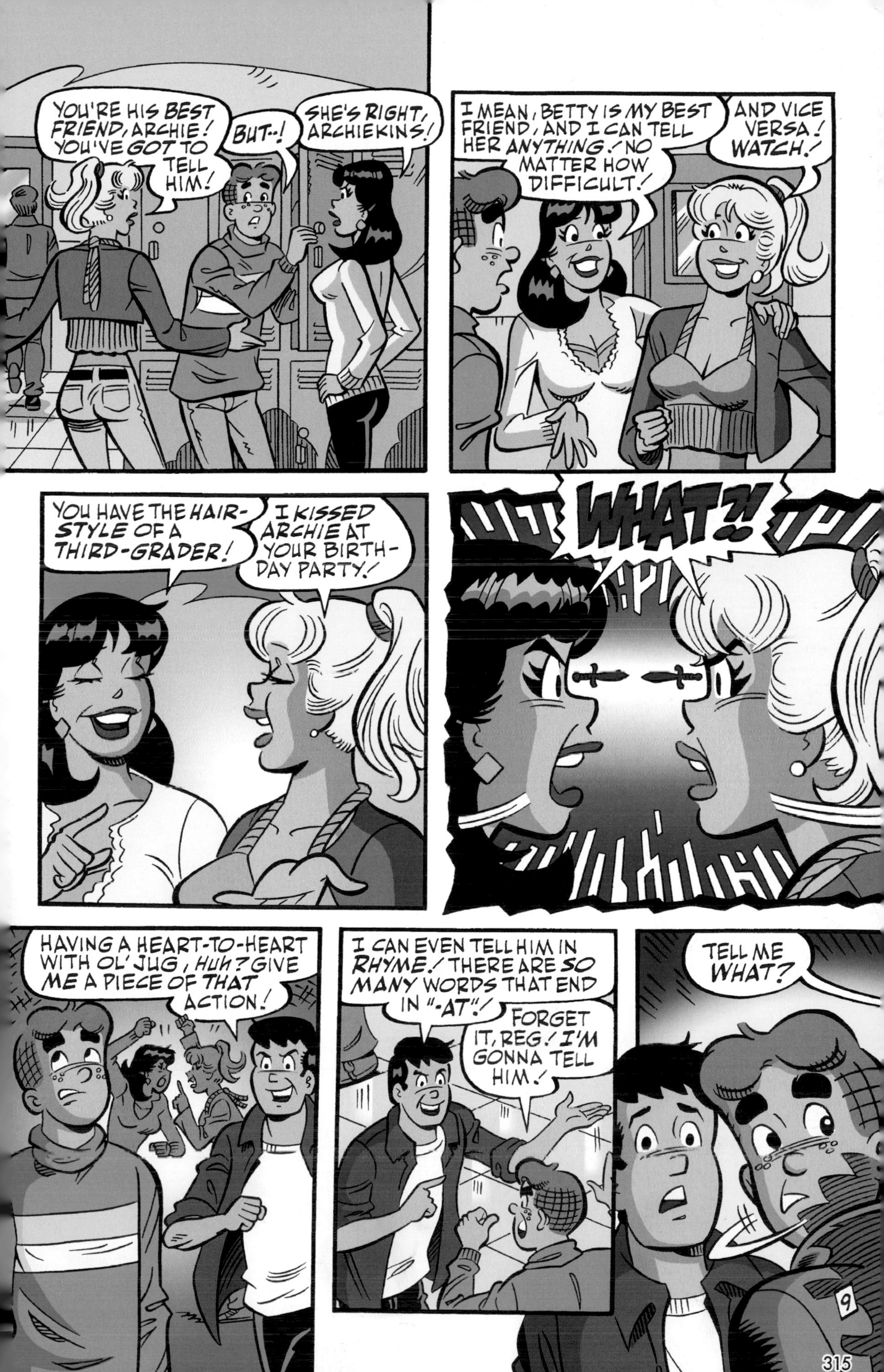
YOU'RE HIS BEST FRIEND, ARCHIE! YOU'VE GOT TO TELL HIM!
BUT--!
SHE'S RIGHT, ARCHIEKINS!
I MEAN, BETTY IS MY BEST FRIEND, AND I CAN TELL HER ANYTHING! NO MATTER HOW DIFFICULT!
AND VICE VERSA! WATCH!
YOU HAVE THE HAIR-STYLE OF A THIRD-GRADER!
I KISSED ARCHIE AT YOUR BIRTH-DAY PARTY!
WHAT?!
HAVING A HEART-TO-HEART WITH OL' JUG, HUH? GIVE ME A PIECE OF THAT ACTION!
I CAN EVEN TELL HIM IN RHYME! THERE ARE SO MANY WORDS THAT END IN "-AT"!
FORGET IT, REG! I'M GONNA TELL HIM!
TELL ME WHAT?
9

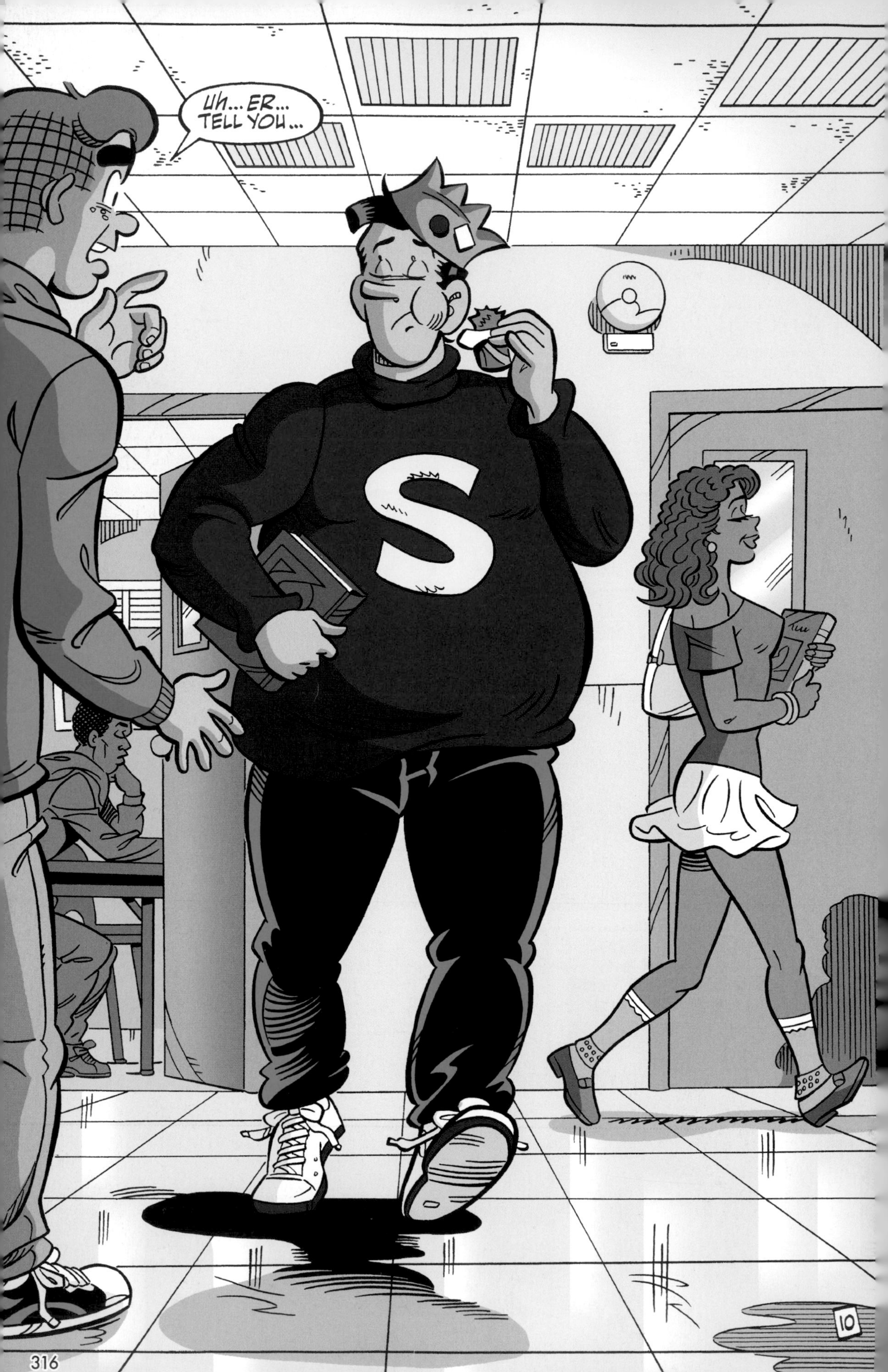
UH... ER... TELL YOU...
10

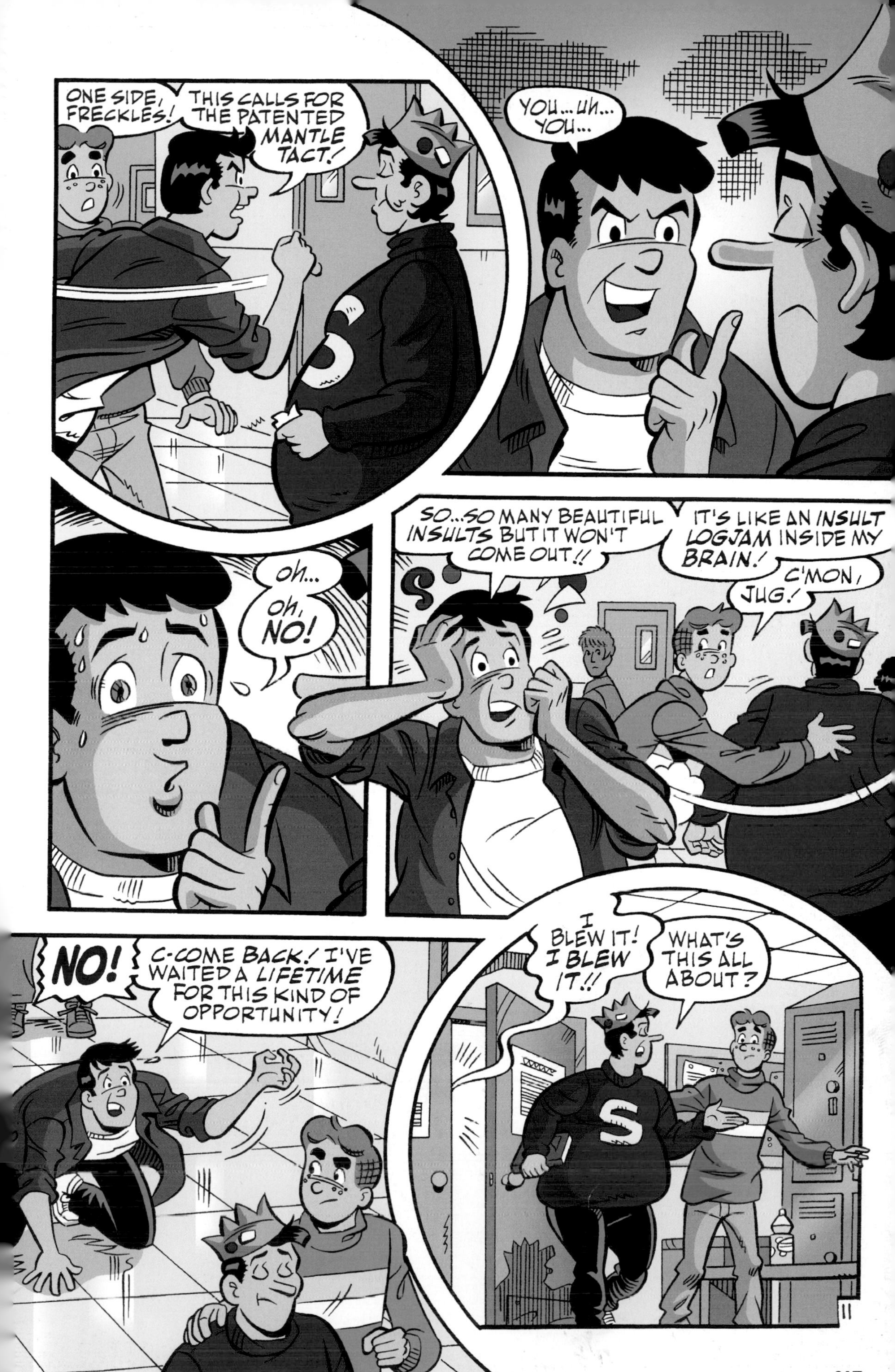

ONE SIDE, FRECKLES!
THIS CALLS FOR THE PATENTED MANTLE TACT!
YOU... UH... YOU...
OH... OH, NO!
SO...SO MANY BEAUTIFUL INSULTS BUT IT WON'T COME OUT!!
IT'S LIKE AN INSULT LOGJAM INSIDE MY BRAIN!
C'MON, JUG!
NO!
C-COME BACK! I'VE WAITED A LIFETIME FOR THIS KIND OF OPPORTUNITY!
I BLEW IT! I BLEW IT!!
WHAT'S THIS ALL ABOUT?
11

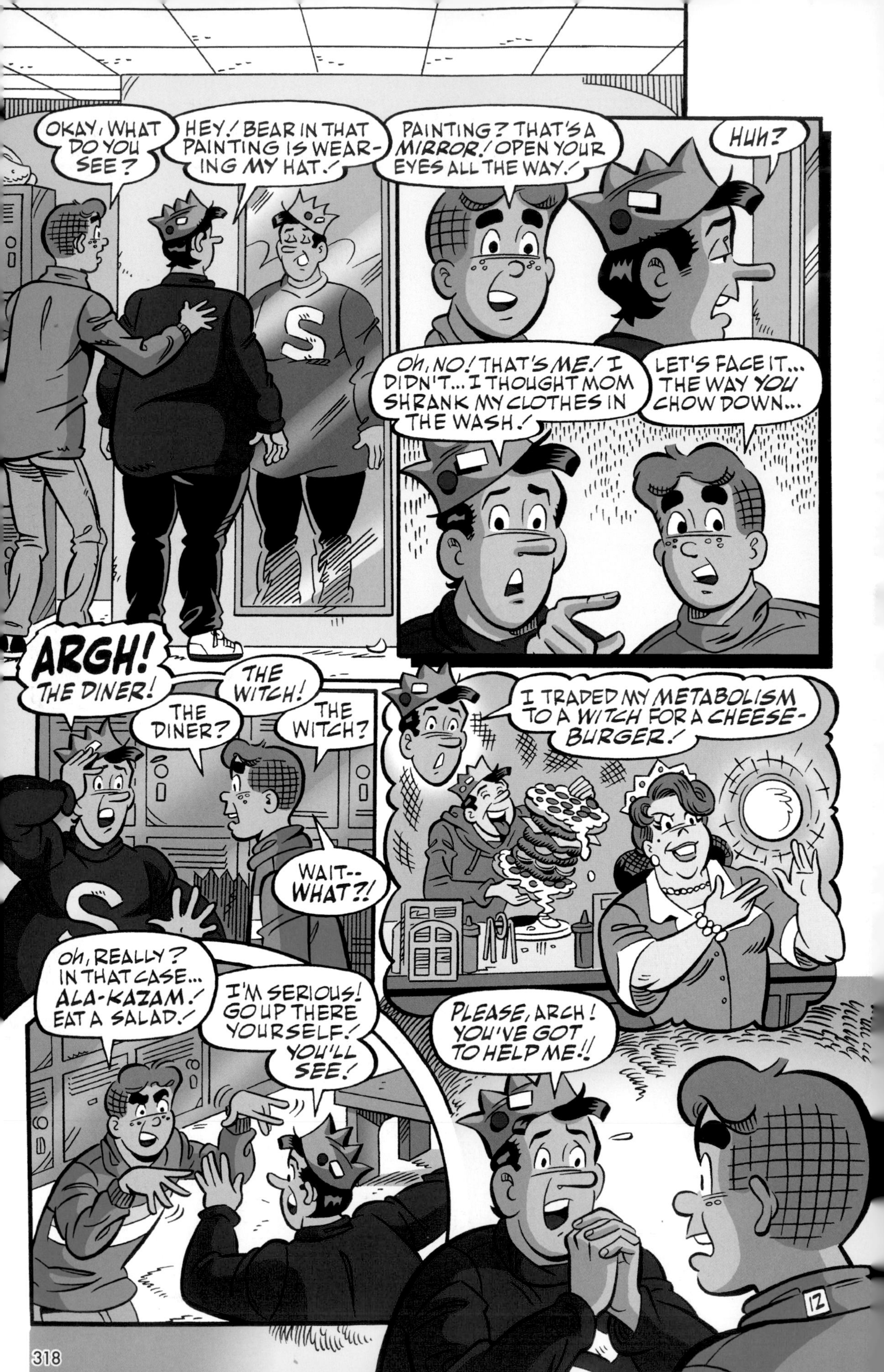

OKAY, WHAT DO YOU SEE?
HEY! BEAR IN THAT PAINTING IS WEARING MY HAT!
PAINTING? THAT'S A MIRROR! OPEN YOUR EYES ALL THE WAY!
HUH?
Oh, NO! THAT'S ME! I DIDN'T... I THOUGHT MOM SHRANK MY CLOTHES IN THE WASH!
LET'S FACE IT... THE WAY YOU CHOW DOWN...
ARGH! THE DINER!
THE DINER?
THE WITCH!
THE WITCH?
WAIT-- WHAT?!
I TRADED MY METABOLISM TO A WITCH FOR A CHEESE-BURGER!
Oh, REALLY? IN THAT CASE... ALA-KAZAM! EAT A SALAD!
I'M SERIOUS! GO UP THERE YOURSELF! YOU'LL SEE!
PLEASE, ARCH! YOU'VE GOT TO HELP ME!!
12

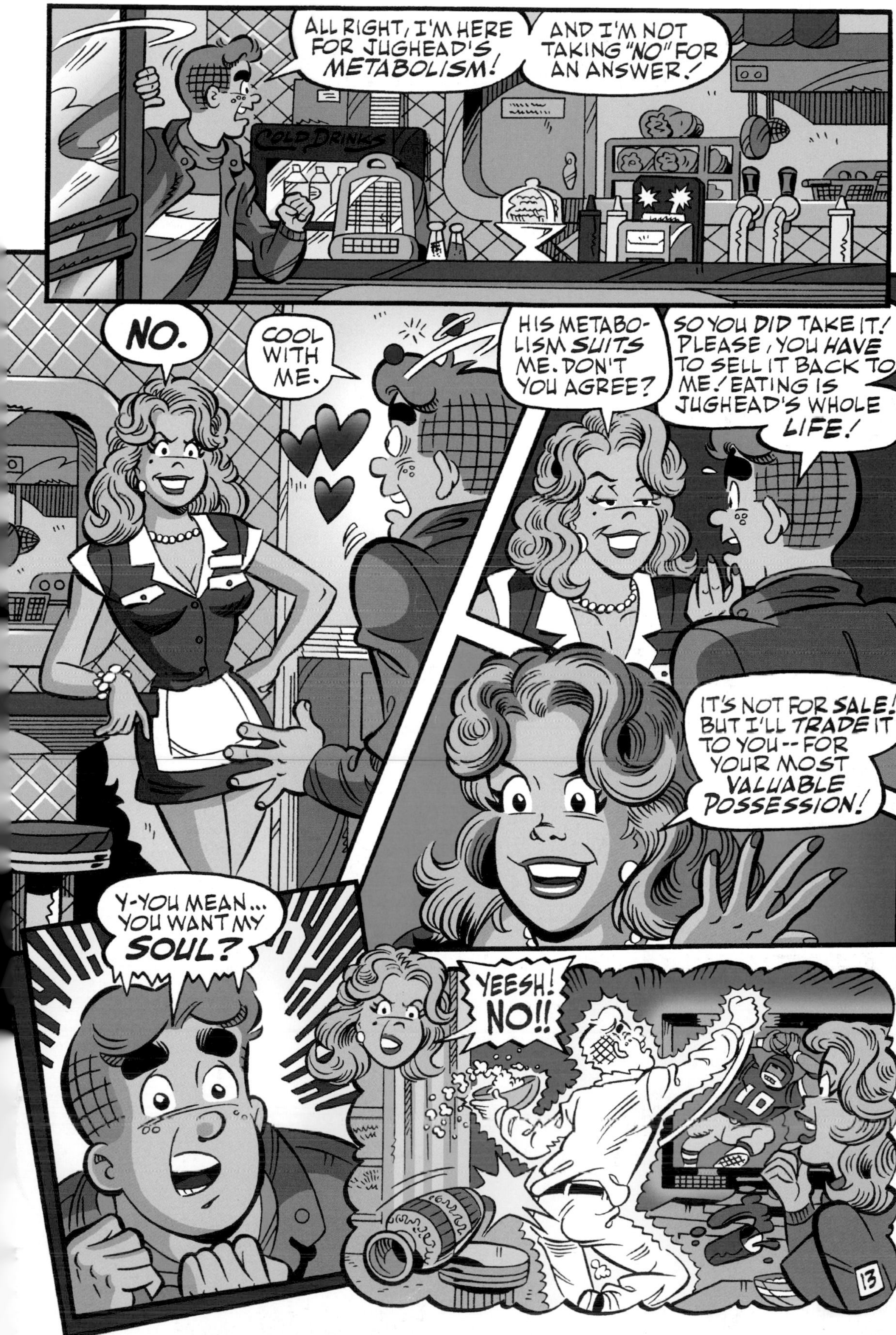
ALL RIGHT, I'M HERE FOR JUGHEAD'S METABOLISM!
AND I'M NOT TAKING "NO" FOR AN ANSWER!
COLD DRINKS
NO.
COOL WITH ME.
HIS METABOLISM SUITS ME. DON'T YOU AGREE?
SO YOU DID TAKE IT! PLEASE, YOU HAVE TO SELL IT BACK TO ME! EATING IS JUGHEAD'S WHOLE LIFE!
IT'S NOT FOR SALE! BUT I'LL TRADE IT TO YOU -- FOR YOUR MOST VALUABLE POSSESSION!
Y-YOU MEAN... YOU WANT MY SOUL?
YEESH! NO!!
13

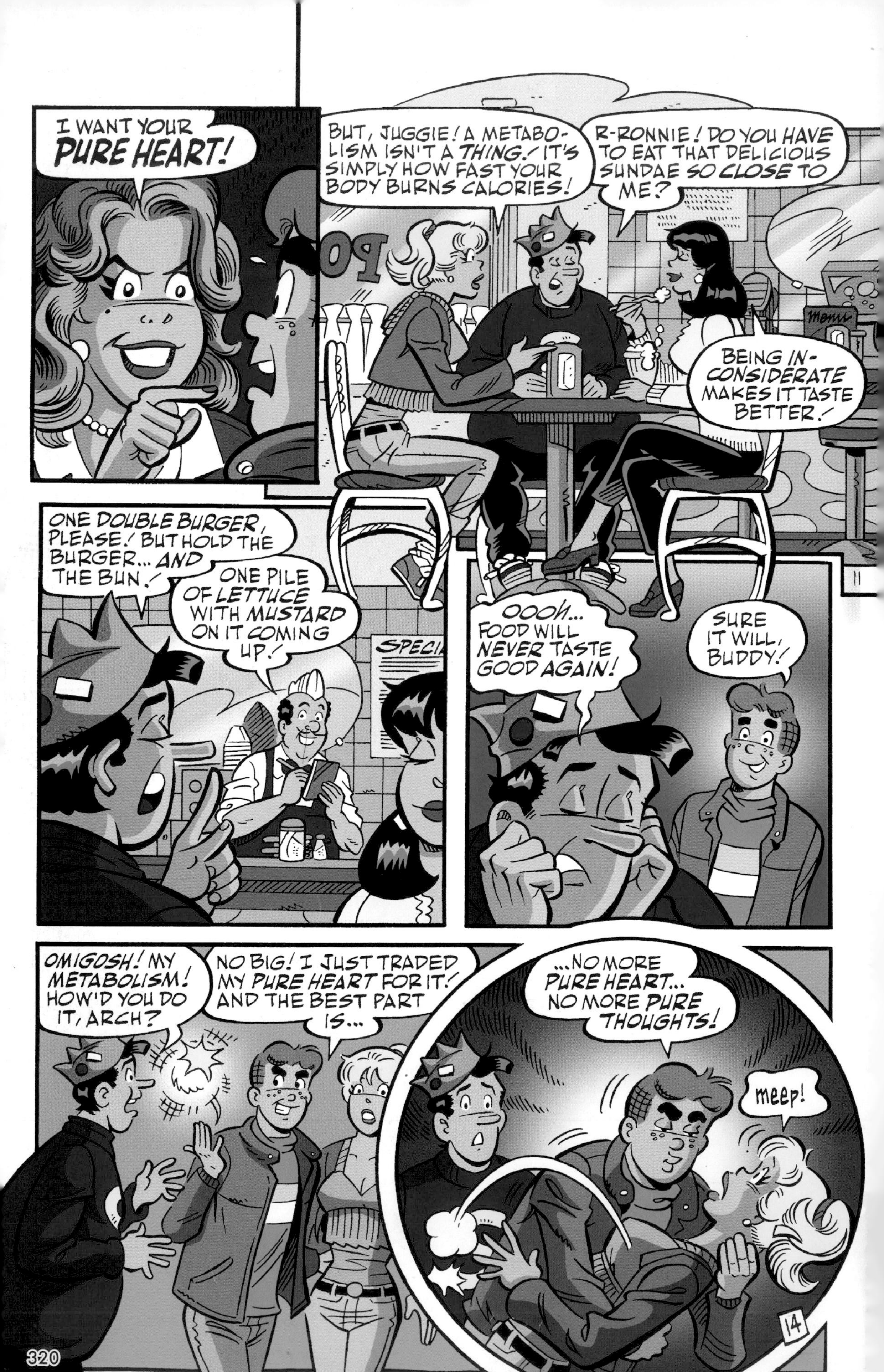
I WANT YOUR PURE HEART!
BUT, JUGGIE! A METABOLISM ISN'T A THING! IT'S SIMPLY HOW FAST YOUR BODY BURNS CALORIES!
R-RONNIE! DO YOU HAVE TO EAT THAT DELICIOUS SUNDAE SO CLOSE TO ME?
BEING INCONSIDERATE MAKES IT TASTE BETTER!
ONE DOUBLE BURGER, PLEASE! BUT HOLD THE BURGER... AND THE BUN!
ONE PILE OF LETTUCE WITH MUSTARD ON IT COMING UP!
OOOH... FOOD WILL NEVER TASTE GOOD AGAIN!
SURE IT WILL, BUDDY!
OMIGOSH! MY METABOLISM! HOW'D YOU DO IT, ARCH?
NO BIG! I JUST TRADED MY PURE HEART FOR IT! AND THE BEST PART IS...
...NO MORE PURE HEART... NO MORE PURE THOUGHTS!
meep!
14

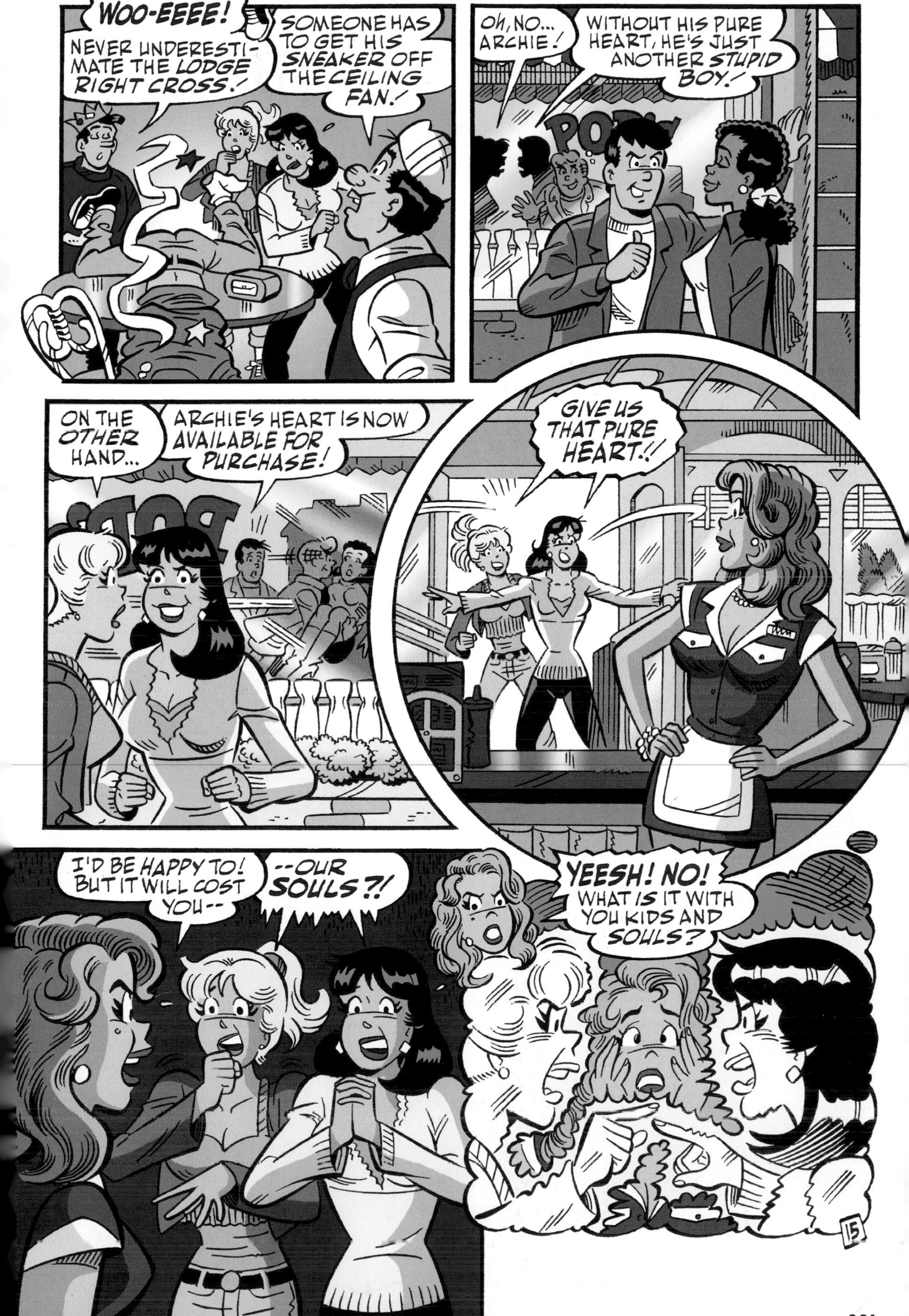
WOO-EEEE!
NEVER UNDERESTIMATE THE LODGE RIGHT CROSS!
SOMEONE HAS TO GET HIS SNEAKER OFF THE CEILING FAN!
OH, NO... ARCHIE!
WITHOUT HIS PURE HEART, HE'S JUST ANOTHER STUPID BOY!
ON THE OTHER HAND...
ARCHIE'S HEART IS NOW AVAILABLE FOR PURCHASE!
GIVE US THAT PURE HEART!!
I'D BE HAPPY TO! BUT IT WILL COST YOU--
--OUR SOULS?!
YEESH! NO! WHAT IS IT WITH YOU KIDS AND SOULS?
15

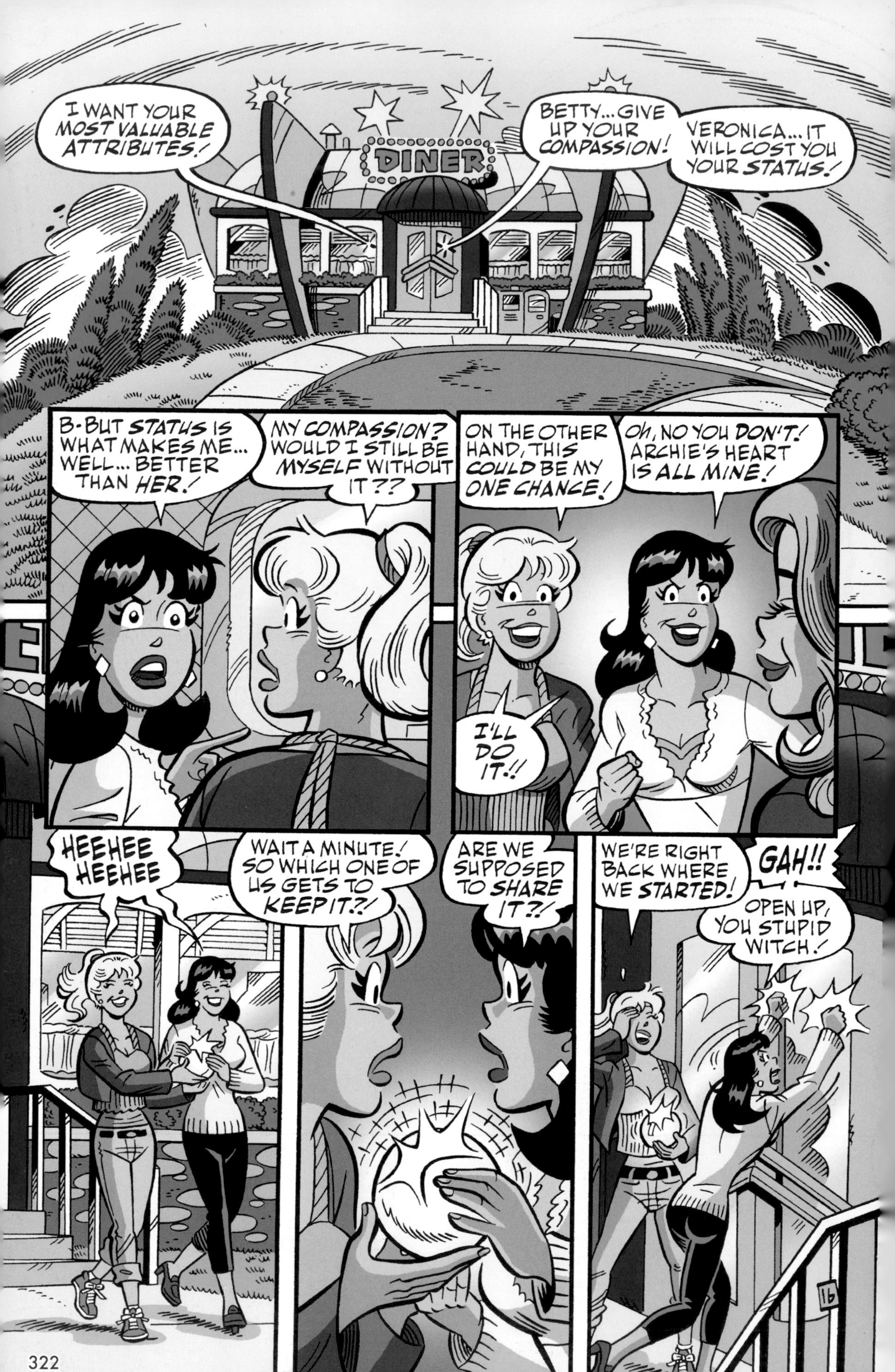
I WANT YOUR MOST VALUABLE ATTRIBUTES!
BETTY... GIVE UP YOUR COMPASSION!
VERONICA... IT WILL COST YOU YOUR STATUS!
B-BUT STATUS IS WHAT MAKES ME... WELL... BETTER THAN HER!
MY COMPASSION? WOULD I STILL BE MYSELF WITHOUT IT??
ON THE OTHER HAND, THIS COULD BE MY ONE CHANCE!
Oh, NO YOU DON'T! ARCHIE'S HEART IS ALL MINE!
I'LL DO IT!!
HEEHEE HEEHEE
WAIT A MINUTE! SO WHICH ONE OF US GETS TO KEEP IT?!
ARE WE SUPPOSED TO SHARE IT?!
WE'RE RIGHT BACK WHERE WE STARTED!
GAH!!
OPEN UP, YOU STUPID WITCH!
16

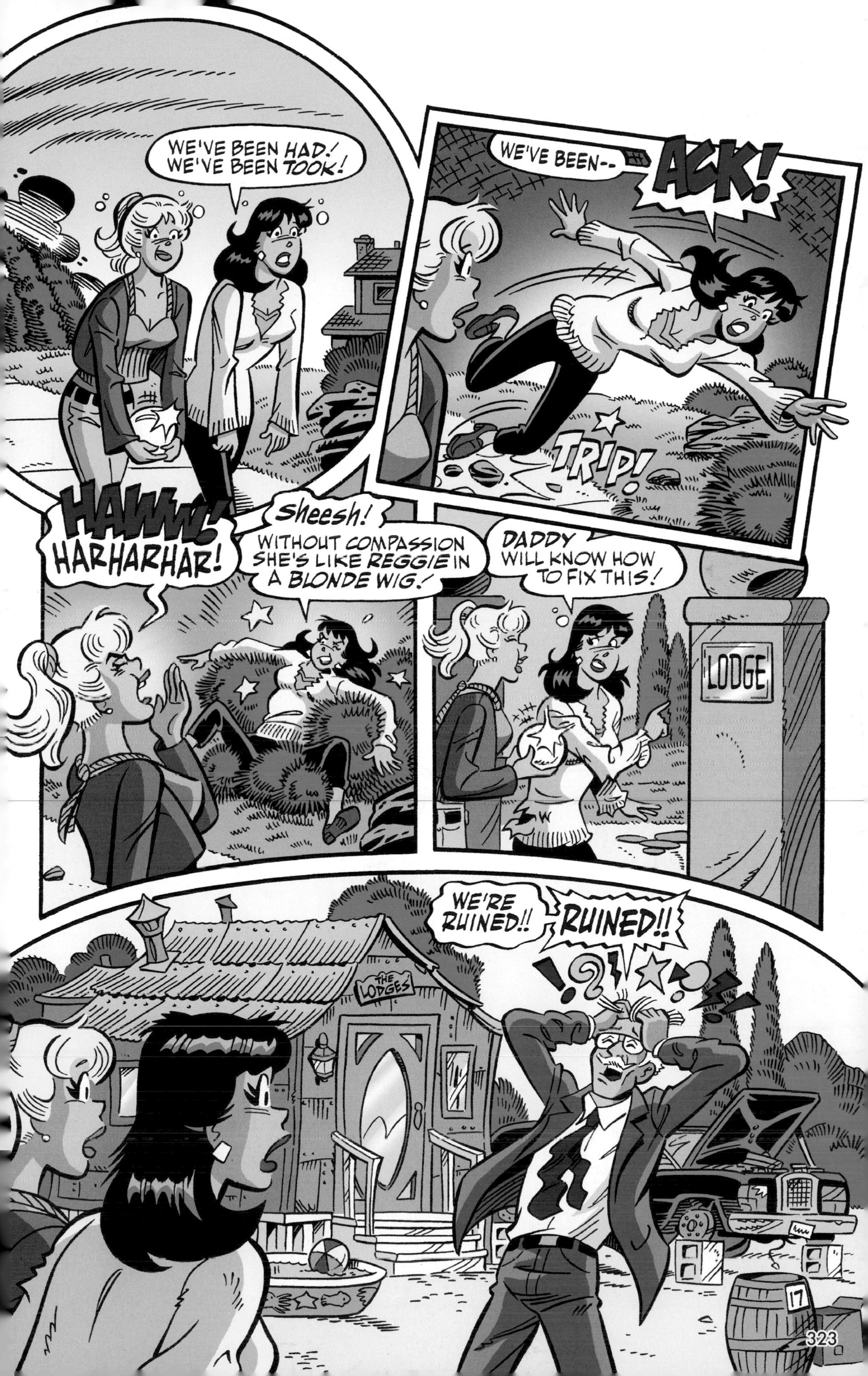
WE'VE BEEN HAD! WE'VE BEEN TOOK!
WE'VE BEEN--
ACK!
TRIP!
HAWW! HARHARHAR!
Sheesh! WITHOUT COMPASSION SHE'S LIKE REGGIE IN A BLONDE WIG!
DADDY WILL KNOW HOW TO FIX THIS!
LODGE
WE'RE RUINED!!
RUINED!!
THE LODGES
17

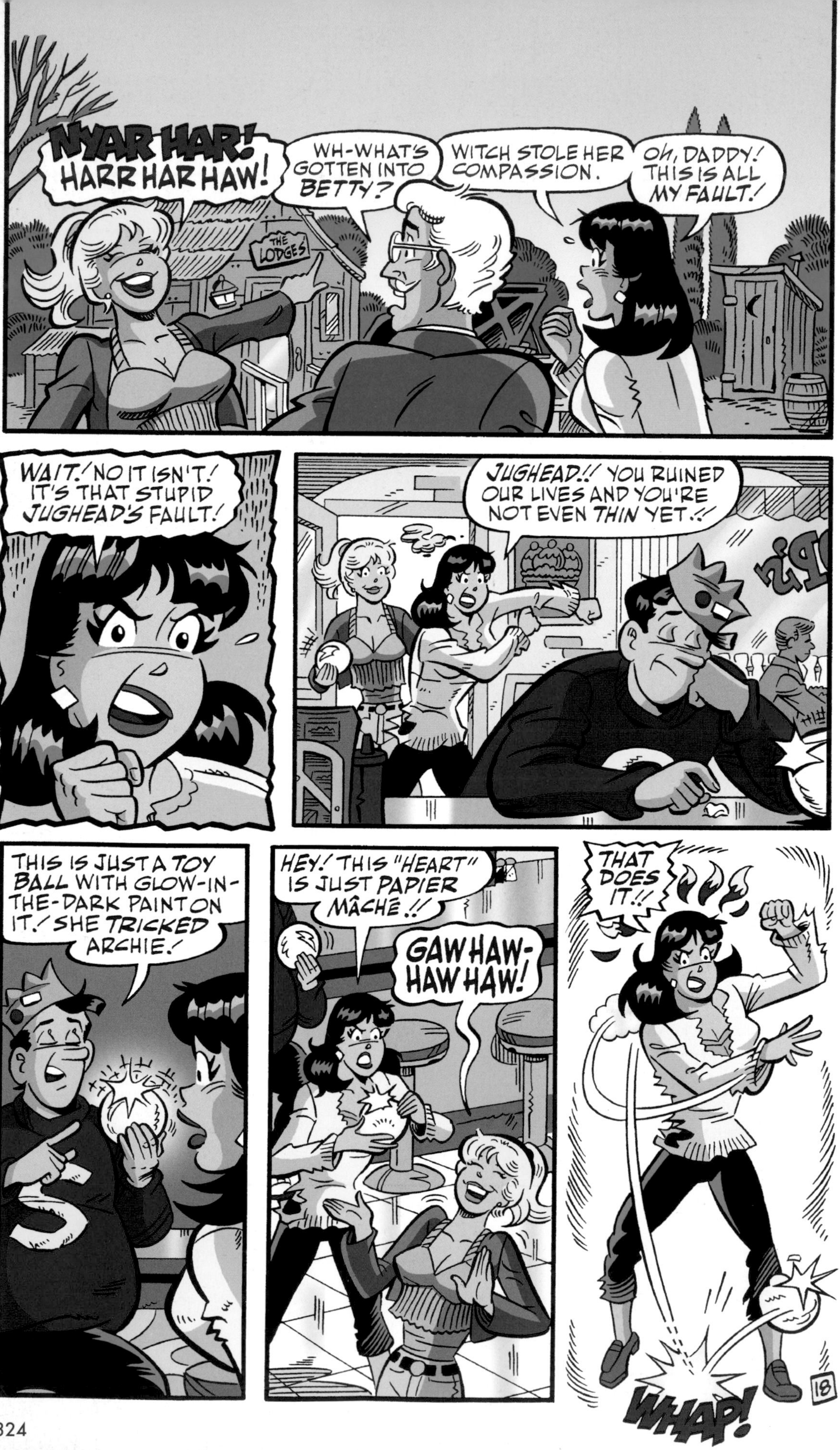
NYAR HAR! HARR HAR HAW!
WH-WHAT'S GOTTEN INTO BETTY?
WITCH STOLE HER COMPASSION.
OH, DADDY! THIS IS ALL MY FAULT!
THE LODGES
WAIT! NO IT ISN'T! IT'S THAT STUPID JUGHEAD'S FAULT!
JUGHEAD!! YOU RUINED OUR LIVES AND YOU'RE NOT EVEN THIN YET.!!
THIS IS JUST A TOY BALL WITH GLOW-IN-THE-DARK PAINT ON IT! SHE TRICKED ARCHIE!
HEY! THIS "HEART" IS JUST PAPIER MÂCHÉ!!
GAW HAW-HAW HAW!
THAT DOES IT!!
WHAP!
18

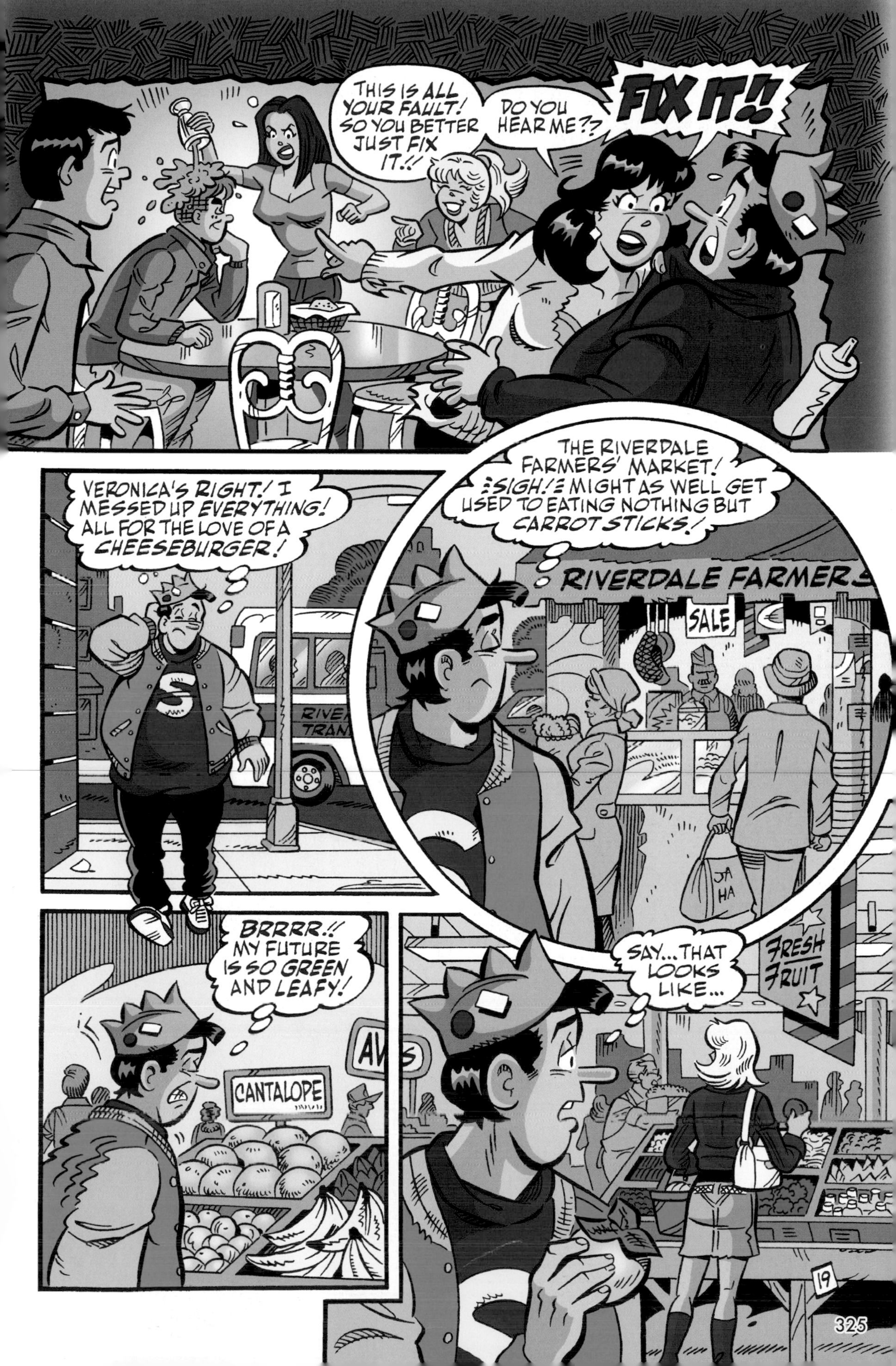
THIS IS ALL YOUR FAULT! SO YOU BETTER JUST FIX IT!!
DO YOU HEAR ME??
FIX IT!!
VERONICA'S RIGHT! I MESSED UP EVERYTHING! ALL FOR THE LOVE OF A CHEESEBURGER!
RIVER TRAN
THE RIVERDALE FARMERS' MARKET! SIGH! MIGHT AS WELL GET USED TO EATING NOTHING BUT CARROT STICKS!
RIVERDALE FARMERS
SALE
BRRRR!! MY FUTURE IS SO GREEN AND LEAFY!
CANTALOPE
SAY...THAT LOOKS LIKE...
FRESH FRUIT
19

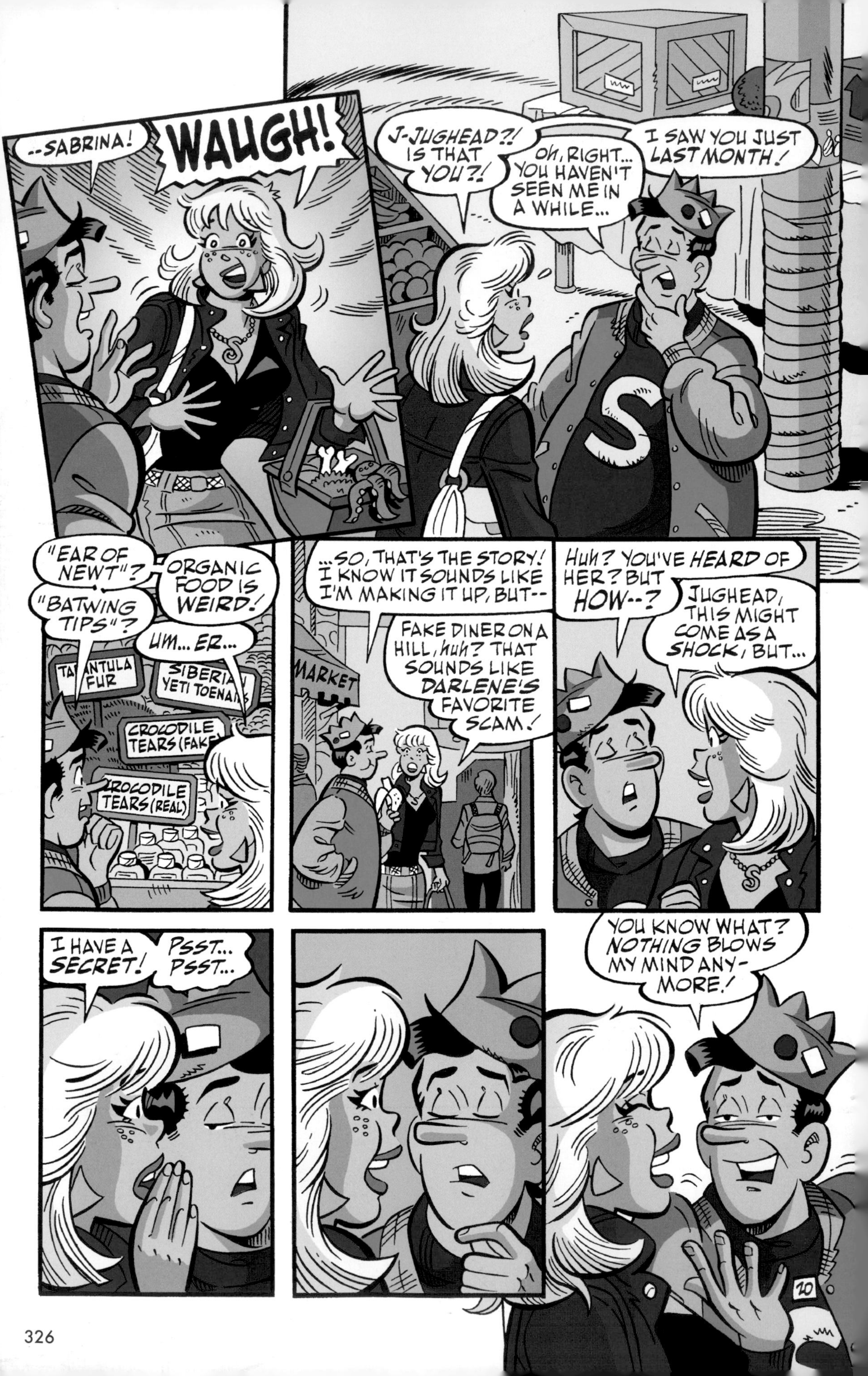
--SABRINA!
WAUGH!
J-JUGHEAD?! IS THAT YOU?!
OH, RIGHT... YOU HAVEN'T SEEN ME IN A WHILE...
I SAW YOU JUST LAST MONTH!
"EAR OF NEWT"?
"BATWING TIPS"?
ORGANIC FOOD IS WEIRD!
UM... ER...
TARANTULA FUR
SIBERIAN YETI TOENAILS
CROCODILE TEARS (FAKE)
CROCODILE TEARS (REAL)
...SO, THAT'S THE STORY! I KNOW IT SOUNDS LIKE I'M MAKING IT UP, BUT--
MARKET
FAKE DINER ON A HILL, HUH? THAT SOUNDS LIKE DARLENE'S FAVORITE SCAM!
HUH? YOU'VE HEARD OF HER? BUT HOW--?
JUGHEAD, THIS MIGHT COME AS A SHOCK, BUT...
I HAVE A SECRET!
PSST... PSST...
YOU KNOW WHAT? NOTHING BLOWS MY MIND ANY-MORE!
20

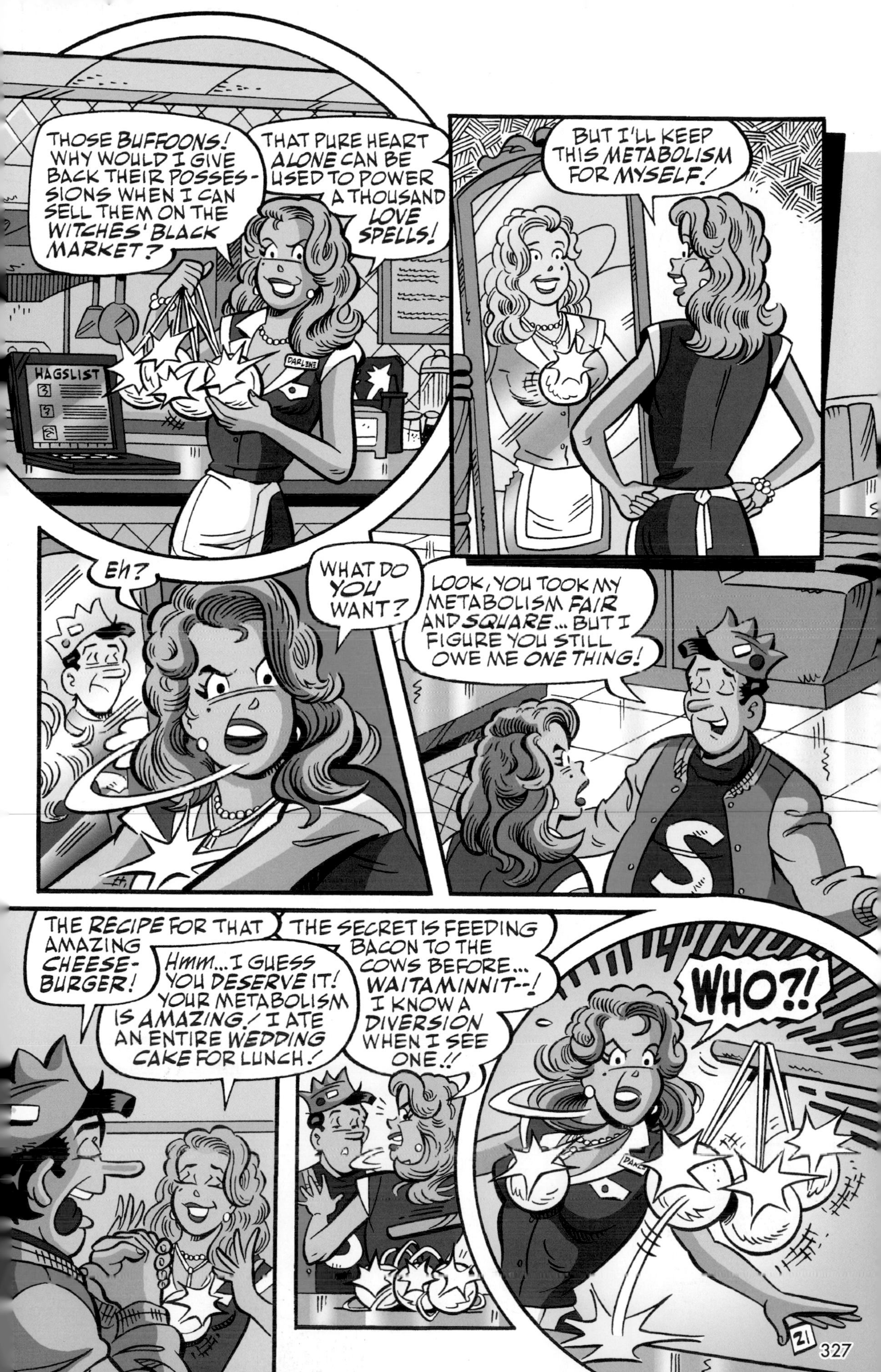

THOSE BUFFOONS! WHY WOULD I GIVE BACK THEIR POSSES-SIONS WHEN I CAN SELL THEM ON THE WITCHES' BLACK MARKET?
THAT PURE HEART ALONE CAN BE USED TO POWER A THOUSAND LOVE SPELLS!
HAGSLIST
DARLENE
BUT I'LL KEEP THIS METABOLISM FOR MYSELF!
Eh?
WHAT DO YOU WANT?
LOOK, YOU TOOK MY METABOLISM FAIR AND SQUARE... BUT I FIGURE YOU STILL OWE ME ONE THING!
THE RECIPE FOR THAT AMAZING CHEESE-BURGER!
Hmm... I GUESS YOU DESERVE IT! YOUR METABOLISM IS AMAZING! I ATE AN ENTIRE WEDDING CAKE FOR LUNCH!
THE SECRET IS FEEDING BACON TO THE COWS BEFORE... WAITAMINNIT--! I KNOW A DIVERSION WHEN I SEE ONE!!
WHO?!
21

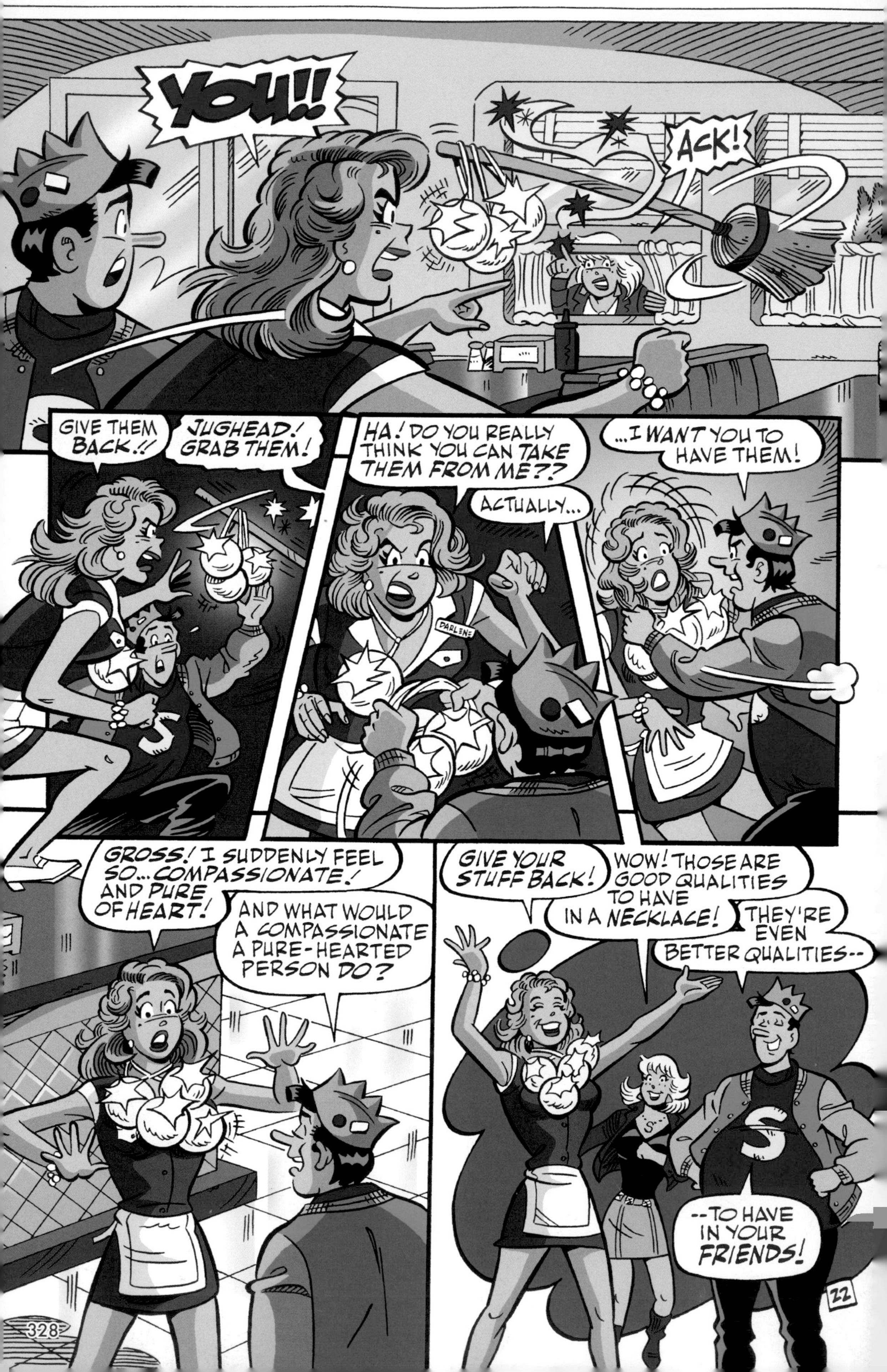

YOU!!
ACK!
GIVE THEM BACK.!!
JUGHEAD! GRAB THEM!
HA! DO YOU REALLY THINK YOU CAN TAKE THEM FROM ME??
ACTUALLY...
...I WANT YOU TO HAVE THEM!
DARLENE
GROSS! I SUDDENLY FEEL SO...COMPASSIONATE! AND PURE OF HEART!
AND WHAT WOULD A COMPASSIONATE A PURE-HEARTED PERSON DO?
GIVE YOUR STUFF BACK!
WOW! THOSE ARE GOOD QUALITIES TO HAVE IN A NECKLACE!
THEY'RE EVEN BETTER QUALITIES--
--TO HAVE IN YOUR FRIENDS!
22

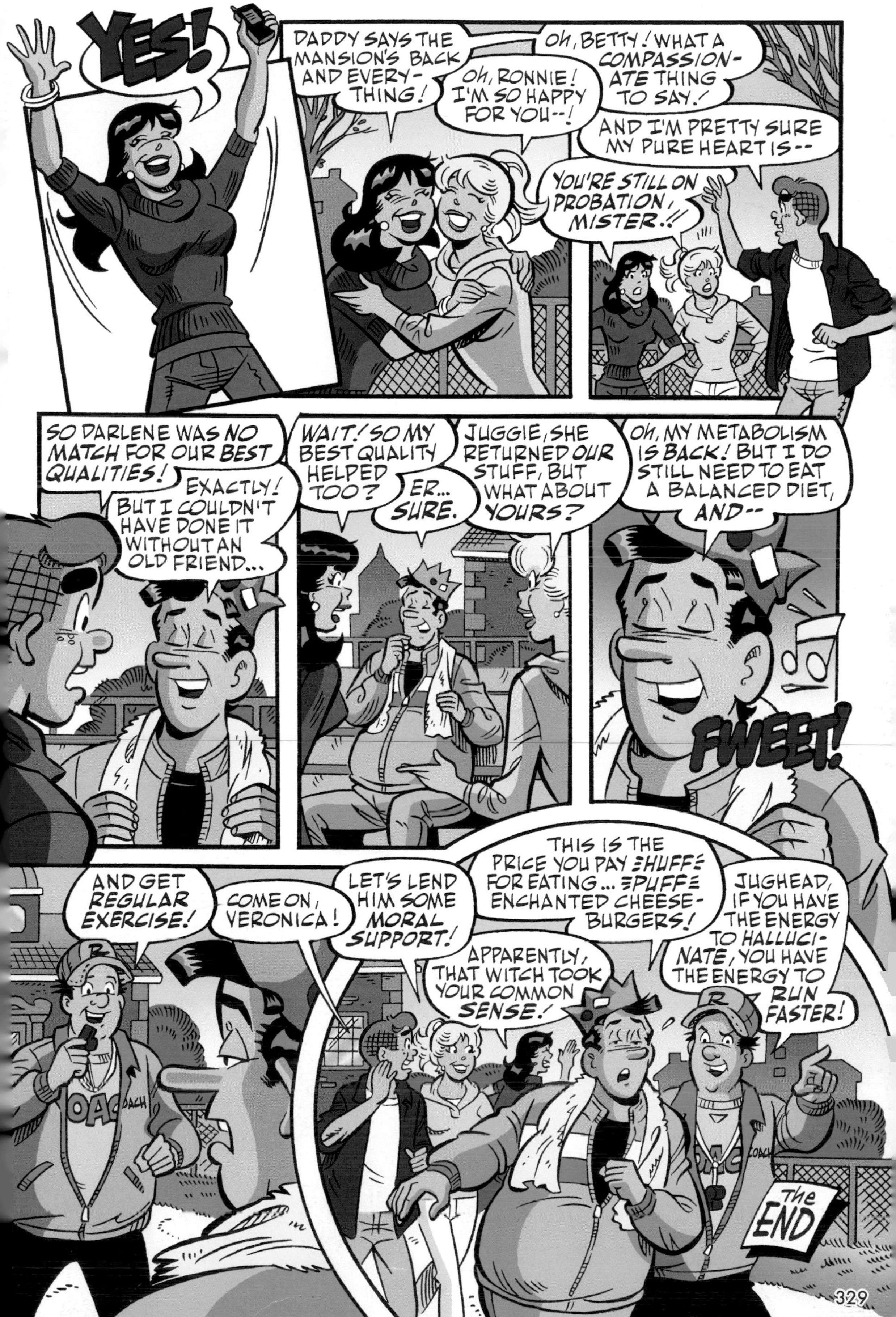
YES!
DADDY SAYS THE MANSION'S BACK AND EVERY-THING!
OH, RONNIE! I'M SO HAPPY FOR YOU--!
OH, BETTY! WHAT A COMPASSION-ATE THING TO SAY!
AND I'M PRETTY SURE MY PURE HEART IS--
YOU'RE STILL ON PROBATION, MISTER!!
SO DARLENE WAS NO MATCH FOR OUR BEST QUALITIES!
EXACTLY! BUT I COULDN'T HAVE DONE IT WITHOUT AN OLD FRIEND...
WAIT! SO MY BEST QUALITY HELPED TOO?
ER... SURE.
JUGGIE, SHE RETURNED OUR STUFF, BUT WHAT ABOUT YOURS?
OH, MY METABOLISM IS BACK! BUT I DO STILL NEED TO EAT A BALANCED DIET, AND--
FWEET!
AND GET REGULAR EXERCISE!
COME ON, VERONICA!
LET'S LEND HIM SOME MORAL SUPPORT!
THIS IS THE PRICE YOU PAY =HUFF= FOR EATING... =PUFF= ENCHANTED CHEESE-BURGERS!
APPARENTLY, THAT WITCH TOOK YOUR COMMON SENSE!
JUGHEAD, IF YOU HAVE THE ENERGY TO HALLUCI-NATE, YOU HAVE THE ENERGY TO RUN FASTER!
The END

THE GREAT SWITCHEROO
ARCHIE #636, 2012
BY TANIA DEL RIO, GISELE, RICH KOSLOWSKI, JACK MORELLI & DIGIKORE STUDIOS

"The Great Switcheroo", known affectionately amongst fans as "Reversedale," was the result of a brainstorming session where I tried to think of a way to do something new and unusual in the Archie universe. Once I had the idea to switch the genders of all the cast, inspiration and jokes came to me in droves! It was so much fun to imagine how Archina, Billy, Ronnie, Regina, and JJ would relate to their more traditional counterparts. With Gisele's amazing art bringing my wacky ideas to life, the result is a fun romp in Archie bizarro-land. It even features a cameo by one of my personal favorites: Sabrina the Teenage Witch!

—*Tania del Rio*
Writer & Artist,
Archie Comics

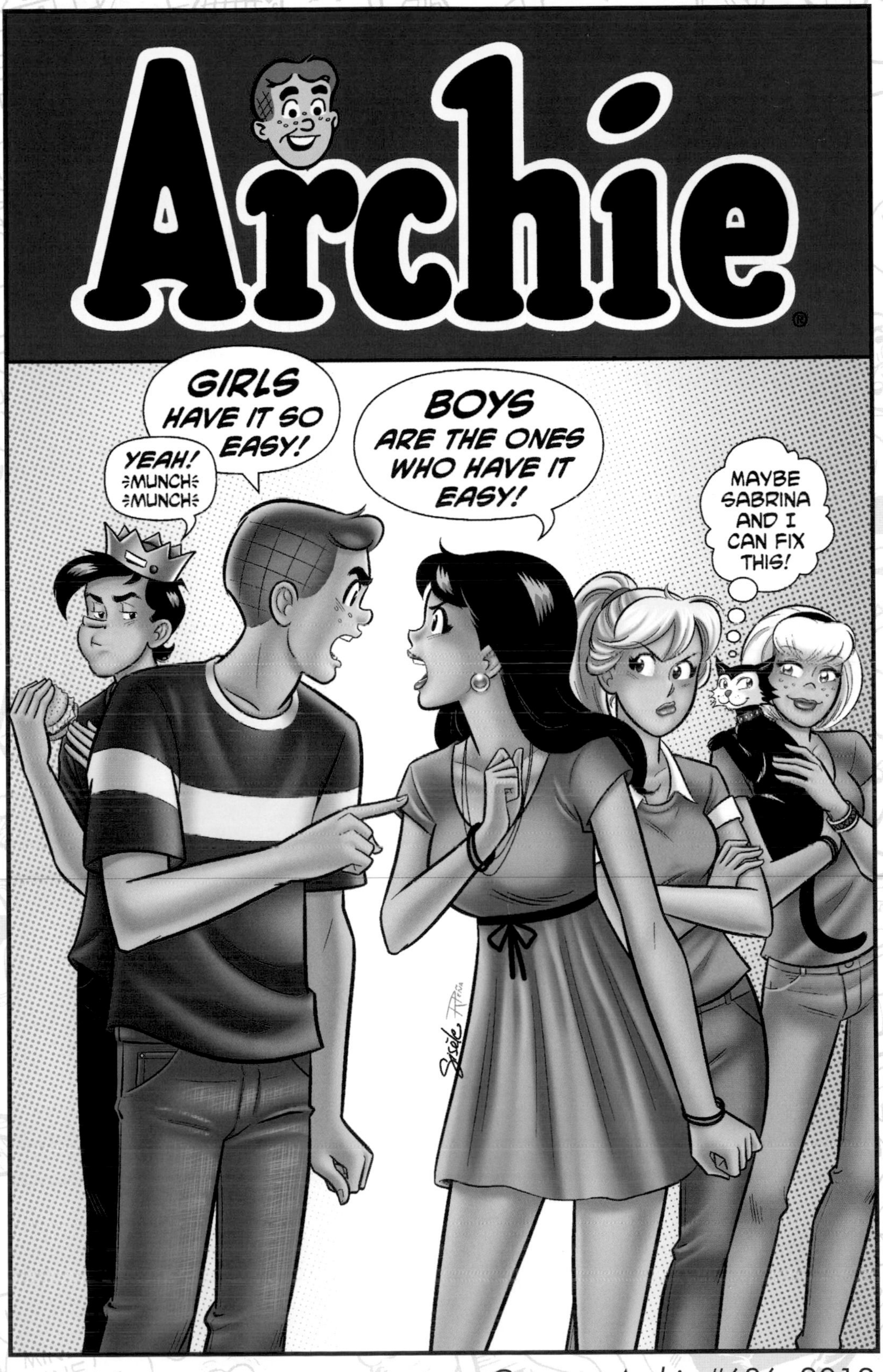
Archie
GIRLS HAVE IT SO EASY!
YEAH! MUNCH MUNCH
BOYS ARE THE ONES WHO HAVE IT EASY!
MAYBE SABRINA AND I CAN FIX THIS!

Cover to *Archie* #636, 2012
art by Gisele

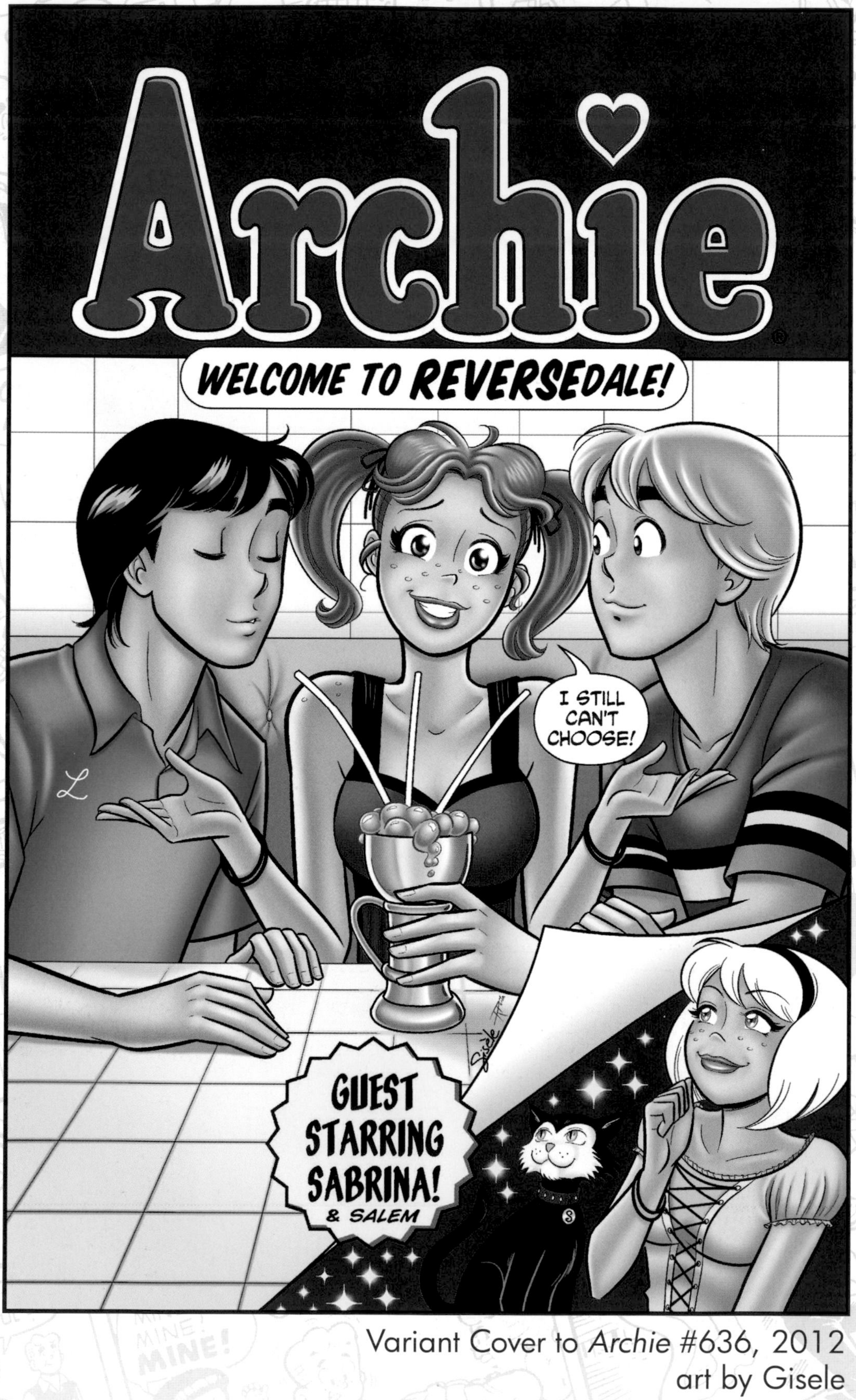
Archie
WELCOME TO REVERSEDALE!
I STILL CAN'T CHOOSE!
GUEST STARRING SABRINA!
& SALEM

Variant Cover to *Archie* #636, 2012
art by Gisele

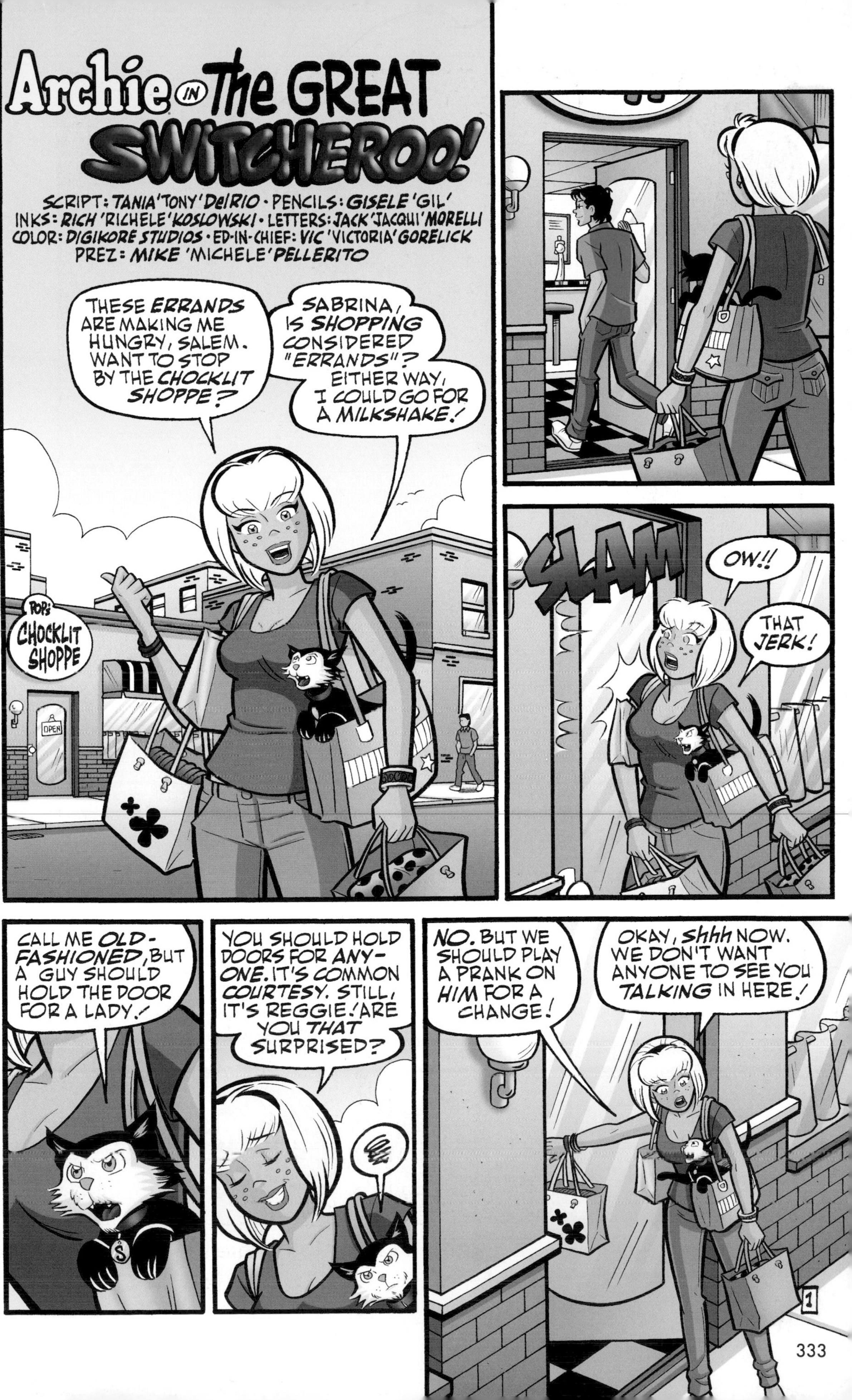
Archie IN The GREAT SWITCHEROO!
SCRIPT: TANIA 'TONY' DelRIO · PENCILS: GISELE 'GIL'
INKS: RICH 'RICHELE' KOSLOWSKI · LETTERS: JACK 'JACQUI' MORELLI
COLOR: DIGIKORE STUDIOS · ED-IN-CHIEF: VIC 'VICTORIA' GORELICK
PREZ: MIKE 'MICHELE' PELLERITO
THESE ERRANDS ARE MAKING ME HUNGRY, SALEM. WANT TO STOP BY THE CHOCKLIT SHOPPE?
SABRINA, IS SHOPPING CONSIDERED "ERRANDS"? EITHER WAY, I COULD GO FOR A MILKSHAKE!
POP'S CHOCKLIT SHOPPE
OPEN
SLAM
OW!!
THAT JERK!
CALL ME OLD-FASHIONED, BUT A GUY SHOULD HOLD THE DOOR FOR A LADY!
YOU SHOULD HOLD DOORS FOR ANYONE. IT'S COMMON COURTESY. STILL, IT'S REGGIE! ARE YOU THAT SURPRISED?
NO. BUT WE SHOULD PLAY A PRANK ON HIM FOR A CHANGE!
OKAY, shhh NOW. WE DON'T WANT ANYONE TO SEE YOU TALKING IN HERE!
1

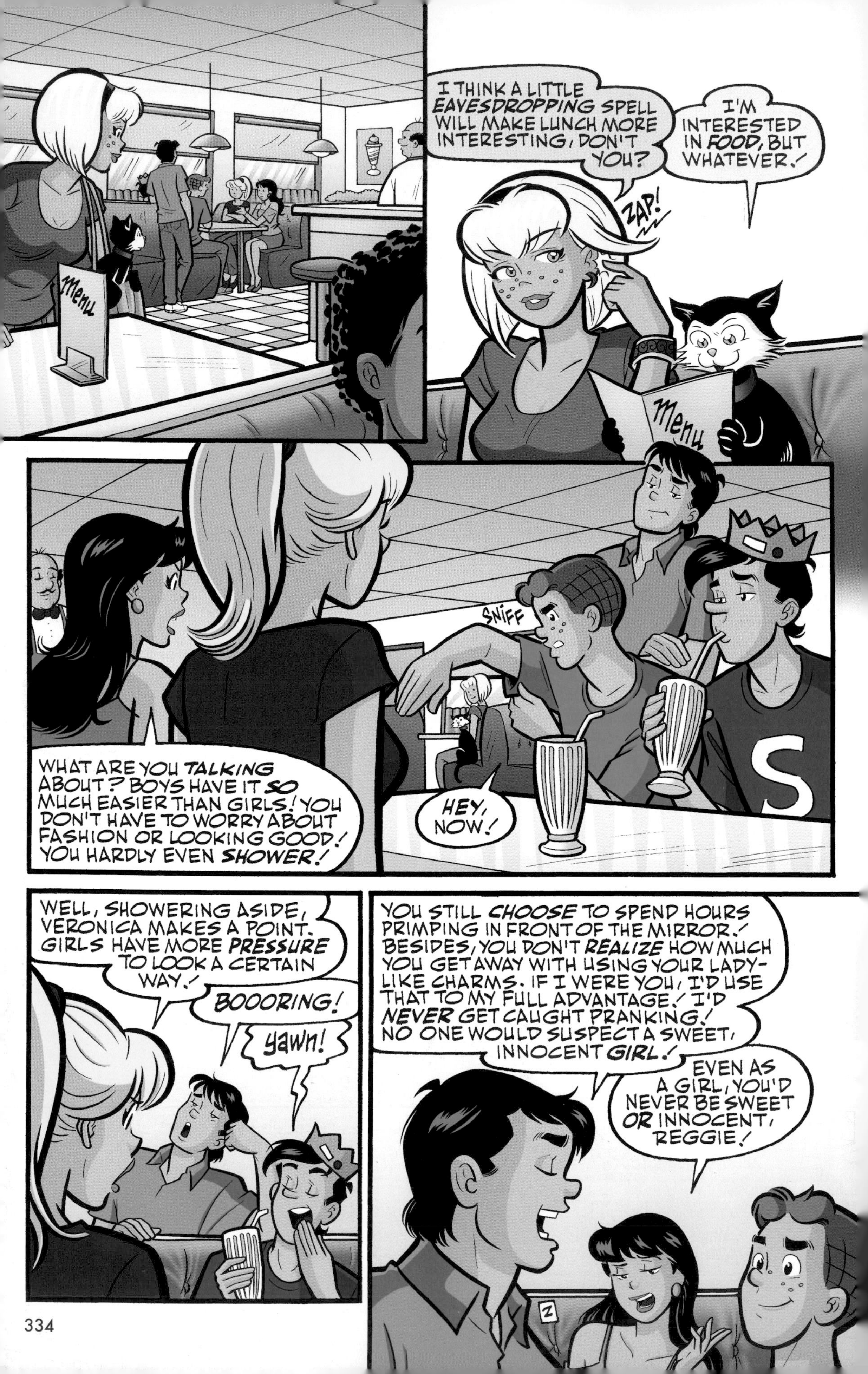
Menu
I THINK A LITTLE EAVESDROPPING SPELL WILL MAKE LUNCH MORE INTERESTING, DON'T YOU?
I'M INTERESTED IN FOOD, BUT WHATEVER.!
ZAP!
Menu
SNIFF
WHAT ARE YOU TALKING ABOUT? BOYS HAVE IT SO MUCH EASIER THAN GIRLS! YOU DON'T HAVE TO WORRY ABOUT FASHION OR LOOKING GOOD! YOU HARDLY EVEN SHOWER!
HEY, NOW!
S
WELL, SHOWERING ASIDE, VERONICA MAKES A POINT. GIRLS HAVE MORE PRESSURE TO LOOK A CERTAIN WAY.!
BOOORING!
yawn!
YOU STILL CHOOSE TO SPEND HOURS PRIMPING IN FRONT OF THE MIRROR.! BESIDES, YOU DON'T REALIZE HOW MUCH YOU GET AWAY WITH USING YOUR LADY-LIKE CHARMS. IF I WERE YOU, I'D USE THAT TO MY FULL ADVANTAGE.! I'D NEVER GET CAUGHT PRANKING.! NO ONE WOULD SUSPECT A SWEET, INNOCENT GIRL.!
EVEN AS A GIRL, YOU'D NEVER BE SWEET OR INNOCENT, REGGIE.!

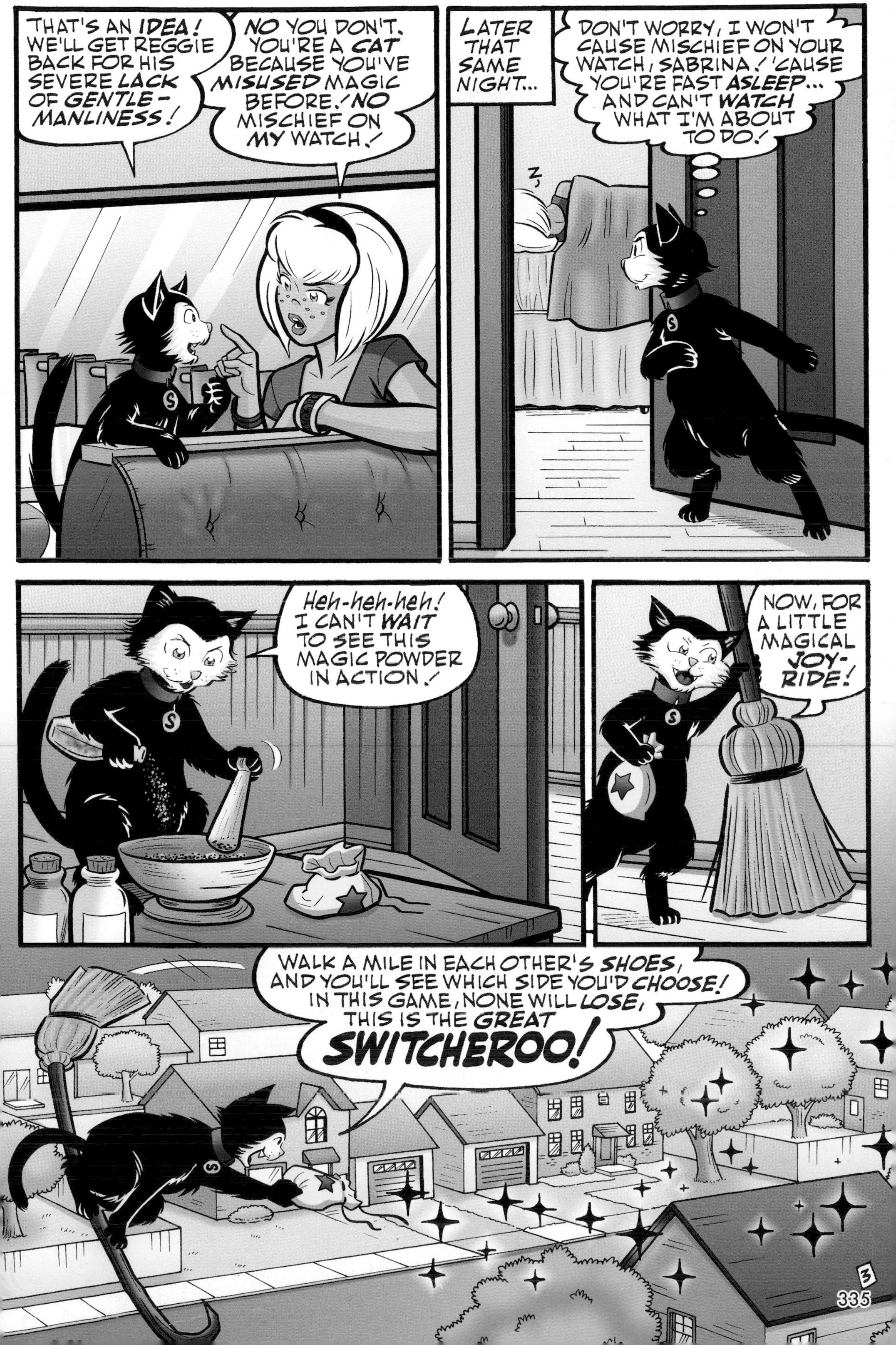
THAT'S AN IDEA! WE'LL GET REGGIE BACK FOR HIS SEVERE LACK OF GENTLE-MANLINESS!
NO YOU DON'T. YOU'RE A CAT BECAUSE YOU'VE MISUSED MAGIC BEFORE! NO MISCHIEF ON MY WATCH!
LATER THAT SAME NIGHT...
DON'T WORRY, I WON'T CAUSE MISCHIEF ON YOUR WATCH, SABRINA! 'CAUSE YOU'RE FAST ASLEEP... AND CAN'T WATCH WHAT I'M ABOUT TO DO!
Z
Heh-heh-heh! I CAN'T WAIT TO SEE THIS MAGIC POWDER IN ACTION!
NOW, FOR A LITTLE MAGICAL JOY-RIDE!
WALK A MILE IN EACH OTHER'S SHOES, AND YOU'LL SEE WHICH SIDE YOU'D CHOOSE! IN THIS GAME, NONE WILL LOSE, THIS IS THE GREAT SWITCHEROO!
3

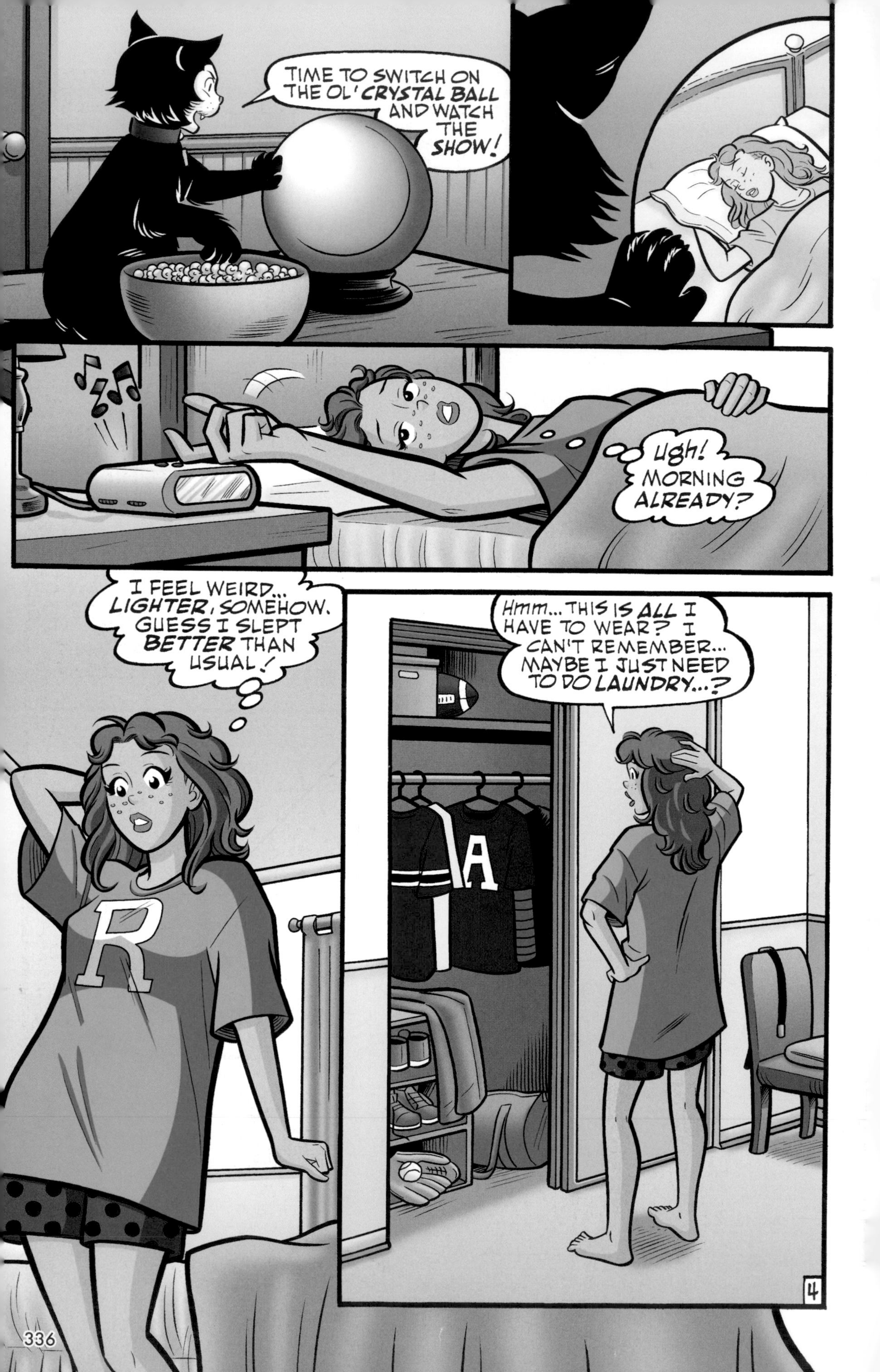
TIME TO SWITCH ON THE OL' CRYSTAL BALL AND WATCH THE SHOW!
Ugh! MORNING ALREADY?
I FEEL WEIRD... LIGHTER, SOMEHOW. GUESS I SLEPT BETTER THAN USUAL!
Hmm... THIS IS ALL I HAVE TO WEAR? I CAN'T REMEMBER... MAYBE I JUST NEED TO DO LAUNDRY...?
4

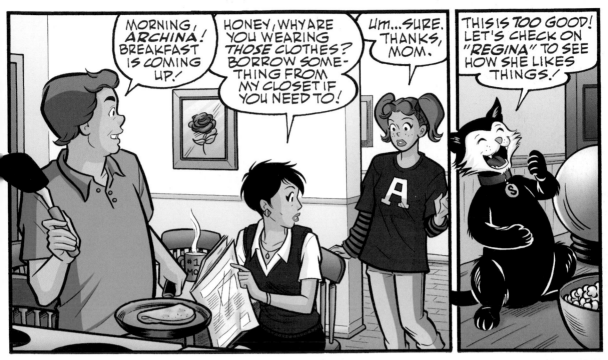

MORNING, *ARCHINA!* BREAKFAST IS COMING UP!

HONEY, WHY ARE YOU WEARING *THOSE* CLOTHES? BORROW SOMETHING FROM MY CLOSET IF YOU NEED TO!

Um... SURE. THANKS, MOM.

THIS IS *TOO GOOD!* LET'S CHECK ON *"REGINA"* TO SEE HOW SHE LIKES THINGS!

*Hmm...*WHAT *PRANKS* FOR TODAY? BEING THE MOST BEAUTIFUL GIRL IN SCHOOL JUST MAKES IT *THAT* MUCH EASIER FOR ME TO PULL THE WOOL OVER SOMEONE'S EYES! TODAY, I'M THINKING *FIREWORKS!*

Hmph! REGGIE JUST *DOESN'T* LEARN!

NOW... *WHERE* WERE WE?

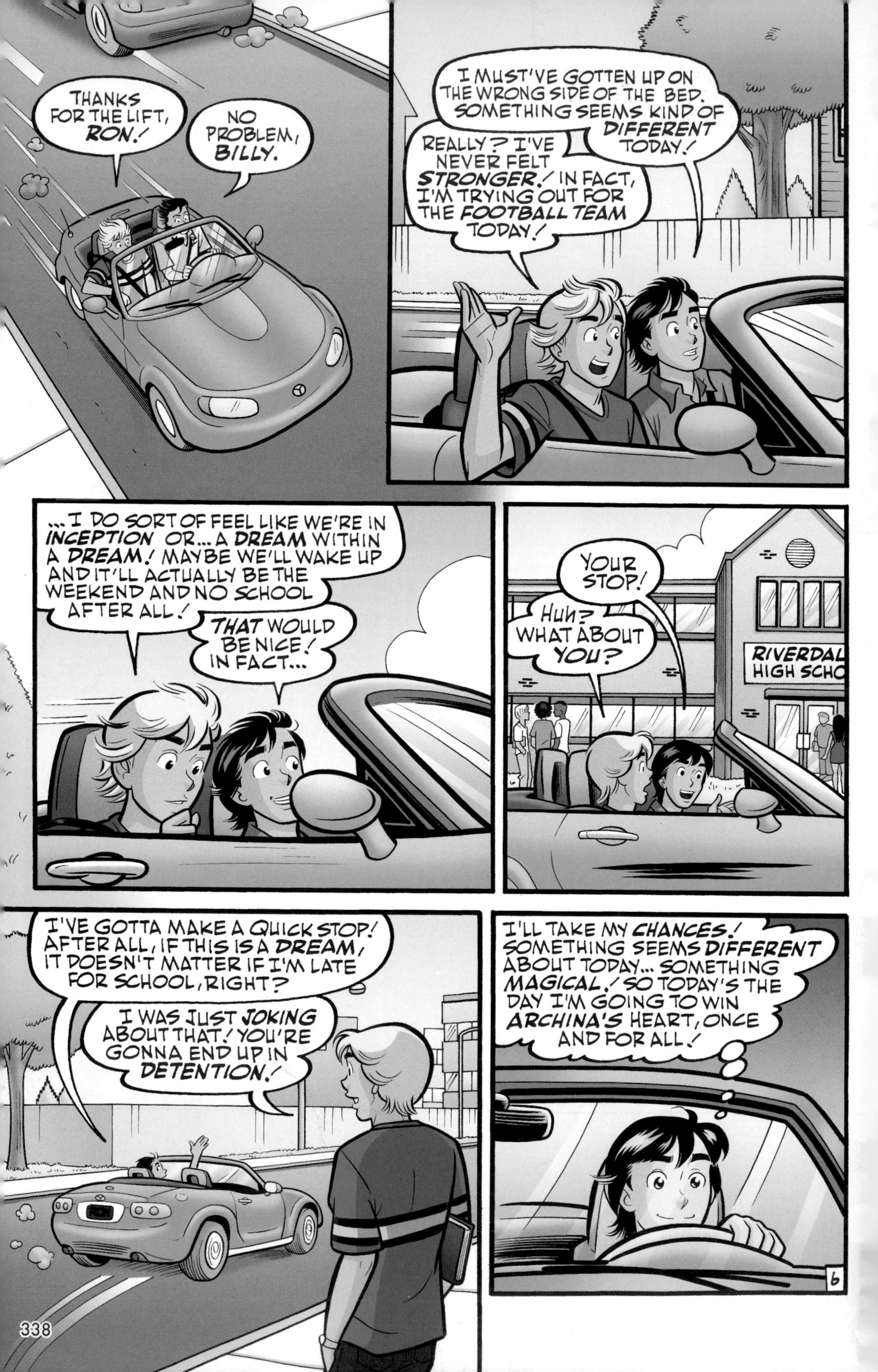

THANKS FOR THE LIFT, RON.!
NO PROBLEM, BILLY.
I MUST'VE GOTTEN UP ON THE WRONG SIDE OF THE BED. SOMETHING SEEMS KIND OF DIFFERENT TODAY!
REALLY? I'VE NEVER FELT STRONGER! IN FACT, I'M TRYING OUT FOR THE FOOTBALL TEAM TODAY!
...I DO SORT OF FEEL LIKE WE'RE IN INCEPTION OR... A DREAM WITHIN A DREAM! MAYBE WE'LL WAKE UP AND IT'LL ACTUALLY BE THE WEEKEND AND NO SCHOOL AFTER ALL!
THAT WOULD BE NICE! IN FACT...
YOUR STOP!
HUH? WHAT ABOUT YOU?
RIVERDAL
HIGH SCHO
I'VE GOTTA MAKE A QUICK STOP! AFTER ALL, IF THIS IS A DREAM, IT DOESN'T MATTER IF I'M LATE FOR SCHOOL, RIGHT?
I WAS JUST JOKING ABOUT THAT! YOU'RE GONNA END UP IN DETENTION!
RON
I'LL TAKE MY CHANCES! SOMETHING SEEMS DIFFERENT ABOUT TODAY... SOMETHING MAGICAL! SO TODAY'S THE DAY I'M GOING TO WIN ARCHINA'S HEART, ONCE AND FOR ALL!
6

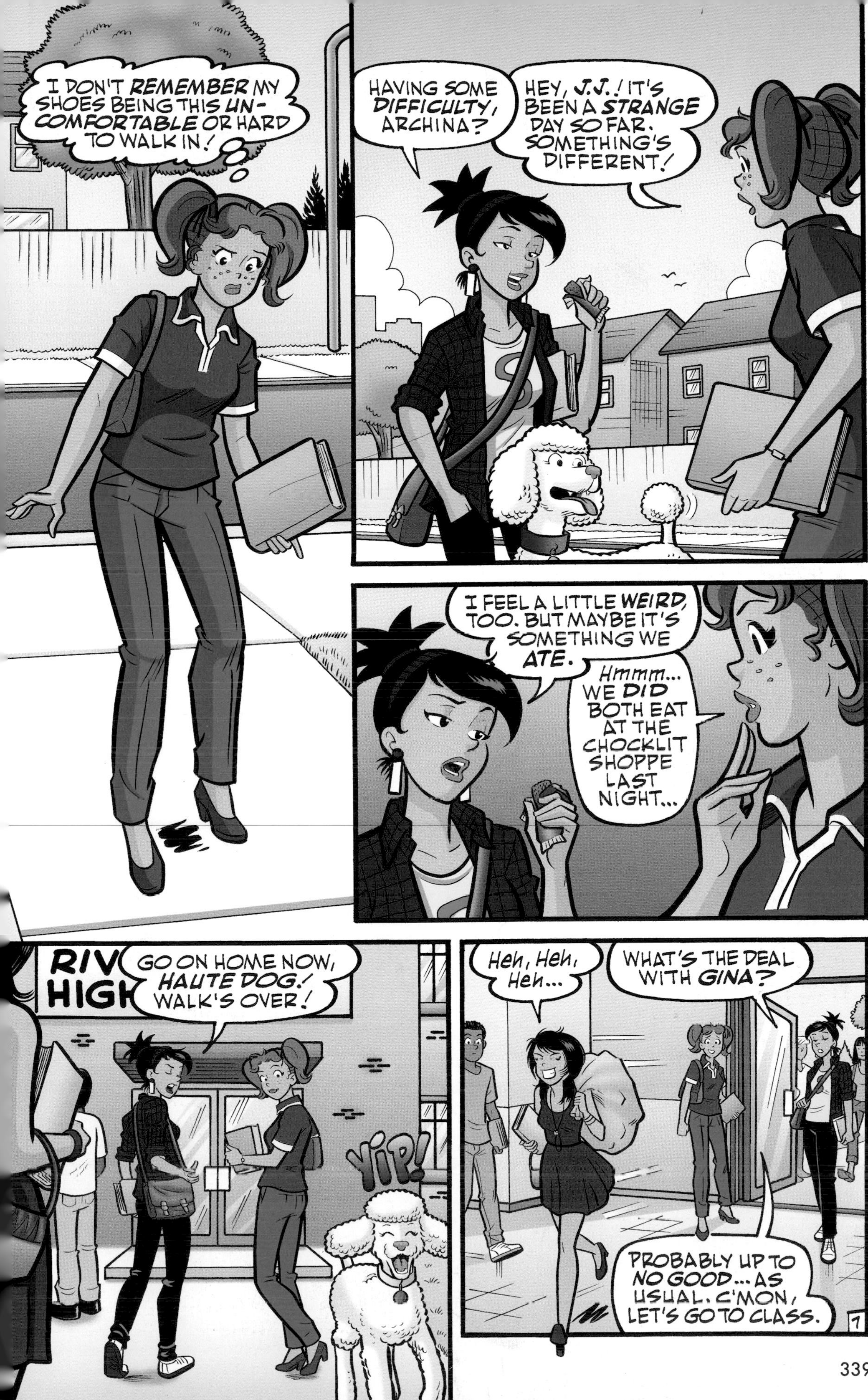
I DON'T REMEMBER MY SHOES BEING THIS UN-COMFORTABLE OR HARD TO WALK IN!
HAVING SOME DIFFICULTY, ARCHINA?
HEY, J.J.! IT'S BEEN A STRANGE DAY SO FAR. SOMETHING'S DIFFERENT!
I FEEL A LITTLE WEIRD, TOO. BUT MAYBE IT'S SOMETHING WE ATE.
Hmmm... WE DID BOTH EAT AT THE CHOCKLIT SHOPPE LAST NIGHT...
GO ON HOME NOW, HAUTE DOG! WALK'S OVER!
YIP!
Heh, Heh, Heh...
WHAT'S THE DEAL WITH GINA?
PROBABLY UP TO NO GOOD... AS USUAL. C'MON, LET'S GO TO CLASS.
7

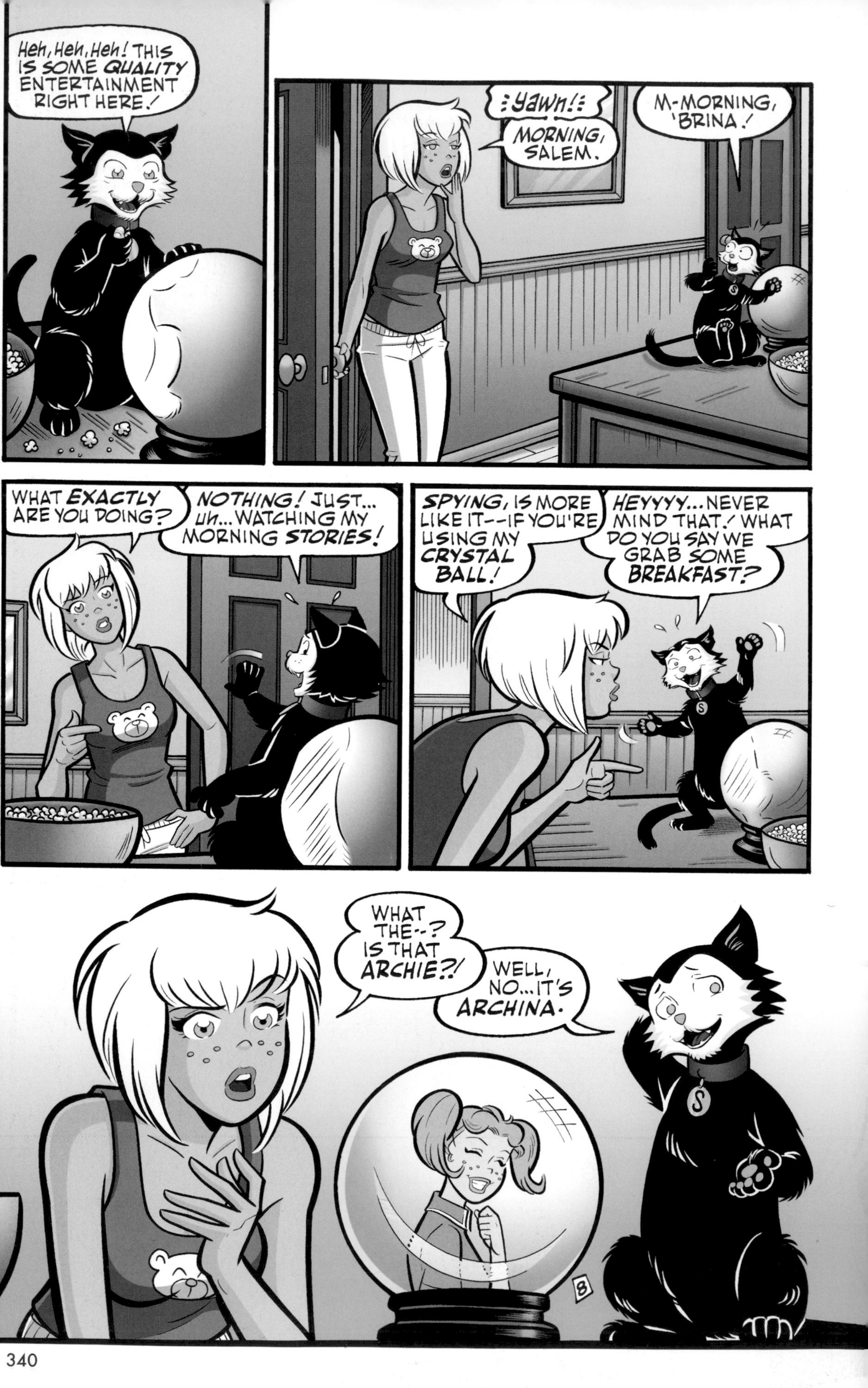
Heh, Heh, Heh! THIS IS SOME QUALITY ENTERTAINMENT RIGHT HERE!
:YAWN!:
MORNING, SALEM.
M-MORNING, 'BRINA!
WHAT EXACTLY ARE YOU DOING?
NOTHING! JUST... UH... WATCHING MY MORNING STORIES!
SPYING, IS MORE LIKE IT--IF YOU'RE USING MY CRYSTAL BALL!
HEYYYY... NEVER MIND THAT! WHAT DO YOU SAY WE GRAB SOME BREAKFAST?
WHAT THE--? IS THAT ARCHIE?!
WELL, NO... IT'S ARCHINA.
8

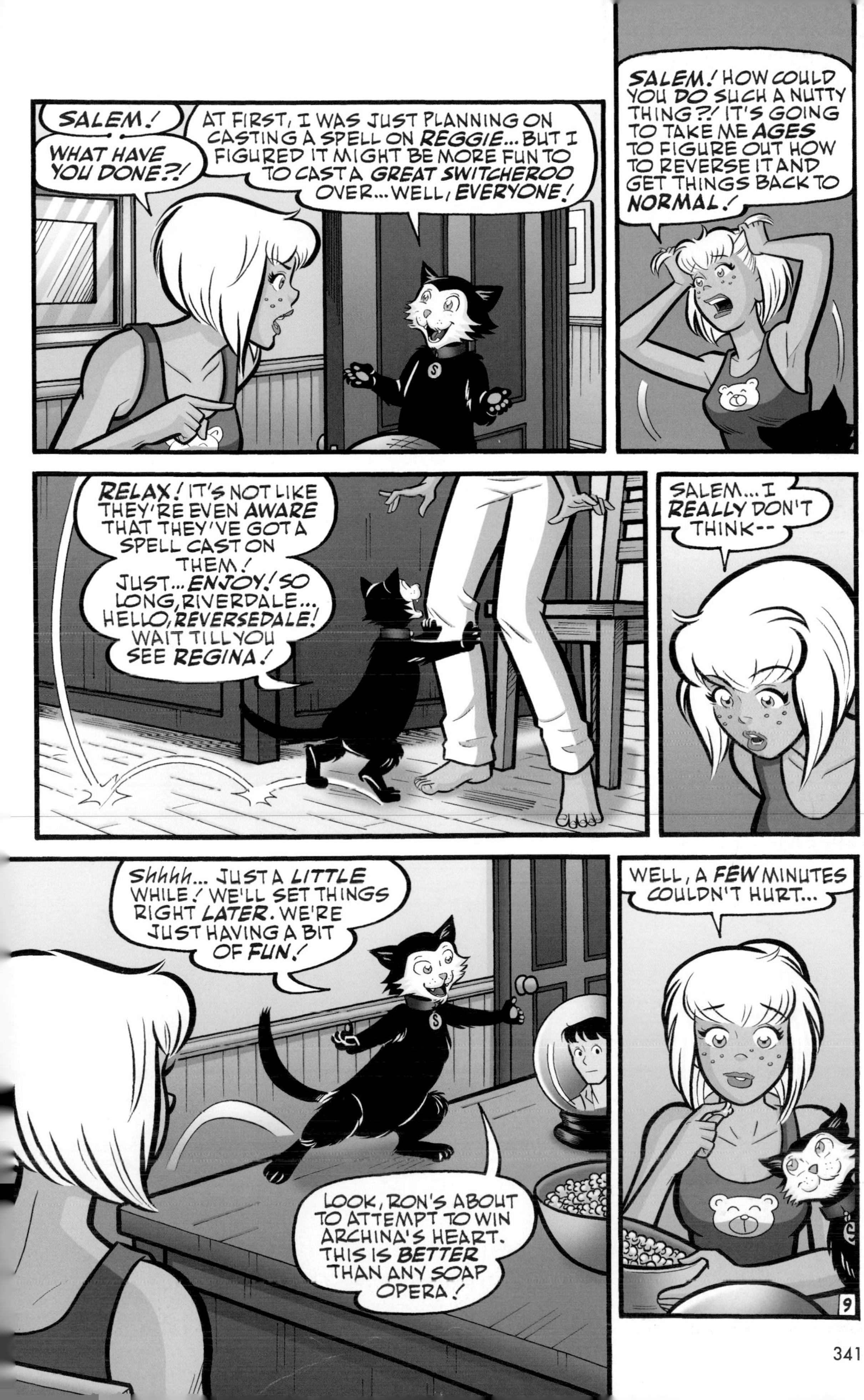
SALEM!
WHAT HAVE YOU DONE?!
AT FIRST, I WAS JUST PLANNING ON CASTING A SPELL ON REGGIE... BUT I FIGURED IT MIGHT BE MORE FUN TO TO CAST A GREAT SWITCHEROO OVER... WELL, EVERYONE!
SALEM! HOW COULD YOU DO SUCH A NUTTY THING?! IT'S GOING TO TAKE ME AGES TO FIGURE OUT HOW TO REVERSE IT AND GET THINGS BACK TO NORMAL!
RELAX! IT'S NOT LIKE THEY'RE EVEN AWARE THAT THEY'VE GOT A SPELL CAST ON THEM! JUST... ENJOY! SO LONG, RIVERDALE... HELLO, REVERSEDALE! WAIT TILL YOU SEE REGINA!
SALEM... I REALLY DON'T THINK--
Shhhh... JUST A LITTLE WHILE! WE'LL SET THINGS RIGHT LATER. WE'RE JUST HAVING A BIT OF FUN!
LOOK, RON'S ABOUT TO ATTEMPT TO WIN ARCHINA'S HEART. THIS IS BETTER THAN ANY SOAP OPERA!
WELL, A FEW MINUTES COULDN'T HURT...
9

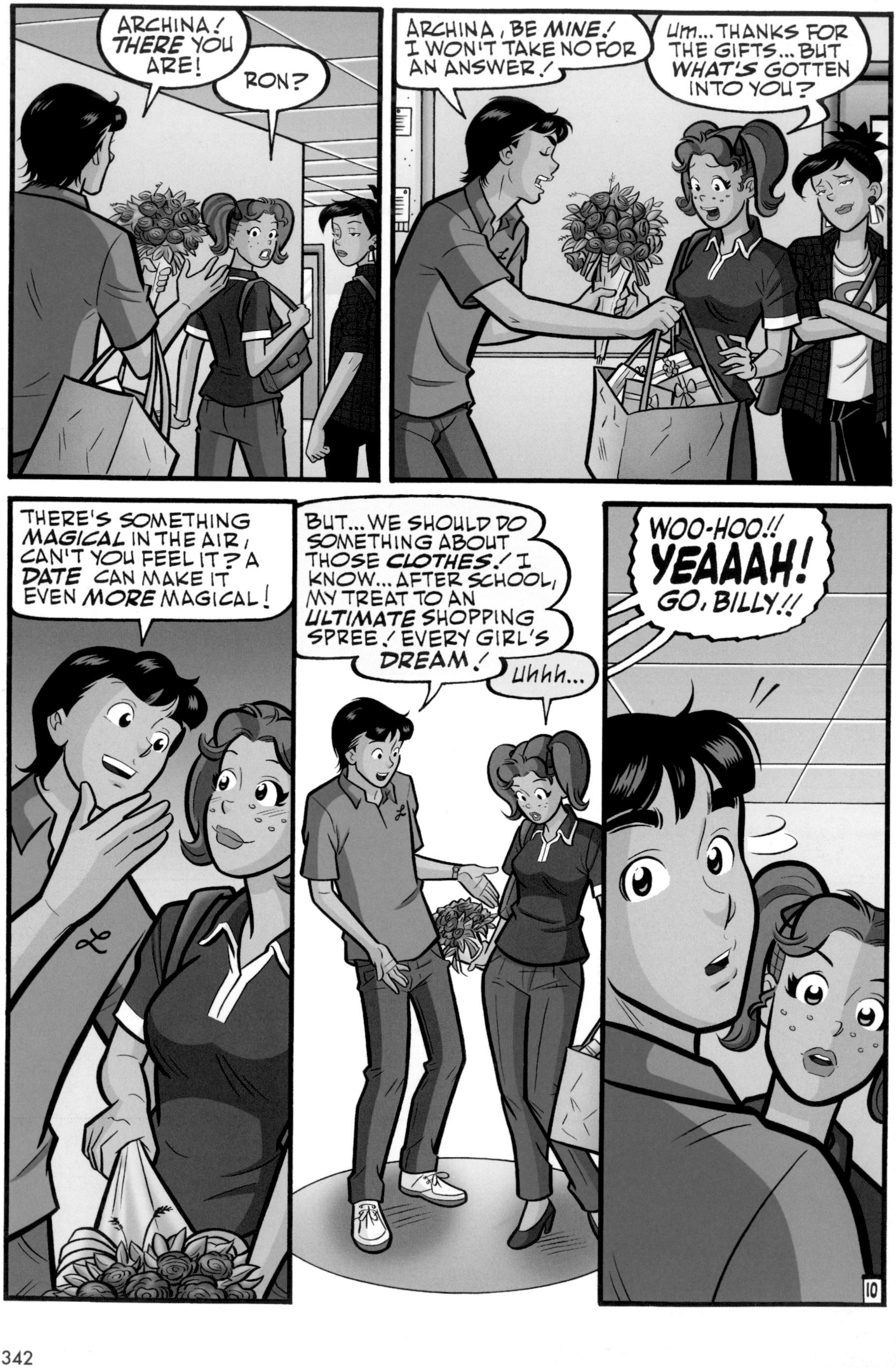
ARCHINA! THERE YOU ARE!
RON?
ARCHINA, BE MINE! I WON'T TAKE NO FOR AN ANSWER!
Um... THANKS FOR THE GIFTS... BUT WHAT'S GOTTEN INTO YOU?
THERE'S SOMETHING MAGICAL IN THE AIR, CAN'T YOU FEEL IT? A DATE CAN MAKE IT EVEN MORE MAGICAL!
BUT... WE SHOULD DO SOMETHING ABOUT THOSE CLOTHES! I KNOW... AFTER SCHOOL, MY TREAT TO AN ULTIMATE SHOPPING SPREE! EVERY GIRL'S DREAM!
Uhhh...
WOO-HOO!! YEAAAH! GO, BILLY!!
10

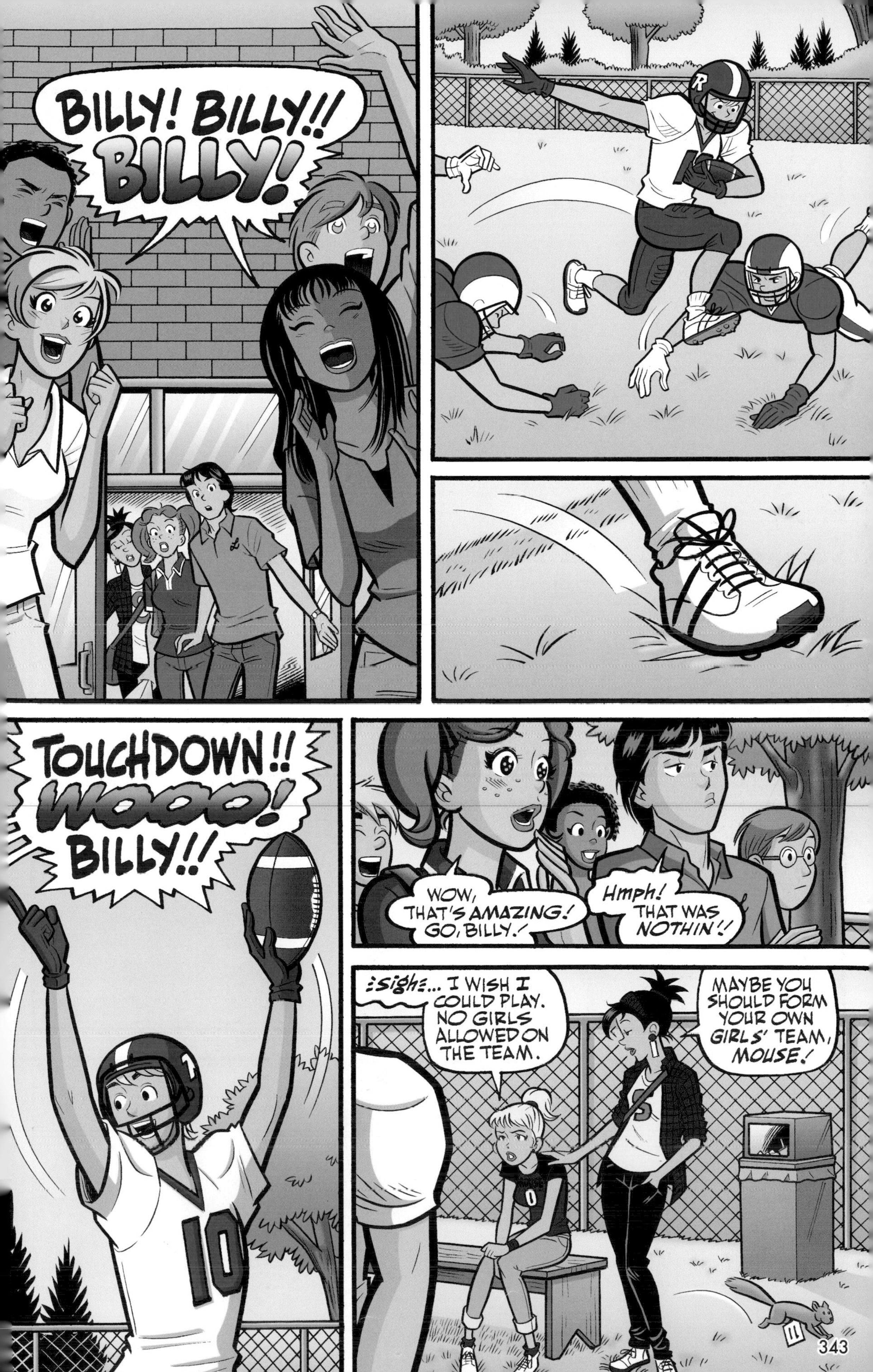
BILLY! BILLY!! BILLY!
TOUCHDOWN!! WOOO! BILLY!!
WOW, THAT'S AMAZING! GO, BILLY!
Hmph! THAT WAS NOTHIN'!
:sigh:... I WISH I COULD PLAY. NO GIRLS ALLOWED ON THE TEAM.
MAYBE YOU SHOULD FORM YOUR OWN GIRLS' TEAM, MOUSE!

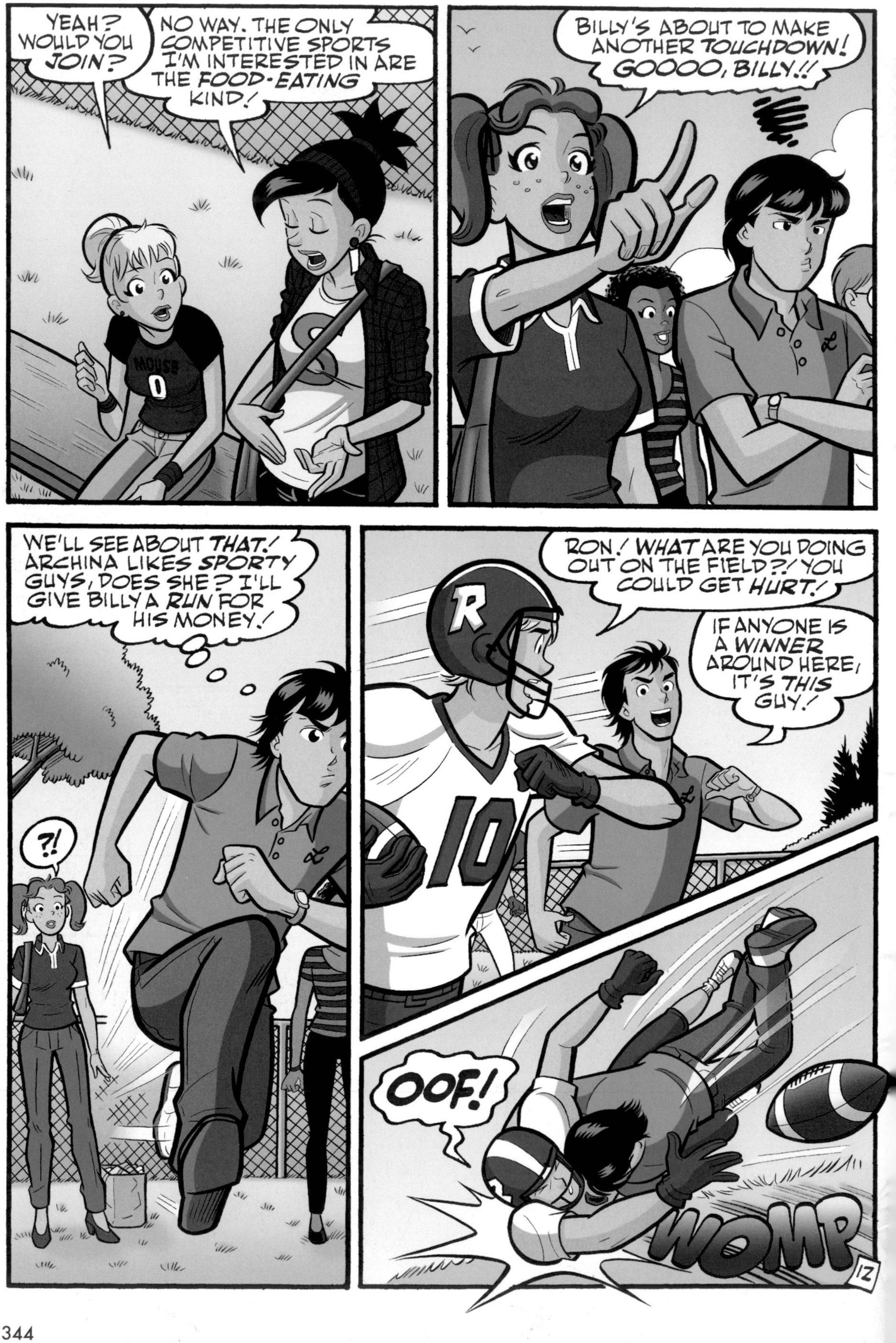

YEAH? WOULD YOU JOIN?
NO WAY. THE ONLY COMPETITIVE SPORTS I'M INTERESTED IN ARE THE FOOD-EATING KIND!
BILLY'S ABOUT TO MAKE ANOTHER TOUCHDOWN! GOOOO, BILLY!!
WE'LL SEE ABOUT THAT! ARCHINA LIKES SPORTY GUYS, DOES SHE? I'LL GIVE BILLY A RUN FOR HIS MONEY!
?!
RON! WHAT ARE YOU DOING OUT ON THE FIELD?! YOU COULD GET HURT!
IF ANYONE IS A WINNER AROUND HERE, IT'S THIS GUY!
OOF!
WOMP
12

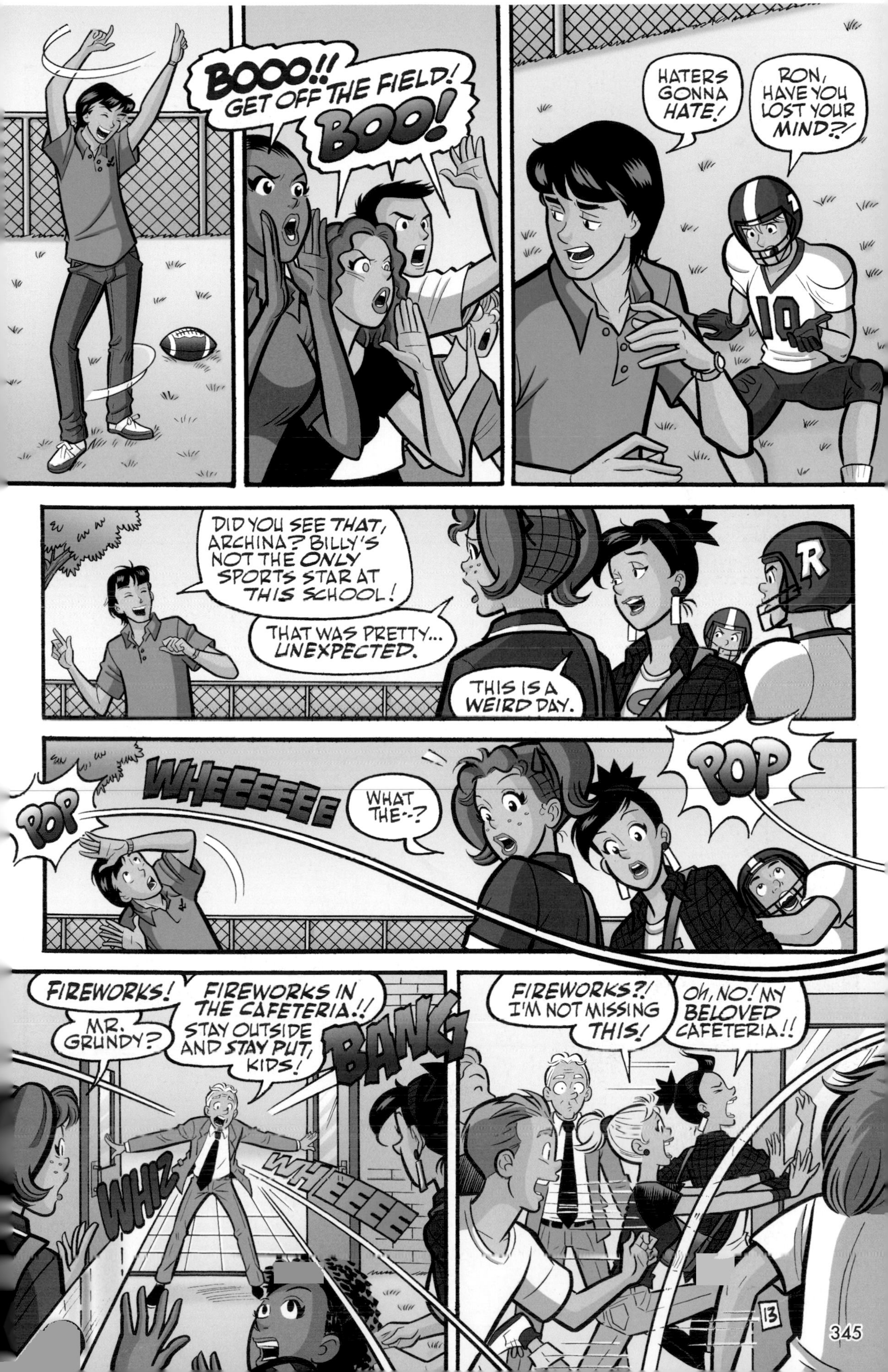
BOOO!!
GET OFF THE FIELD!
BOO!
HATERS GONNA HATE!
RON, HAVE YOU LOST YOUR MIND?!
DID YOU SEE THAT, ARCHINA? BILLY'S NOT THE ONLY SPORTS STAR AT THIS SCHOOL!
THAT WAS PRETTY... UNEXPECTED.
THIS IS A WEIRD DAY.
POP
WHEEEEEEE
WHAT THE--?
POP
FIREWORKS!
MR. GRUNDY?
FIREWORKS IN THE CAFETERIA!!
STAY OUTSIDE AND STAY PUT, KIDS!
BANG
WHIZ
WHEEEEE
FIREWORKS?! I'M NOT MISSING THIS!
OH, NO! MY BELOVED CAFETERIA!!
13

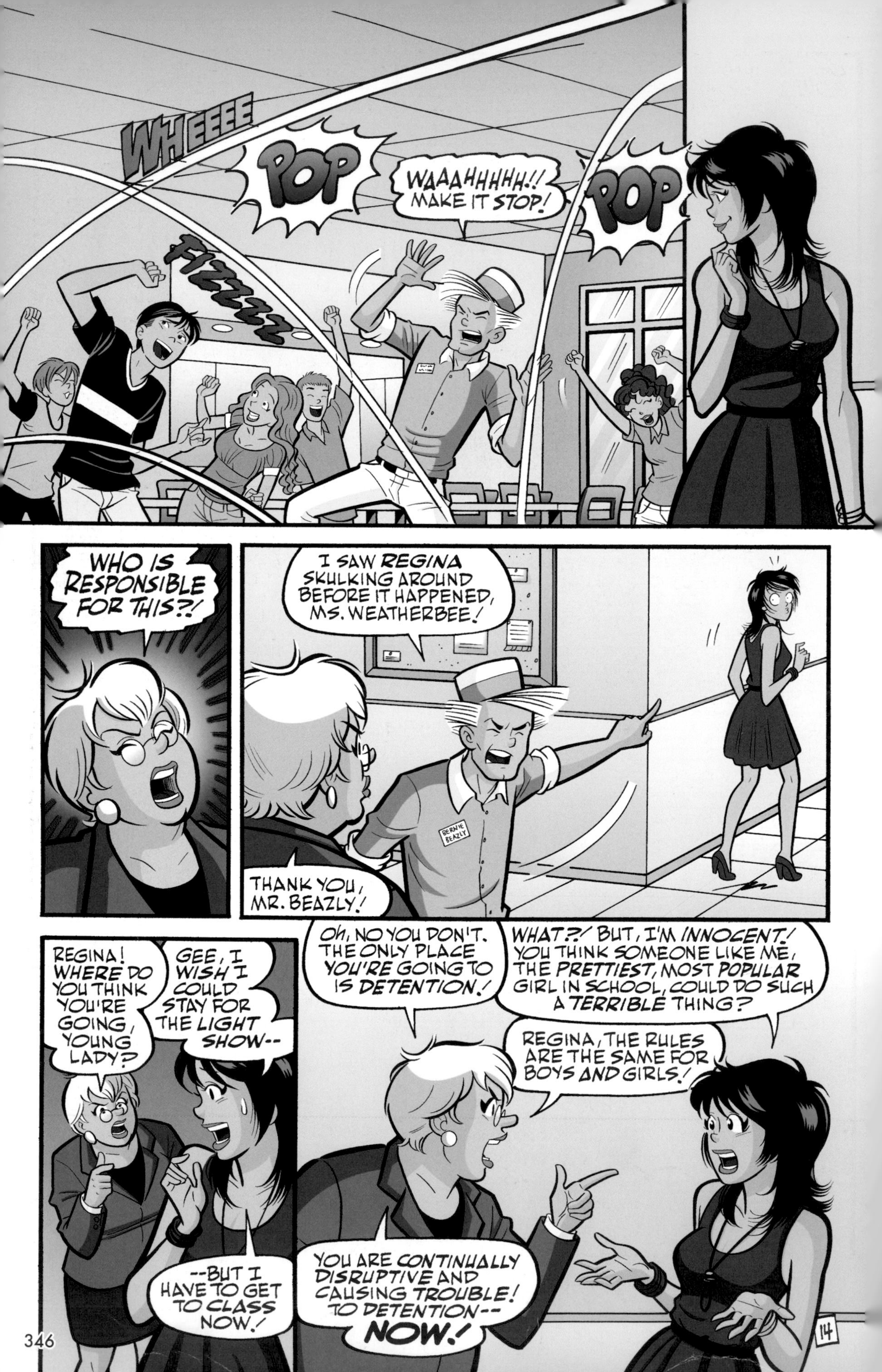
WHEEEE
POP
WAAAHHHHH!! MAKE IT STOP!
POP
FIZZZZZ
WHO IS RESPONSIBLE FOR THIS?!
I SAW REGINA SKULKING AROUND BEFORE IT HAPPENED, MS. WEATHERBEE!
BERNIE BEAZLY
THANK YOU, MR. BEAZLY!
REGINA! WHERE DO YOU THINK YOU'RE GOING, YOUNG LADY?
GEE, I WISH I COULD STAY FOR THE LIGHT SHOW--
--BUT I HAVE TO GET TO CLASS NOW!
OH, NO YOU DON'T. THE ONLY PLACE YOU'RE GOING TO IS DETENTION!
WHAT?! BUT, I'M INNOCENT! YOU THINK SOMEONE LIKE ME, THE PRETTIEST, MOST POPULAR GIRL IN SCHOOL, COULD DO SUCH A TERRIBLE THING?
REGINA, THE RULES ARE THE SAME FOR BOYS AND GIRLS!
YOU ARE CONTINUALLY DISRUPTIVE AND CAUSING TROUBLE! TO DETENTION-- NOW!
14

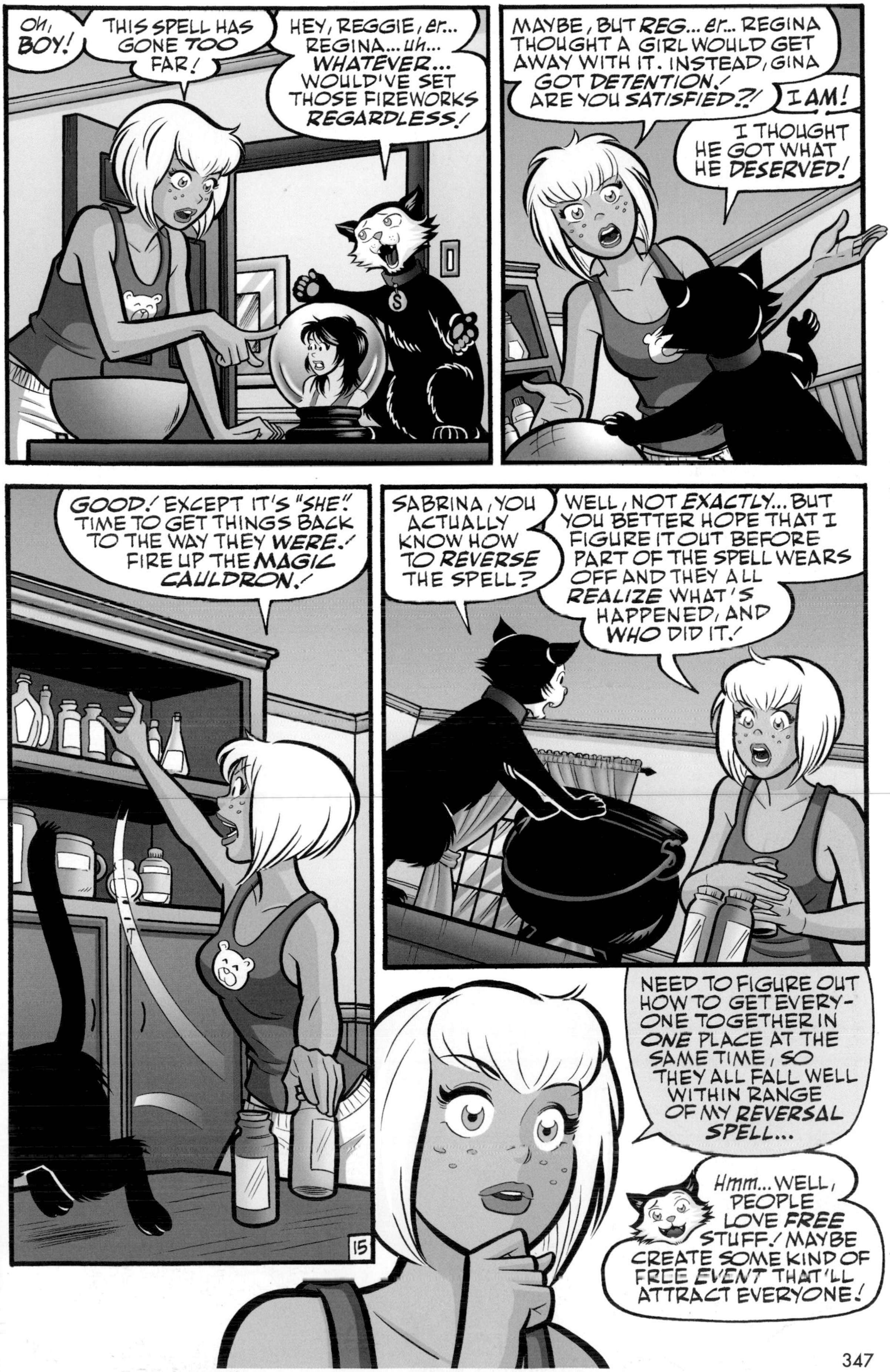
Oh, BOY!
THIS SPELL HAS GONE TOO FAR!
HEY, REGGIE, er... REGINA... uh... WHATEVER... WOULD'VE SET THOSE FIREWORKS REGARDLESS!
MAYBE, BUT REG... er... REGINA THOUGHT A GIRL WOULD GET AWAY WITH IT. INSTEAD, GINA GOT DETENTION! ARE YOU SATISFIED?!
I AM!
I THOUGHT HE GOT WHAT HE DESERVED!
GOOD! EXCEPT IT'S "SHE." TIME TO GET THINGS BACK TO THE WAY THEY WERE! FIRE UP THE MAGIC CAULDRON!
15
SABRINA, YOU ACTUALLY KNOW HOW TO REVERSE THE SPELL?
WELL, NOT EXACTLY... BUT YOU BETTER HOPE THAT I FIGURE IT OUT BEFORE PART OF THE SPELL WEARS OFF AND THEY ALL REALIZE WHAT'S HAPPENED, AND WHO DID IT!
NEED TO FIGURE OUT HOW TO GET EVERY-ONE TOGETHER IN ONE PLACE AT THE SAME TIME, SO THEY ALL FALL WELL WITHIN RANGE OF MY REVERSAL SPELL...
Hmm... WELL, PEOPLE LOVE FREE STUFF! MAYBE CREATE SOME KIND OF FREE EVENT THAT'LL ATTRACT EVERYONE!

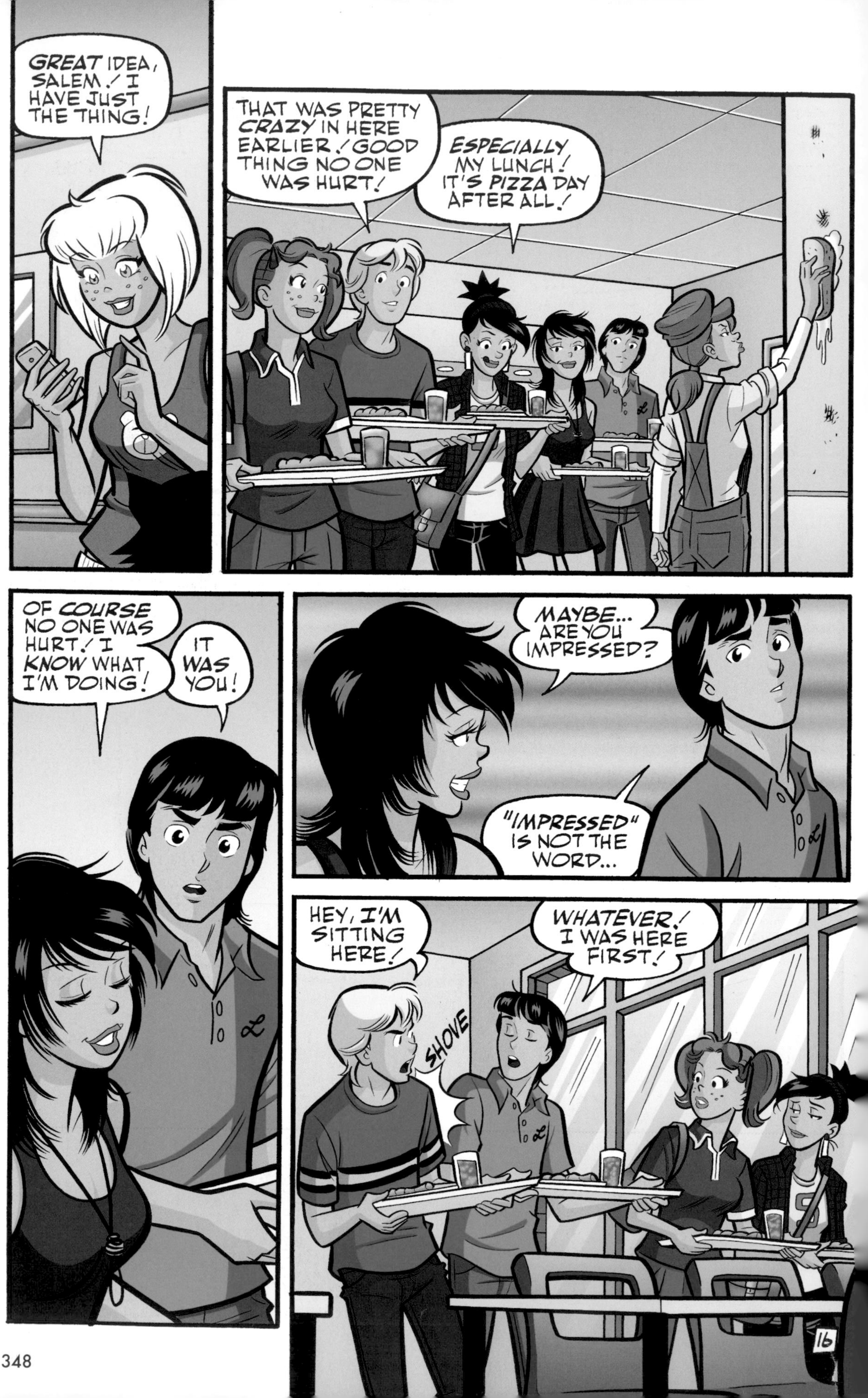
GREAT IDEA, SALEM! I HAVE JUST THE THING!
THAT WAS PRETTY CRAZY IN HERE EARLIER! GOOD THING NO ONE WAS HURT!
ESPECIALLY MY LUNCH! IT'S PIZZA DAY AFTER ALL!
OF COURSE NO ONE WAS HURT! I KNOW WHAT I'M DOING!
IT WAS YOU!
MAYBE... ARE YOU IMPRESSED?
"IMPRESSED" IS NOT THE WORD...
HEY, I'M SITTING HERE!
WHATEVER! I WAS HERE FIRST!
SHOVE
16

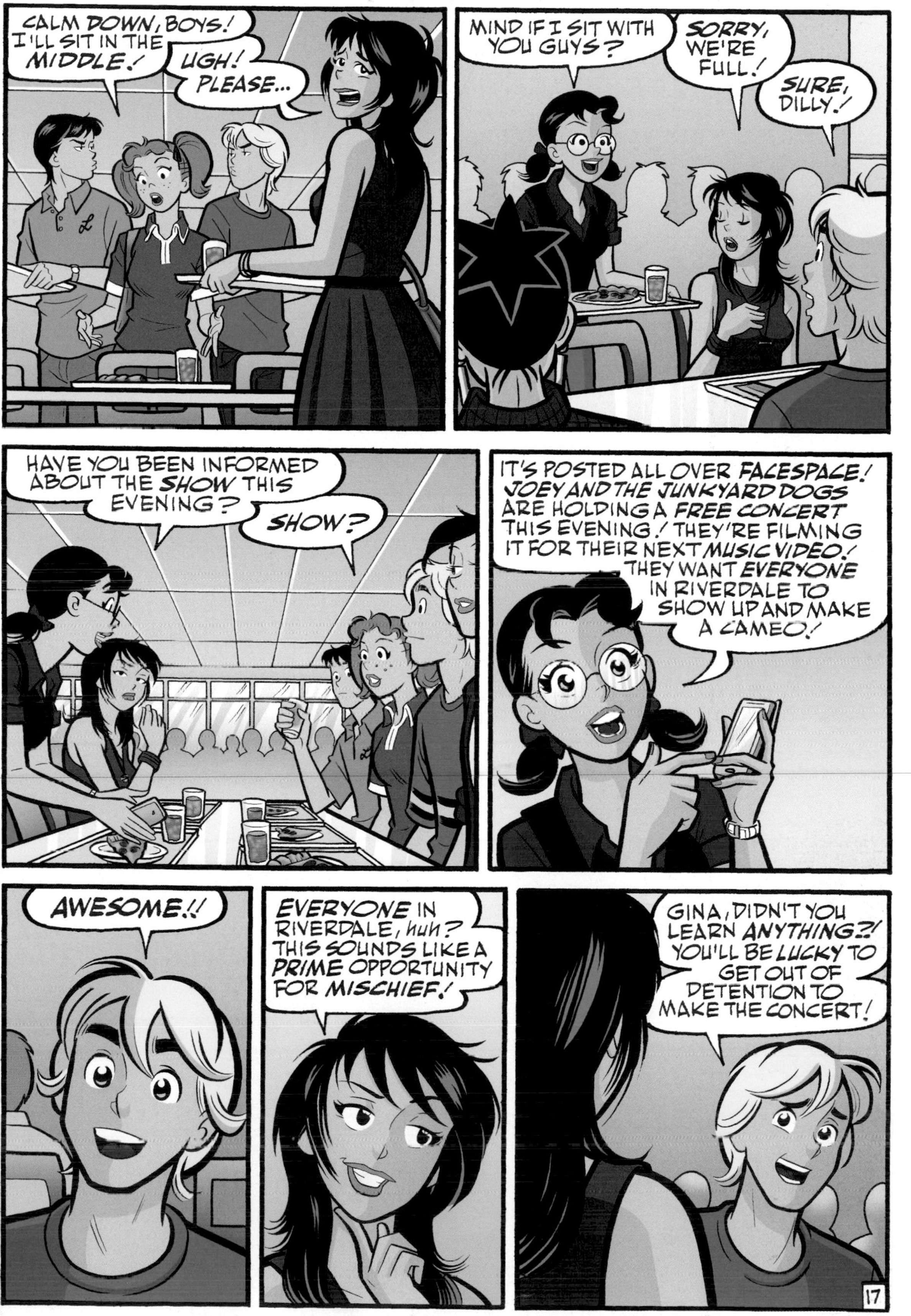
CALM DOWN, BOYS! I'LL SIT IN THE MIDDLE!
UGH! PLEASE...
MIND IF I SIT WITH YOU GUYS?
SORRY, WE'RE FULL!
SURE, DILLY!
HAVE YOU BEEN INFORMED ABOUT THE SHOW THIS EVENING?
SHOW?
IT'S POSTED ALL OVER FACESPACE! JOEY AND THE JUNKYARD DOGS ARE HOLDING A FREE CONCERT THIS EVENING! THEY'RE FILMING IT FOR THEIR NEXT MUSIC VIDEO! THEY WANT EVERYONE IN RIVERDALE TO SHOW UP AND MAKE A CAMEO!
AWESOME!!
EVERYONE IN RIVERDALE, huh? THIS SOUNDS LIKE A PRIME OPPORTUNITY FOR MISCHIEF!
GINA, DIDN'T YOU LEARN ANYTHING?! YOU'LL BE LUCKY TO GET OUT OF DETENTION TO MAKE THE CONCERT!
17

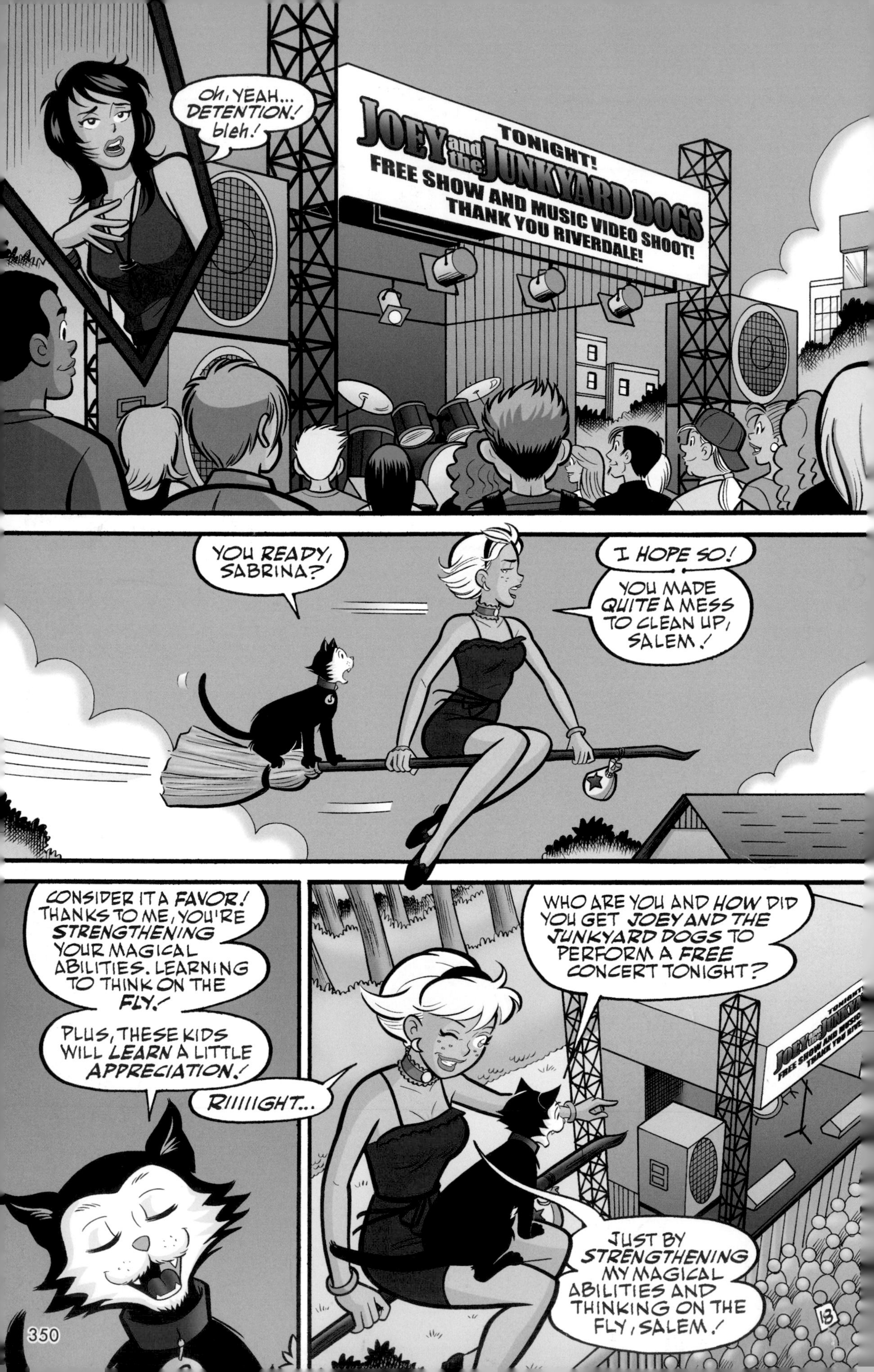

Oh, YEAH... DETENTION! bleh!
TONIGHT!
JOEY and the JUNKYARD DOGS
FREE SHOW AND MUSIC VIDEO SHOOT!
THANK YOU RIVERDALE!
YOU READY, SABRINA?
I HOPE SO!
YOU MADE QUITE A MESS TO CLEAN UP, SALEM!
CONSIDER IT A FAVOR! THANKS TO ME, YOU'RE STRENGTHENING YOUR MAGICAL ABILITIES. LEARNING TO THINK ON THE FLY!
PLUS, THESE KIDS WILL LEARN A LITTLE APPRECIATION!
RIIIIIGHT...
WHO ARE YOU AND HOW DID YOU GET JOEY AND THE JUNKYARD DOGS TO PERFORM A FREE CONCERT TONIGHT?
JUST BY STRENGTHENING MY MAGICAL ABILITIES AND THINKING ON THE FLY, SALEM!
18

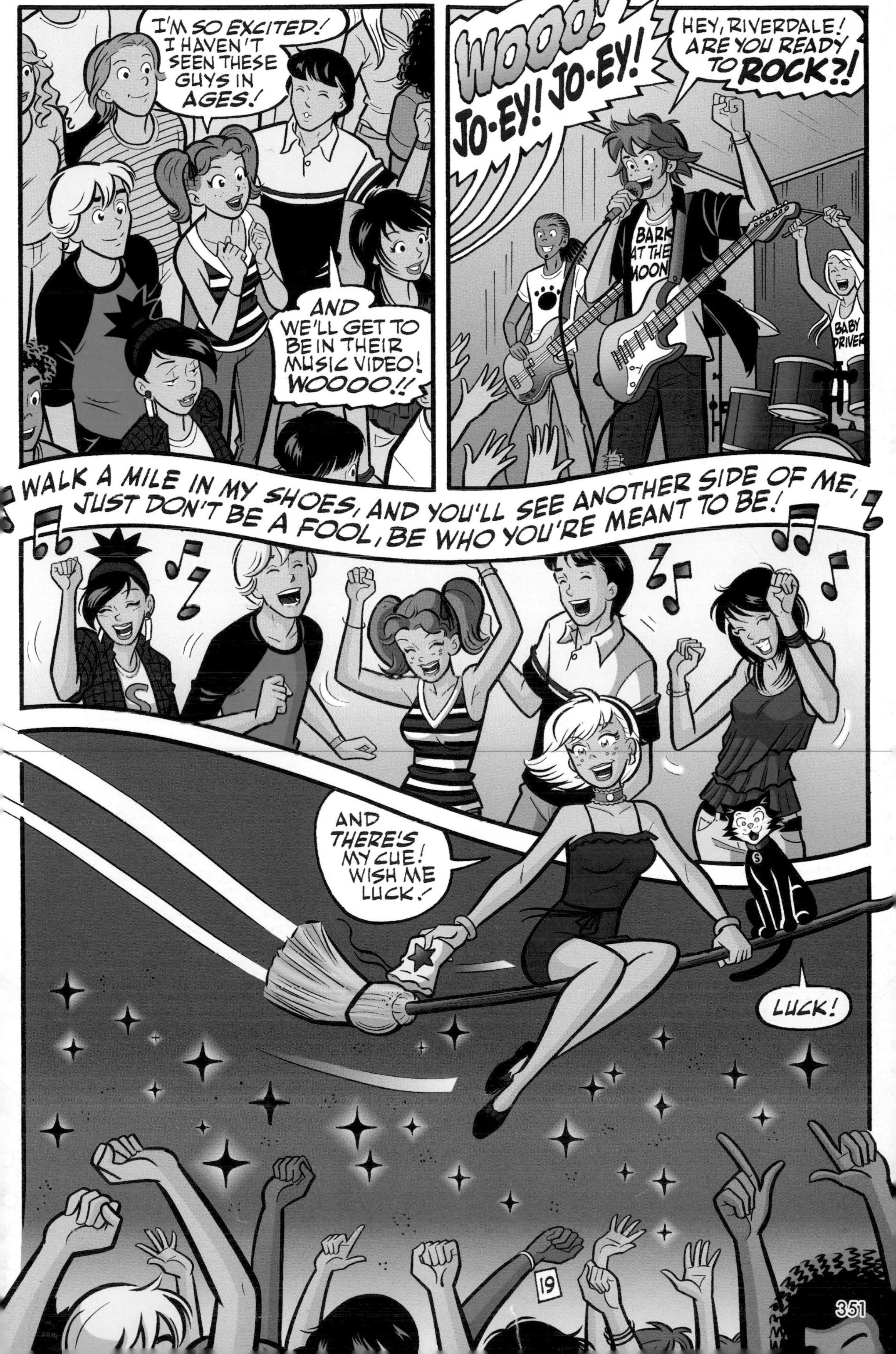
I'M SO EXCITED! I HAVEN'T SEEN THESE GUYS IN AGES!
AND WE'LL GET TO BE IN THEIR MUSIC VIDEO! WOOOO!!
WOOO! JO-EY! JO-EY!
HEY, RIVERDALE! ARE YOU READY TO ROCK?!
BARK AT THE MOON
BABY DRIVER
WALK A MILE IN MY SHOES, AND YOU'LL SEE ANOTHER SIDE OF ME, JUST DON'T BE A FOOL, BE WHO YOU'RE MEANT TO BE!
AND THERE'S MY CUE! WISH ME LUCK!
LUCK!
19

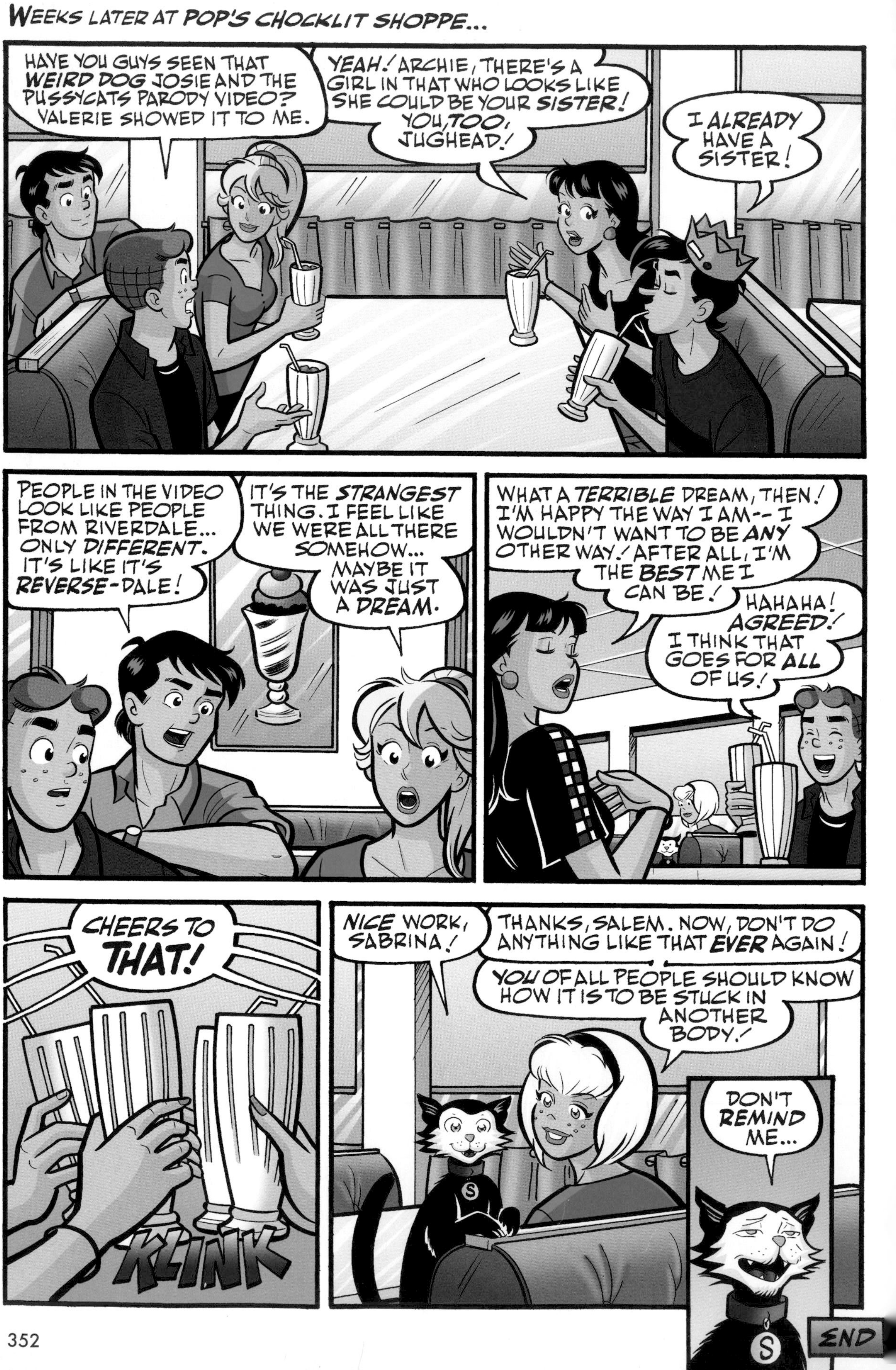
WEEKS LATER AT POP'S CHOCKLIT SHOPPE...
HAVE YOU GUYS SEEN THAT WEIRD DOG JOSIE AND THE PUSSYCATS PARODY VIDEO? VALERIE SHOWED IT TO ME.
YEAH! ARCHIE, THERE'S A GIRL IN THAT WHO LOOKS LIKE SHE COULD BE YOUR SISTER! YOU, TOO, JUGHEAD!
I ALREADY HAVE A SISTER!
PEOPLE IN THE VIDEO LOOK LIKE PEOPLE FROM RIVERDALE... ONLY DIFFERENT. IT'S LIKE IT'S REVERSE-DALE!
IT'S THE STRANGEST THING. I FEEL LIKE WE WERE ALL THERE SOMEHOW... MAYBE IT WAS JUST A DREAM.
WHAT A TERRIBLE DREAM, THEN! I'M HAPPY THE WAY I AM-- I WOULDN'T WANT TO BE ANY OTHER WAY! AFTER ALL, I'M THE BEST ME I CAN BE!
HAHAHA! AGREED! I THINK THAT GOES FOR ALL OF US!
CHEERS TO THAT!
KLINK
NICE WORK, SABRINA!
THANKS, SALEM. NOW, DON'T DO ANYTHING LIKE THAT EVER AGAIN!
YOU OF ALL PEOPLE SHOULD KNOW HOW IT IS TO BE STUCK IN ANOTHER BODY!
DON'T REMIND ME...
END

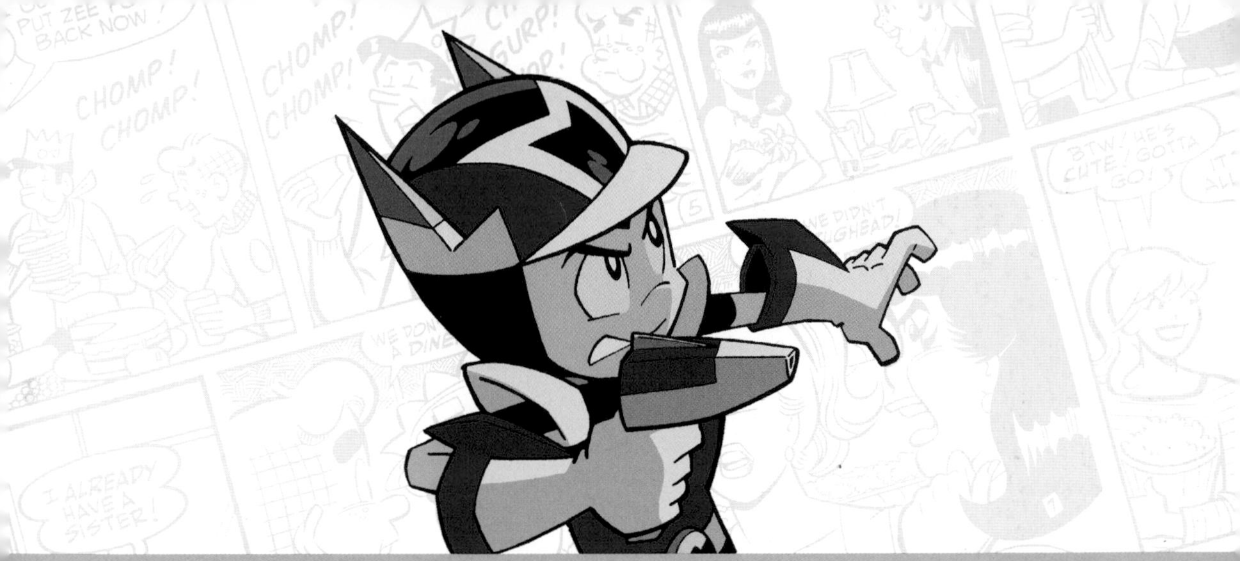
CHOMP! CHOMP!
CHOMP! CHOMP!
I ALREADY HAVE A SISTER!

COSMO

COSMO #1, 2018

BY IAN FLYNN, TRACY YARDLEY, JACK MORELLI & MATT HERMS

The original *Cosmo the Merry Martian* series was printed way back in 1958. A lot of things have changed since then: our understanding of our Solar System, our understanding of each other, our collective sense of humor, and more. But one underlying element remained eternal: Cosmo was weird, and that was fantastic. Jump ahead sixty years and Cosmo's crew launches once again. Cosmo's still our brave leader, but he's a bit more thoughtful this time. Astra's the pilot now, and we see what drives Orbi. Prof. Thimk is out and Dr. Medulla is in (but is there a relation?) The Queen of Venus is looking far less human, and far more threatening. But things are still wonderfully weird—and limitless! Here you'll read about the Cosmo crew's adventures on the Moon, but what about the queendom of Venus? The vegetable people of Saturn? The eternal golf course that is the Kuiper Belt? Our Solar System is a treasure trove of alien worlds that can be spun in all sorts of wacky ways. And the galaxy beyond? The universe? Every star, ever y comet, and ever y lump of space rock out there has something fun going on. I really hope that, one day, we'll be able to take you there.

—Ian Flynn
Writer, Archie Comics

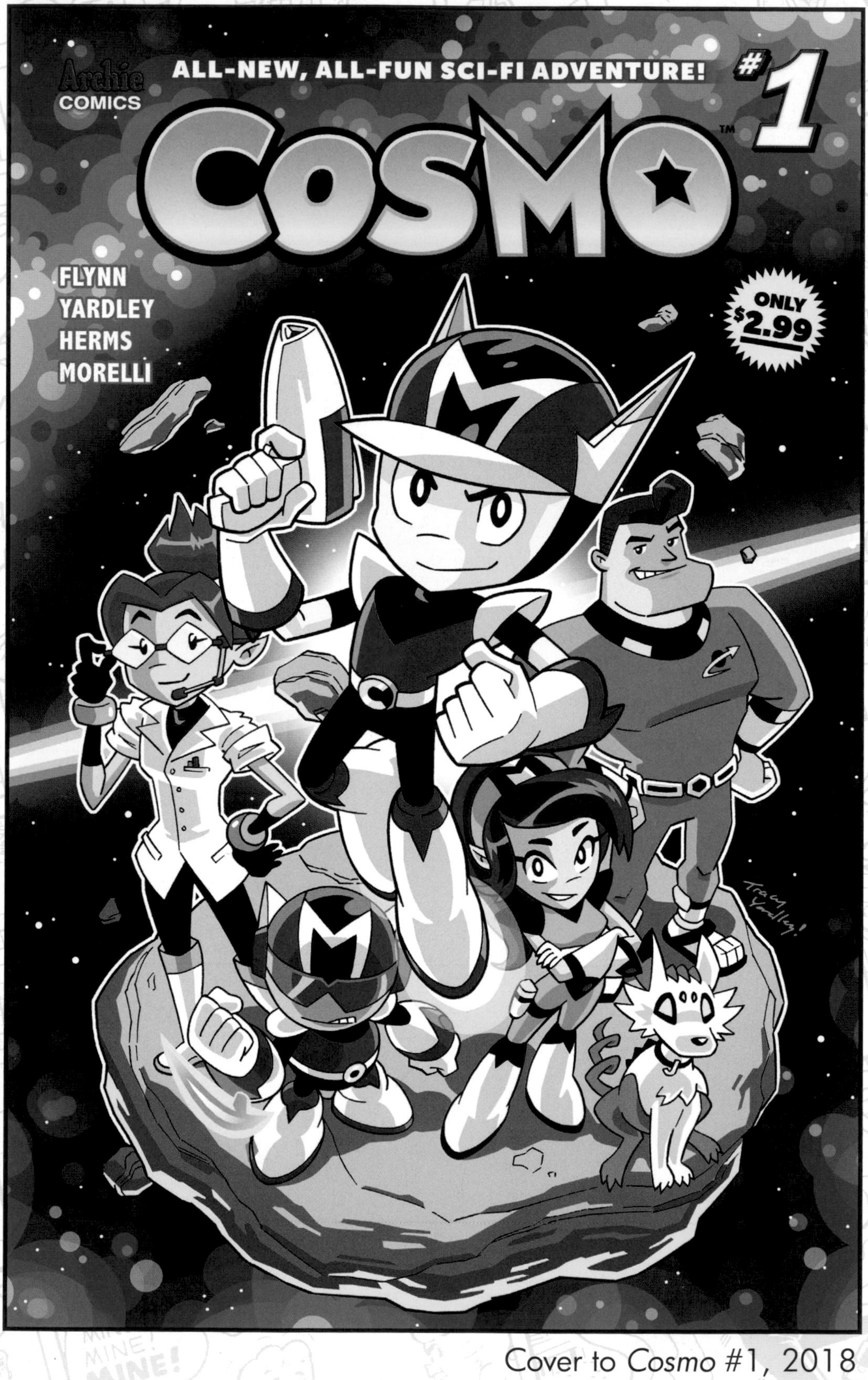
Archie COMICS
ALL-NEW, ALL-FUN SCI-FI ADVENTURE!
#1
COSMO™
FLYNN
YARDLEY
HERMS
MORELLI
ONLY $2.99
Tracy Yardley!

Cover to *Cosmo* #1, 2018
art by Tracy Yardley

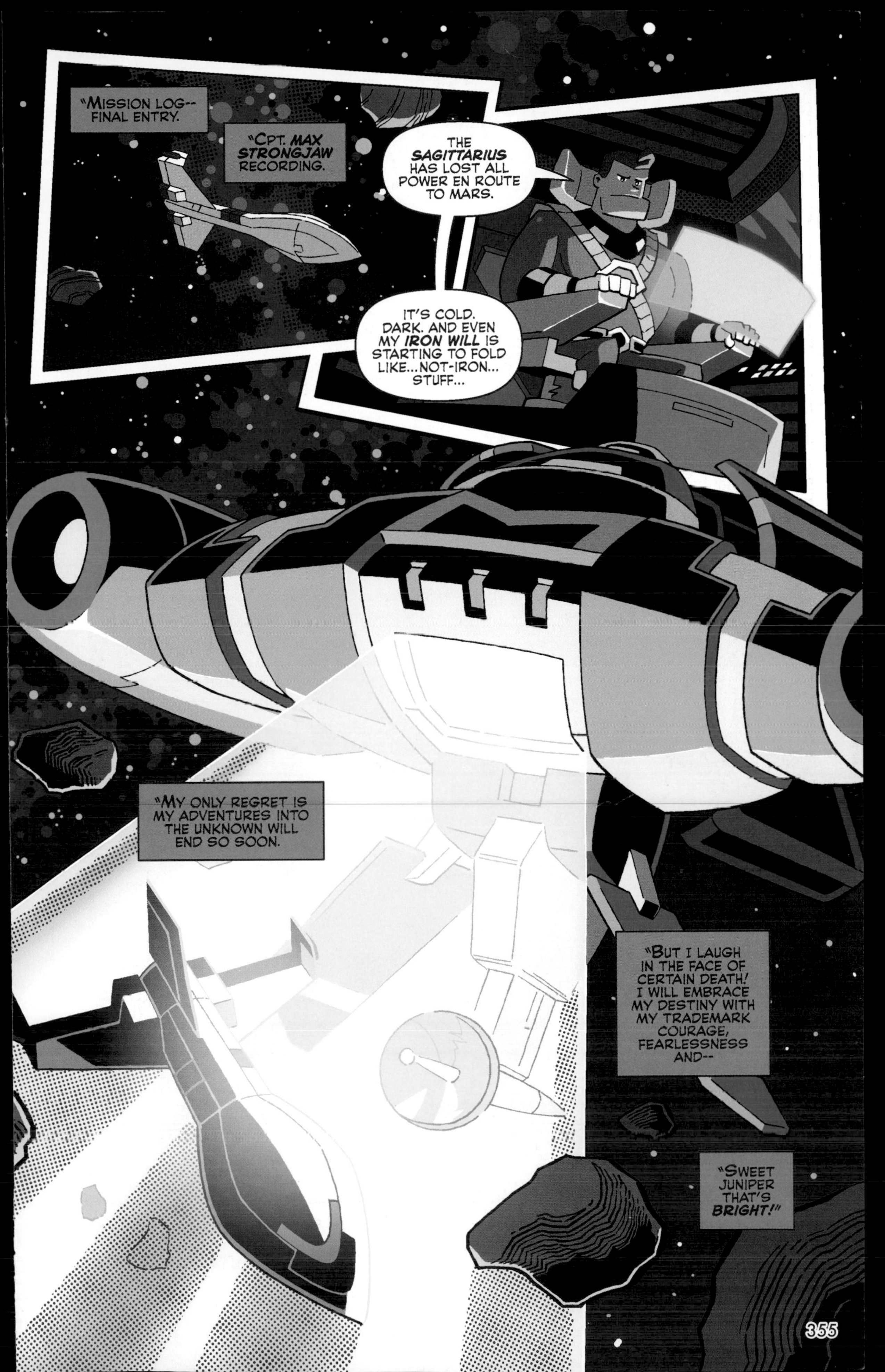
"MISSION LOG--
FINAL ENTRY.
"CPT. MAX STRONGJAW RECORDING.
THE SAGITTARIUS HAS LOST ALL POWER EN ROUTE TO MARS.
IT'S COLD. DARK. AND EVEN MY IRON WILL IS STARTING TO FOLD LIKE...NOT-IRON... STUFF...
"MY ONLY REGRET IS MY ADVENTURES INTO THE UNKNOWN WILL END SO SOON.
"BUT I LAUGH IN THE FACE OF CERTAIN DEATH! I WILL EMBRACE MY DESTINY WITH MY TRADEMARK COURAGE, FEARLESSNESS AND--
"SWEET JUNIPER THAT'S BRIGHT!"

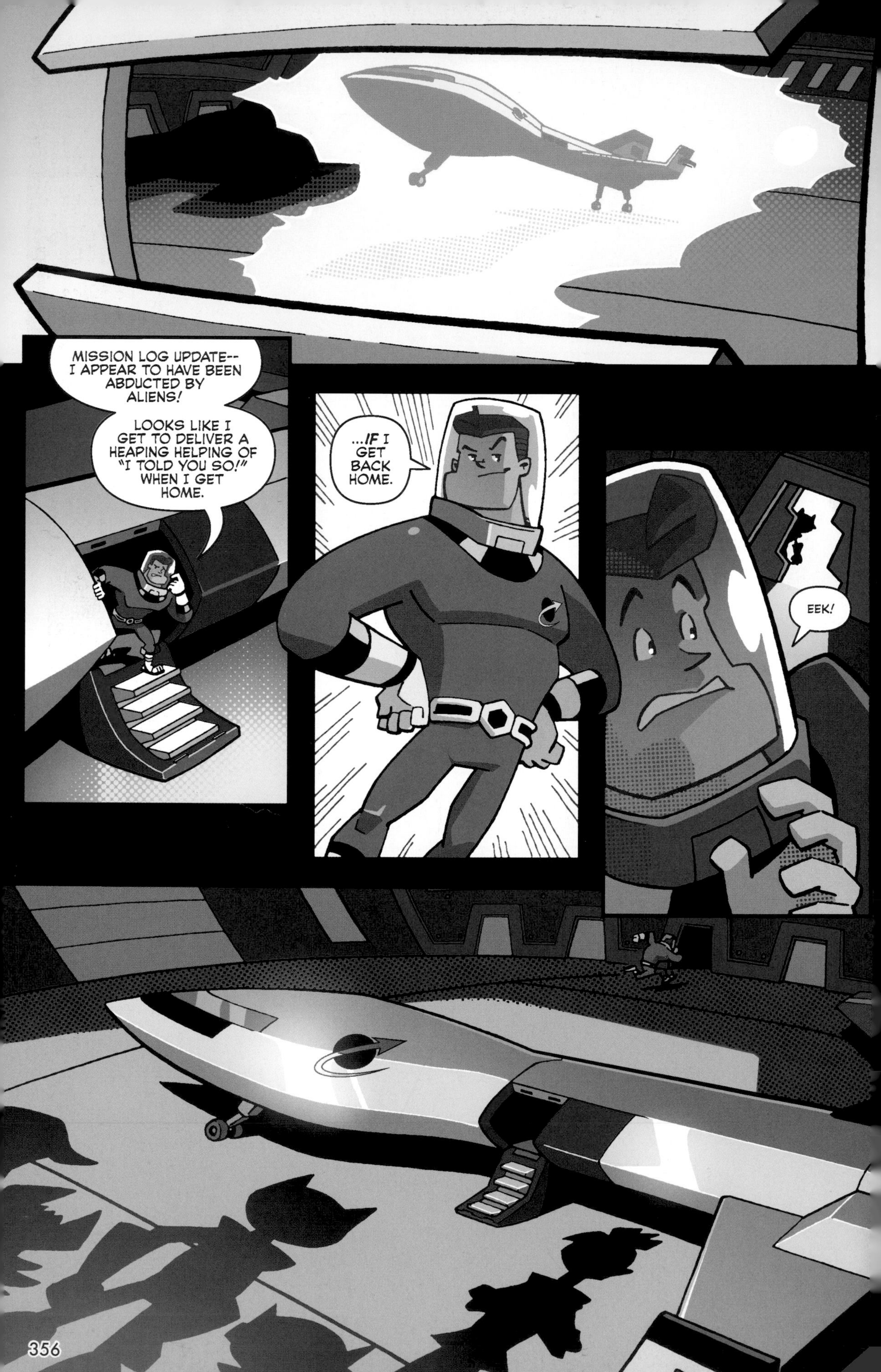
MISSION LOG UPDATE-- I APPEAR TO HAVE BEEN ABDUCTED BY ALIENS!
LOOKS LIKE I GET TO DELIVER A HEAPING HELPING OF "I TOLD YOU SO!" WHEN I GET HOME.
...IF I GET BACK HOME.
EEK!

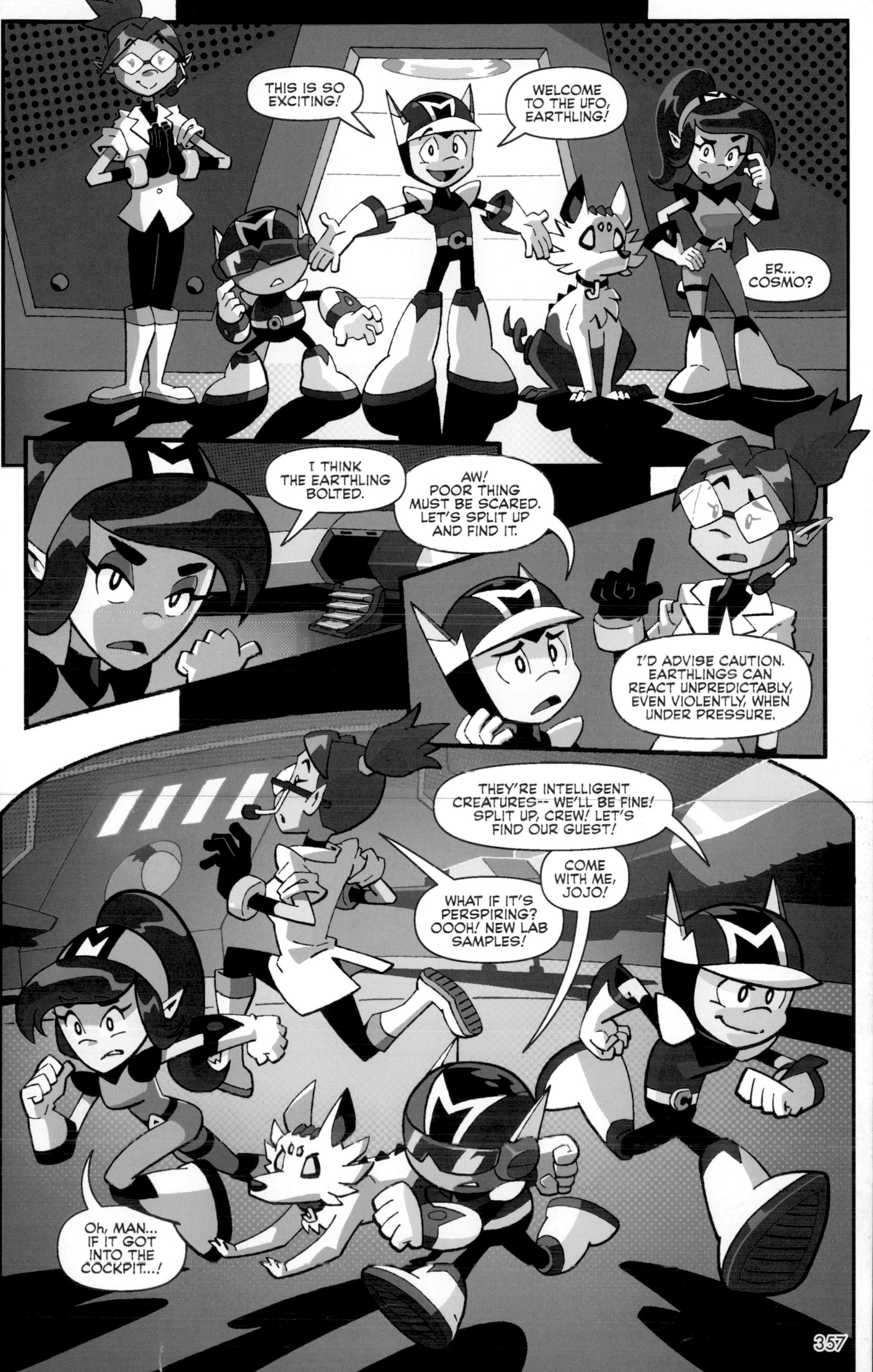
THIS IS SO EXCITING!
WELCOME TO THE UFO, EARTHLING!
ER... COSMO?
I THINK THE EARTHLING BOLTED.
AW! POOR THING MUST BE SCARED. LET'S SPLIT UP AND FIND IT.
I'D ADVISE CAUTION. EARTHLINGS CAN REACT UNPREDICTABLY, EVEN VIOLENTLY, WHEN UNDER PRESSURE.
THEY'RE INTELLIGENT CREATURES-- WE'LL BE FINE! SPLIT UP, CREW! LET'S FIND OUR GUEST!
COME WITH ME, JOJO!
WHAT IF IT'S PERSPIRING? OOOH! NEW LAB SAMPLES!
Oh, MAN... IF IT GOT INTO THE COCKPIT...!

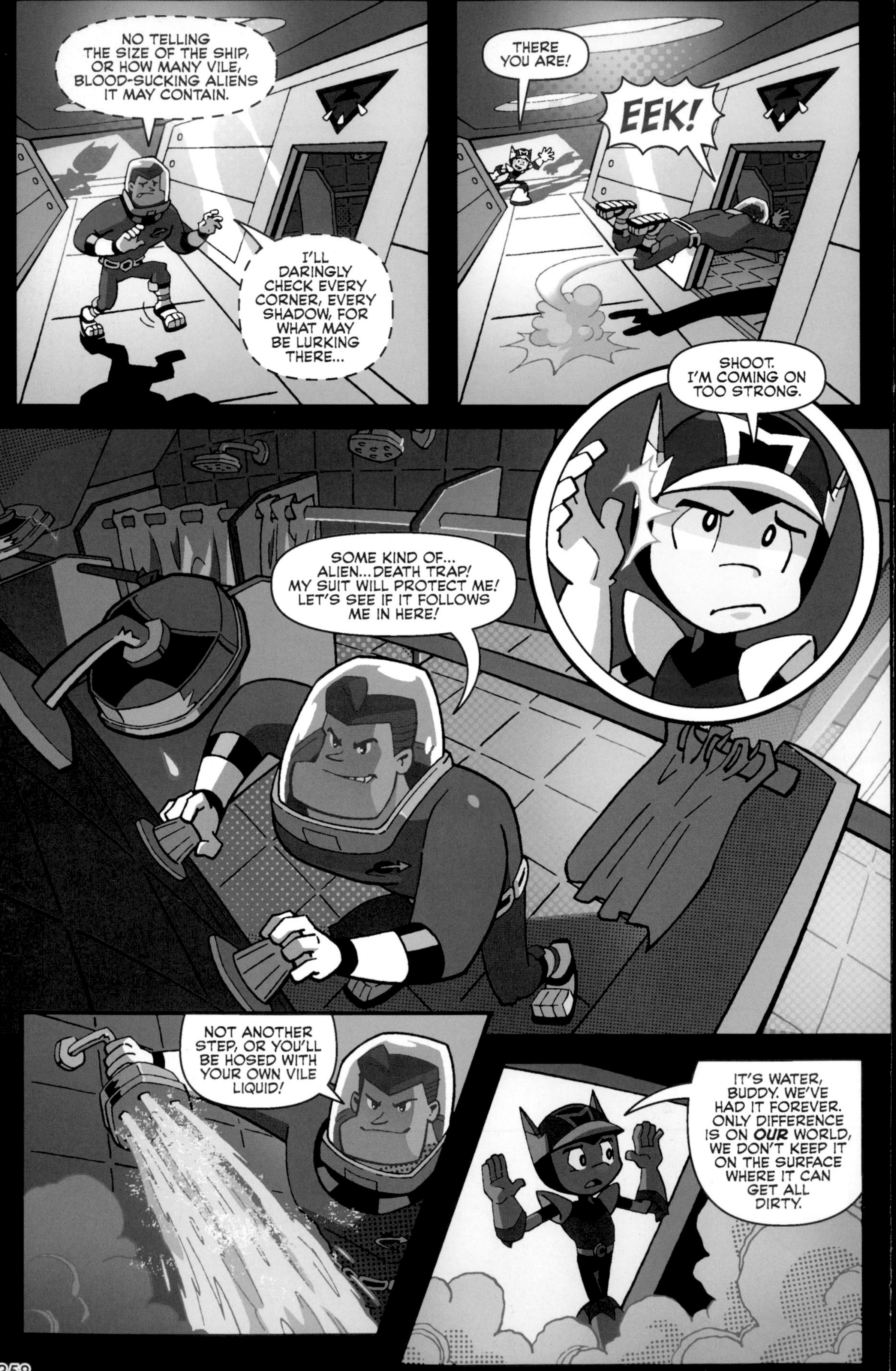
NO TELLING THE SIZE OF THE SHIP, OR HOW MANY VILE, BLOOD-SUCKING ALIENS IT MAY CONTAIN.
I'LL DARINGLY CHECK EVERY CORNER, EVERY SHADOW, FOR WHAT MAY BE LURKING THERE...
THERE YOU ARE!
EEK!
SHOOT. I'M COMING ON TOO STRONG.
SOME KIND OF... ALIEN...DEATH TRAP! MY SUIT WILL PROTECT ME! LET'S SEE IF IT FOLLOWS ME IN HERE!
NOT ANOTHER STEP, OR YOU'LL BE HOSED WITH YOUR OWN VILE LIQUID!
IT'S WATER, BUDDY. WE'VE HAD IT FOREVER. ONLY DIFFERENCE IS ON ***OUR*** WORLD, WE DON'T KEEP IT ON THE SURFACE WHERE IT CAN GET ALL DIRTY.

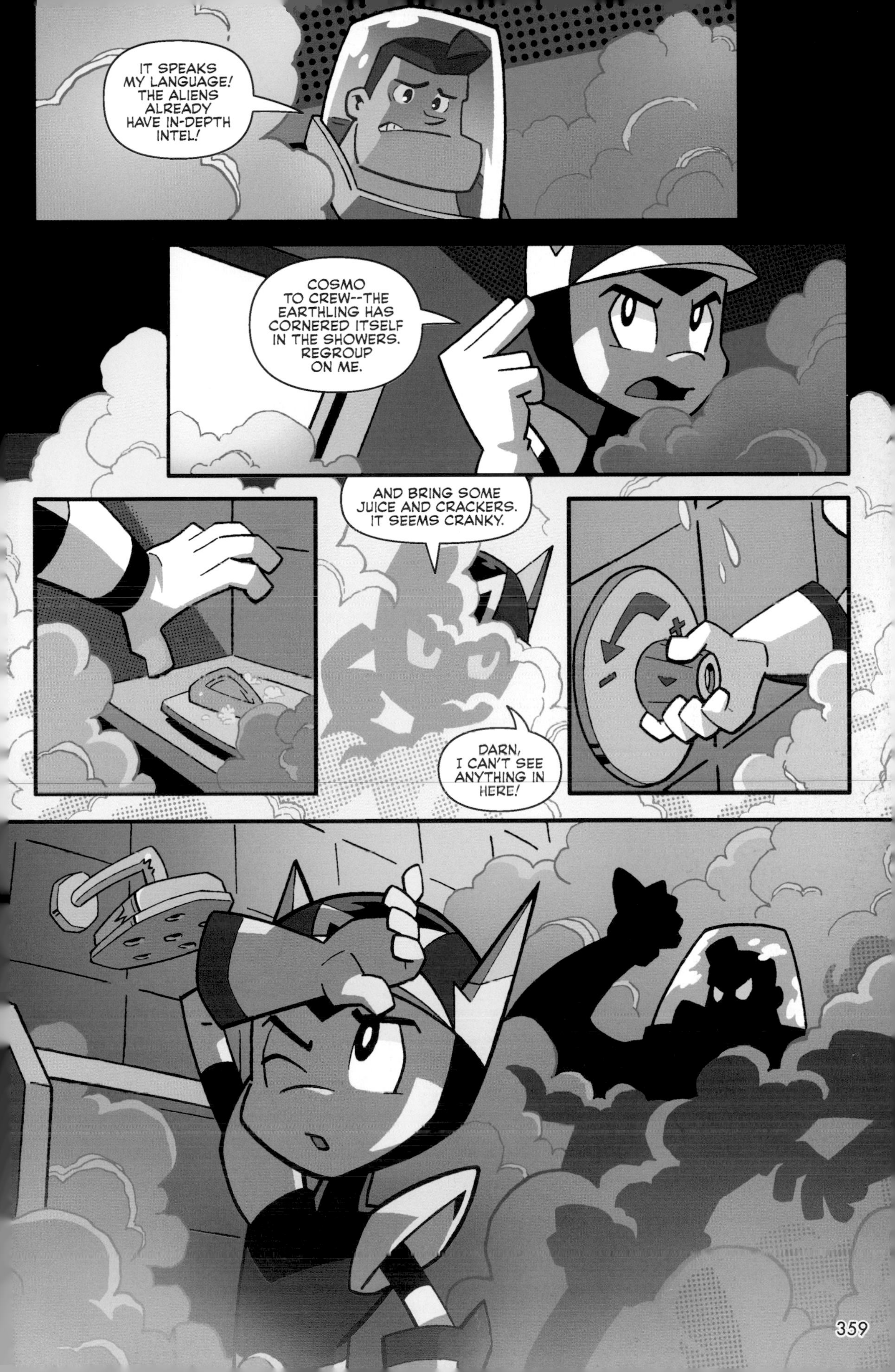
IT SPEAKS MY LANGUAGE! THE ALIENS ALREADY HAVE IN-DEPTH INTEL!
COSMO TO CREW--THE EARTHLING HAS CORNERED ITSELF IN THE SHOWERS. REGROUP ON ME.
AND BRING SOME JUICE AND CRACKERS. IT SEEMS CRANKY.
DARN, I CAN'T SEE ANYTHING IN HERE!

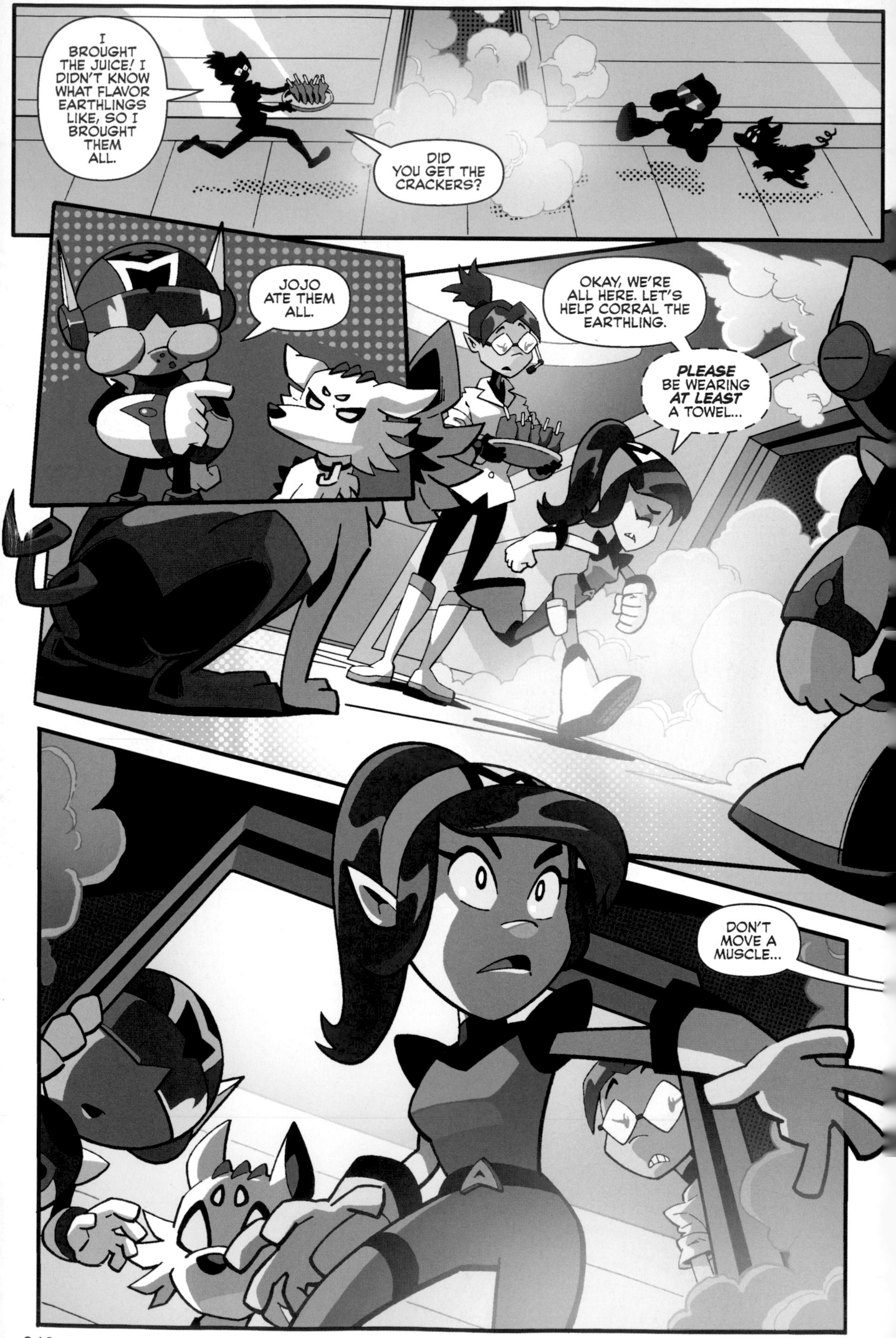
I BROUGHT THE JUICE! I DIDN'T KNOW WHAT FLAVOR EARTHLINGS LIKE, SO I BROUGHT THEM ALL.
DID YOU GET THE CRACKERS?
JOJO ATE THEM ALL.
OKAY, WE'RE ALL HERE. LET'S HELP CORRAL THE EARTHLING.
PLEASE BE WEARING *AT LEAST* A TOWEL...
DON'T MOVE A MUSCLE...

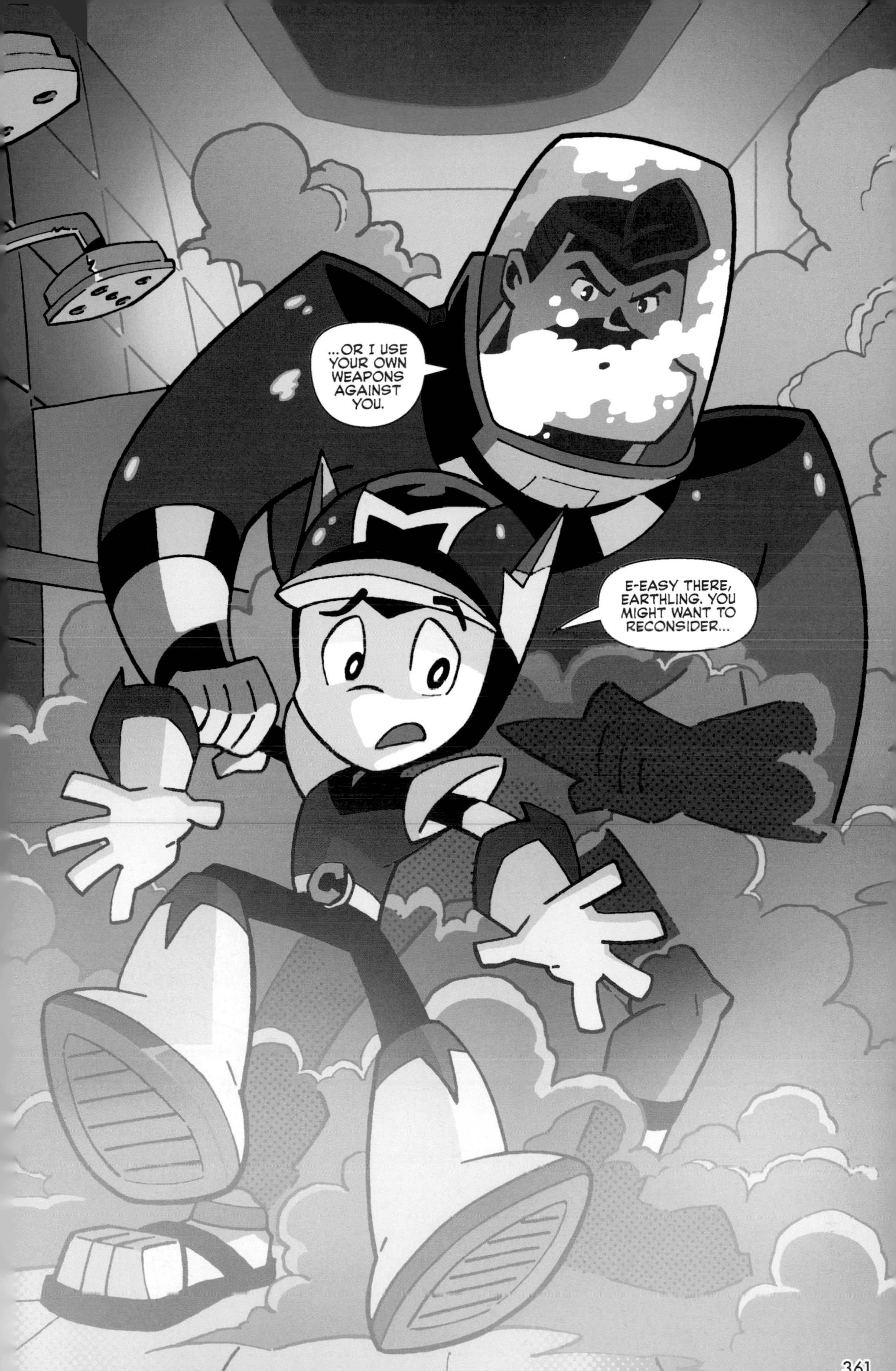
...OR I USE YOUR OWN WEAPONS AGAINST YOU.
E-EASY THERE, EARTHLING. YOU MIGHT WANT TO RECONSIDER...

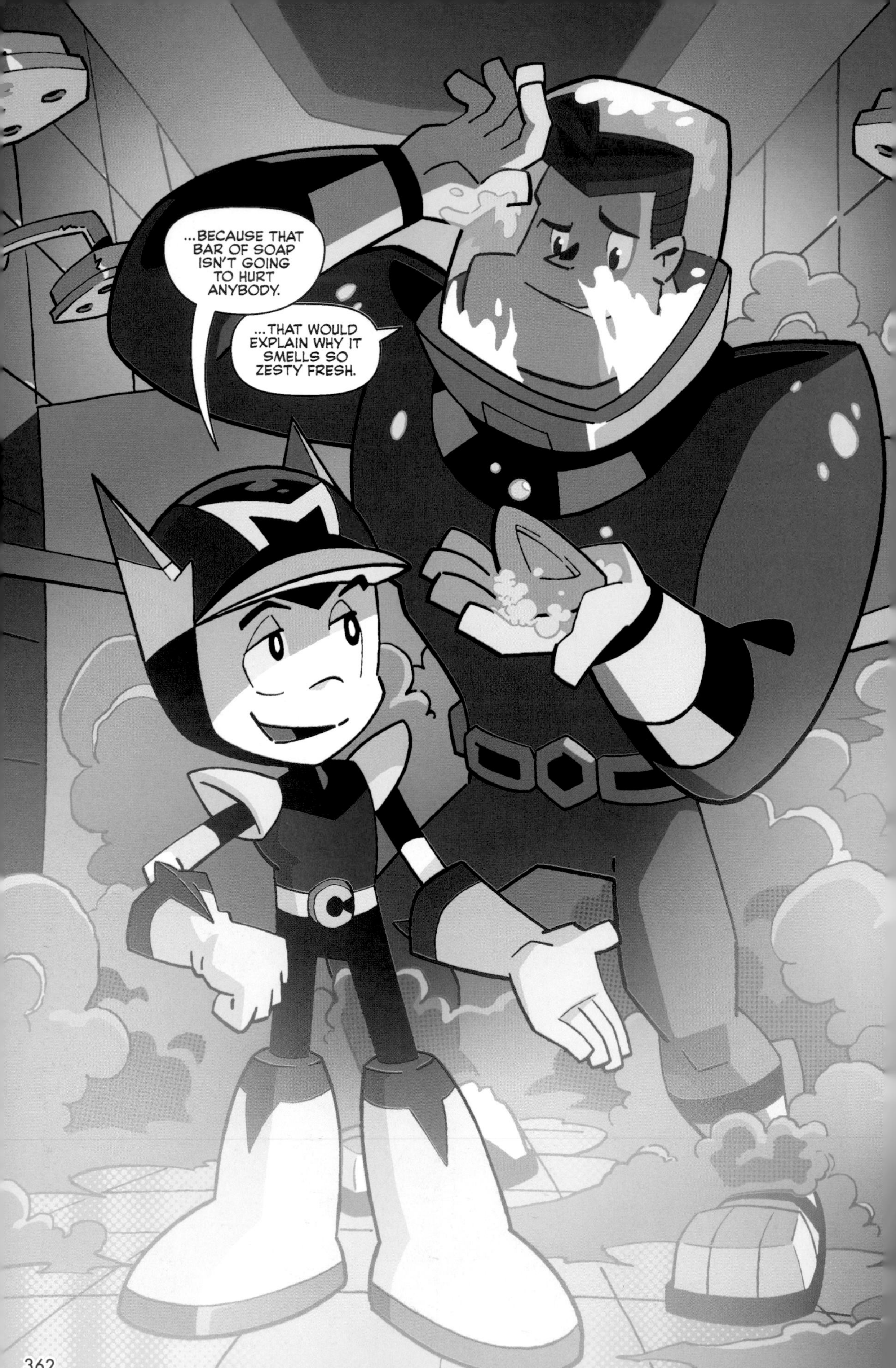
...BECAUSE THAT BAR OF SOAP ISN'T GOING TO HURT ANYBODY.
...THAT WOULD EXPLAIN WHY IT SMELLS SO ZESTY FRESH.

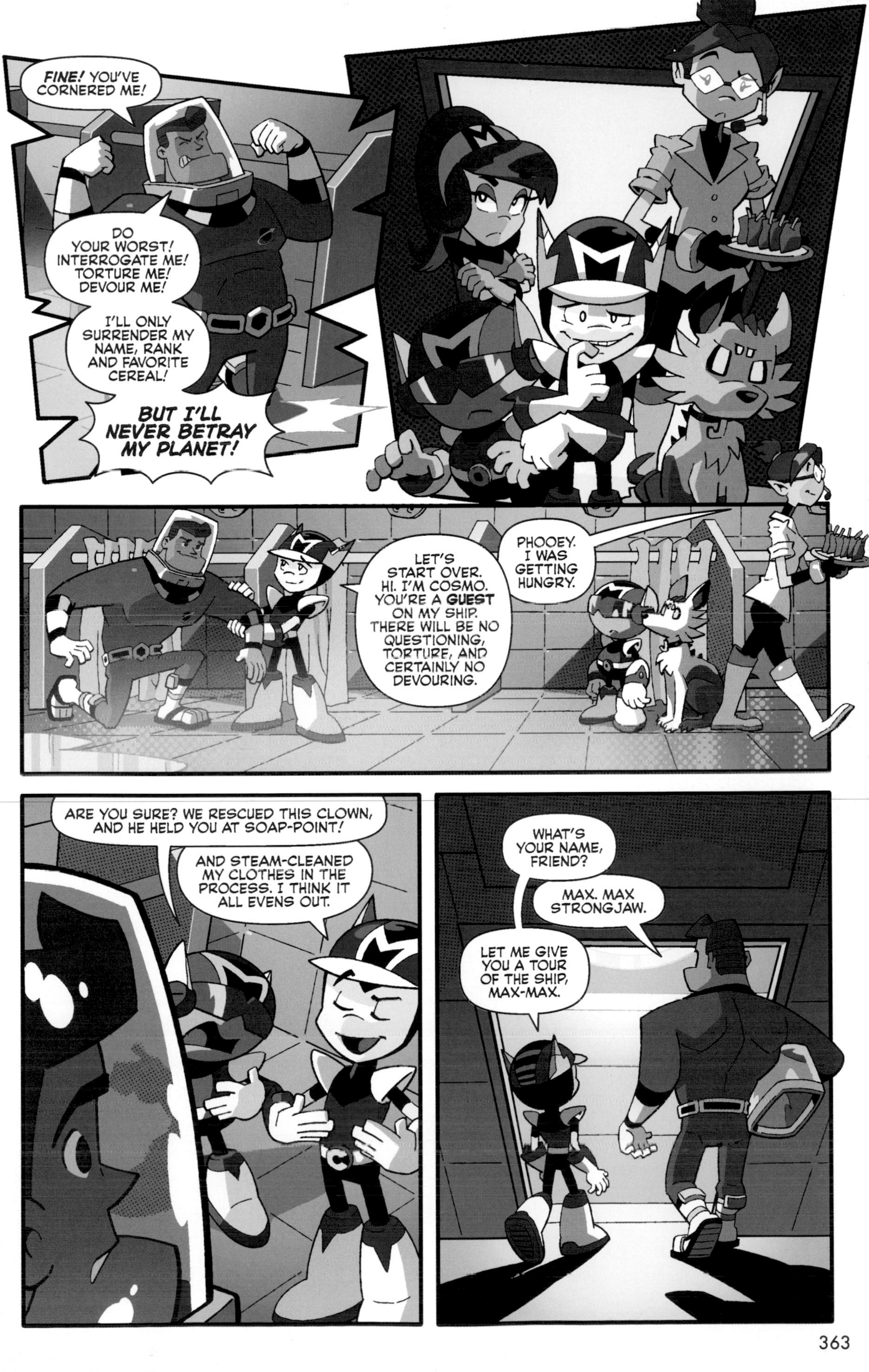
FINE! YOU'VE CORNERED ME!
DO YOUR WORST! INTERROGATE ME! TORTURE ME! DEVOUR ME!
I'LL ONLY SURRENDER MY NAME, RANK AND FAVORITE CEREAL!
BUT I'LL NEVER BETRAY MY PLANET!
LET'S START OVER. HI. I'M COSMO. YOU'RE A GUEST ON MY SHIP. THERE WILL BE NO QUESTIONING, TORTURE, AND CERTAINLY NO DEVOURING.
PHOOEY. I WAS GETTING HUNGRY.
ARE YOU SURE? WE RESCUED THIS CLOWN, AND HE HELD YOU AT SOAP-POINT!
AND STEAM-CLEANED MY CLOTHES IN THE PROCESS. I THINK IT ALL EVENS OUT.
WHAT'S YOUR NAME, FRIEND?
MAX. MAX STRONGJAW.
LET ME GIVE YOU A TOUR OF THE SHIP, MAX-MAX.

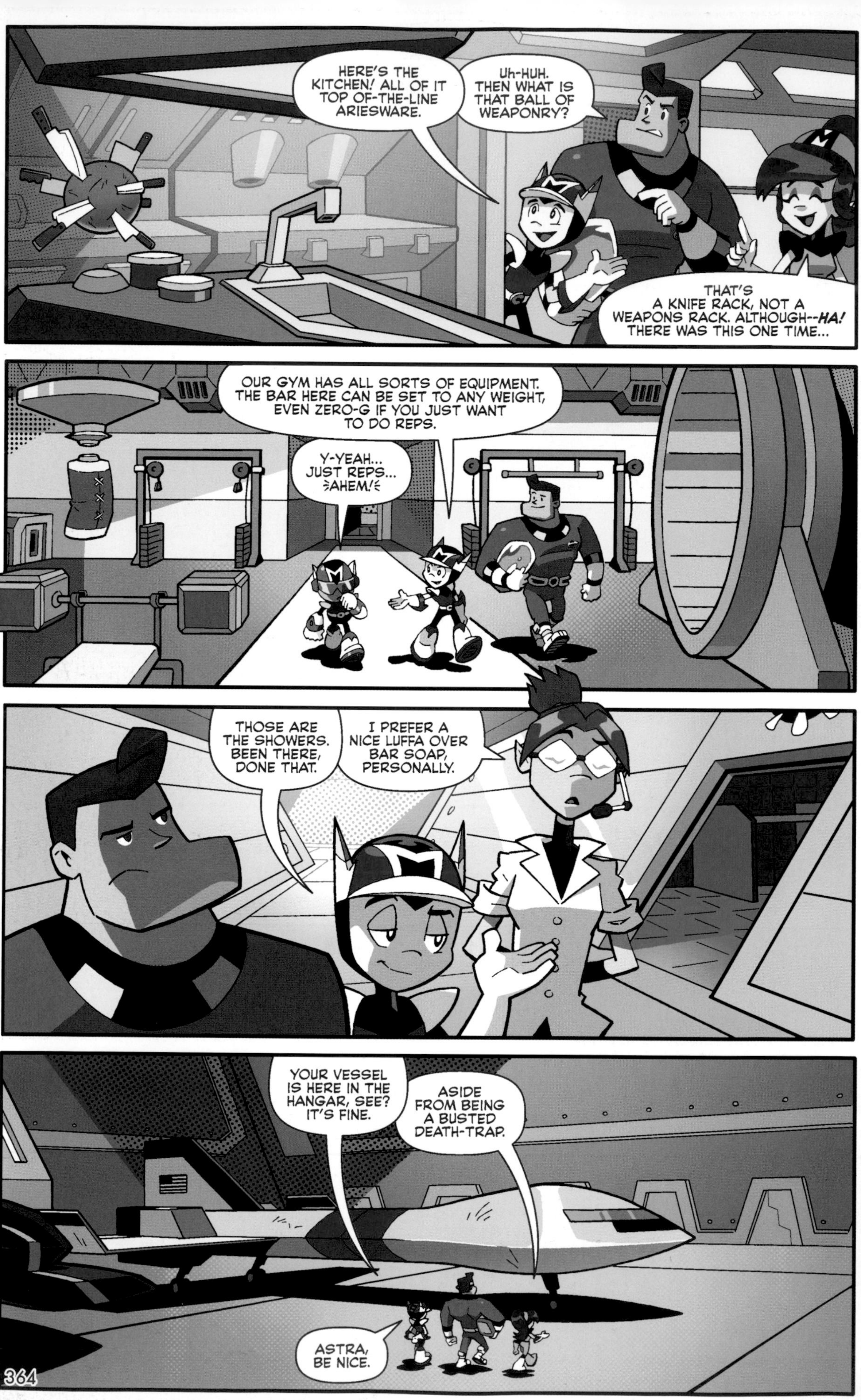
HERE'S THE KITCHEN! ALL OF IT TOP OF-THE-LINE ARIESWARE.
UH-HUH. THEN WHAT IS THAT BALL OF WEAPONRY?
THAT'S A KNIFE RACK, NOT A WEAPONS RACK. ALTHOUGH--HA! THERE WAS THIS ONE TIME...
OUR GYM HAS ALL SORTS OF EQUIPMENT. THE BAR HERE CAN BE SET TO ANY WEIGHT, EVEN ZERO-G IF YOU JUST WANT TO DO REPS.
Y-YEAH... JUST REPS... *AHEM!*
THOSE ARE THE SHOWERS. BEEN THERE, DONE THAT.
I PREFER A NICE LUFFA OVER BAR SOAP, PERSONALLY.
YOUR VESSEL IS HERE IN THE HANGAR, SEE? IT'S FINE.
ASIDE FROM BEING A BUSTED DEATH-TRAP.
ASTRA, BE NICE.

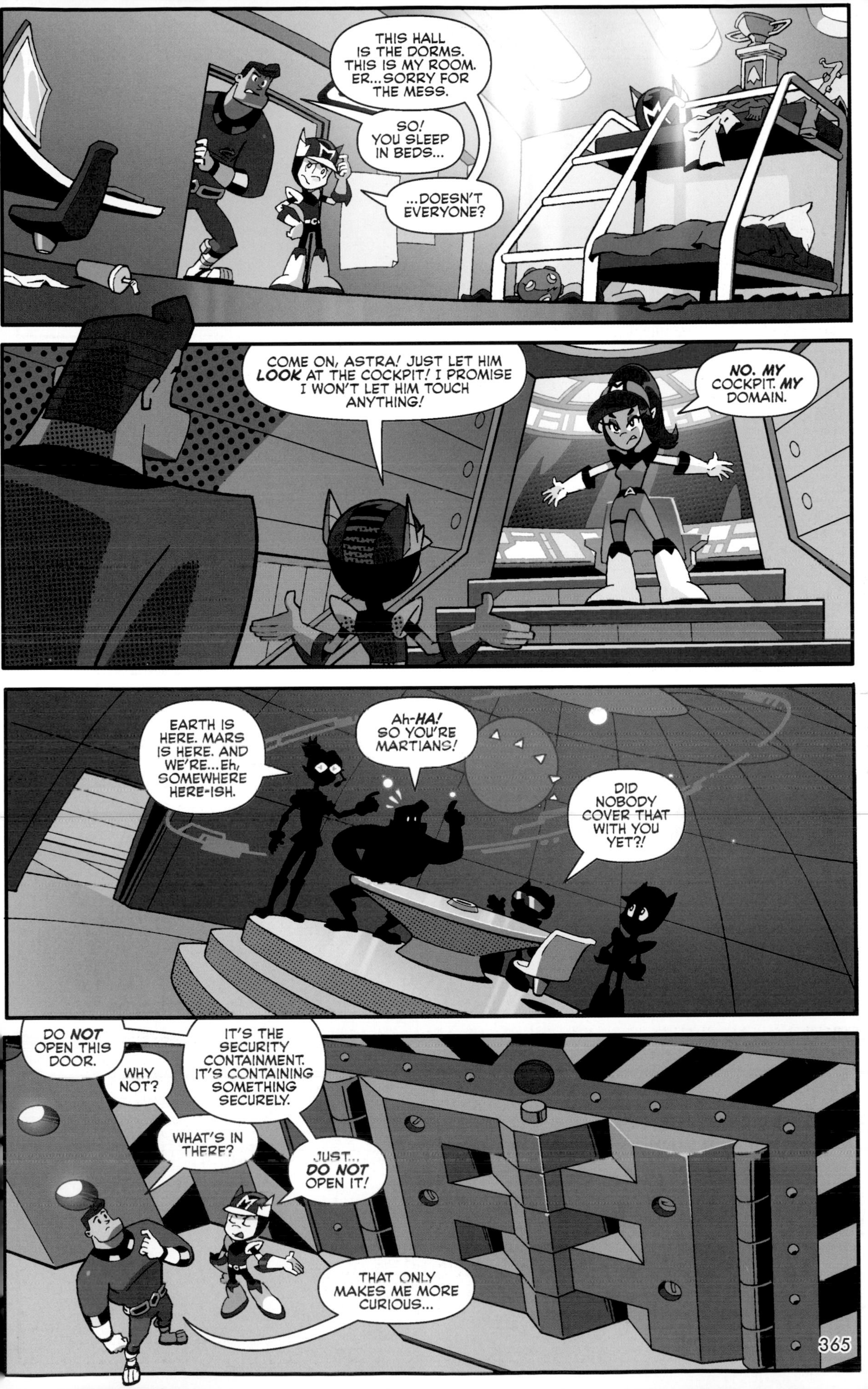
THIS HALL IS THE DORMS. THIS IS MY ROOM. ER...SORRY FOR THE MESS.
SO! YOU SLEEP IN BEDS...
...DOESN'T EVERYONE?
COME ON, ASTRA! JUST LET HIM LOOK AT THE COCKPIT! I PROMISE I WON'T LET HIM TOUCH ANYTHING!
NO. MY COCKPIT. MY DOMAIN.
EARTH IS HERE. MARS IS HERE. AND WE'RE...Eh, SOMEWHERE HERE-ISH.
Ah-HA! SO YOU'RE MARTIANS!
DID NOBODY COVER THAT WITH YOU YET?!
DO NOT OPEN THIS DOOR.
WHY NOT?
IT'S THE SECURITY CONTAINMENT. IT'S CONTAINING SOMETHING SECURELY.
WHAT'S IN THERE?
JUST... DO NOT OPEN IT!
THAT ONLY MAKES ME MORE CURIOUS...

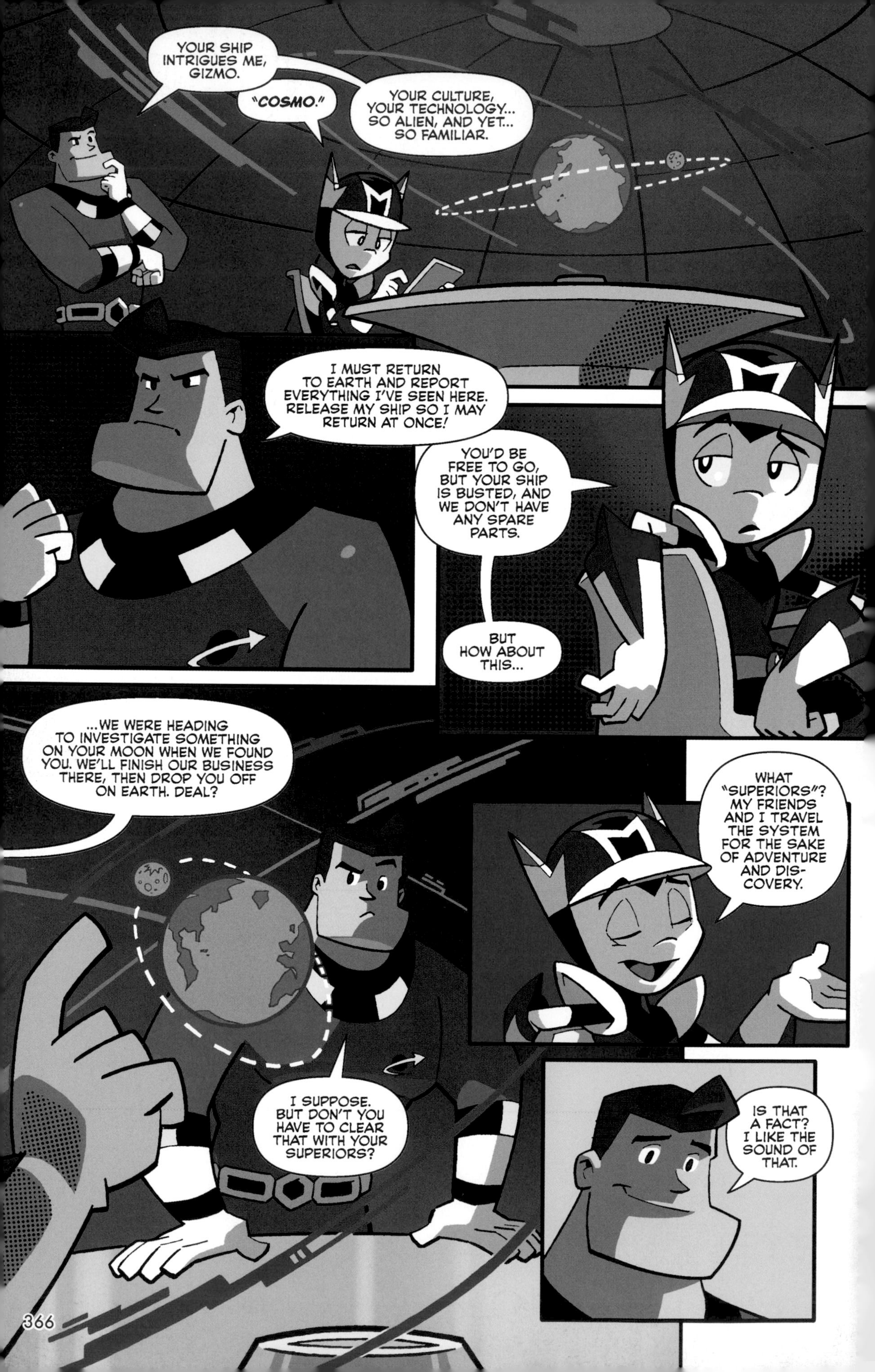
YOUR SHIP INTRIGUES ME, GIZMO.
"COSMO."
YOUR CULTURE, YOUR TECHNOLOGY... SO ALIEN, AND YET... SO FAMILIAR.
I MUST RETURN TO EARTH AND REPORT EVERYTHING I'VE SEEN HERE. RELEASE MY SHIP SO I MAY RETURN AT ONCE!
YOU'D BE FREE TO GO, BUT YOUR SHIP IS BUSTED, AND WE DON'T HAVE ANY SPARE PARTS.
BUT HOW ABOUT THIS...
...WE WERE HEADING TO INVESTIGATE SOMETHING ON YOUR MOON WHEN WE FOUND YOU. WE'LL FINISH OUR BUSINESS THERE, THEN DROP YOU OFF ON EARTH. DEAL?
I SUPPOSE. BUT DON'T YOU HAVE TO CLEAR THAT WITH YOUR SUPERIORS?
WHAT "SUPERIORS"? MY FRIENDS AND I TRAVEL THE SYSTEM FOR THE SAKE OF ADVENTURE AND DISCOVERY.
IS THAT A FACT? I LIKE THE SOUND OF THAT.

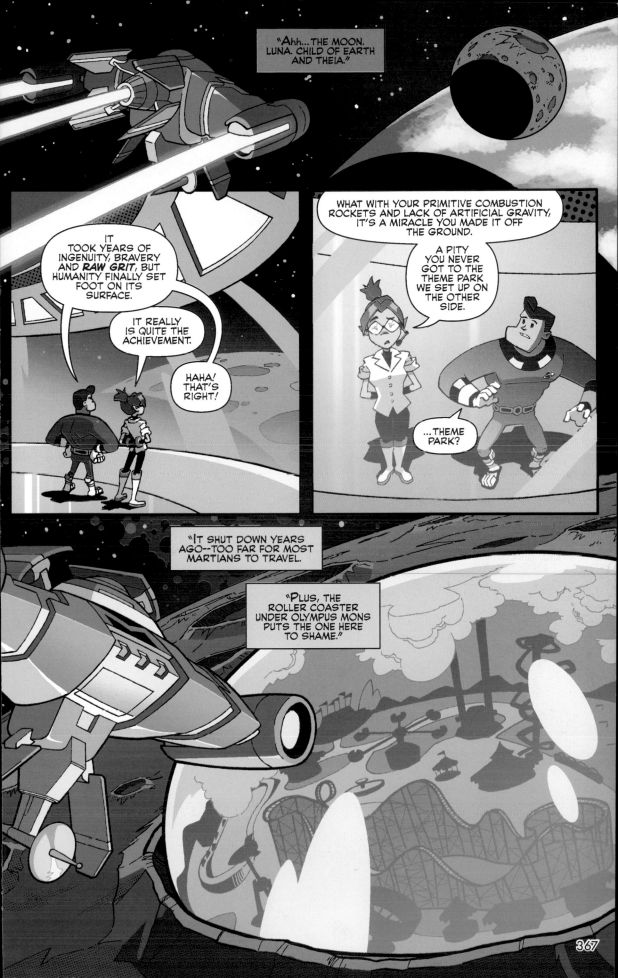

"Ahh... THE MOON. LUNA. CHILD OF EARTH AND THEIA."

IT TOOK YEARS OF INGENUITY, BRAVERY AND *RAW GRIT*, BUT HUMANITY FINALLY SET FOOT ON ITS SURFACE.

IT REALLY IS QUITE THE ACHIEVEMENT.

HAHA! THAT'S RIGHT!

WHAT WITH YOUR PRIMITIVE COMBUSTION ROCKETS AND LACK OF ARTIFICIAL GRAVITY, IT'S A MIRACLE YOU MADE IT OFF THE GROUND.

A PITY YOU NEVER GOT TO THE THEME PARK WE SET UP ON THE OTHER SIDE.

...THEME PARK?

"IT SHUT DOWN YEARS AGO--TOO FAR FOR MOST MARTIANS TO TRAVEL.

"PLUS, THE ROLLER COASTER UNDER OLYMPUS MONS PUTS THE ONE HERE TO SHAME."

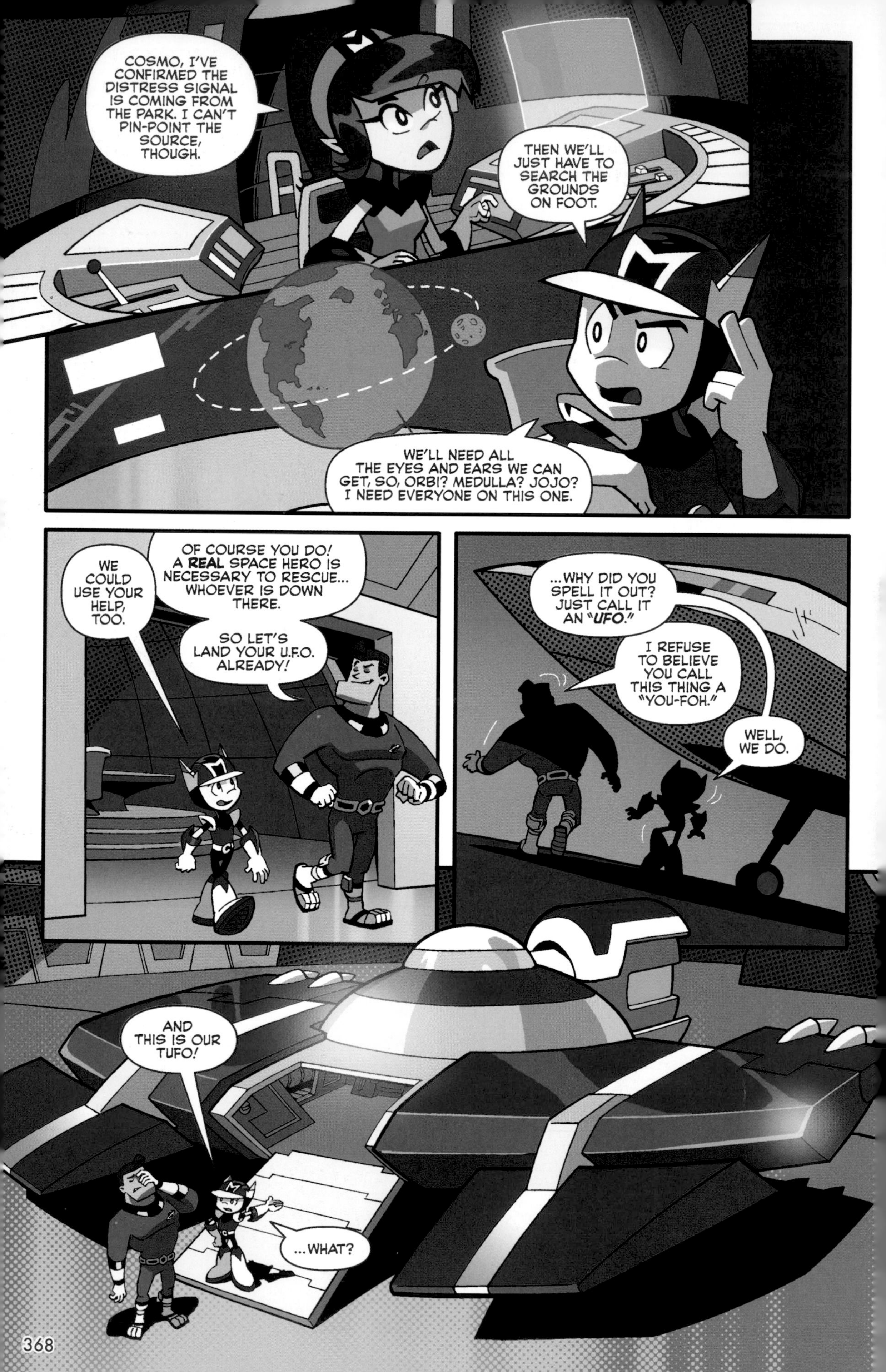
COSMO, I'VE CONFIRMED THE DISTRESS SIGNAL IS COMING FROM THE PARK. I CAN'T PIN-POINT THE SOURCE, THOUGH.
THEN WE'LL JUST HAVE TO SEARCH THE GROUNDS ON FOOT.
WE'LL NEED ALL THE EYES AND EARS WE CAN GET, SO, ORBI? MEDULLA? JOJO? I NEED EVERYONE ON THIS ONE.
WE COULD USE YOUR HELP, TOO.
OF COURSE YOU DO! A **REAL** SPACE HERO IS NECESSARY TO RESCUE... WHOEVER IS DOWN THERE.
SO LET'S LAND YOUR U.F.O. ALREADY!
...WHY DID YOU SPELL IT OUT? JUST CALL IT AN "*UFO*."
I REFUSE TO BELIEVE YOU CALL THIS THING A "YOU-FOH."
WELL, WE DO.
AND THIS IS OUR TUFO!
...WHAT?

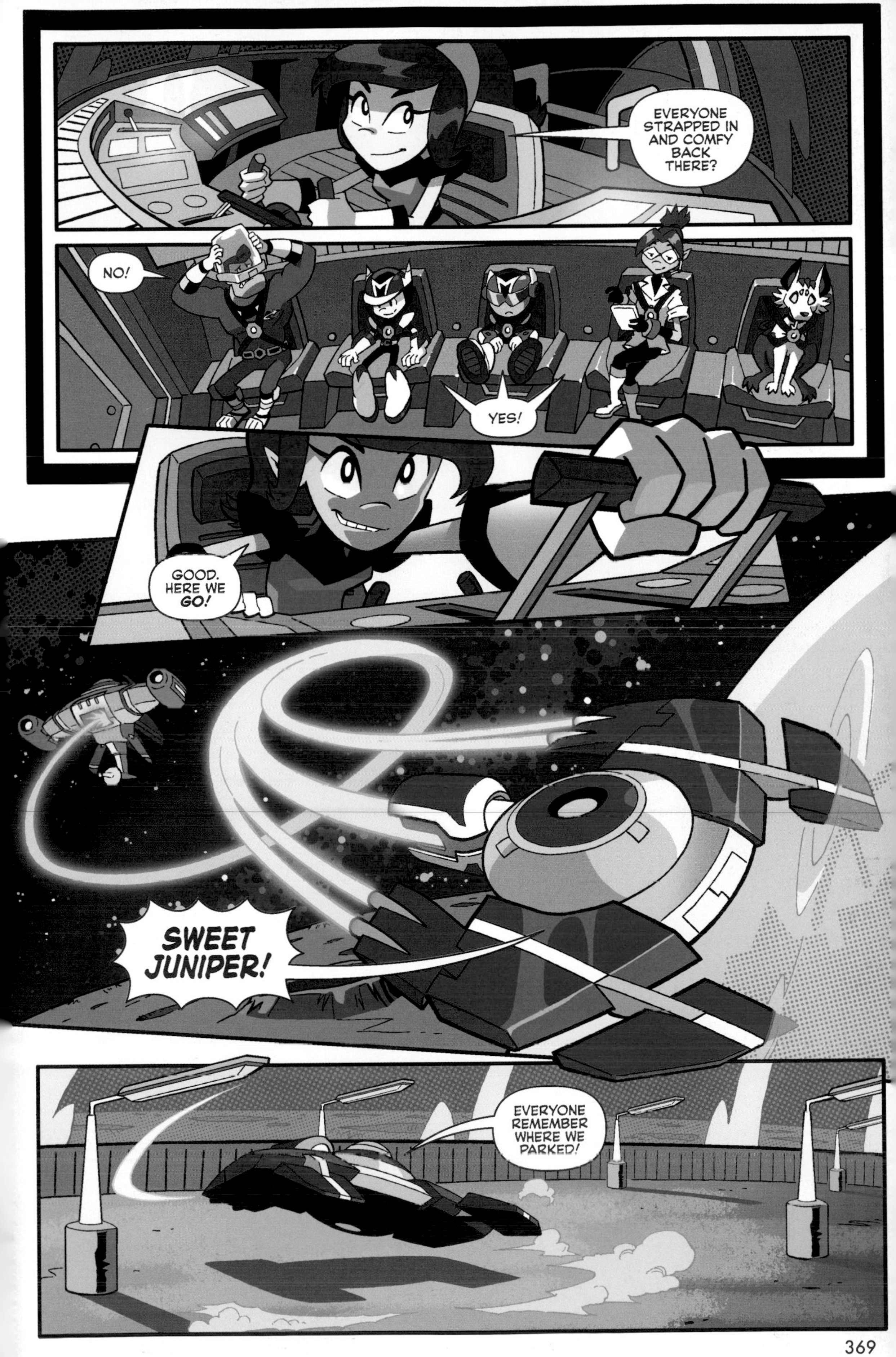
EVERYONE STRAPPED IN AND COMFY BACK THERE?
NO!
YES!
GOOD. HERE WE GO!
SWEET JUNIPER!
EVERYONE REMEMBER WHERE WE PARKED!

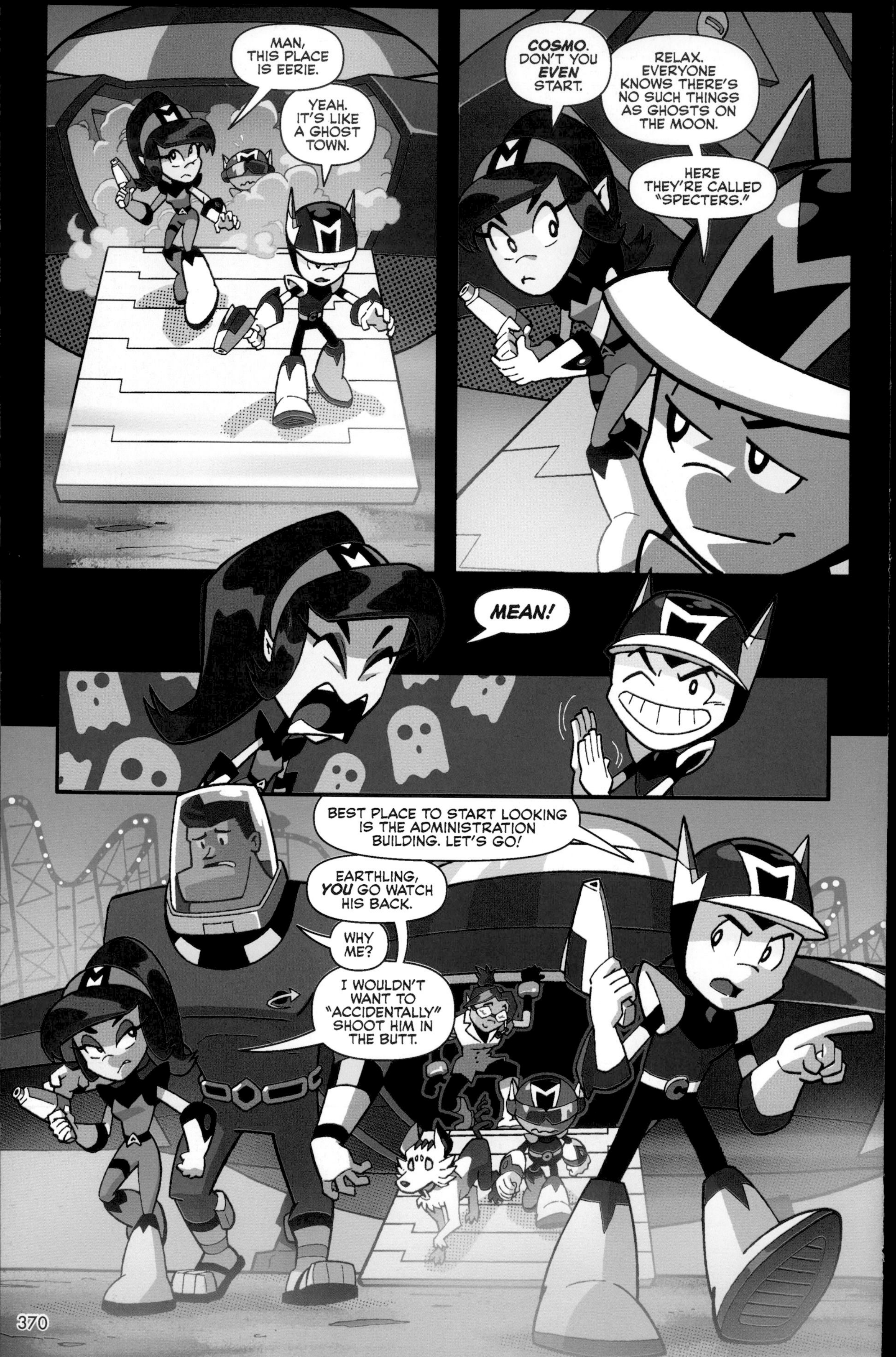

MAN, THIS PLACE IS EERIE.
YEAH. IT'S LIKE A GHOST TOWN.
COSMO. DON'T YOU EVEN START.
RELAX. EVERYONE KNOWS THERE'S NO SUCH THINGS AS GHOSTS ON THE MOON.
HERE THEY'RE CALLED "SPECTERS."
MEAN!
BEST PLACE TO START LOOKING IS THE ADMINISTRATION BUILDING. LET'S GO!
EARTHLING, YOU GO WATCH HIS BACK.
WHY ME?
I WOULDN'T WANT TO "ACCIDENTALLY" SHOOT HIM IN THE BUTT.

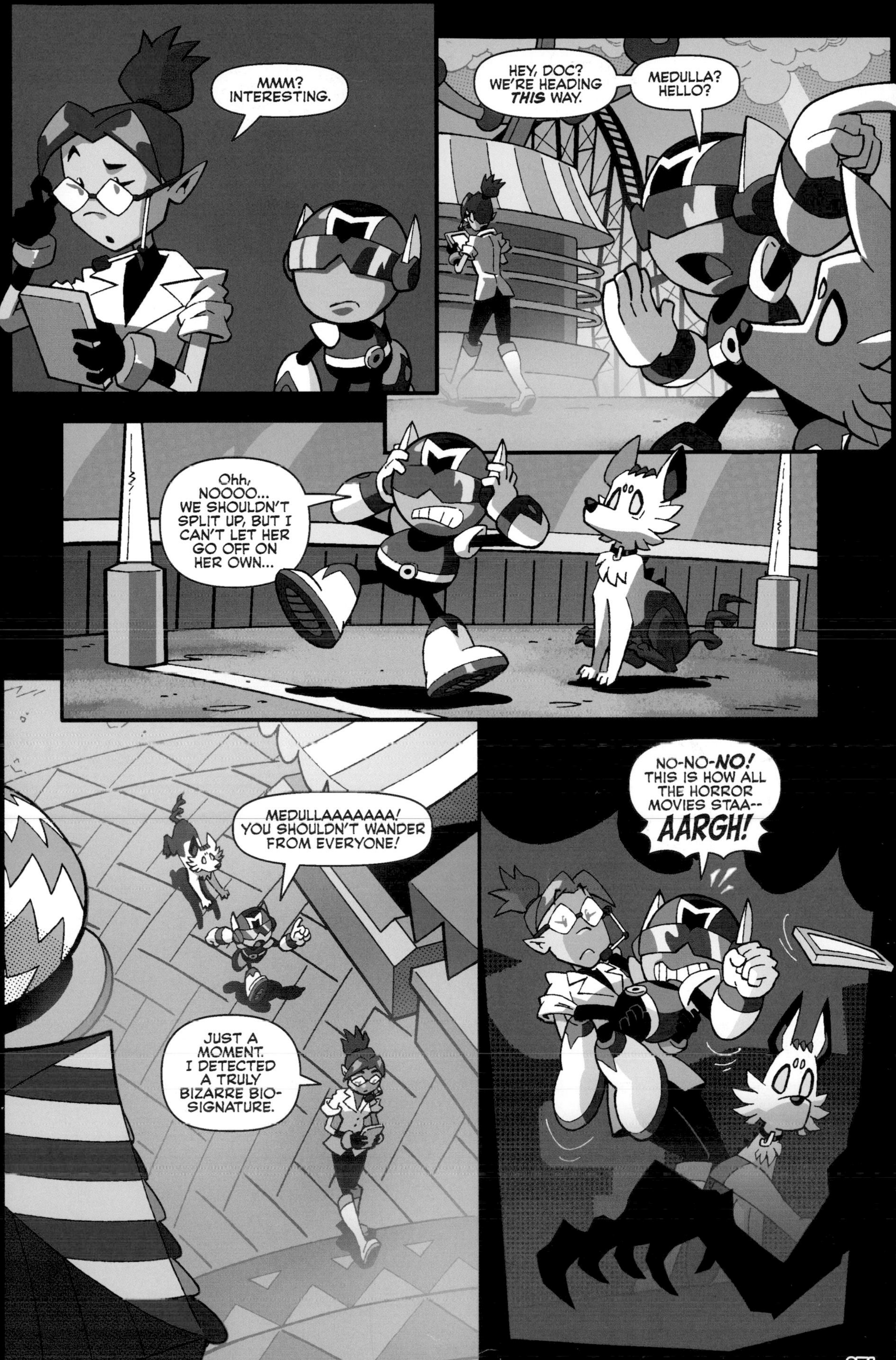
MMM? INTERESTING.
HEY, DOC? WE'RE HEADING *THIS* WAY.
MEDULLA? HELLO?
Ohh, NOOOO... WE SHOULDN'T SPLIT UP, BUT I CAN'T LET HER GO OFF ON HER OWN...
MEDULLAAAAAAA! YOU SHOULDN'T WANDER FROM EVERYONE!
JUST A MOMENT. I DETECTED A TRULY BIZARRE BIO-SIGNATURE.
NO-NO-*NO*! THIS IS HOW ALL THE HORROR MOVIES STAA--
AARGH!

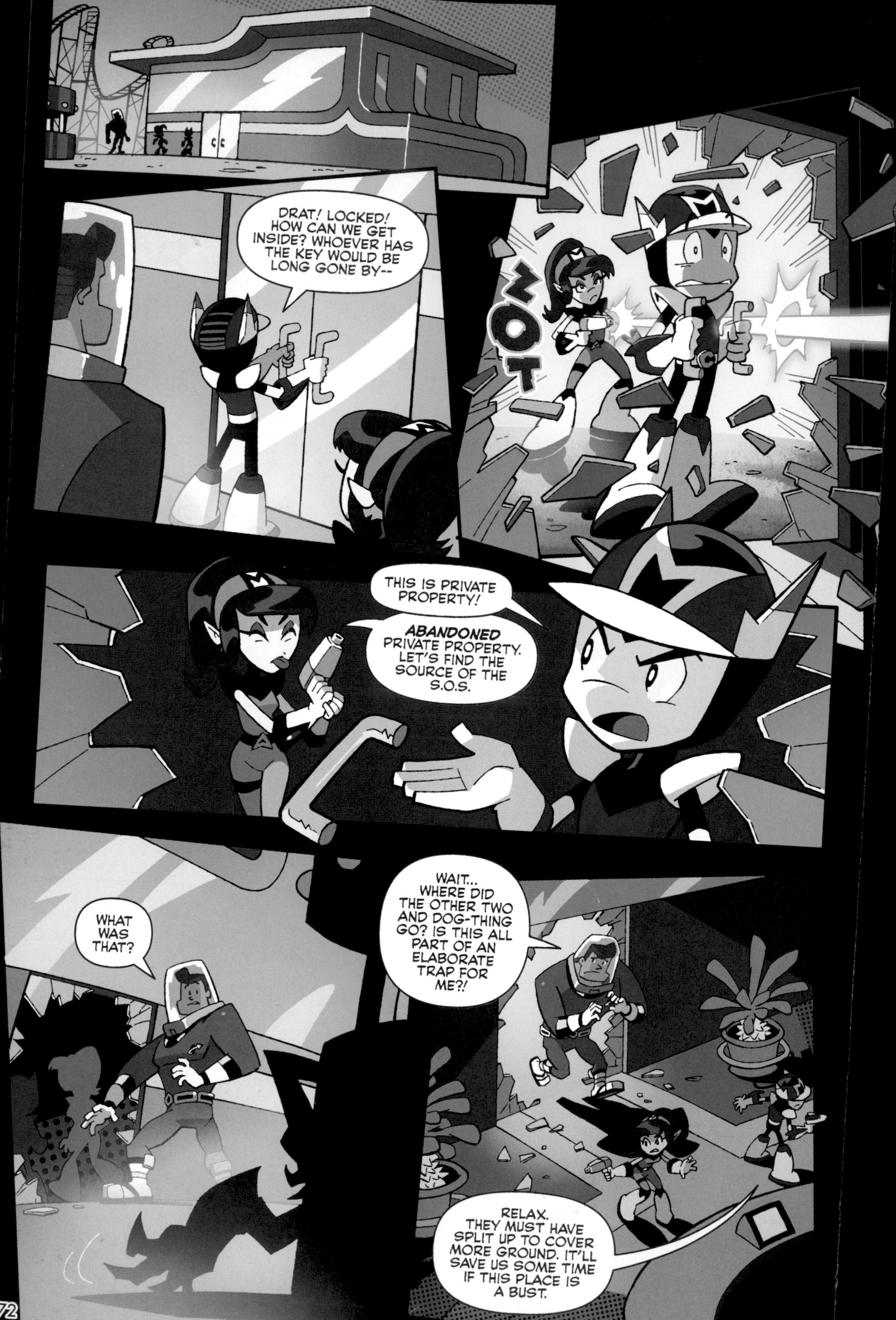
DRAT! LOCKED! HOW CAN WE GET INSIDE? WHOEVER HAS THE KEY WOULD BE LONG GONE BY--
ZOT
THIS IS PRIVATE PROPERTY!
ABANDONED PRIVATE PROPERTY. LET'S FIND THE SOURCE OF THE S.O.S.
WHAT WAS THAT?
WAIT... WHERE DID THE OTHER TWO AND DOG-THING GO? IS THIS ALL PART OF AN ELABORATE TRAP FOR ME?!
RELAX. THEY MUST HAVE SPLIT UP TO COVER MORE GROUND. IT'LL SAVE US SOME TIME IF THIS PLACE IS A BUST.

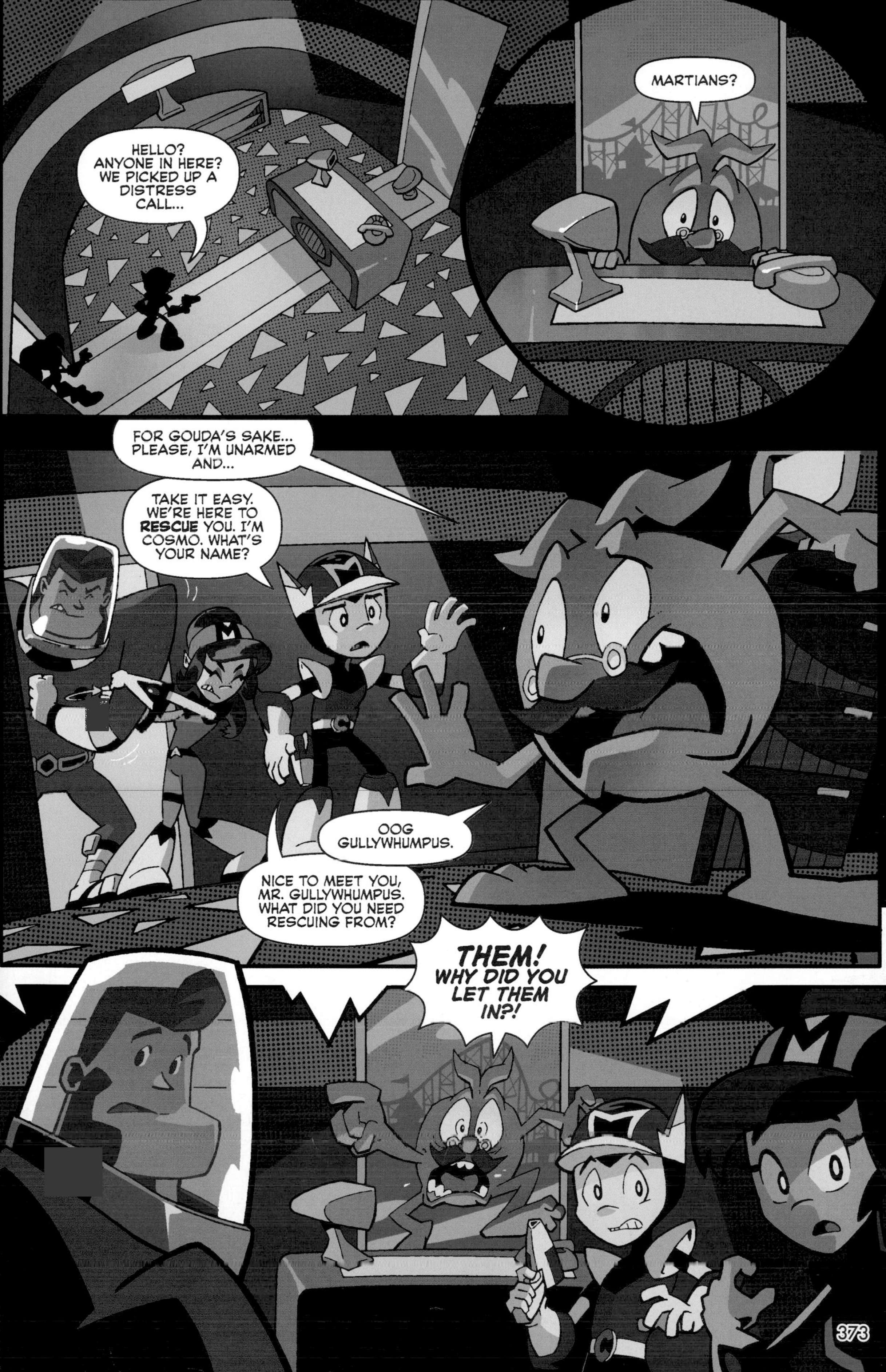
HELLO? ANYONE IN HERE? WE PICKED UP A DISTRESS CALL...
MARTIANS?
FOR GOUDA'S SAKE... PLEASE, I'M UNARMED AND...
TAKE IT EASY. WE'RE HERE TO **RESCUE** YOU. I'M COSMO. WHAT'S YOUR NAME?
OOG GULLYWHUMPUS.
NICE TO MEET YOU, MR. GULLYWHUMPUS. WHAT DID YOU NEED RESCUING FROM?
THEM! WHY DID YOU LET THEM IN?!

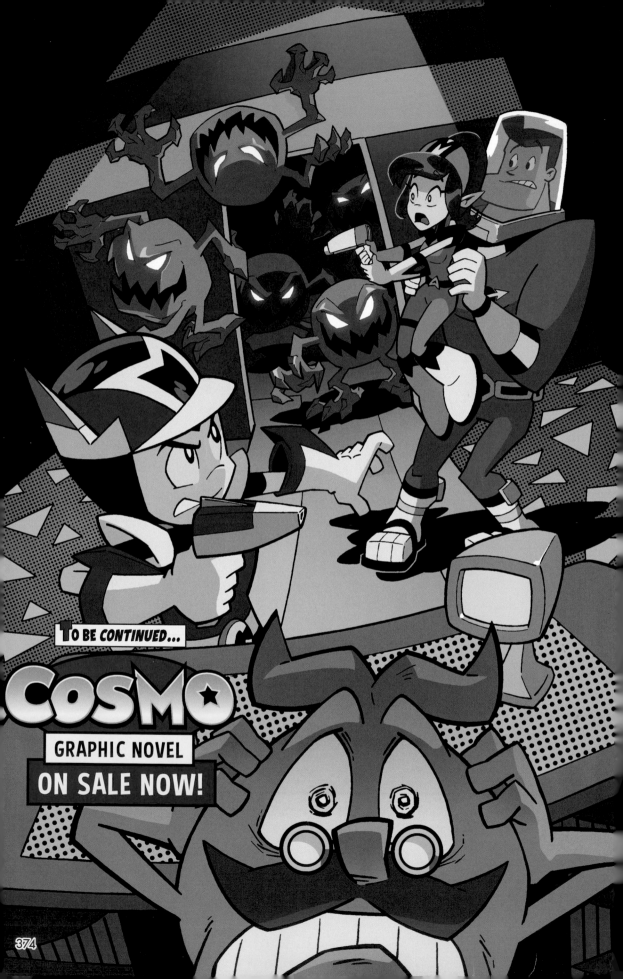

TO BE CONTINUED...

COSMO ★

GRAPHIC NOVEL
ON SALE NOW!

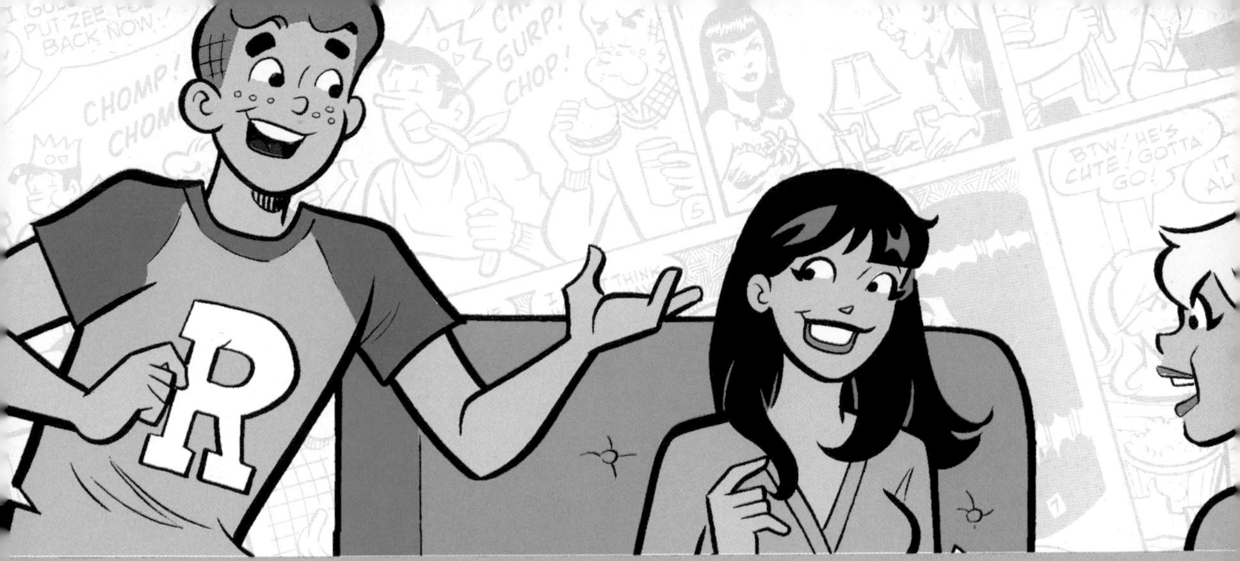
CHOMP!
GURP! CHOP!
BTW! HE'S CUTE! GOTTA GO!

RIOT ON THE SET!
& MOVIE MIX UP!

BETTY AND VERONICA FRIENDS FOREVER: AT THE MOVIES #1, 2018

BY BILL GOLLIHER, DAN PARENT, RICH KOSLOWSKI, GLENN WHITMORE & JACK MORELLI

As a fan of *Riverdale* and the new things going on at Archie, I'm glad to keep the classic style going, too. It's what I love and what feels natural to me, and I'm so glad our fans support it! I also love doing the classic five-page stories; they bring back memories of the stories I grew up on. It's especially great working with my old partner in crime, Bill Golliher. And Rich Koslowski always knocks it out of the park with his inking. Glenn Whitmore also does a bang-up job, and like Bill, we go all the way back to the Joe Kubert School years (make that decades) ago! Here's to many more classic adventures with Betty and Veronica!

—Dan Parent
Writer and Artist,
Archie Comics

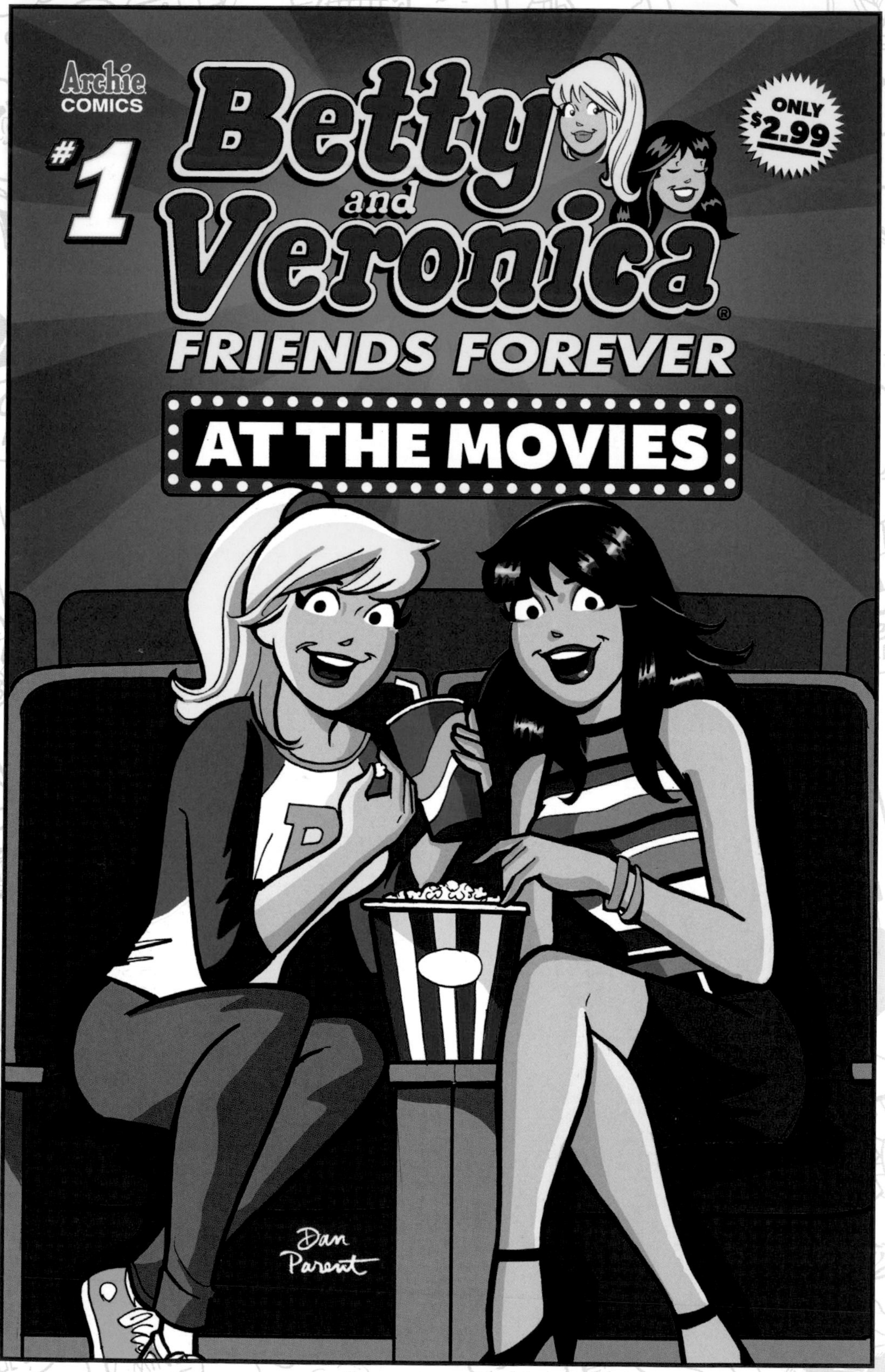
Archie
COMICS
#1
Betty
and
Veronica®
FRIENDS FOREVER
AT THE MOVIES
ONLY
$2.99
Dan
Parent

Cover to *Betty & Veronica Friends Forever: At The Movies* #1, 2018
art by Dan Parent

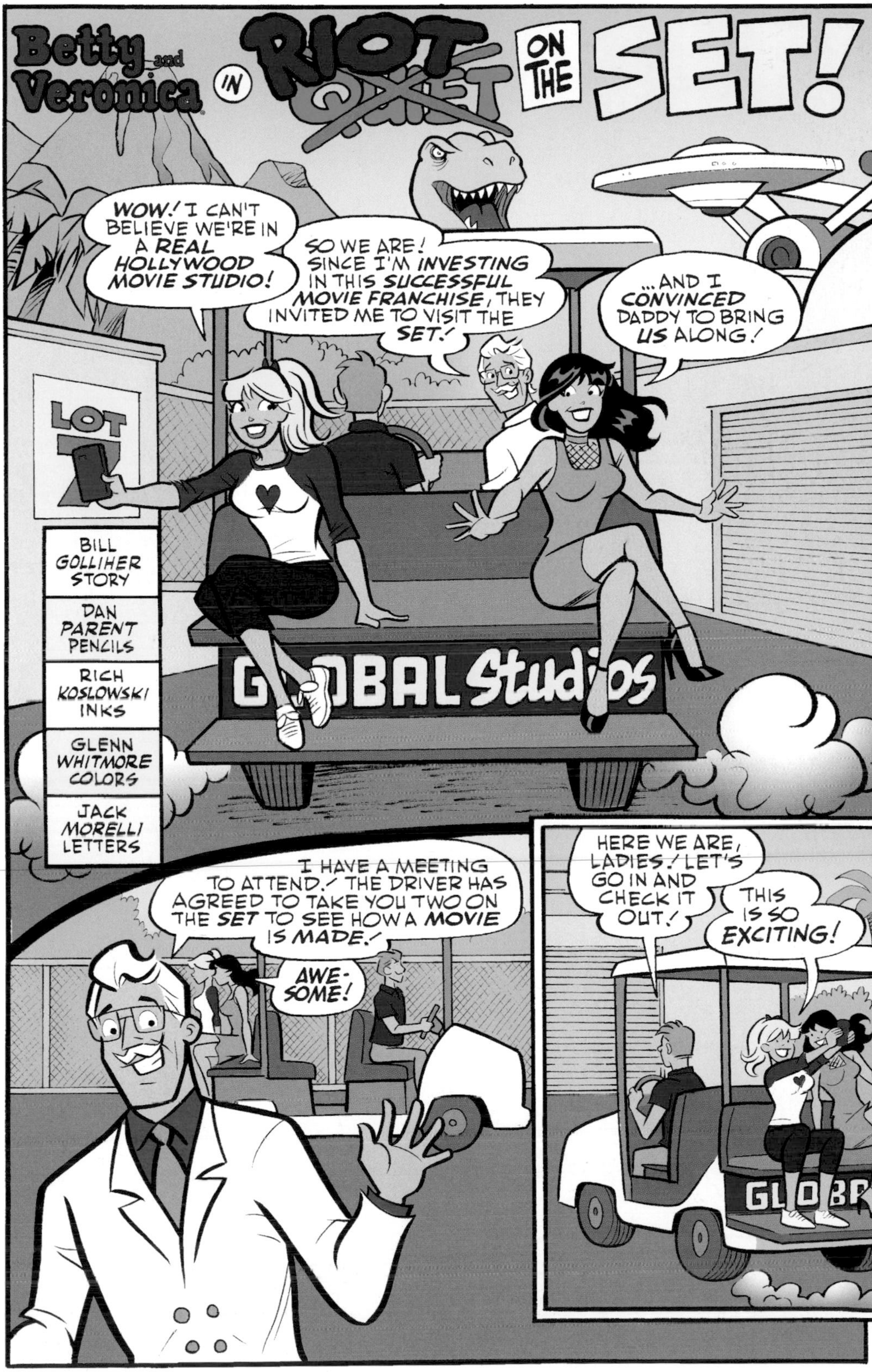

Betty and Veronica in RIOT QUIET ON THE SET!
WOW! I CAN'T BELIEVE WE'RE IN A REAL HOLLYWOOD MOVIE STUDIO!
SO WE ARE! SINCE I'M INVESTING IN THIS SUCCESSFUL MOVIE FRANCHISE, THEY INVITED ME TO VISIT THE SET!
...AND I CONVINCED DADDY TO BRING US ALONG!
LOT 7
BILL GOLLIHER STORY
DAN PARENT PENCILS
RICH KOSLOWSKI INKS
GLENN WHITMORE COLORS
JACK MORELLI LETTERS
GLOBAL Studios
I HAVE A MEETING TO ATTEND! THE DRIVER HAS AGREED TO TAKE YOU TWO ON THE SET TO SEE HOW A MOVIE IS MADE!
AWE-SOME!
HERE WE ARE, LADIES! LET'S GO IN AND CHECK IT OUT!
THIS IS SO EXCITING!
GLOBAL

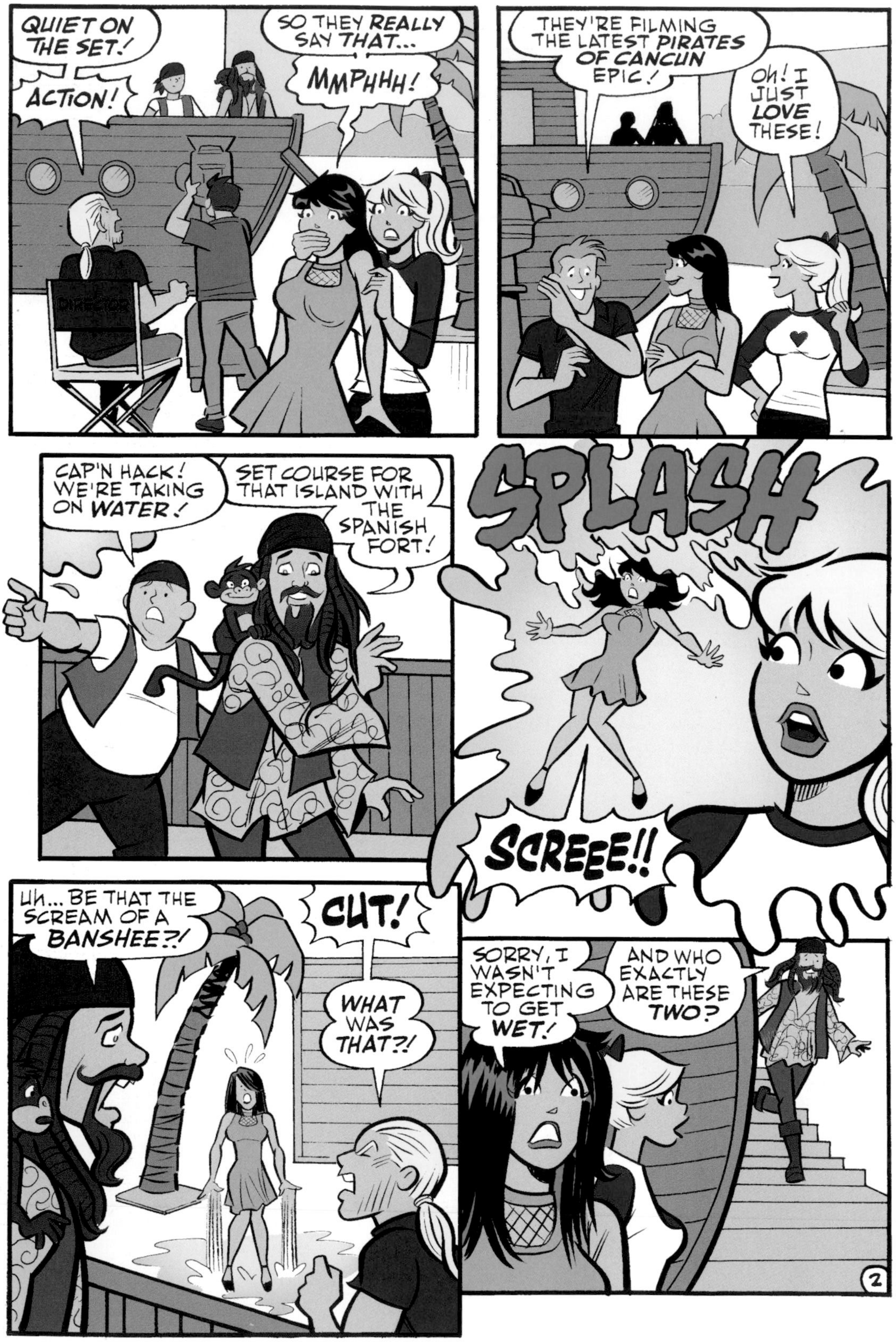
QUIET ON THE SET!
ACTION!
SO THEY REALLY SAY THAT...
MMPHHH!
DIRECTOR
THEY'RE FILMING THE LATEST PIRATES OF CANCUN EPIC!
OH! I JUST LOVE THESE!
CAP'N HACK! WE'RE TAKING ON WATER!
SET COURSE FOR THAT ISLAND WITH THE SPANISH FORT!
SPLASH
SCREEE!!
UH... BE THAT THE SCREAM OF A BANSHEE?!
CUT!
WHAT WAS THAT?!
SORRY, I WASN'T EXPECTING TO GET WET!
AND WHO EXACTLY ARE THESE TWO?
2

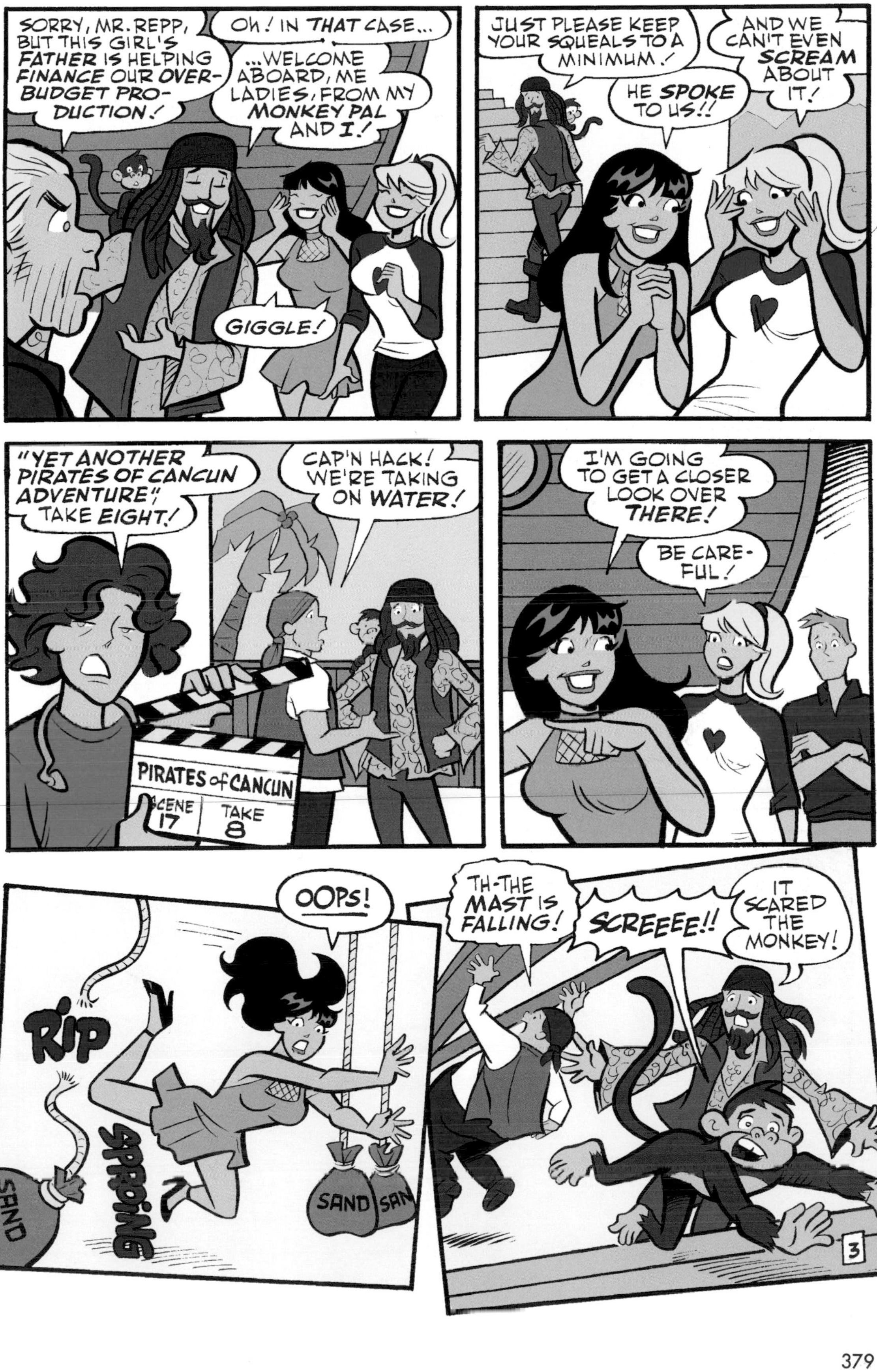
SORRY, MR. REPP, BUT THIS GIRL'S FATHER IS HELPING FINANCE OUR OVER-BUDGET PRODUCTION!
OH! IN THAT CASE...
...WELCOME ABOARD, ME LADIES, FROM MY MONKEY PAL AND I!
GIGGLE!
JUST PLEASE KEEP YOUR SQUEALS TO A MINIMUM!
HE SPOKE TO US!!
AND WE CAN'T EVEN SCREAM ABOUT IT!
"YET ANOTHER PIRATES OF CANCUN ADVENTURE", TAKE EIGHT!
CAP'N HACK! WE'RE TAKING ON WATER!
PIRATES of CANCUN
SCENE 17
TAKE 8
I'M GOING TO GET A CLOSER LOOK OVER THERE!
BE CAREFUL!
OOPS!
RIP
SPRONG
SAND
SAND
SAN
TH-THE MAST IS FALLING!
SCREEEE!!
IT SCARED THE MONKEY!
3

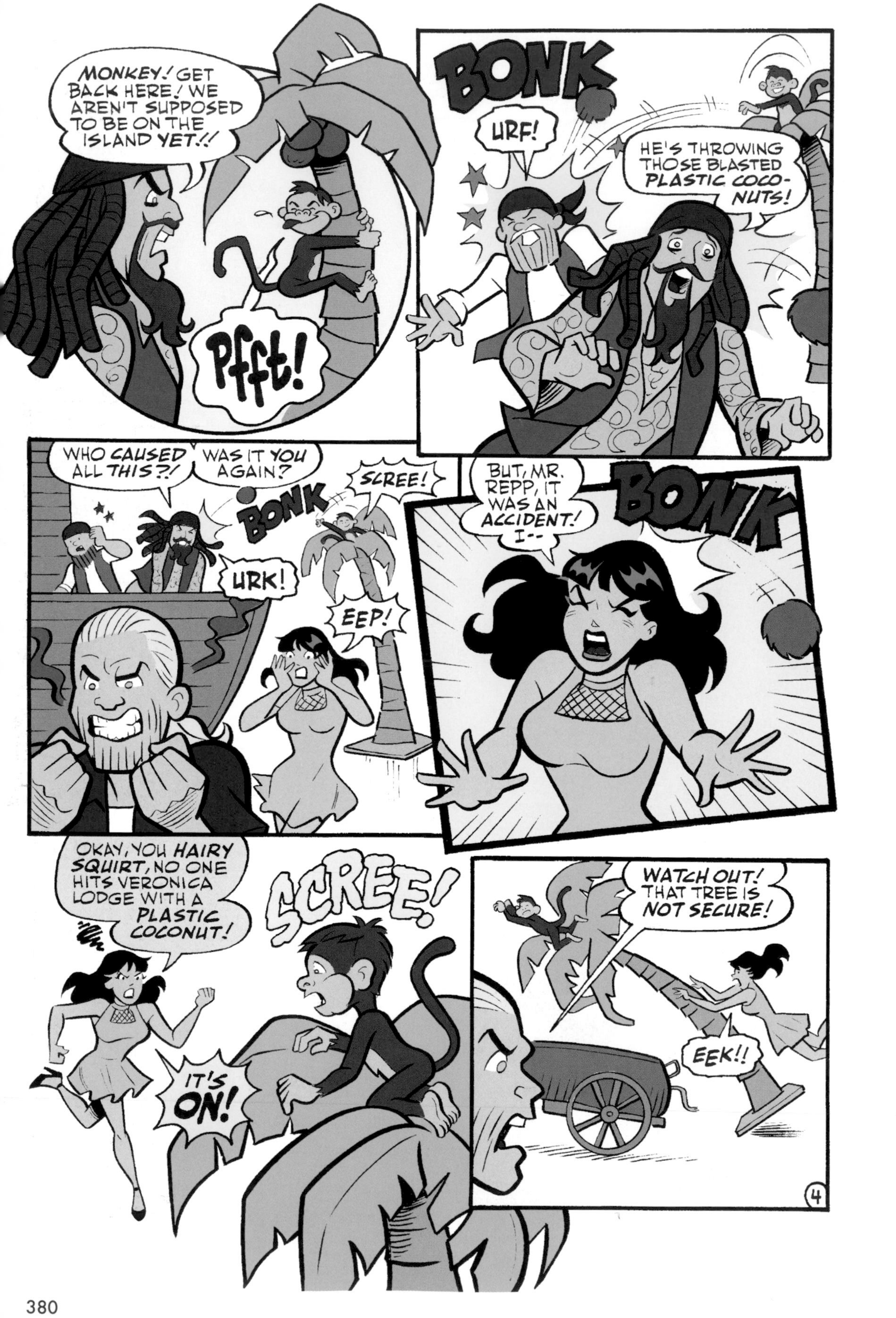
MONKEY! GET BACK HERE! WE AREN'T SUPPOSED TO BE ON THE ISLAND YET!!
Pffft!
BONK
URF!
HE'S THROWING THOSE BLASTED PLASTIC COCO-NUTS!
WHO CAUSED ALL THIS?!
WAS IT YOU AGAIN?
BONK
SCREE!
URK!
EEP!
BUT, MR. REPP, IT WAS AN ACCIDENT! I--
BONK
OKAY, YOU HAIRY SQUIRT, NO ONE HITS VERONICA LODGE WITH A PLASTIC COCONUT!
SCREE!
IT'S ON!
WATCH OUT! THAT TREE IS NOT SECURE!
EEK!!
4

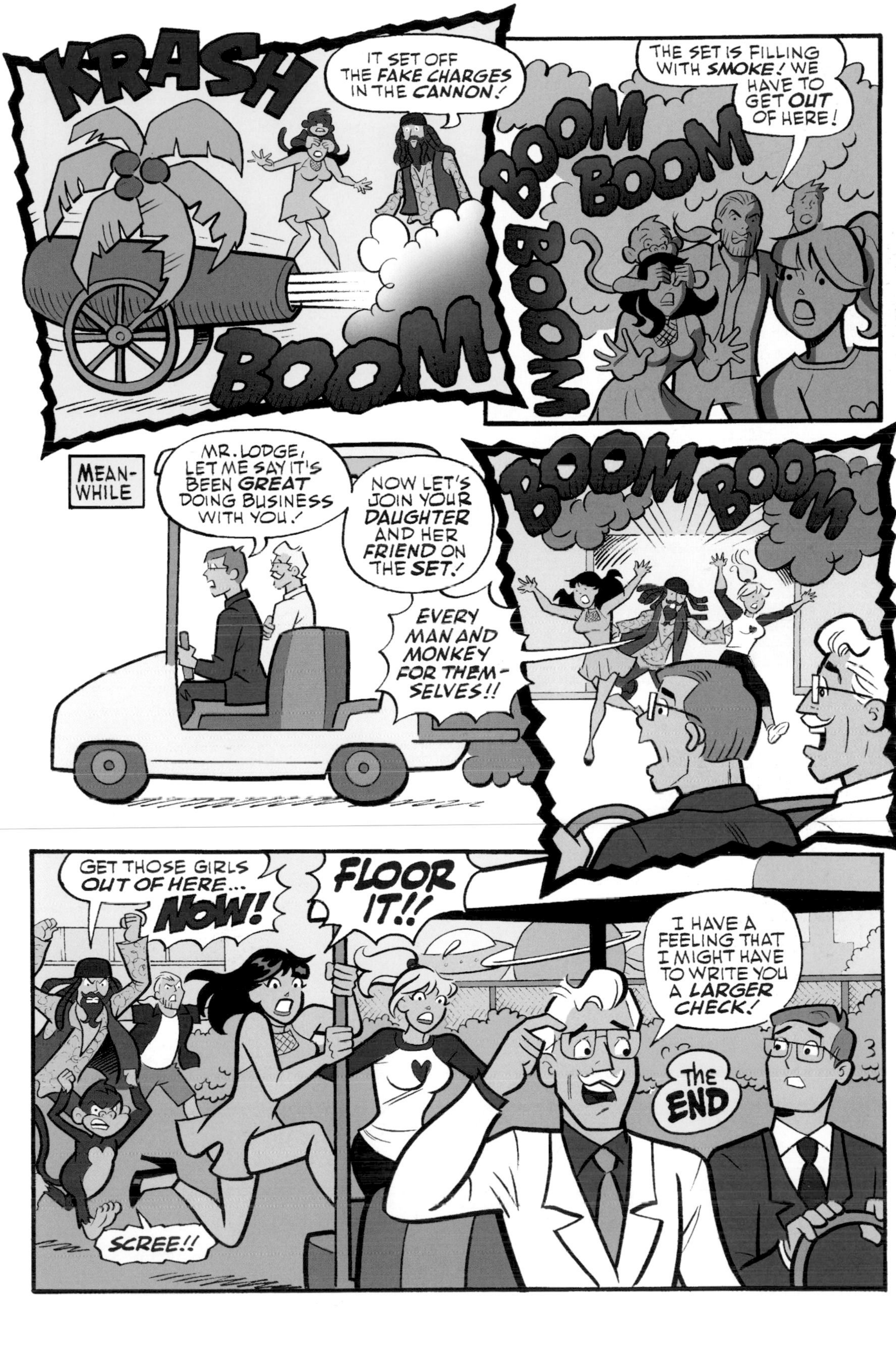
KRASH
IT SET OFF THE FAKE CHARGES IN THE CANNON!
BOOM
THE SET IS FILLING WITH SMOKE! WE HAVE TO GET OUT OF HERE!
BOOM BOOM BOOM
MEAN-WHILE
MR. LODGE, LET ME SAY IT'S BEEN GREAT DOING BUSINESS WITH YOU!
NOW LET'S JOIN YOUR DAUGHTER AND HER FRIEND ON THE SET!
EVERY MAN AND MONKEY FOR THEM-SELVES!!
BOOM BOOM
GET THOSE GIRLS OUT OF HERE... NOW!
FLOOR IT!!
I HAVE A FEELING THAT I MIGHT HAVE TO WRITE YOU A LARGER CHECK!
THE END
SCREE!!

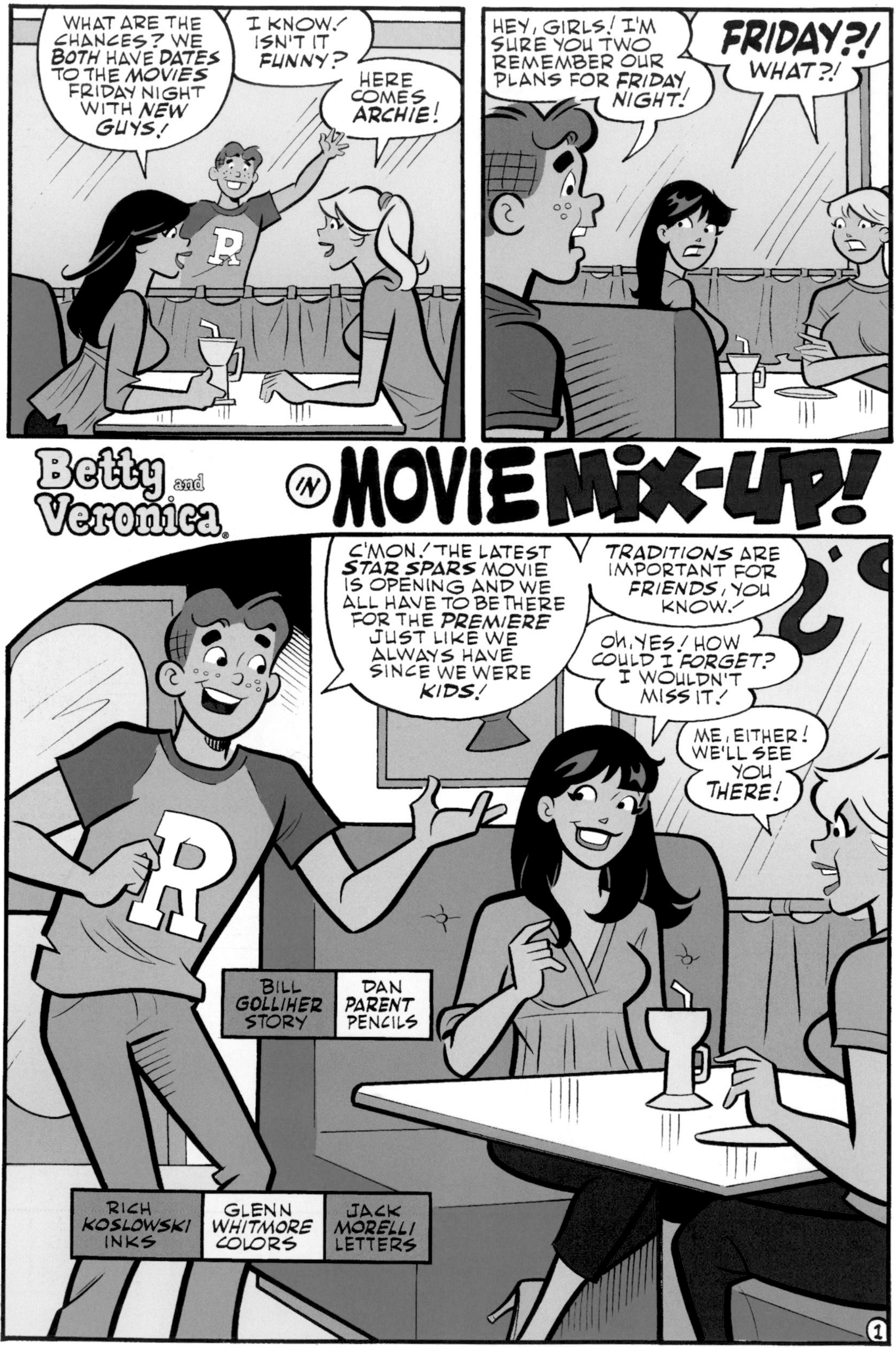
WHAT ARE THE CHANCES? WE BOTH HAVE DATES TO THE MOVIES FRIDAY NIGHT WITH NEW GUYS!
I KNOW! ISN'T IT FUNNY?
HERE COMES ARCHIE!
HEY, GIRLS! I'M SURE YOU TWO REMEMBER OUR PLANS FOR FRIDAY NIGHT!
FRIDAY?! WHAT?!
Betty and Veronica
IN MOVIE MIX-UP!
C'MON! THE LATEST STAR SPARS MOVIE IS OPENING AND WE ALL HAVE TO BE THERE FOR THE PREMIERE JUST LIKE WE ALWAYS HAVE SINCE WE WERE KIDS!
TRADITIONS ARE IMPORTANT FOR FRIENDS, YOU KNOW!
OH, YES! HOW COULD I FORGET? I WOULDN'T MISS IT!
ME, EITHER! WE'LL SEE YOU THERE!
BILL GOLLIHER STORY
DAN PARENT PENCILS
RICH KOSLOWSKI INKS
GLENN WHITMORE COLORS
JACK MORELLI LETTERS
1

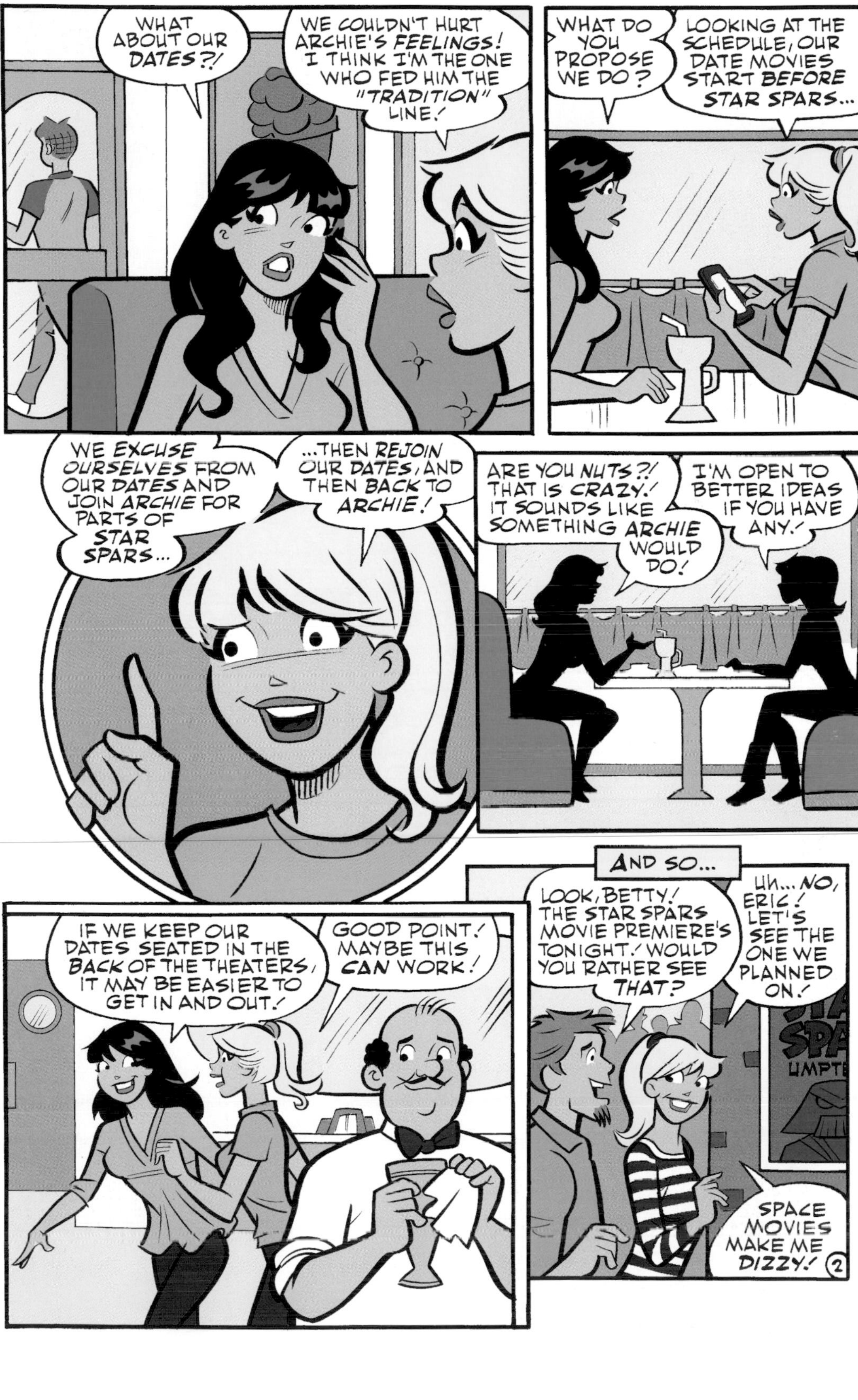
WHAT ABOUT OUR DATES?!
WE COULDN'T HURT ARCHIE'S FEELINGS! I THINK I'M THE ONE WHO FED HIM THE "TRADITION" LINE!
WHAT DO YOU PROPOSE WE DO?
LOOKING AT THE SCHEDULE, OUR DATE MOVIES START BEFORE STAR SPARS...
WE EXCUSE OURSELVES FROM OUR DATES AND JOIN ARCHIE FOR PARTS OF STAR SPARS...
...THEN REJOIN OUR DATES, AND THEN BACK TO ARCHIE!
ARE YOU NUTS?! THAT IS CRAZY! IT SOUNDS LIKE SOMETHING ARCHIE WOULD DO!
I'M OPEN TO BETTER IDEAS IF YOU HAVE ANY!
IF WE KEEP OUR DATES SEATED IN THE BACK OF THE THEATERS, IT MAY BE EASIER TO GET IN AND OUT!
GOOD POINT! MAYBE THIS CAN WORK!
AND SO...
LOOK, BETTY! THE STAR SPARS MOVIE PREMIERE'S TONIGHT! WOULD YOU RATHER SEE THAT?
UH... NO, ERIC! LET'S SEE THE ONE WE PLANNED ON!
SPACE MOVIES MAKE ME DIZZY!
2

MEANWHILE... VERONICA, WOULD YOU CARE TO SEE *STAR SPARS* INSTEAD?

NO, PAUL! I INSIST ON SEEING WHATEVER IS IN THE THEATER *ACROSS* FROM IT!

OKAY!

TICKETS

SOON... WHERE ARE YOU *GOING*, BETTY? THE MOVIE IS JUST GETTING INTERESTING!

UH... IT'S THE *POPCORN!* IT NEEDS MUCH MORE *BUTTER!*

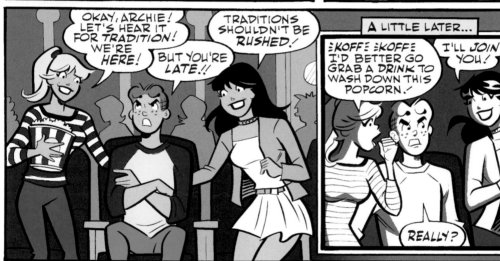

OKAY, ARCHIE! LET'S HEAR IT FOR *TRADITION!* WE'RE *HERE!*

BUT YOU'RE *LATE!!*

TRADITIONS SHOULDN'T BE *RUSHED!*

A LITTLE LATER...

≿KOFF≿ ≿KOFF≿ I'D BETTER GO GRAB A *DRINK* TO WASH DOWN THIS POPCORN!

I'LL *JOIN* YOU!

REALLY?

≿Whew!≿ I HAVE TO GET BACK TO MY *THEATER!*

I THINK I'LL GO GRAB A DRINK, SO I'LL HAVE A GOOD *EXCUSE* FOR PAUL!

IT'S DARK IN HERE!

OKAY, WHAT DID I *MISS?*

DO I *KNOW* YOU? I'M *PAUL!*

3

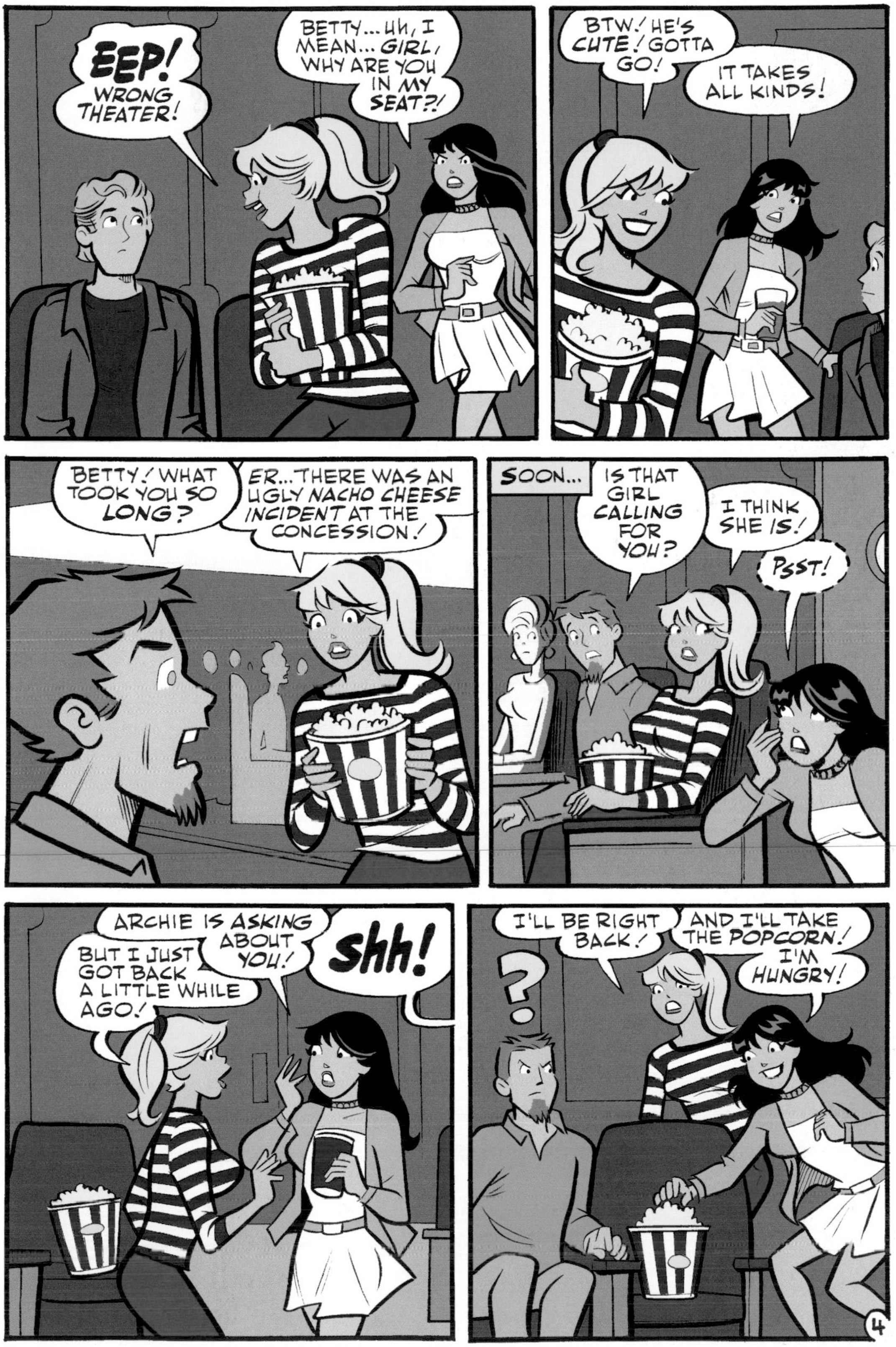
EEP! WRONG THEATER!
BETTY... UH, I MEAN... GIRL, WHY ARE YOU IN MY SEAT?!
BTW! HE'S CUTE! GOTTA GO!
IT TAKES ALL KINDS!
BETTY! WHAT TOOK YOU SO LONG?
ER... THERE WAS AN UGLY NACHO CHEESE INCIDENT AT THE CONCESSION!
SOON...
IS THAT GIRL CALLING FOR YOU?
I THINK SHE IS!
PSST!
ARCHIE IS ASKING ABOUT YOU!
BUT I JUST GOT BACK A LITTLE WHILE AGO!
SHH!
I'LL BE RIGHT BACK!
AND I'LL TAKE THE POPCORN! I'M HUNGRY!
?
4

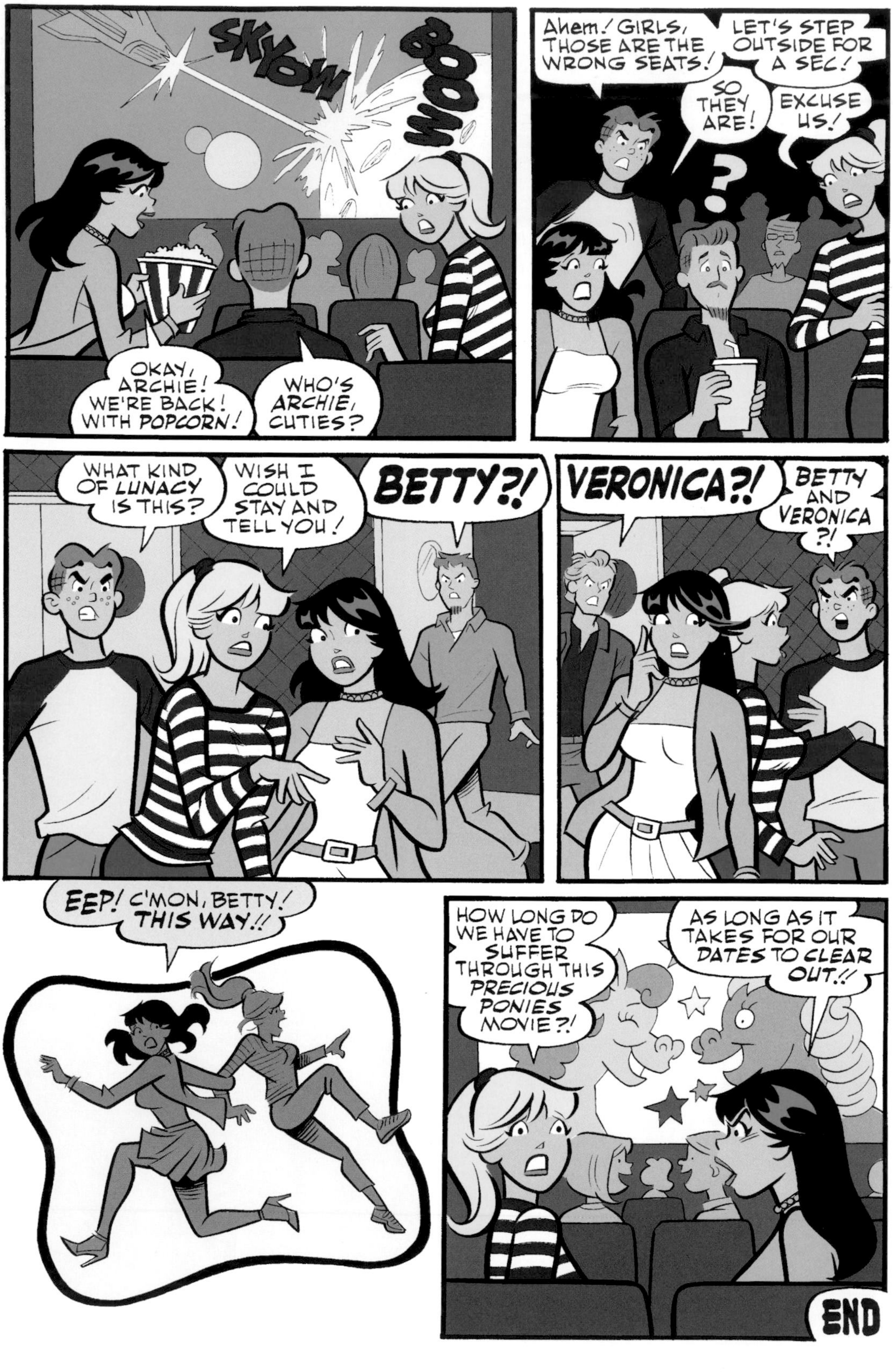
SKYOW
BOOOM
OKAY, ARCHIE! WE'RE BACK! WITH POPCORN!
WHO'S ARCHIE, CUTIES?
Ahem! GIRLS, THOSE ARE THE WRONG SEATS!
LET'S STEP OUTSIDE FOR A SEC!
SO THEY ARE!
EXCUSE US!
WHAT KIND OF LUNACY IS THIS?
WISH I COULD STAY AND TELL YOU!
BETTY?!
VERONICA?!
BETTY AND VERONICA ?!
EEP! C'MON, BETTY! THIS WAY!!
HOW LONG DO WE HAVE TO SUFFER THROUGH THIS PRECIOUS PONIES MOVIE?!
AS LONG AS IT TAKES FOR OUR DATES TO CLEAR OUT!!
END

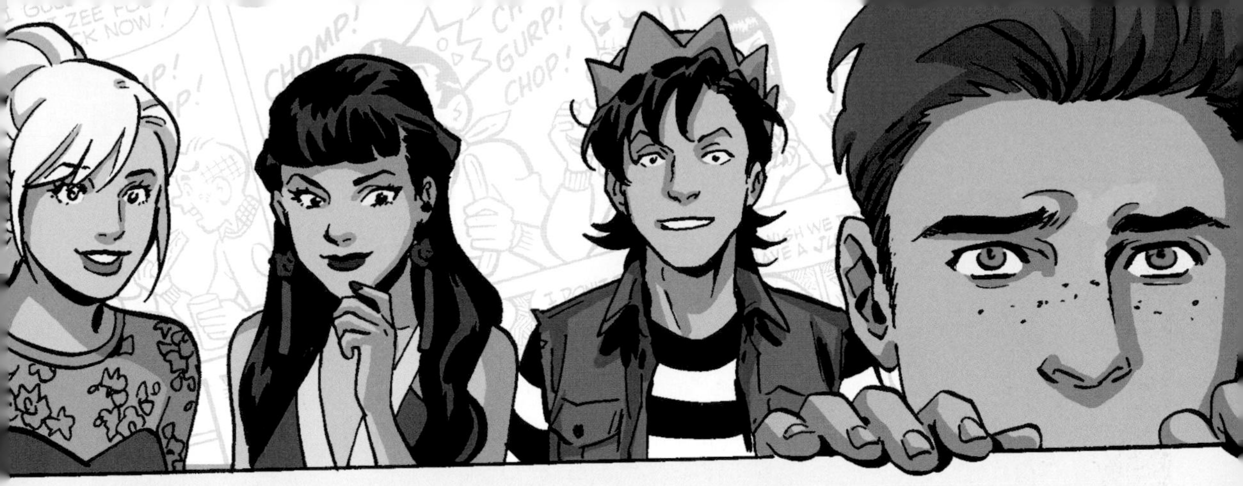
CHOMP!
GURP!
CHOP!

ARCHIE

ARCHIE #32, 2018

BY MARK WAID, IAN FLYNN, AUDREY MOK, KELLY FITZPATRICK & JACK MORELLI

In 1941 (that's over 75 years ago!), a lot changed in the world, and even more was to come. Also in that year, a little company called MLJ Comics that created superhero comics after years of publishing pulp novels introduced a brand new character: seemingly out of the blue, a red-headed everyday teen character showed up in their comics... and everything changed.

The teen, named Archie Andrews, was so influential on the company that MLJ actually changed its name to Archie Comics! Archie, the character, lived in the perfect any town known as "Riverdale," which for the past 75 years has remained the same—while simultaneously changing and evolving, just like the world around us.

As you have seen in The CW *Riverdale* TV series, the characters are versatile, strong-willed, likable and enthralling—and the same can be said for the cast and stories that appear in our comics. When it comes to passion, intrigue and emotion—Archie has it all.

—Mike Pellerito
Co-President, Archie Comics

ARCHIE COVER

ARCHIE #700, 2018

ART BY MARGUERITE SAUVAGE

This isn't a reboot... what you'll see is a change of pace and a little zooming out to include some core Archie characters that maybe haven't popped up before. We'll also see the drama level increase a bit, but not to the point where the humor and familiar character beats go away. It also makes for a great, fresh jumping on point for fans of the *Riverdale* show or any comic readers who may have drifted away from the series.

—Alex Segura
Co-President, Archie Comics

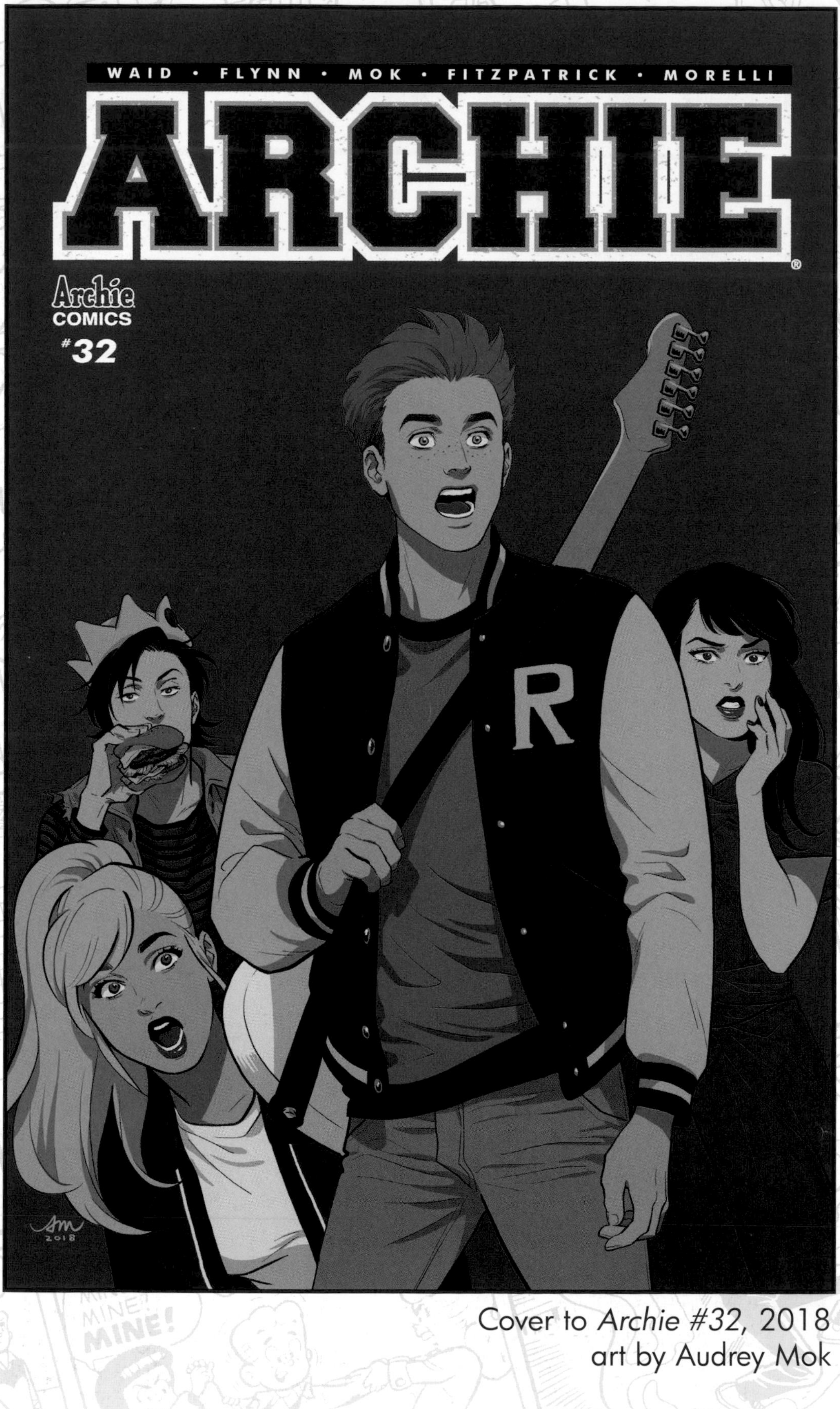
WAID • FLYNN • MOK • FITZPATRICK • MORELLI
ARCHIE
Archie COMICS
#32
R

Cover to *Archie #32*, 2018
art by Audrey Mok

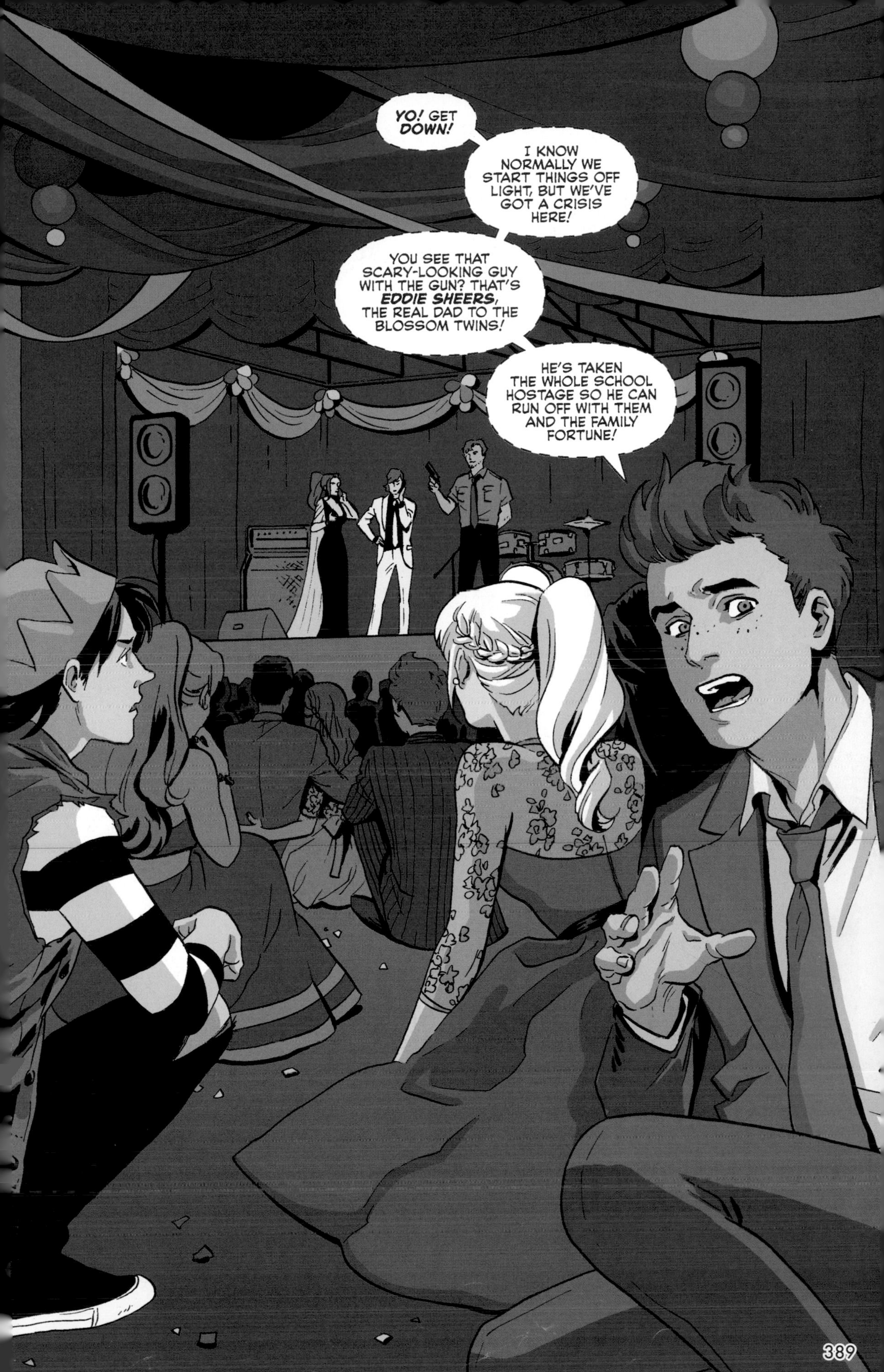
YO! GET DOWN!
I KNOW NORMALLY WE START THINGS OFF LIGHT, BUT WE'VE GOT A CRISIS HERE!
YOU SEE THAT SCARY-LOOKING GUY WITH THE GUN? THAT'S EDDIE SHEERS, THE REAL DAD TO THE BLOSSOM TWINS!
HE'S TAKEN THE WHOLE SCHOOL HOSTAGE SO HE CAN RUN OFF WITH THEM AND THE FAMILY FORTUNE!

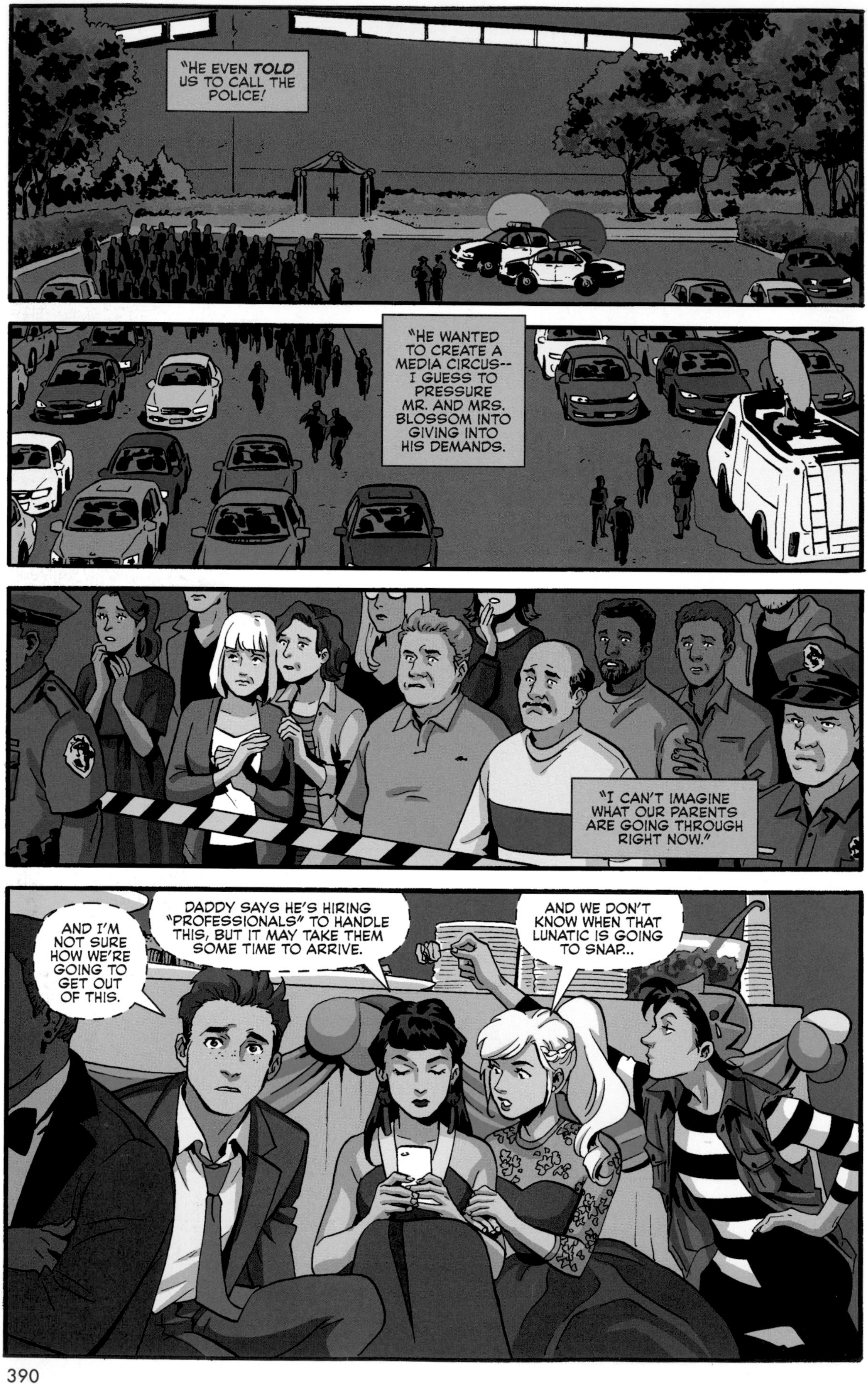
"HE EVEN TOLD US TO CALL THE POLICE!
"HE WANTED TO CREATE A MEDIA CIRCUS-- I GUESS TO PRESSURE MR. AND MRS. BLOSSOM INTO GIVING INTO HIS DEMANDS.
"I CAN'T IMAGINE WHAT OUR PARENTS ARE GOING THROUGH RIGHT NOW."
AND I'M NOT SURE HOW WE'RE GOING TO GET OUT OF THIS.
DADDY SAYS HE'S HIRING "PROFESSIONALS" TO HANDLE THIS, BUT IT MAY TAKE THEM SOME TIME TO ARRIVE.
AND WE DON'T KNOW WHEN THAT LUNATIC IS GOING TO SNAP...

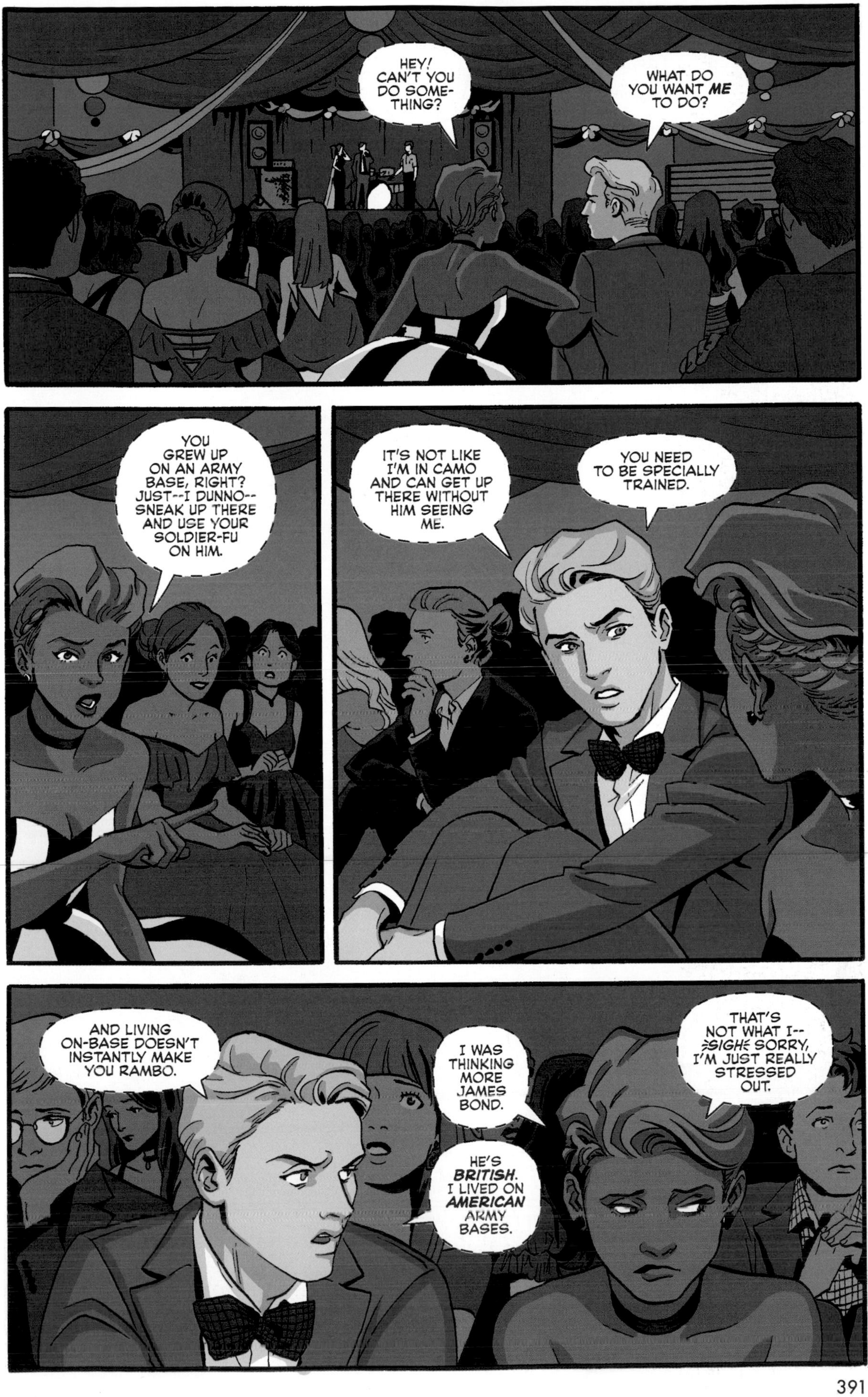
HEY! CAN'T YOU DO SOME-THING?
WHAT DO YOU WANT ME TO DO?
YOU GREW UP ON AN ARMY BASE, RIGHT? JUST--I DUNNO--SNEAK UP THERE AND USE YOUR SOLDIER-FU ON HIM.
IT'S NOT LIKE I'M IN CAMO AND CAN GET UP THERE WITHOUT HIM SEEING ME.
YOU NEED TO BE SPECIALLY TRAINED.
AND LIVING ON-BASE DOESN'T INSTANTLY MAKE YOU RAMBO.
I WAS THINKING MORE JAMES BOND.
HE'S BRITISH. I LIVED ON AMERICAN ARMY BASES.
THAT'S NOT WHAT I-- ≶SIGH≶ SORRY, I'M JUST REALLY STRESSED OUT.

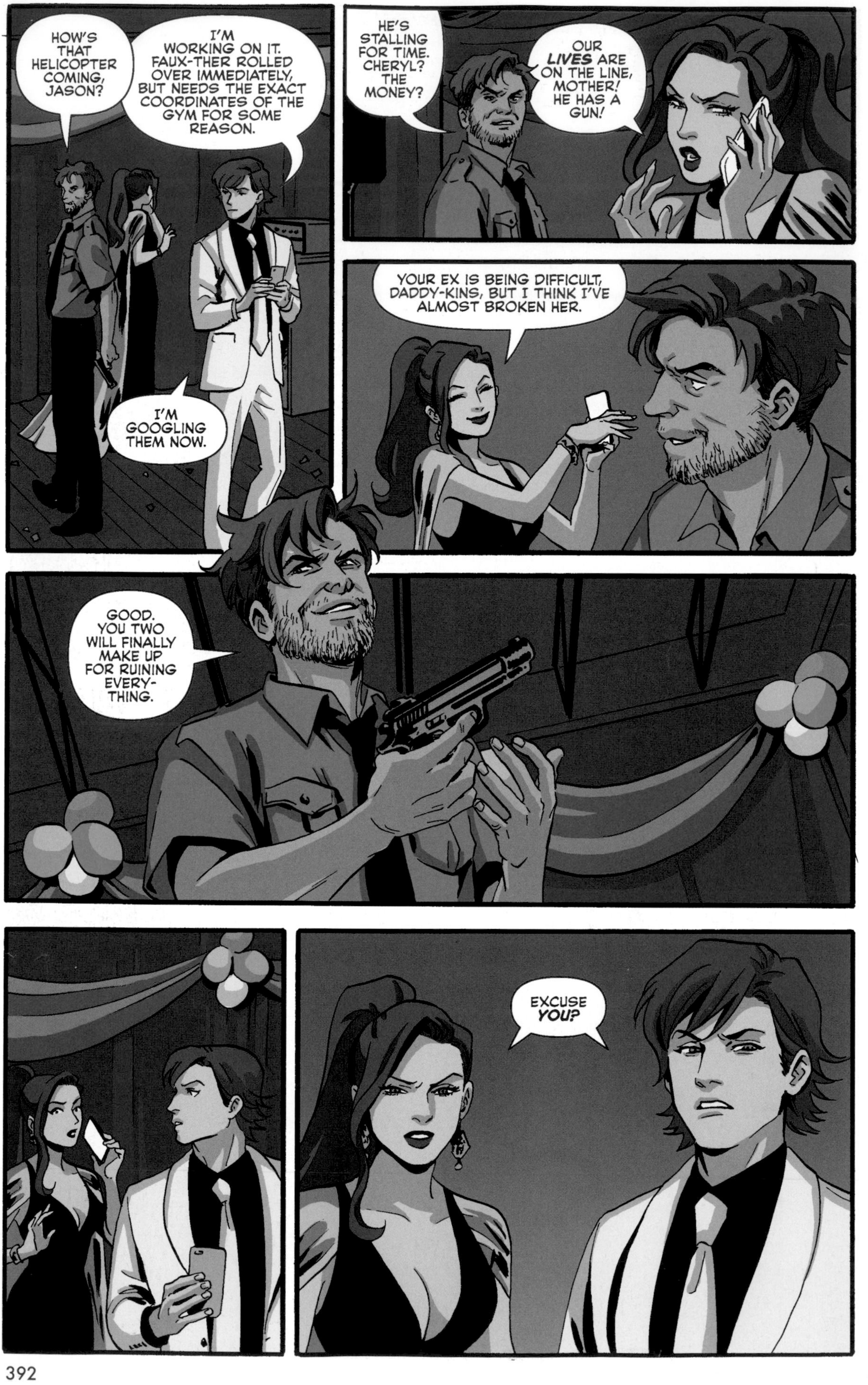
HOW'S THAT HELICOPTER COMING, JASON?
I'M WORKING ON IT. FAUX-THER ROLLED OVER IMMEDIATELY, BUT NEEDS THE EXACT COORDINATES OF THE GYM FOR SOME REASON.
I'M GOOGLING THEM NOW.
HE'S STALLING FOR TIME. CHERYL? THE MONEY?
OUR LIVES ARE ON THE LINE, MOTHER! HE HAS A GUN!
YOUR EX IS BEING DIFFICULT, DADDY-KINS, BUT I THINK I'VE ALMOST BROKEN HER.
GOOD. YOU TWO WILL FINALLY MAKE UP FOR RUINING EVERY-THING.
EXCUSE YOU?

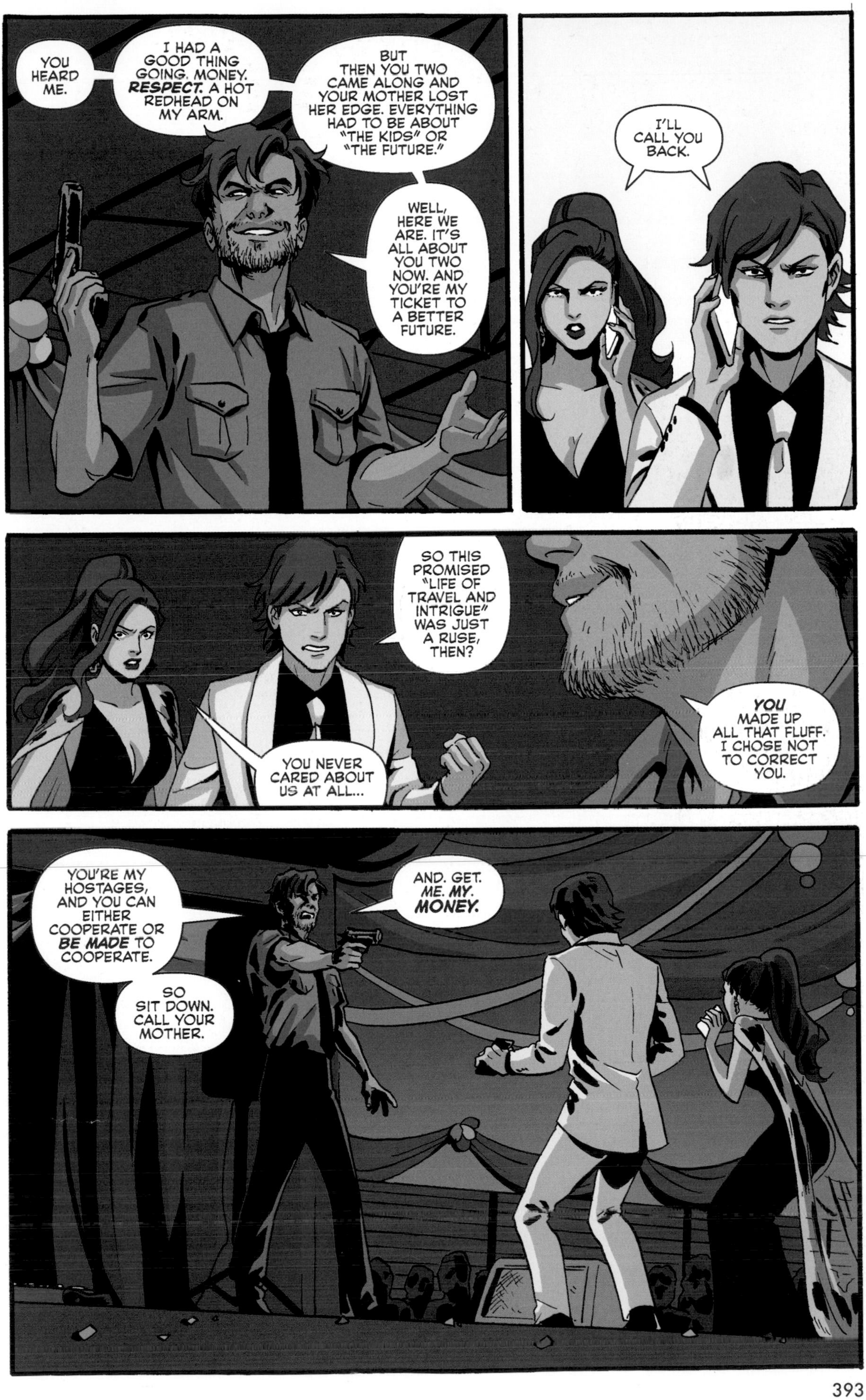
YOU HEARD ME.
I HAD A GOOD THING GOING. MONEY. RESPECT. A HOT REDHEAD ON MY ARM.
BUT THEN YOU TWO CAME ALONG AND YOUR MOTHER LOST HER EDGE. EVERYTHING HAD TO BE ABOUT "THE KIDS" OR "THE FUTURE."
WELL, HERE WE ARE. IT'S ALL ABOUT YOU TWO NOW. AND YOU'RE MY TICKET TO A BETTER FUTURE.
I'LL CALL YOU BACK.
SO THIS PROMISED "LIFE OF TRAVEL AND INTRIGUE" WAS JUST A RUSE, THEN?
YOU NEVER CARED ABOUT US AT ALL...
YOU MADE UP ALL THAT FLUFF. I CHOSE NOT TO CORRECT YOU.
YOU'RE MY HOSTAGES, AND YOU CAN EITHER COOPERATE OR BE MADE TO COOPERATE.
SO SIT DOWN. CALL YOUR MOTHER.
AND. GET. ME. MY. MONEY.

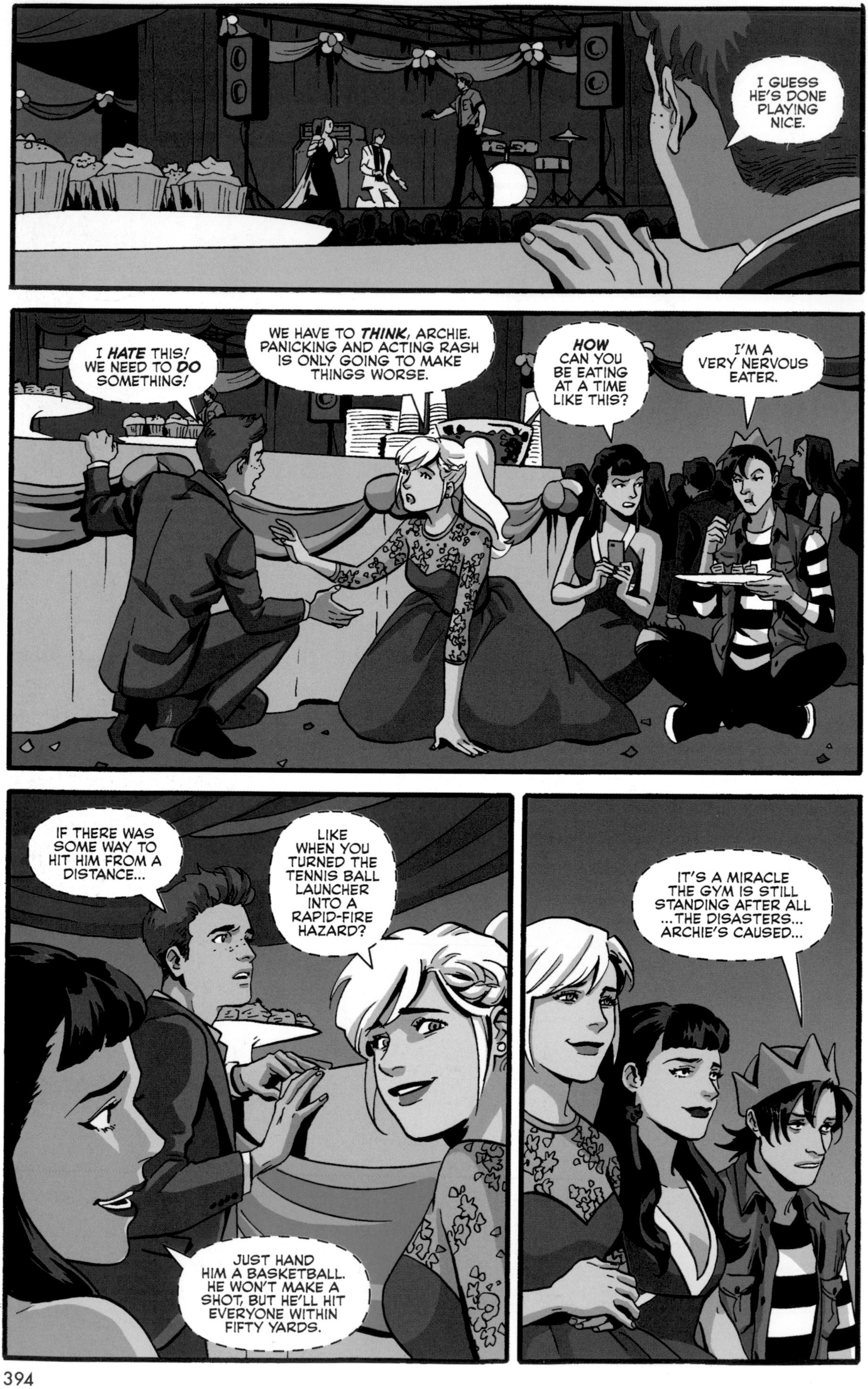
I GUESS HE'S DONE PLAYING NICE.
I HATE THIS! WE NEED TO DO SOMETHING!
WE HAVE TO THINK, ARCHIE. PANICKING AND ACTING RASH IS ONLY GOING TO MAKE THINGS WORSE.
HOW CAN YOU BE EATING AT A TIME LIKE THIS?
I'M A VERY NERVOUS EATER.
IF THERE WAS SOME WAY TO HIT HIM FROM A DISTANCE...
LIKE WHEN YOU TURNED THE TENNIS BALL LAUNCHER INTO A RAPID-FIRE HAZARD?
JUST HAND HIM A BASKETBALL. HE WON'T MAKE A SHOT, BUT HE'LL HIT EVERYONE WITHIN FIFTY YARDS.
IT'S A MIRACLE THE GYM IS STILL STANDING AFTER ALL ...THE DISASTERS... ARCHIE'S CAUSED...

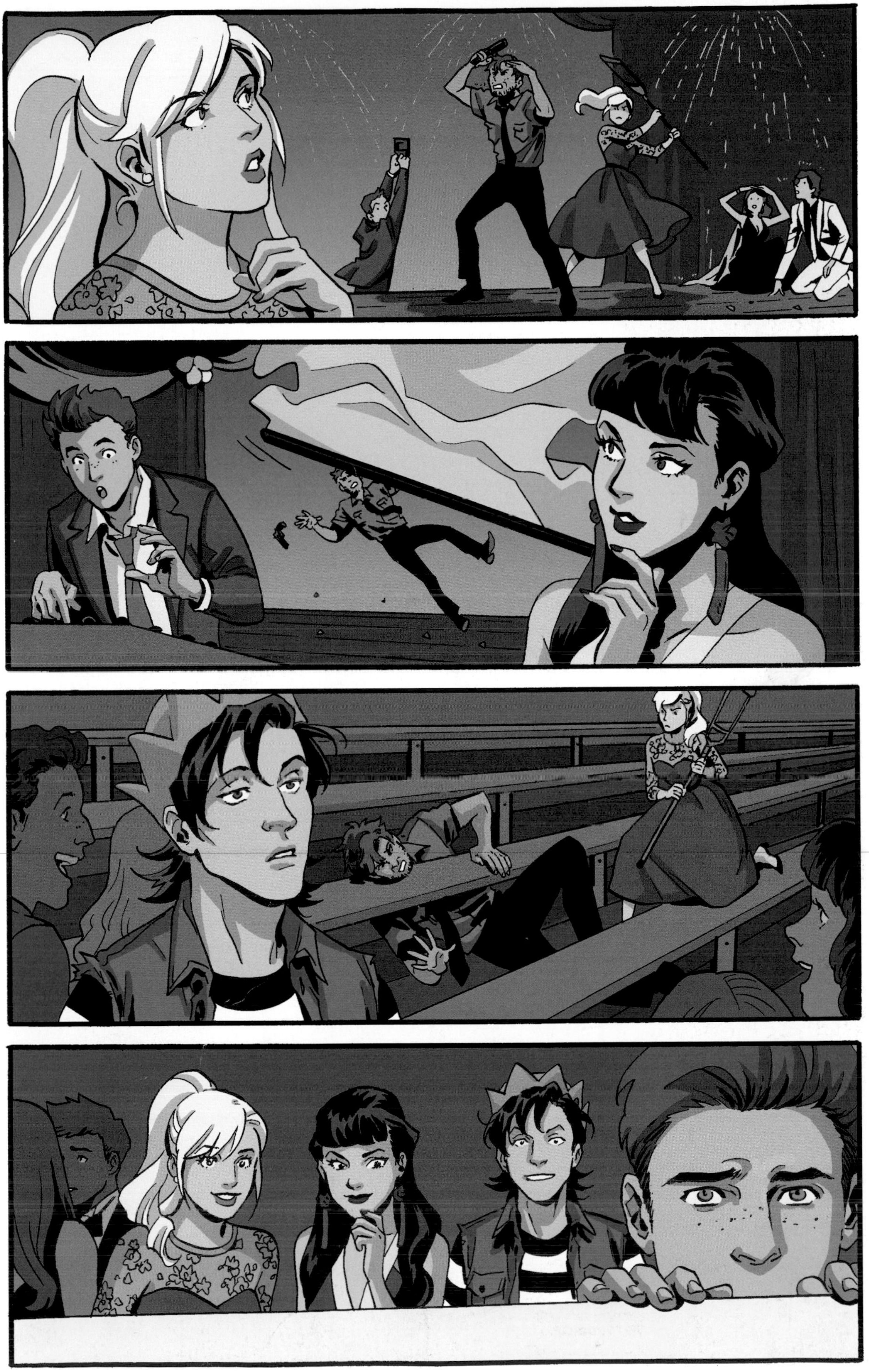

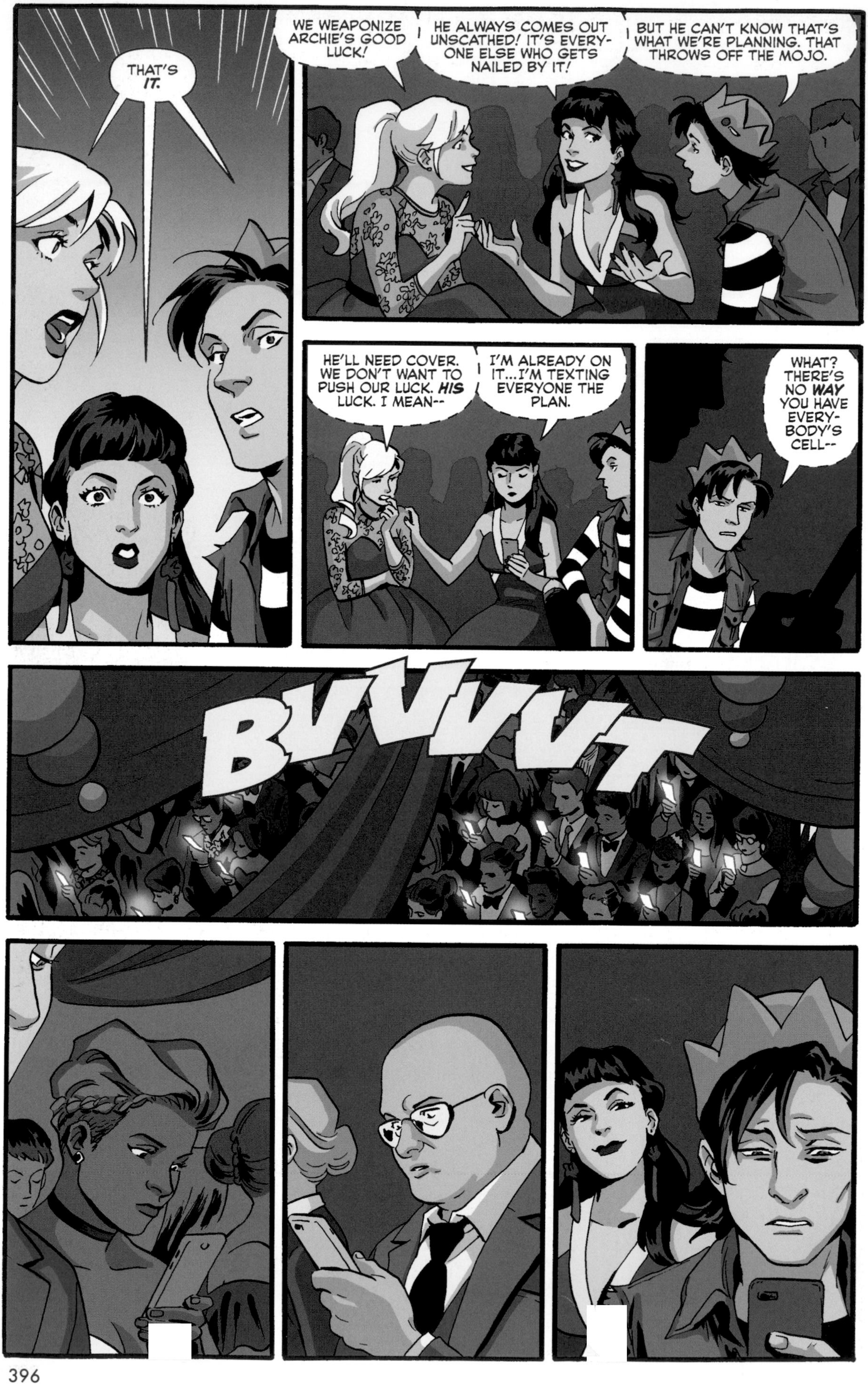
THAT'S *IT.*
WE WEAPONIZE ARCHIE'S GOOD LUCK!
HE ALWAYS COMES OUT UNSCATHED! IT'S EVERYONE ELSE WHO GETS NAILED BY IT!
BUT HE CAN'T KNOW THAT'S WHAT WE'RE PLANNING. THAT THROWS OFF THE MOJO.
HE'LL NEED COVER. WE DON'T WANT TO PUSH OUR LUCK. ***HIS*** LUCK. I MEAN--
I'M ALREADY ON IT...I'M TEXTING EVERYONE THE PLAN.
WHAT? THERE'S NO ***WAY*** YOU HAVE EVERYBODY'S CELL--
BVVVVT

OF COURSE SHE DOES.

ARCHIE! WE HAVE A PLAN!

WE DO?

RONNIE IS ORGANIZING A DISTRACTION. WHEN IT HAPPENS, YOU GET TO THE STAGE AND CRANK THE SPEAKERS. ONE CHORD ON YOUR GUITAR SHOULD BE ENOUGH TO DISARM THE GUNMAN SO WE CAN RUSH HIM.

BUT WHATEVER YOU DO...

"...*DON'T* GO NEAR THE TOUCHY FIRE ALARM...

FIRE ALARM

PULL DOWN

"...*DO NOT* CUE THE FINICKY PROJECTOR SCREEN...

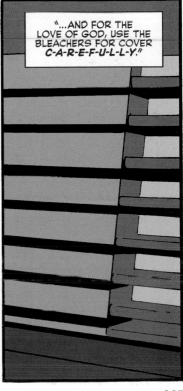

"...AND FOR THE LOVE OF GOD, USE THE BLEACHERS FOR COVER *C-A-R-E-F-U-L-L-Y.*"

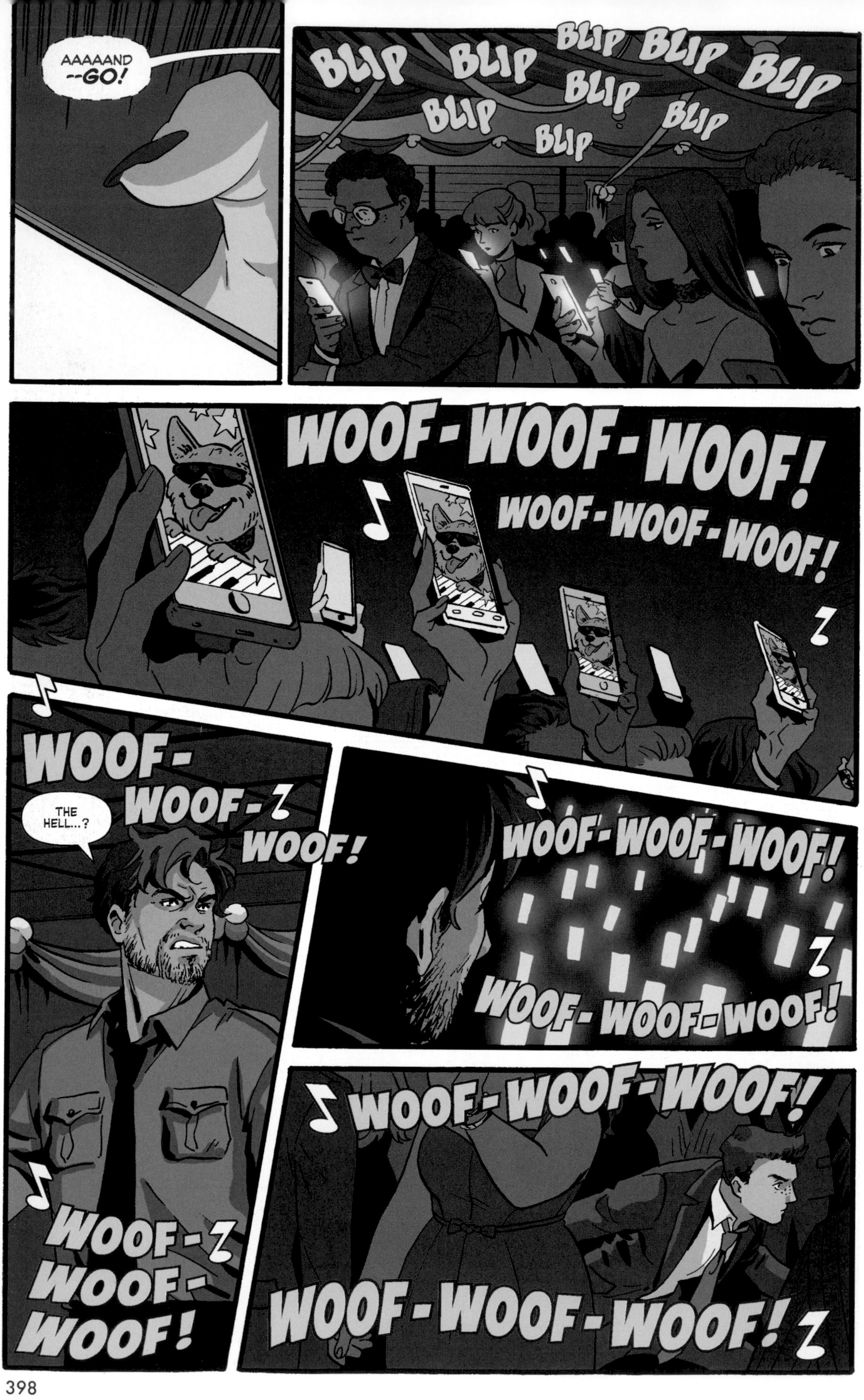
AAAAAND --GO!
BLIP BLIP BLIP BLIP BLIP BLIP BLIP BLIP BLIP
WOOF-WOOF-WOOF!
WOOF-WOOF-WOOF!
WOOF-WOOF-WOOF!
THE HELL...?
WOOF-WOOF-WOOF!
WOOF-WOOF-WOOF!
WOOF-WOOF-WOOF!
WOOF-WOOF-WOOF!
WOOF-WOOF-WOOF!

...DID HE COME OUT *CLEANER*...?

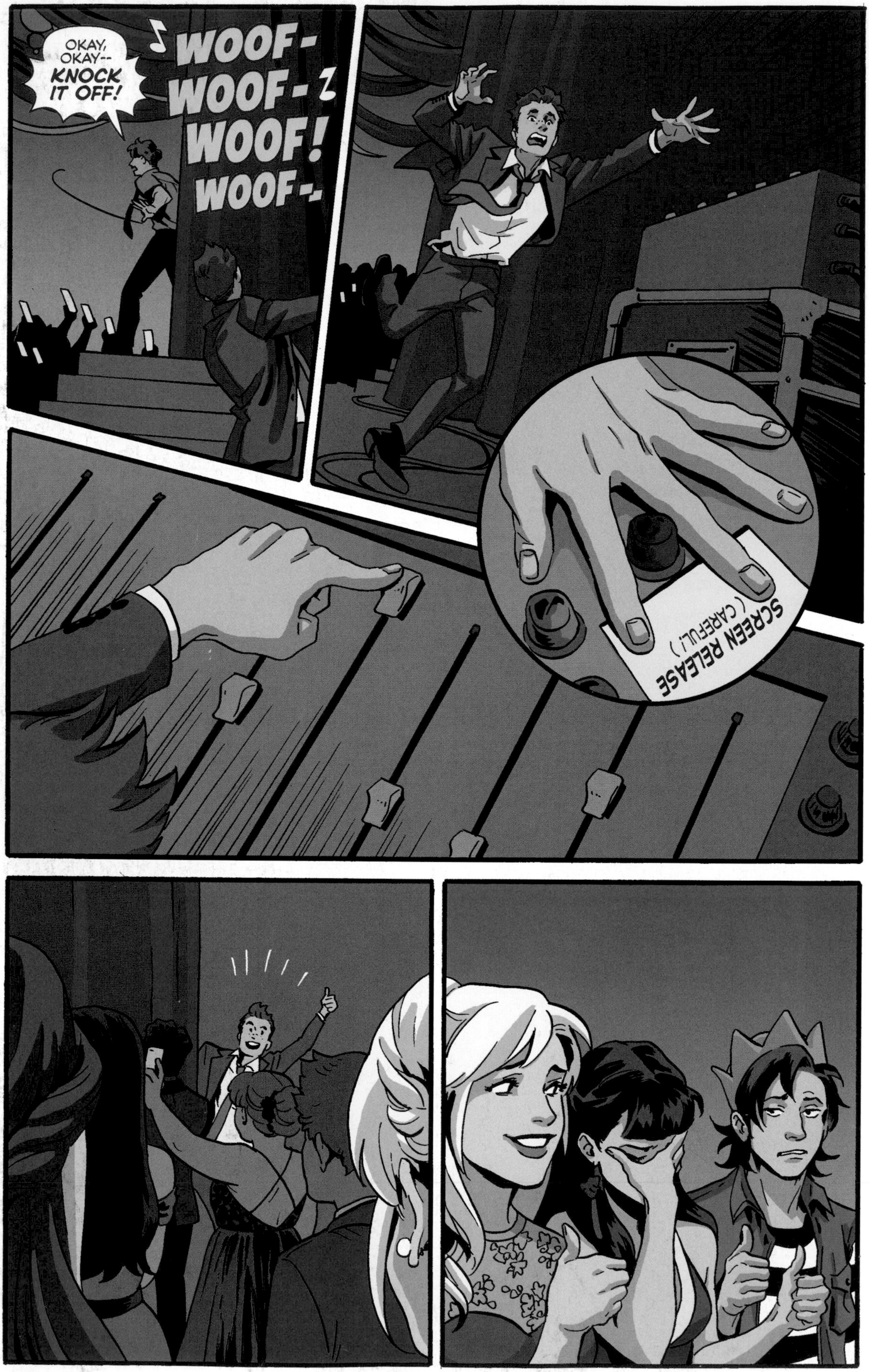

OKAY, OKAY-- KNOCK IT OFF!
WOOF-WOOF-WOOF! WOOF-
SCREEN RELEASE
(CAREFUL!)

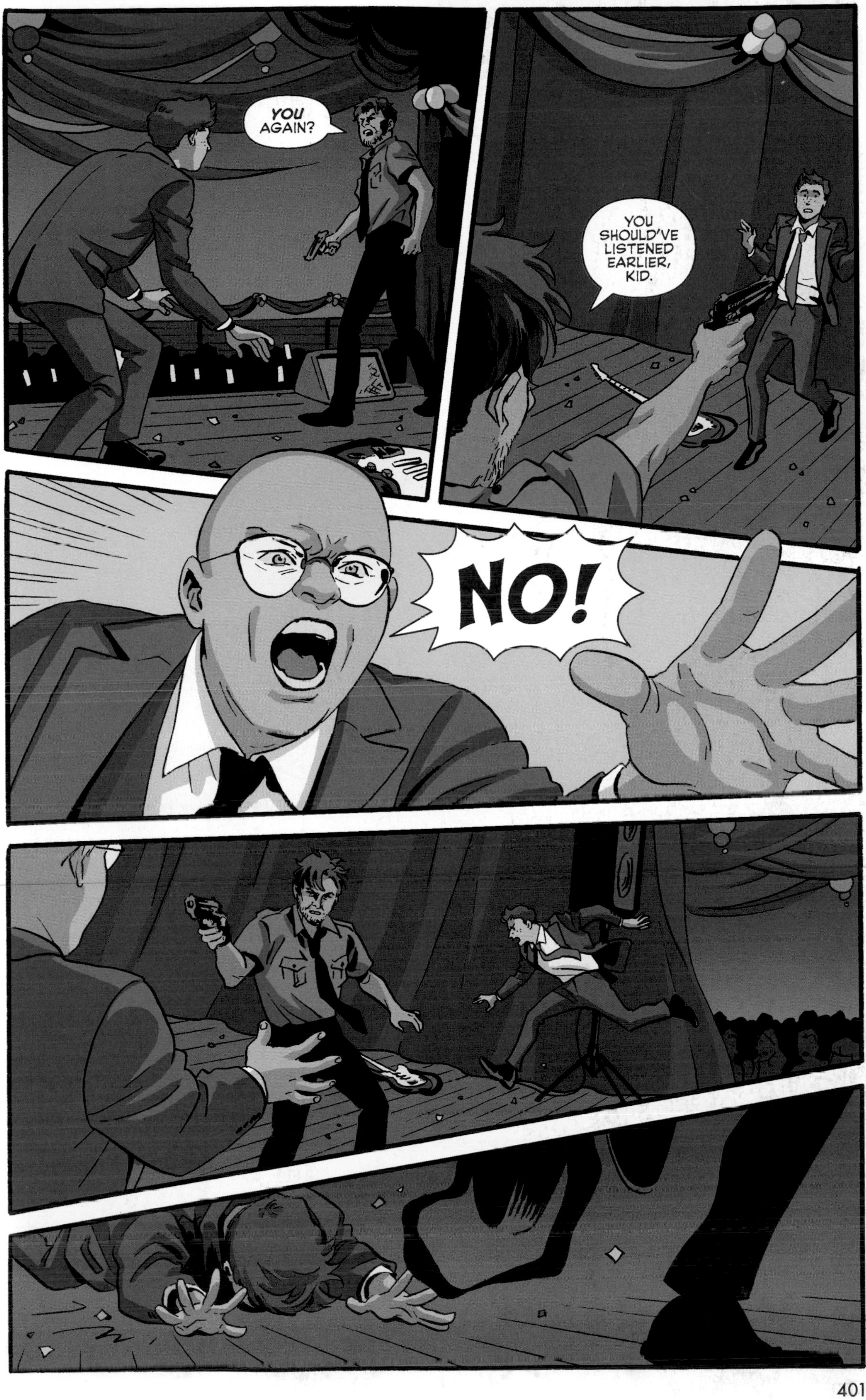
YOU AGAIN?
YOU SHOULD'VE LISTENED EARLIER, KID.
NO!

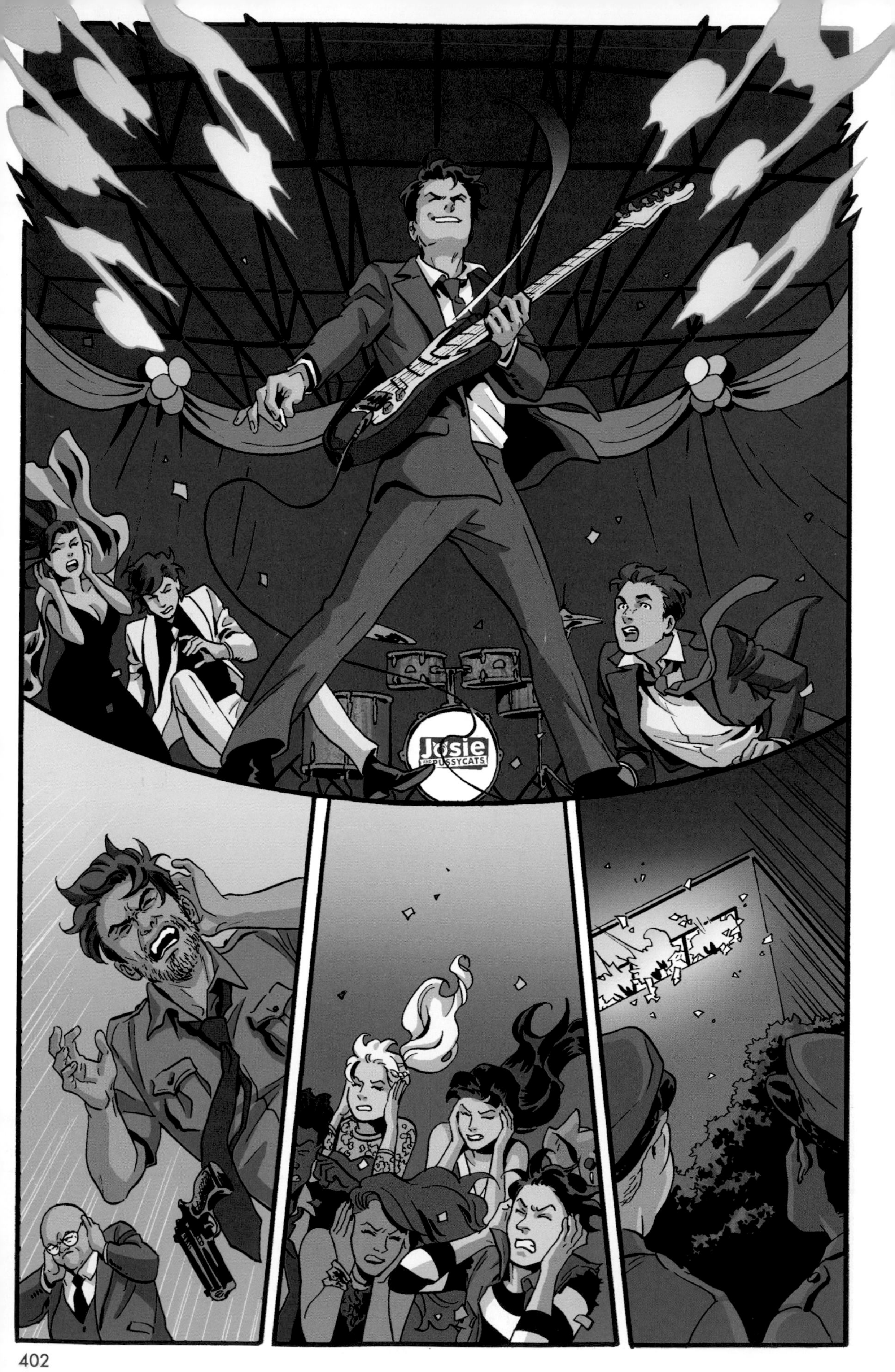
Josie
AND THE PUSSYCATS

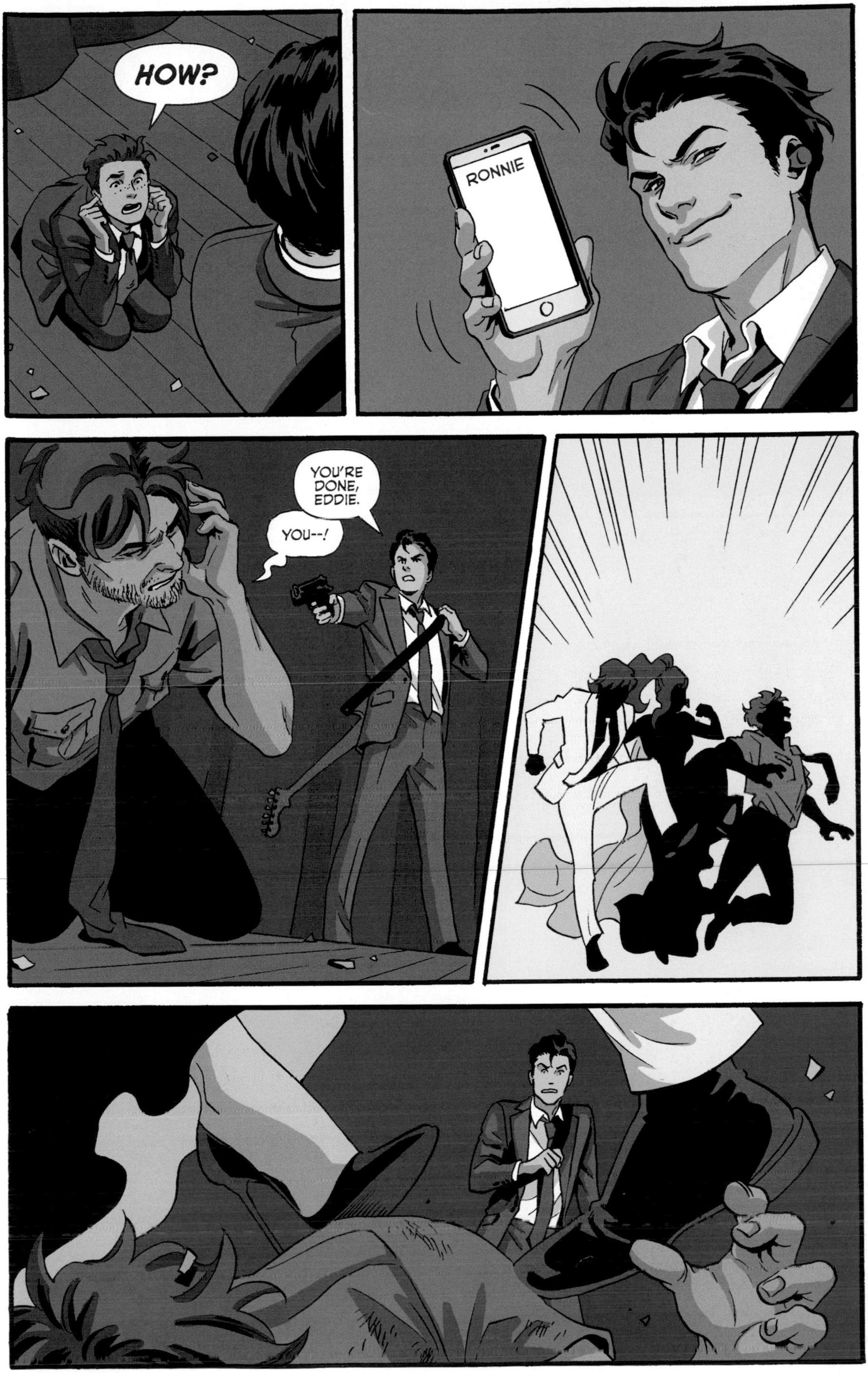
HOW?
RONNIE
YOU'RE DONE, EDDIE.
YOU--!

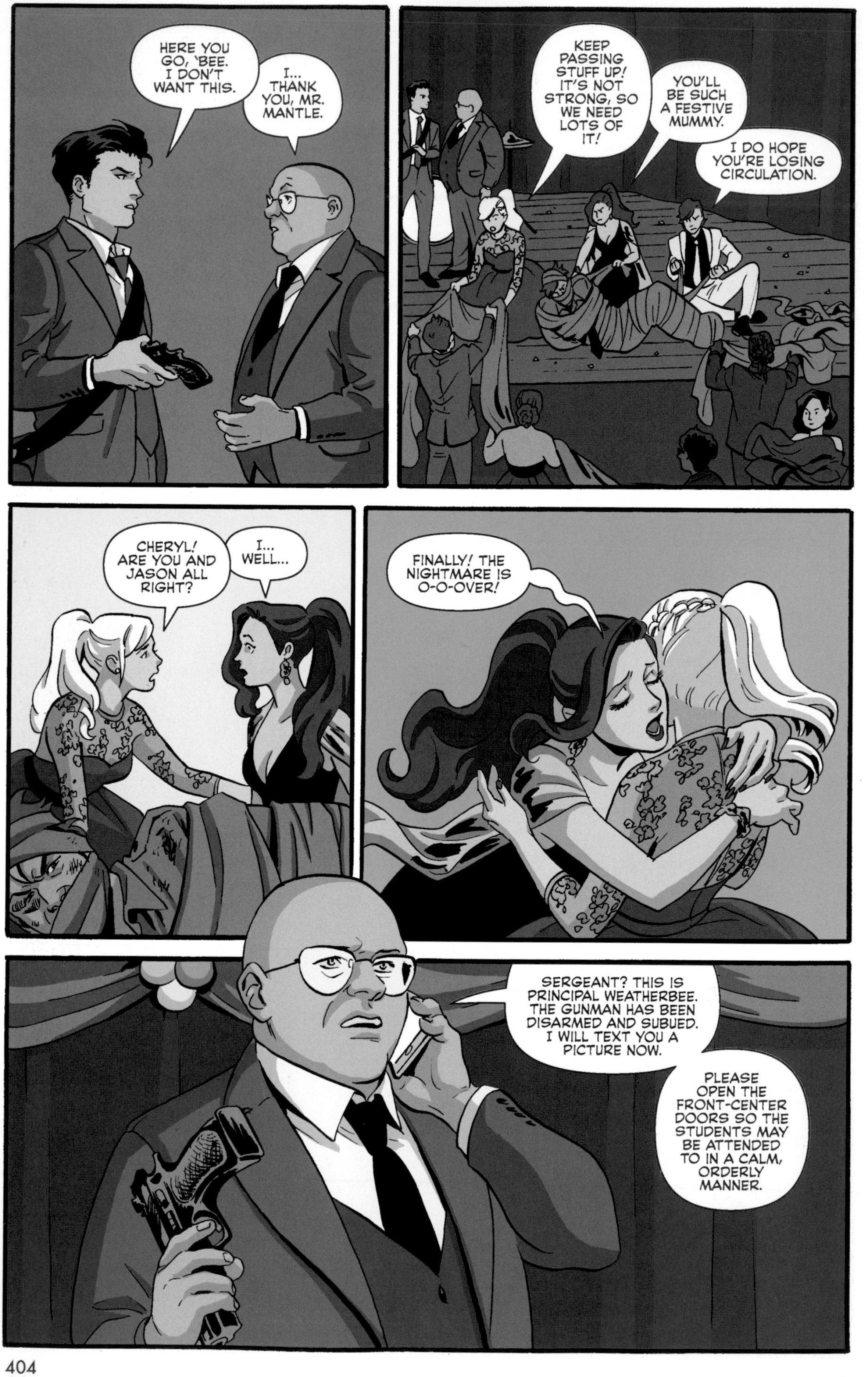
HERE YOU GO, 'BEE. I DON'T WANT THIS.
I... THANK YOU, MR. MANTLE.
KEEP PASSING STUFF UP! IT'S NOT STRONG, SO WE NEED LOTS OF IT!
YOU'LL BE SUCH A FESTIVE MUMMY.
I DO HOPE YOU'RE LOSING CIRCULATION.
CHERYL! ARE YOU AND JASON ALL RIGHT?
I... WELL...
FINALLY! THE NIGHTMARE IS O-O-OVER!
SERGEANT? THIS IS PRINCIPAL WEATHERBEE. THE GUNMAN HAS BEEN DISARMED AND SUBUED. I WILL TEXT YOU A PICTURE NOW.
PLEASE OPEN THE FRONT-CENTER DOORS SO THE STUDENTS MAY BE ATTENDED TO IN A CALM, ORDERLY MANNER.

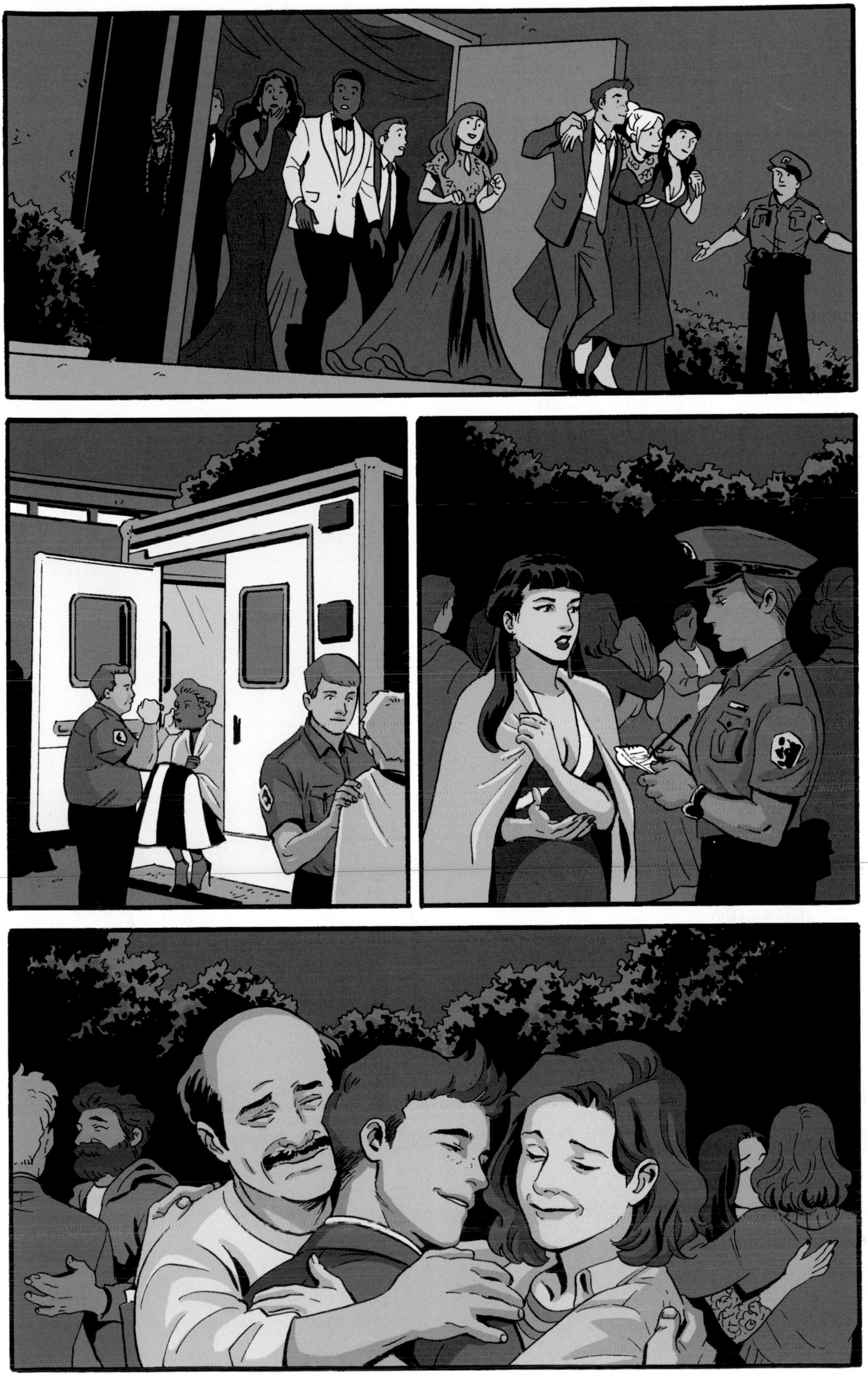

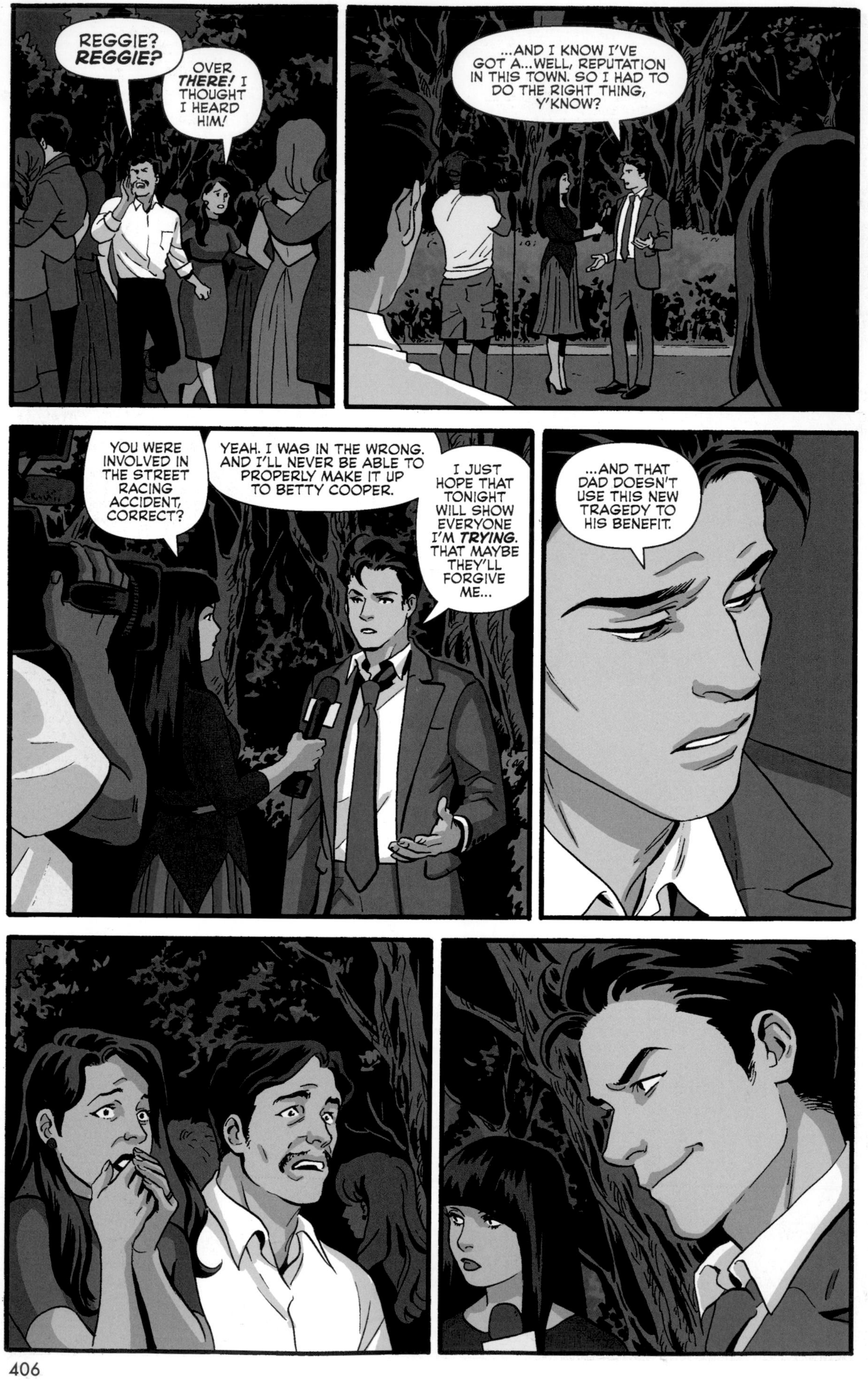
REGGIE? REGGIE?
OVER THERE! I THOUGHT I HEARD HIM!
...AND I KNOW I'VE GOT A...WELL, REPUTATION IN THIS TOWN. SO I HAD TO DO THE RIGHT THING, Y'KNOW?
YOU WERE INVOLVED IN THE STREET RACING ACCIDENT, CORRECT?
YEAH. I WAS IN THE WRONG. AND I'LL NEVER BE ABLE TO PROPERLY MAKE IT UP TO BETTY COOPER.
I JUST HOPE THAT TONIGHT WILL SHOW EVERYONE I'M TRYING. THAT MAYBE THEY'LL FORGIVE ME...
...AND THAT DAD DOESN'T USE THIS NEW TRAGEDY TO HIS BENEFIT.

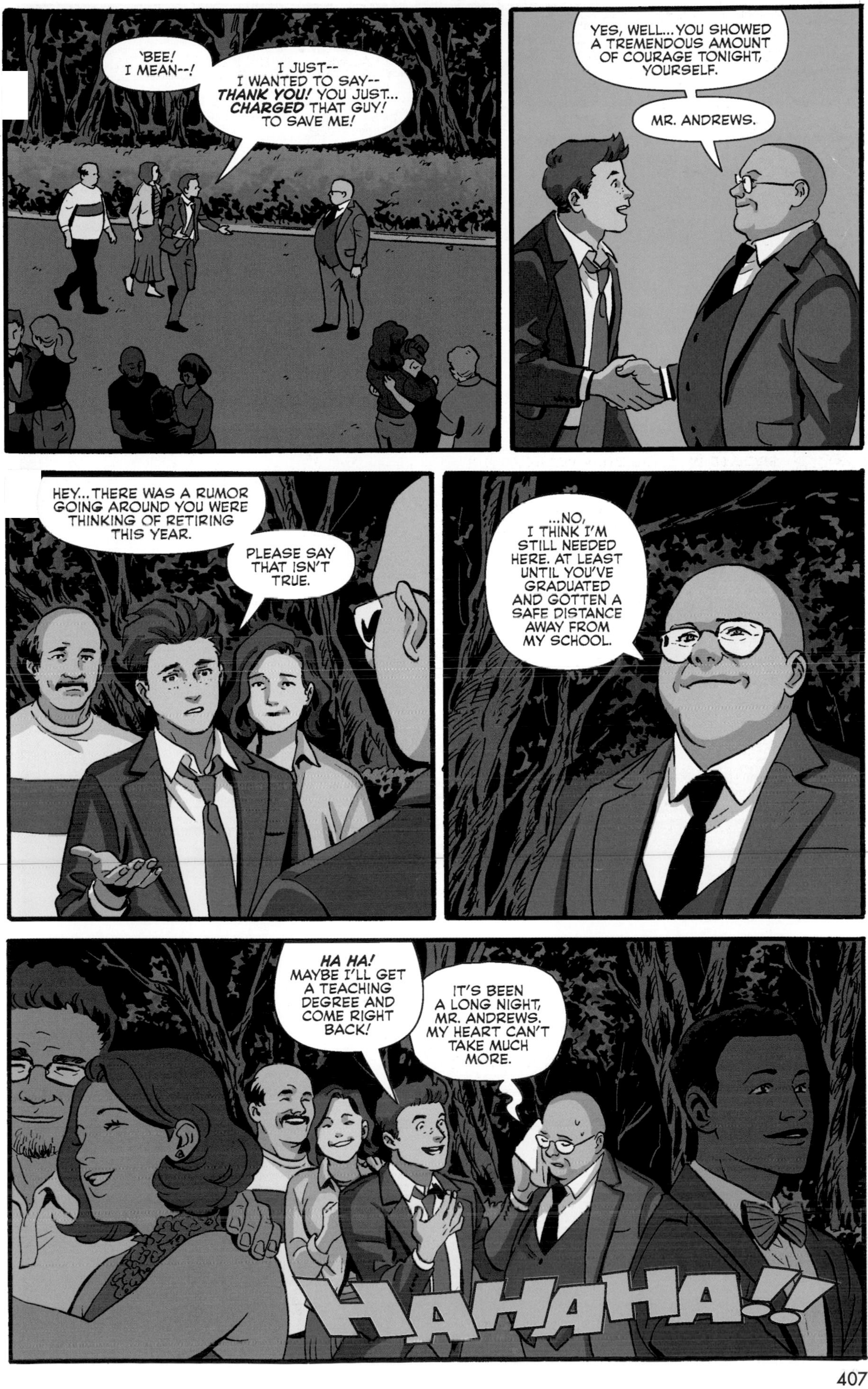
'BEE! I MEAN--!
I JUST-- I WANTED TO SAY-- *THANK YOU!* YOU JUST... *CHARGED* THAT GUY! TO SAVE ME!
YES, WELL... YOU SHOWED A TREMENDOUS AMOUNT OF COURAGE TONIGHT, YOURSELF.
MR. ANDREWS.
HEY... THERE WAS A RUMOR GOING AROUND YOU WERE THINKING OF RETIRING THIS YEAR.
PLEASE SAY THAT ISN'T TRUE.
...NO, I THINK I'M STILL NEEDED HERE. AT LEAST UNTIL YOU'VE GRADUATED AND GOTTEN A SAFE DISTANCE AWAY FROM MY SCHOOL.
HA HA! MAYBE I'LL GET A TEACHING DEGREE AND COME RIGHT BACK!
IT'S BEEN A LONG NIGHT, MR. ANDREWS. MY HEART CAN'T TAKE MUCH MORE.
HAHAHA!!

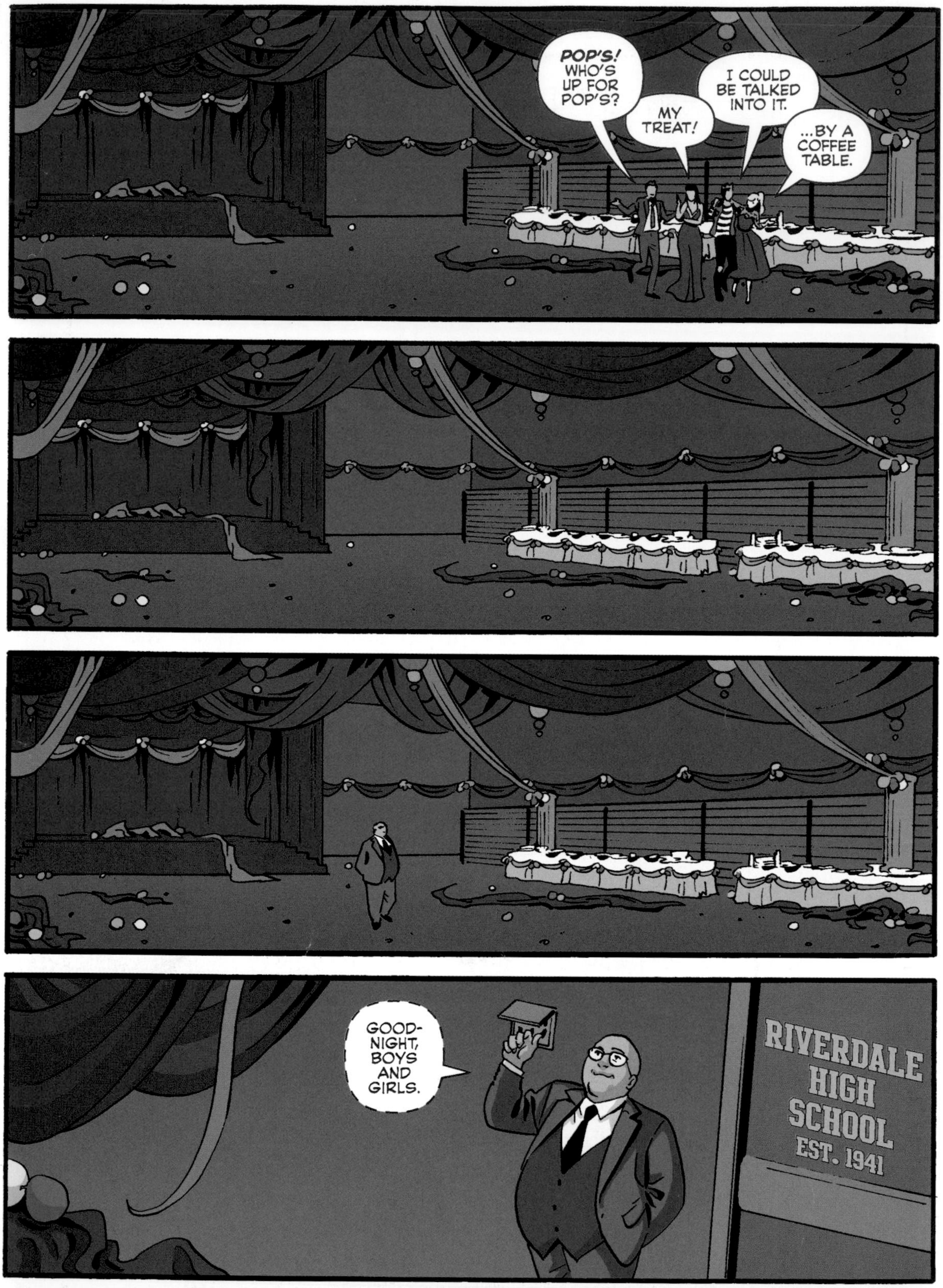
POP'S! WHO'S UP FOR POP'S?
MY TREAT!
I COULD BE TALKED INTO IT.
...BY A COFFEE TABLE.
GOOD-NIGHT, BOYS AND GIRLS.
RIVERDALE HIGH SCHOOL EST. 1941

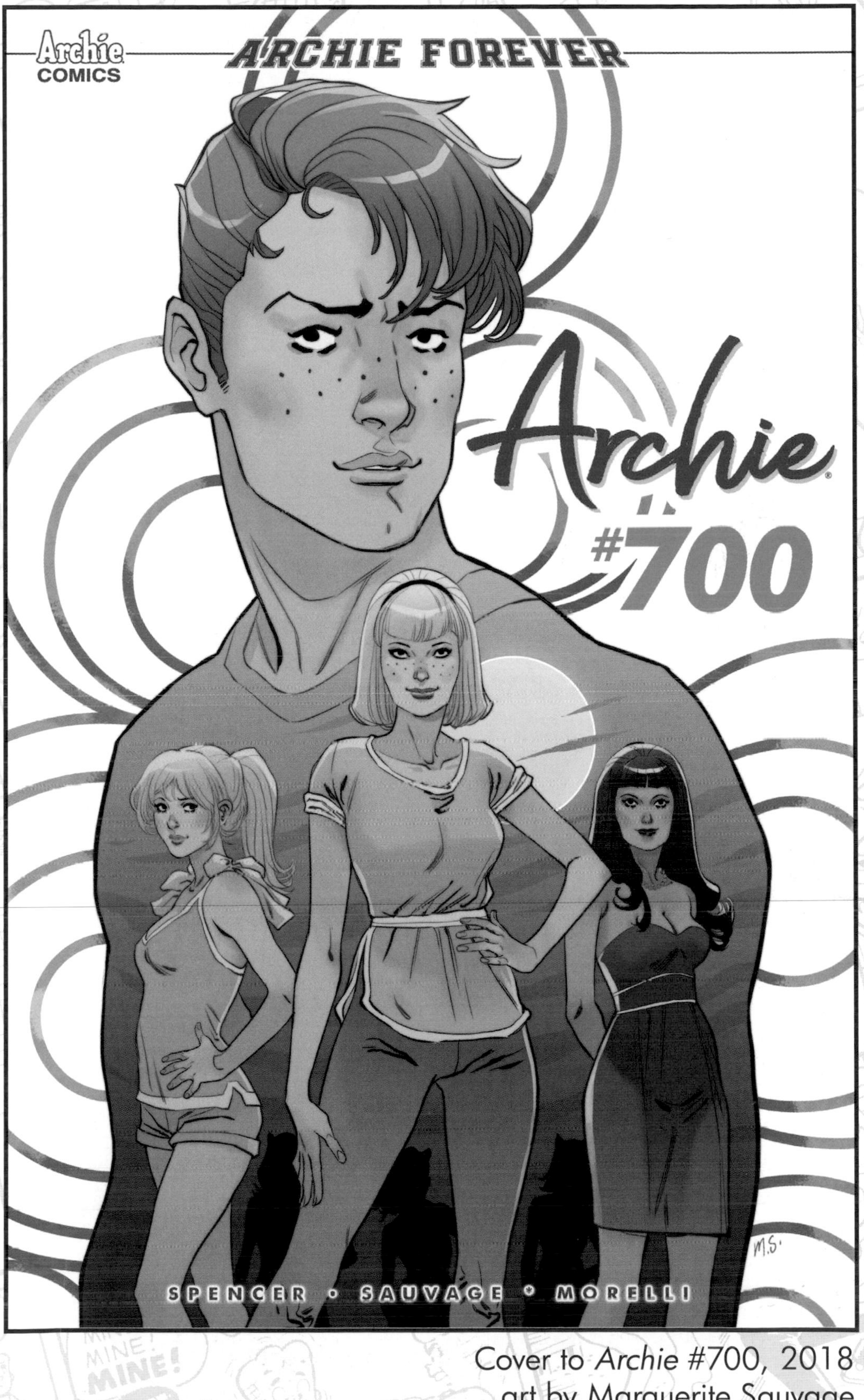
Archie COMICS
ARCHIE FOREVER
Archie
#700
M.S.
SPENCER • SAUVAGE • MORELLI

Cover to *Archie* #700, 2018
art by Marguerite Sauvage

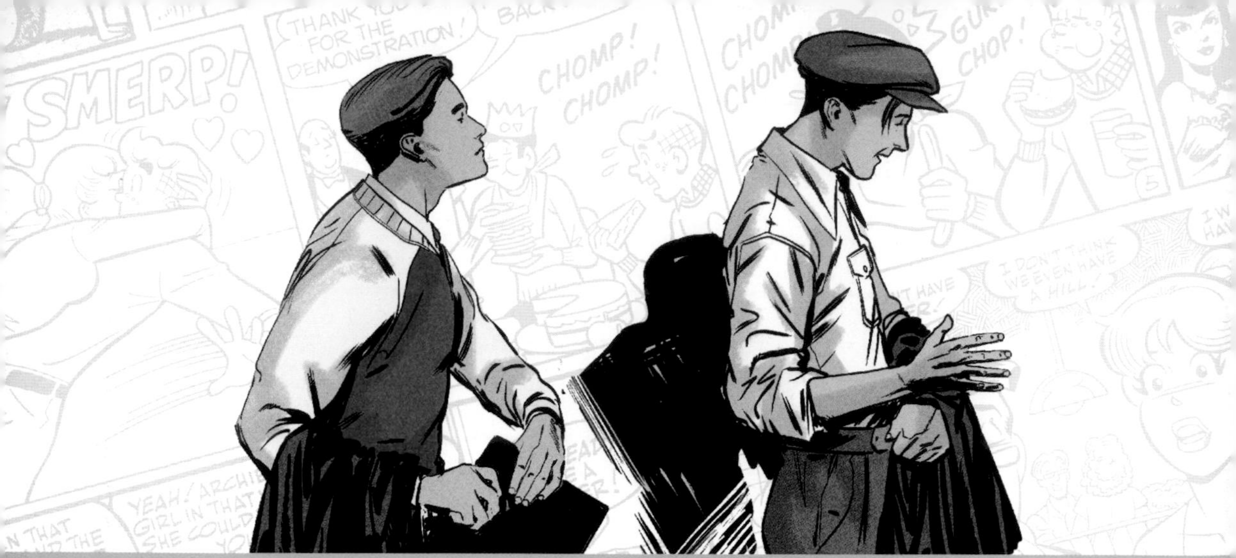
SMERP!
CHOMP! CHOMP!
I DON'T THINK WE EVEN HAVE A HILL!

ARCHIE 1941

ARCHIE 1941 #1, 2018

BY MARK WAID, BRIAN AUGUSTYN, PETER KRAUSE, KELLY FITZPATRICK & JACK MORELLI

This is the sweeping epic Archie fans have been looking forward to for years. *Archie 1941* finds Archie and the gang set against the dramatic back drop of WWII, taking things back to the year they were created to tell a story for the ages. Hats off to Mark, Brian, Pete, Kelly and Jack—they've created a masterpiece.

—Mike Pellerito
Co-President,
Archie Comics

I think *1941* is one of the best books Archie's ever done. Maybe even THE best.

—Victor Gorelick
Co-President/Editor-in-Chief,
Archie Comics

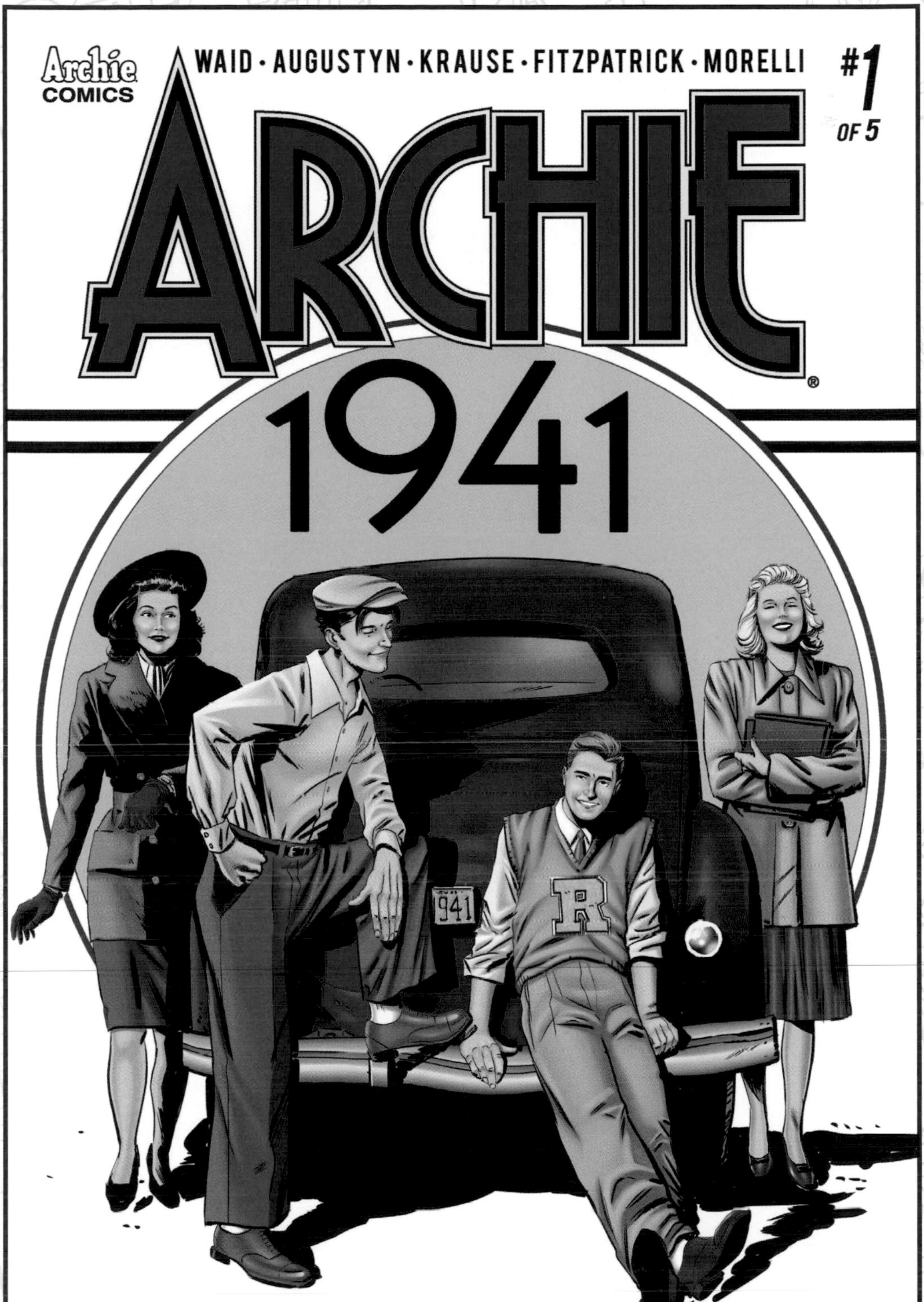
Archie COMICS
WAID · AUGUSTYN · KRAUSE · FITZPATRICK · MORELLI
#1 OF 5
ARCHIE®
1941
941
R

Cover to *Archie 1941* #1, 2018
art by Peter Krause

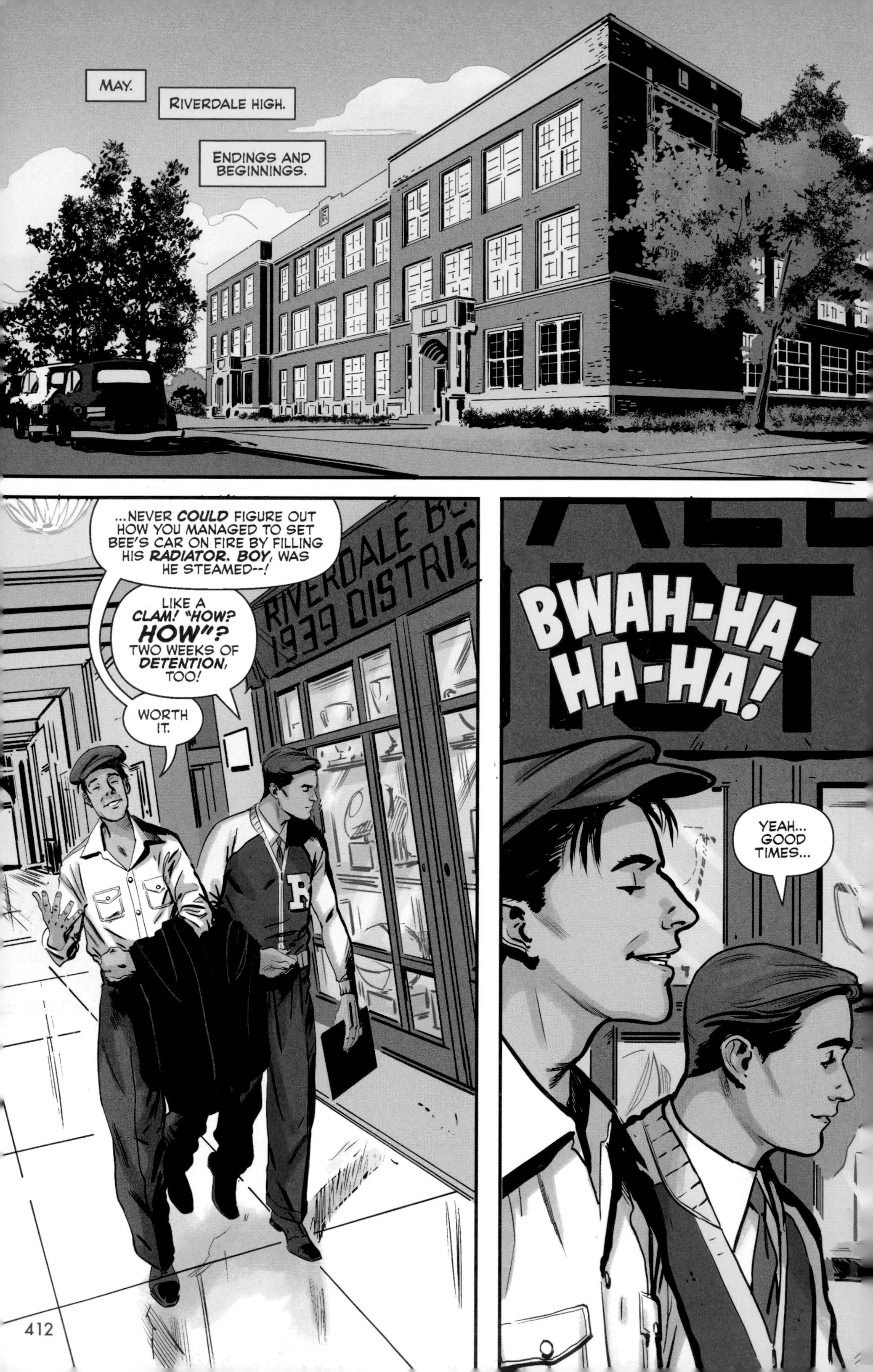
MAY.
RIVERDALE HIGH.
ENDINGS AND BEGINNINGS.
...NEVER COULD FIGURE OUT HOW YOU MANAGED TO SET BEE'S CAR ON FIRE BY FILLING HIS RADIATOR. BOY, WAS HE STEAMED--!
LIKE A CLAM! "HOW? HOW"? TWO WEEKS OF DETENTION, TOO!
WORTH IT.
BWAH-HA-HA-HA!
YEAH... GOOD TIMES...

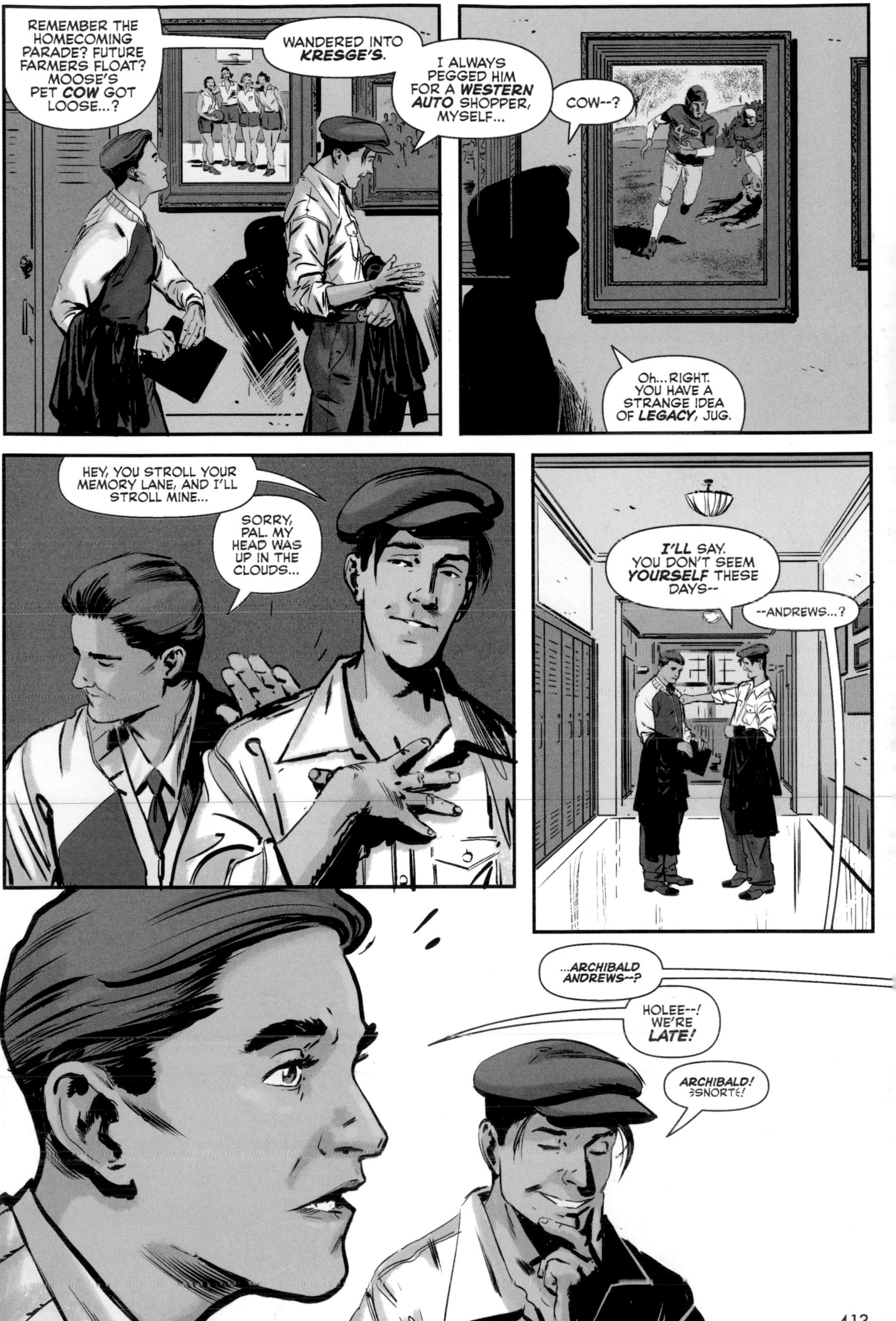
REMEMBER THE HOMECOMING PARADE? FUTURE FARMERS FLOAT? MOOSE'S PET COW GOT LOOSE...?
WANDERED INTO KRESGE'S.
I ALWAYS PEGGED HIM FOR A WESTERN AUTO SHOPPER, MYSELF...
COW--?
Oh... RIGHT. YOU HAVE A STRANGE IDEA OF LEGACY, JUG.
HEY, YOU STROLL YOUR MEMORY LANE, AND I'LL STROLL MINE...
SORRY, PAL. MY HEAD WAS UP IN THE CLOUDS...
I'LL SAY. YOU DON'T SEEM YOURSELF THESE DAYS--
--ANDREWS...?
...ARCHIBALD ANDREWS--?
HOLEE--! WE'RE LATE!
ARCHIBALD! SNORT!

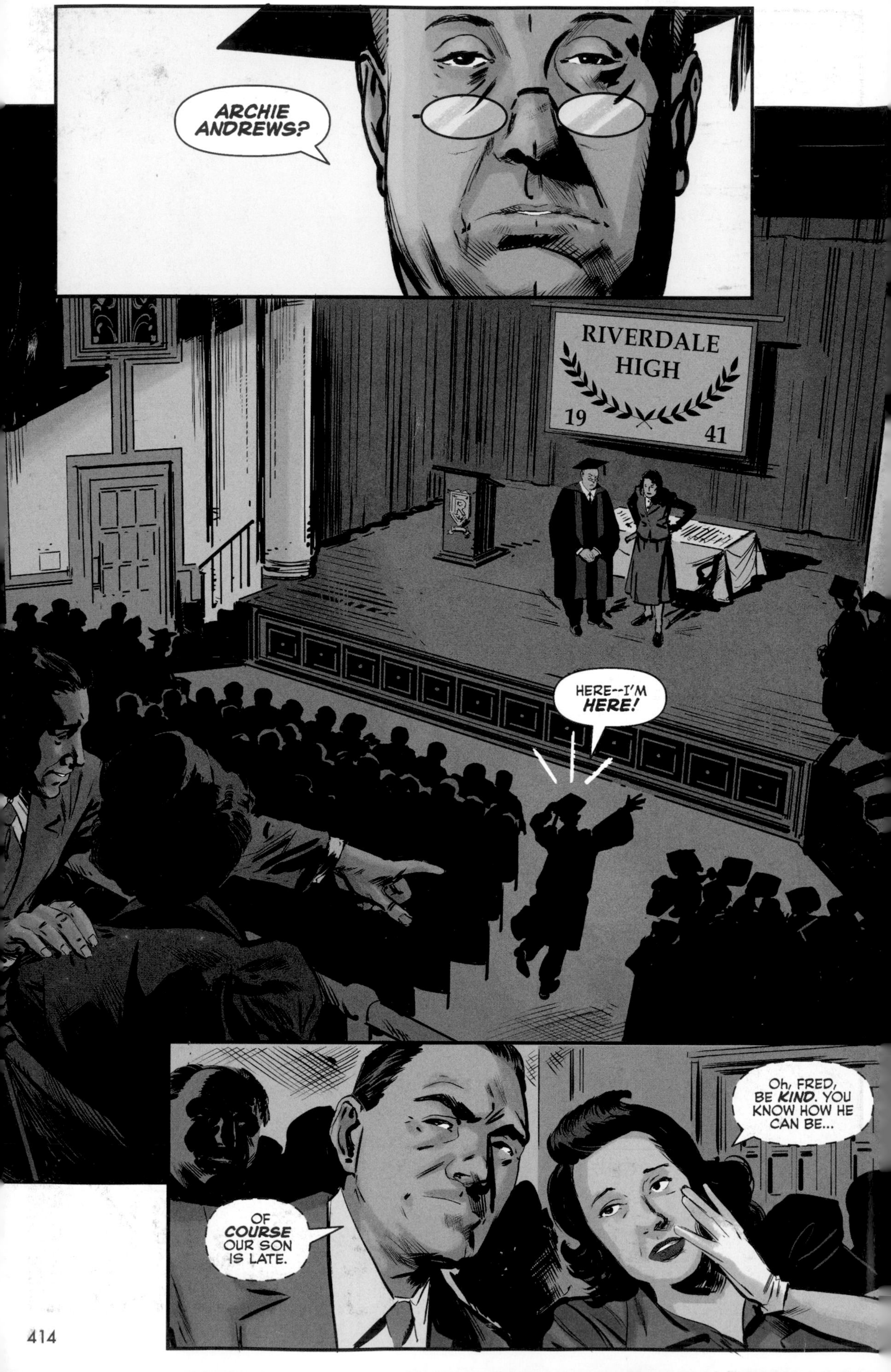
ARCHIE ANDREWS?
RIVERDALE HIGH 19 41
HERE--I'M HERE!
Oh, FRED, BE KIND. YOU KNOW HOW HE CAN BE...
OF COURSE OUR SON IS LATE.

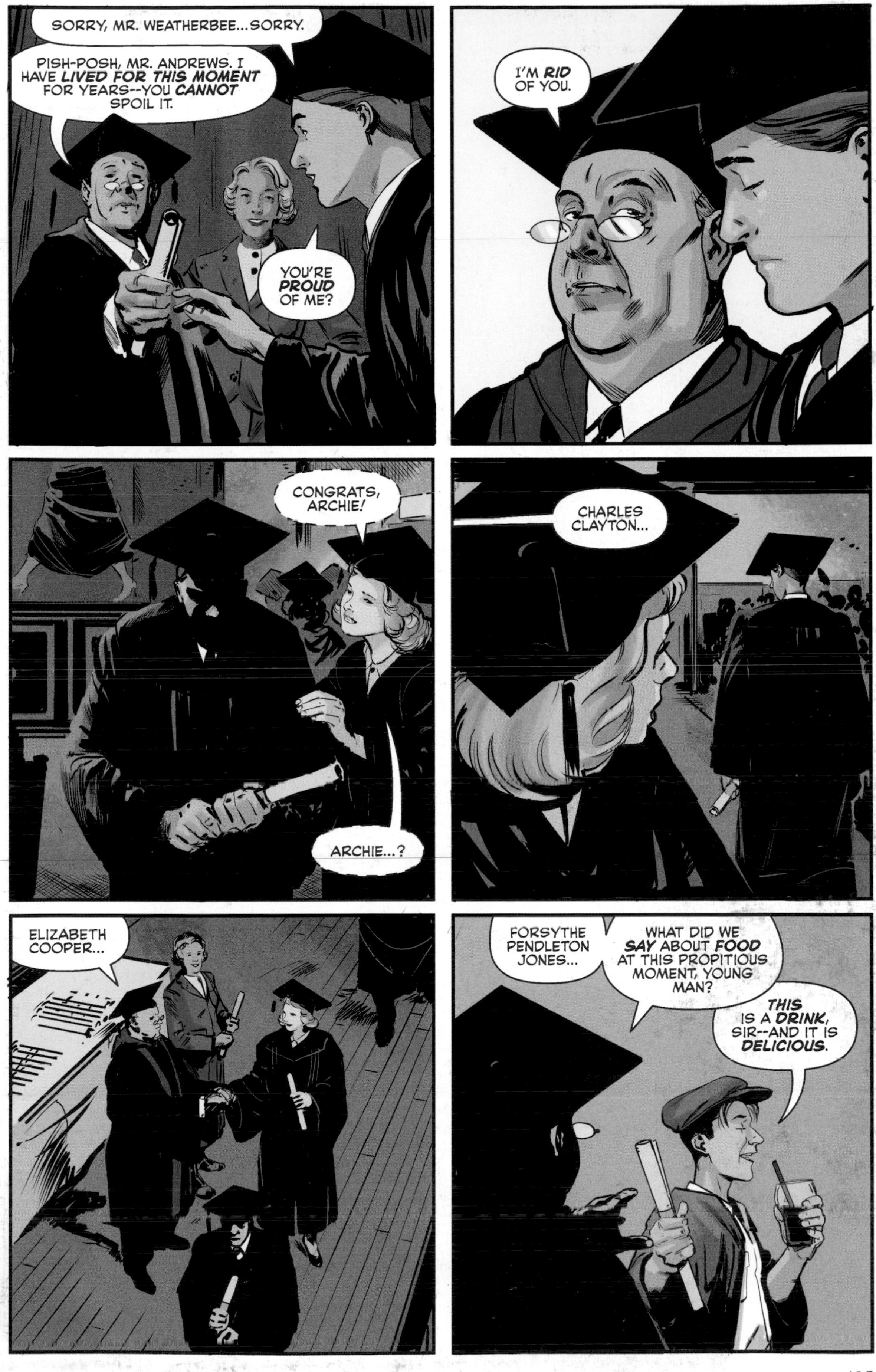
SORRY, MR. WEATHERBEE...SORRY.
PISH-POSH, MR. ANDREWS. I HAVE LIVED FOR THIS MOMENT FOR YEARS--YOU CANNOT SPOIL IT.
YOU'RE PROUD OF ME?
I'M RID OF YOU.
CONGRATS, ARCHIE!
ARCHIE...?
CHARLES CLAYTON...
ELIZABETH COOPER...
FORSYTHE PENDLETON JONES...
WHAT DID WE SAY ABOUT FOOD AT THIS PROPITIOUS MOMENT, YOUNG MAN?
THIS IS A DRINK, SIR--AND IT IS DELICIOUS.

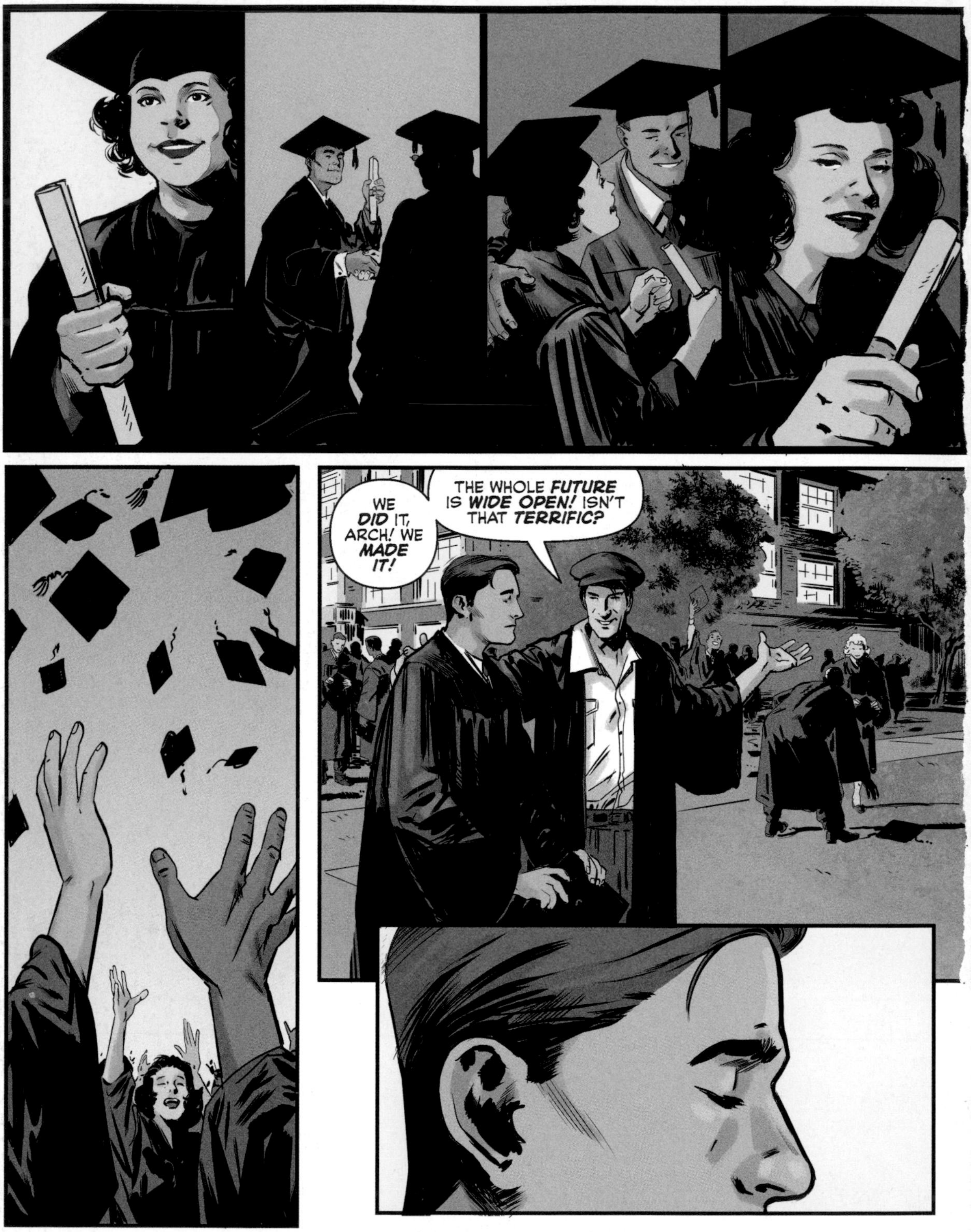

WE DID IT, ARCH! WE MADE IT!
THE WHOLE FUTURE IS WIDE OPEN! ISN'T THAT TERRIFIC?